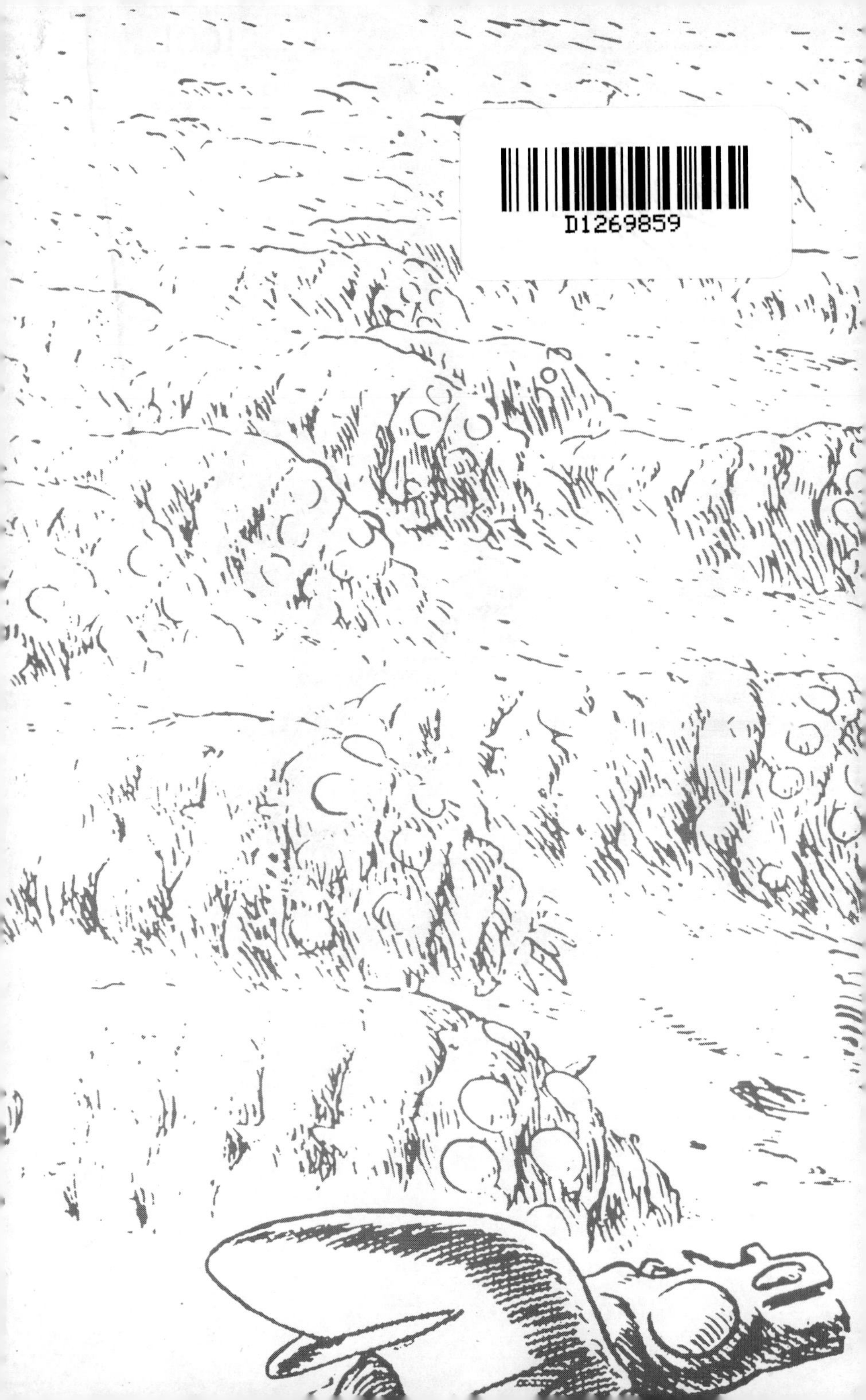

NAUSICAÄ OF THE VALLEY OF WIND™

PERFECT COLLECTION

3

STORY AND ART BY
HAYAO MIYAZAKI

This volume contains NAUSICAÄ OF THE VALLEY OF WIND, Vol. 5 and the first two-thirds of Vol. 6 in their entirety.

Story & Art by Hayao Miyazaki

Translation/Matt Thorn
Lettering & Retouch/Wayne Truman
Cover Design/Viz Graphics
Editor/Annette Roman

Senior Editor/Trish Ledoux
Director of Sales and Marketing/Oliver Chin
Editor-in-Chief/Satoru Fujii
Publisher/Seiji Horibuchi

For the purposes of publication in English, the artwork in this publication is in reverse from the original Japanese version.

Printed in Canada

Published by Viz Communications, Inc.
P.O. Box 77010, San Francisco, CA 94107

10 9 8 7 6 5 4 3
First printing, April 1996

NAUSICAÄ PERFECT COLLECTION GRAPHIC NOVELS

Volume 1
Volume 2
Volume 3
Volume 4

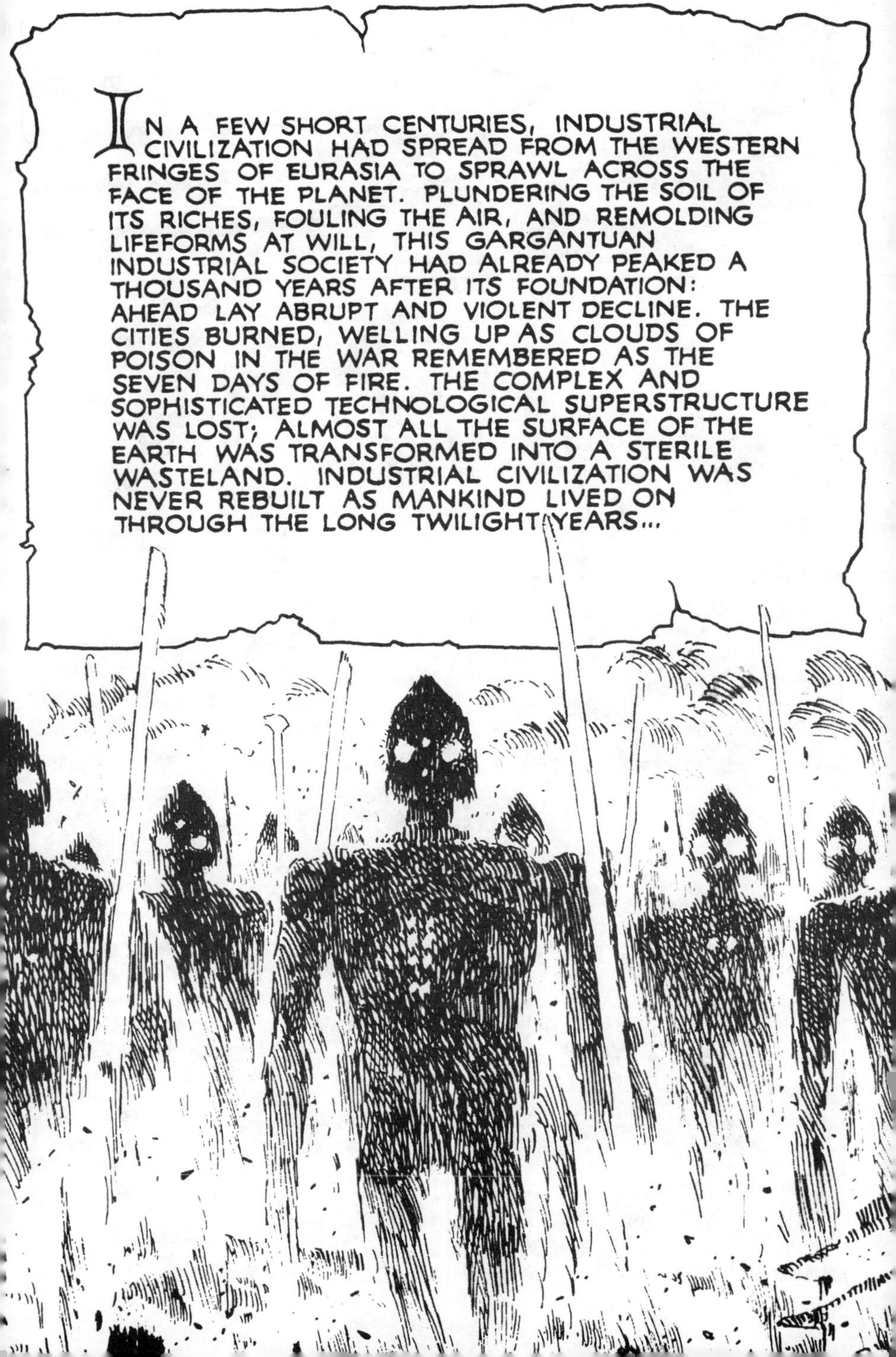
IN A FEW SHORT CENTURIES, INDUSTRIAL CIVILIZATION HAD SPREAD FROM THE WESTERN FRINGES OF EURASIA TO SPRAWL ACROSS THE FACE OF THE PLANET. PLUNDERING THE SOIL OF ITS RICHES, FOULING THE AIR, AND REMOLDING LIFEFORMS AT WILL, THIS GARGANTUAN INDUSTRIAL SOCIETY HAD ALREADY PEAKED A THOUSAND YEARS AFTER ITS FOUNDATION: AHEAD LAY ABRUPT AND VIOLENT DECLINE. THE CITIES BURNED, WELLING UP AS CLOUDS OF POISON IN THE WAR REMEMBERED AS THE SEVEN DAYS OF FIRE. THE COMPLEX AND SOPHISTICATED TECHNOLOGICAL SUPERSTRUCTURE WAS LOST; ALMOST ALL THE SURFACE OF THE EARTH WAS TRANSFORMED INTO A STERILE WASTELAND. INDUSTRIAL CIVILIZATION WAS NEVER REBUILT AS MANKIND LIVED ON THROUGH THE LONG TWILIGHT YEARS...

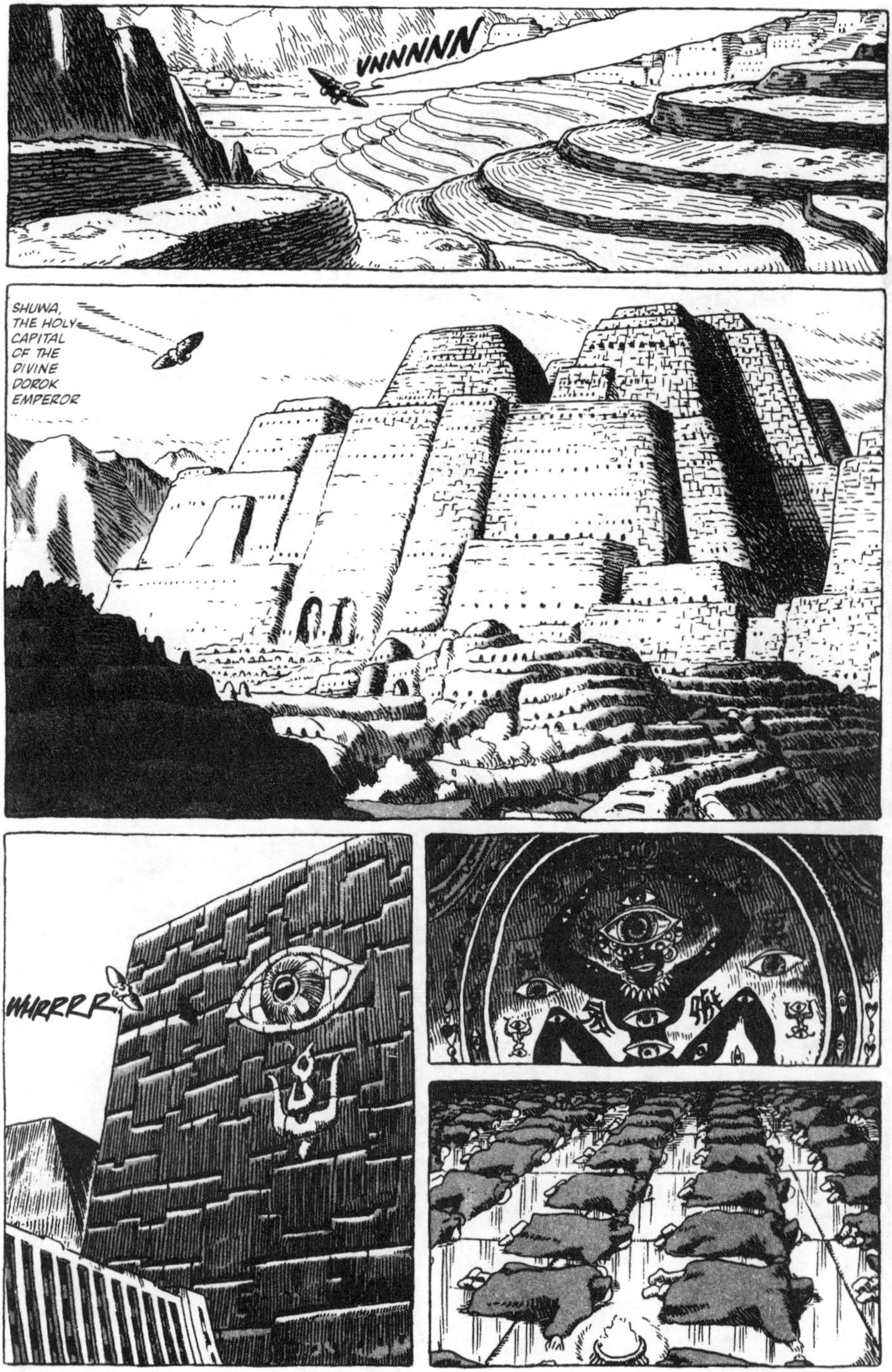
VNNNNN
SHUWA, THE HOLY CAPITAL OF THE DIVINE DOROK EMPEROR
WHRRRR

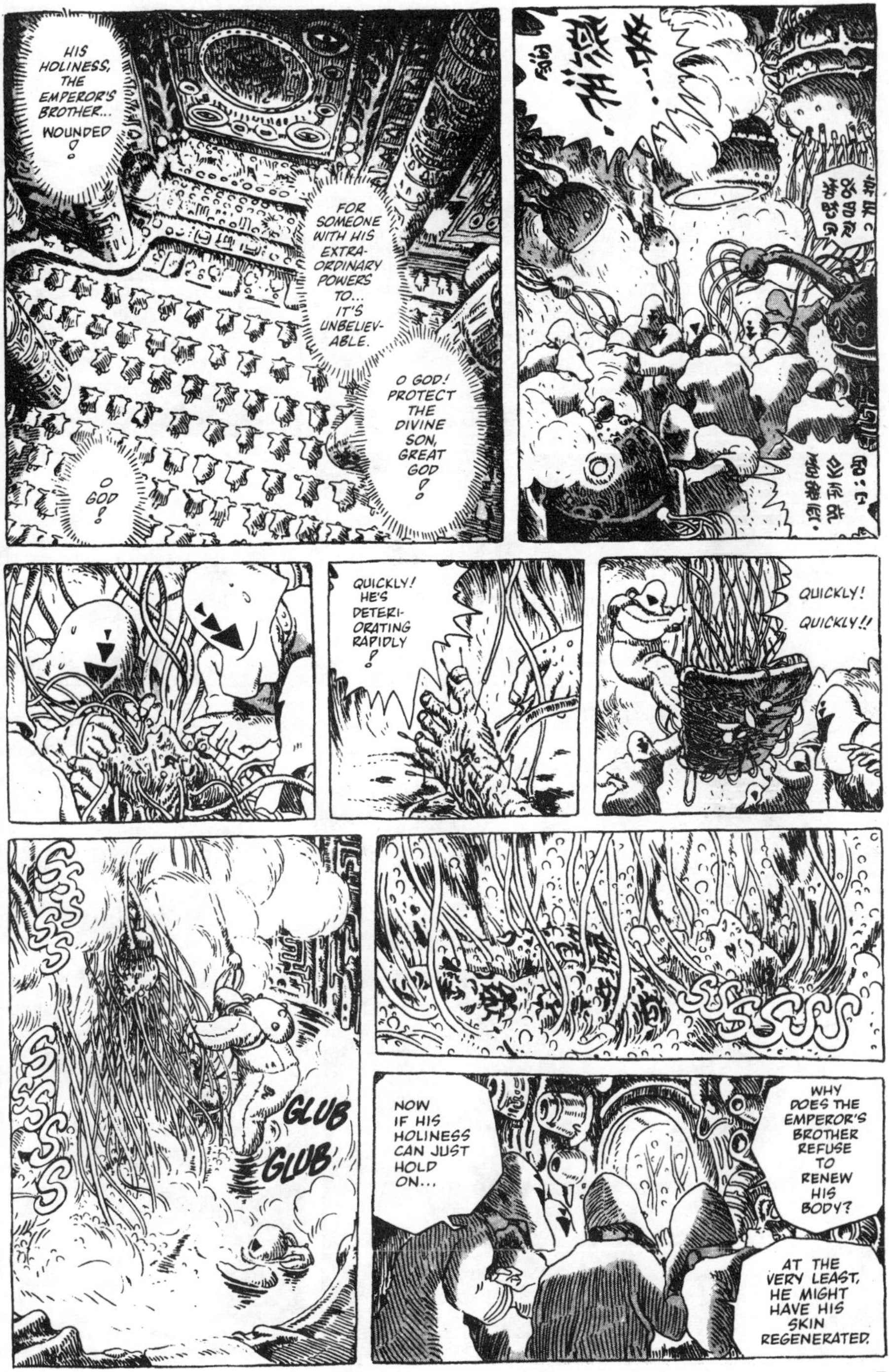
HIS HOLINESS, THE EMPEROR'S BROTHER... WOUNDED!?
FOR SOMEONE WITH HIS EXTRA-ORDINARY POWERS TO... IT'S UNBELIEV-ABLE.
O GOD! PROTECT THE DIVINE SON, GREAT GOD!!
O GOD!
QUICKLY! HE'S DETERI-ORATING RAPIDLY!
QUICKLY!
QUICKLY!!
SSSSS
GLUB
GLUB
SSSSSSS
SSSSS
NOW IF HIS HOLINESS CAN JUST HOLD ON...
WHY DOES THE EMPEROR'S BROTHER REFUSE TO RENEW HIS BODY?
AT THE VERY LEAST, HE MIGHT HAVE HIS SKIN REGENERATED.

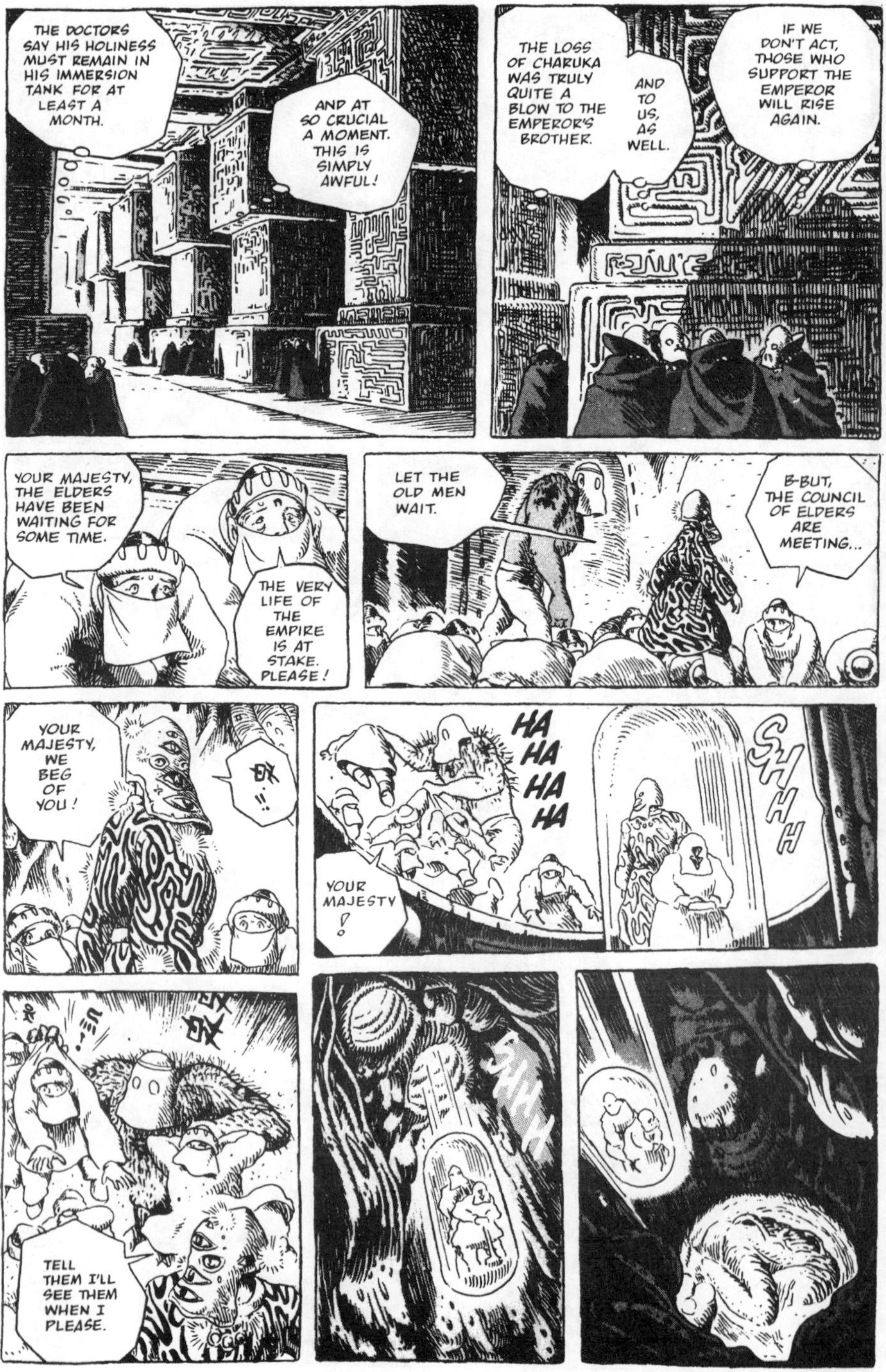
THE DOCTORS SAY HIS HOLINESS MUST REMAIN IN HIS IMMERSION TANK FOR AT LEAST A MONTH.
AND AT SO CRUCIAL A MOMENT. THIS IS SIMPLY AWFUL!
THE LOSS OF CHARUKA WAS TRULY QUITE A BLOW TO THE EMPEROR'S BROTHER.
AND TO US, AS WELL.
IF WE DON'T ACT, THOSE WHO SUPPORT THE EMPEROR WILL RISE AGAIN.
YOUR MAJESTY, THE ELDERS HAVE BEEN WAITING FOR SOME TIME.
THE VERY LIFE OF THE EMPIRE IS AT STAKE. PLEASE!
LET THE OLD MEN WAIT.
B-BUT, THE COUNCIL OF ELDERS ARE MEETING...
YOUR MAJESTY, WE BEG OF YOU!
HA HA HA HA
YOUR MAJESTY!
SHHHH
TELL THEM I'LL SEE THEM WHEN I PLEASE.
SHHH

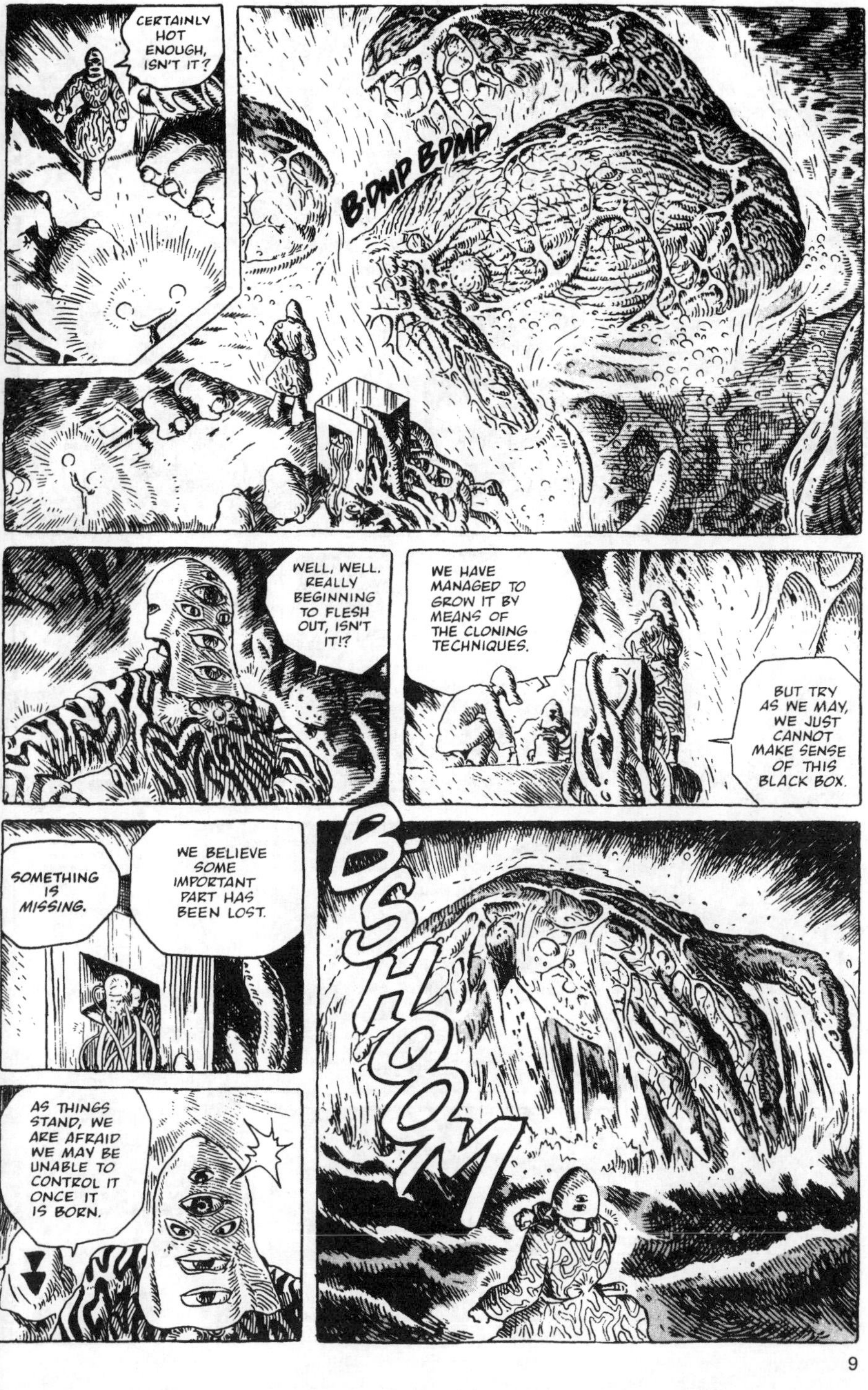
CERTAINLY HOT ENOUGH, ISN'T IT?
B-DMP B-DMP
WELL, WELL. REALLY BEGINNING TO FLESH OUT, ISN'T IT!?
WE HAVE MANAGED TO GROW IT BY MEANS OF THE CLONING TECHNIQUES.
BUT TRY AS WE MAY, WE JUST CANNOT MAKE SENSE OF THIS BLACK BOX.
SOMETHING IS MISSING.
WE BELIEVE SOME IMPORTANT PART HAS BEEN LOST.
AS THINGS STAND, WE ARE AFRAID WE MAY BE UNABLE TO CONTROL IT ONCE IT IS BORN.
B-SHOOM

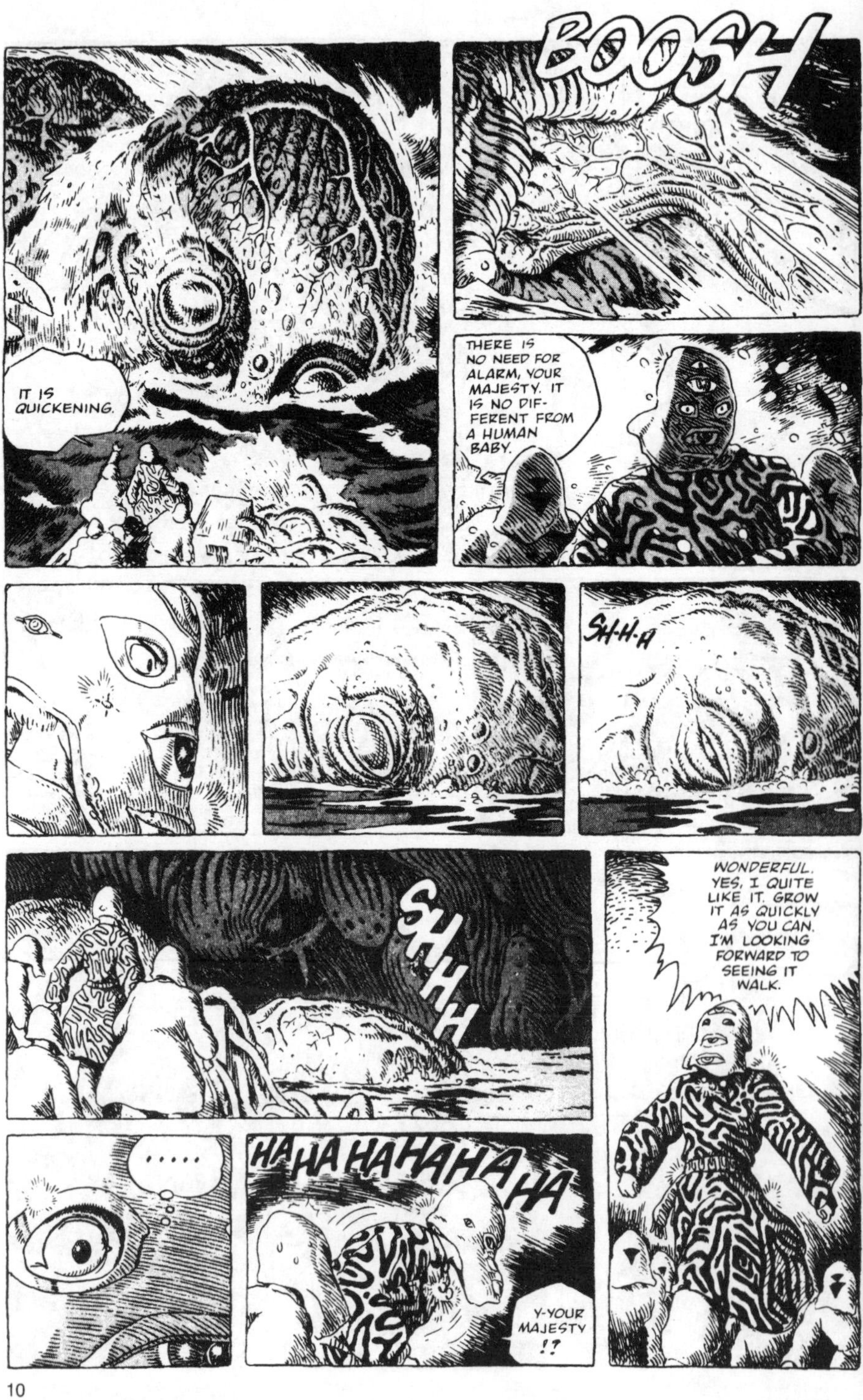

IT IS QUICKENING.
BOOSH
THERE IS NO NEED FOR ALARM, YOUR MAJESTY. IT IS NO DIFFERENT FROM A HUMAN BABY.
SH-H-H
SHHHH
WONDERFUL. YES, I QUITE LIKE IT. GROW IT AS QUICKLY AS YOU CAN. I'M LOOKING FORWARD TO SEEING IT WALK.
.....
HA HA HA HA HA HA HA HA HA
Y-YOUR MAJESTY !?

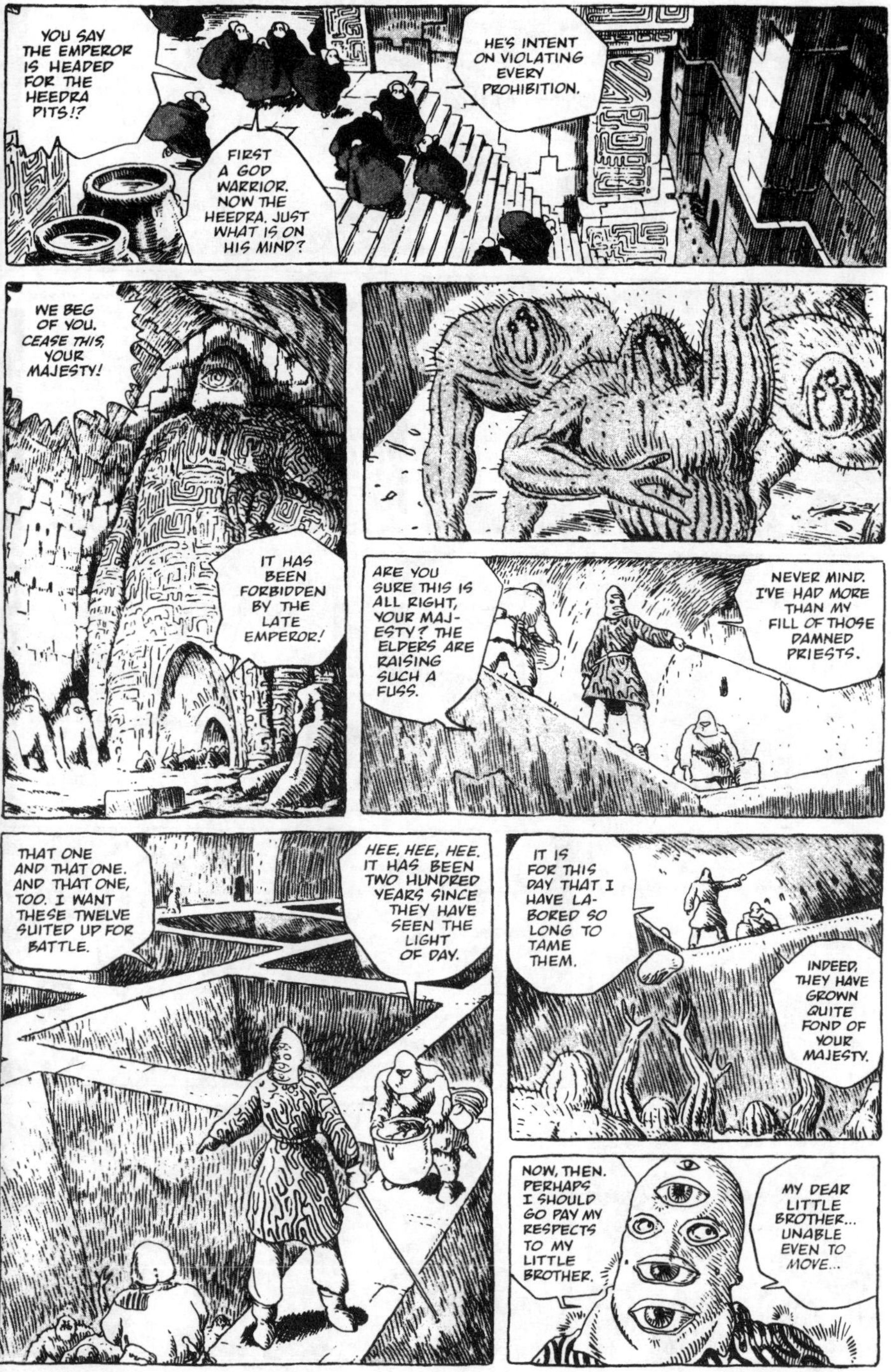
YOU SAY THE EMPEROR IS HEADED FOR THE HEEDRA PITS!?
HE'S INTENT ON VIOLATING EVERY PROHIBITION.
FIRST A GOD WARRIOR. NOW THE HEEDRA. JUST WHAT IS ON HIS MIND?
WE BEG OF YOU. CEASE THIS, YOUR MAJESTY!
IT HAS BEEN FORBIDDEN BY THE LATE EMPEROR!
ARE YOU SURE THIS IS ALL RIGHT, YOUR MAJ-ESTY? THE ELDERS ARE RAISING SUCH A FUSS.
NEVER MIND. I'VE HAD MORE THAN MY FILL OF THOSE DAMNED PRIESTS.
THAT ONE AND THAT ONE. AND THAT ONE, TOO. I WANT THESE TWELVE SUITED UP FOR BATTLE.
HEE, HEE, HEE. IT HAS BEEN TWO HUNDRED YEARS SINCE THEY HAVE SEEN THE LIGHT OF DAY.
IT IS FOR THIS DAY THAT I HAVE LA-BORED SO LONG TO TAME THEM.
INDEED, THEY HAVE GROWN QUITE FOND OF YOUR MAJESTY.
NOW, THEN. PERHAPS I SHOULD GO PAY MY RESPECTS TO MY LITTLE BROTHER.
MY DEAR LITTLE BROTHER... UNABLE EVEN TO MOVE...

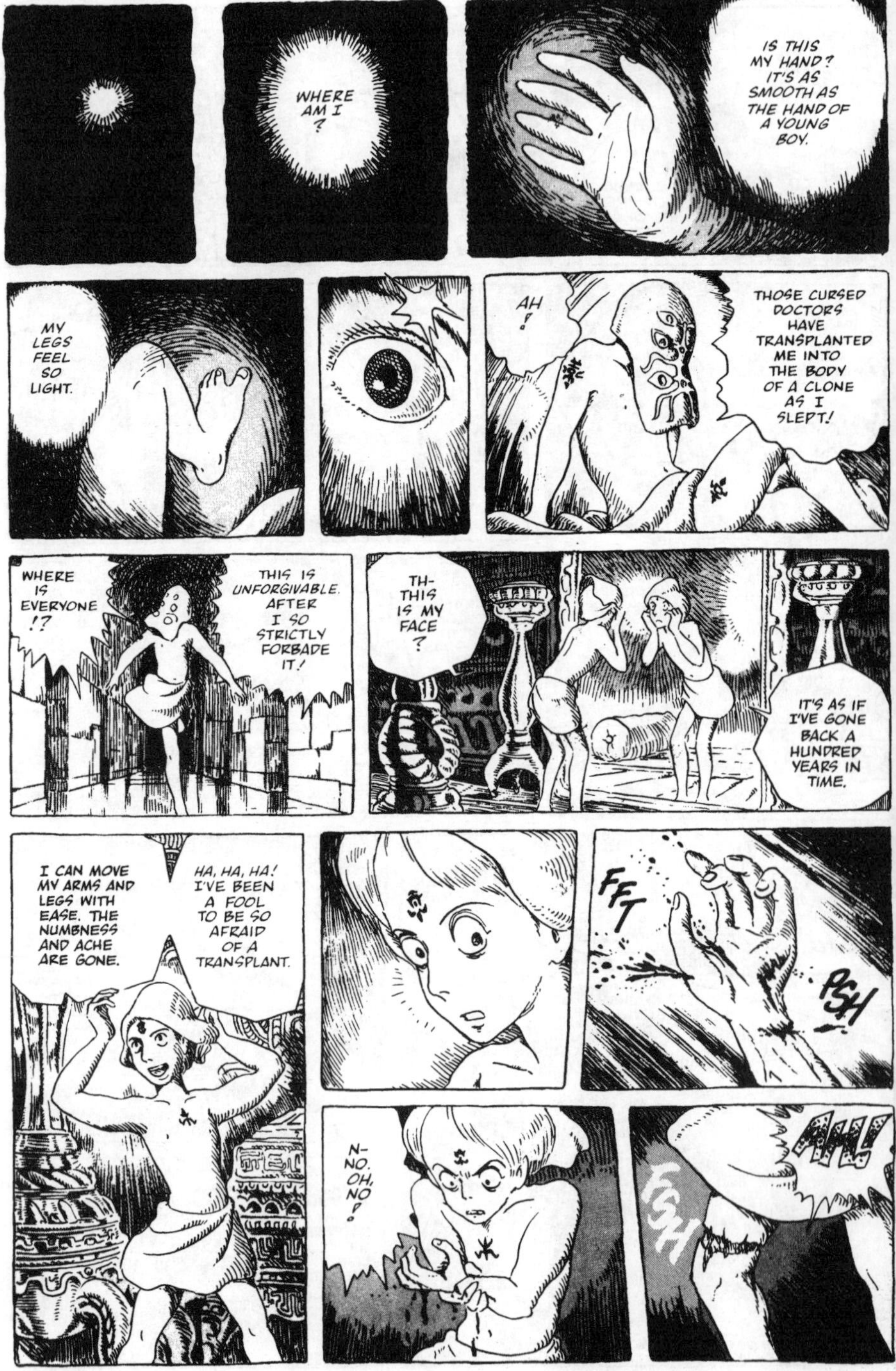
WHERE AM I ?
IS THIS MY HAND? IT'S AS SMOOTH AS THE HAND OF A YOUNG BOY.
MY LEGS FEEL SO LIGHT.
AH !
THOSE CURSED DOCTORS HAVE TRANSPLANTED ME INTO THE BODY OF A CLONE AS I SLEPT!
WHERE IS EVERYONE !?
THIS IS UNFORGIVABLE. AFTER I SO STRICTLY FORBADE IT!
TH- THIS IS MY FACE ?
IT'S AS IF I'VE GONE BACK A HUNDRED YEARS IN TIME.
I CAN MOVE MY ARMS AND LEGS WITH EASE. THE NUMBNESS AND ACHE ARE GONE.
HA, HA, HA! I'VE BEEN A FOOL TO BE SO AFRAID OF A TRANSPLANT.
FFT
PSH
N- NO, OH, NO !
AH!
FSH

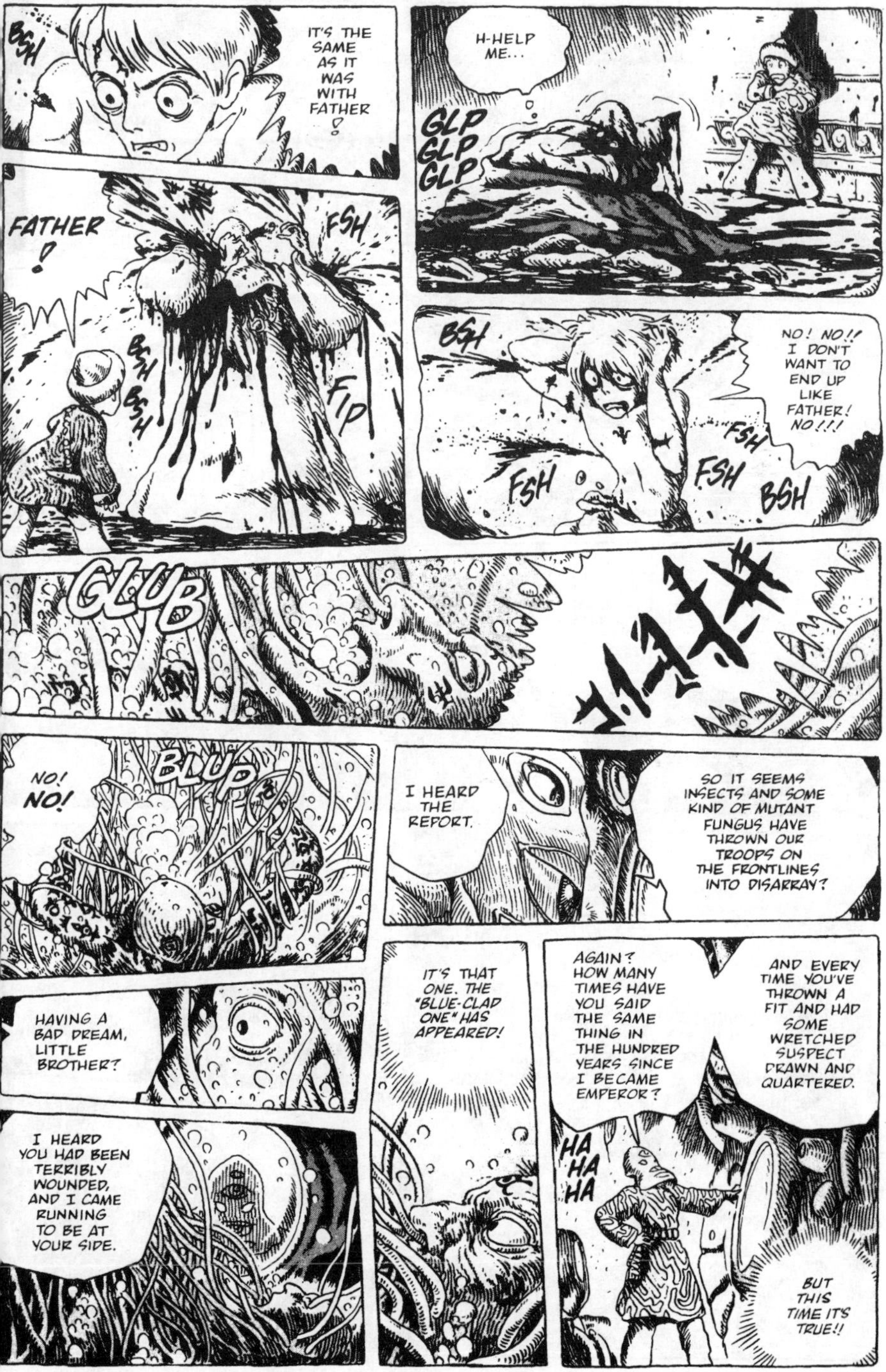
BSH
IT'S THE SAME AS IT WAS WITH FATHER!
H-HELP ME...
GLP GLP GLP
FATHER!
FSH
BSH BSH
FIP
BSH
NO! NO!! I DON'T WANT TO END UP LIKE FATHER! NO!!!
FSH
FSH
FSH
BSH
GLUB
NO! NO!
BLUP
I HEARD THE REPORT.
SO IT SEEMS INSECTS AND SOME KIND OF MUTANT FUNGUS HAVE THROWN OUR TROOPS ON THE FRONTLINES INTO DISARRAY?
HAVING A BAD DREAM, LITTLE BROTHER?
IT'S THAT ONE. THE "BLUE-CLAD ONE" HAS APPEARED!
AGAIN? HOW MANY TIMES HAVE YOU SAID THE SAME THING IN THE HUNDRED YEARS SINCE I BECAME EMPEROR?
AND EVERY TIME YOU'VE THROWN A FIT AND HAD SOME WRETCHED SUSPECT DRAWN AND QUARTERED.
I HEARD YOU HAD BEEN TERRIBLY WOUNDED, AND I CAME RUNNING TO BE AT YOUR SIDE.
HA HA HA
BUT THIS TIME IT'S TRUE!!

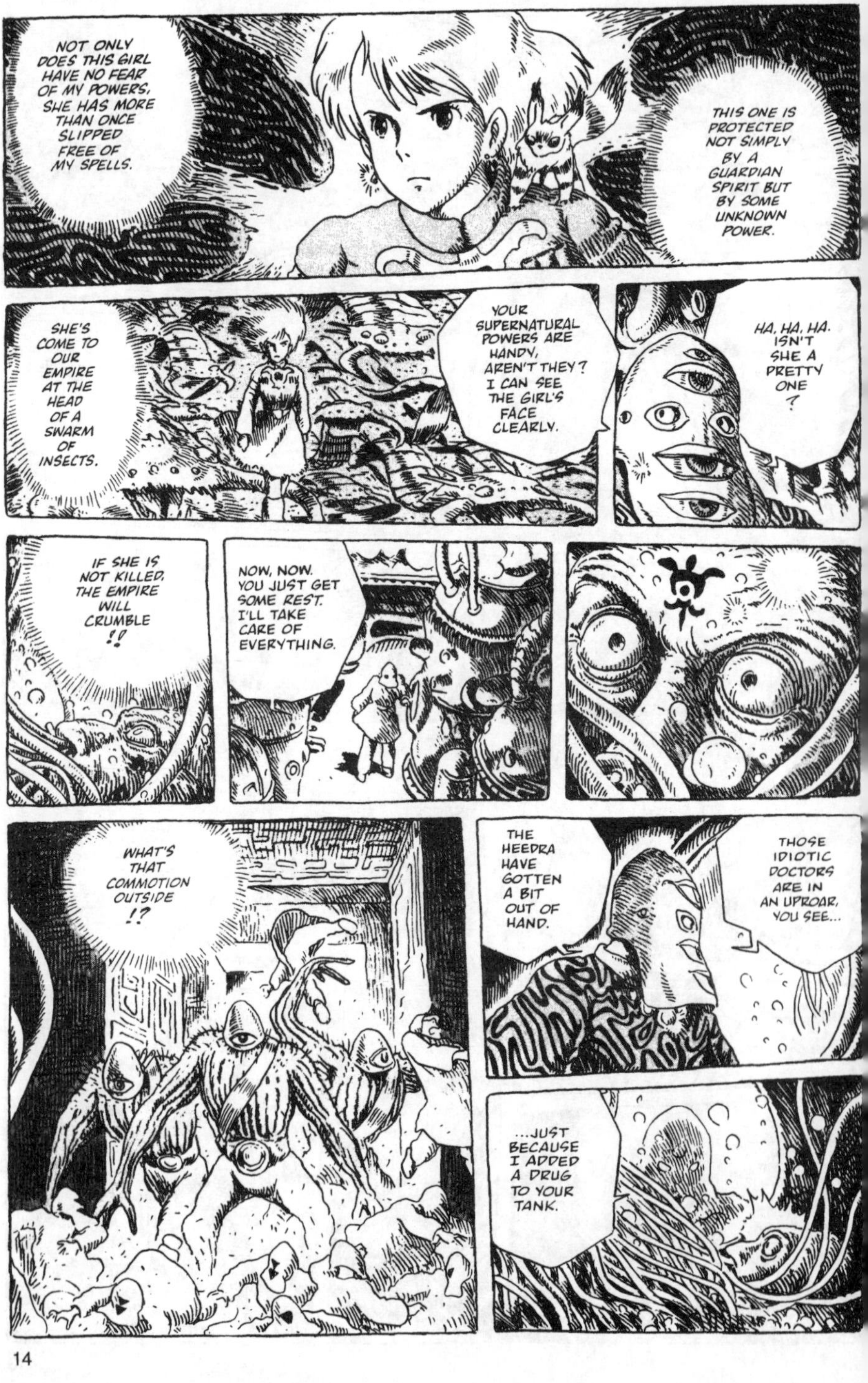
NOT ONLY DOES THIS GIRL HAVE NO FEAR OF MY POWERS, SHE HAS MORE THAN ONCE SLIPPED FREE OF MY SPELLS.
THIS ONE IS PROTECTED NOT SIMPLY BY A GUARDIAN SPIRIT BUT BY SOME UNKNOWN POWER.
SHE'S COME TO OUR EMPIRE AT THE HEAD OF A SWARM OF INSECTS.
YOUR SUPERNATURAL POWERS ARE HANDY, AREN'T THEY? I CAN SEE THE GIRL'S FACE CLEARLY.
HA, HA, HA. ISN'T SHE A PRETTY ONE ?
IF SHE IS NOT KILLED, THE EMPIRE WILL CRUMBLE !!
NOW, NOW. YOU JUST GET SOME REST. I'LL TAKE CARE OF EVERYTHING.
WHAT'S THAT COMMOTION OUTSIDE !?
THE HEEDRA HAVE GOTTEN A BIT OUT OF HAND.
THOSE IDIOTIC DOCTORS ARE IN AN UPROAR, YOU SEE...
...JUST BECAUSE I ADDED A DRUG TO YOUR TANK.

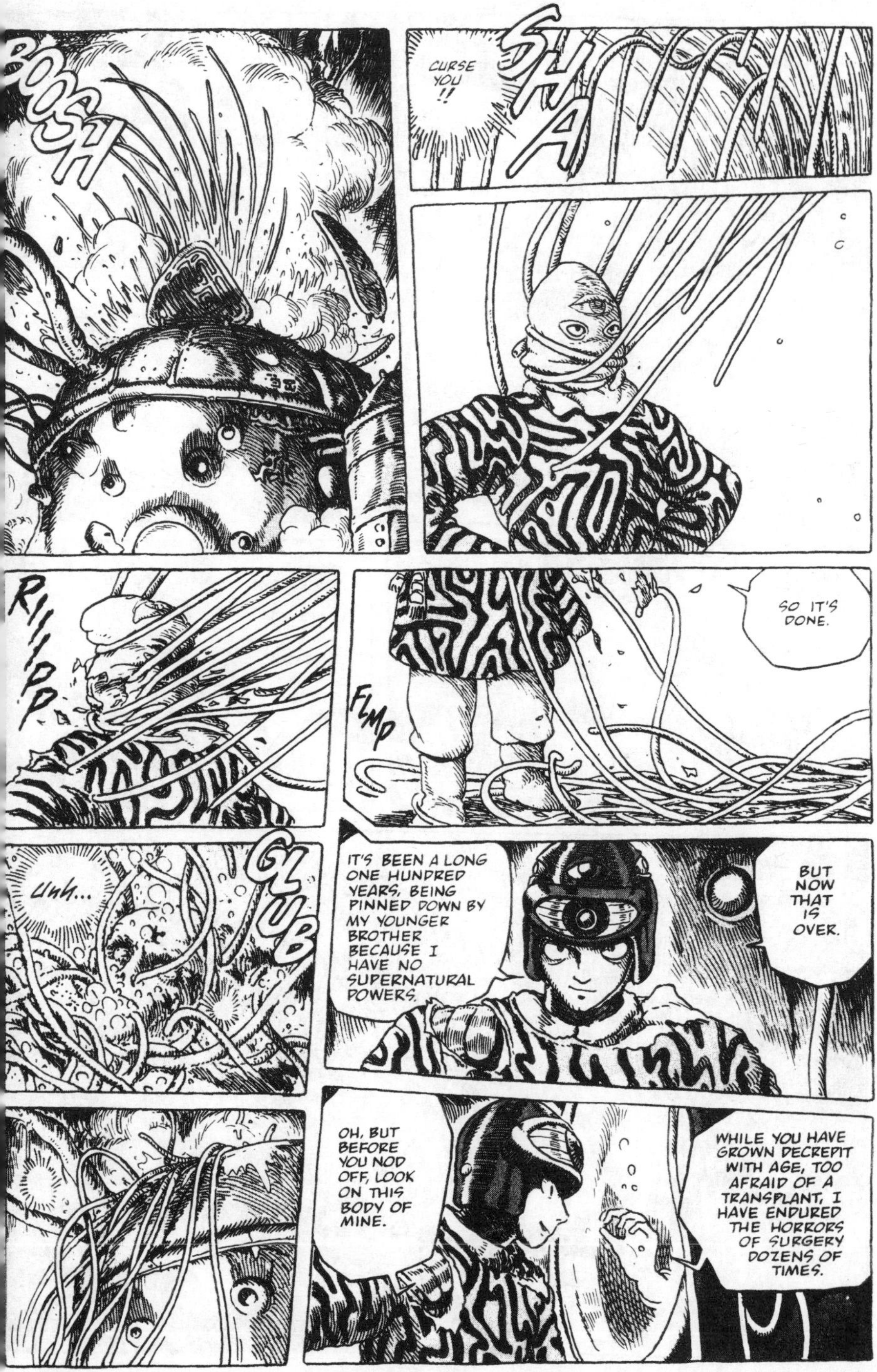
BOOSH
CURSE YOU !!
SHAA
RIIIPP
FLMP
SO IT'S DONE.
GLUB
unh...
IT'S BEEN A LONG ONE HUNDRED YEARS, BEING PINNED DOWN BY MY YOUNGER BROTHER BECAUSE I HAVE NO SUPERNATURAL POWERS.
BUT NOW THAT IS OVER.
OH, BUT BEFORE YOU NOD OFF, LOOK ON THIS BODY OF MINE.
WHILE YOU HAVE GROWN DECREPIT WITH AGE, TOO AFRAID OF A TRANSPLANT, I HAVE ENDURED THE HORRORS OF SURGERY DOZENS OF TIMES.

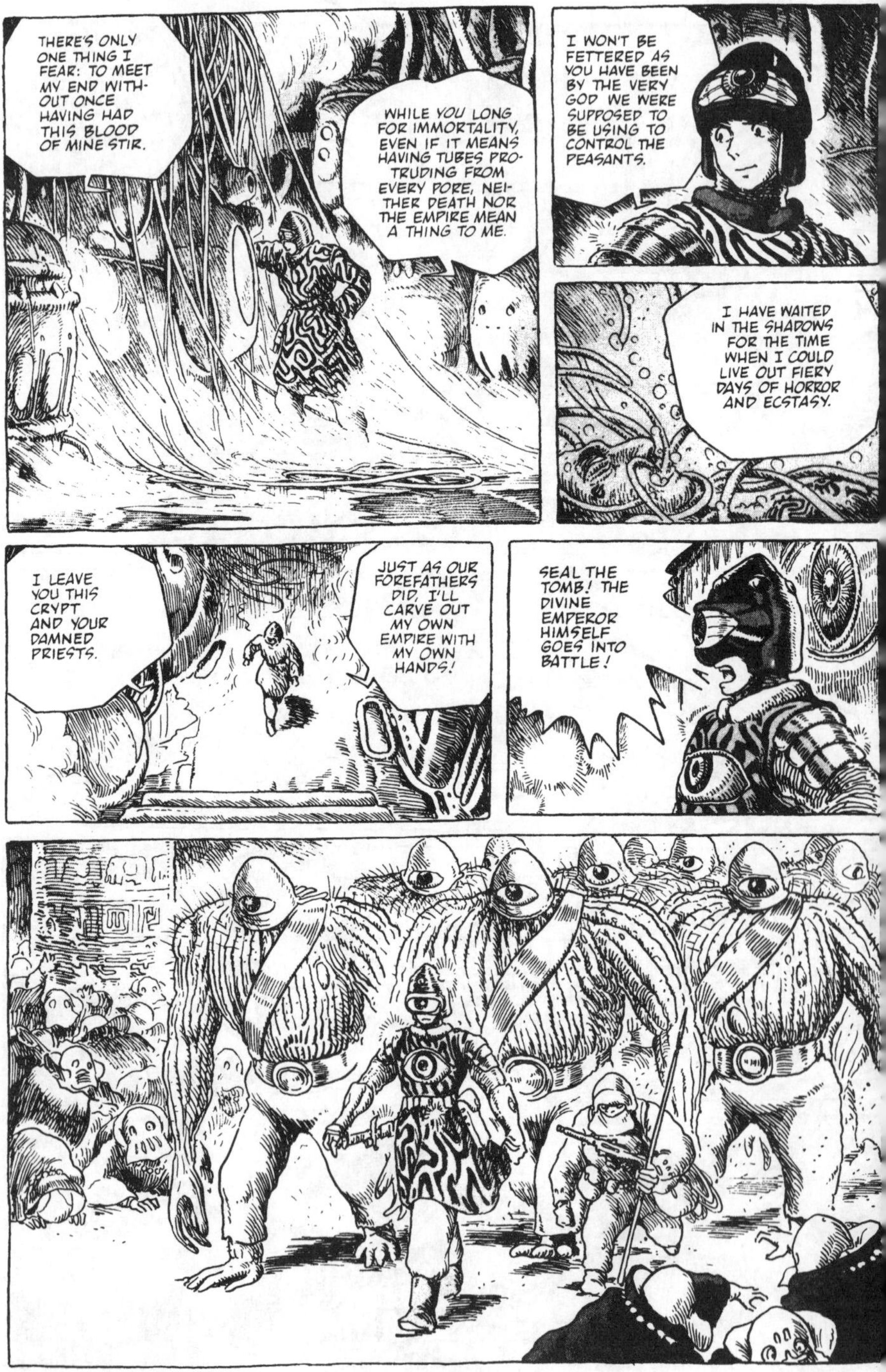
THERE'S ONLY ONE THING I FEAR: TO MEET MY END WITH-OUT ONCE HAVING HAD THIS BLOOD OF MINE STIR.
WHILE YOU LONG FOR IMMORTALITY, EVEN IF IT MEANS HAVING TUBES PRO-TRUDING FROM EVERY PORE, NEI-THER DEATH NOR THE EMPIRE MEAN A THING TO ME.
I WON'T BE FETTERED AS YOU HAVE BEEN BY THE VERY GOD WE WERE SUPPOSED TO BE USING TO CONTROL THE PEASANTS.
I HAVE WAITED IN THE SHADOWS FOR THE TIME WHEN I COULD LIVE OUT FIERY DAYS OF HORROR AND ECSTASY.
I LEAVE YOU THIS CRYPT AND YOUR DAMNED PRIESTS.
JUST AS OUR FOREFATHERS DID, I'LL CARVE OUT MY OWN EMPIRE WITH MY OWN HANDS!
SEAL THE TOMB! THE DIVINE EMPEROR HIMSELF GOES INTO BATTLE!

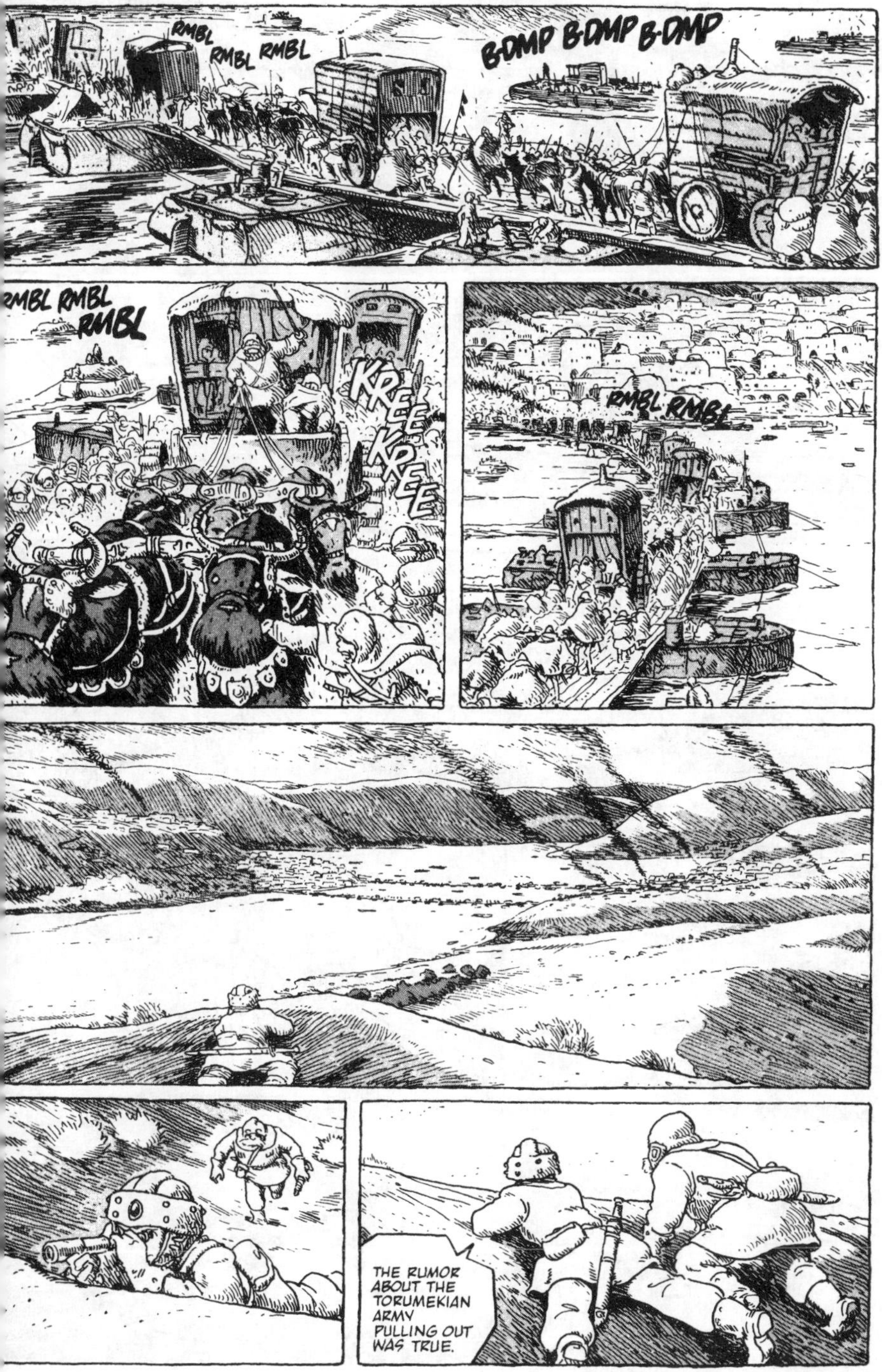
RMBL
RMBL RMBL
B-DMP B-DMP B-DMP
RMBL RMBL
RMBL
KREEE
KREEE
RMBL RMBL
THE RUMOR ABOUT THE TORUMEKIAN ARMY PULLING OUT WAS TRUE.

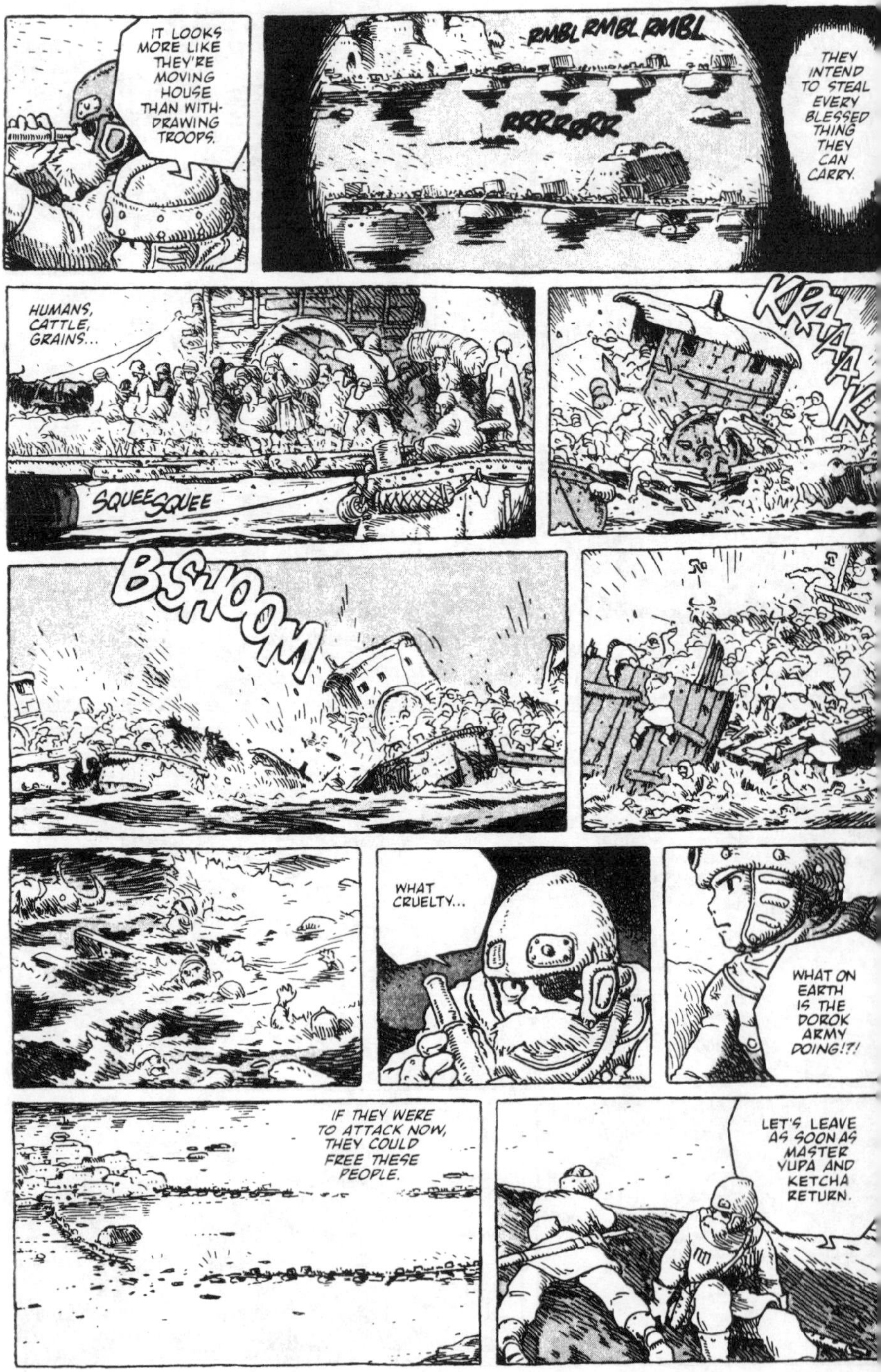
IT LOOKS MORE LIKE THEY'RE MOVING HOUSE THAN WITH-DRAWING TROOPS.
RMBL RMBL RMBL
RRRRRRR
THEY INTEND TO STEAL EVERY BLESSED THING THEY CAN CARRY.
HUMANS, CATTLE, GRAINS...
SQUEE SQUEE
KRAAAK
BSHOOM
WHAT CRUELTY...
WHAT ON EARTH IS THE DOROK ARMY DOING!?!
IF THEY WERE TO ATTACK NOW, THEY COULD FREE THESE PEOPLE.
LET'S LEAVE AS SOON AS MASTER YUPA AND KETCHA RETURN.

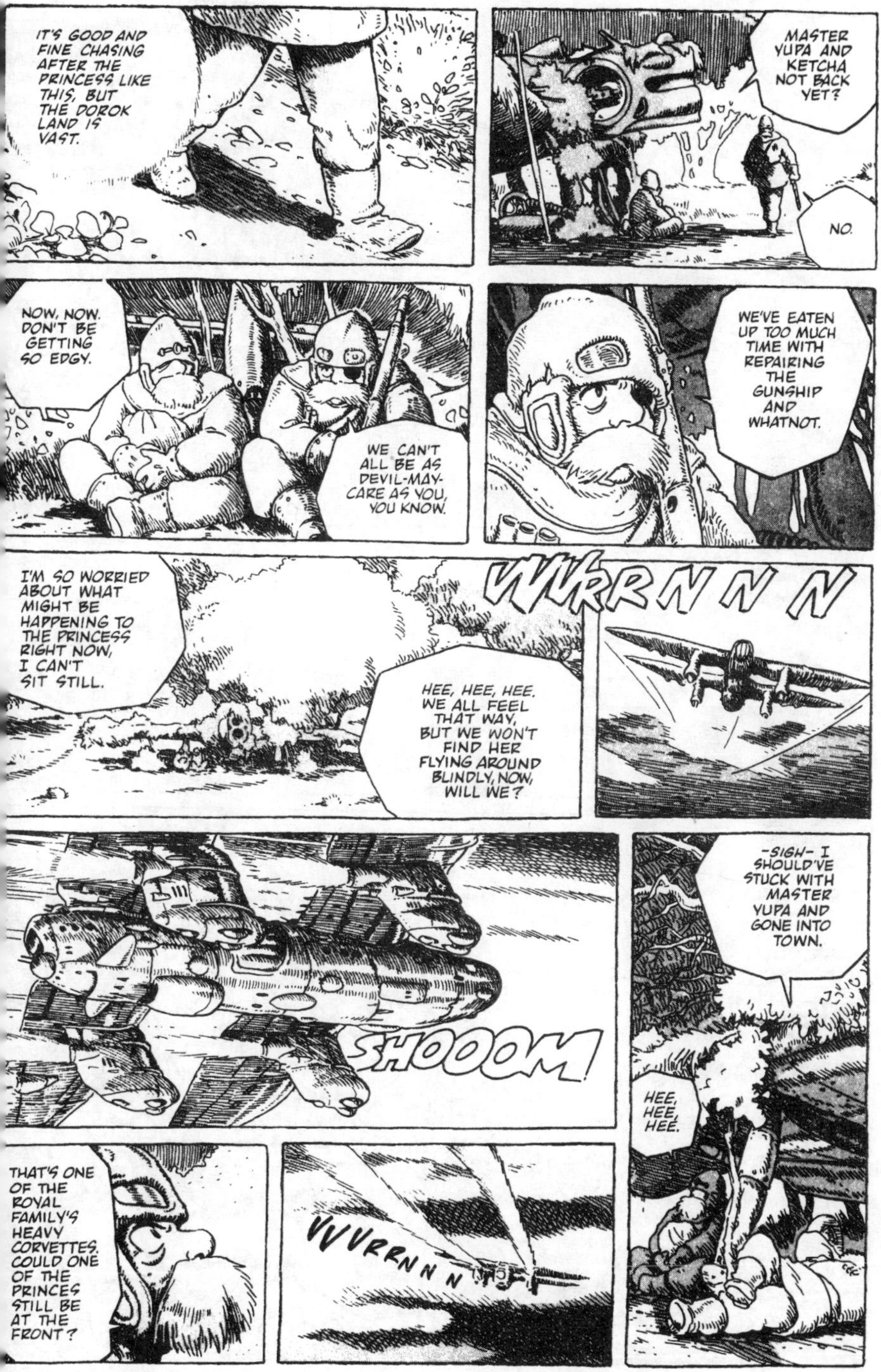
IT'S GOOD AND FINE CHASING AFTER THE PRINCESS LIKE THIS, BUT THE DOROK LAND IS VAST.
MASTER YUPA AND KETCHA NOT BACK YET?
NO.
NOW, NOW. DON'T BE GETTING SO EDGY.
WE CAN'T ALL BE AS DEVIL-MAY-CARE AS YOU, YOU KNOW.
WE'VE EATEN UP TOO MUCH TIME WITH REPAIRING THE GUNSHIP AND WHATNOT.
I'M SO WORRIED ABOUT WHAT MIGHT BE HAPPENING TO THE PRINCESS RIGHT NOW, I CAN'T SIT STILL.
HEE, HEE, HEE. WE ALL FEEL THAT WAY, BUT WE WON'T FIND HER FLYING AROUND BLINDLY, NOW, WILL WE?
VVURRNNN
SHOOOM
-SIGH- I SHOULD'VE STUCK WITH MASTER YUPA AND GONE INTO TOWN.
HEE, HEE, HEE.
THAT'S ONE OF THE ROYAL FAMILY'S HEAVY CORVETTES. COULD ONE OF THE PRINCES STILL BE AT THE FRONT?
VVURRNNN

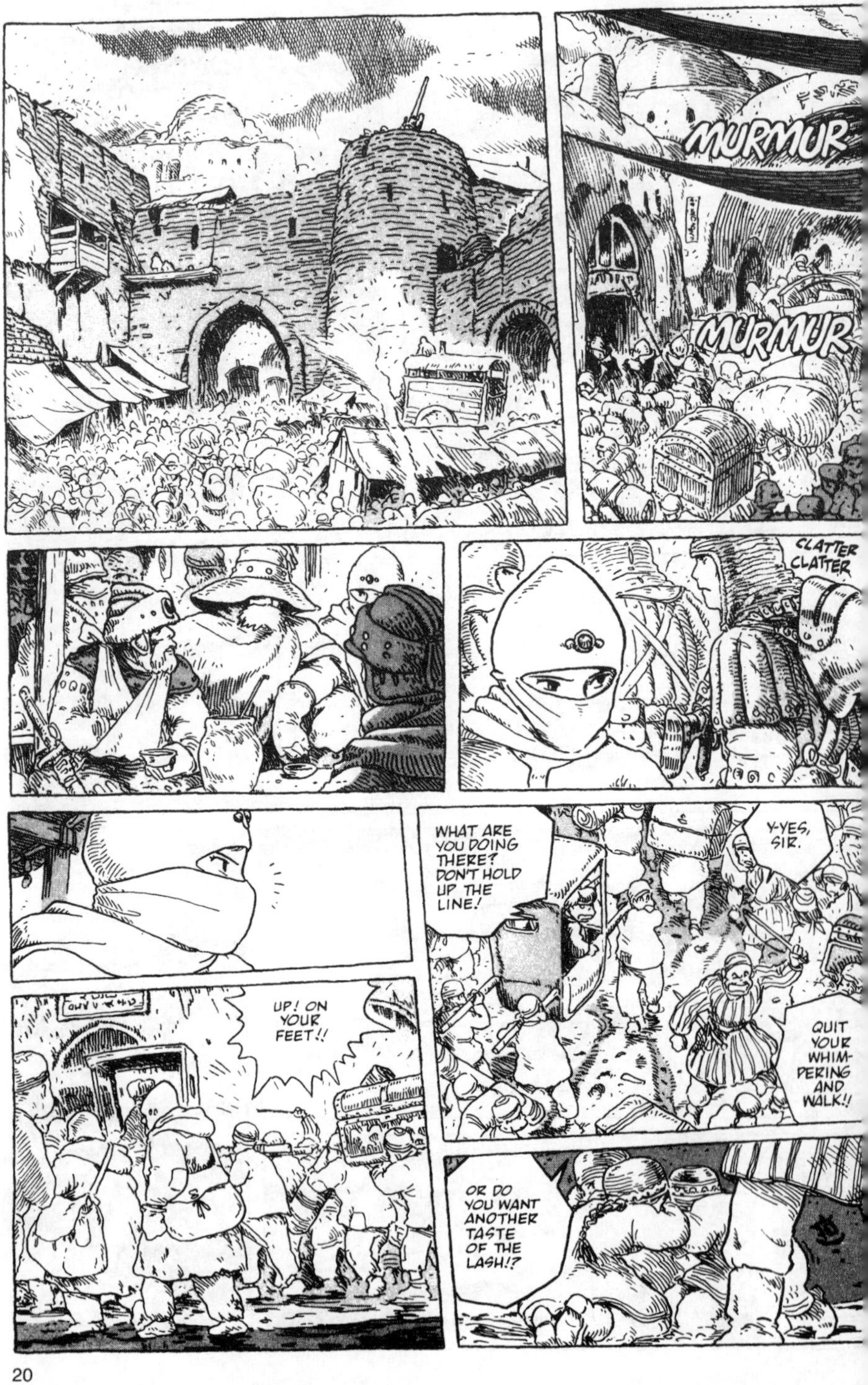
MURMUR
MURMUR
CLATTER CLATTER
WHAT ARE YOU DOING THERE? DON'T HOLD UP THE LINE!
Y-YES, SIR.
QUIT YOUR WHIMPERING AND WALK!!
UP! ON YOUR FEET!!
OR DO YOU WANT ANOTHER TASTE OF THE LASH!?

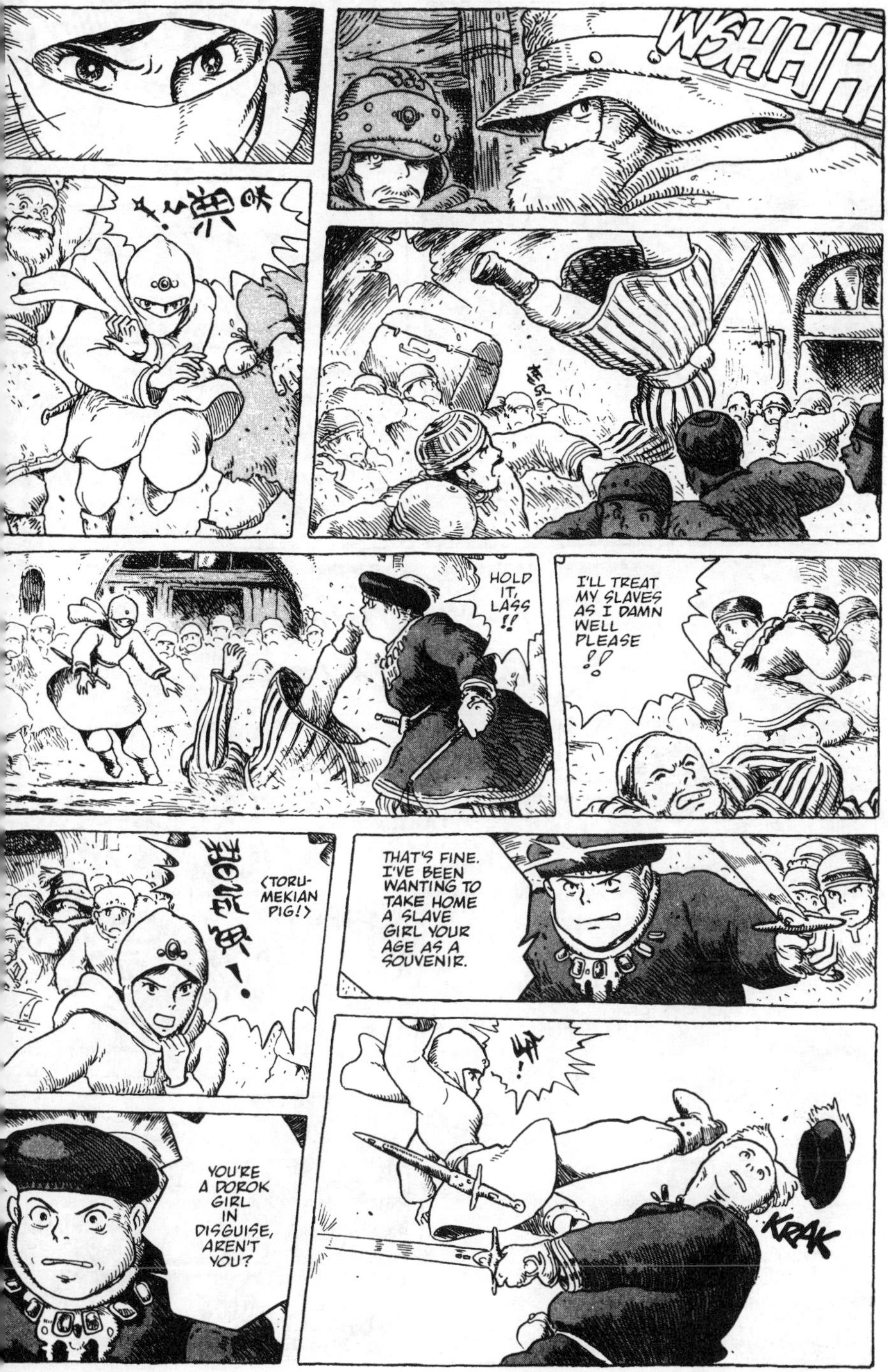
WSHHH
HOLD IT, LASS!!
I'LL TREAT MY SLAVES AS I DAMN WELL PLEASE!!
<TORU-MEKIAN PIG!>
THAT'S FINE. I'VE BEEN WANTING TO TAKE HOME A SLAVE GIRL YOUR AGE AS A SOUVENIR.
YOU'RE A DOROK GIRL IN DISGUISE, AREN'T YOU?
KRAK

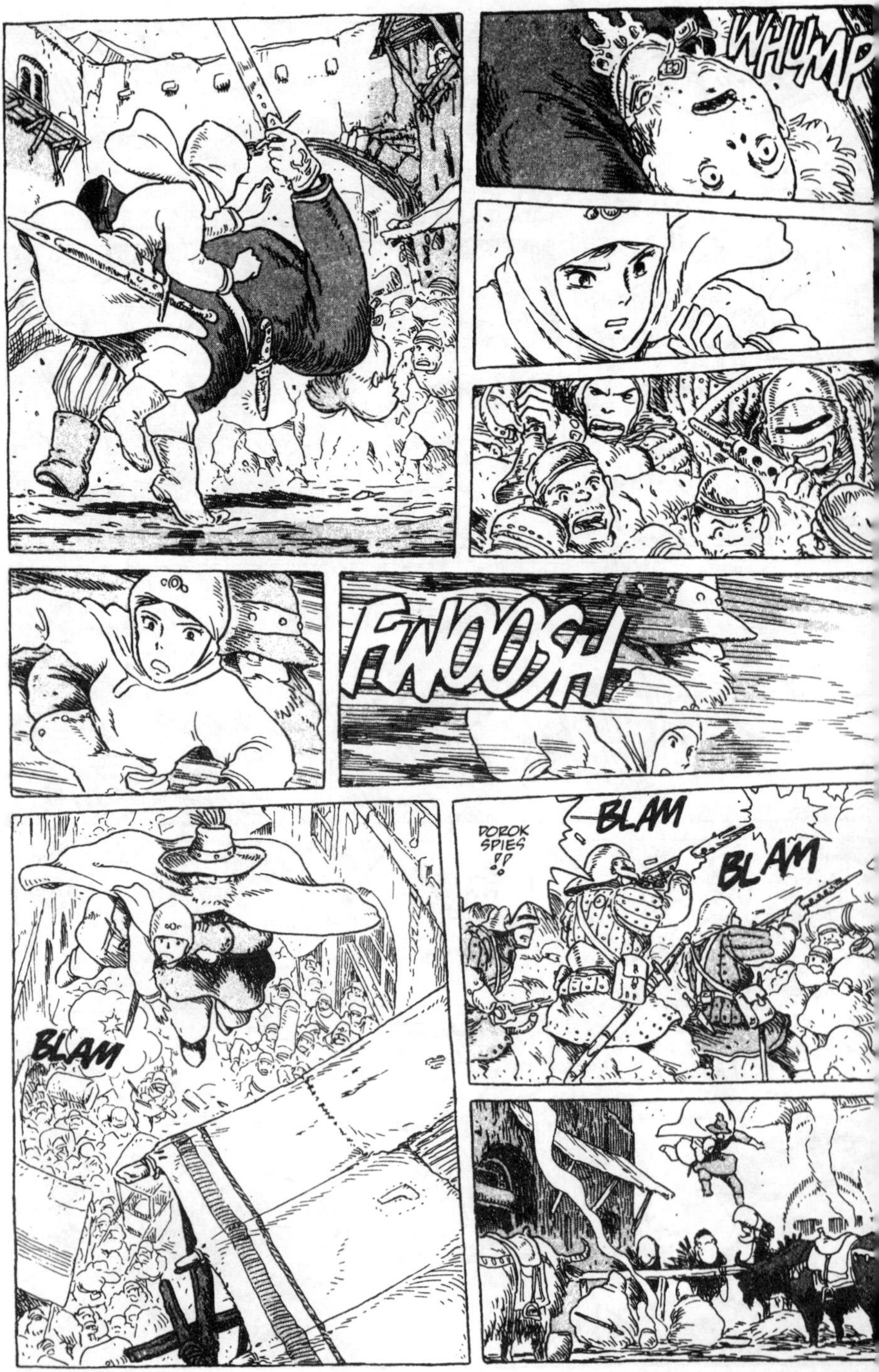
WHUMP
FWOOSH
BLAM
DOROK SPIES !!
BLAM
BLAM

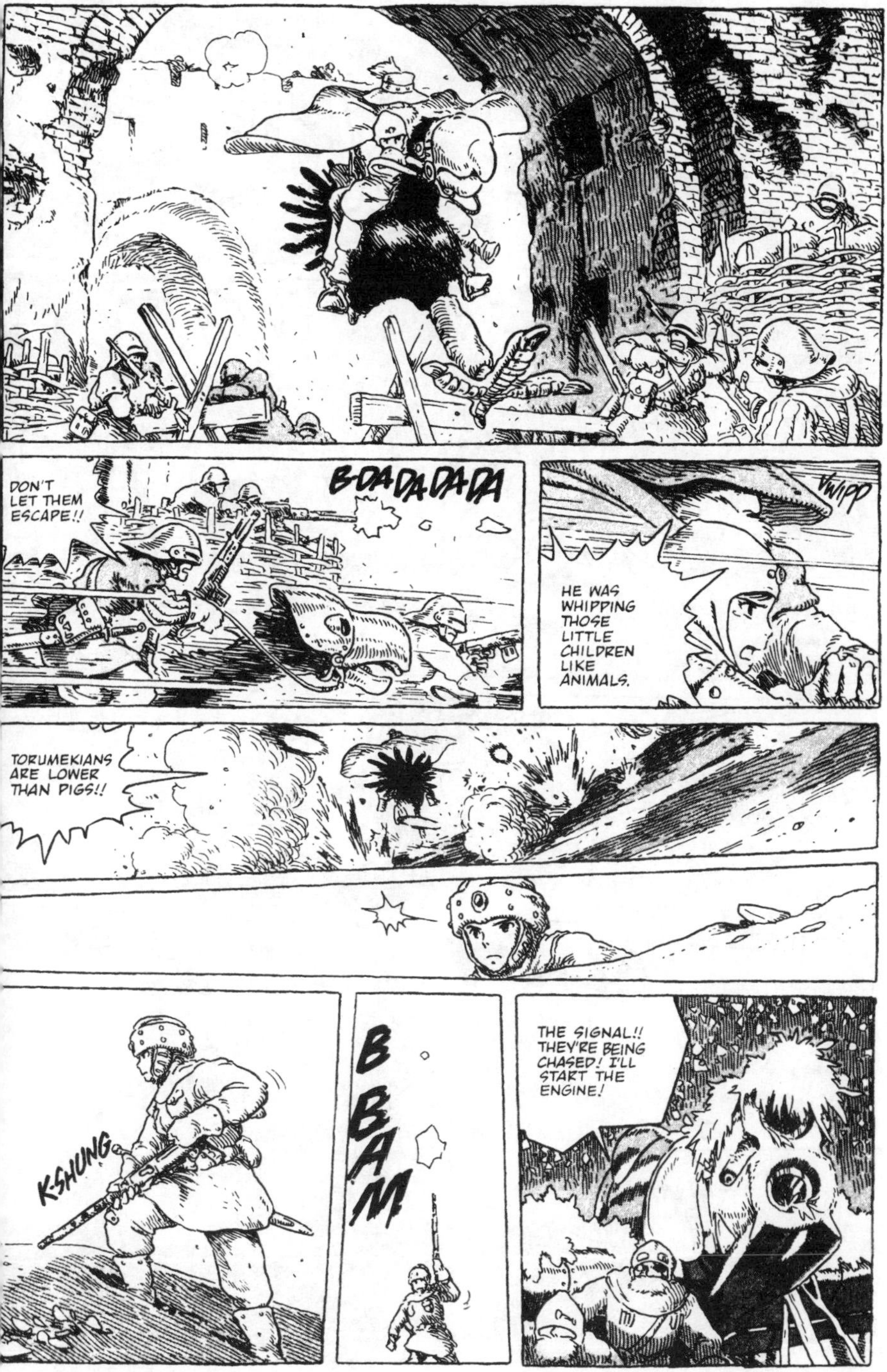
DON'T LET THEM ESCAPE!!
B-DA DA DA DA
VWIPP
HE WAS WHIPPING THOSE LITTLE CHILDREN LIKE ANIMALS.
TORUMEKIANS ARE LOWER THAN PIGS!!
K-SHUNG
B BAM
THE SIGNAL!! THEY'RE BEING CHASED! I'LL START THE ENGINE!

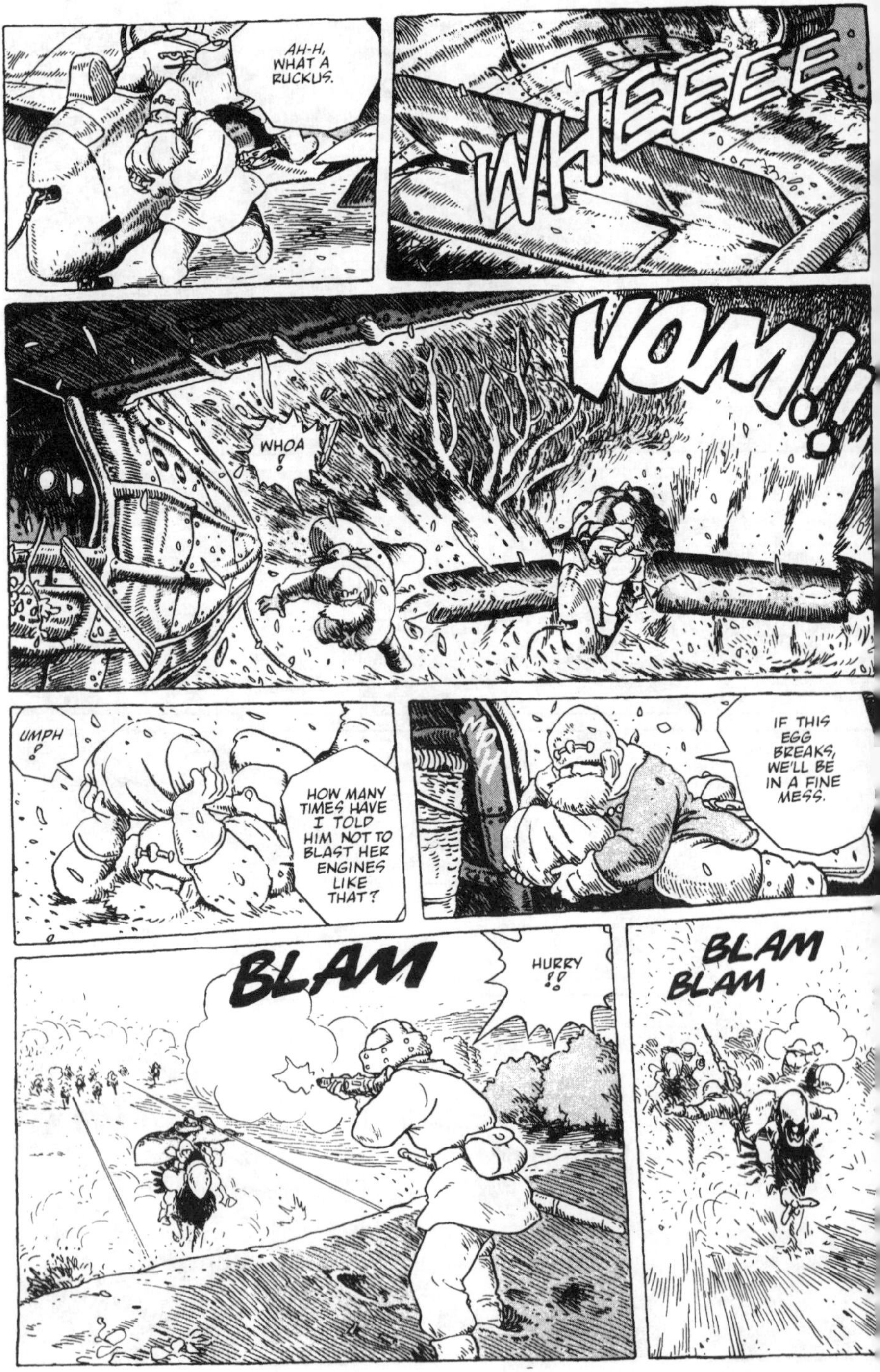
AH-H, WHAT A RUCKUS.
WHEEEEE
VOM!!
WHOA!
UMPH!
HOW MANY TIMES HAVE I TOLD HIM NOT TO BLAST HER ENGINES LIKE THAT?
IF THIS EGG BREAKS, WE'LL BE IN A FINE MESS.
BLAM
HURRY!!
BLAM
BLAM

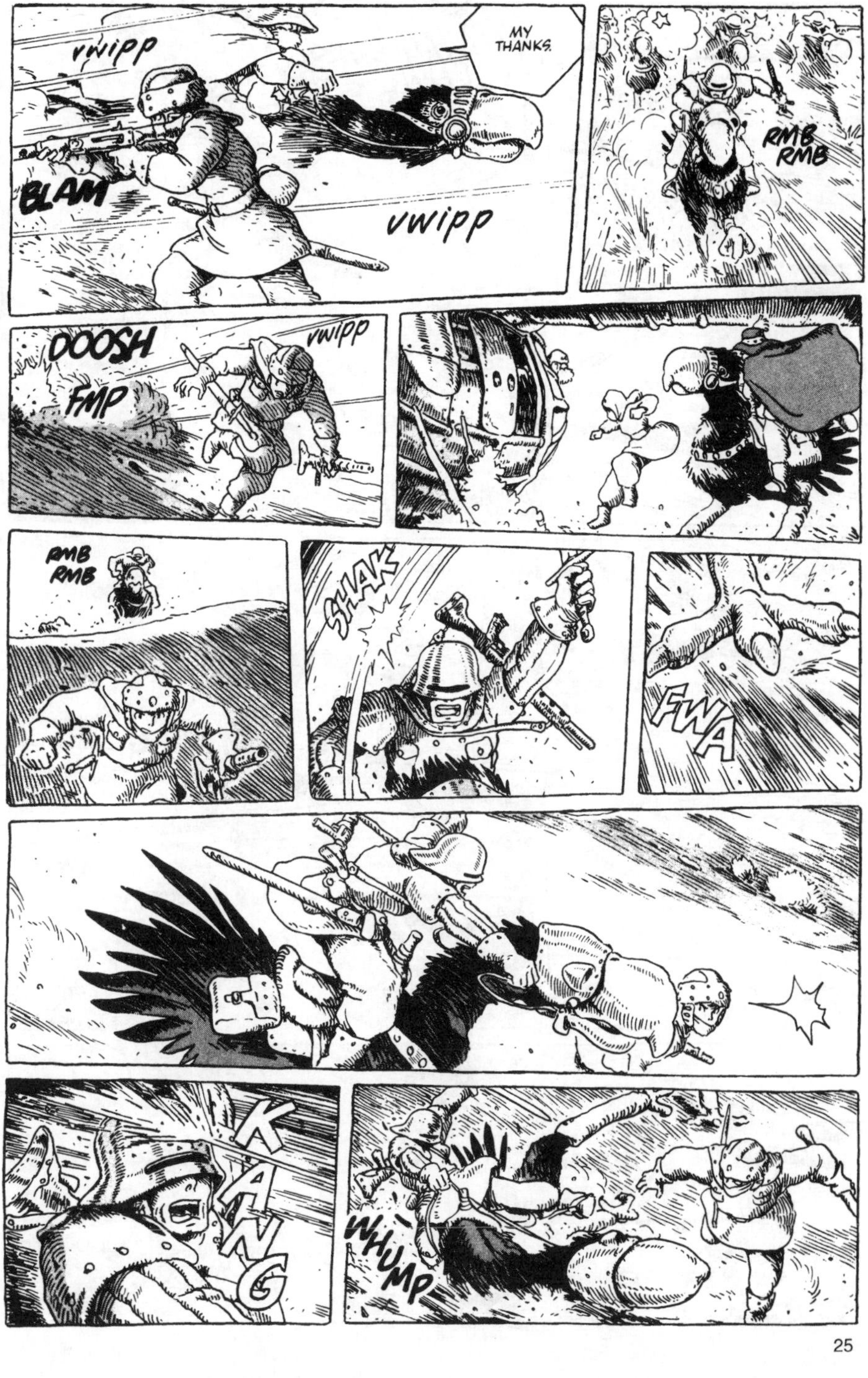
vwipp
MY THANKS.
BLAM
vwipp
RMB RMB
DOOSH
FMP
vwipp
RMB RMB
SHAK
FWA
KANG
WHUMP

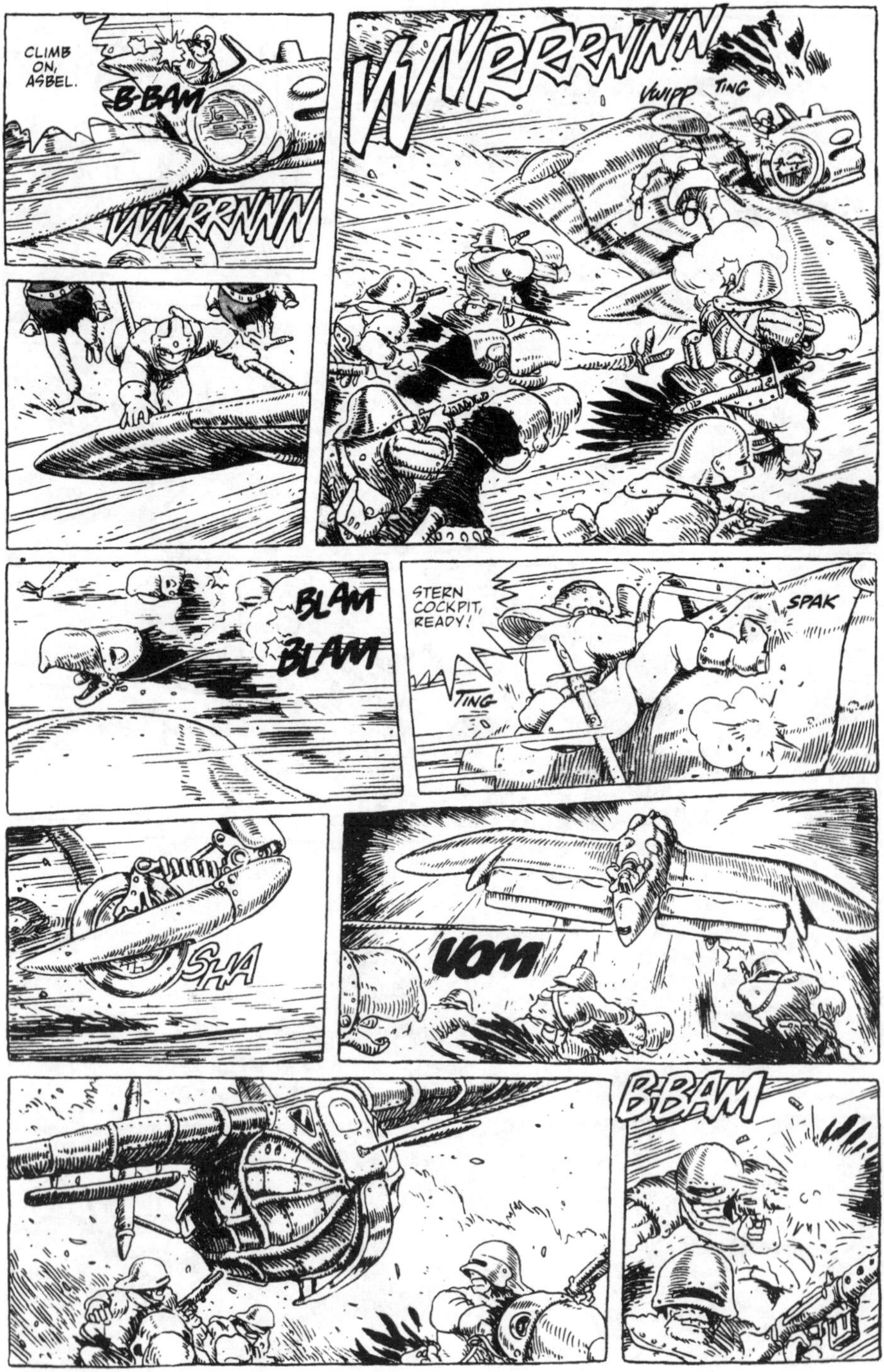
CLIMB ON, ASBEL.
B-BAM
VVVRRRNNN
VVVRRRNNNN
VWIPP
TING
BLAM
BLAM
STERN COCKPIT, READY!
SPAK
TING
SHA
VOM
B-BAM

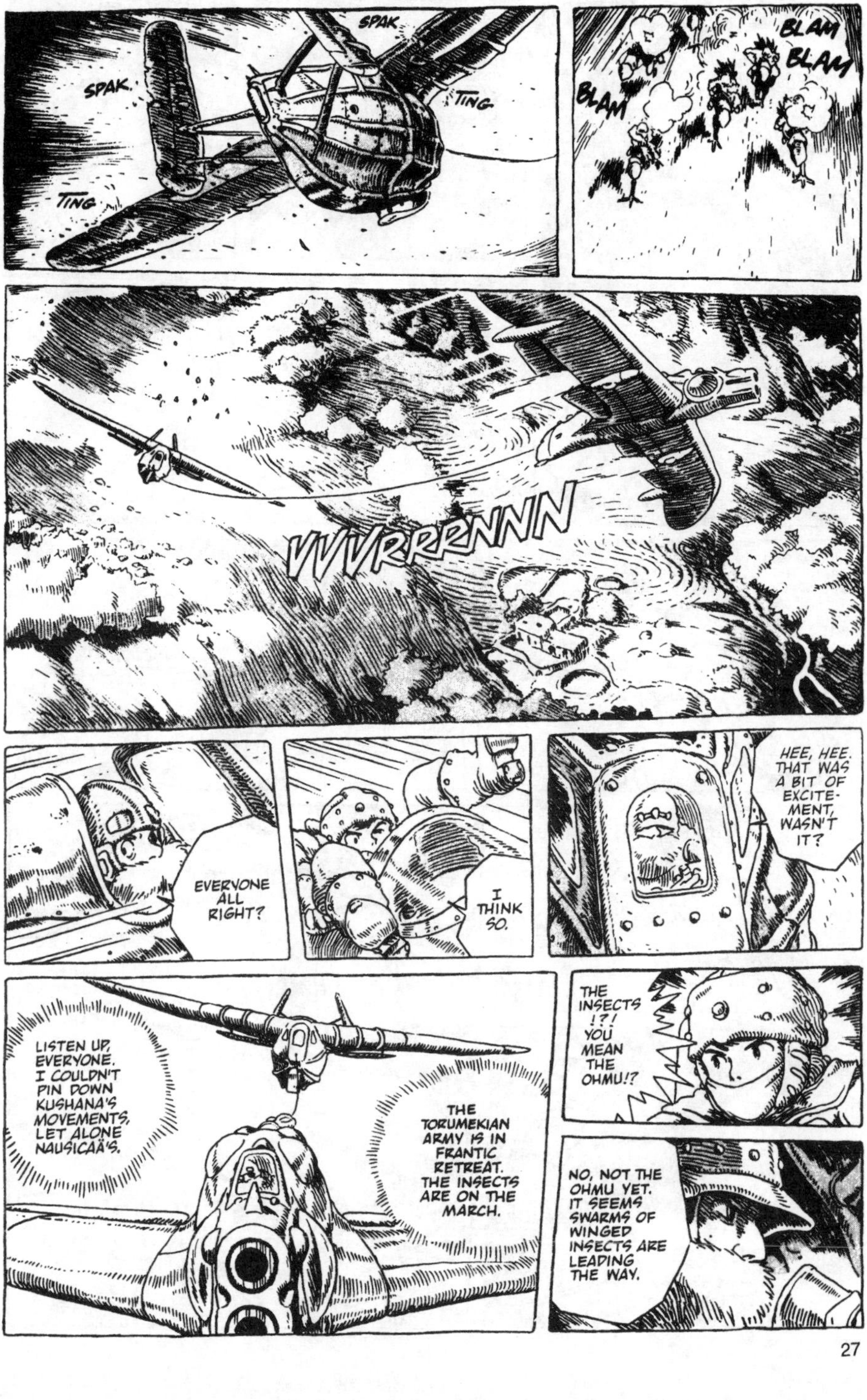
SPAK
SPAK
TING
TING
BLAM
BLAM
BLAM
VVVRRRNNN
EVERYONE ALL RIGHT?
I THINK SO.
HEE, HEE. THAT WAS A BIT OF EXCITE- MENT, WASN'T IT?
LISTEN UP, EVERYONE. I COULDN'T PIN DOWN KUSHANA'S MOVEMENTS, LET ALONE NAUSICAÄ'S.
THE TORUMEKIAN ARMY IS IN FRANTIC RETREAT. THE INSECTS ARE ON THE MARCH.
THE INSECTS!?! YOU MEAN THE OHMU!?
NO, NOT THE OHMU YET. IT SEEMS SWARMS OF WINGED INSECTS ARE LEADING THE WAY.

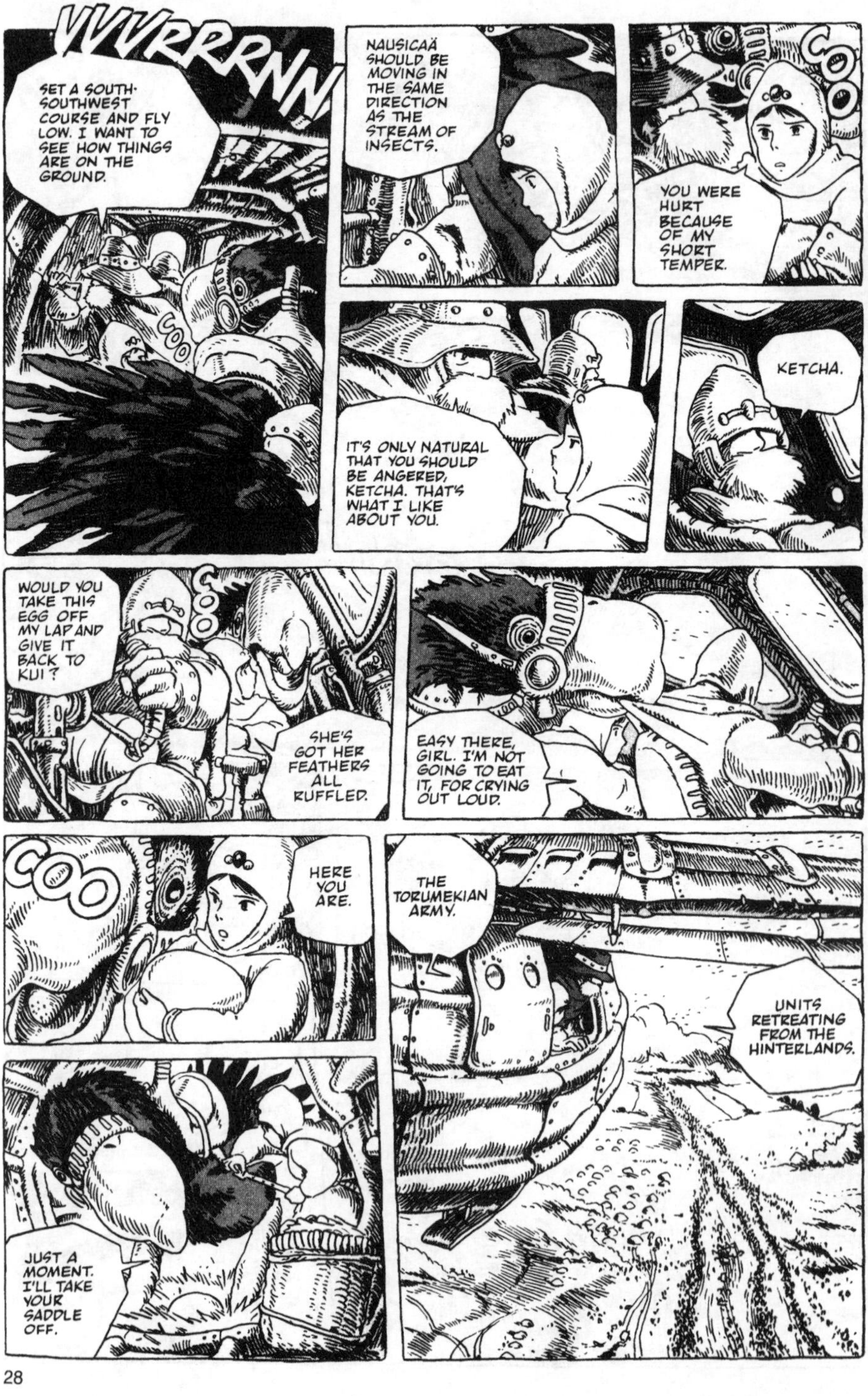
VVVRRRNN
SET A SOUTH-SOUTHWEST COURSE AND FLY LOW. I WANT TO SEE HOW THINGS ARE ON THE GROUND.
COO
NAUSICAÄ SHOULD BE MOVING IN THE SAME DIRECTION AS THE STREAM OF INSECTS.
COO
YOU WERE HURT BECAUSE OF MY SHORT TEMPER.
IT'S ONLY NATURAL THAT YOU SHOULD BE ANGERED, KETCHA. THAT'S WHAT I LIKE ABOUT YOU.
KETCHA.
WOULD YOU TAKE THIS EGG OFF MY LAP AND GIVE IT BACK TO KUI?
COO
SHE'S GOT HER FEATHERS ALL RUFFLED.
EASY THERE, GIRL. I'M NOT GOING TO EAT IT, FOR CRYING OUT LOUD.
COO
HERE YOU ARE.
JUST A MOMENT. I'LL TAKE YOUR SADDLE OFF.
THE TORUMEKIAN ARMY.
UNITS RETREATING FROM THE HINTERLANDS.

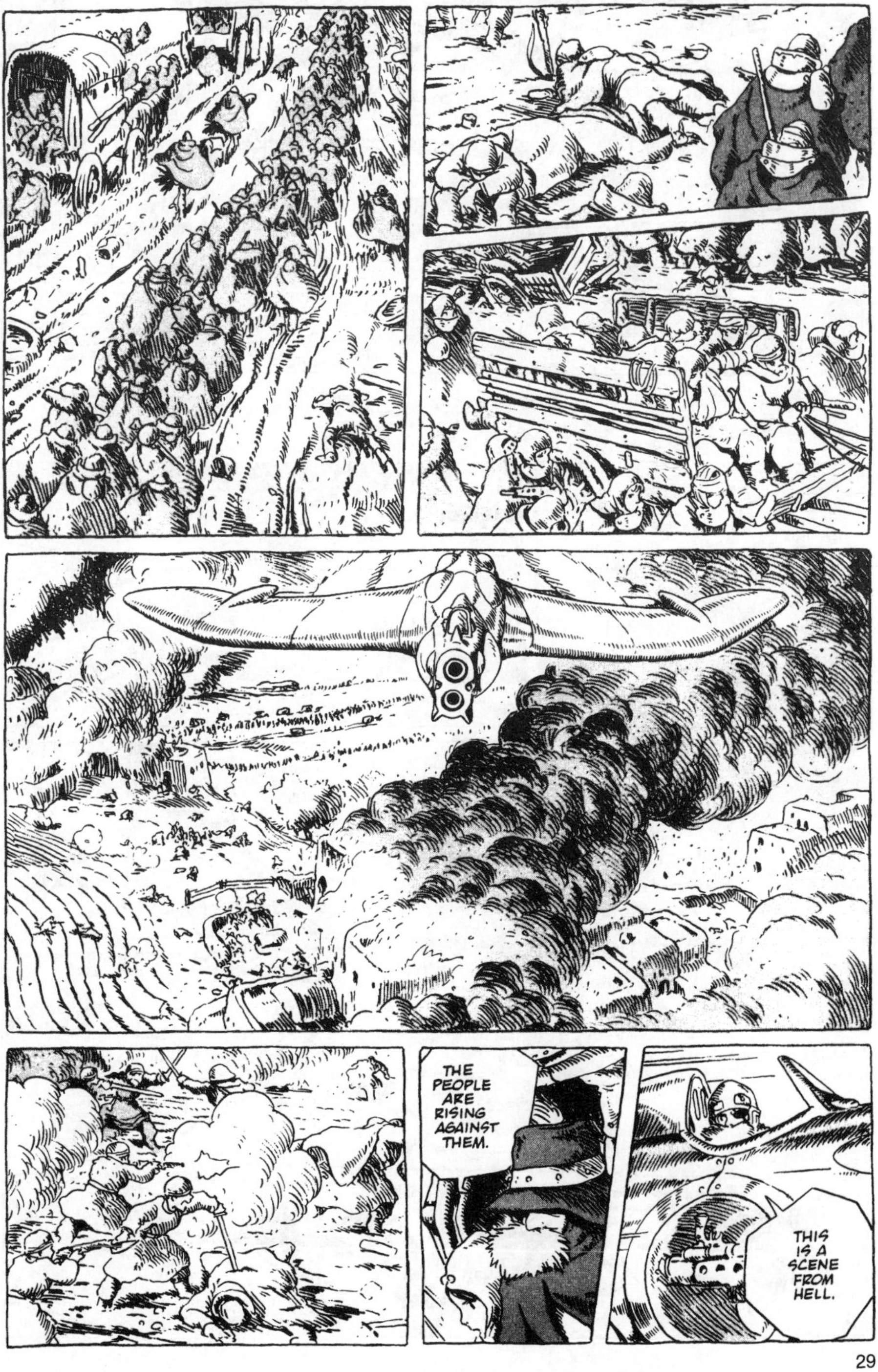
THE PEOPLE ARE RISING AGAINST THEM.
THIS IS A SCENE FROM HELL.

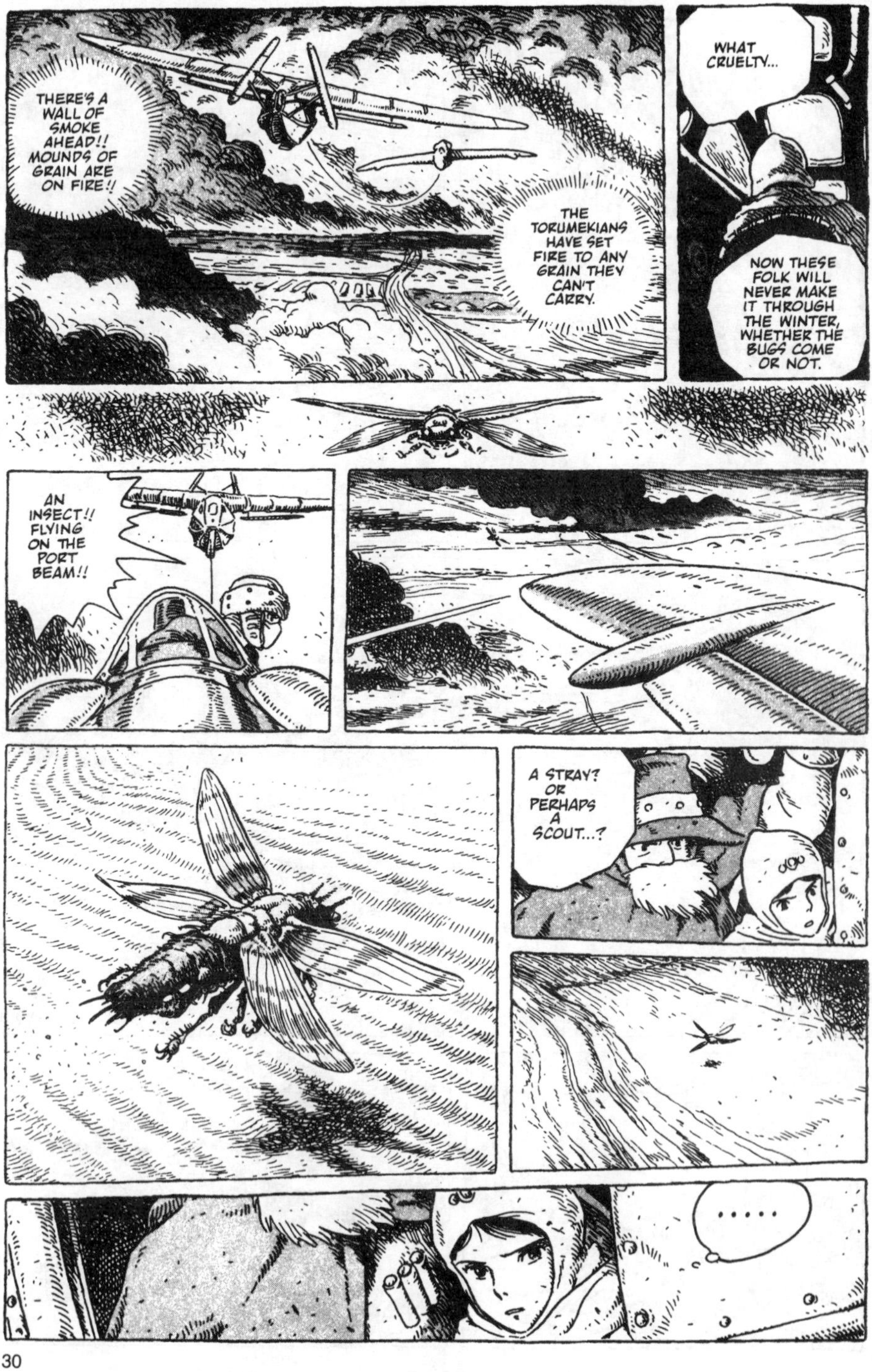
THERE'S A WALL OF SMOKE AHEAD!! MOUNDS OF GRAIN ARE ON FIRE!!
THE TORUMEKIANS HAVE SET FIRE TO ANY GRAIN THEY CAN'T CARRY.
WHAT CRUELTY...
NOW THESE FOLK WILL NEVER MAKE IT THROUGH THE WINTER, WHETHER THE BUGS COME OR NOT.
AN INSECT!! FLYING ON THE PORT BEAM!!
A STRAY? OR PERHAPS A SCOUT...?
......

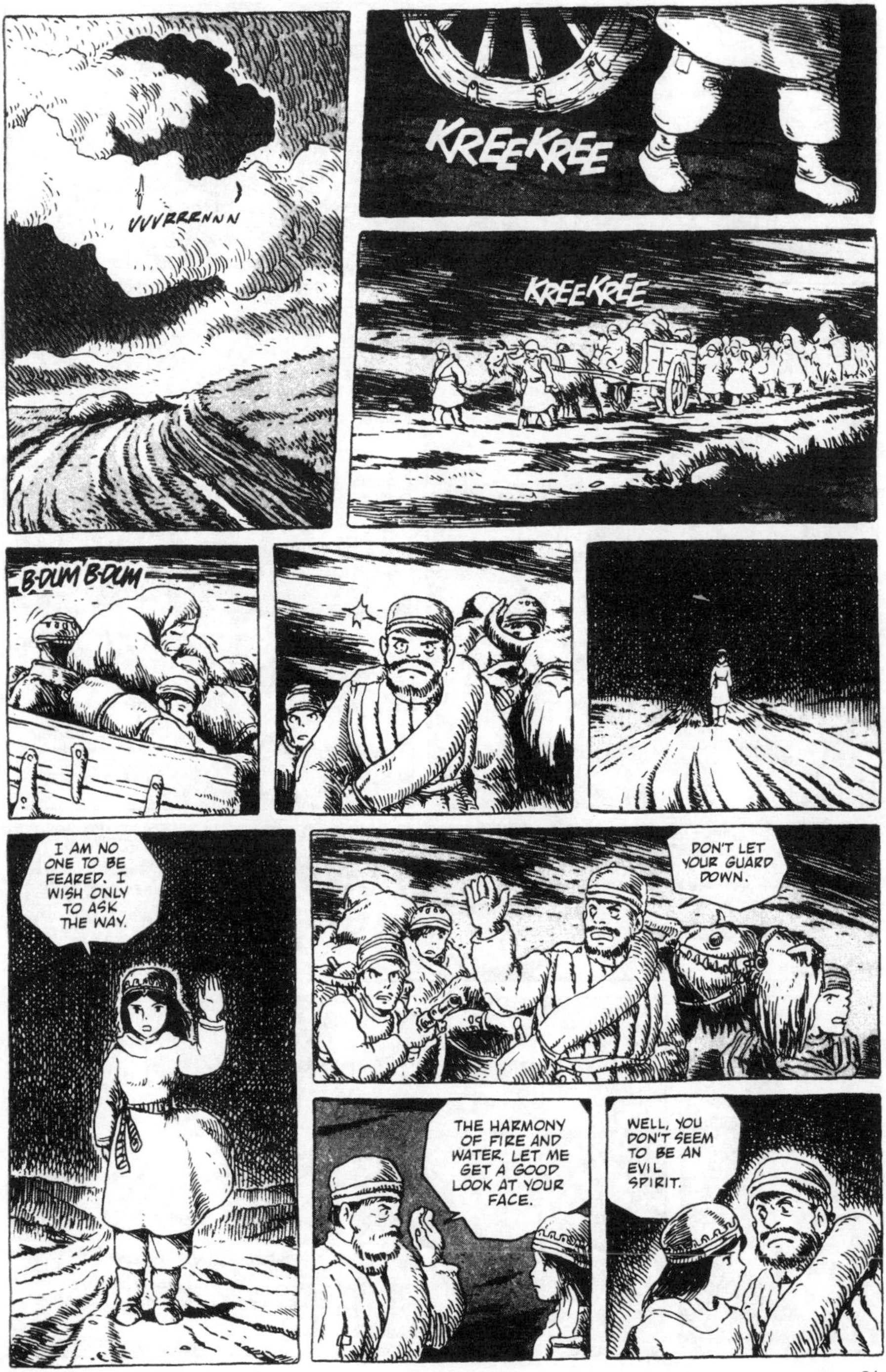
VUVRRRNNN
KREEKREE
KREEKREE
B-DUM B-DUM
I AM NO ONE TO BE FEARED. I WISH ONLY TO ASK THE WAY.
DON'T LET YOUR GUARD DOWN.
THE HARMONY OF FIRE AND WATER. LET ME GET A GOOD LOOK AT YOUR FACE.
WELL, YOU DON'T SEEM TO BE AN EVIL SPIRIT.

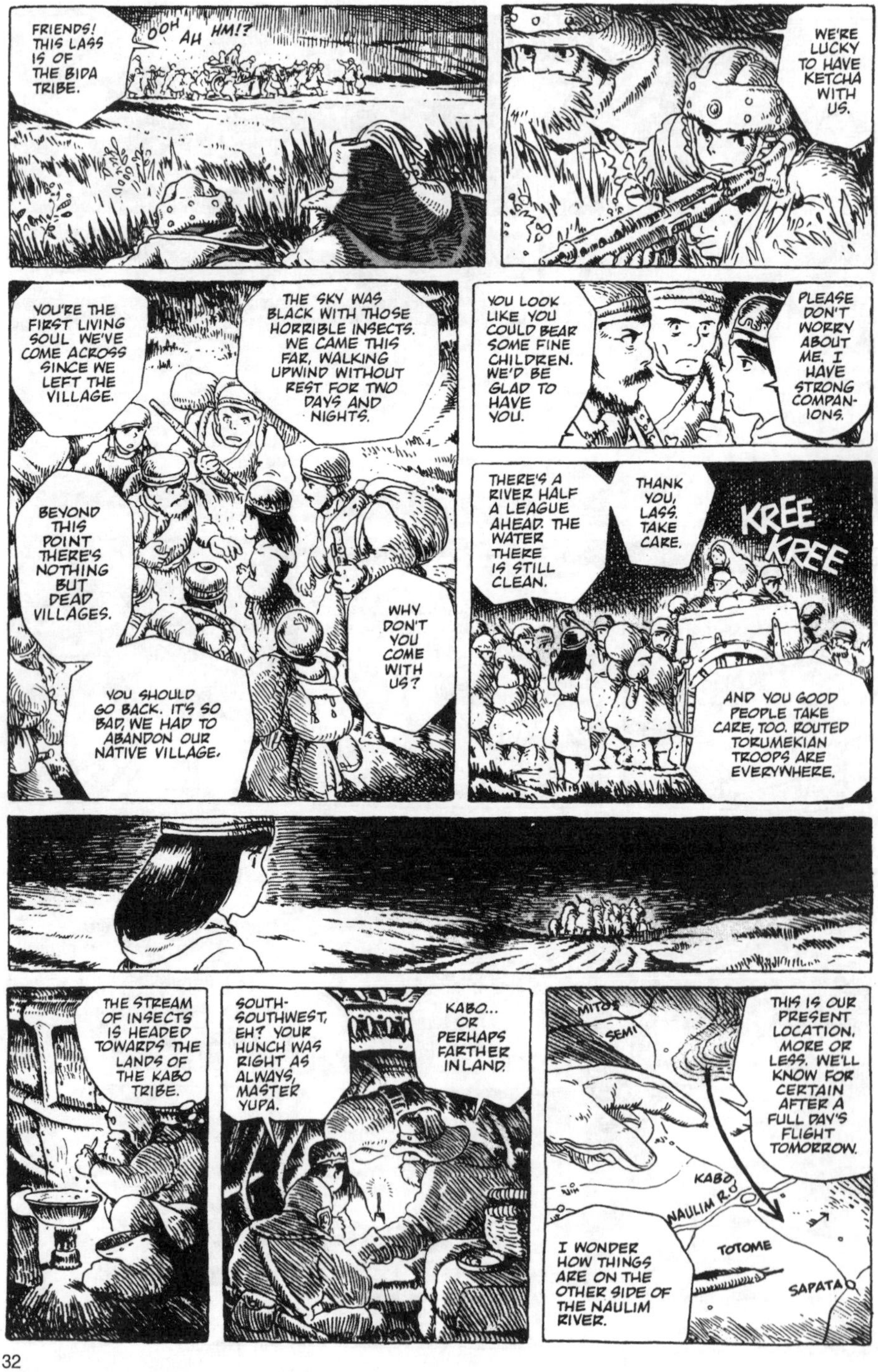
FRIENDS! THIS LASS IS OF THE BIDA TRIBE.
OOH
AH
HM!?
WE'RE LUCKY TO HAVE KETCHA WITH US.
YOU'RE THE FIRST LIVING SOUL WE'VE COME ACROSS SINCE WE LEFT THE VILLAGE.
THE SKY WAS BLACK WITH THOSE HORRIBLE INSECTS. WE CAME THIS FAR, WALKING UPWIND WITHOUT REST FOR TWO DAYS AND NIGHTS.
BEYOND THIS POINT THERE'S NOTHING BUT DEAD VILLAGES.
YOU SHOULD GO BACK. IT'S SO BAD, WE HAD TO ABANDON OUR NATIVE VILLAGE.
WHY DON'T YOU COME WITH US?
YOU LOOK LIKE YOU COULD BEAR SOME FINE CHILDREN. WE'D BE GLAD TO HAVE YOU.
PLEASE DON'T WORRY ABOUT ME. I HAVE STRONG COMPANIONS.
THERE'S A RIVER HALF A LEAGUE AHEAD. THE WATER THERE IS STILL CLEAN.
THANK YOU, LASS. TAKE CARE.
KREE KREE
AND YOU GOOD PEOPLE TAKE CARE, TOO. ROUTED TORUMEKIAN TROOPS ARE EVERYWHERE.
THE STREAM OF INSECTS IS HEADED TOWARDS THE LANDS OF THE KABO TRIBE.
SOUTH-SOUTHWEST, EH? YOUR HUNCH WAS RIGHT AS ALWAYS, MASTER YUPA.
KABO... OR PERHAPS FARTHER INLAND.
THIS IS OUR PRESENT LOCATION, MORE OR LESS. WE'LL KNOW FOR CERTAIN AFTER A FULL DAY'S FLIGHT TOMORROW.
MITO'S
SEMI
KABO
NAULIM R.
TOTOME
SAPATA
I WONDER HOW THINGS ARE ON THE OTHER SIDE OF THE NAULIM RIVER.

THOSE PEOPLE WERE CARRYING CAREFULLY WRAPPED SEED STOCK FOR CROPS.

THEY SAID THEY WOULD PLANT THEM WHEN THEY HAD FOUND NEW LAND.

BUT NO MATTER WHERE THEY GO...

IT'S TOO LATE TO DO ANYTHING AT ALL.

THE PRINCESS SAW FAR BEYOND WHAT WE COULD HAVE, BUT STILL SHE KEEPS ON FIGHTING.

THAT SMELLS SO GOOD I CAN BARELY STAND IT!

HEE, HEE, HEE. ALWAYS READY TO EAT, EH? AH, YOUTH.

VVVRRRNNN

ONE HOUR TO THE NAULIM RIVER. WE'VE ENTERED THE KABO LANDS.

BRING US UP, EVERYONE! PUT YOUR MASKS ON.

C-COO

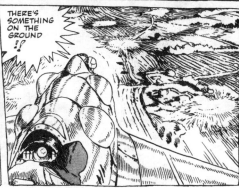
THERE'S SOMETHING ON THE GROUND !?

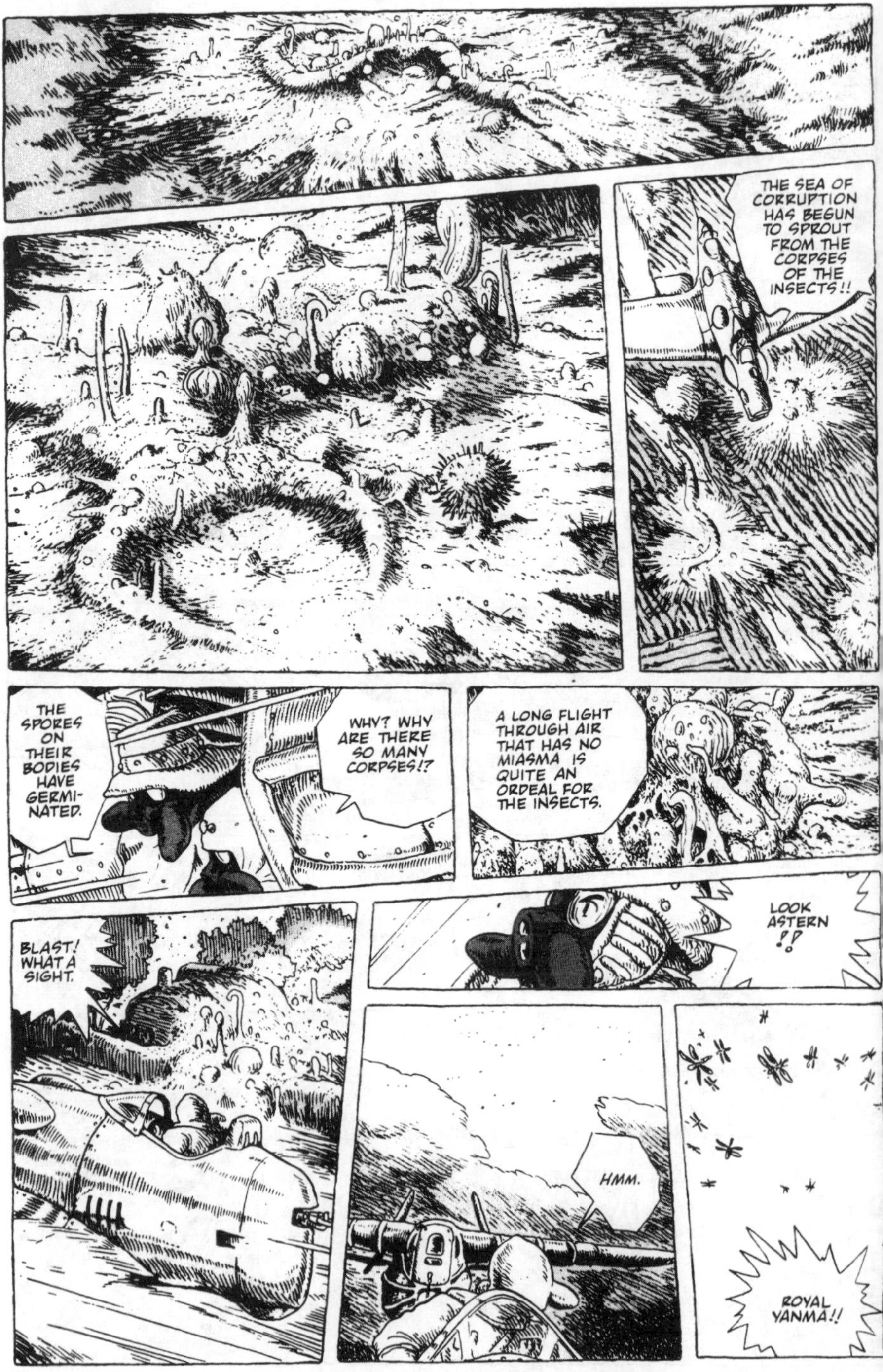
THE SEA OF CORRUPTION HAS BEGUN TO SPROUT FROM THE CORPSES OF THE INSECTS!!
THE SPORES ON THEIR BODIES HAVE GERMINATED.
WHY? WHY ARE THERE SO MANY CORPSES!?
A LONG FLIGHT THROUGH AIR THAT HAS NO MIASMA IS QUITE AN ORDEAL FOR THE INSECTS.
LOOK ASTERN!?
BLAST! WHAT A SIGHT.
HMM.
ROYAL YANMA!!

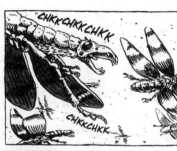

CHKKCHKKCHKK

CHKKCHKK

THEY'VE COME TO WATCH OVER THE NEW FOREST ALREADY.

THEY'RE ON THE GROUND, TOO. DON'T EXCITE THEM.

IT'S THE KABO CASTLE TOWN. BE ON YOUR GUARD.

THERE MIGHT BE SURVIVORS. SLOW HER DOWN.

VVVRRRNNN

THIS IS AWFUL.

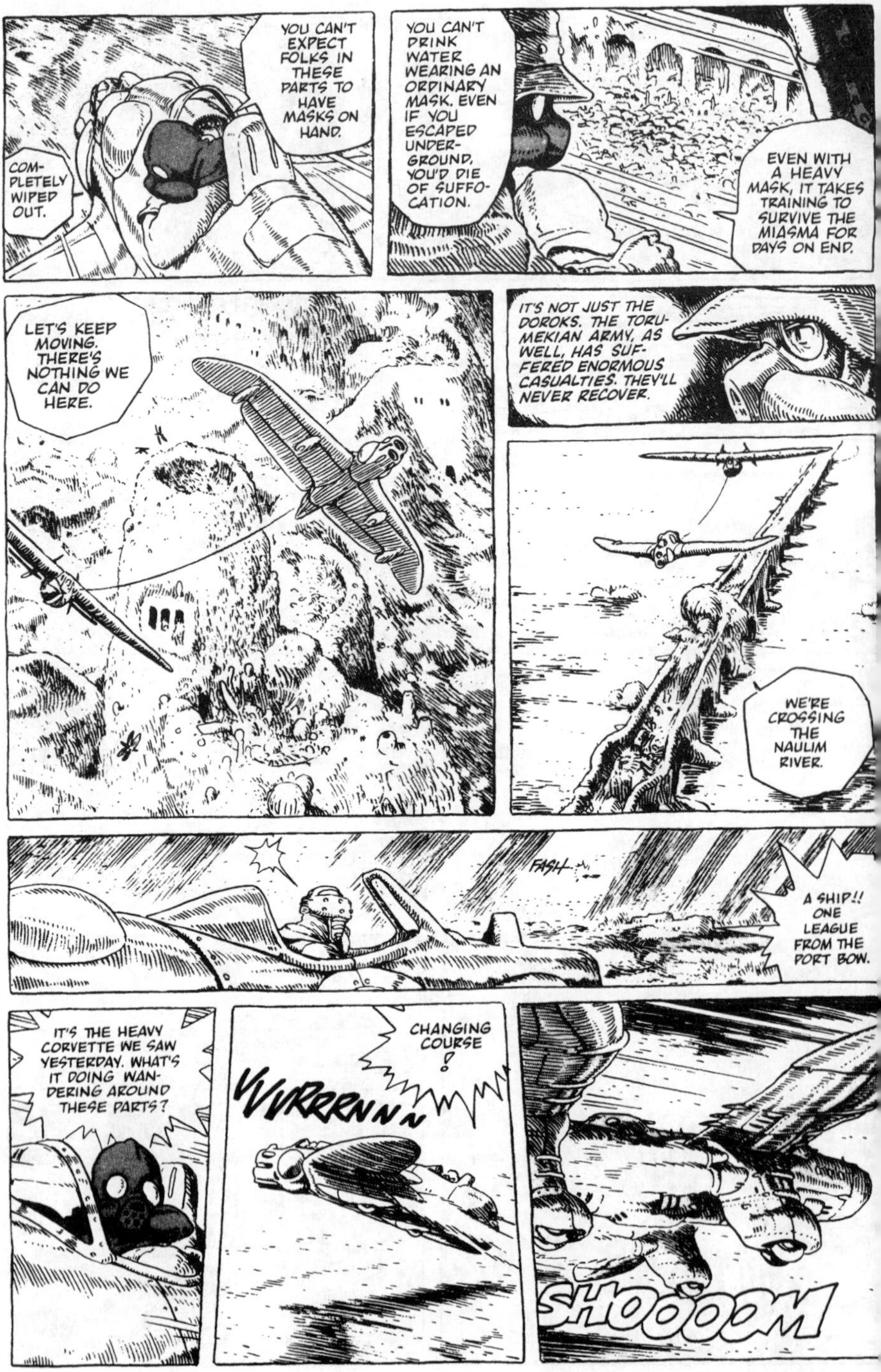
YOU CAN'T EXPECT FOLKS IN THESE PARTS TO HAVE MASKS ON HAND.
COMPLETELY WIPED OUT.
YOU CAN'T DRINK WATER WEARING AN ORDINARY MASK. EVEN IF YOU ESCAPED UNDERGROUND, YOU'D DIE OF SUFFOCATION.
EVEN WITH A HEAVY MASK, IT TAKES TRAINING TO SURVIVE THE MIASMA FOR DAYS ON END.
LET'S KEEP MOVING. THERE'S NOTHING WE CAN DO HERE.
IT'S NOT JUST THE DOROKS. THE TORUMEKIAN ARMY, AS WELL, HAS SUFFERED ENORMOUS CASUALTIES. THEY'LL NEVER RECOVER.
WE'RE CROSSING THE NAULIM RIVER.
FASH
A SHIP!! ONE LEAGUE FROM THE PORT BOW.
IT'S THE HEAVY CORVETTE WE SAW YESTERDAY. WHAT'S IT DOING WANDERING AROUND THESE PARTS?
CHANGING COURSE!
VVVRRRNNN
SHOOOOOM

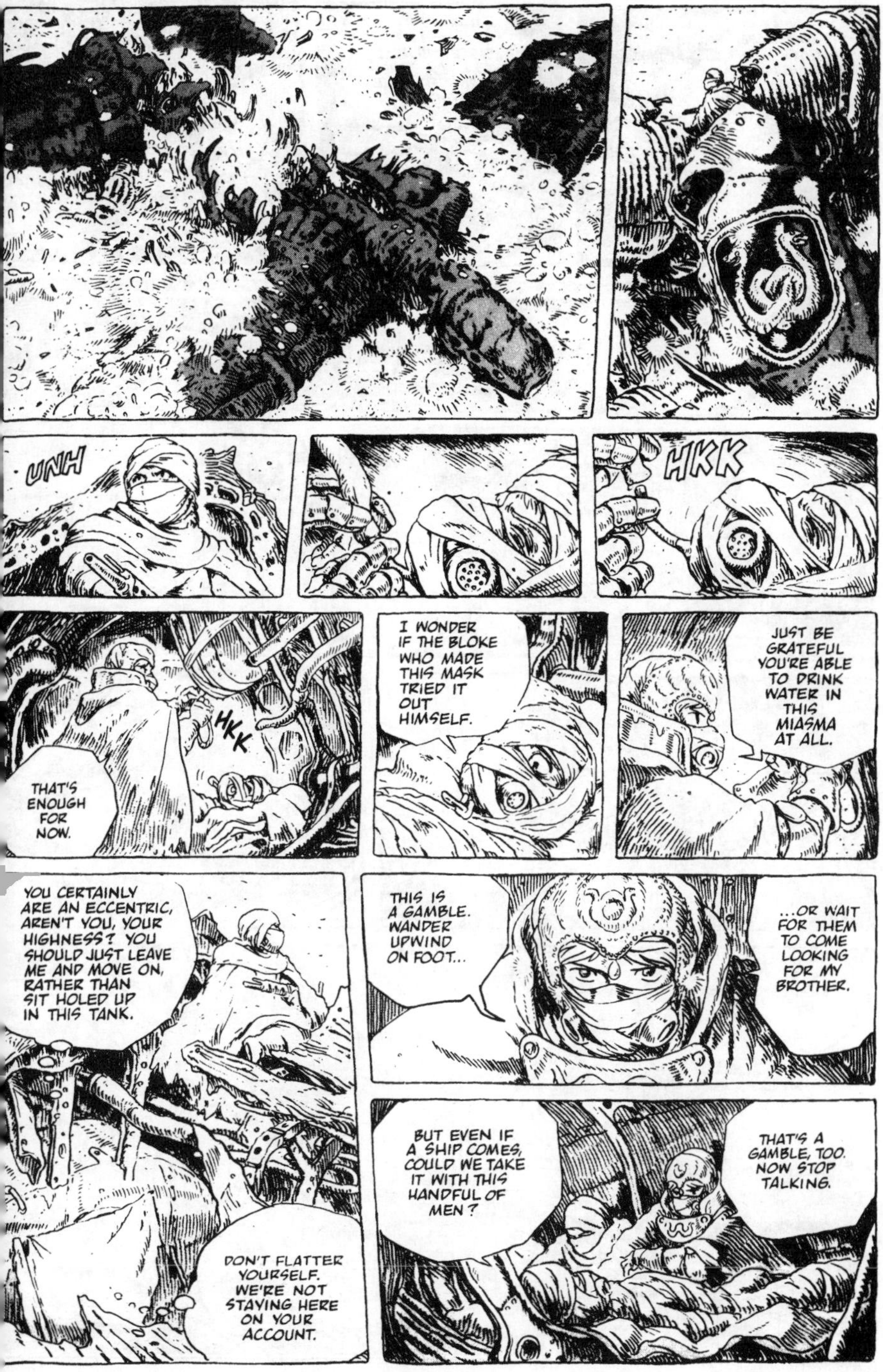
UNH
HKK
HKK
THAT'S ENOUGH FOR NOW.
I WONDER IF THE BLOKE WHO MADE THIS MASK TRIED IT OUT HIMSELF.
JUST BE GRATEFUL YOU'RE ABLE TO DRINK WATER IN THIS MIASMA AT ALL.
YOU CERTAINLY ARE AN ECCENTRIC, AREN'T YOU, YOUR HIGHNESS? YOU SHOULD JUST LEAVE ME AND MOVE ON, RATHER THAN SIT HOLED UP IN THIS TANK.
DON'T FLATTER YOURSELF. WE'RE NOT STAYING HERE ON YOUR ACCOUNT.
THIS IS A GAMBLE. WANDER UPWIND ON FOOT...
...OR WAIT FOR THEM TO COME LOOKING FOR MY BROTHER.
BUT EVEN IF A SHIP COMES, COULD WE TAKE IT WITH THIS HANDFUL OF MEN?
THAT'S A GAMBLE, TOO. NOW STOP TALKING.

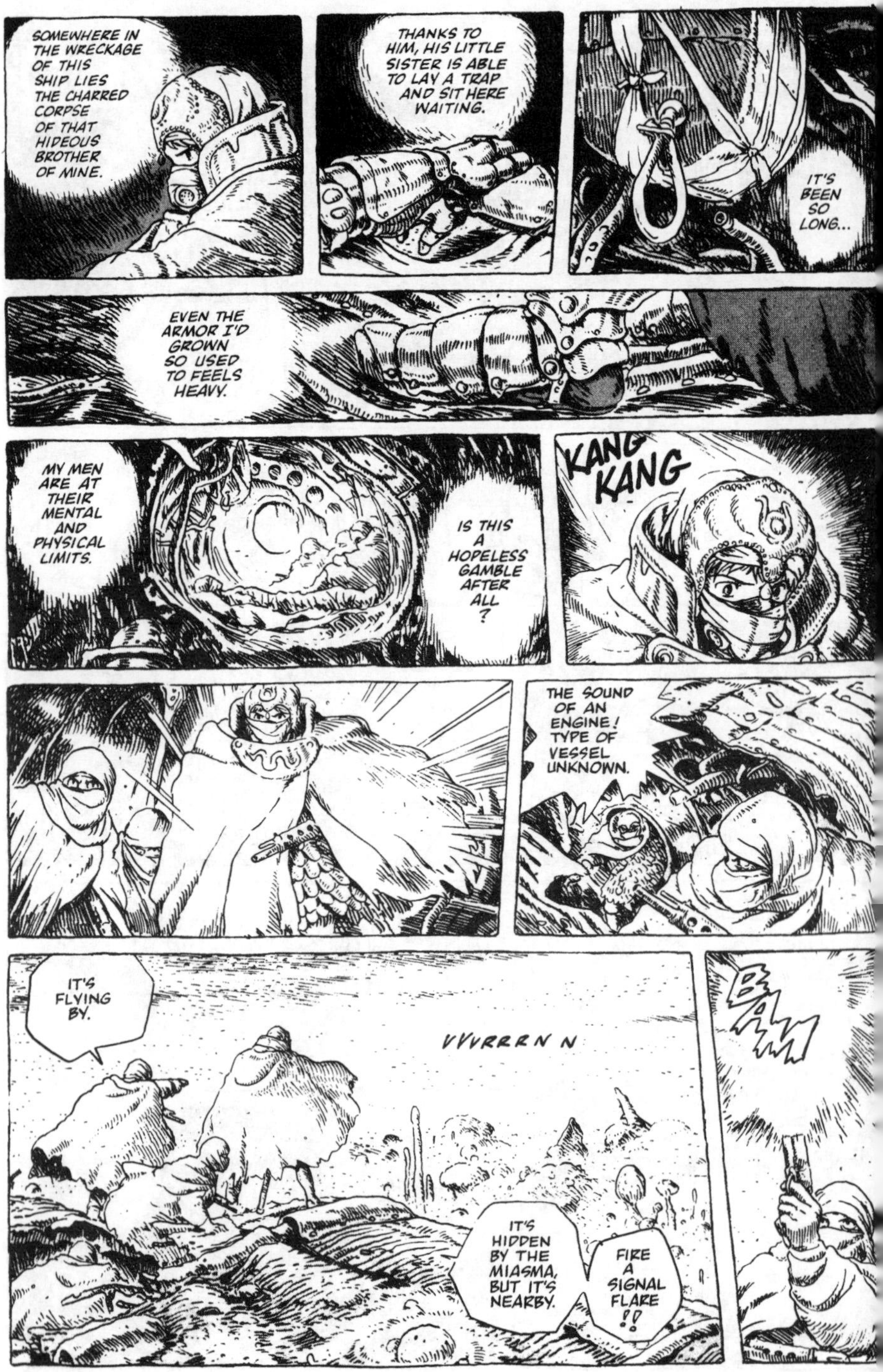
SOMEWHERE IN THE WRECKAGE OF THIS SHIP LIES THE CHARRED CORPSE OF THAT HIDEOUS BROTHER OF MINE.
THANKS TO HIM, HIS LITTLE SISTER IS ABLE TO LAY A TRAP AND SIT HERE WAITING.
IT'S BEEN SO LONG...
EVEN THE ARMOR I'D GROWN SO USED TO FEELS HEAVY.
MY MEN ARE AT THEIR MENTAL AND PHYSICAL LIMITS.
IS THIS A HOPELESS GAMBLE AFTER ALL?
KANG KANG
THE SOUND OF AN ENGINE! TYPE OF VESSEL UNKNOWN.
IT'S FLYING BY.
VVVRRRRN N
IT'S HIDDEN BY THE MIASMA, BUT IT'S NEARBY.
FIRE A SIGNAL FLARE!!
BAM

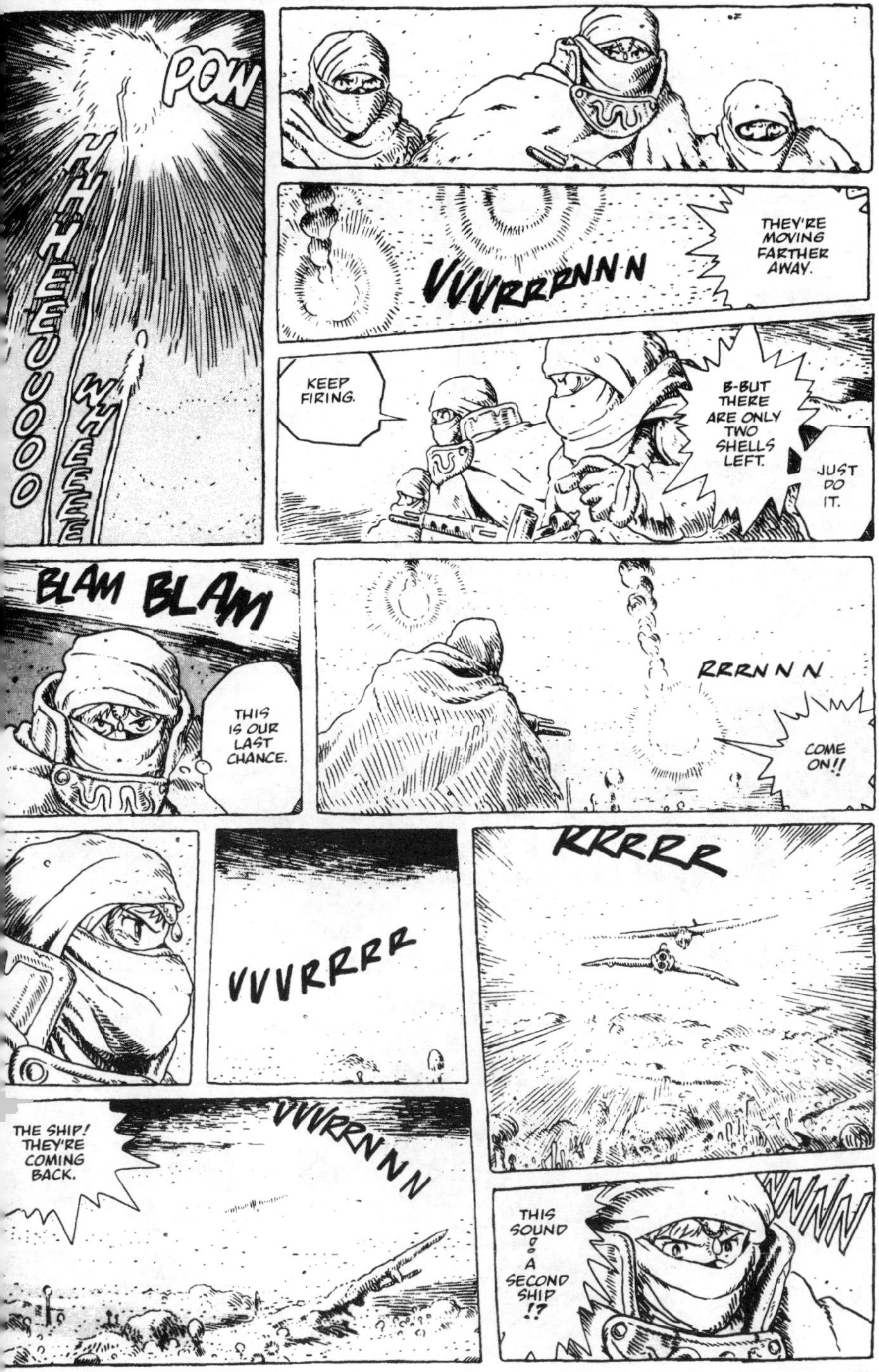
POW
HHHHEEEUUOOO
WHEEEE
THEY'RE MOVING FARTHER AWAY.
VVVRRRRNNN
KEEP FIRING.
B-BUT THERE ARE ONLY TWO SHELLS LEFT.
JUST DO IT.
BLAM BLAM
THIS IS OUR LAST CHANCE.
RRRNNN
COME ON!!
VVVRRRR
KRRRRR
THE SHIP! THEY'RE COMING BACK.
VVVRRNNNN
THIS SOUND... A SECOND SHIP!?

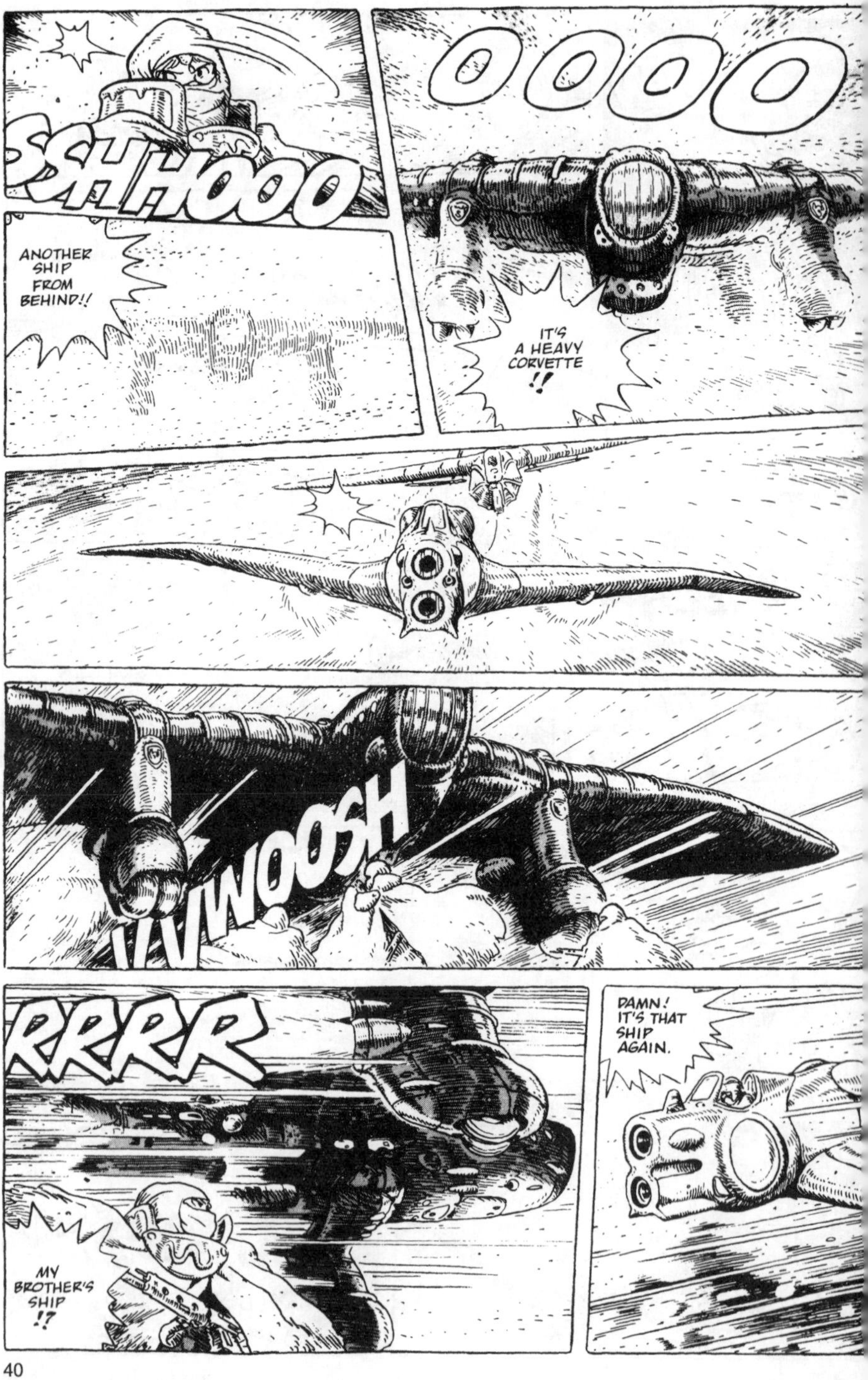
SSHHOOO
OOOO
ANOTHER SHIP FROM BEHIND!!
IT'S A HEAVY CORVETTE !!
VVWOOSH
RRRR
MY BROTHER'S SHIP !?
DAMN! IT'S THAT SHIP AGAIN.

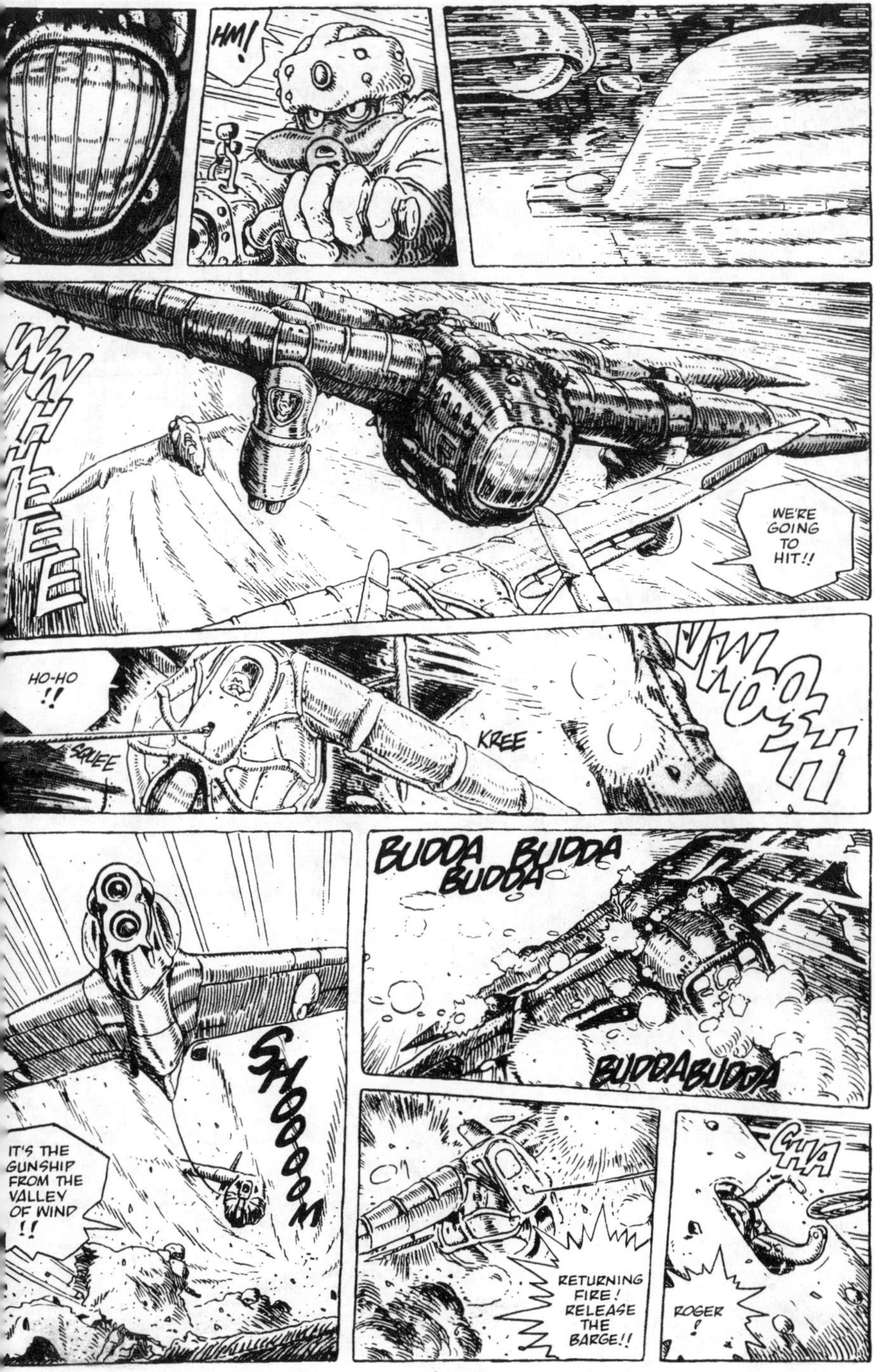
HM!
WHHEEEE
WE'RE GOING TO HIT!!
HO-HO !!
SQUEE
KREE
VWOOOH
BUDDA BUDDA BUDDA
BUDDABUDDA
IT'S THE GUNSHIP FROM THE VALLEY OF WIND !!
GHOOOOOM
RETURNING FIRE! RELEASE THE BARGE!!
GHA
ROGER!

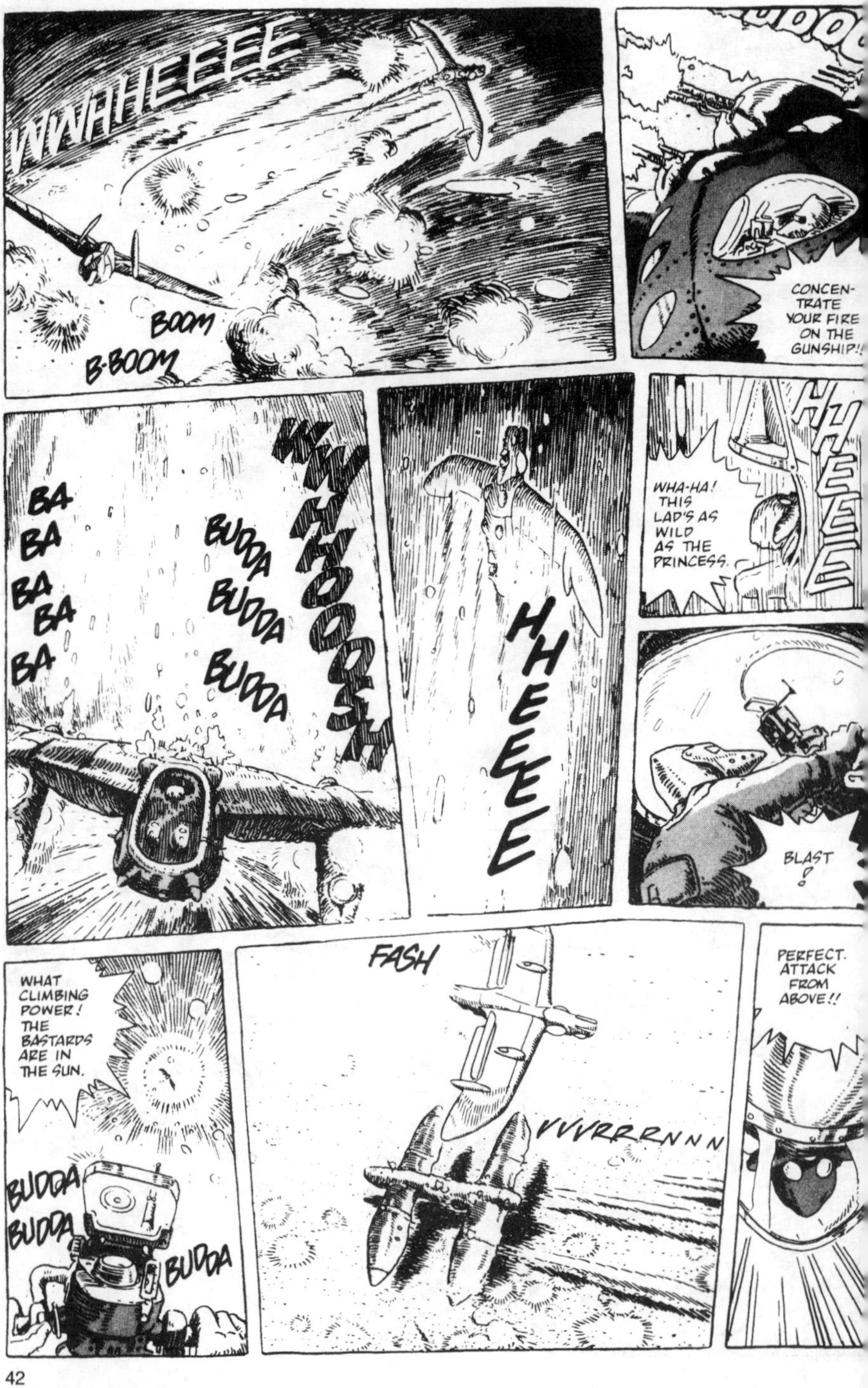
WWHEEEEE
BOOM
B-BOOM
CONCEN-TRATE YOUR FIRE ON THE GUNSHIP!!
BA BA BA BA BA
BUDDA BUDDA BUDDA
WWHOOOSH
HHEEEEE
WHA-HA! THIS LAD'S AS WILD AS THE PRINCESS.
HHEEEE
BLAST!
WHAT CLIMBING POWER! THE BASTARDS ARE IN THE SUN.
BUDDA BUDDA BUDDA
FASH
VVVRRRNNN
PERFECT. ATTACK FROM ABOVE!!

BOW COCKPIT! THOSE DEVILS HAVE THICK ARMOR. AIM FOR THE BASE OF THEIR WINGS!

ROGER!

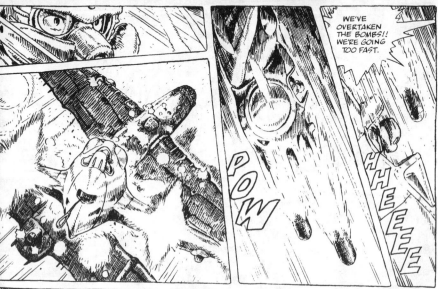

WE'VE OVERTAKEN THE BOMBS!! WE'RE GOING TOO FAST.

POW

HHEEEE

HHEEEE

PULL UP!!

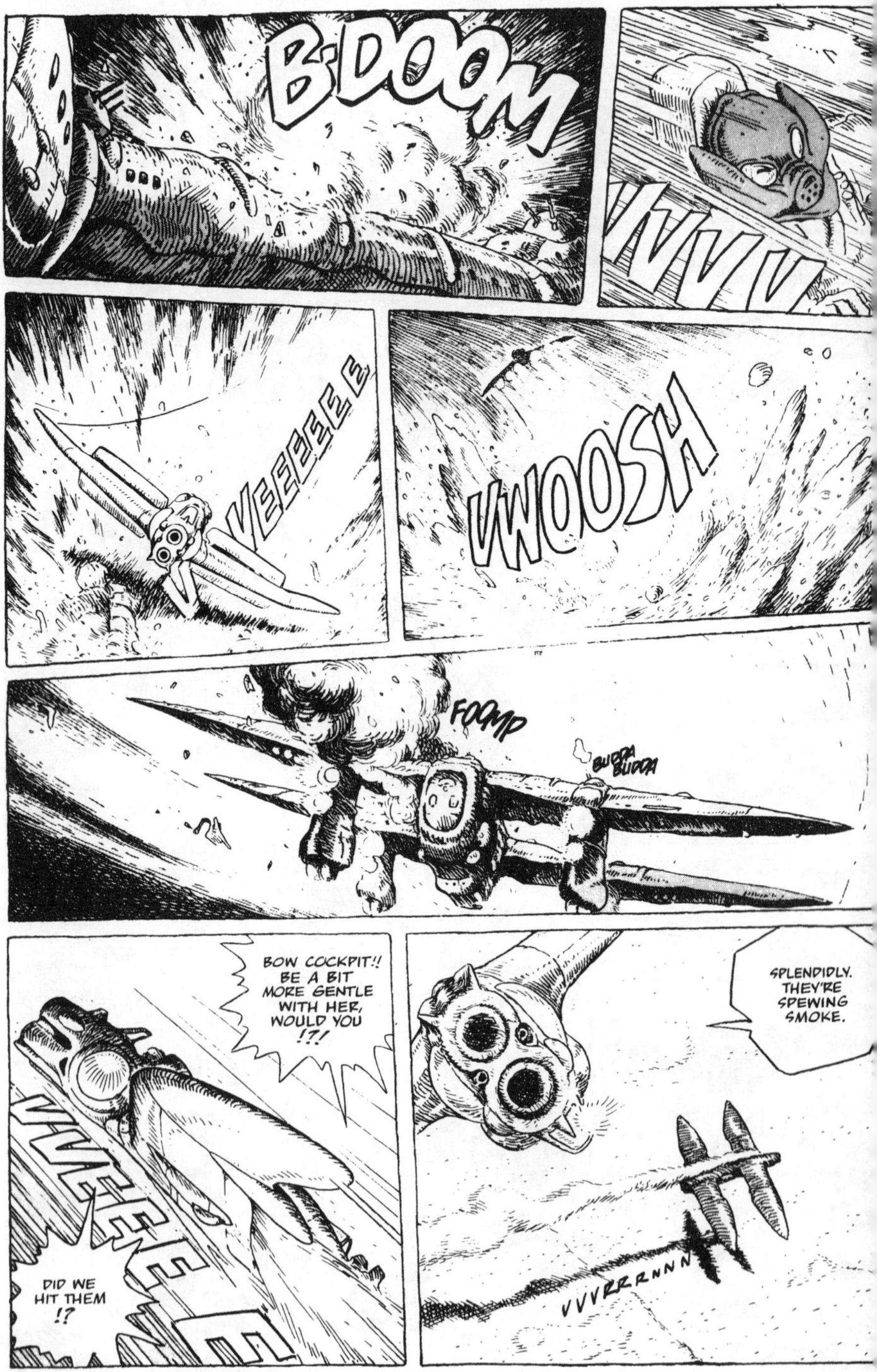
B-DOOM
VWOOSH
FOOMP
BUDDA BUDDA
DID WE HIT THEM !?
BOW COCKPIT!! BE A BIT MORE GENTLE WITH HER, WOULD YOU !?!
SPLENDIDLY. THEY'RE SPEWING SMOKE.
VVVRRRNNN

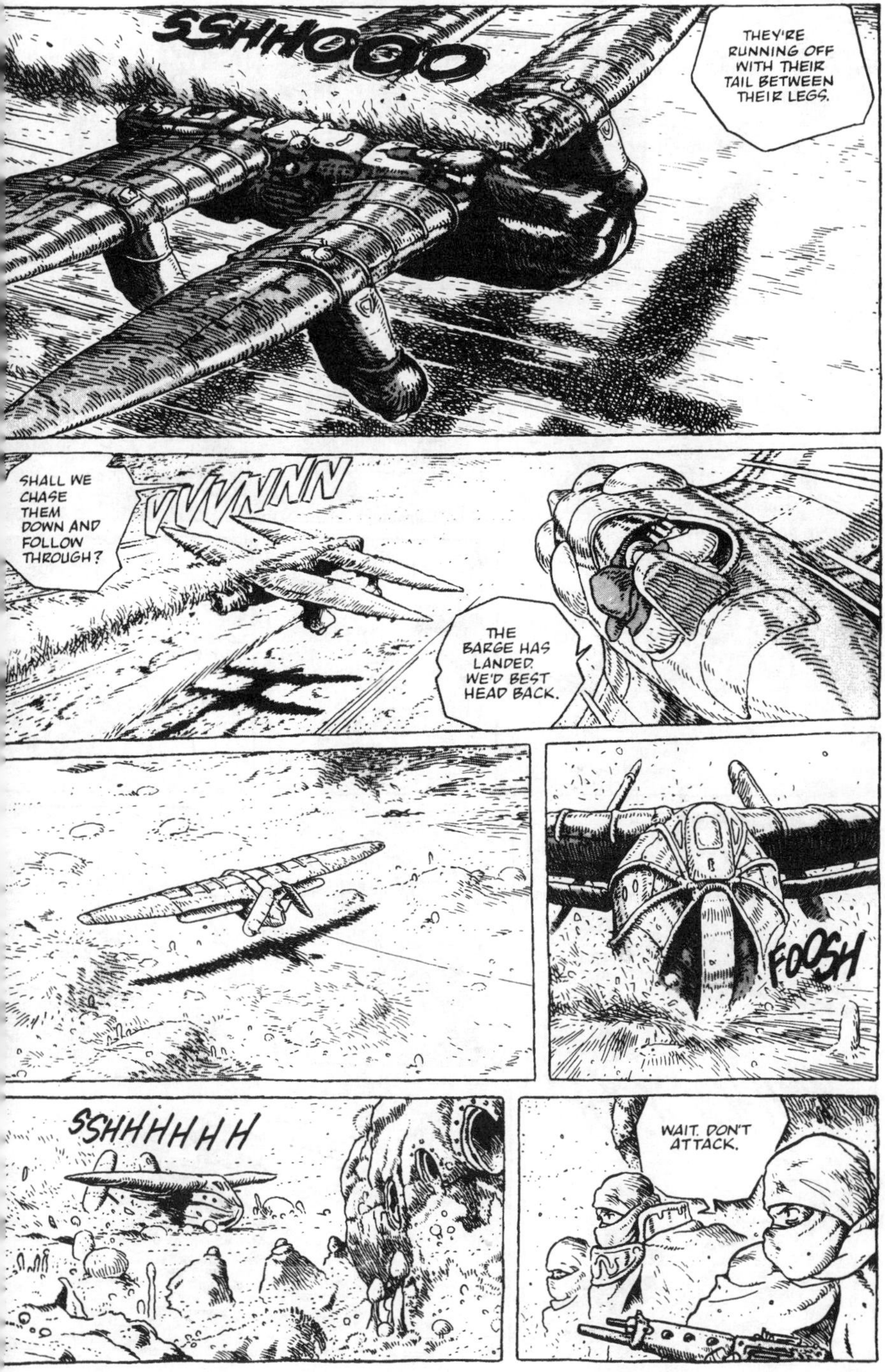
SSHHOOOO
THEY'RE RUNNING OFF WITH THEIR TAIL BETWEEN THEIR LEGS.
SHALL WE CHASE THEM DOWN AND FOLLOW THROUGH?
VVVNNNN
THE BARGE HAS LANDED. WE'D BEST HEAD BACK.
FOOSH
SSHHHHHH
WAIT. DON'T ATTACK.

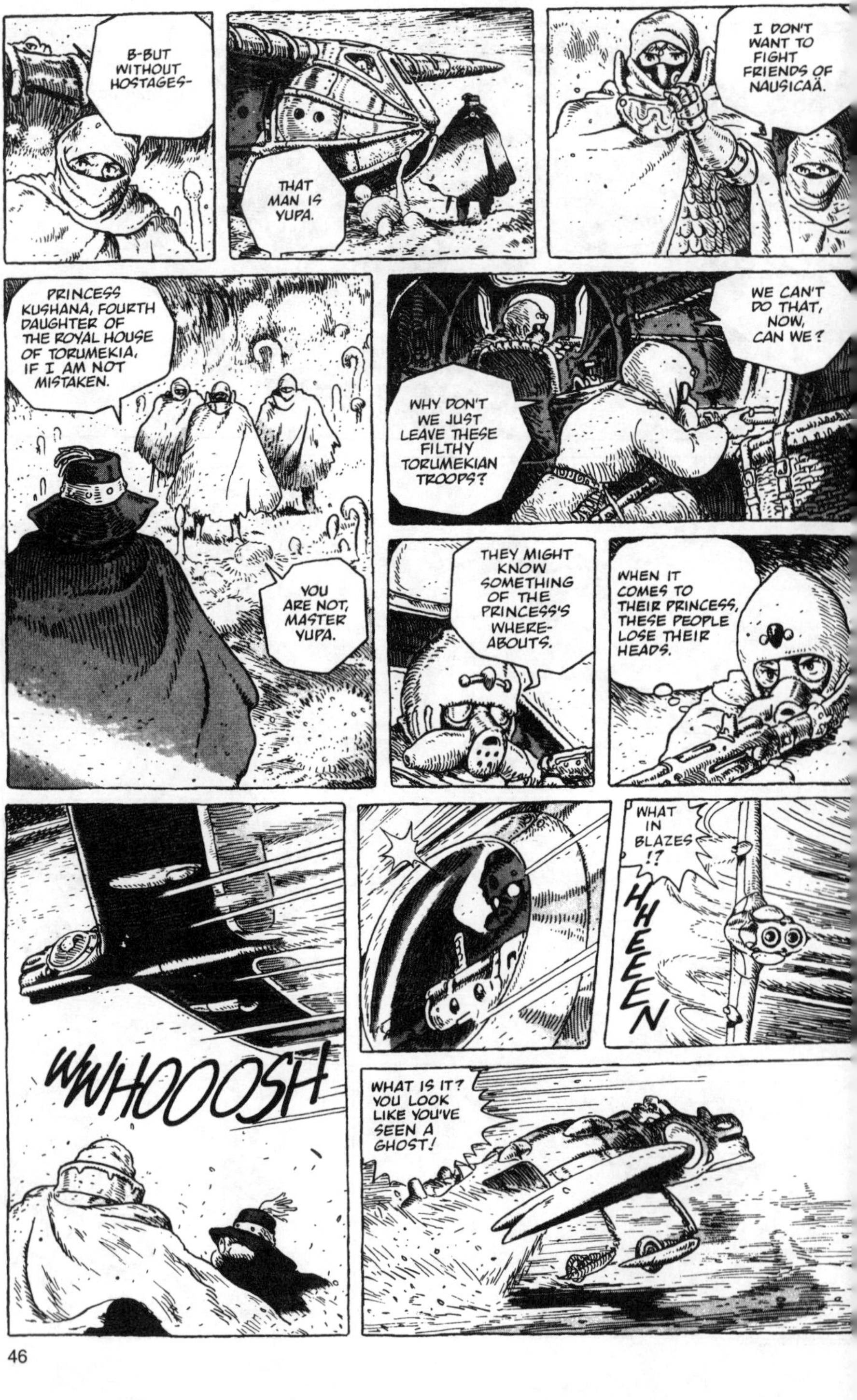

B-BUT WITHOUT HOSTAGES-
THAT MAN IS YUPA.
I DON'T WANT TO FIGHT FRIENDS OF NAUSICAÄ.
PRINCESS KUSHANA, FOURTH DAUGHTER OF THE ROYAL HOUSE OF TORUMEKIA, IF I AM NOT MISTAKEN.
YOU ARE NOT, MASTER YUPA.
WHY DON'T WE JUST LEAVE THESE FILTHY TORUMEKIAN TROOPS?
WE CAN'T DO THAT, NOW, CAN WE?
THEY MIGHT KNOW SOMETHING OF THE PRINCESS'S WHERE-ABOUTS.
WHEN IT COMES TO THEIR PRINCESS, THESE PEOPLE LOSE THEIR HEADS.
WWHOOOSH
WHAT IN BLAZES !?
HHEEEEN
WHAT IS IT? YOU LOOK LIKE YOU'VE SEEN A GHOST!

ASBEL! WAIT!

ASBEL OF PEJITEI

STOP, ASBEL.

LET ME GO! THIS IS THE WOMAN WHO DESTROYED PEJITEI

CALM YOURSELF, ASBEL, AND LISTEN TO ME.

PRINCESS KUSHANA JUST NOW OFFERED TO SURRENDER IN EXCHANGE FOR SAVING HER MEN.

SHE BURNED THE TOWN AND MURDERED EVERYONE!

SHE MERCILESSLY SLAUGHTERED NONCOMBATANTS-- WOMEN, CHILDREN, THE OLD!!

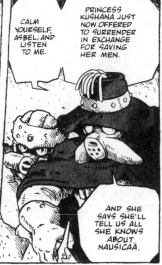

AND SHE SAYS SHE'LL TELL US ALL SHE KNOWS ABOUT NAUSICAÄ.

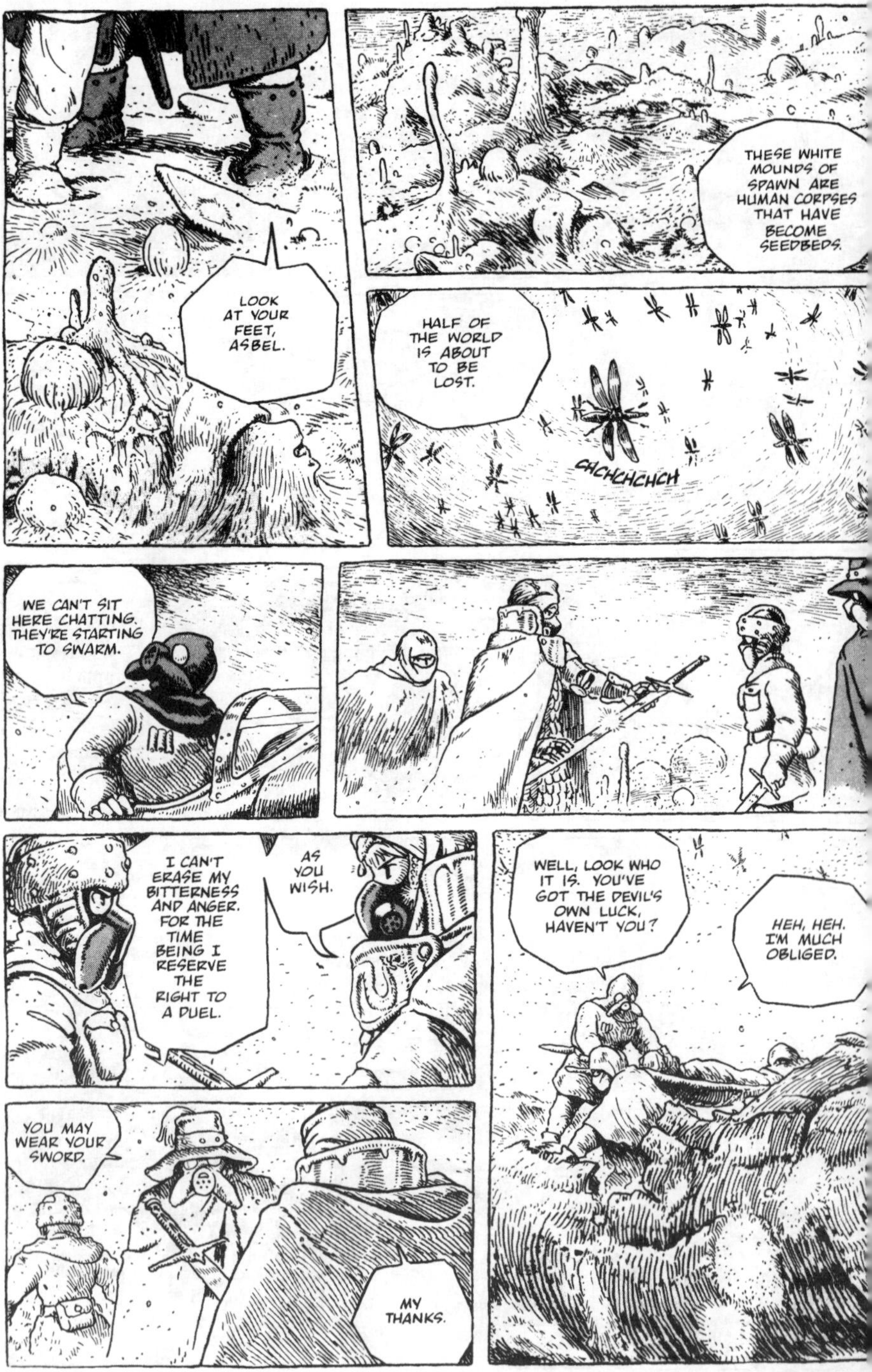
LOOK AT YOUR FEET, ASBEL.
THESE WHITE MOUNDS OF SPAWN ARE HUMAN CORPSES THAT HAVE BECOME SEEDBEDS.
HALF OF THE WORLD IS ABOUT TO BE LOST.
CHCHCHCHCH
WE CAN'T SIT HERE CHATTING. THEY'RE STARTING TO SWARM.
I CAN'T ERASE MY BITTERNESS AND ANGER. FOR THE TIME BEING I RESERVE THE RIGHT TO A DUEL.
AS YOU WISH.
YOU MAY WEAR YOUR SWORD.
MY THANKS.
WELL, LOOK WHO IT IS. YOU'VE GOT THE DEVIL'S OWN LUCK, HAVEN'T YOU?
HEH, HEH. I'M MUCH OBLIGED.

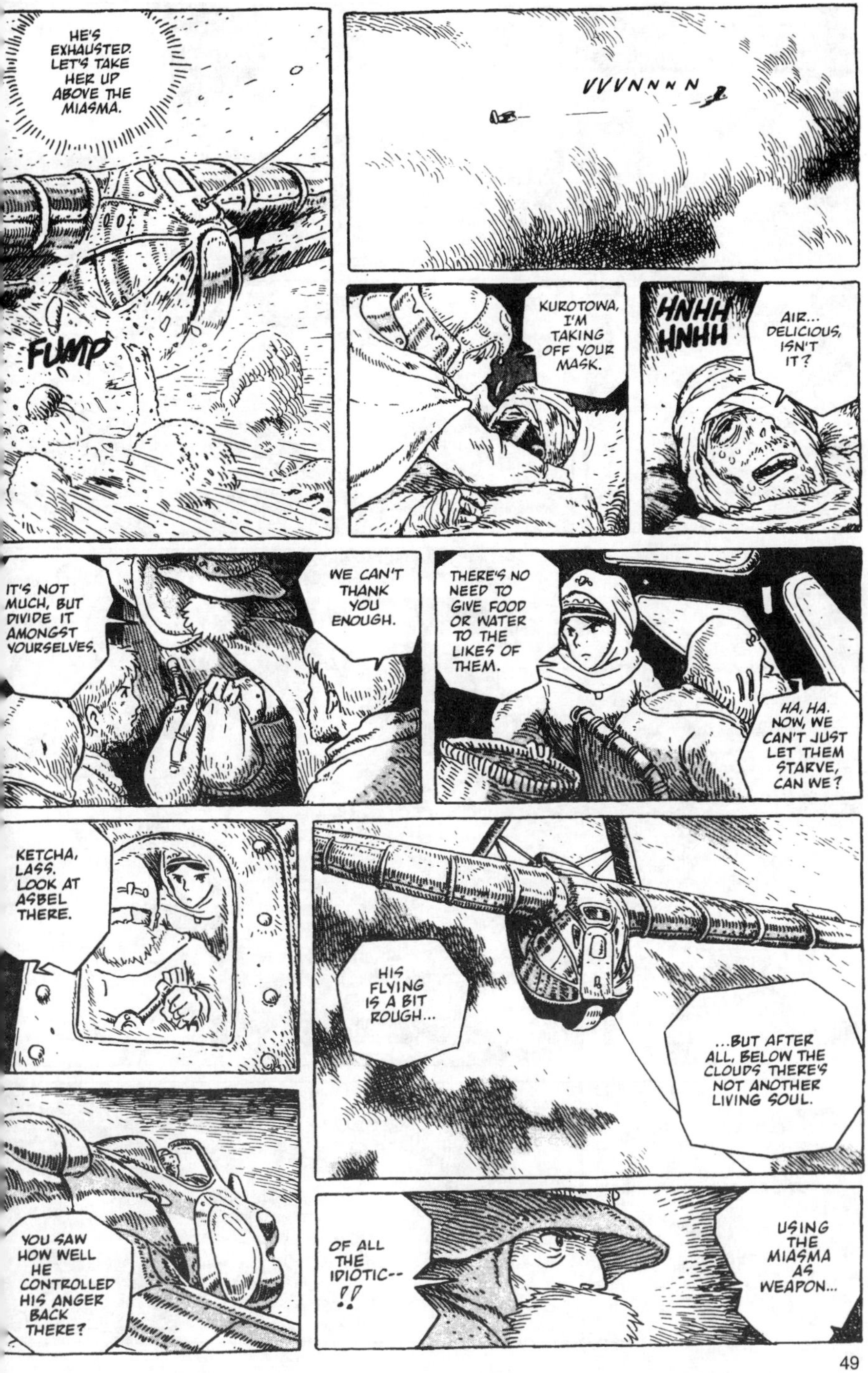
HE'S EXHAUSTED. LET'S TAKE HER UP ABOVE THE MIASMA.
FUMP
VVVNNNN
KUROTOWA, I'M TAKING OFF YOUR MASK.
HNHH HNHH
AIR... DELICIOUS, ISN'T IT?
IT'S NOT MUCH, BUT DIVIDE IT AMONGST YOURSELVES.
WE CAN'T THANK YOU ENOUGH.
THERE'S NO NEED TO GIVE FOOD OR WATER TO THE LIKES OF THEM.
HA, HA. NOW, WE CAN'T JUST LET THEM STARVE, CAN WE?
KETCHA, LASS. LOOK AT ASBEL THERE.
HIS FLYING IS A BIT ROUGH...
...BUT AFTER ALL, BELOW THE CLOUDS THERE'S NOT ANOTHER LIVING SOUL.
YOU SAW HOW WELL HE CONTROLLED HIS ANGER BACK THERE?
OF ALL THE IDIOTIC--
!!
USING THE MIASMA AS WEAPON...

IS THERE NOT A SINGLE ECOLOGIST ON THE COUNCIL OF PRIESTS?

I HAVE NO DOUBT THAT THE TORUMEKIAN EMPEROR WOULD HAVE DONE THE SAME THING UNDER THE CIRCUMSTANCES.

SQUEE

THE DOROK EMPEROR IS NOT THE ONLY FOOL. I'M THE SAME MYSELF.

THERE'S NOT MUCH DIFFERENCE BETWEEN BEING AT THE MERCY OF DESIRE AND BEING A PRISONER OF HATRED.

HHKK

WHEN THE INSECTS CAME...

...ONE OF THE OBJECTS OF MY VENGEANCE DIED ALL TOO EASILY, RIGHT BEFORE MY EYES. HIS DEATH WAS ALL I HAD BEEN LIVING FOR.

I WAS COMPLETELY EMPTY. I WAS OBLIVIOUS TO THE TERRIBLE SCENE BEFORE ME...

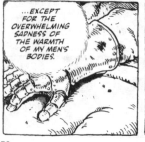

...EXCEPT FOR THE OVERWHELMING SADNESS OF THE WARMTH OF MY MEN'S BODIES.

SUDDENLY I FOUND MYSELF DOING JUST AS NAUSICAÄ HAD SAID.

SHE SAID THAT IF YOU CAST ASIDE YOUR HATRED AND FEAR, THE INSECTS WILL NOT ATTACK.

WHEN THE INSECTS HAD LEFT, I BECAME AWARE FOR THE FIRST TIME...THAT I HAD BEEN SINGING THROUGHOUT THE ENTIRE EPISODE.

A LULLABYE, OF ALL THINGS!!

IT SEEMS I'VE SOLVED THE PUZZLE OF YOUR PRINCESS TO SOME EXTENT.

BUT I COULD NEVER DO IT AGAIN.

NO, I DON'T EVEN WANT TO TRY TO EMULATE HER.

WITH ALL OF THIS FIERCE, BURNING ANGER INSIDE, FOR ME TO HAVE FELT NOT CONTEMPT AND HATRED... BUT SORROW...

EAT TOO FAST, AND YOUR EMPTY STOMACH WON'T BE ABLE TO TAKE IT.

MUNCH MUNCH

CHEW IT SLOWLY.

I WONDER IF EVEN A SMALL PORTION OF THE EARTH WILL BE LEFT TO HUMANKIND.

IF SO, THEN IT LOOKS LIKE THE DAY IS COMING WHEN THE LIVING WILL ENVY THE DEAD, DOESN'T IT?

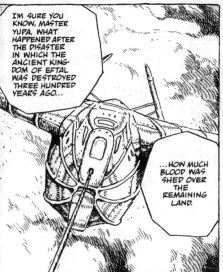

I'M SURE YOU KNOW, MASTER YUPA, WHAT HAPPENED AFTER THE DISASTER IN WHICH THE ANCIENT KINGDOM OF EFTAL WAS DESTROYED THREE HUNDRED YEARS AGO...

...HOW MUCH BLOOD WAS SHED OVER THE REMAINING LAND.

I'VE NEVER BEFORE HEARD THAT RECORDS OF THE SEA OF CORRUPTION HAVE SURVIVED IN TORUMEKIA, TOO.

THE CHRONICLES RECORD THAT MORE LIVES WERE LOST IN THE SUBSEQUENT FIGHTING FOR EVERY INCH OF REMAINING LAND THAN IN THE DAIKAISHO ITSELF.

IT WAS MERE CONJECTURE ON MY PART, BUT I WAS RIGHT, WASN'T I? AND THE SAME THING WILL PROBABLY HAPPEN THIS TIME AROUND.

Gulp

THE HORRIBLE SCENE BELOW IS ONLY THE BEGINNING.

THE SURVIVING DOROKS WILL SET THEIR SIGHTS ON TORUMEKIA AND MAKE THEIR MOVE. THE FLAMES OF WAR WILL BE REIGNITED, AND IF THE COUNCIL OF PRIESTS IS STILL INTACT, THEY MAY WIELD THE MIASMA AS A WEAPON ONCE AGAIN. PERHAPS EVEN A GOD WARRIOR.

SO THIS WOMAN HAS ALREADY FORSEEN THESE THINGS, HAS SHE?

BOTH THE TORUMEKIAN AND DOROK EMPERORS ARE NOTHING MORE THAN RUTHLESS, EVIL COWARDS.

THE MORE DIFFICULT THINGS BECOME, THE WORSE THEIR FOLLY BECOMES.

WE NEED A NEW KING.

IF ONE WHO WILL TREAD THE TRUE PATH OF RIGHTEOUS RULE DOES NOT APPEAR, HUMANITY WILL BE DESTROYED.

HOLD YOUR TONGUE!!

THIS WOULD NEVER HAVE HAPPENED IF YOU AND YOUR PEOPLE HADN'T GONE TO WAR.

...IT IS INDEED AS YOU SAY.

FORGIVE THE RAMBLINGS OF A PRISONER.

WHO ARE YOU TO SPEAK SO SELF-RIGHTEOUSLY, WOMAN OF TORUMEKIA!?

WE DO NOT EVEN COMPREHEND THE SCALE OF THE DESTRUCTION THAT WILL BE WROUGHT.

ATTENTION BARGE!!

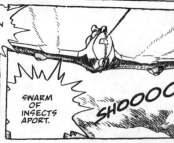

SWARM OF INSECTS APORT.

SHOOOO

NO NEED FOR ALARM. IT'S A SMALL SWARM.

FOR THE SAKE OF CAUTION, I'M TAKING COVER. TURNING HELM TO STARBOARD.

THE DAIKAISHO HAS ONLY JUST BEGUN.

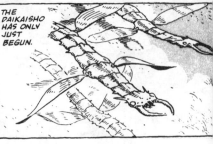

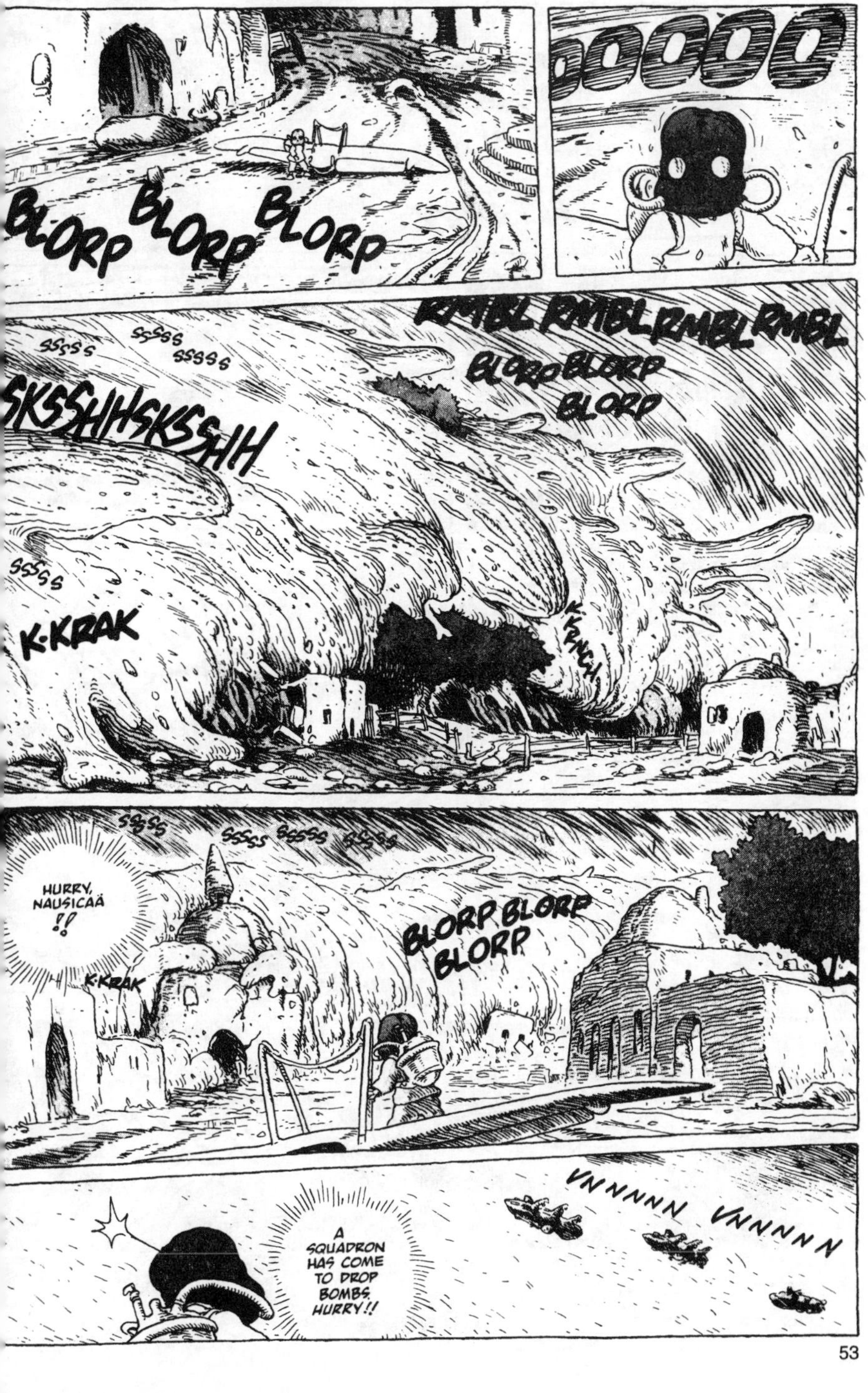
BLORP BLORP BLORP
OOOOOO
RMBL RMBL RMBL RMBL
BLORP BLORP
BLORP
SSSSS
SSSSS
SSSSS
SKSSHHSKSSHH
SSSSS
K-KRAK
K-RNCH
SSSSS
SSSSS SSSSS SSSSS
HURRY, NAUSICAÄ !!
K-KRAK
BLORP BLORP
BLORP
VNNNNN VNNNNN
A SQUADRON HAS COME TO DROP BOMBS. HURRY!!

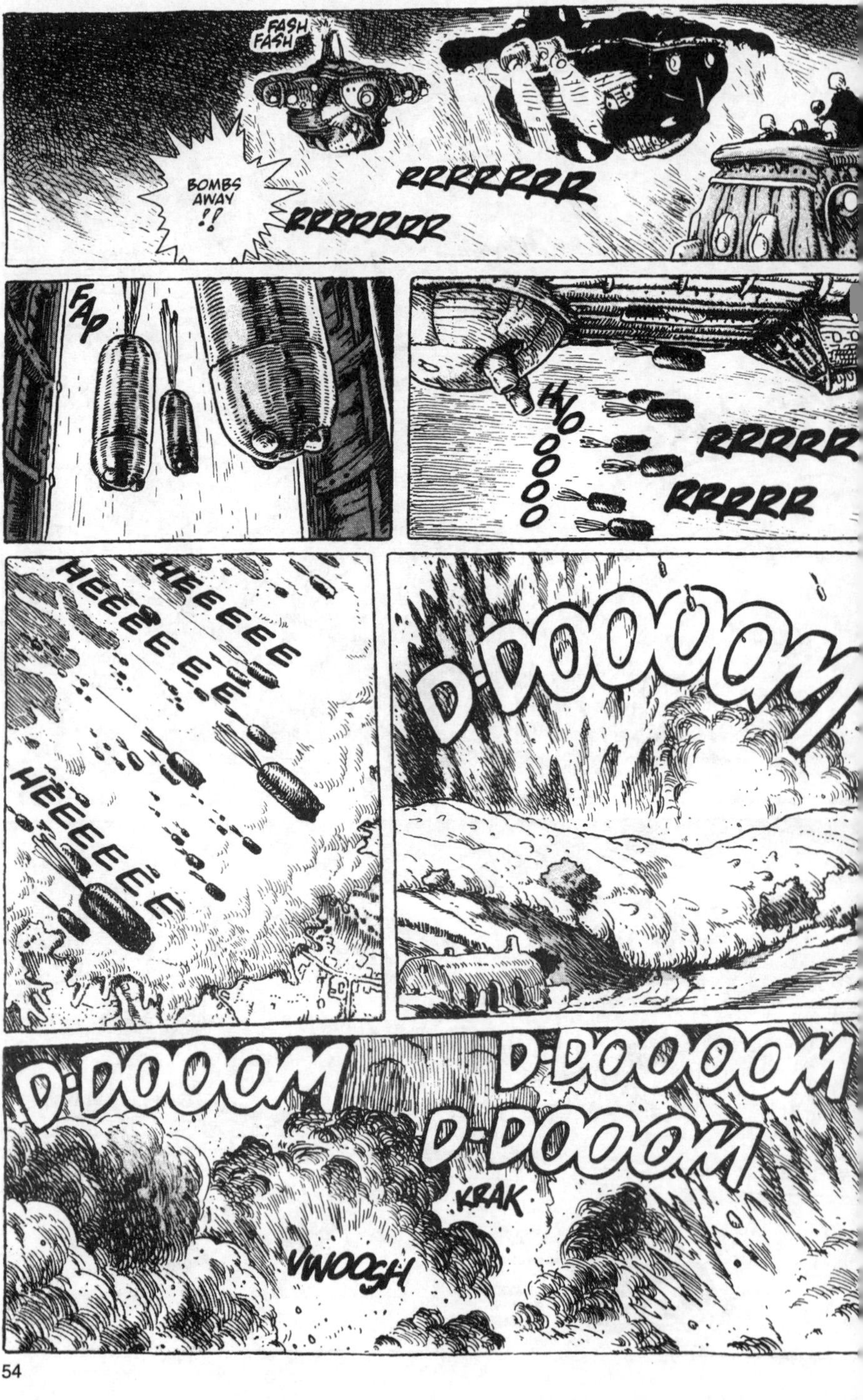
FASH FASH
BOMBS AWAY !!
RRRRRRRR
RRRRRRRR
FAP
HWOOOOOO
RRRRRR
RRRRR
HEEEEEE
HEEEEE EEE
HEEEEEEEE
D-DOOOOM
D-DOOOM
D-DOOOOOM
D-DOOOM
KRAK
VWOOSH

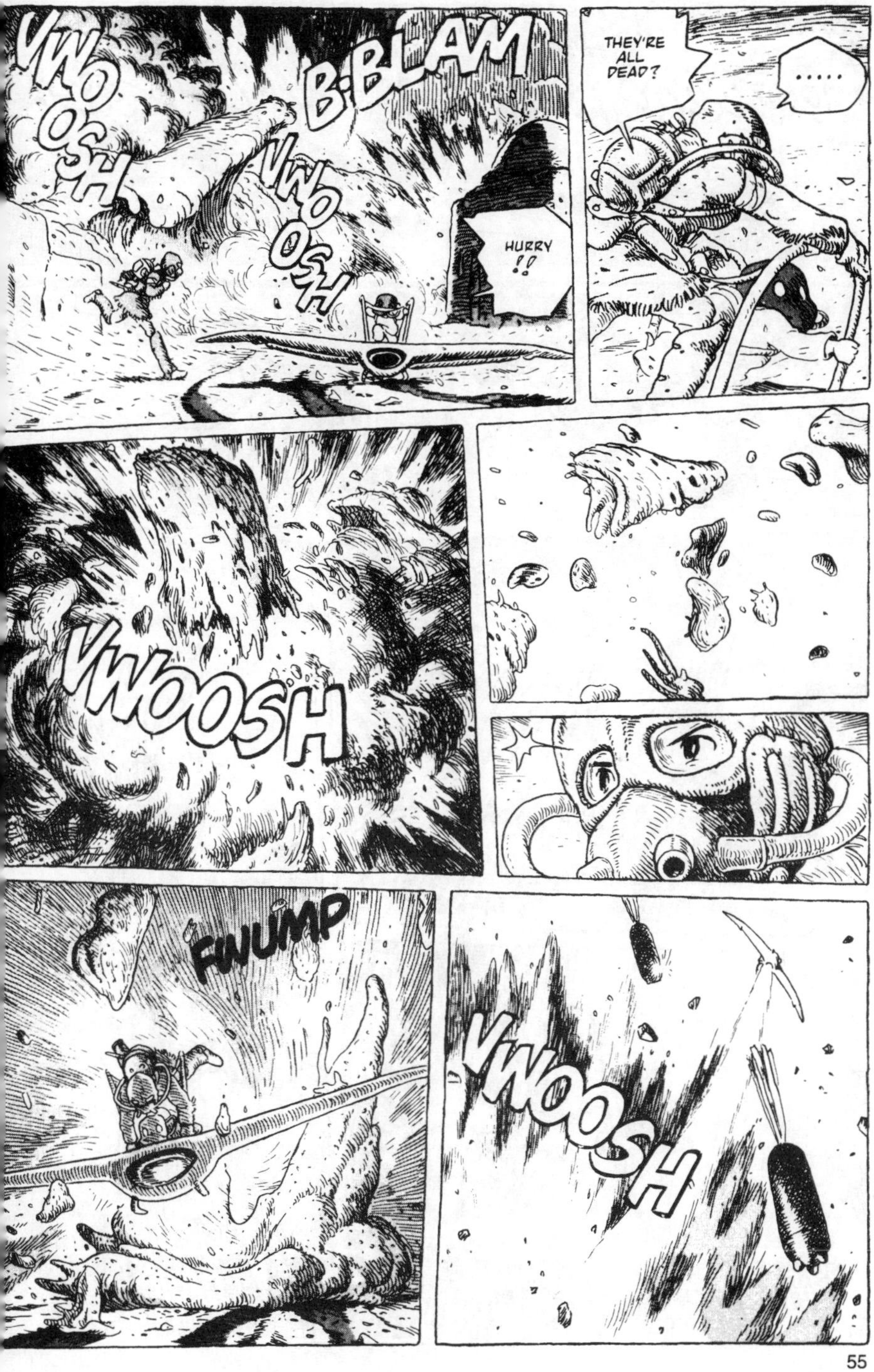
VWOOSH
B-BLAM
VWOOSH
HURRY !!
THEY'RE ALL DEAD?
......
VWOOSH
FWUMP
VWOOSH

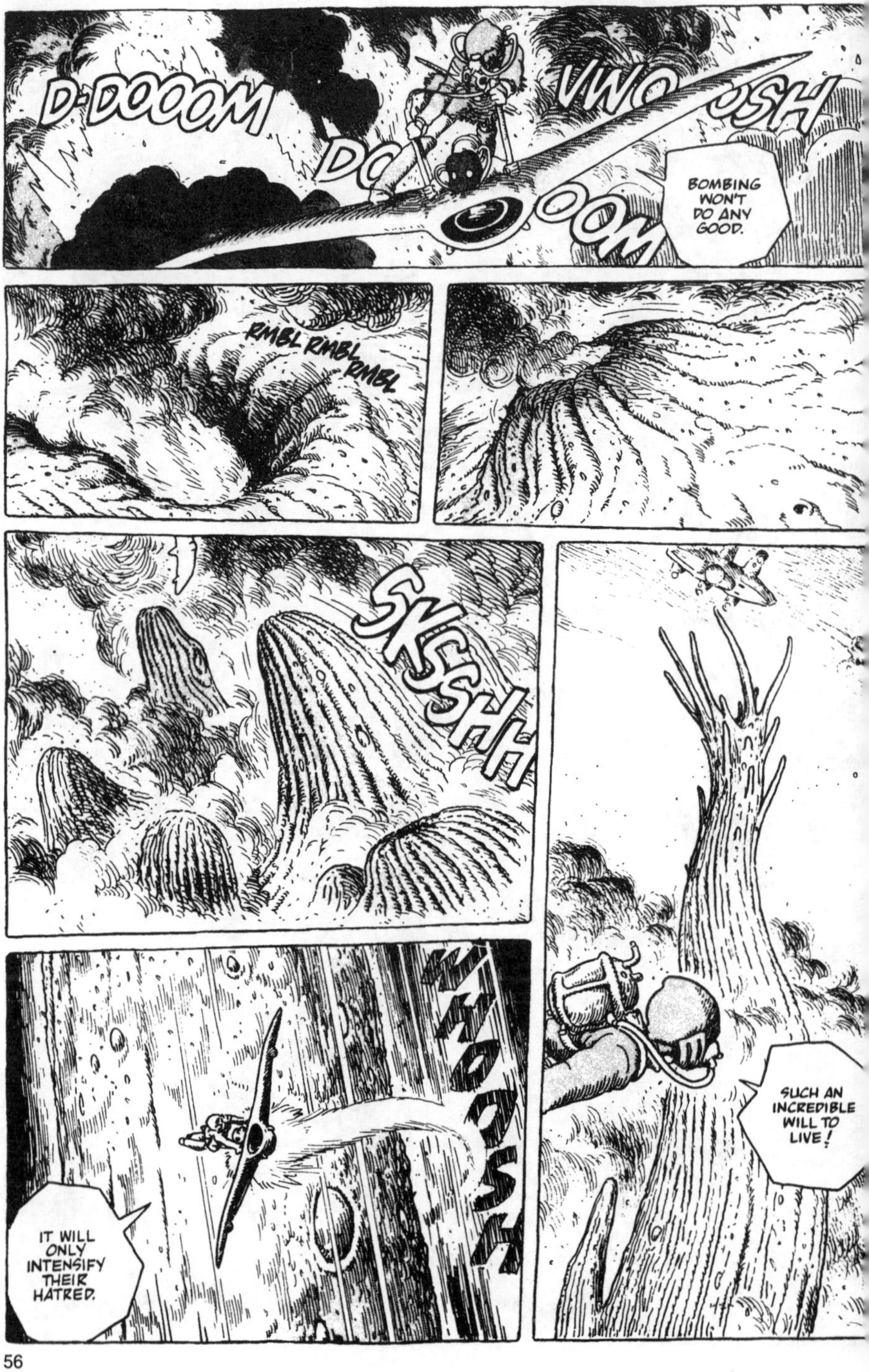
D-DOOOM
DO
VWOOSH
BOMBING WON'T DO ANY GOOD.
OOOM
RMBL RMBL RMBL
SKSSHH
SUCH AN INCREDIBLE WILL TO LIVE!
WHOOSH
IT WILL ONLY INTENSIFY THEIR HATRED.

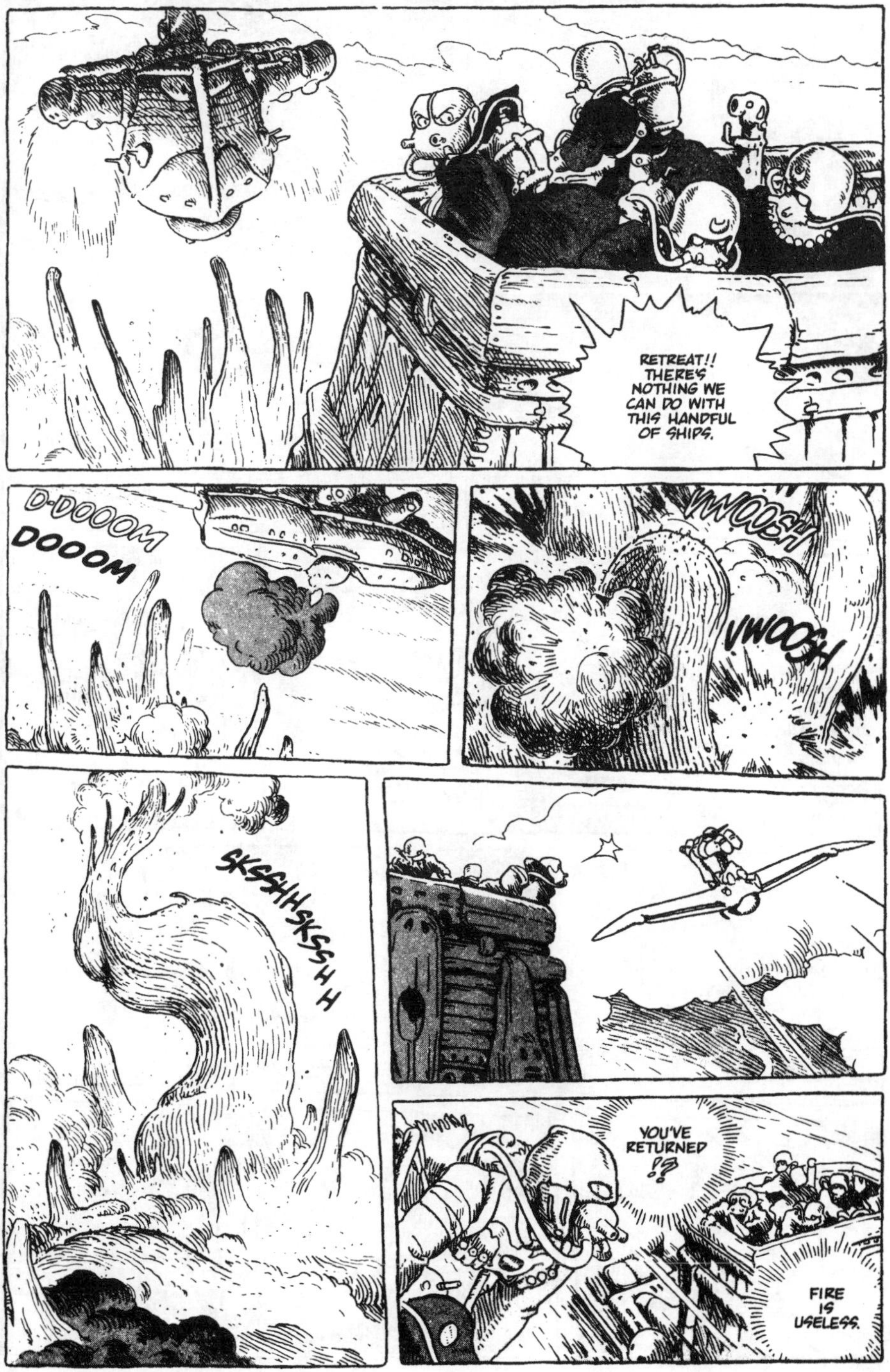
RETREAT!! THERE'S NOTHING WE CAN DO WITH THIS HANDFUL OF SHIPS.
D-DOOOM
DOOOM
VWOOSH
VWOOSH
SKSSHH SKSSHH
YOU'VE RETURNED !?
FIRE IS USELESS.

I FOUND SOME PEOPLE WHO HAVE TAKEN REFUGE IN THE HIGHLANDS.

THEY JUST BECOME ANGRY AND SPEW MIASMA EVEN MORE FIERCELY.

HEAD THREE POINTS EAST AT FULL SPEED.

WE WILL.

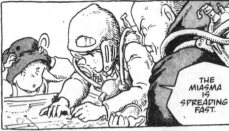

AN ORDER TO ALL SHIPS: FOLLOW US. CHANGING COURSE. FULL SPEED. THREE POINTS EAST.

YOU'VE COME BACK, TOO!?

CHIKUKU WON'T RUN AWAY.

A MAP! I'VE TRACED THE MOVEMENT OF THE MOLD.

THIS WAY.

THE MIASMA IS SPREADING FAST.

THE BLOOD'S GONE OUT OF HER HANDS.

HER FACE, TOO. SHE'S DEATHLY PALE.

IT'S ONLY TO BE EXPECTED. THIS YOUNG GIRL HAS JUST LOOKED INTO HELL.

FOUR DIFFERENT BODIES OF MOLD HAVE BEEN SPAWNED. THEY'RE MOVING ALONG, EXPELLING HEAVY MIASMA AND EATING EVERYTHING IN THEIR PATHS AS THEY GO.

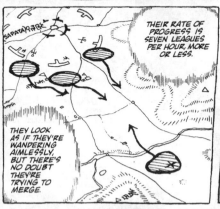

THEIR RATE OF PROGRESS IS SEVEN LEAGUES PER HOUR, MORE OR LESS.

THEY LOOK AS IF THEY'RE WANDERING AIMLESSLY, BUT THERE'S NO DOUBT THEY'RE TRYING TO MERGE.

THE MIASMA IS DIFFUSING FAIRLY QUICKLY.

THE GRANARIES OF SAPATA HAVE BEEN WIPED OUT.

WHAT ON EARTH COULD THESE THINGS HOPE TO ACCOMPLISH BY MERGING?

I'VE SEEN SMALL MOLDS IN THE FOREST NEAR MY VALLEY.

THE CELLS GATHER TOGETHER AND MOVE AROUND IN SEARCH OF FOOD.

INDIVIDUAL CELLS NEVER MOVE AROUND BY THEMSELVES.

WHEN THERE'S NO MORE FOOD TO BE FOUND OR THEY GROW OLD, THEY GATHER INTO A BALL AND SLEEP.

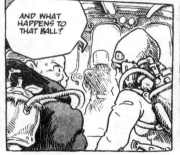

AND WHAT HAPPENS TO THAT BALL?

IN TIME IT BURSTS OPEN...

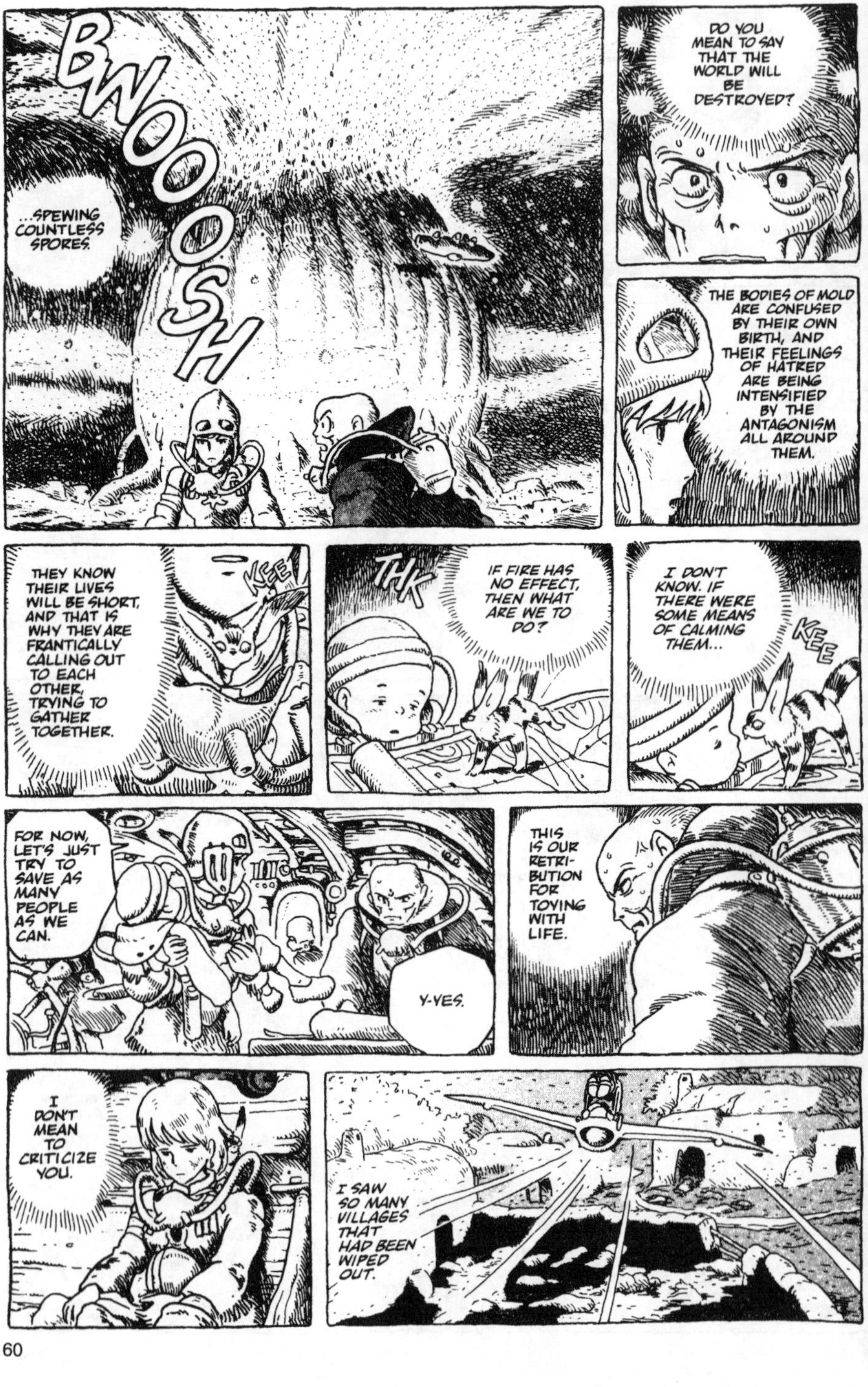
BWOOOSH
...SPEWING COUNTLESS SPORES.
DO YOU MEAN TO SAY THAT THE WORLD WILL BE DESTROYED?
THE BODIES OF MOLD ARE CONFUSED BY THEIR OWN BIRTH, AND THEIR FEELINGS OF HATRED ARE BEING INTENSIFIED BY THE ANTAGONISM ALL AROUND THEM.
THEY KNOW THEIR LIVES WILL BE SHORT, AND THAT IS WHY THEY ARE FRANTICALLY CALLING OUT TO EACH OTHER, TRYING TO GATHER TOGETHER.
KEE
THK
IF FIRE HAS NO EFFECT, THEN WHAT ARE WE TO DO?
I DON'T KNOW. IF THERE WERE SOME MEANS OF CALMING THEM...
KEE
FOR NOW, LET'S JUST TRY TO SAVE AS MANY PEOPLE AS WE CAN.
Y-YES.
THIS IS OUR RETRIBUTION FOR TOYING WITH LIFE.
I DON'T MEAN TO CRITICIZE YOU.
I SAW SO MANY VILLAGES THAT HAD BEEN WIPED OUT.

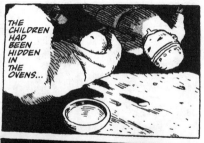

THE CHILDREN HAD BEEN HIDDEN IN THE OVENS...

THE ROADS ARE FULL OF THE CORPSES OF THOSE WHO TRIED TO ESCAPE AND FAILED.

...AND DIED AS THEY WAITED TO BE SAVED.

I HEARD THE VOICE OF THE MOLD'S HEART, AS WELL.

I'VE NEVER ENCOUNTERED SO WRETCHED A CREATURE.

ANY FORM OF LIFE KNOWS JOY AND SATISFACTION...

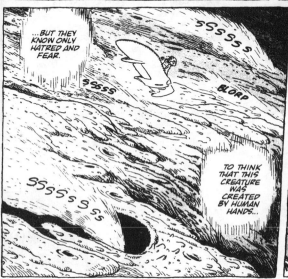

...BUT THEY KNOW ONLY HATRED AND FEAR.

SSSSSS

SSSSS

BLORP

TO THINK THAT THIS CREATURE WAS CREATED BY HUMAN HANDS...

SSSSSSSS

WHY DID THEY BREAK THE SEAL TO THE CRYPTS OF SHUWA?

ARE WE A CURSED RACE, DESTINED TO BE DESTROYED?

61

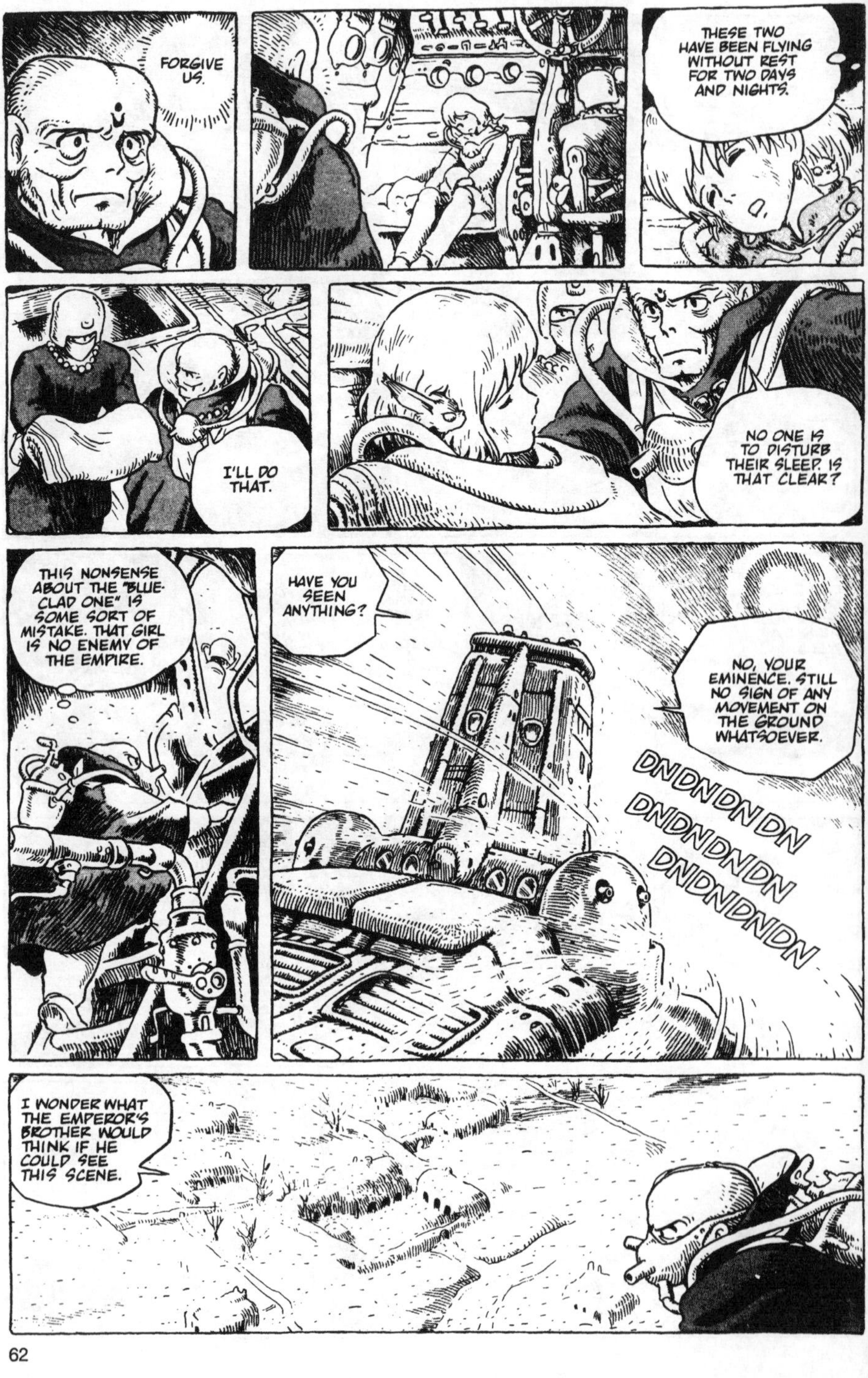

FORGIVE US.
THESE TWO HAVE BEEN FLYING WITHOUT REST FOR TWO DAYS AND NIGHTS.
I'LL DO THAT.
NO ONE IS TO DISTURB THEIR SLEEP. IS THAT CLEAR?
THIS NONSENSE ABOUT THE "BLUE-CLAD ONE" IS SOME SORT OF MISTAKE. THAT GIRL IS NO ENEMY OF THE EMPIRE.
HAVE YOU SEEN ANYTHING?
NO, YOUR EMINENCE. STILL NO SIGN OF ANY MOVEMENT ON THE GROUND WHATSOEVER.
DNDNDNDN DNDNDNDN DNDNDNDN DNDNDNDN
I WONDER WHAT THE EMPEROR'S BROTHER WOULD THINK IF HE COULD SEE THIS SCENE.

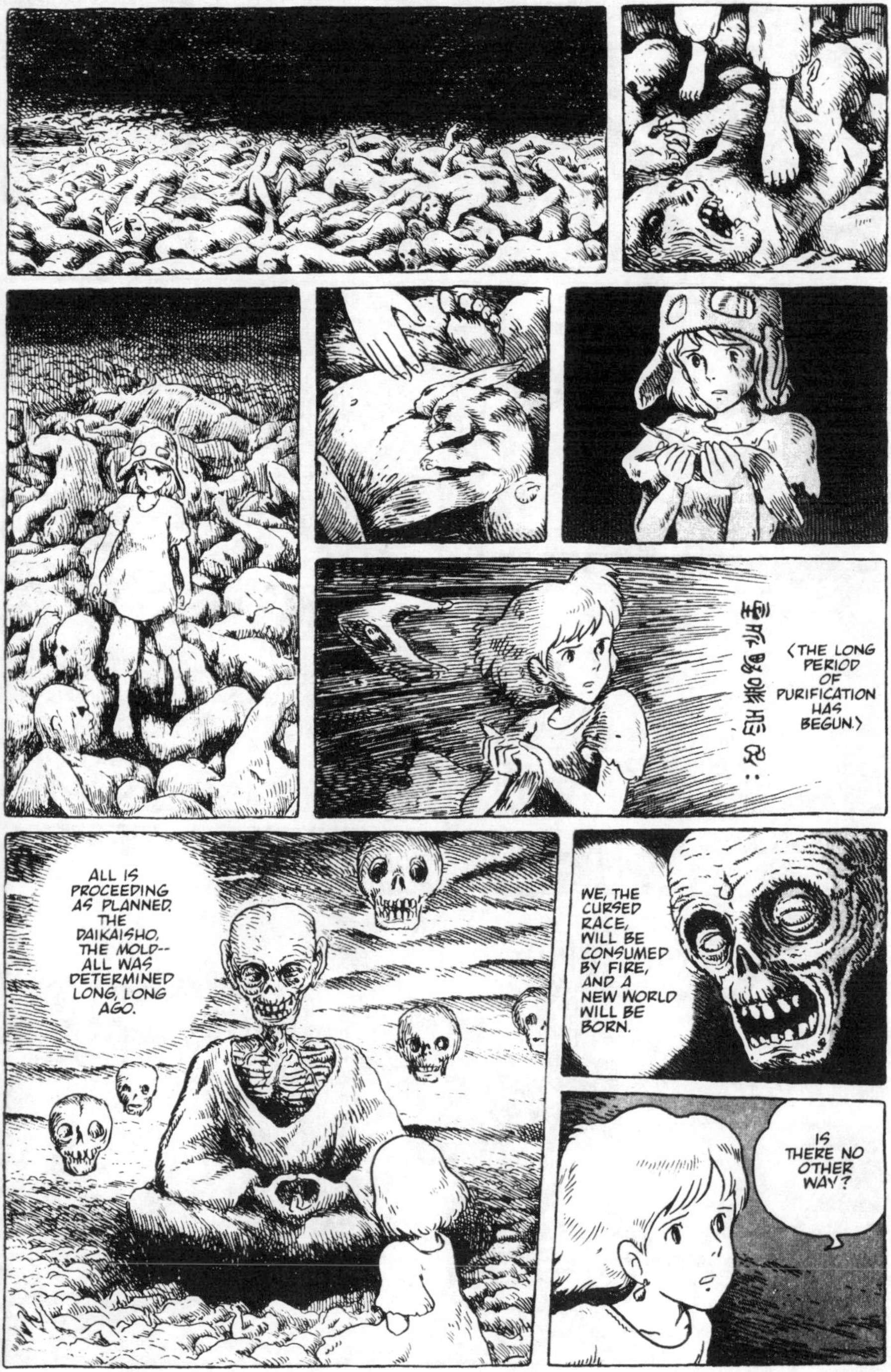
〈THE LONG PERIOD OF PURIFICATION HAS BEGUN.〉
ALL IS PROCEEDING AS PLANNED. THE DAIKAISHO, THE MOLD-- ALL WAS DETERMINED LONG, LONG AGO.
WE, THE CURSED RACE, WILL BE CONSUMED BY FIRE, AND A NEW WORLD WILL BE BORN.
IS THERE NO OTHER WAY?

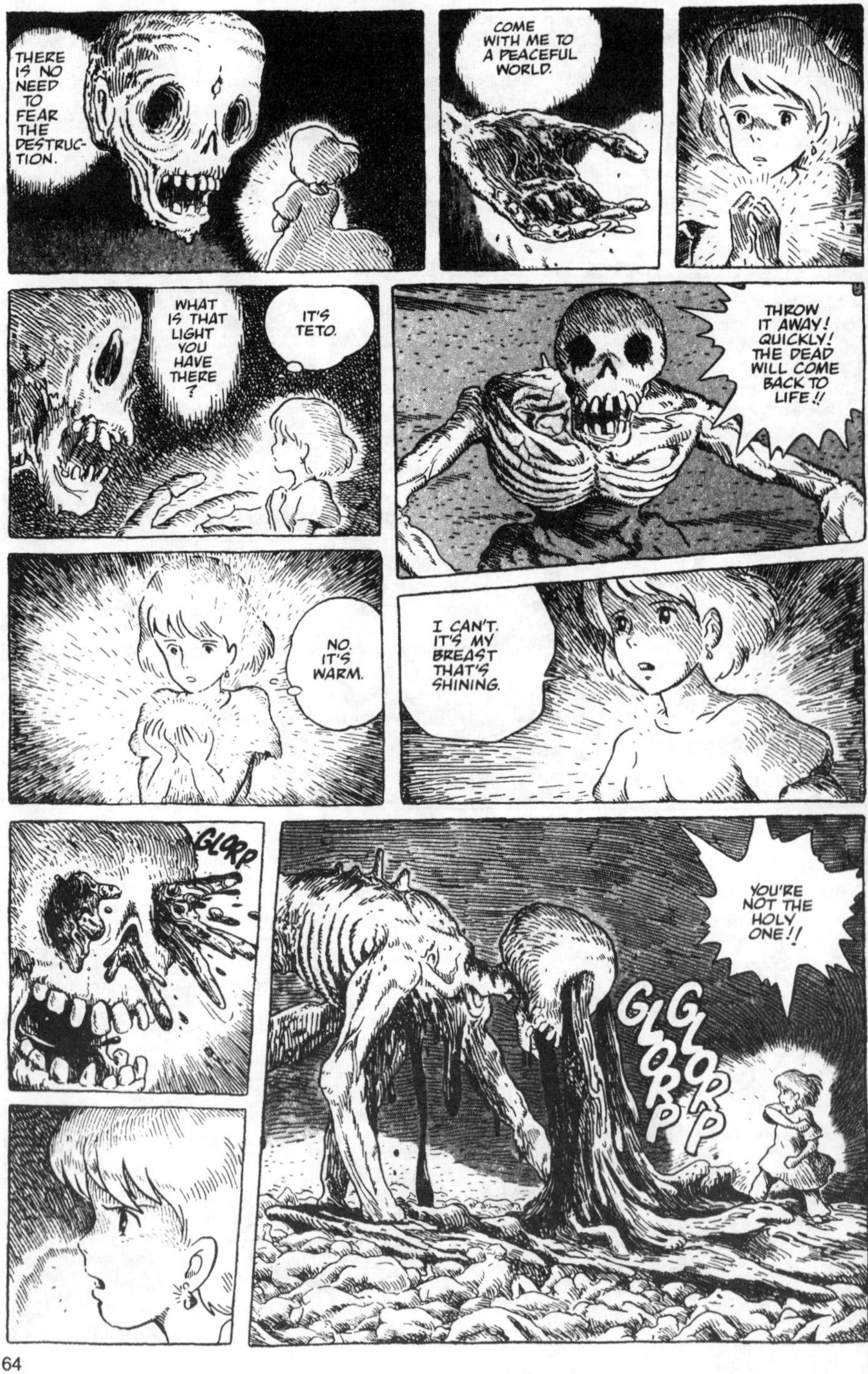
THERE IS NO NEED TO FEAR THE DESTRUCTION.
COME WITH ME TO A PEACEFUL WORLD.
WHAT IS THAT LIGHT YOU HAVE THERE?
IT'S TETO.
THROW IT AWAY! QUICKLY! THE DEAD WILL COME BACK TO LIFE!!
NO. IT'S WARM.
I CAN'T. IT'S MY BREAST THAT'S SHINING.
GLORP
YOU'RE NOT THE HOLY ONE!!
GLORP GLORP

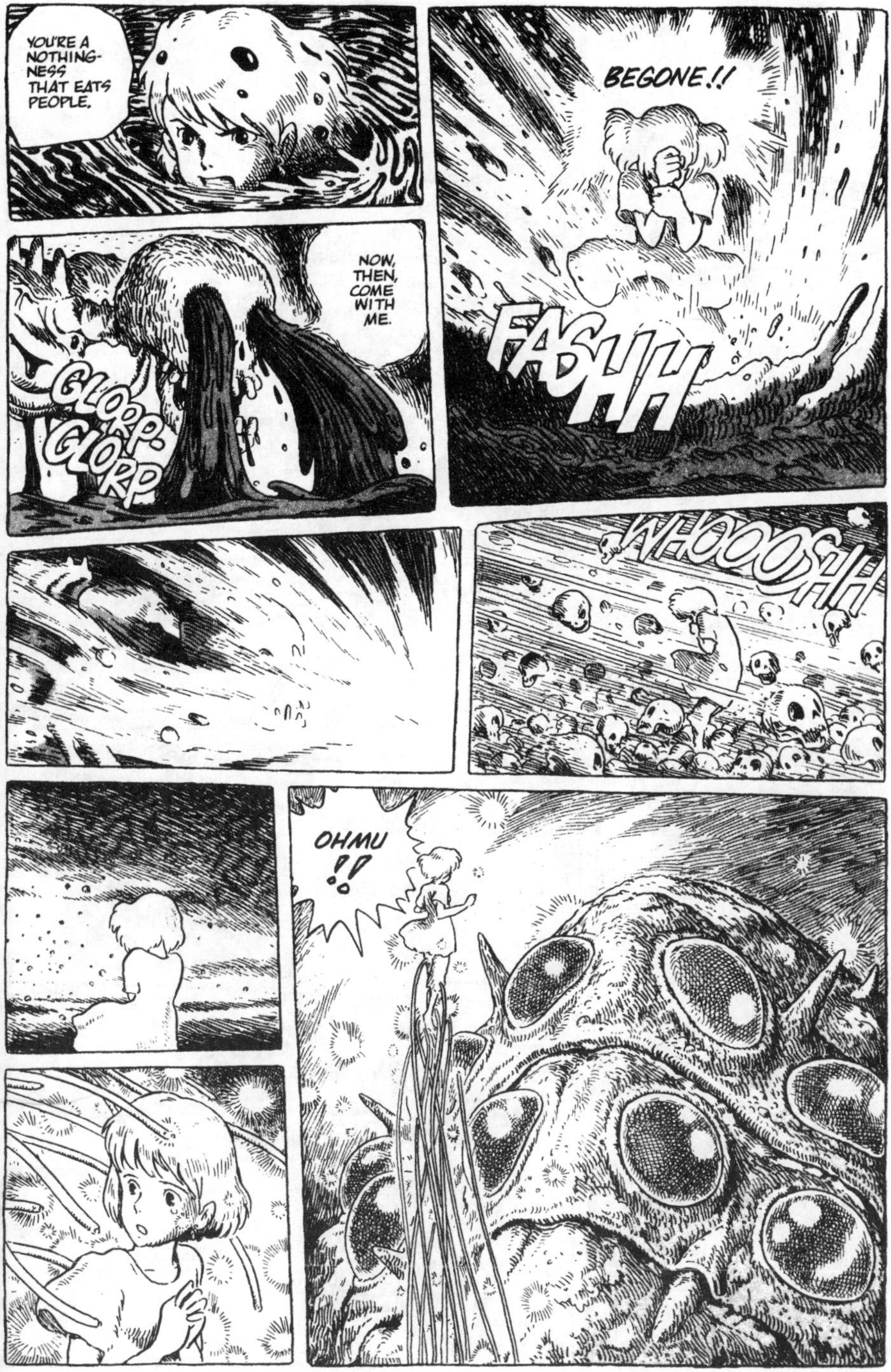
YOU'RE A NOTHING-NESS THAT EATS PEOPLE.
BEGONE!!
NOW, THEN, COME WITH ME.
GLORP GLORP
FASHH
WHOOOSHH
OHMU!!

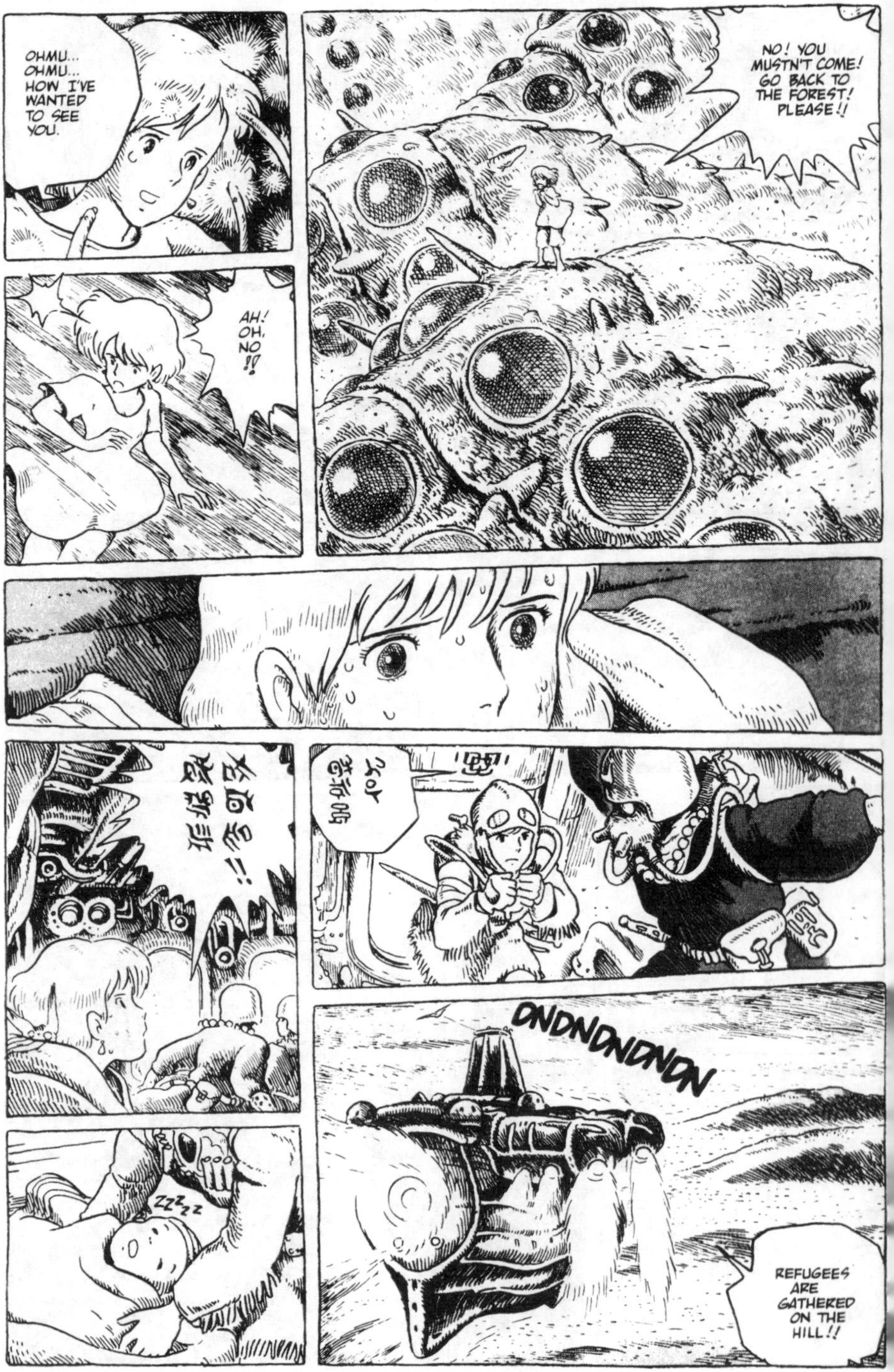
OHMU... OHMU... HOW I'VE WANTED TO SEE YOU.
NO! YOU MUSTN'T COME! GO BACK TO THE FOREST! PLEASE!!
AH! OH, NO!!
DNDNDNDNDNDN
REFUGEES ARE GATHERED ON THE HILL!!

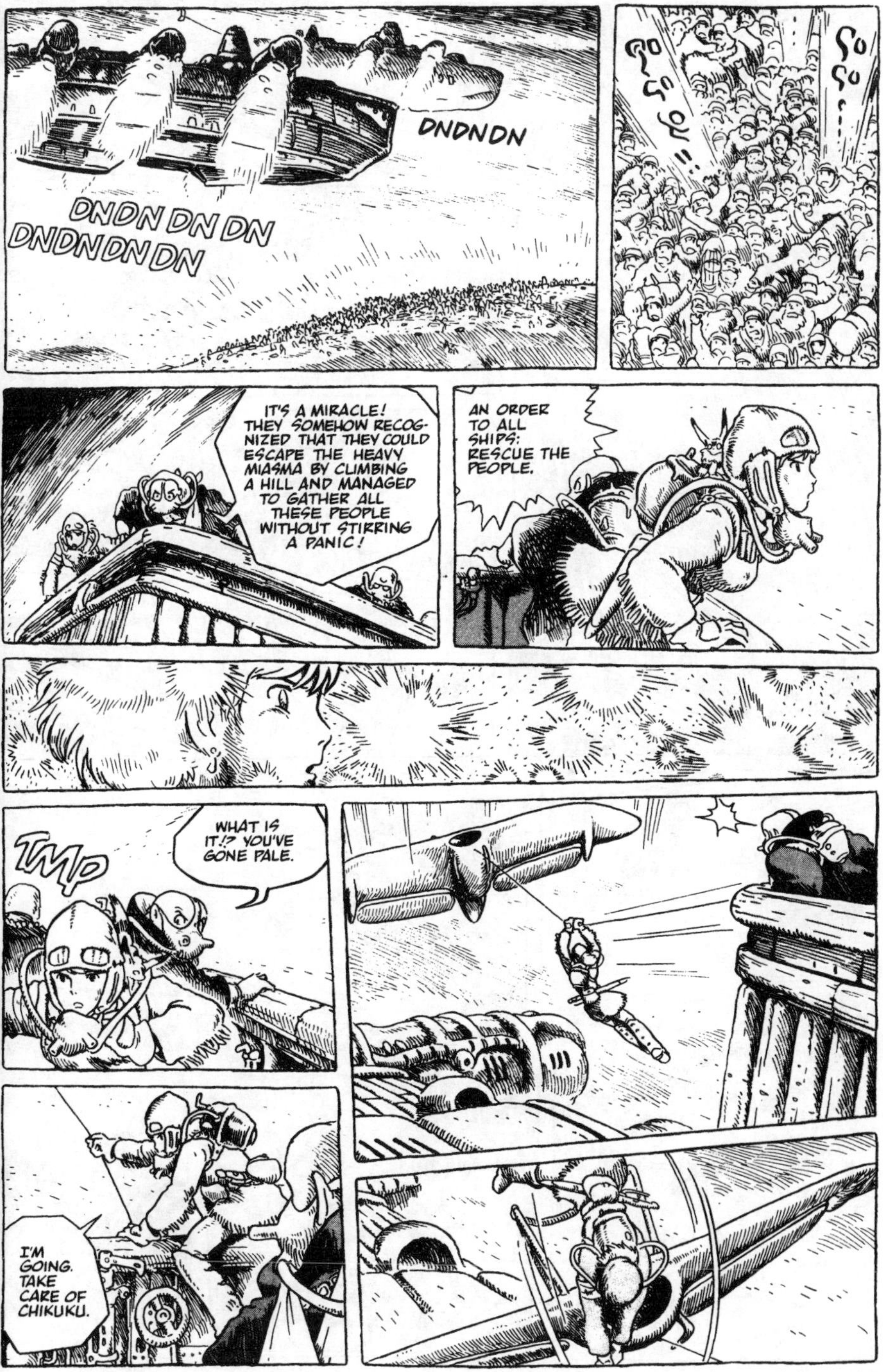
DNDNDN
DNDN DN DN
DNDNDN DN
IT'S A MIRACLE! THEY SOMEHOW RECOGNIZED THAT THEY COULD ESCAPE THE HEAVY MIASMA BY CLIMBING A HILL AND MANAGED TO GATHER ALL THESE PEOPLE WITHOUT STIRRING A PANIC!
AN ORDER TO ALL SHIPS: RESCUE THE PEOPLE.
WHAT IS IT!? YOU'VE GONE PALE.
I'M GOING. TAKE CARE OF CHIKUKU.

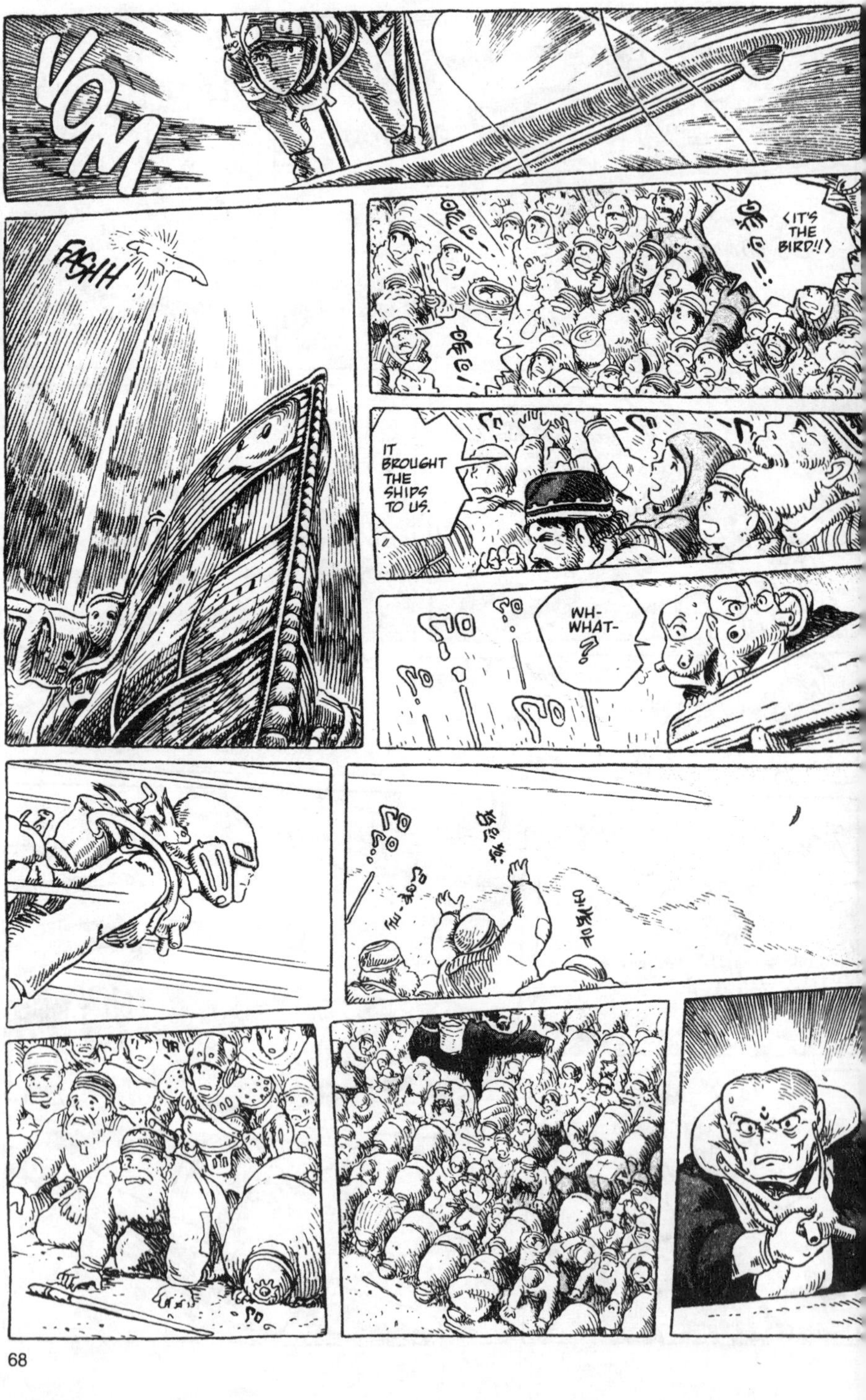
VOM
FASHH
<IT'S THE BIRD!!>
IT BROUGHT THE SHIPS TO US.
WH-WHAT-?

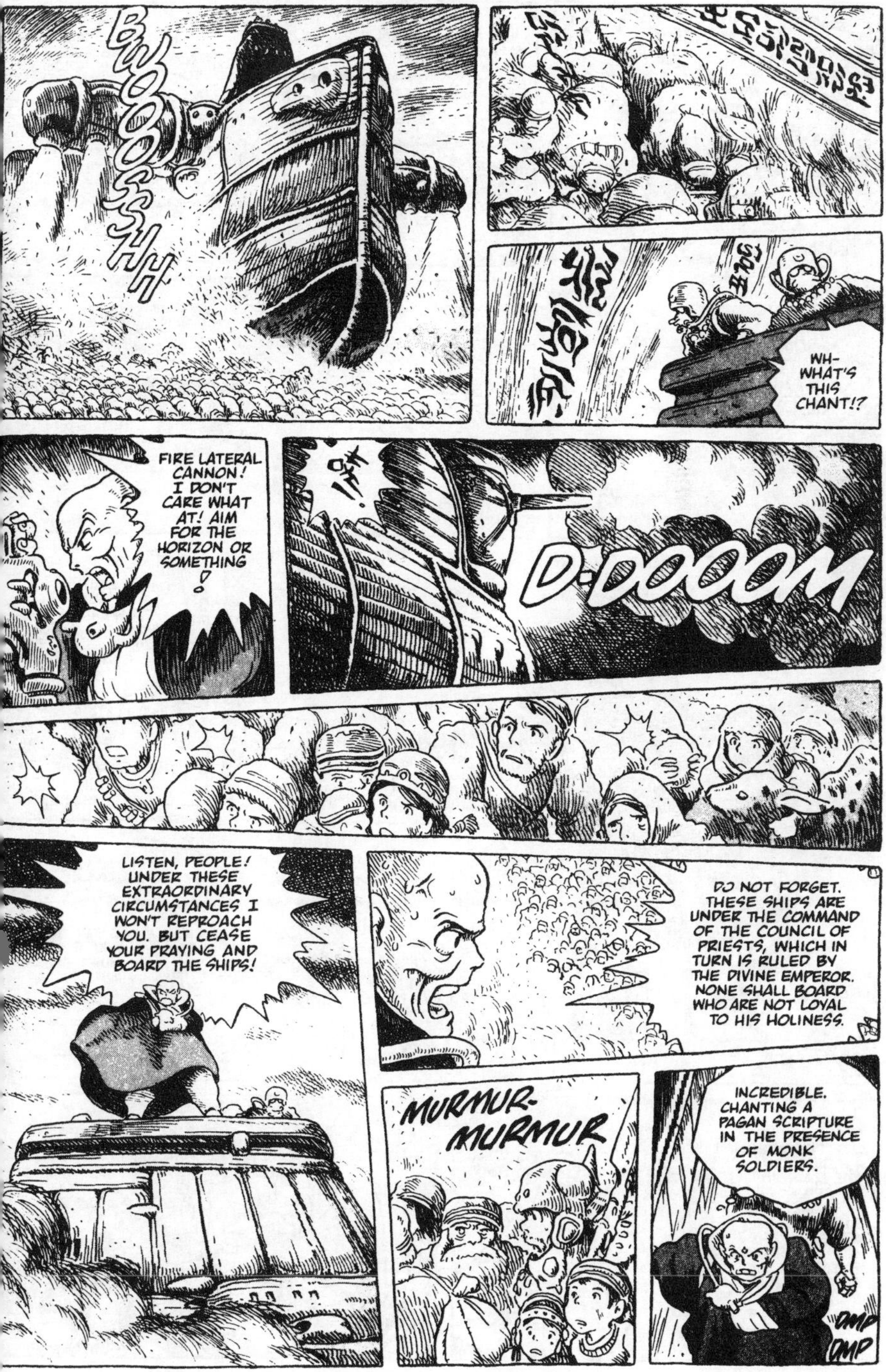
BWOOOSSHH
WH-WHAT'S THIS CHANT!?
FIRE LATERAL CANNON! I DON'T CARE WHAT AT! AIM FOR THE HORIZON OR SOMETHING!
D-DOOOM
LISTEN, PEOPLE! UNDER THESE EXTRAORDINARY CIRCUMSTANCES I WON'T REPROACH YOU. BUT CEASE YOUR PRAYING AND BOARD THE SHIPS!
DO NOT FORGET. THESE SHIPS ARE UNDER THE COMMAND OF THE COUNCIL OF PRIESTS, WHICH IN TURN IS RULED BY THE DIVINE EMPEROR. NONE SHALL BOARD WHO ARE NOT LOYAL TO HIS HOLINESS.
MURMUR-MURMUR
INCREDIBLE. CHANTING A PAGAN SCRIPTURE IN THE PRESENCE OF MONK SOLDIERS.
OMP OMP

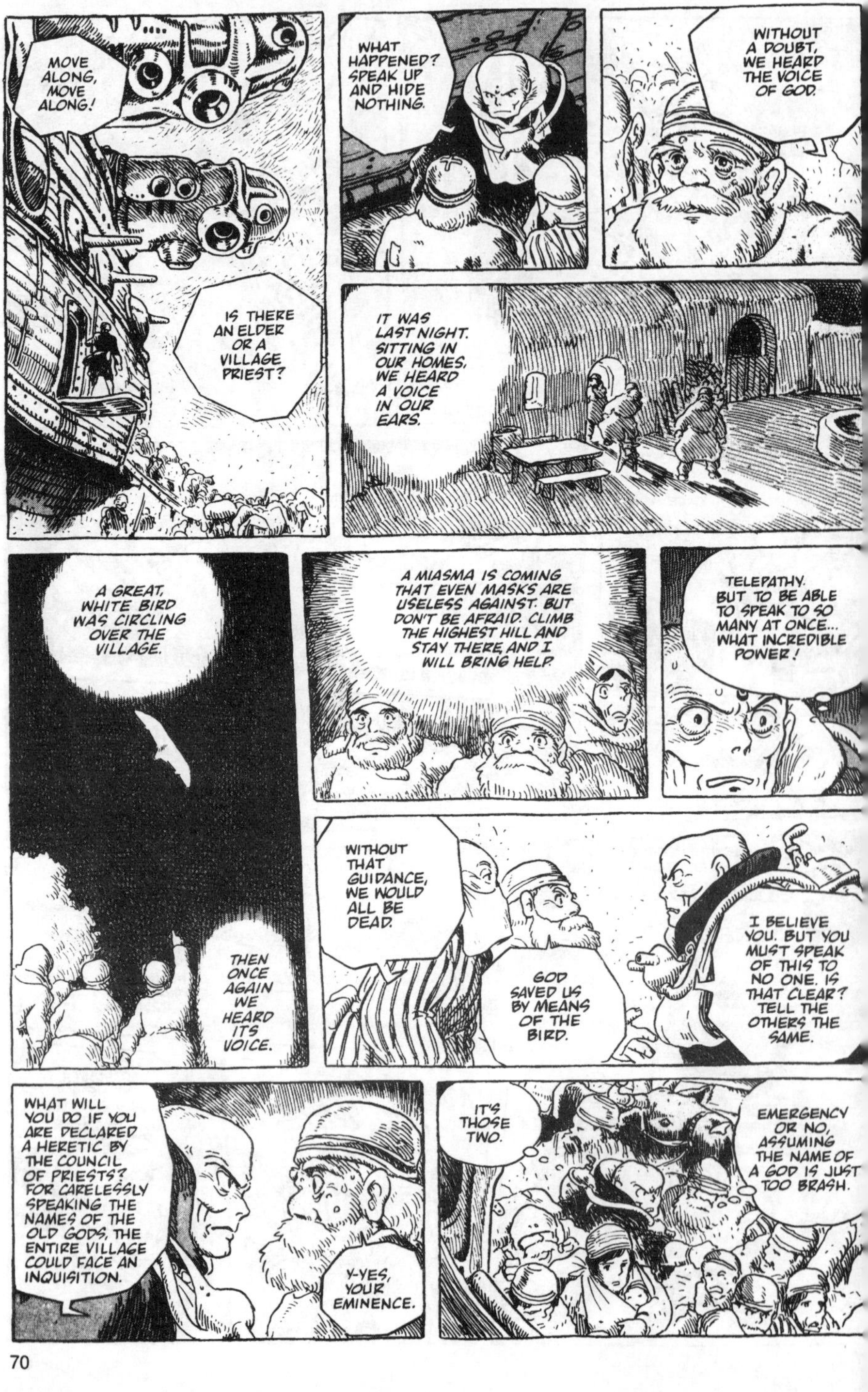
MOVE ALONG, MOVE ALONG!
IS THERE AN ELDER OR A VILLAGE PRIEST?
WHAT HAPPENED? SPEAK UP AND HIDE NOTHING.
WITHOUT A DOUBT, WE HEARD THE VOICE OF GOD.
IT WAS LAST NIGHT. SITTING IN OUR HOMES, WE HEARD A VOICE IN OUR EARS.
A GREAT, WHITE BIRD WAS CIRCLING OVER THE VILLAGE.
THEN ONCE AGAIN WE HEARD ITS VOICE.
A MIASMA IS COMING THAT EVEN MASKS ARE USELESS AGAINST. BUT DON'T BE AFRAID. CLIMB THE HIGHEST HILL AND STAY THERE, AND I WILL BRING HELP.
TELEPATHY. BUT TO BE ABLE TO SPEAK TO SO MANY AT ONCE... WHAT INCREDIBLE POWER!
WITHOUT THAT GUIDANCE, WE WOULD ALL BE DEAD.
GOD SAVED US BY MEANS OF THE BIRD.
I BELIEVE YOU. BUT YOU MUST SPEAK OF THIS TO NO ONE. IS THAT CLEAR? TELL THE OTHERS THE SAME.
WHAT WILL YOU DO IF YOU ARE DECLARED A HERETIC BY THE COUNCIL OF PRIESTS? FOR CARELESSLY SPEAKING THE NAMES OF THE OLD GODS, THE ENTIRE VILLAGE COULD FACE AN INQUISITION.
Y-YES, YOUR EMINENCE.
IT'S THOSE TWO.
EMERGENCY OR NO, ASSUMING THE NAME OF A GOD IS JUST TOO BRASH.

THAT'S RIGHT. CHIKUKU DID IT.

ALL YOU HAVE TO SAY IS: "THAT'S RIGHT"?

CHIKUKU'S TIRED.

WH-!? DON'T FALL ASLEEP!

YOU'RE STILL A CHILD, SO PERHAPS YOU DON'T KNOW, BUT MANY HAVE BURNED AT THE STAKE ON SUSPICION OF PREACHING HERETICAL RELIGION.

NAUSICAÄ ISN'T A PREACHER. SHE'S THE APOSTLE.

THE APOSTLE!?

THE WHITE-WINGED APOSTLE.

DON'T BE SILLY. THAT GIRL IS JUST A HEATHEN. AND THOSE WINGS ARE A KIND OF KITE USED BY THE PEOPLE OF EFTAL.

OF COURSE. THE APOSTLE IS A HUMAN BEING. IF SHE HAD WINGS GROWING OUT OF HER BACK, SHE'D BE A MONSTER.

CHIKUKU LOVES NAUSICAÄ.

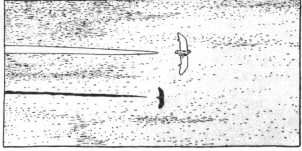

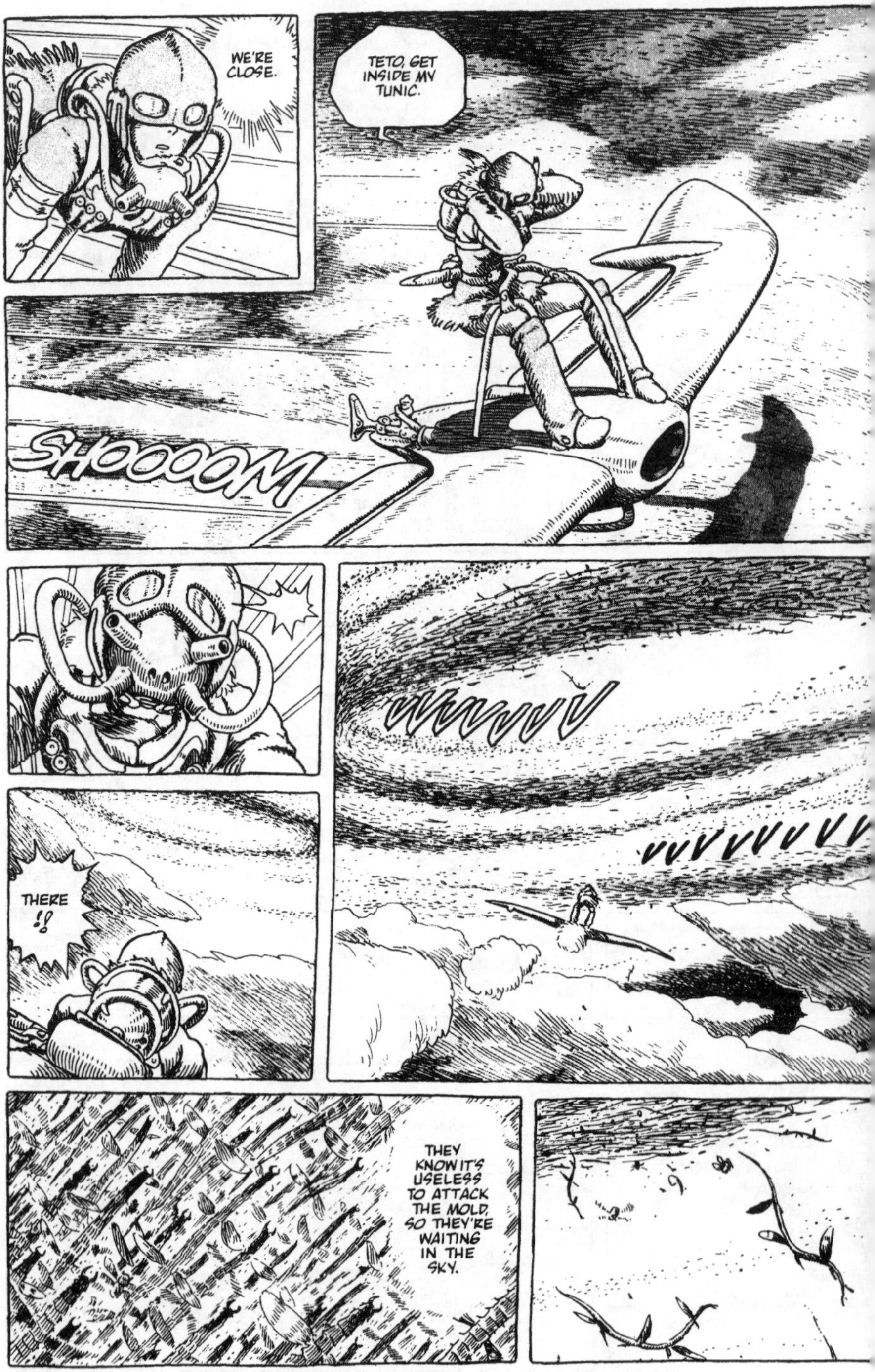
WE'RE CLOSE.
TETO, GET INSIDE MY TUNIC.
SHOOOOM
THERE !!
THEY KNOW IT'S USELESS TO ATTACK THE MOLD, SO THEY'RE WAITING IN THE SKY.

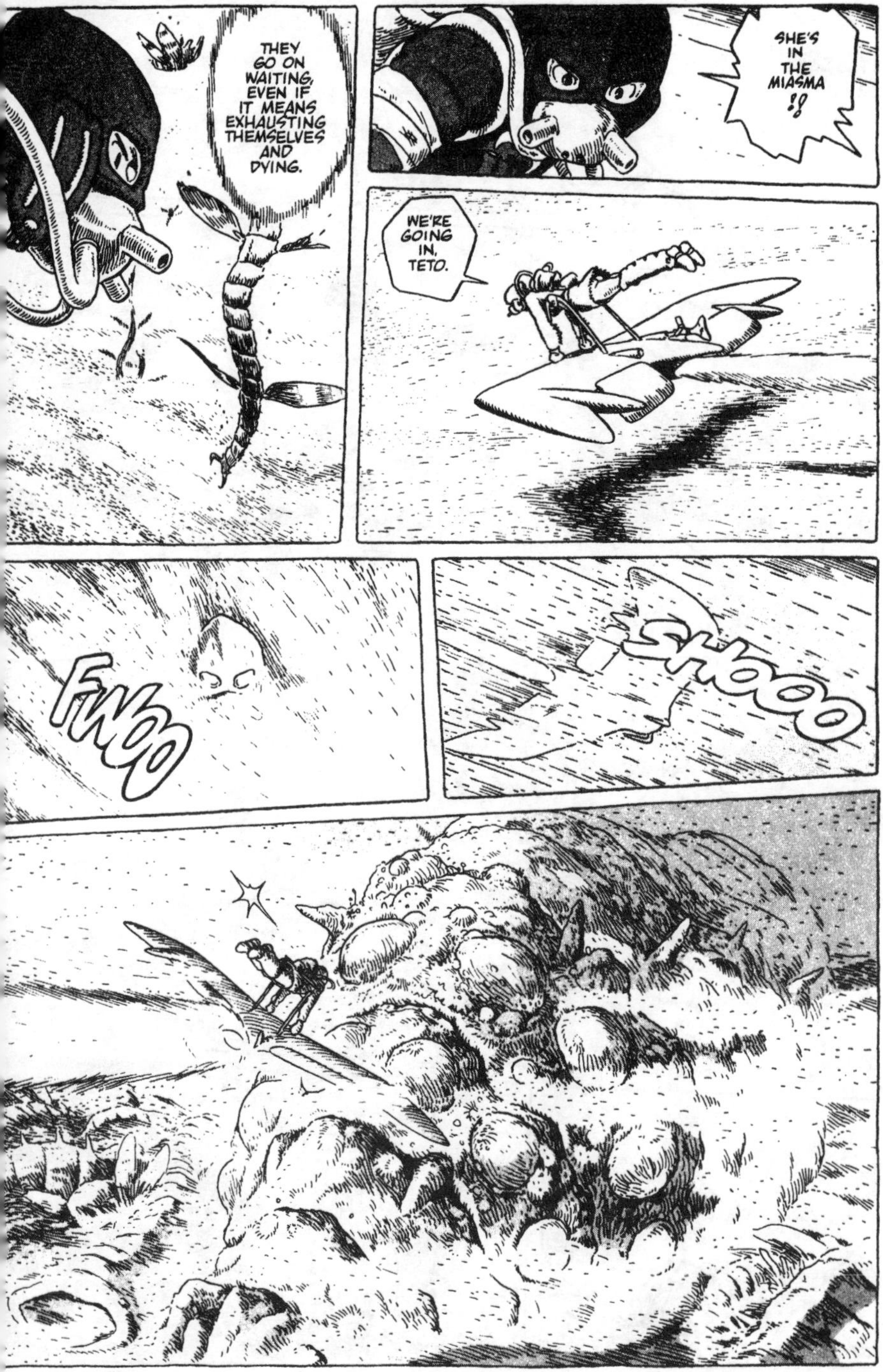
THEY GO ON WAITING, EVEN IF IT MEANS EXHAUSTING THEMSELVES AND DYING.
SHE'S IN THE MIASMA !!
WE'RE GOING IN, TETO.
FWOOO
SHOOO

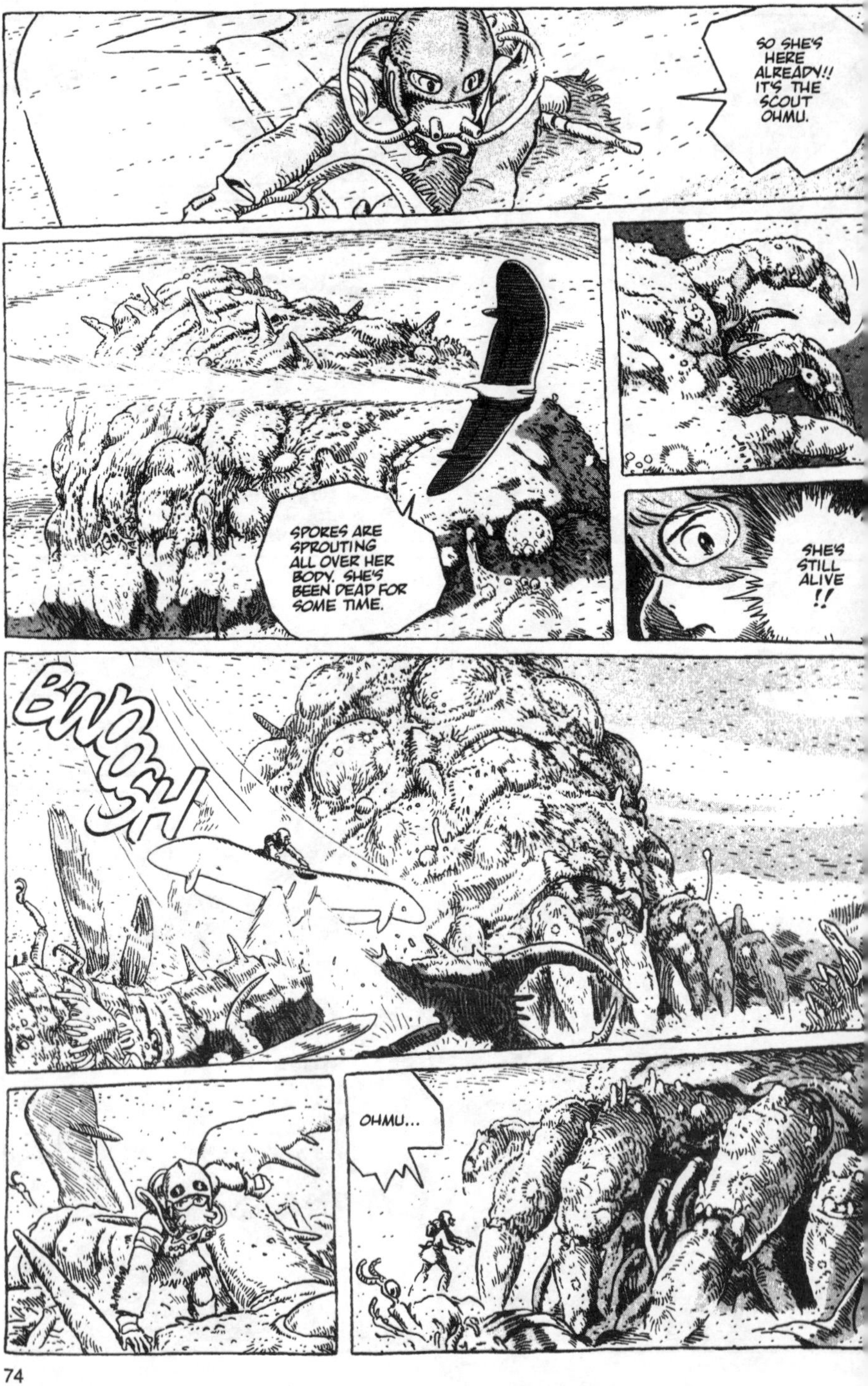
SO SHE'S HERE ALREADY!! IT'S THE SCOUT OHMU.
SPORES ARE SPROUTING ALL OVER HER BODY. SHE'S BEEN DEAD FOR SOME TIME.
SHE'S STILL ALIVE !!
BWOOSH
OHMU...

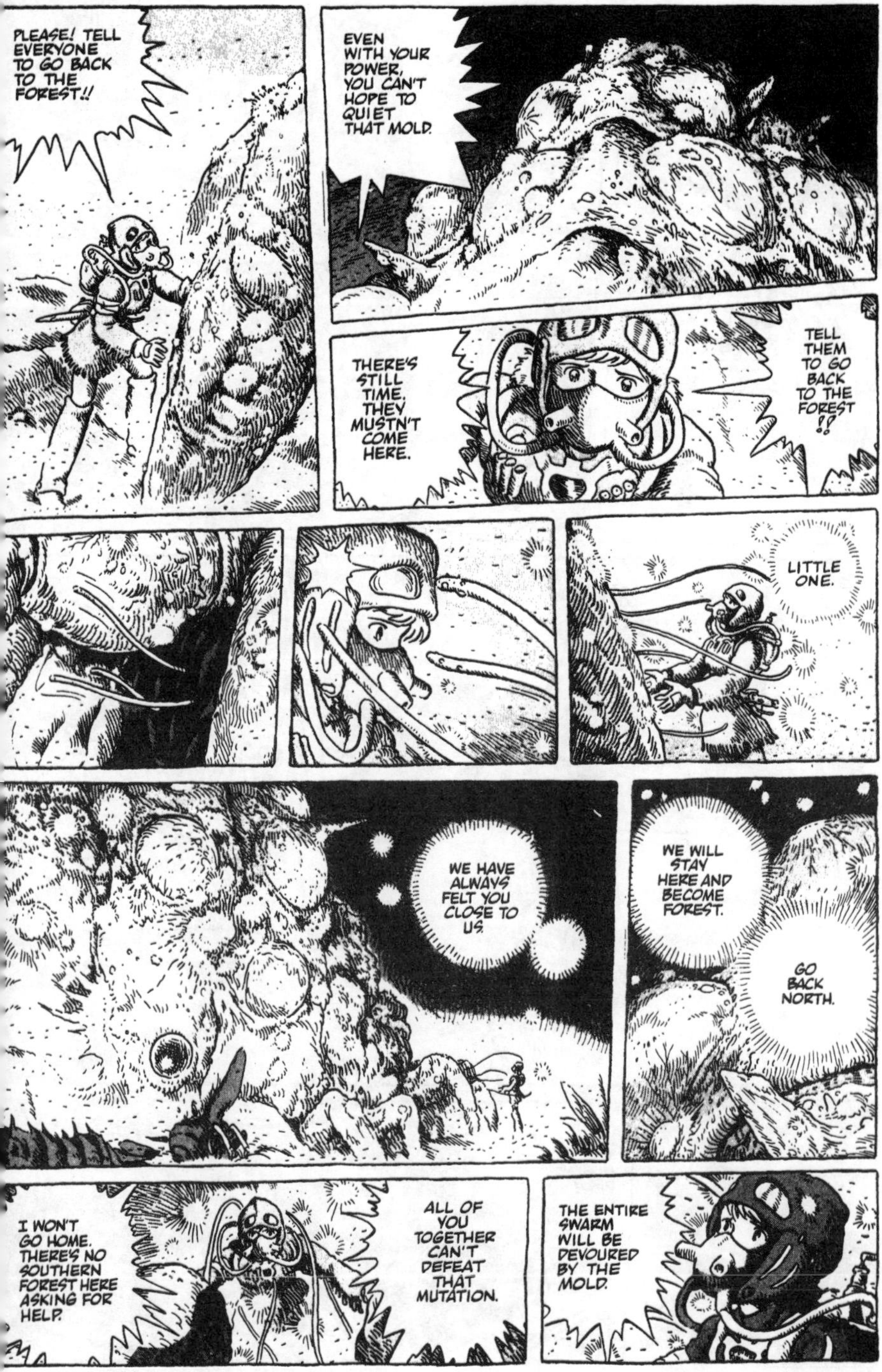
PLEASE! TELL EVERYONE TO GO BACK TO THE FOREST!!
EVEN WITH YOUR POWER, YOU CAN'T HOPE TO QUIET THAT MOLD.
THERE'S STILL TIME. THEY MUSTN'T COME HERE.
TELL THEM TO GO BACK TO THE FOREST!!
LITTLE ONE.
WE HAVE ALWAYS FELT YOU CLOSE TO US.
WE WILL STAY HERE AND BECOME FOREST.
GO BACK NORTH.
I WON'T GO HOME. THERE'S NO SOUTHERN FOREST HERE ASKING FOR HELP.
ALL OF YOU TOGETHER CAN'T DEFEAT THAT MUTATION.
THE ENTIRE SWARM WILL BE DEVOURED BY THE MOLD.

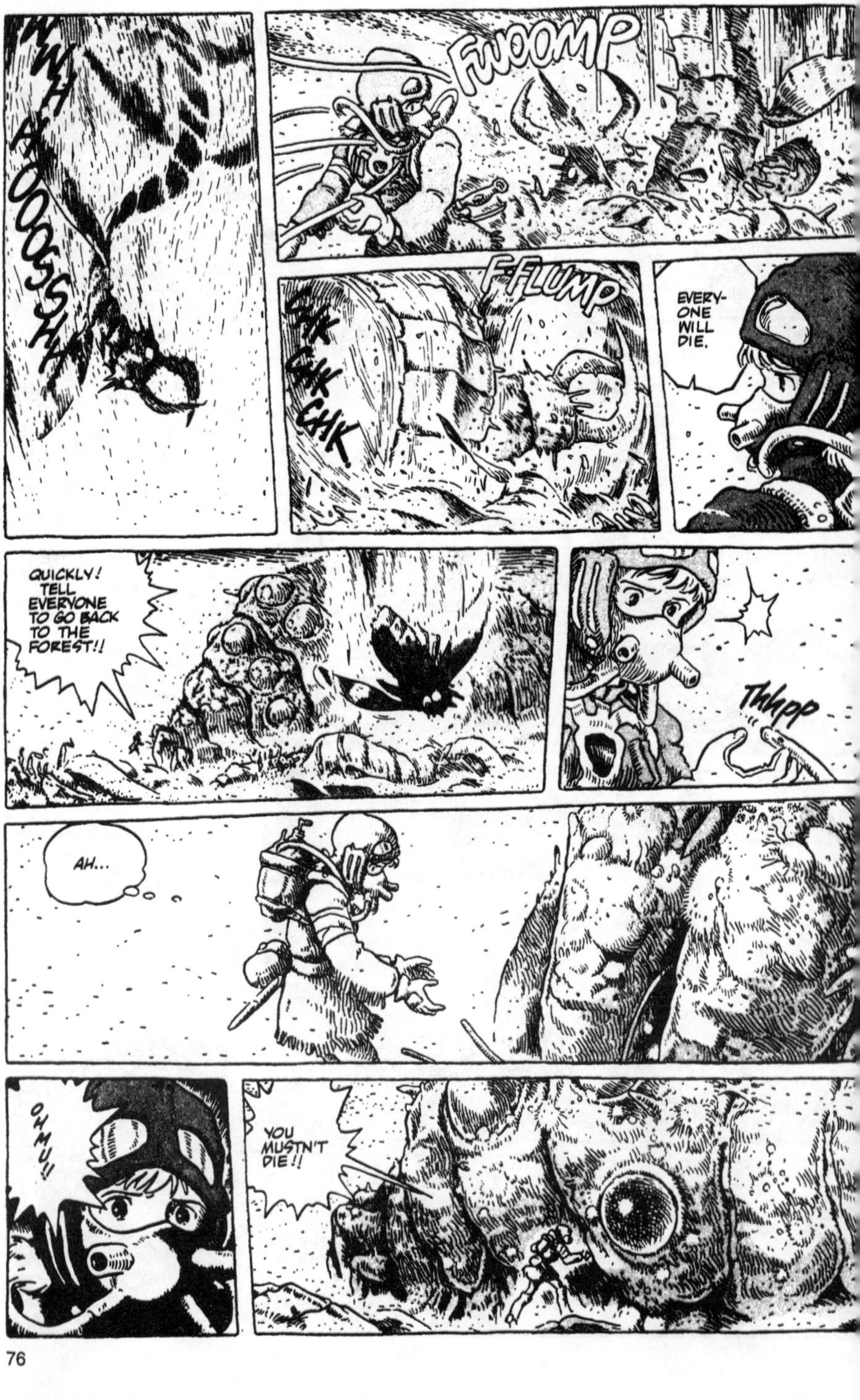
FWOOMP
F-FLUMP
EVERY-ONE WILL DIE.
QUICKLY! TELL EVERYONE TO GO BACK TO THE FOREST!!
THPP
AH...
OHMU!!
YOU MUSTN'T DIE!!

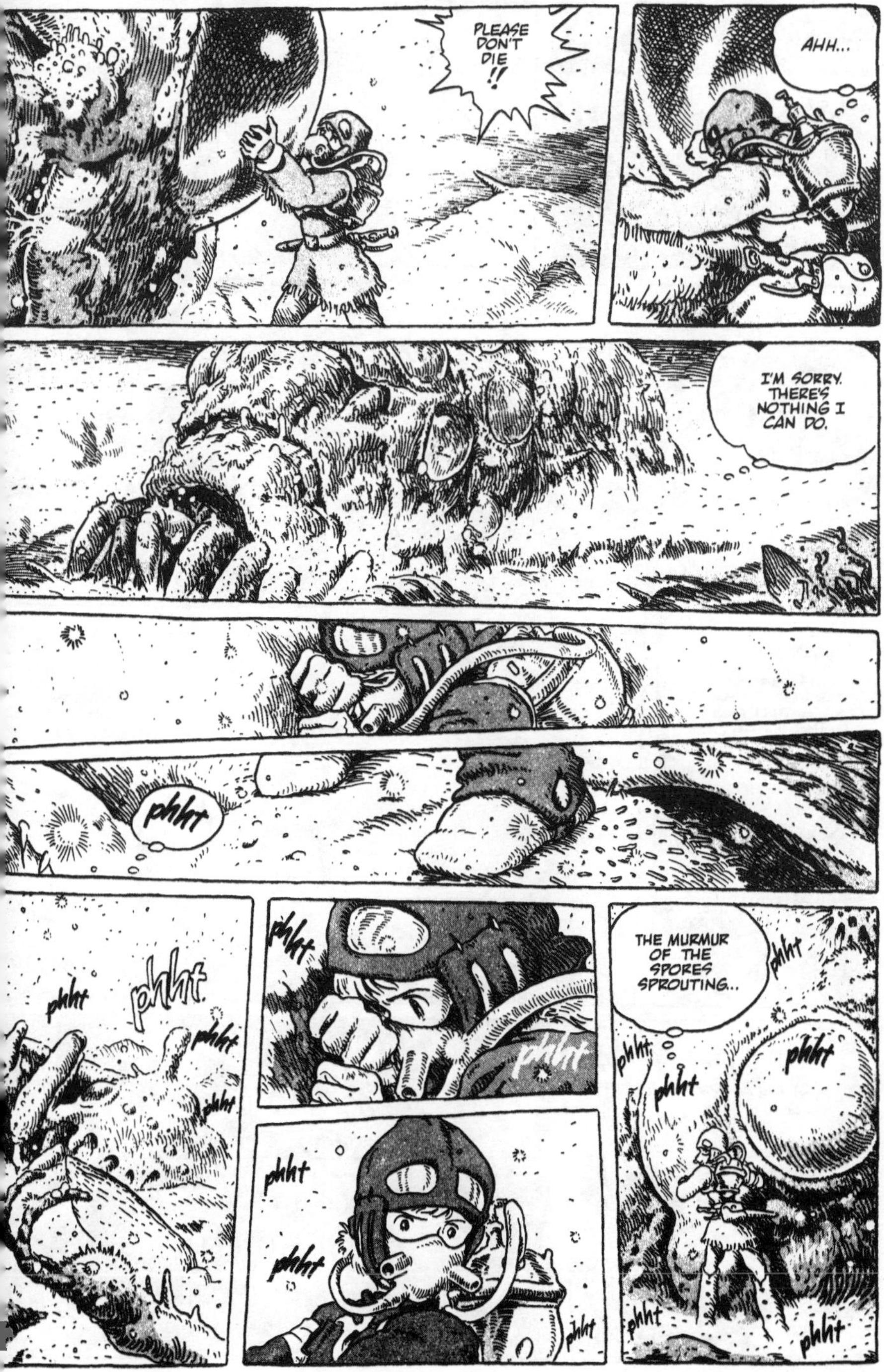
PLEASE DON'T DIE!!
AHH...
I'M SORRY. THERE'S NOTHING I CAN DO.
phht
phht
phht
phht
phht
phht
phht
phht
phht
phht
phht
THE MURMUR OF THE SPORES SPROUTING...
phht
phht
phht
phht
phht
phht

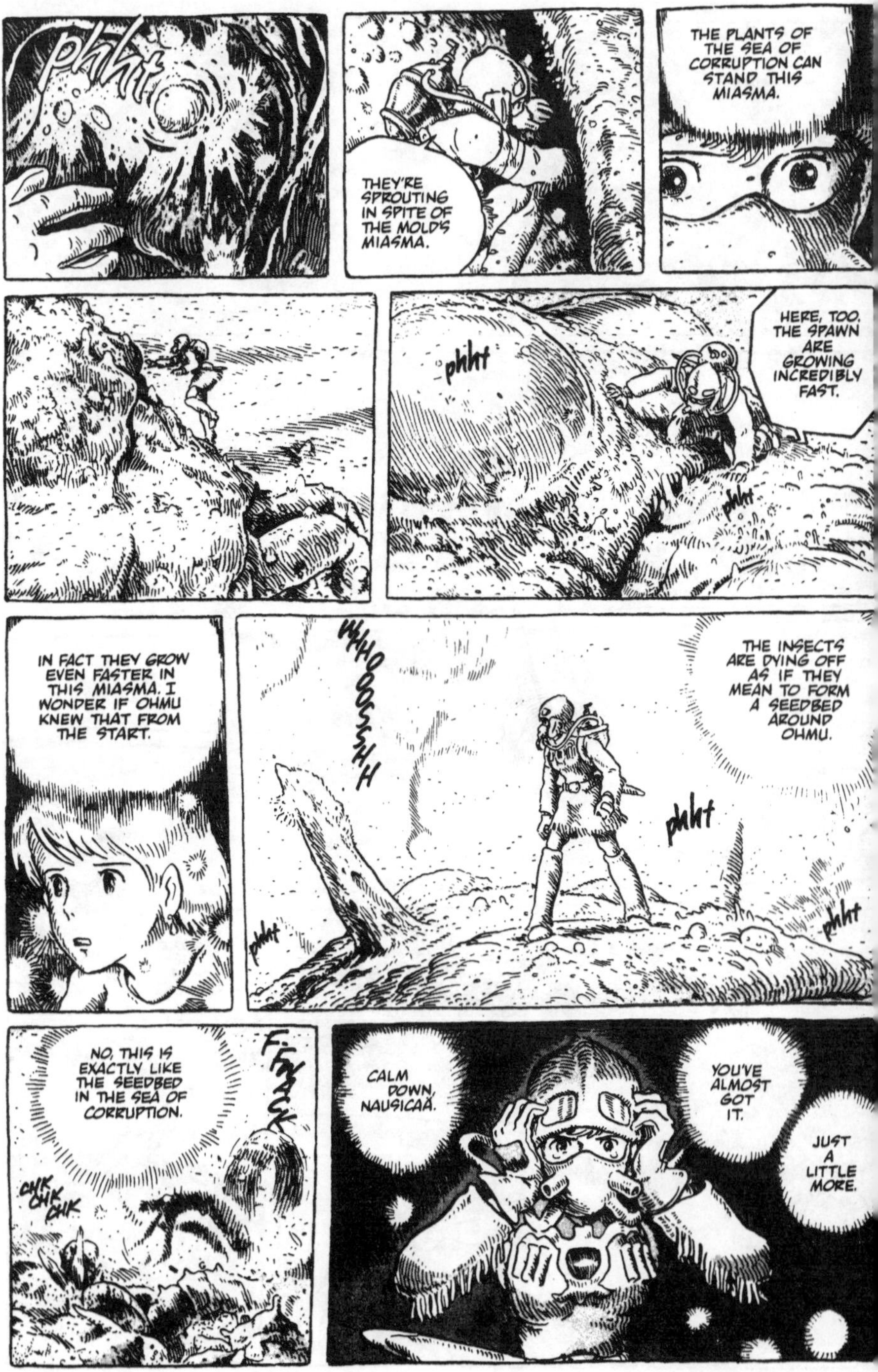
phht
THEY'RE SPROUTING IN SPITE OF THE MOLD'S MIASMA.
THE PLANTS OF THE SEA OF CORRUPTION CAN STAND THIS MIASMA.
phht
HERE, TOO, THE SPAWN ARE GROWING INCREDIBLY FAST.
phht
IN FACT THEY GROW EVEN FASTER IN THIS MIASMA. I WONDER IF OHMU KNEW THAT FROM THE START.
WHHOOOSSHH
THE INSECTS ARE DYING OFF AS IF THEY MEAN TO FORM A SEEDBED AROUND OHMU.
phht
phht
phht
NO, THIS IS EXACTLY LIKE THE SEEDBED IN THE SEA OF CORRUPTION.
CHK CHK CHK
CALM DOWN, NAUSICAÄ.
YOU'VE ALMOST GOT IT.
JUST A LITTLE MORE.

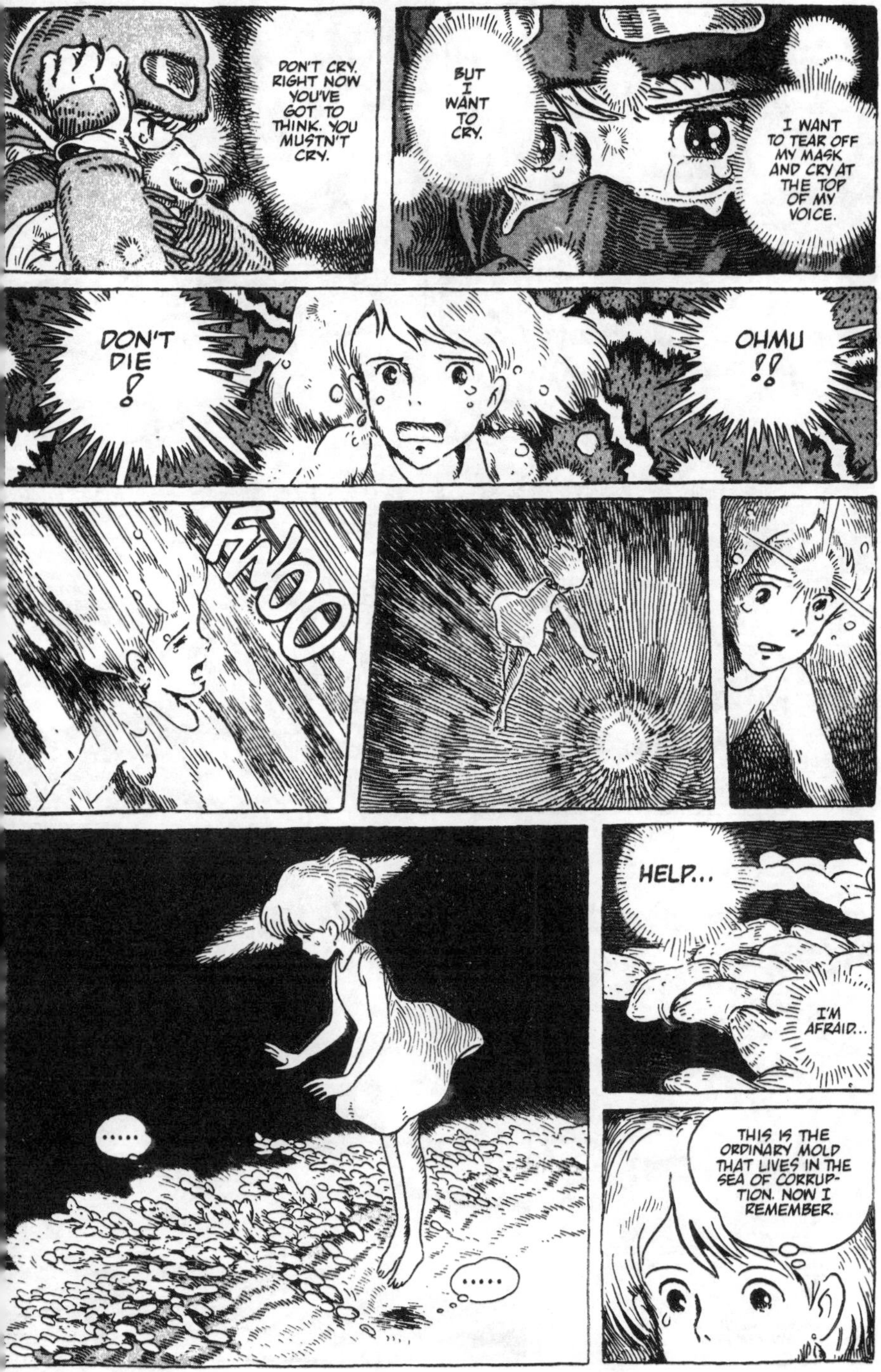
DON'T CRY. RIGHT NOW YOU'VE GOT TO THINK. YOU MUSTN'T CRY.
BUT I WANT TO CRY.
I WANT TO TEAR OFF MY MASK AND CRY AT THE TOP OF MY VOICE.
DON'T DIE!
OHMU!!
FWOO
HELP...
I'M AFRAID...
......
.....
THIS IS THE ORDINARY MOLD THAT LIVES IN THE SEA OF CORRUPTION. NOW I REMEMBER.

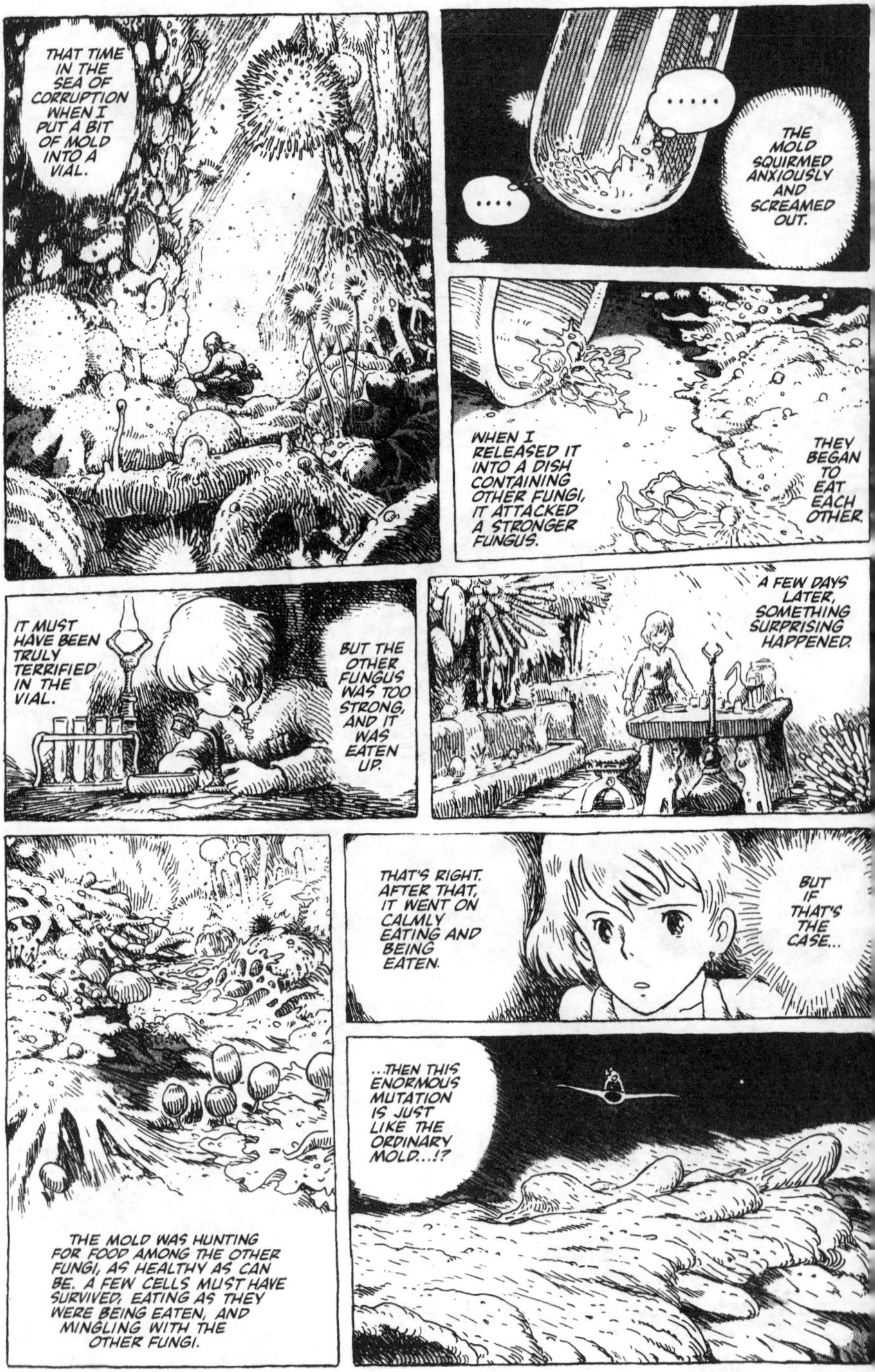
THAT TIME IN THE SEA OF CORRUPTION WHEN I PUT A BIT OF MOLD INTO A VIAL.
.....
....
THE MOLD SQUIRMED ANXIOUSLY AND SCREAMED OUT.
WHEN I RELEASED IT INTO A DISH CONTAINING OTHER FUNGI, IT ATTACKED A STRONGER FUNGUS.
THEY BEGAN TO EAT EACH OTHER.
IT MUST HAVE BEEN TRULY TERRIFIED IN THE VIAL.
BUT THE OTHER FUNGUS WAS TOO STRONG, AND IT WAS EATEN UP.
A FEW DAYS LATER, SOMETHING SURPRISING HAPPENED.
THE MOLD WAS HUNTING FOR FOOD AMONG THE OTHER FUNGI, AS HEALTHY AS CAN BE. A FEW CELLS MUST HAVE SURVIVED, EATING AS THEY WERE BEING EATEN, AND MINGLING WITH THE OTHER FUNGI.
THAT'S RIGHT. AFTER THAT, IT WENT ON CALMLY EATING AND BEING EATEN.
BUT IF THAT'S THE CASE...
...THEN THIS ENORMOUS MUTATION IS JUST LIKE THE ORDINARY MOLD...!?

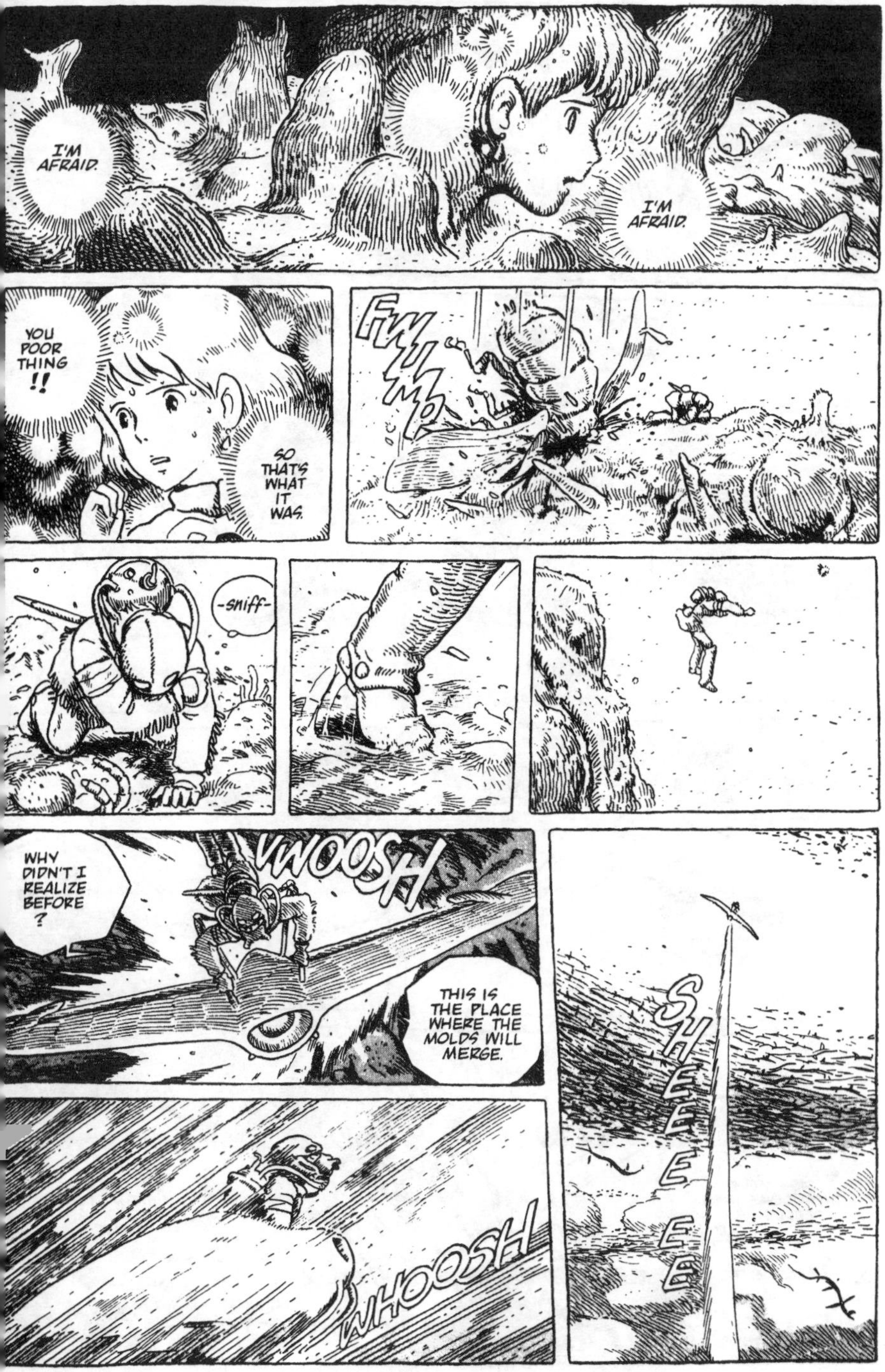
I'M AFRAID.
I'M AFRAID.
YOU POOR THING!!
SO THAT'S WHAT IT WAS.
FWUMP
-sniff-
WHY DIDN'T I REALIZE BEFORE?
WOOSH
THIS IS THE PLACE WHERE THE MOLDS WILL MERGE.
WHOOSH
SHEEEEEE

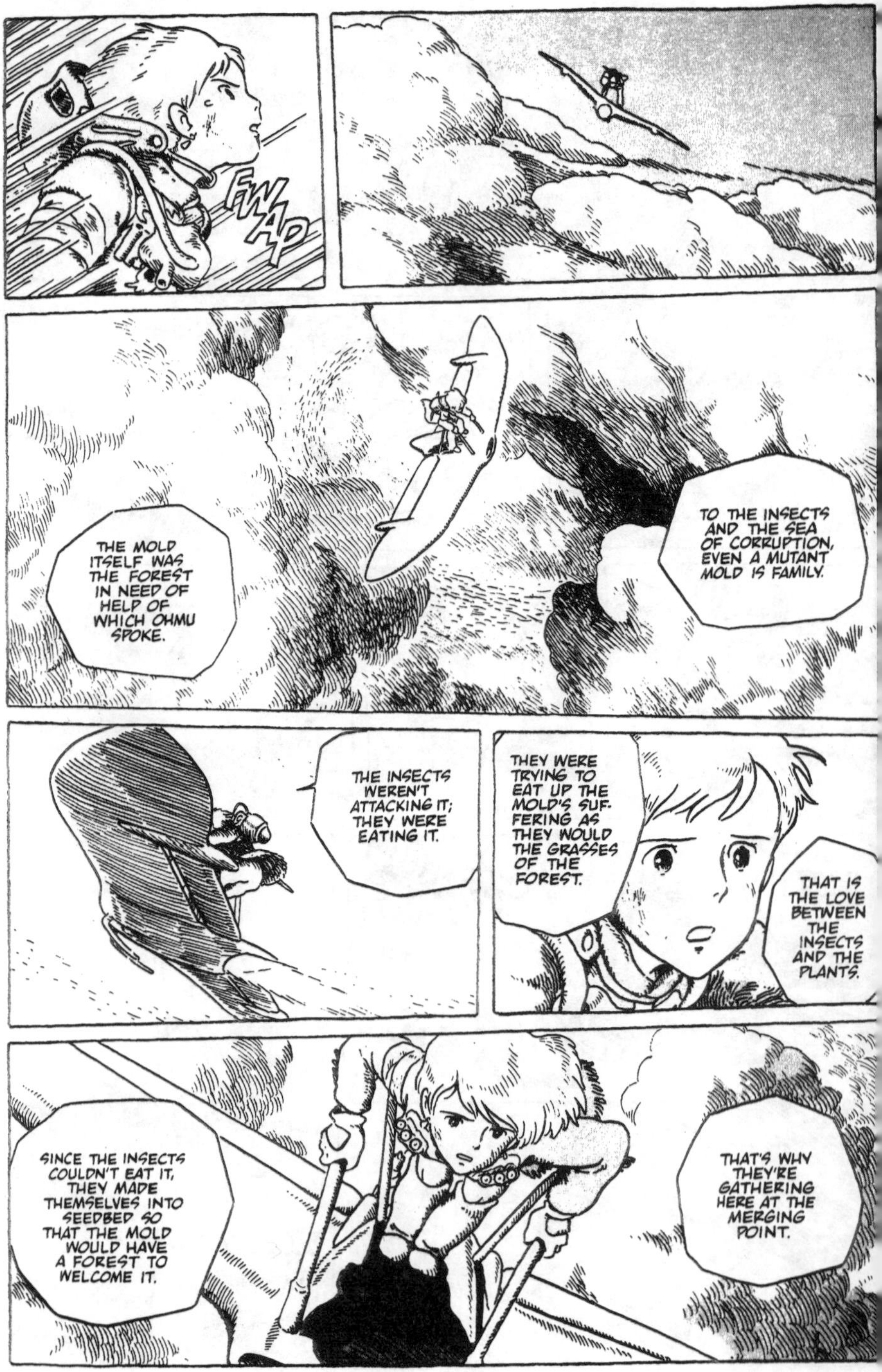
FWAP
THE MOLD ITSELF WAS THE FOREST IN NEED OF HELP OF WHICH OHMU SPOKE.
TO THE INSECTS AND THE SEA OF CORRUPTION, EVEN A MUTANT MOLD IS FAMILY.
THE INSECTS WEREN'T ATTACKING IT; THEY WERE EATING IT.
THEY WERE TRYING TO EAT UP THE MOLD'S SUF- FERING AS THEY WOULD THE GRASSES OF THE FOREST.
THAT IS THE LOVE BETWEEN THE INSECTS AND THE PLANTS.
SINCE THE INSECTS COULDN'T EAT IT, THEY MADE THEMSELVES INTO SEEDBED SO THAT THE MOLD WOULD HAVE A FOREST TO WELCOME IT.
THAT'S WHY THEY'RE GATHERING HERE AT THE MERGING POINT.

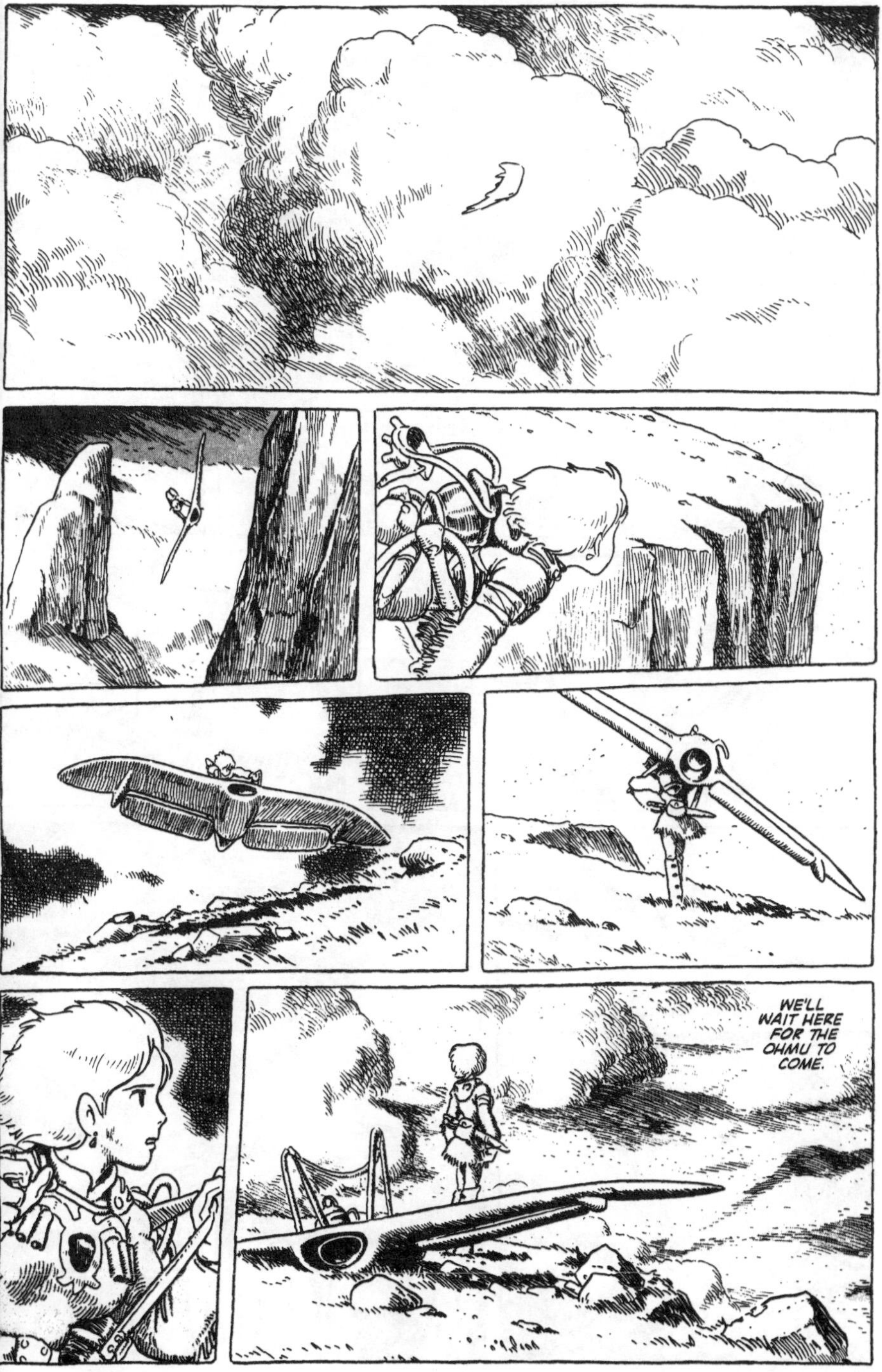
WE'LL WAIT HERE FOR THE OHMU TO COME.

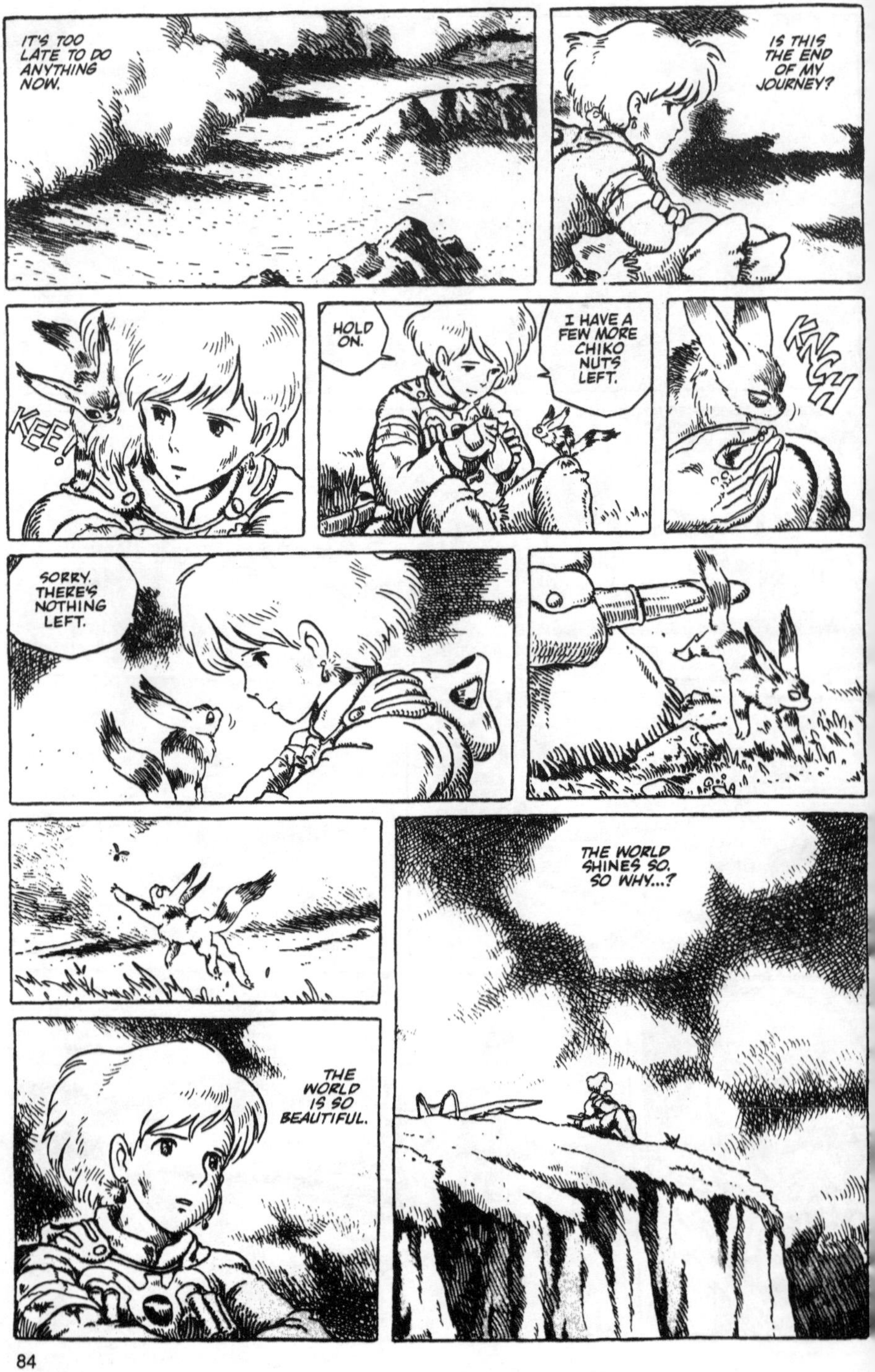
IT'S TOO LATE TO DO ANYTHING NOW.
IS THIS THE END OF MY JOURNEY?
KEE!
HOLD ON.
I HAVE A FEW MORE CHIKO NUTS LEFT.
KNCH
SORRY. THERE'S NOTHING LEFT.
THE WORLD IS SO BEAUTIFUL.
THE WORLD SHINES SO. SO WHY...?

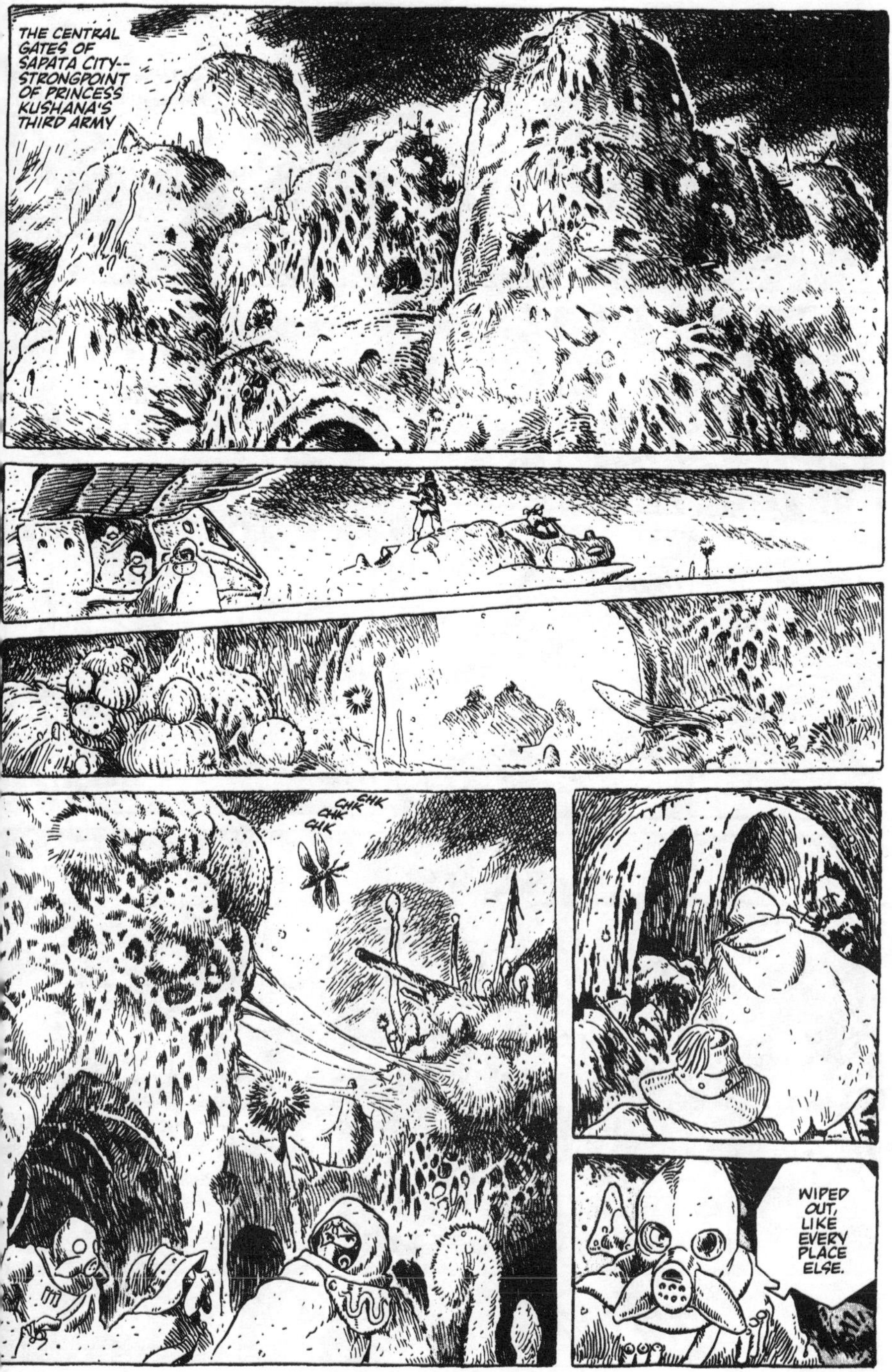
THE CENTRAL GATES OF SAPATA CITY-- STRONGPOINT OF PRINCESS KUSHANA'S THIRD ARMY
CHK CHK CHK CHK
WIPED OUT, LIKE EVERY PLACE ELSE.

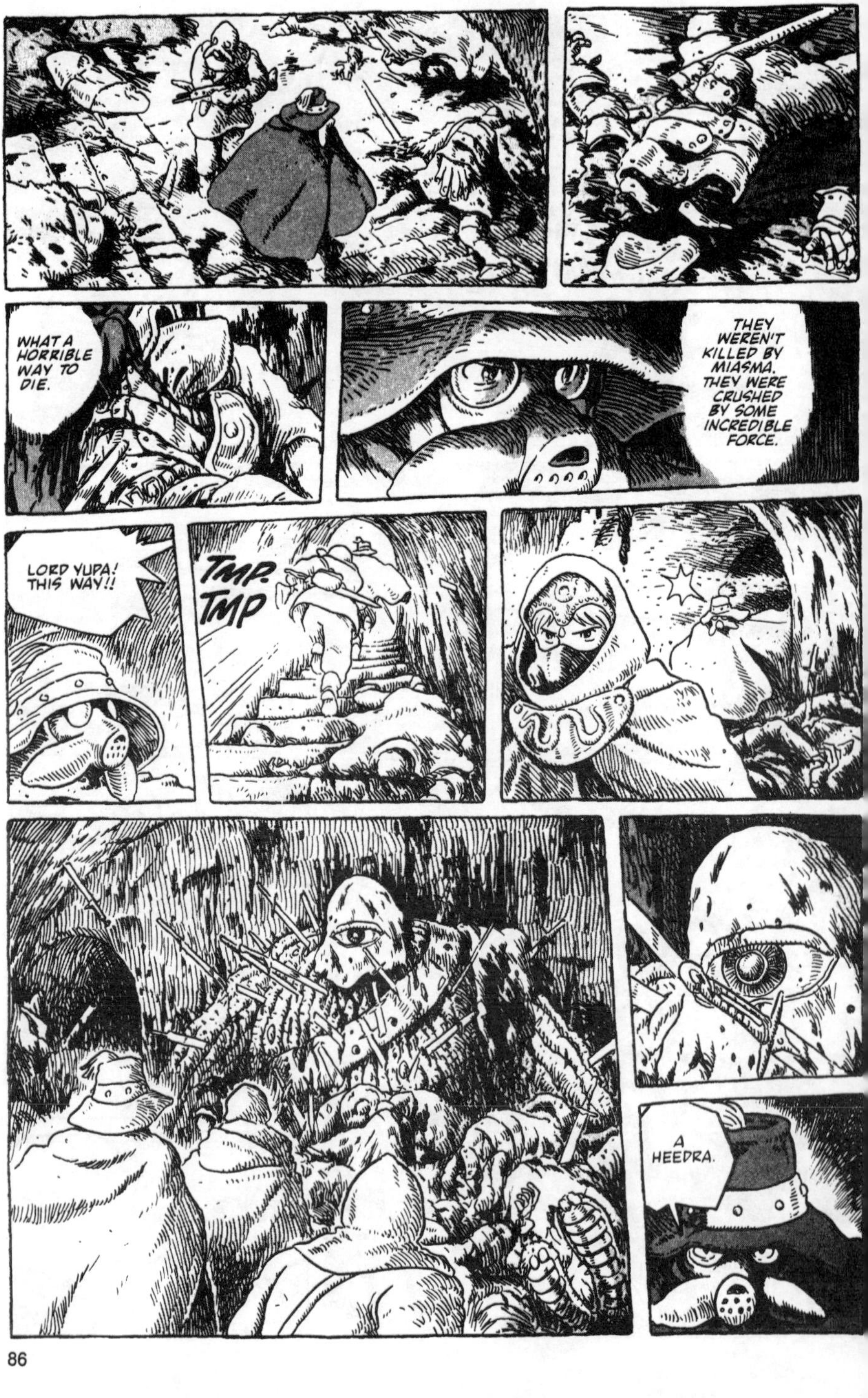
WHAT A HORRIBLE WAY TO DIE.
THEY WEREN'T KILLED BY MIASMA. THEY WERE CRUSHED BY SOME INCREDIBLE FORCE.
LORD YUPA! THIS WAY!!
TMP. TMP
A HEEDRA.

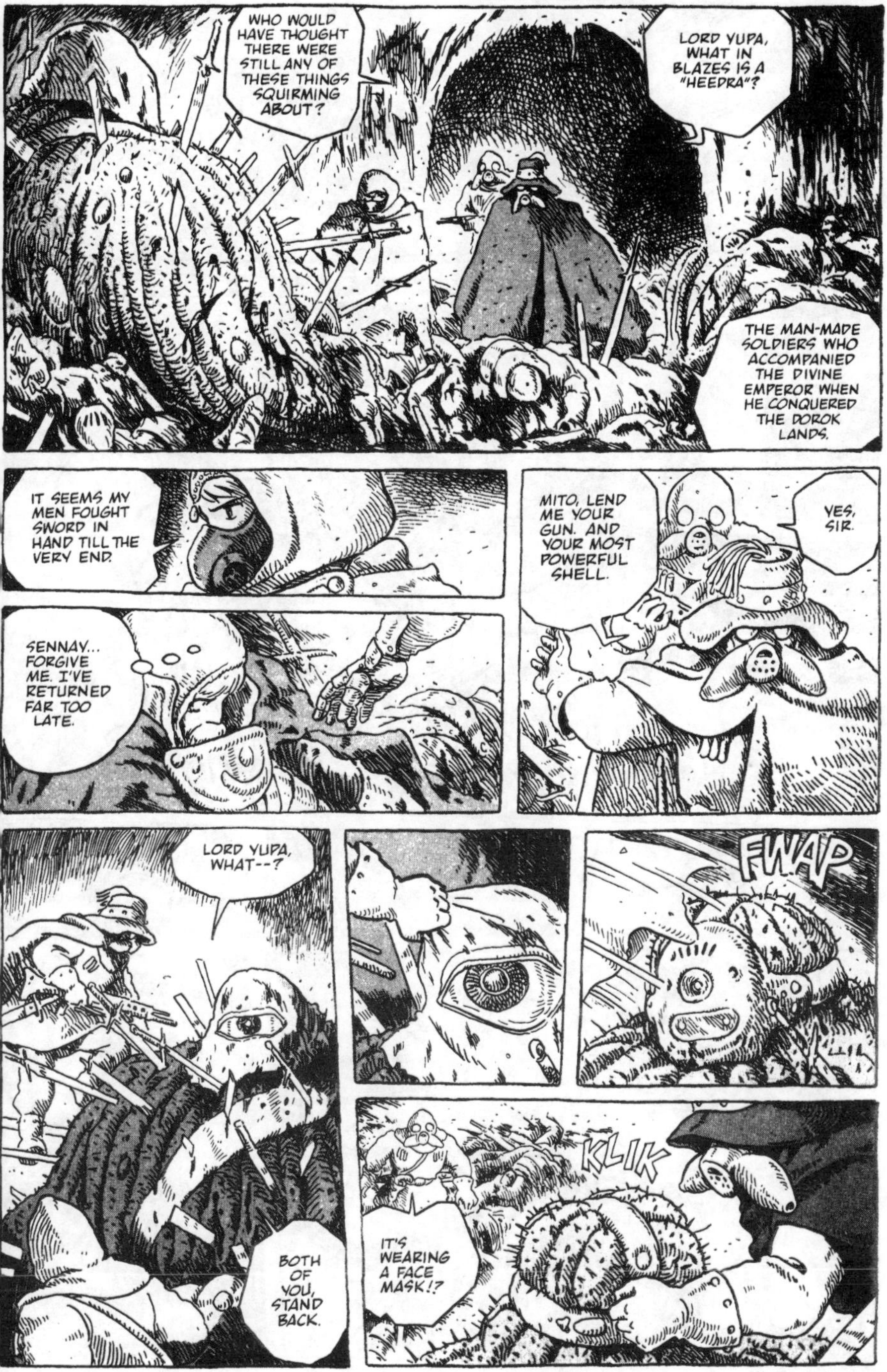
WHO WOULD HAVE THOUGHT THERE WERE STILL ANY OF THESE THINGS SQUIRMING ABOUT?
LORD YUPA, WHAT IN BLAZES IS A "HEEDRA"?
THE MAN-MADE SOLDIERS WHO ACCOMPANIED THE DIVINE EMPEROR WHEN HE CONQUERED THE DOROK LANDS.
IT SEEMS MY MEN FOUGHT SWORD IN HAND TILL THE VERY END.
MITO, LEND ME YOUR GUN. AND YOUR MOST POWERFUL SHELL.
YES, SIR.
SENNAY... FORGIVE ME. I'VE RETURNED FAR TOO LATE.
LORD YUPA, WHAT--?
BOTH OF YOU, STAND BACK.
FWAP
KLIK
IT'S WEARING A FACE MASK!?

LOOK, MITO.

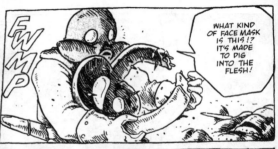

FWMP

WHAT KIND OF FACE MASK IS THIS!? IT'S MADE TO DIG INTO THE FLESH!

GRAARGGH

BLAM

AH!

THESE THINGS ARE IMMORTAL UNLESS YOU DESTROY THEIR CORE. THEY'LL COME BACK TO LIFE AGAIN AND AGAIN.

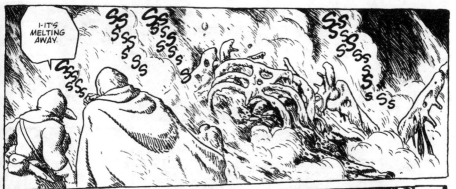

I-IT'S MELTING AWAY.

A SOLDIER!!

YOUR HIGHNESS, YOU'RE STILL ALIVE.

AND SO ARE YOU!!

HANG ON, MAN. TRY TO TELL ME WHAT HAPPENED.

JUST A MOMENT. I'LL HELP YOU TO BREATHE EASIER.

DAMN! IT WON'T WORK THE WAY IT DOES FOR THE PRINCESS.

THE MAIN FORCE ISN'T HERE. THEY ESCAPED TO LANDS UPWIND.

A SWARM OF INSECTS CAME, AND EVERY DAY THE MIASMA GREW THICKER. THEN THAT YOUNG GIRL'S KITE CAME.

SHE DIDN'T LAND. SHE CIRCLED THE SKY ABOVE THE CASTLE ONCE AND LEFT.

BUT EVERY ONE OF US HEARD HER VOICE.

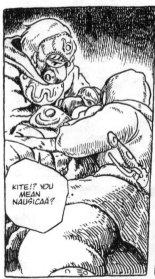

KITE!? YOU MEAN NAUSICAÄ?

"A FATALLY POISONOUS MIASMA IS COMING THAT EVEN MASKS ARE USELESS AGAINST! ESCAPE TO THE EAST AS QUICKLY AS YOU CAN. THAT IS THE ONLY WAY. TRUST ME, HEAD EAST!!"

A MIASMA THAT EVEN MASKS ARE USELESS AGAINST...

OUR COMPANY DECIDED TO WAIT HERE FOR YOUR HIGHNESS ALONE. THEN THIS GANG OF MONSTERS APPEARED.

I SEE. SAY NO MORE.

tmp tmp

90

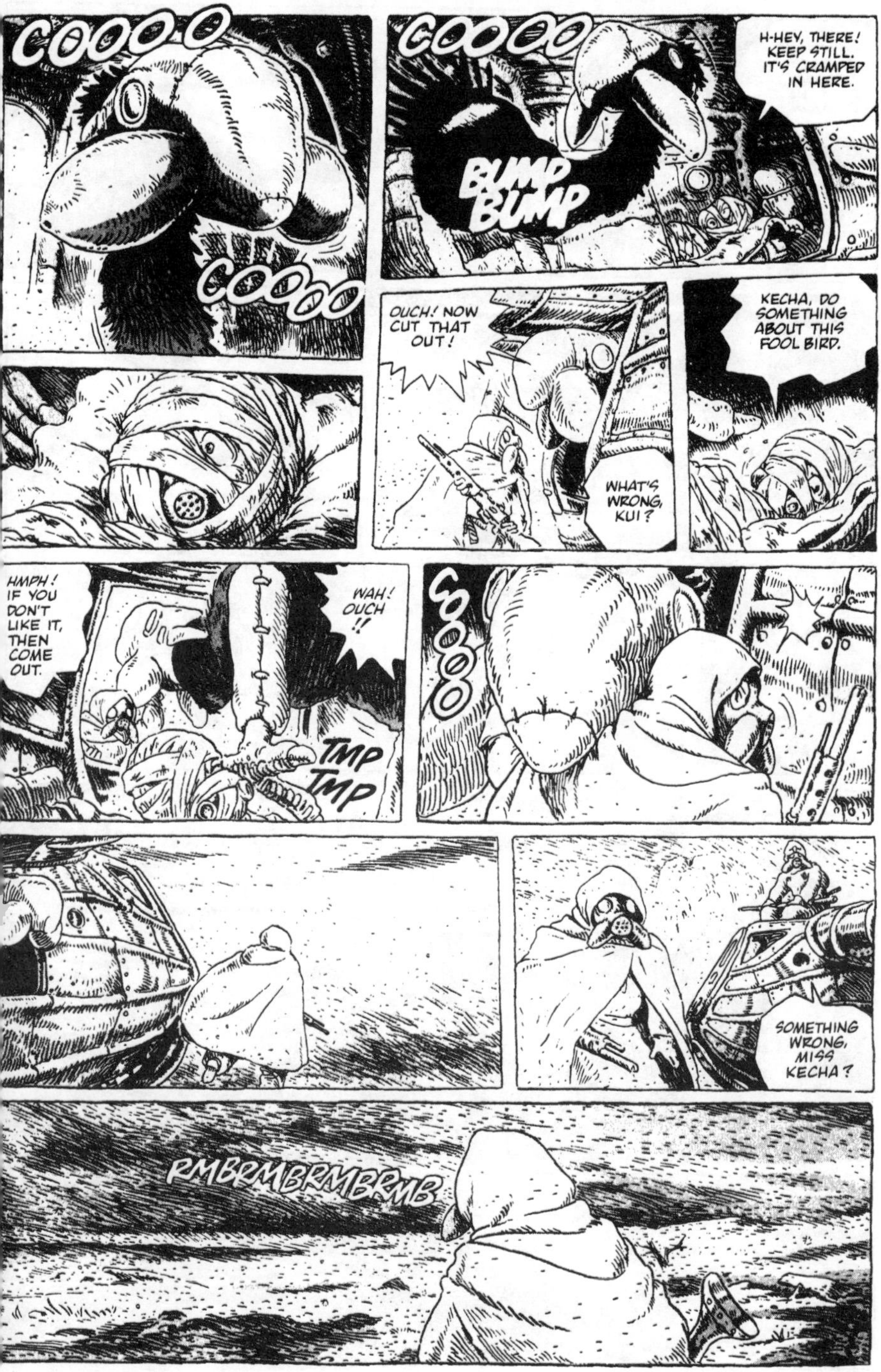
COOOO
COOOO
H-HEY, THERE! KEEP STILL. IT'S CRAMPED IN HERE.
BUMP BUMP
COOOO
OUCH! NOW CUT THAT OUT!
WHAT'S WRONG, KUI?
KECHA, DO SOMETHING ABOUT THIS FOOL BIRD.
HMPH! IF YOU DON'T LIKE IT, THEN COME OUT.
WAH! OUCH!!
TMP TMP
COOOO
SOMETHING WRONG, MISS KECHA?
RMBRMBRMBRMB

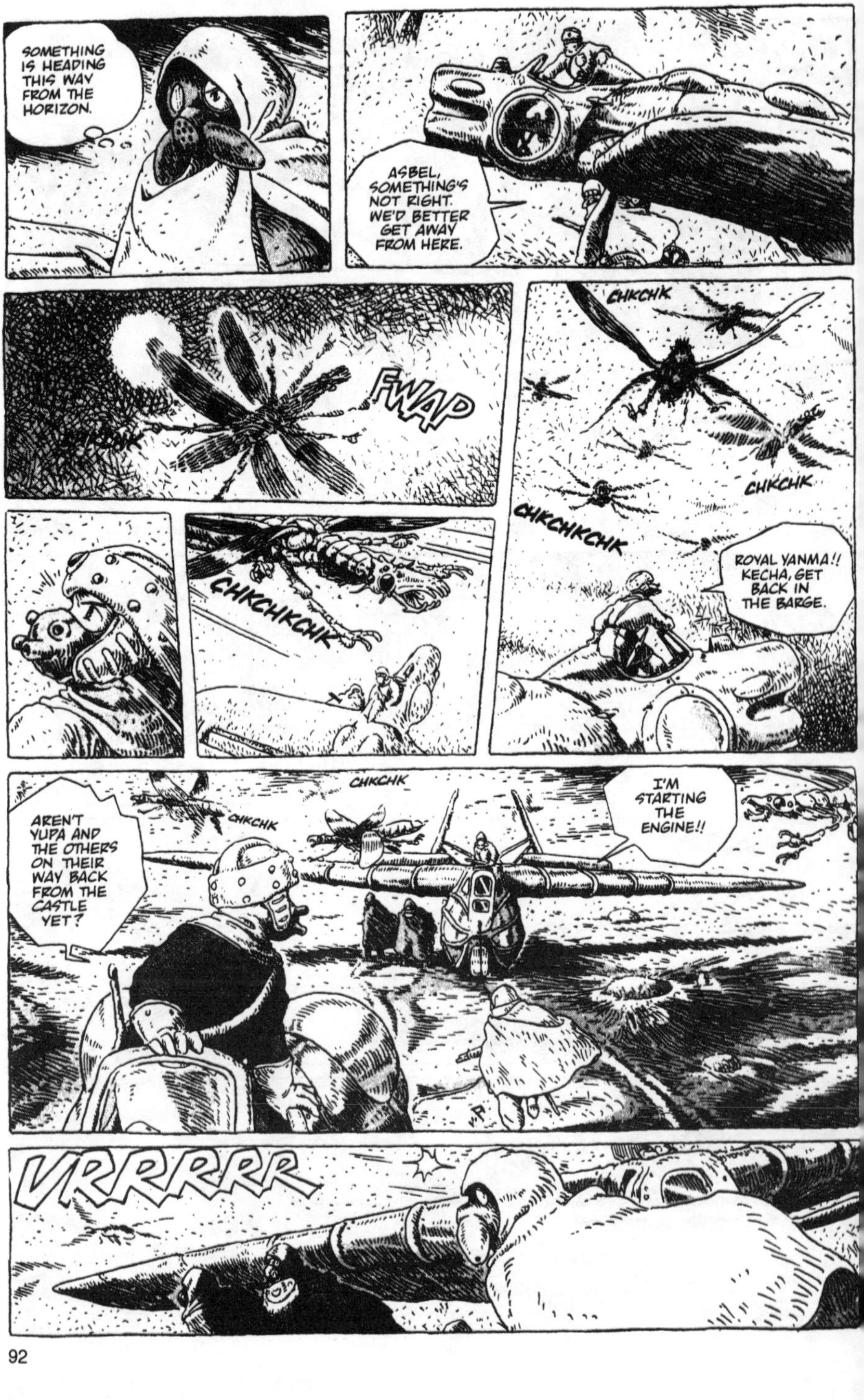
SOMETHING IS HEADING THIS WAY FROM THE HORIZON.
ASBEL, SOMETHING'S NOT RIGHT. WE'D BETTER GET AWAY FROM HERE.
FWAP
CHKCHK
CHKCHK
CHKCHKCHK
CHKCHKCHK
ROYAL YANMA!! KECHA, GET BACK IN THE BARGE.
CHKCHK
CHKCHK
I'M STARTING THE ENGINE!!
AREN'T YUPA AND THE OTHERS ON THEIR WAY BACK FROM THE CASTLE YET?
VRRRRR

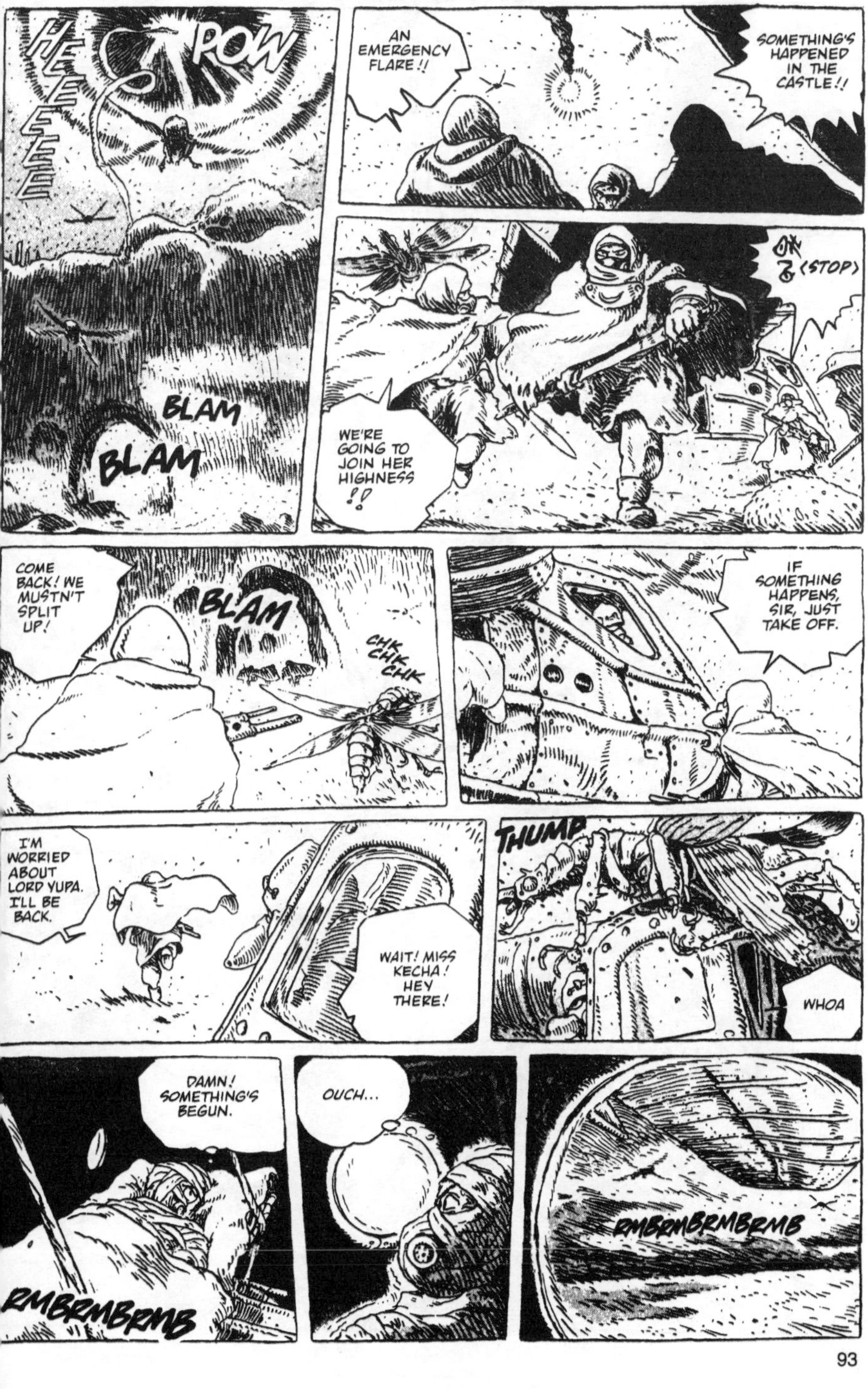
HEEEEEE
POW
BLAM
BLAM
AN EMERGENCY FLARE!!
SOMETHING'S HAPPENED IN THE CASTLE!!
(STOP)
WE'RE GOING TO JOIN HER HIGHNESS!!
COME BACK! WE MUSTN'T SPLIT UP!
BLAM
CHK CHK CHK
IF SOMETHING HAPPENS, SIR, JUST TAKE OFF.
I'M WORRIED ABOUT LORD YUPA. I'LL BE BACK.
WAIT! MISS KECHA! HEY THERE!
THUMP
WHOA
DAMN! SOMETHING'S BEGUN.
RMBRMBRMB
OUCH...
RMBRMBRMBRMB

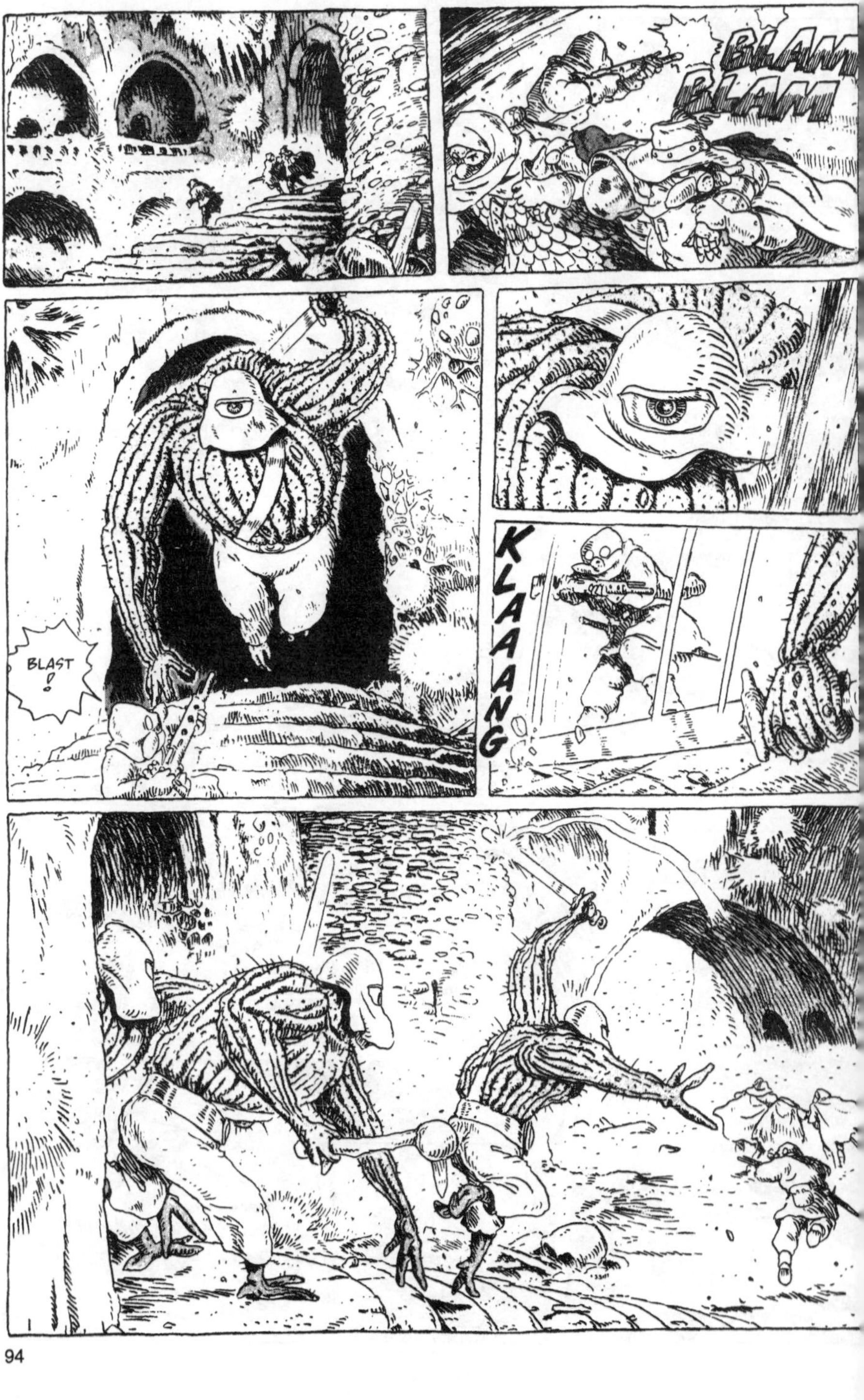
BLAM BLAM
BLAST!
KLAAAANG

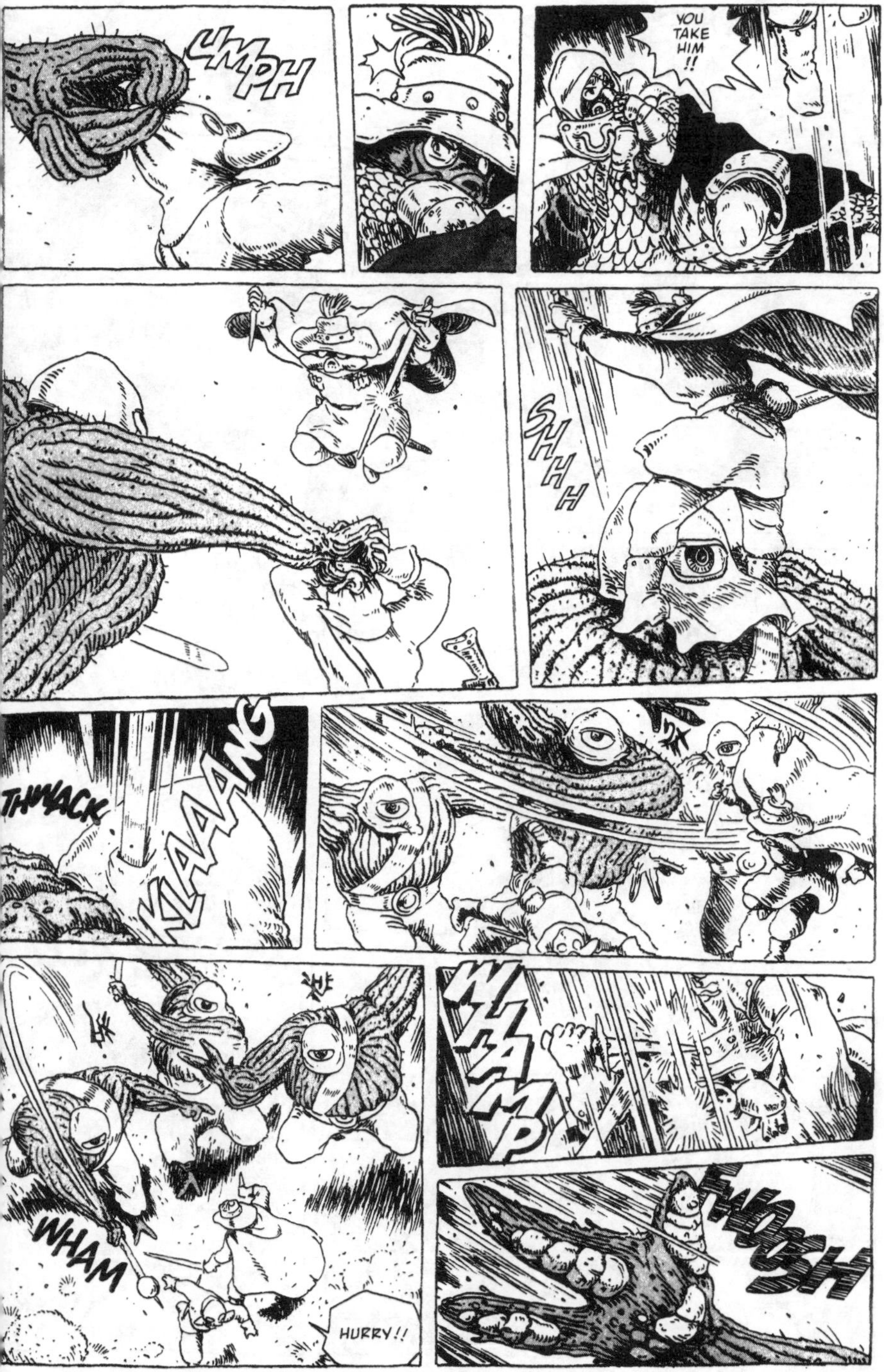
UMPH
YOU TAKE HIM!!
SHHH
THWACK
KLAAANG
WHAM
HURRY!!
WHAMP
WHOOSH

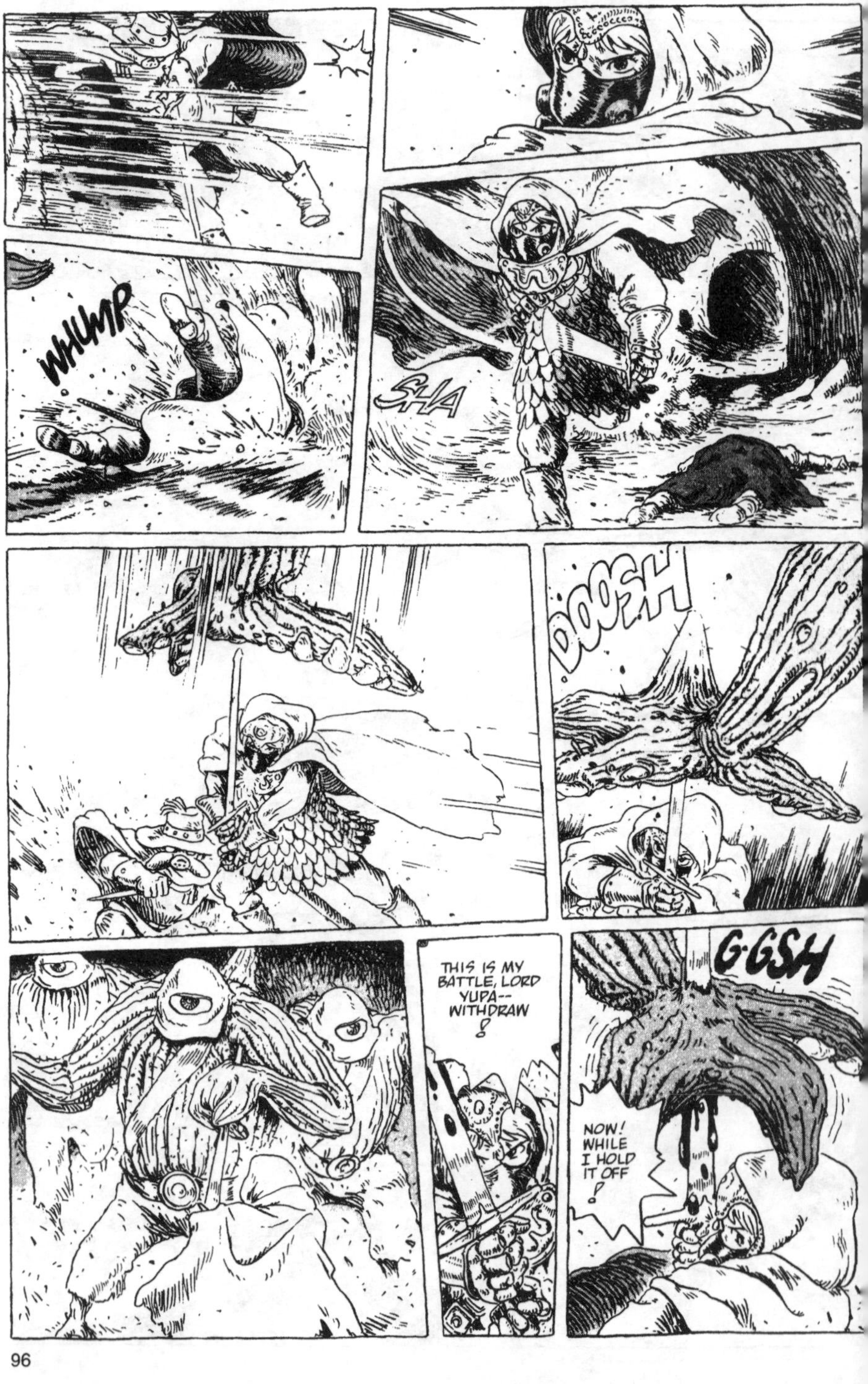
WHUMP
SHA
DOOSH
THIS IS MY BATTLE, LORD YUPA-- WITHDRAW!
G-GSH
NOW! WHILE I HOLD IT OFF!

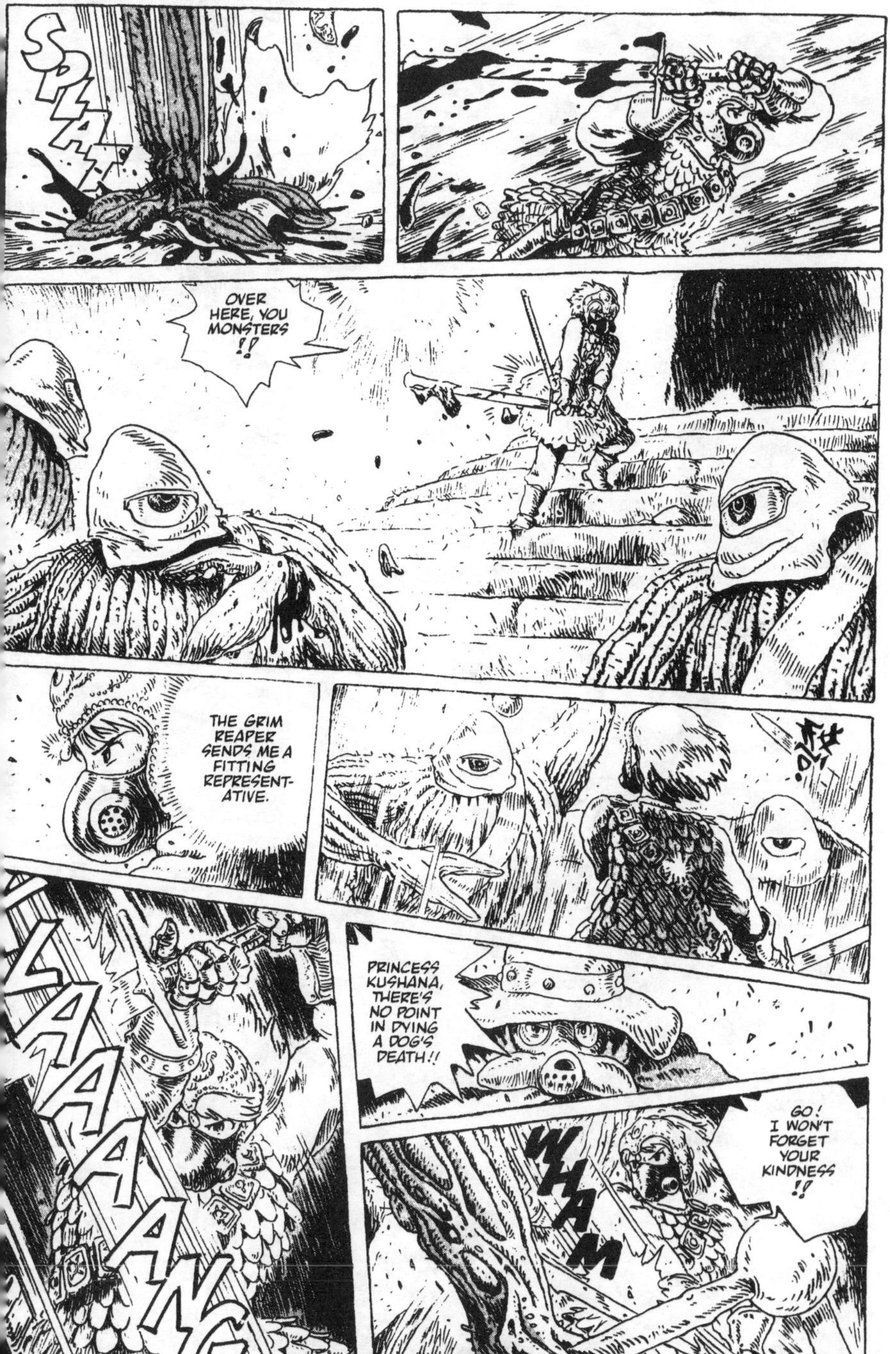
SPLAT
OVER HERE, YOU MONSTERS!!
THE GRIM REAPER SENDS ME A FITTING REPRESENT-ATIVE.
VLAAAAANG
PRINCESS KUSHANA, THERE'S NO POINT IN DYING A DOG'S DEATH!!
GO! I WON'T FORGET YOUR KINDNESS!!
WHAM

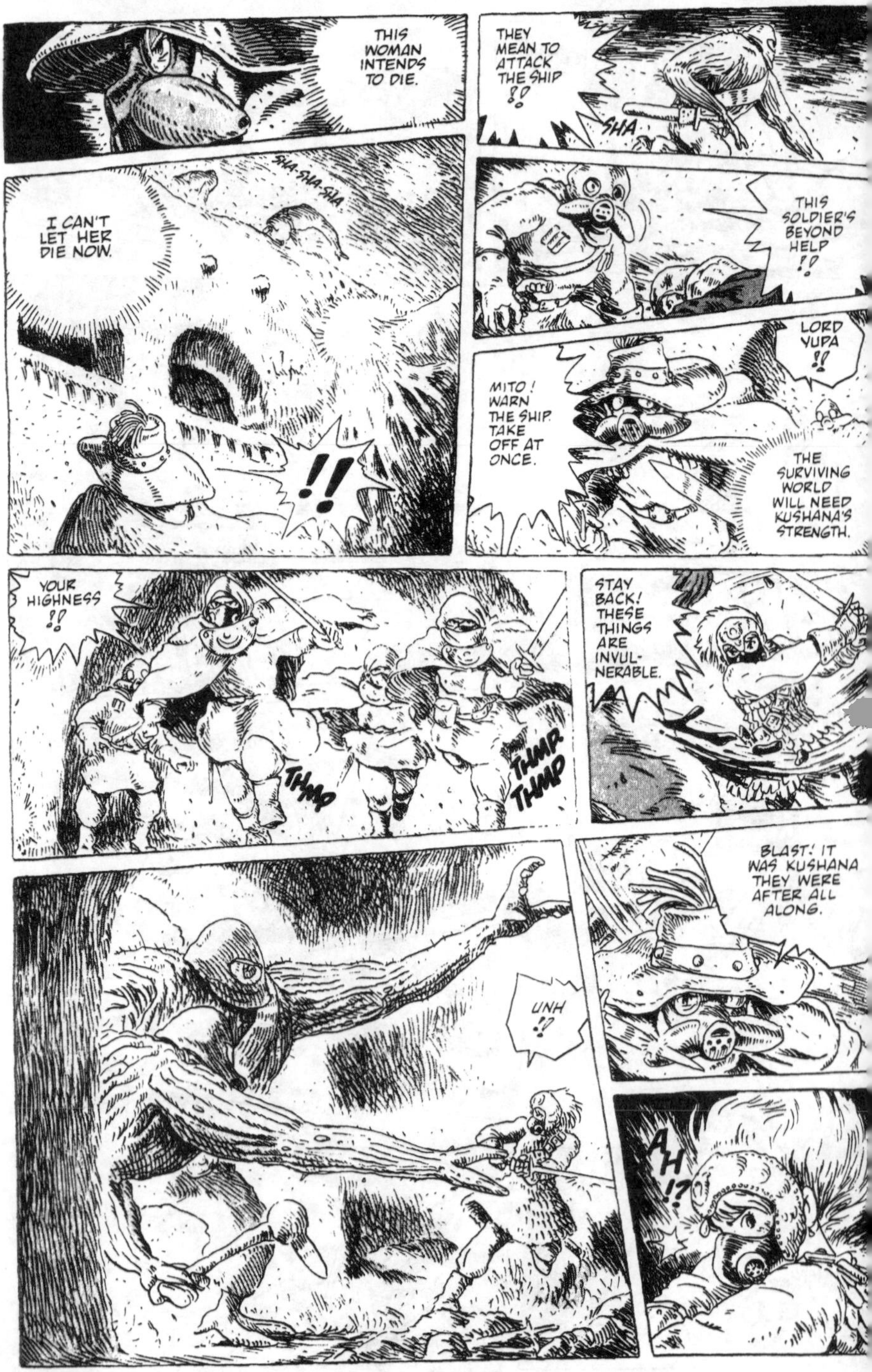
THIS WOMAN INTENDS TO DIE.
THEY MEAN TO ATTACK THE SHIP !?
SHA
SHA-SHA-SHA
I CAN'T LET HER DIE NOW.
!!
THIS SOLDIER'S BEYOND HELP !?
LORD YUPA !!
MITO! WARN THE SHIP. TAKE OFF AT ONCE.
THE SURVIVING WORLD WILL NEED KUSHANA'S STRENGTH.
YOUR HIGHNESS !?
THMP
THMP THMP
STAY BACK! THESE THINGS ARE INVULNERABLE.
BLAST! IT WAS KUSHANA THEY WERE AFTER ALL ALONG.
UNH !?
AH !?

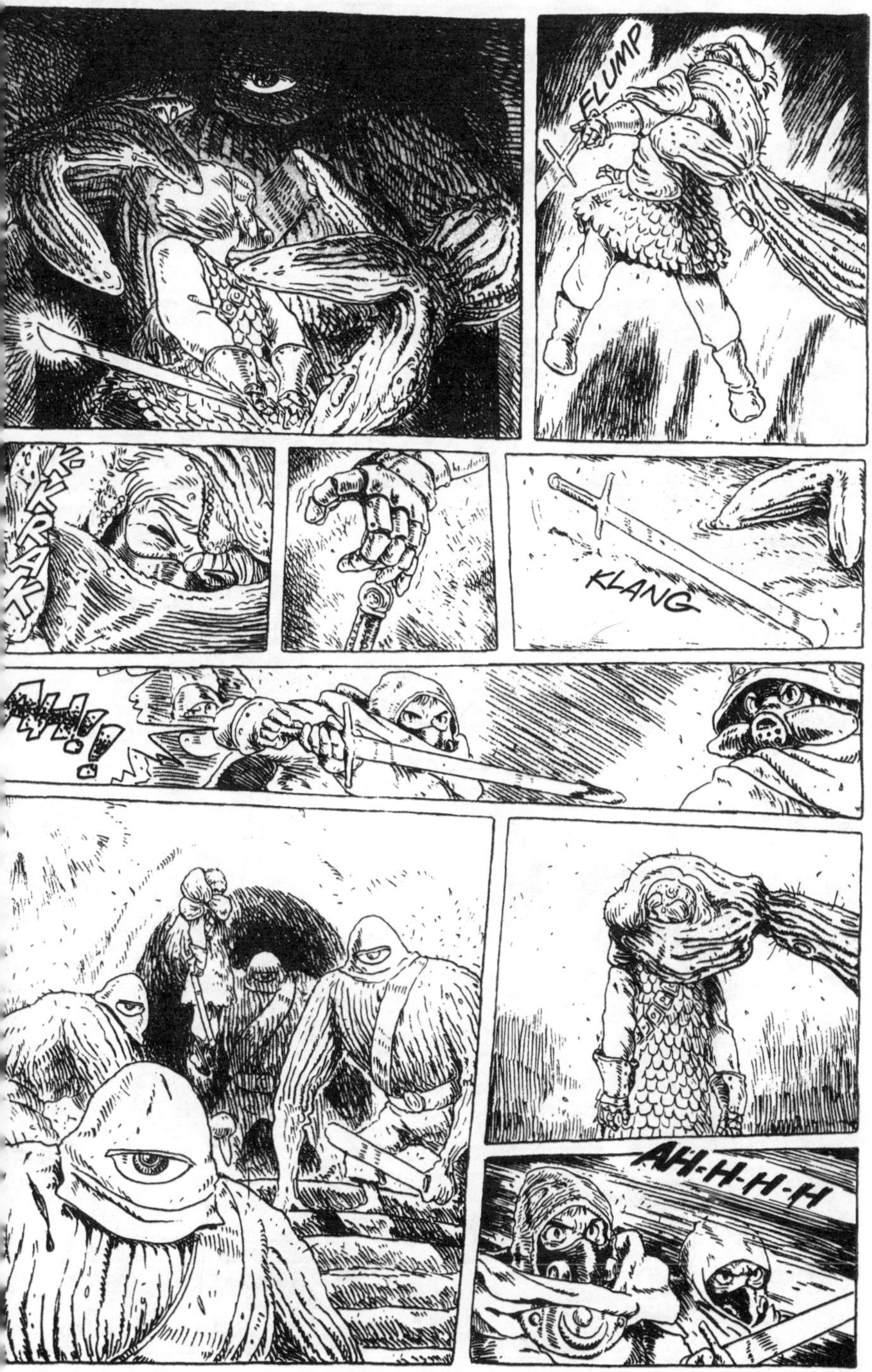
FLUMP
K-KRAK
KLANG
AH!!
AH-H-H-H

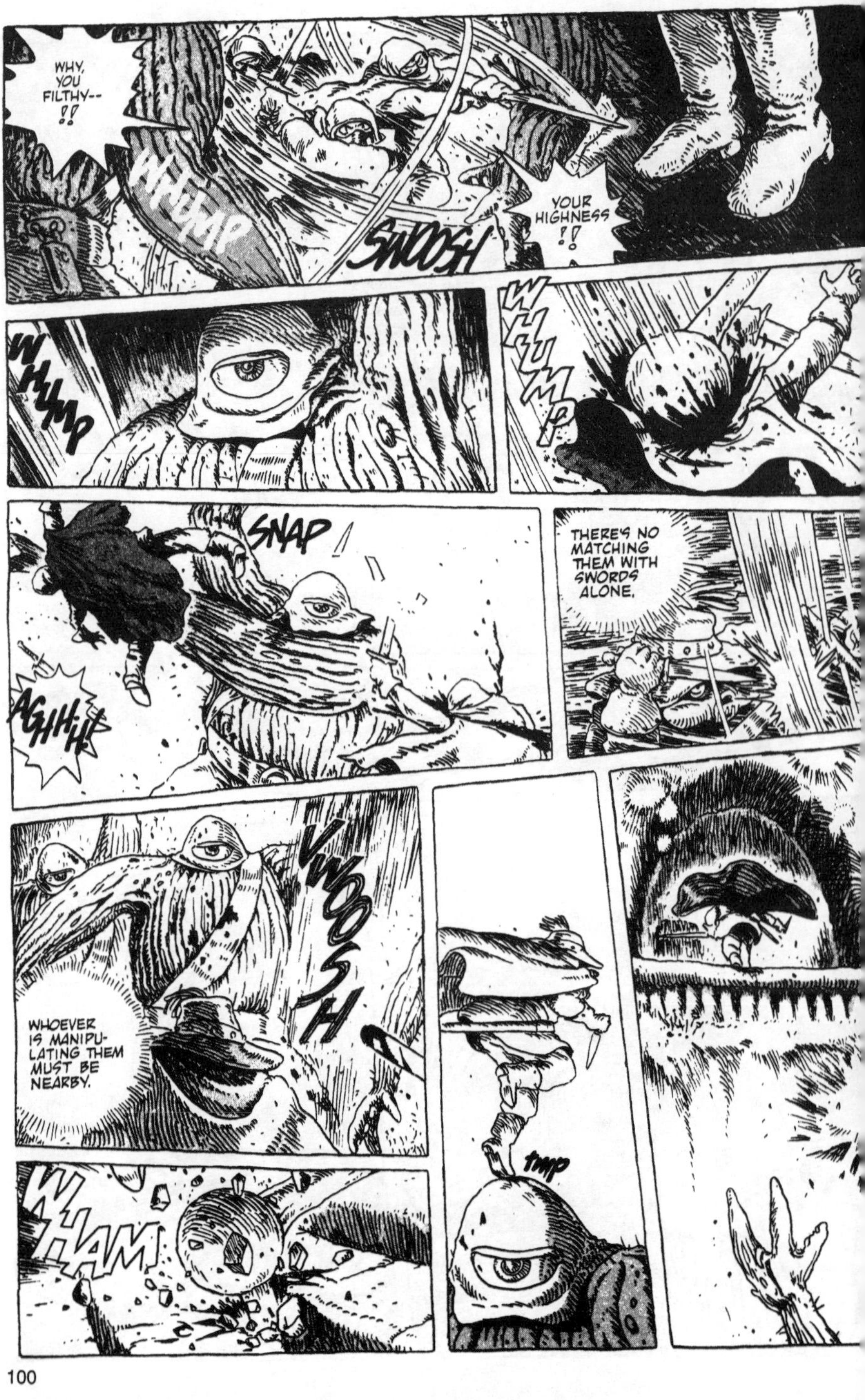
WHY, YOU FILTHY--!!
WHUMP
YOUR HIGHNESS!!
SWOOSH
WHUMP
WHUMP
SNAP
AGHHH
THERE'S NO MATCHING THEM WITH SWORDS ALONE.
VWOOOSH
WHOEVER IS MANIPU-LATING THEM MUST BE NEARBY.
WHAM
tmp

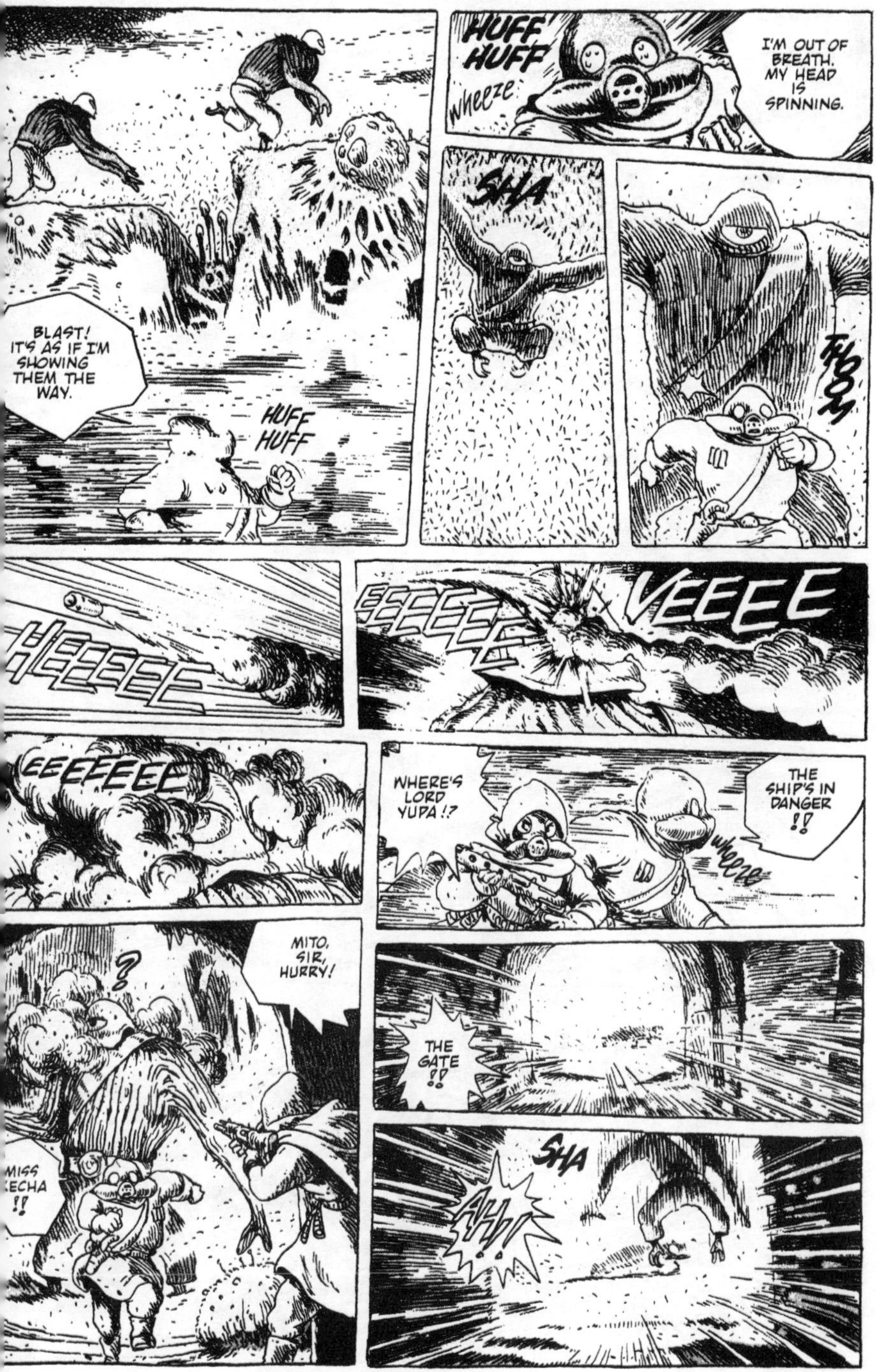
BLAST! IT'S AS IF I'M SHOWING THEM THE WAY.
HUFF HUFF
HUFF HUFF
wheeze
I'M OUT OF BREATH. MY HEAD IS SPINNING.
SHA
FWOOM
HEEEEEE
EEEEEE
VEEEE
EEEEEEE
WHERE'S LORD YUPA!?
THE SHIP'S IN DANGER!!
wheeze
MITO, SIR, HURRY!
?
MISS KECHA!!
THE GATE!!
SHA

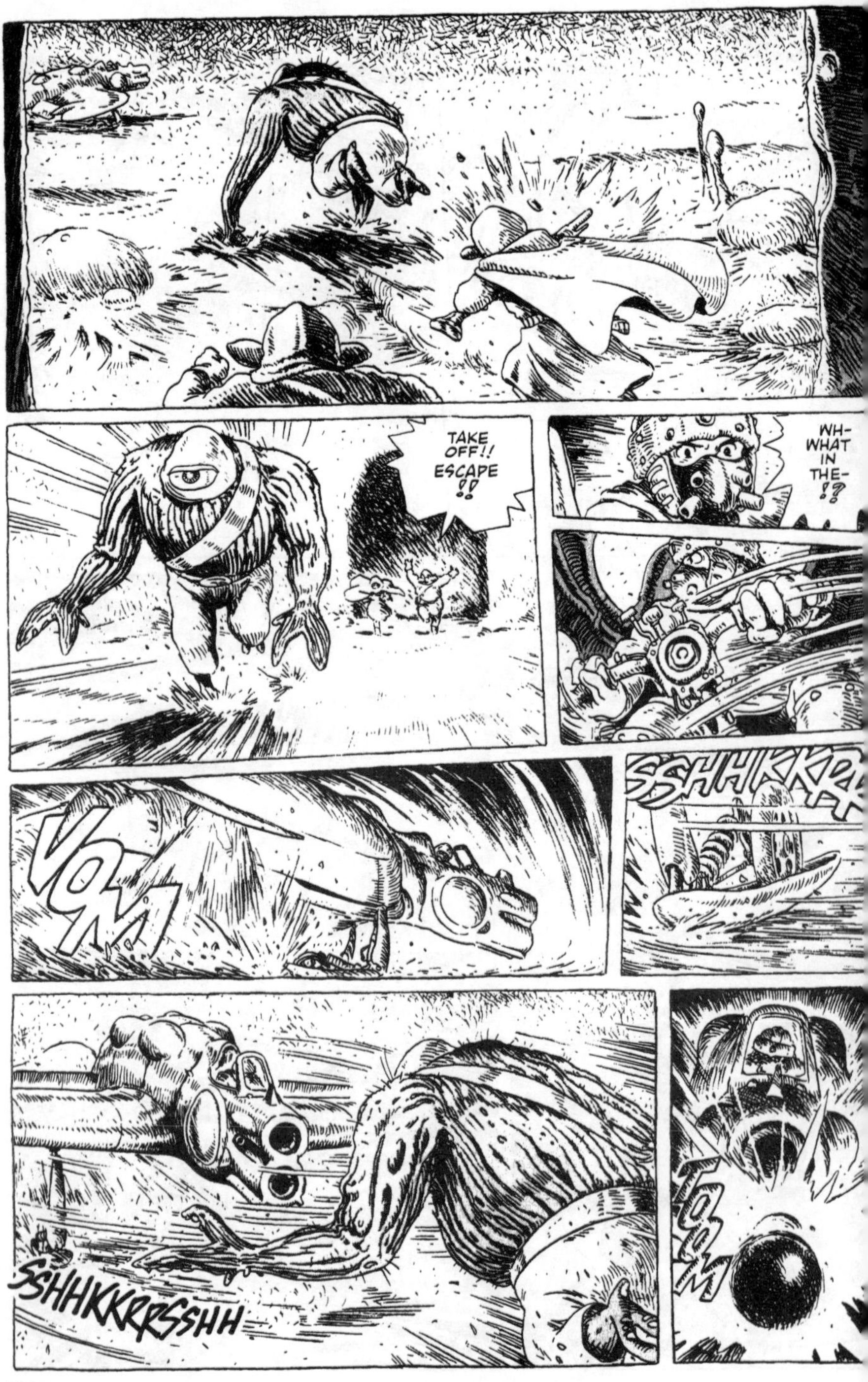

TAKE OFF!! ESCAPE!!
WH- WHAT IN THE-!?
SSHHKKR
VOM
SSHHKKRRSSHH

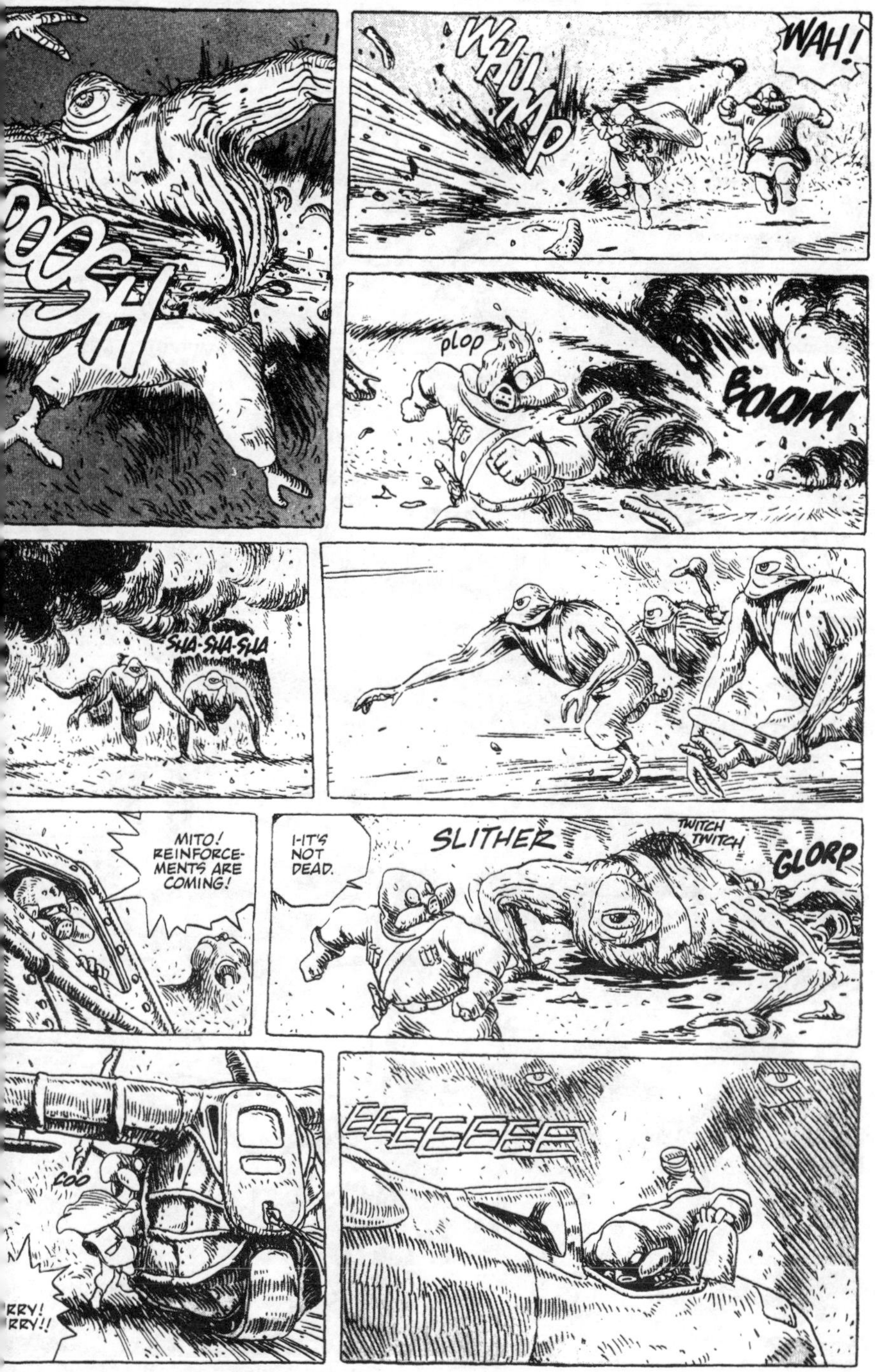
OOOSH
WHUMP
WAH!
plop
BOOM
SHA-SHA-SHA
MITO! REINFORCEMENTS ARE COMING!
I-IT'S NOT DEAD.
SLITHER
TWITCH TWITCH
GLORP
GOO
RRY!
RRY!!
EEEEEEEEE

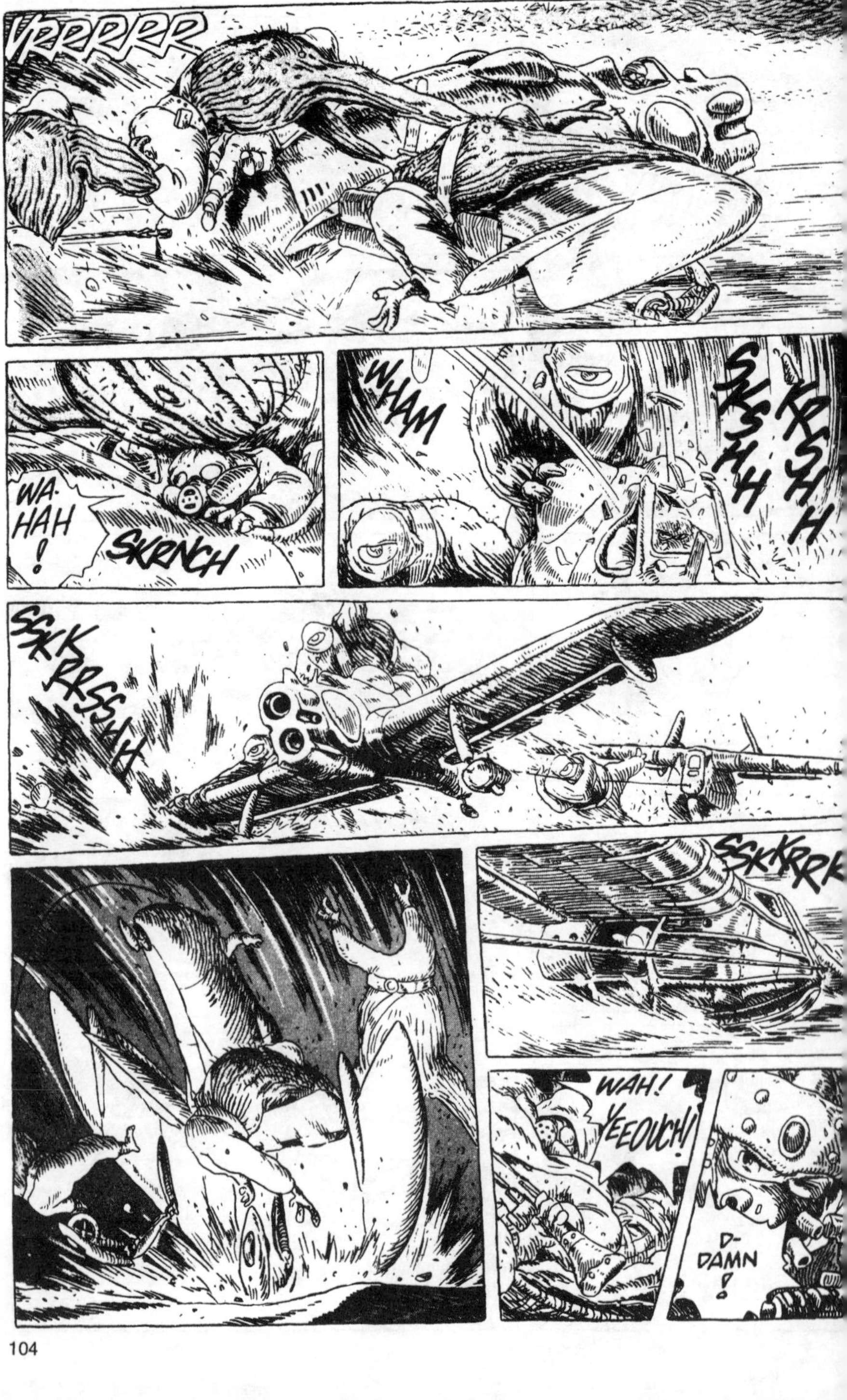
VRRRRRR
WA-HAH!
SKRNCH
WHAM
KRSHHH
SKSHHH
SSKK RRSSHH
SSKKRRK
WAH! YEEOUCH!
D-DAMN!

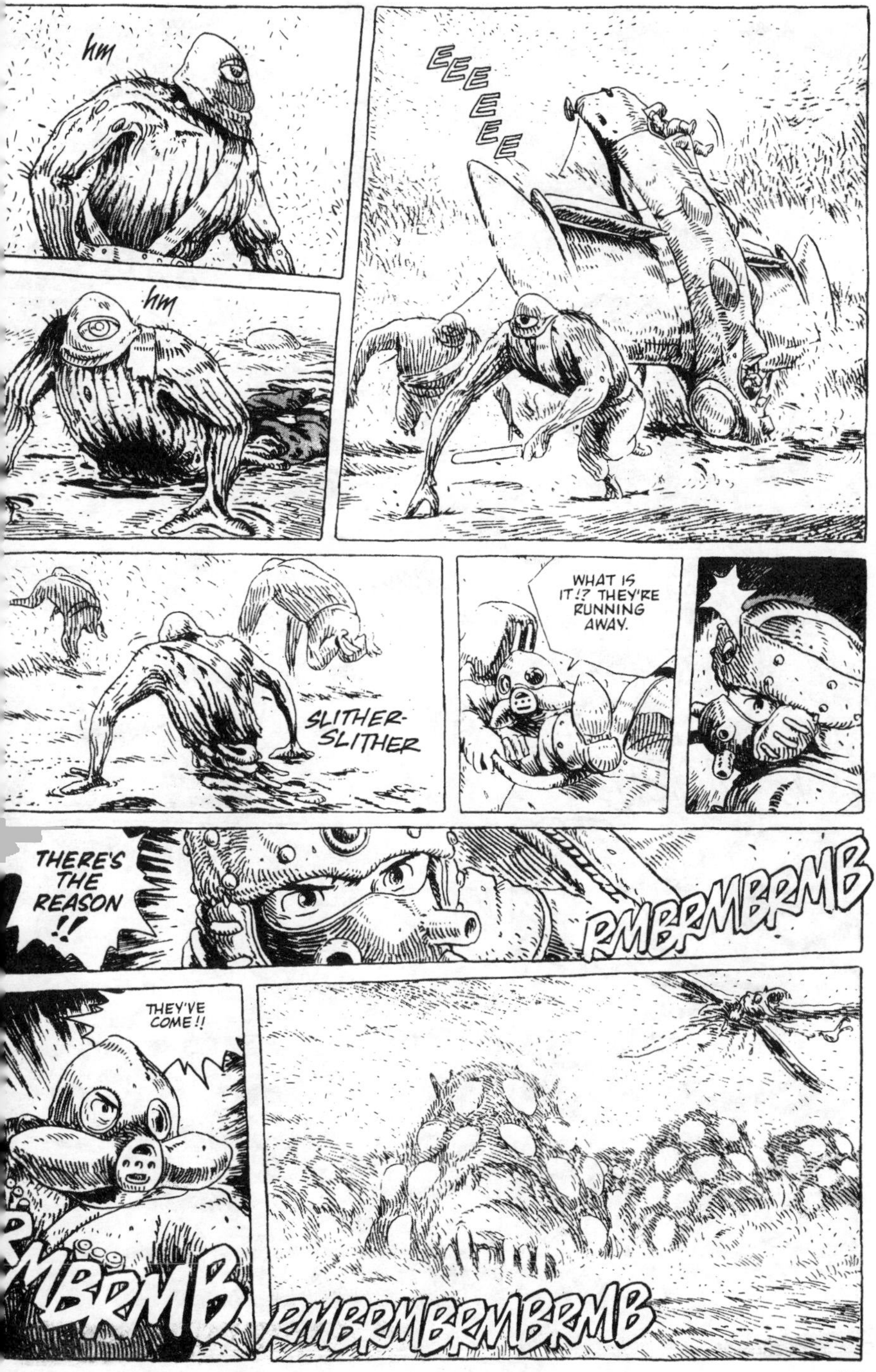
hm
EEEEEEE
hm
SLITHER-SLITHER
WHAT IS IT!? THEY'RE RUNNING AWAY.
THERE'S THE REASON!!
RMBRMBRMB
THEY'VE COME!!
MBRMB
RMBRMBRMBRMB

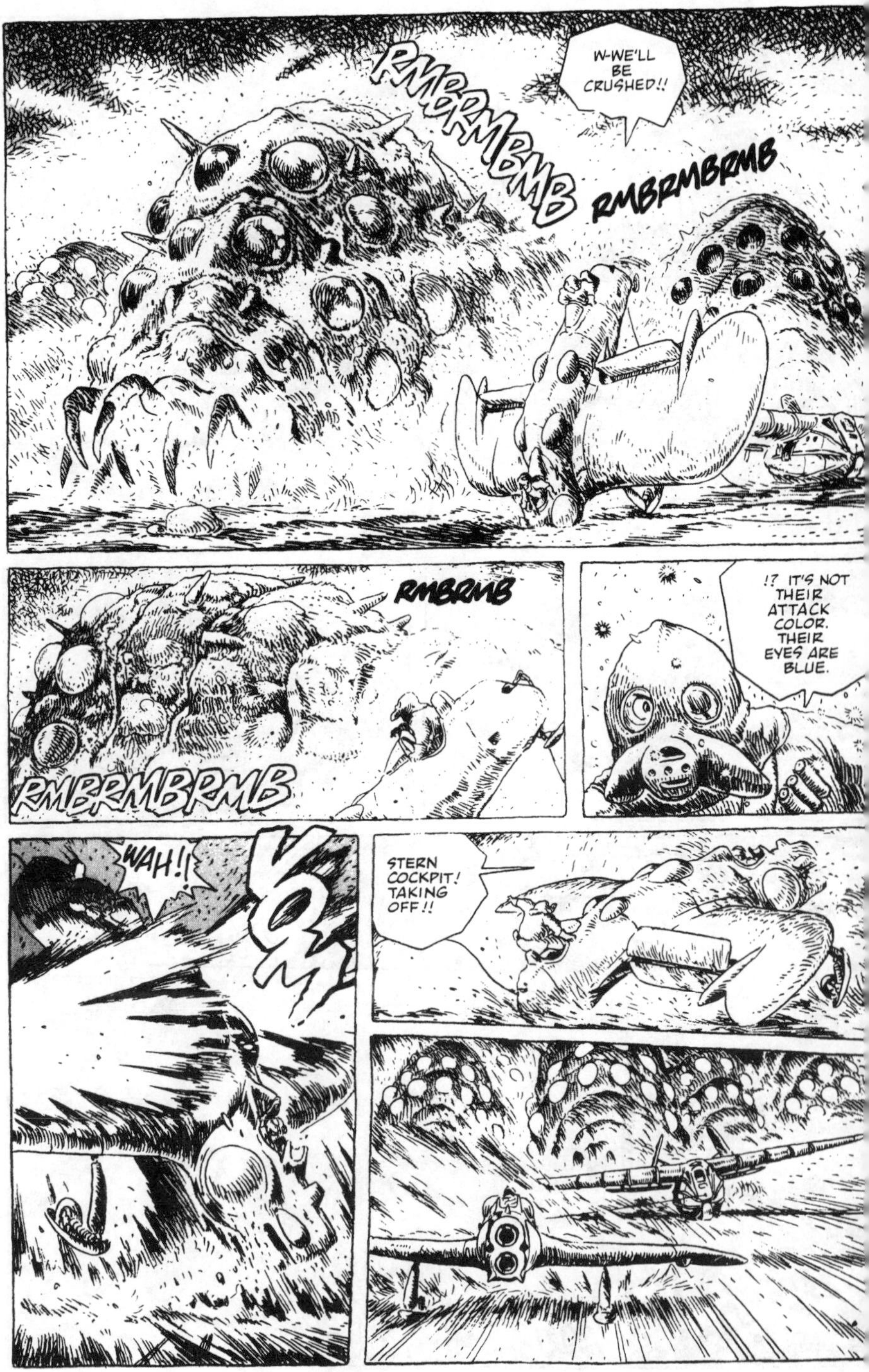
RMBRMBRMB
W-WE'LL BE CRUSHED!!
RMBRMBRMB
RMBRMB
RMBRMBRMB
!? IT'S NOT THEIR ATTACK COLOR. THEIR EYES ARE BLUE.
WAH!!
VOM
STERN COCKPIT! TAKING OFF!!

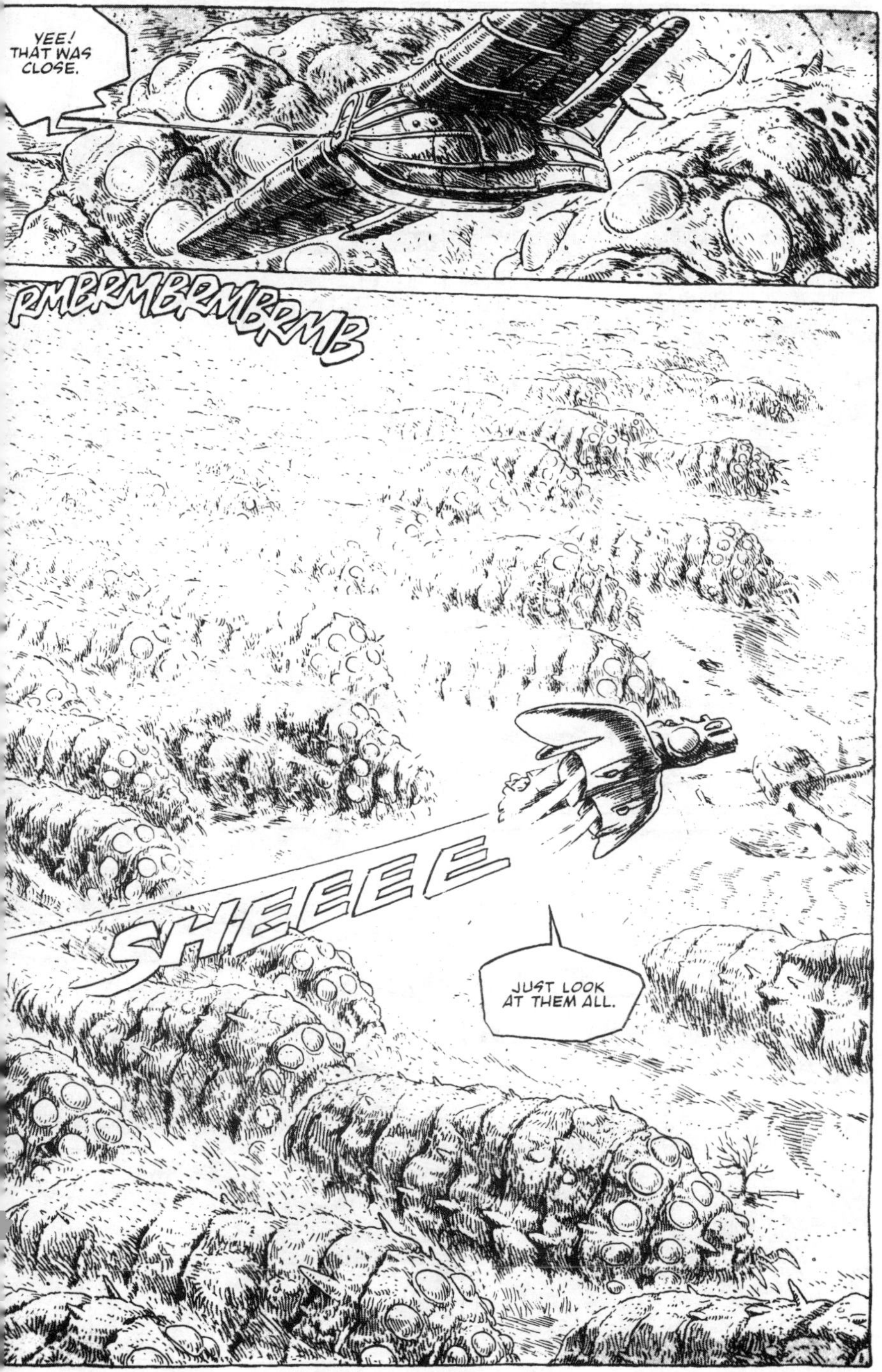
YEE! THAT WAS CLOSE.
RMBRMBRMBRMB
SHEEEEE
JUST LOOK AT THEM ALL.

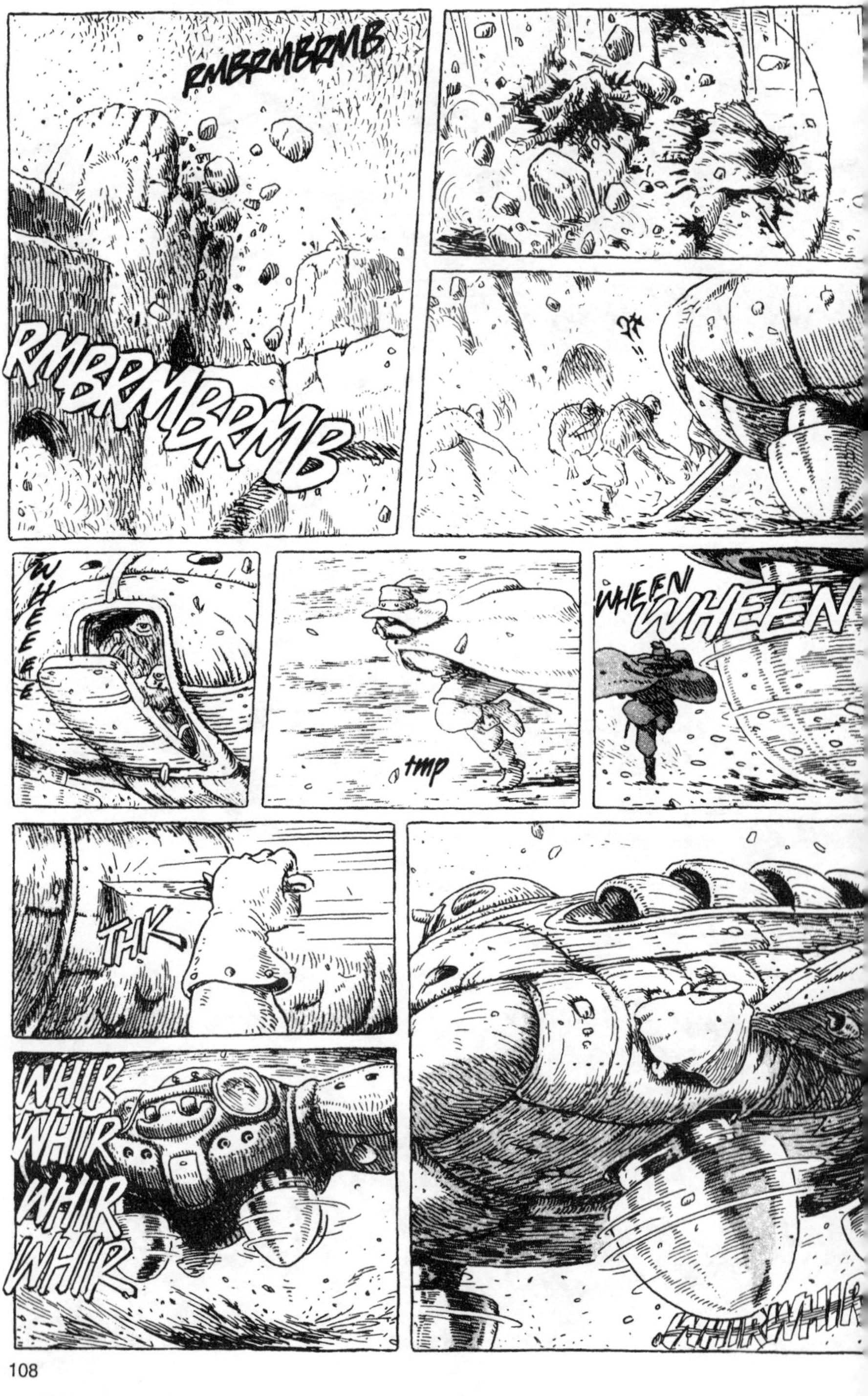
RMBRMBRMB
RMBRMBRMB
WHEEEEE
tmp
WHEEN
WHEEN
THK
WHIR
WHIR
WHIR
WHIR

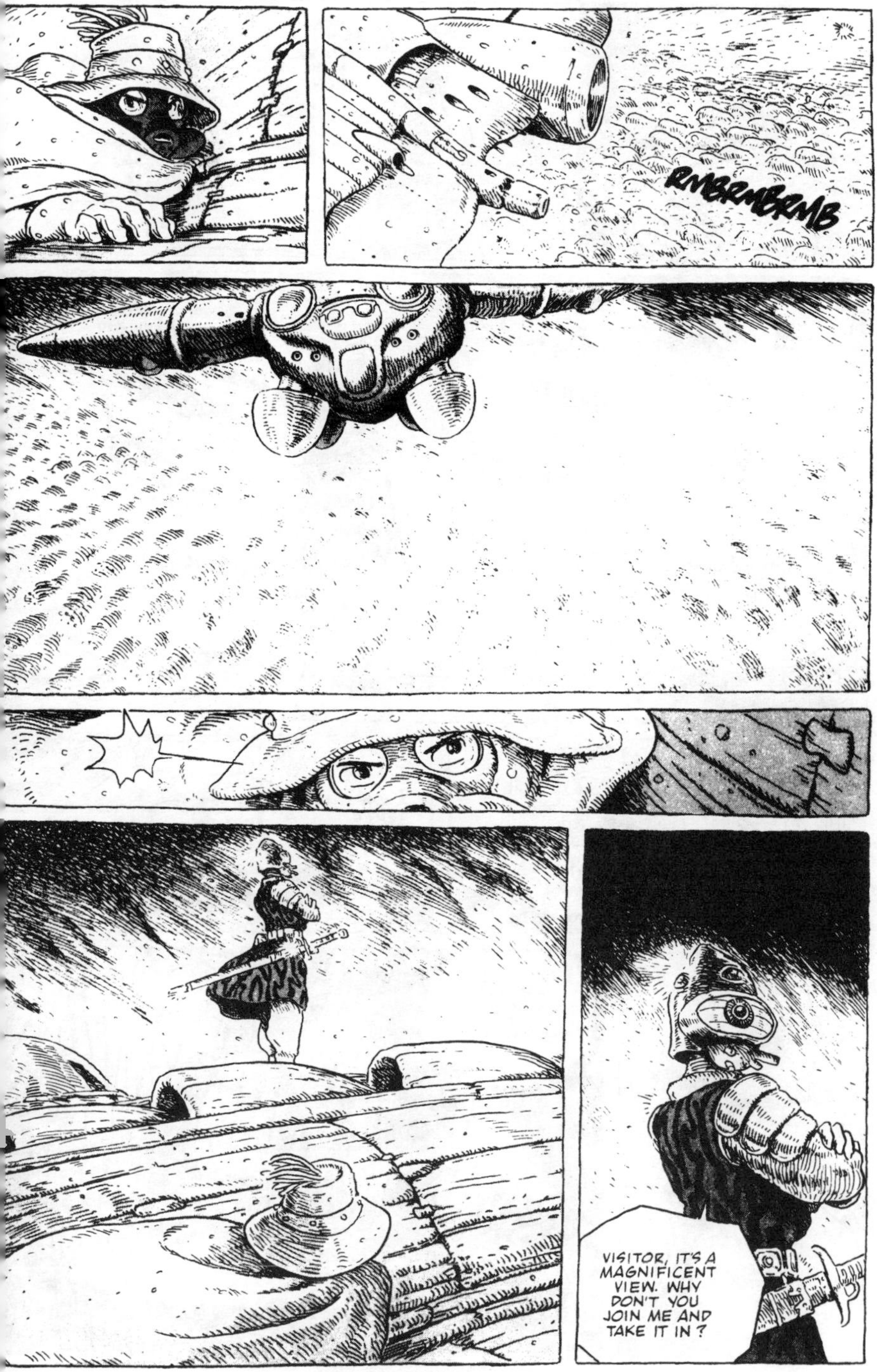
RMBRMBRMB
VISITOR, IT'S A MAGNIFICENT VIEW. WHY DON'T YOU JOIN ME AND TAKE IT IN?

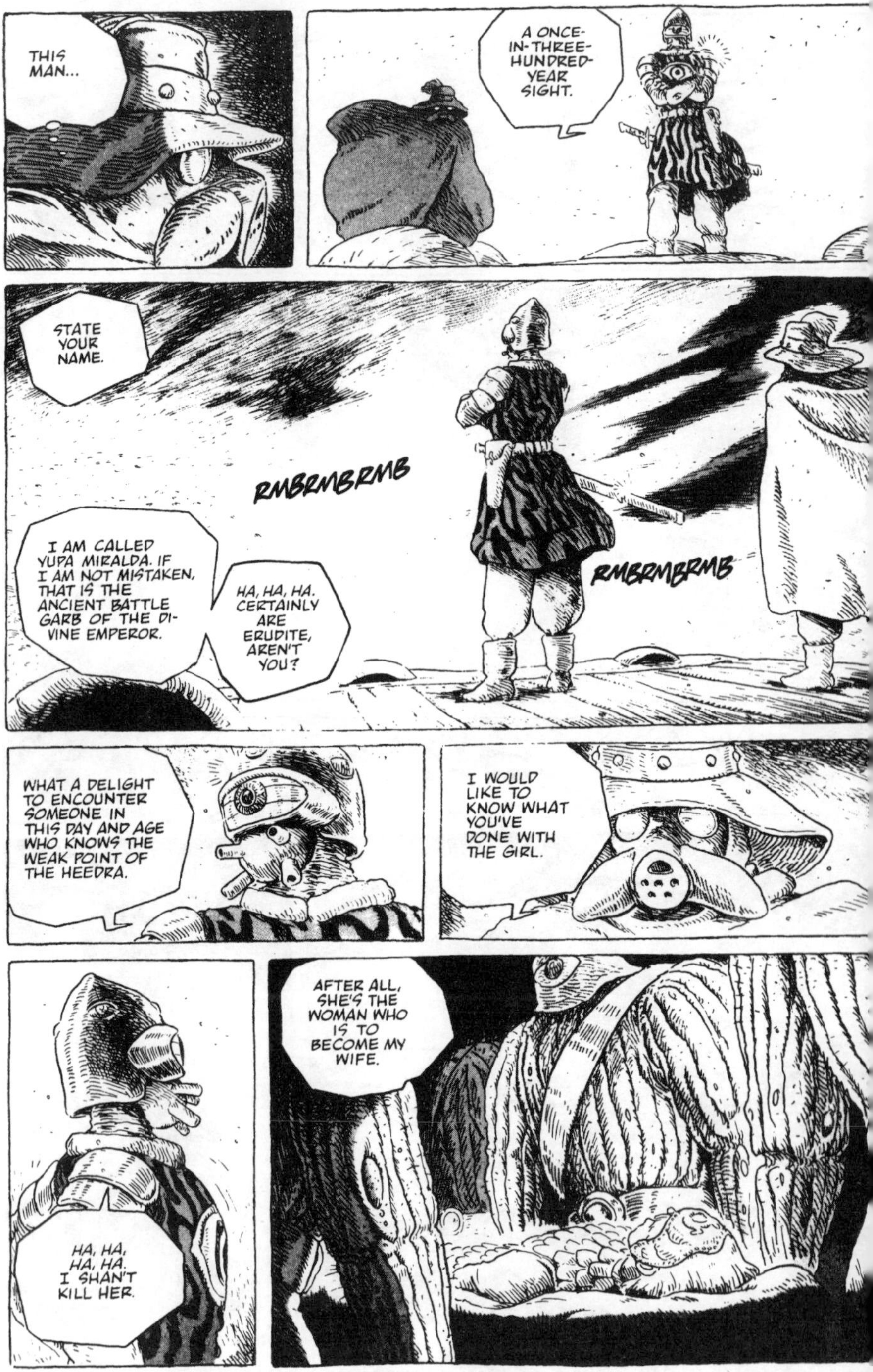
THIS MAN...
A ONCE-IN-THREE-HUNDRED-YEAR SIGHT.
STATE YOUR NAME.
RMBRMBRMB
I AM CALLED YUPA MIRALDA. IF I AM NOT MISTAKEN, THAT IS THE ANCIENT BATTLE GARB OF THE DIVINE EMPEROR.
HA, HA, HA. CERTAINLY ARE ERUDITE, AREN'T YOU?
RMBRMBRMB
WHAT A DELIGHT TO ENCOUNTER SOMEONE IN THIS DAY AND AGE WHO KNOWS THE WEAK POINT OF THE HEEDRA.
I WOULD LIKE TO KNOW WHAT YOU'VE DONE WITH THE GIRL.
HA, HA, HA, HA. I SHAN'T KILL HER.
AFTER ALL, SHE'S THE WOMAN WHO IS TO BECOME MY WIFE.

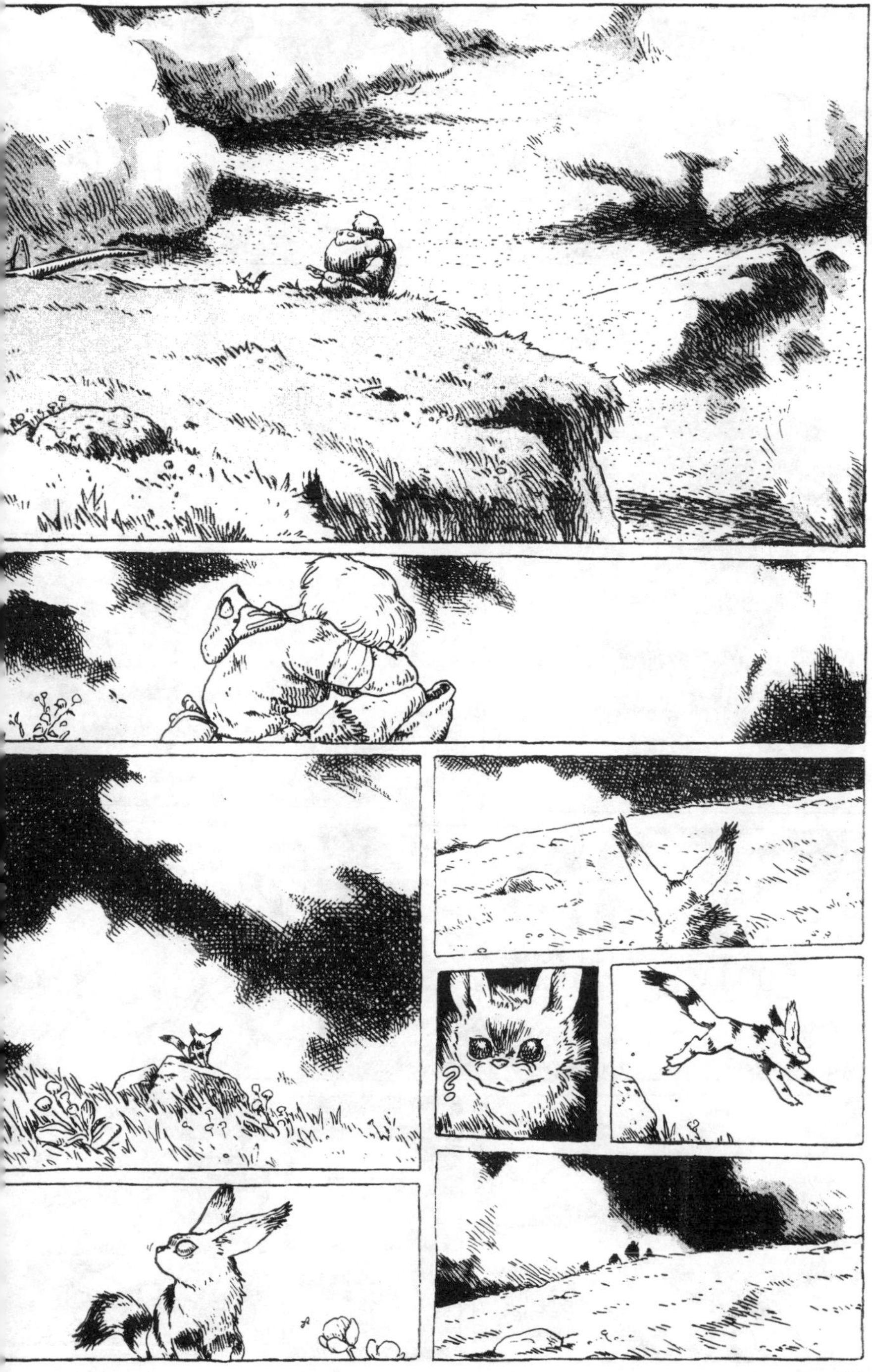

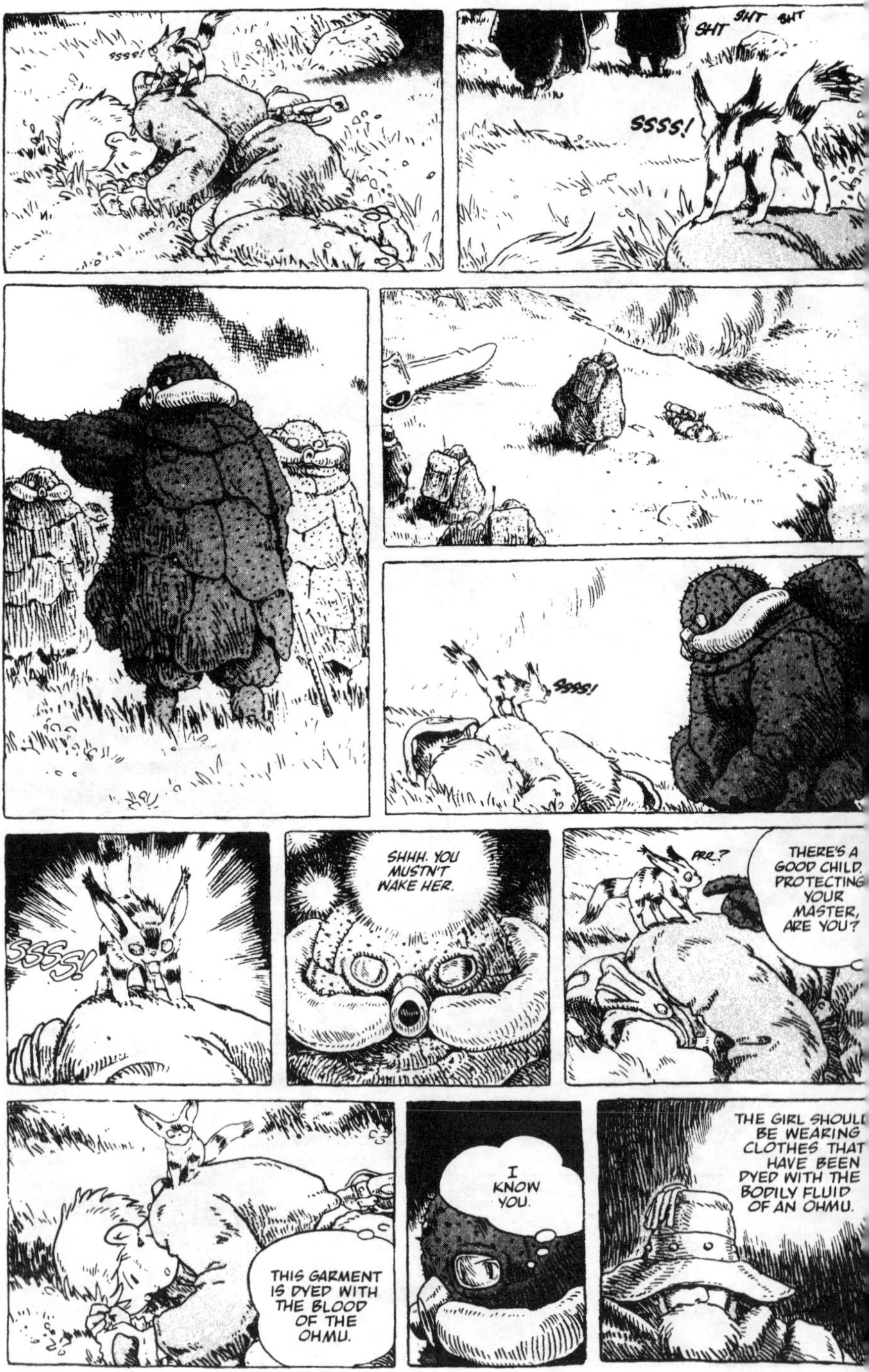
SSSS!
SHT SHT SHT
SSSS!
SSSS!
SSSS!
SHHH. YOU MUSTN'T WAKE HER.
PRR?
THERE'S A GOOD CHILD, PROTECTING YOUR MASTER, ARE YOU?
THIS GARMENT IS DYED WITH THE BLOOD OF THE OHMU.
I KNOW YOU.
THE GIRL SHOULD BE WEARING CLOTHES THAT HAVE BEEN DYED WITH THE BODILY FLUID OF AN OHMU.

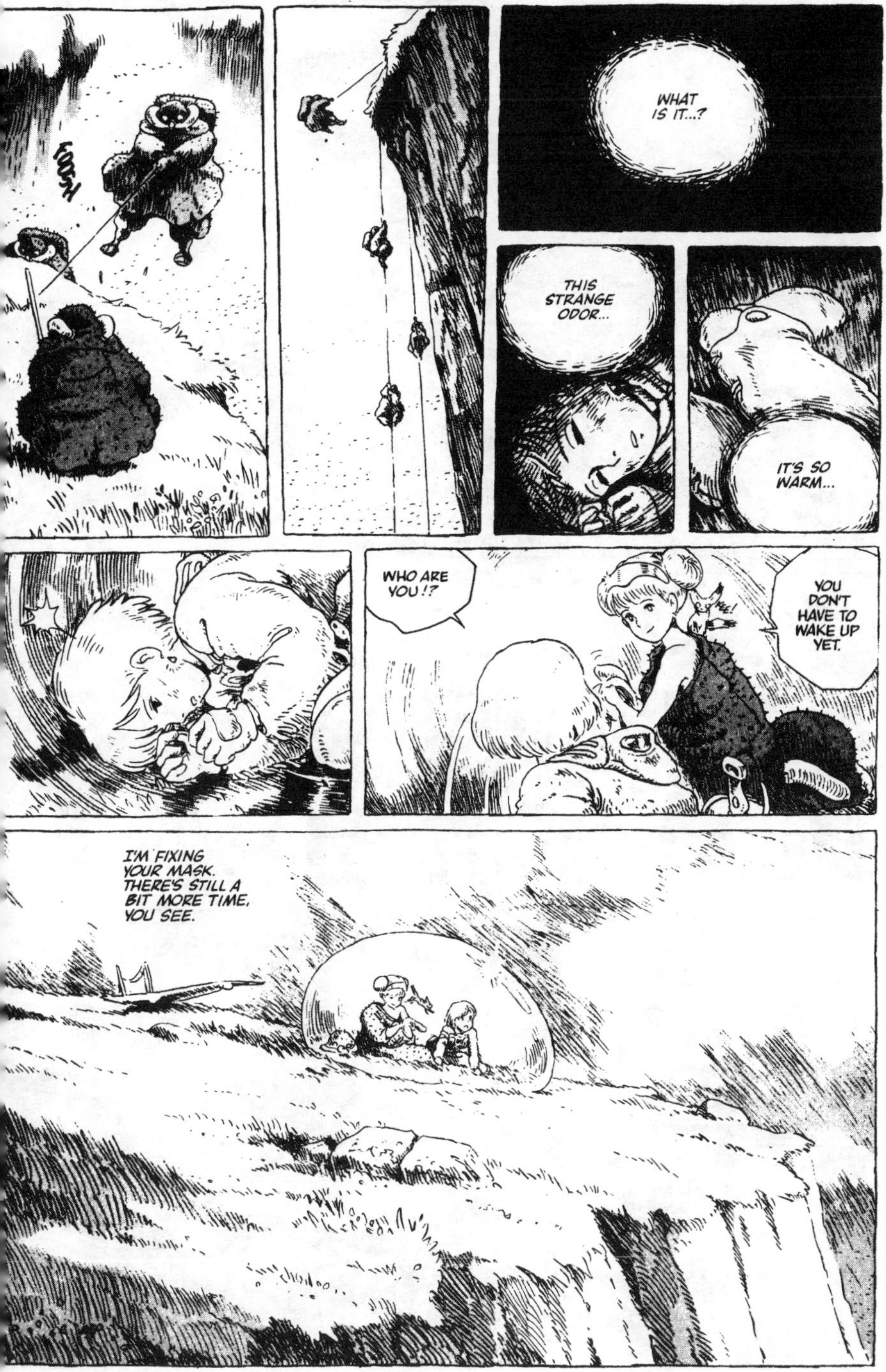
WOOSH
WHAT IS IT...?
THIS STRANGE ODOR...
IT'S SO WARM...
WHO ARE YOU!?
KEE!
YOU DON'T HAVE TO WAKE UP YET.
I'M FIXING YOUR MASK. THERE'S STILL A BIT MORE TIME, YOU SEE.

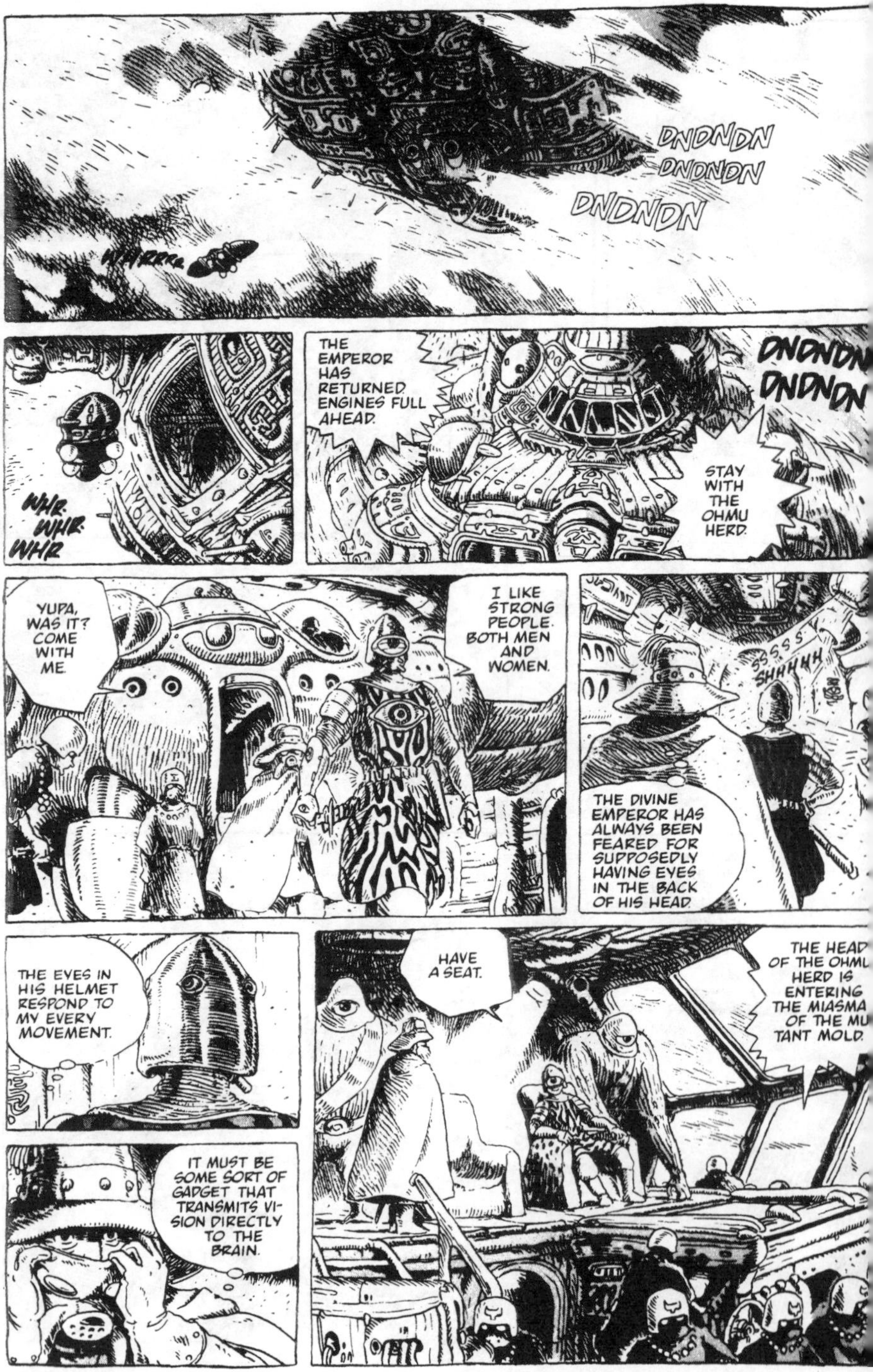
DNDNDN
DNDNDN
DNDNDN
WHRRRR
WHR WHR WHR
THE EMPEROR HAS RETURNED. ENGINES FULL AHEAD.
DNDNDN
DNDNDN
STAY WITH THE OHMU HERD.
YUPA, WAS IT? COME WITH ME.
I LIKE STRONG PEOPLE. BOTH MEN AND WOMEN.
SSSSSS
SHHHHH
THE DIVINE EMPEROR HAS ALWAYS BEEN FEARED FOR SUPPOSEDLY HAVING EYES IN THE BACK OF HIS HEAD.
THE EYES IN HIS HELMET RESPOND TO MY EVERY MOVEMENT.
IT MUST BE SOME SORT OF GADGET THAT TRANSMITS VISION DIRECTLY TO THE BRAIN.
HAVE A SEAT.
THE HEAD OF THE OHMU HERD IS ENTERING THE MIASMA OF THE MUTANT MOLD.

DN DN DN
DN DN DN

RMBL RMBL RMBL

RMBL, RMBL, RMBL

THEY AREN'T STOPPING!! THE OHMU HERD IS PROCEEDING INTO THE MUTANT'S MIASMA.

THE MUTANT'S MIASMA...

YES, THE VERY THING THAT TRIGGERED THE DAIKAISHO. HAVE A LOOK?

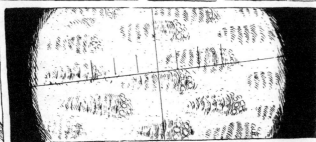

RMBL RMBL RMBL

DN DN DN DN

THE COLOR OF THE MIASMA IS WRONG.

THIS IS THE WORK OF MY CLEVER LITTLE BROTHER AND HIS MINIONS.

THEIR BRILLIANT IDEA TO USE THE SEA OF CORRUPTION HAS RESULTED IN THIS MISERABLE STATE OF AFFAIRS.

DN DN DN DN   DN DN DN

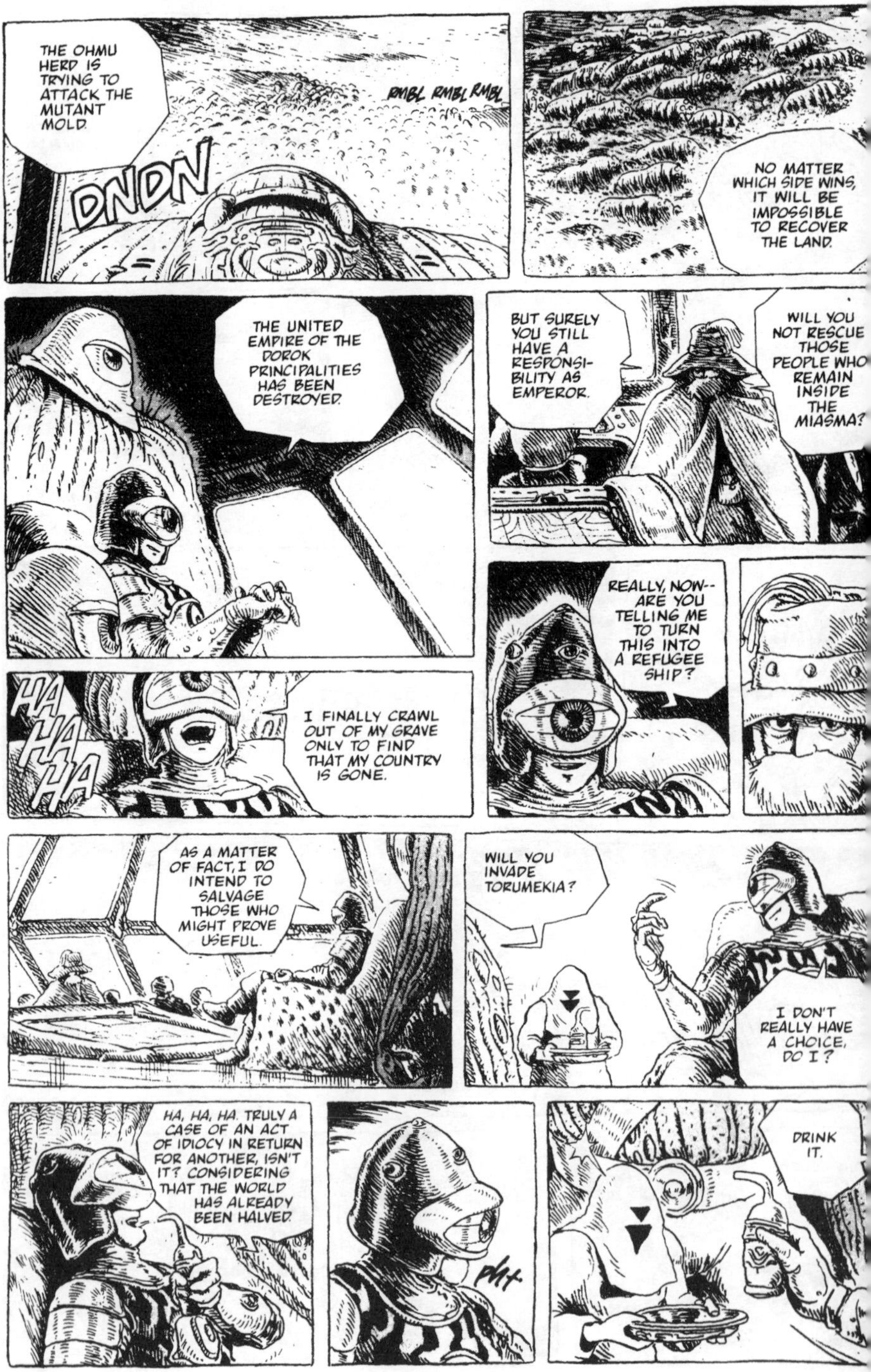
THE OHMU HERD IS TRYING TO ATTACK THE MUTANT MOLD.
RMBL RMBL RMBL
DNDN
NO MATTER WHICH SIDE WINS, IT WILL BE IMPOSSIBLE TO RECOVER THE LAND.
THE UNITED EMPIRE OF THE DOROK PRINCIPALITIES HAS BEEN DESTROYED.
BUT SURELY YOU STILL HAVE A RESPONSIBILITY AS EMPEROR.
WILL YOU NOT RESCUE THOSE PEOPLE WHO REMAIN INSIDE THE MIASMA?
HA HA HA
I FINALLY CRAWL OUT OF MY GRAVE ONLY TO FIND THAT MY COUNTRY IS GONE.
REALLY, NOW-- ARE YOU TELLING ME TO TURN THIS INTO A REFUGEE SHIP?
AS A MATTER OF FACT, I DO INTEND TO SALVAGE THOSE WHO MIGHT PROVE USEFUL.
WILL YOU INVADE TORUMEKIA?
I DON'T REALLY HAVE A CHOICE, DO I?
HA, HA, HA. TRULY A CASE OF AN ACT OF IDIOCY IN RETURN FOR ANOTHER, ISN'T IT? CONSIDERING THAT THE WORLD HAS ALREADY BEEN HALVED.
plut
DRINK IT.

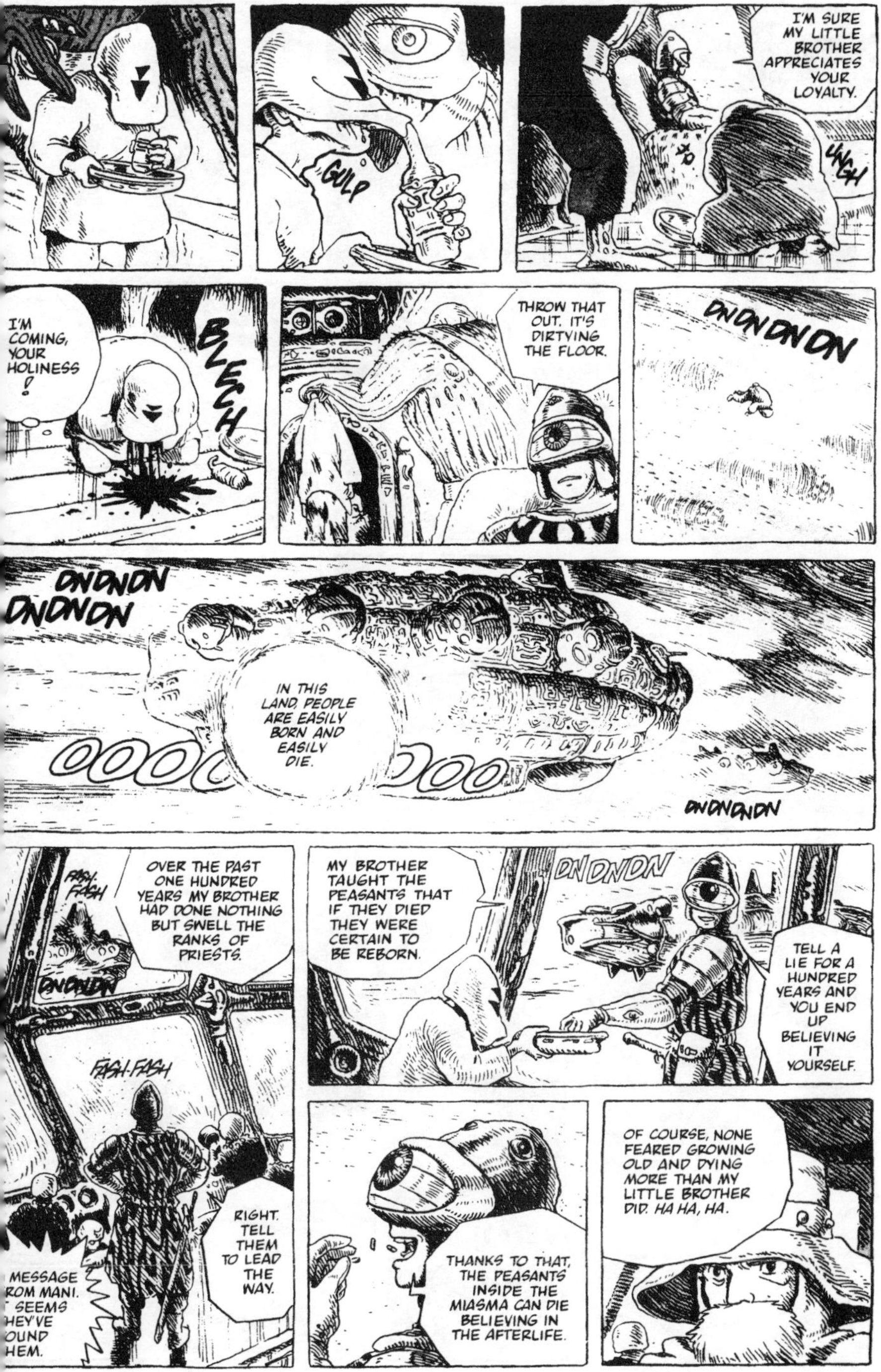
GULP
I'M SURE MY LITTLE BROTHER APPRECIATES YOUR LOYALTY.
UNGH
I'M COMING, YOUR HOLINESS!
BLECH
THROW THAT OUT. IT'S DIRTYING THE FLOOR.
DNDNDNDNDN
DNDNDN
DNDNDN
IN THIS LAND, PEOPLE ARE EASILY BORN AND EASILY DIE.
DNDNDNDN
FASH FASH
OVER THE PAST ONE HUNDRED YEARS MY BROTHER HAD DONE NOTHING BUT SWELL THE RANKS OF PRIESTS.
DNDNDN
FASH FASH
MESSAGE ROM MANI. SEEMS HEY'VE OUND HEM.
RIGHT. TELL THEM TO LEAD THE WAY.
MY BROTHER TAUGHT THE PEASANTS THAT IF THEY DIED THEY WERE CERTAIN TO BE REBORN.
DNDNDN
TELL A LIE FOR A HUNDRED YEARS AND YOU END UP BELIEVING IT YOURSELF.
THANKS TO THAT, THE PEASANTS INSIDE THE MIASMA CAN DIE BELIEVING IN THE AFTERLIFE.
OF COURSE, NONE FEARED GROWING OLD AND DYING MORE THAN MY LITTLE BROTHER DID. HA HA, HA.

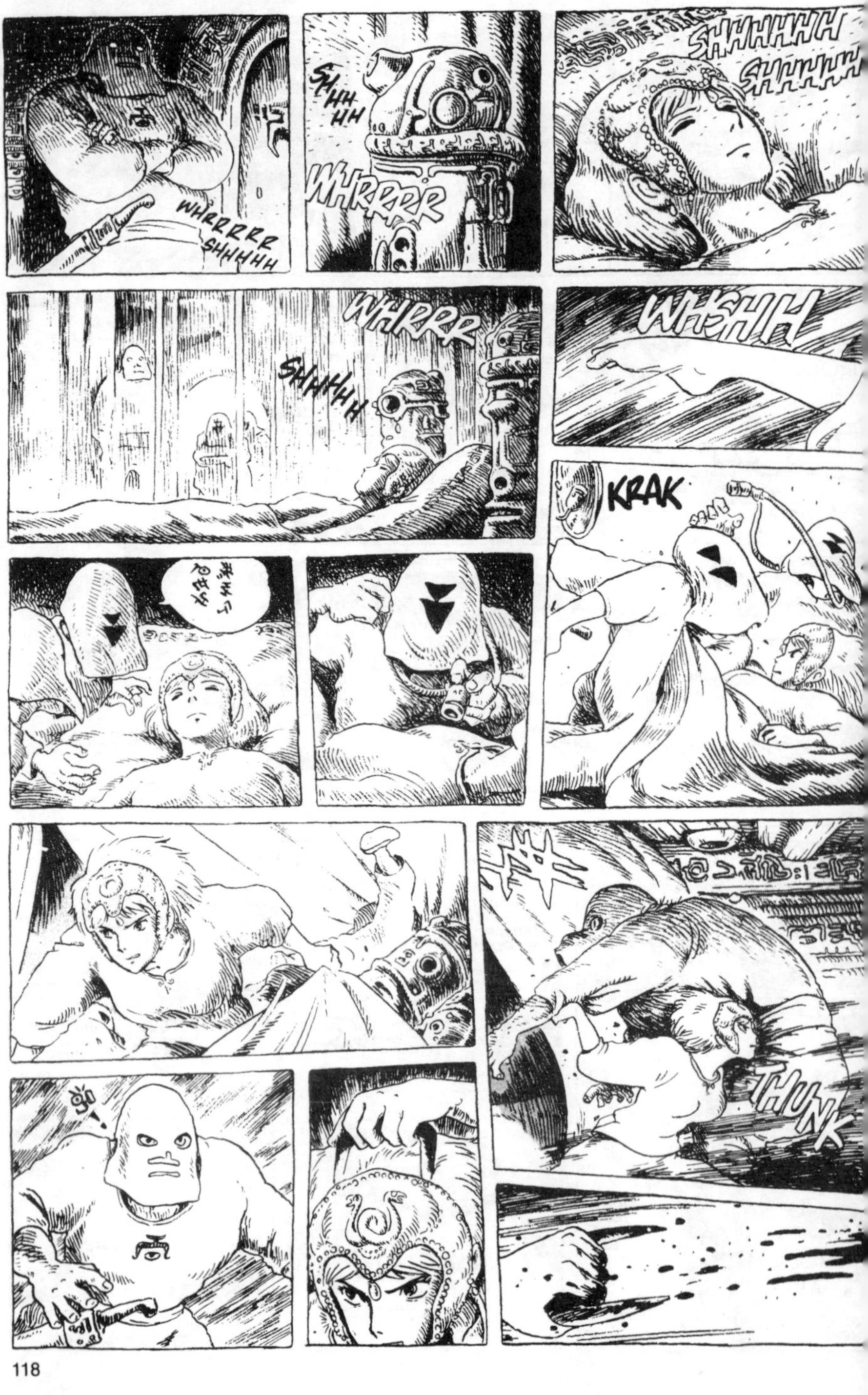
WHRRRRR
SHHHHH
SHHHHH
WHRRRRR
SHHHHHH
SHHHHH
WHRRR
SHHHHH
WHSHH
KRAK
THUNK

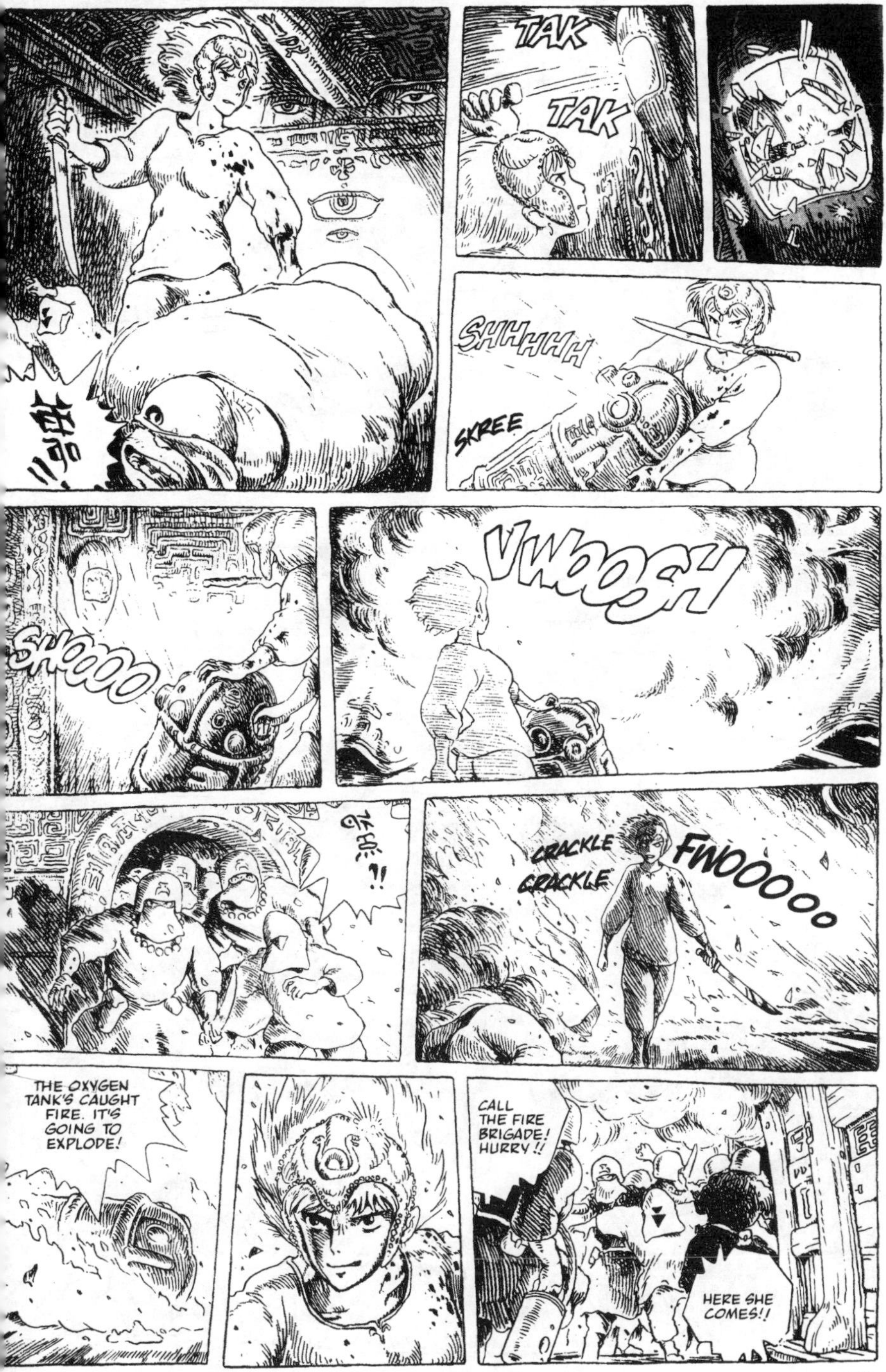
TAK
TAK
SHHHHHH
SKREE
SHOOOO
VWOOSH
CRACKLE
CRACKLE
FWOOOOOO
THE OXYGEN TANK'S CAUGHT FIRE. IT'S GOING TO EXPLODE!
CALL THE FIRE BRIGADE! HURRY!!
HERE SHE COMES!!

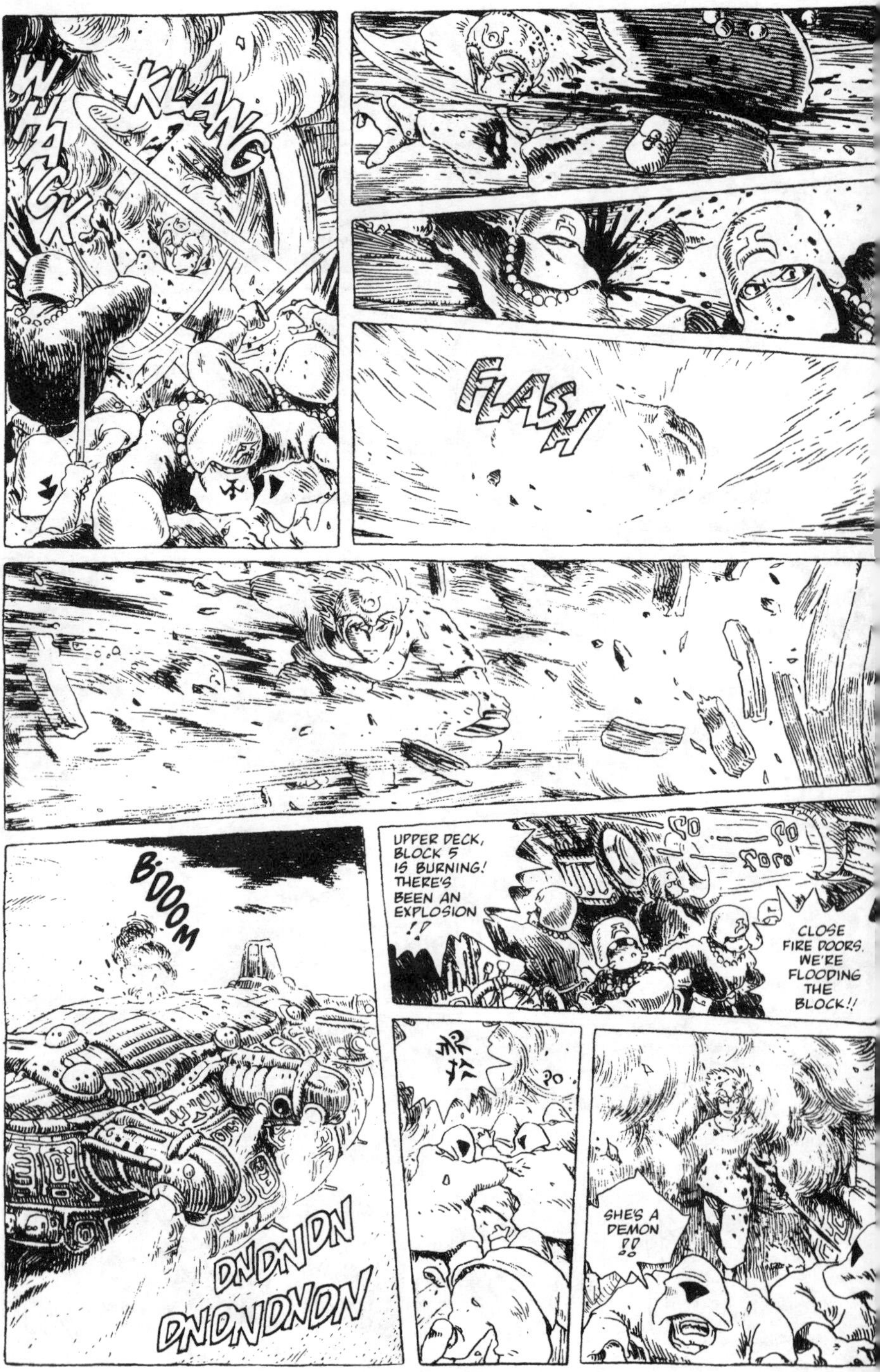
WHACK
KLANG
FLASH
B'DOOM
DNDNDN
DNDNDNDN
UPPER DECK, BLOCK 5 IS BURNING! THERE'S BEEN AN EXPLOSION !!
CLOSE FIRE DOORS. WE'RE FLOODING THE BLOCK!!
SHE'S A DEMON !!

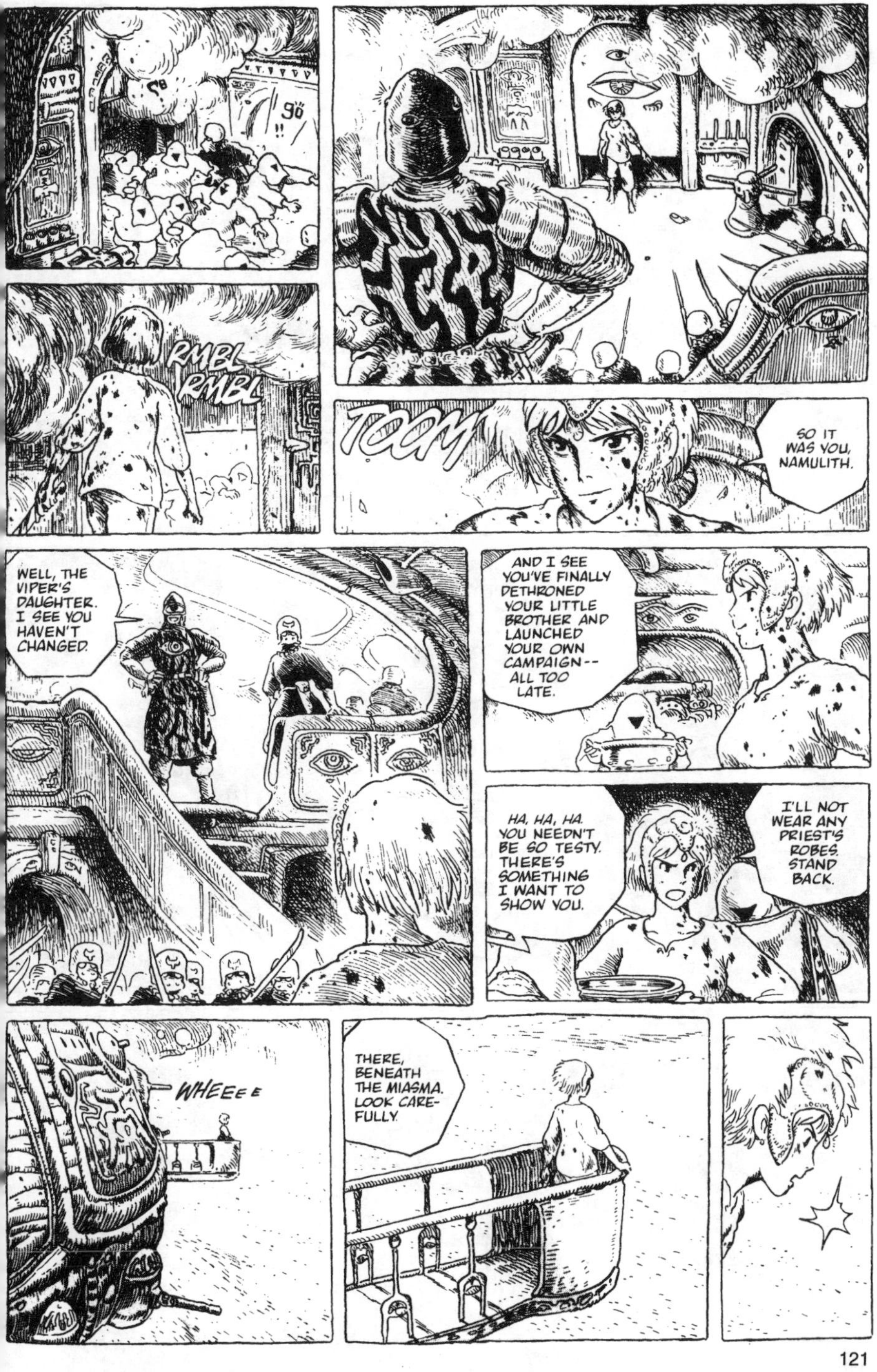

RMBL RMBL
TOOM
SO IT WAS YOU, NAMULITH.
WELL, THE VIPER'S DAUGHTER. I SEE YOU HAVEN'T CHANGED.
AND I SEE YOU'VE FINALLY DETHRONED YOUR LITTLE BROTHER AND LAUNCHED YOUR OWN CAMPAIGN-- ALL TOO LATE.
I'LL NOT WEAR ANY PRIEST'S ROBES. STAND BACK.
HA, HA, HA. YOU NEEDN'T BE SO TESTY. THERE'S SOMETHING I WANT TO SHOW YOU.
WHEEEE
THERE, BENEATH THE MIASMA. LOOK CARE-FULLY.

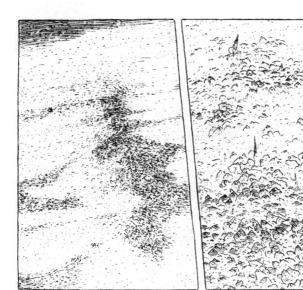

MY MEN.
THEY'RE
ALIVE.

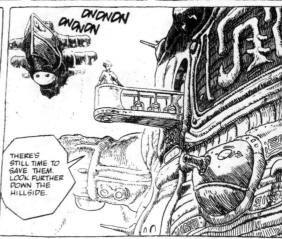

DNDNDN
DNDNDN

THAT'S THE
MAIN FORCE
THAT RETREATED
FROM SAPATA.
I WANT
THOSE
MEN.

THERE'S
STILL TIME TO
SAVE THEM.
LOOK FURTHER
DOWN THE
HILLSIDE.

CAN YOU SEE
SOMETHING
THERE,
INSIDE THE
ODD-COLORED
MIASMA?

BLORP
BLORP
BLORP

122

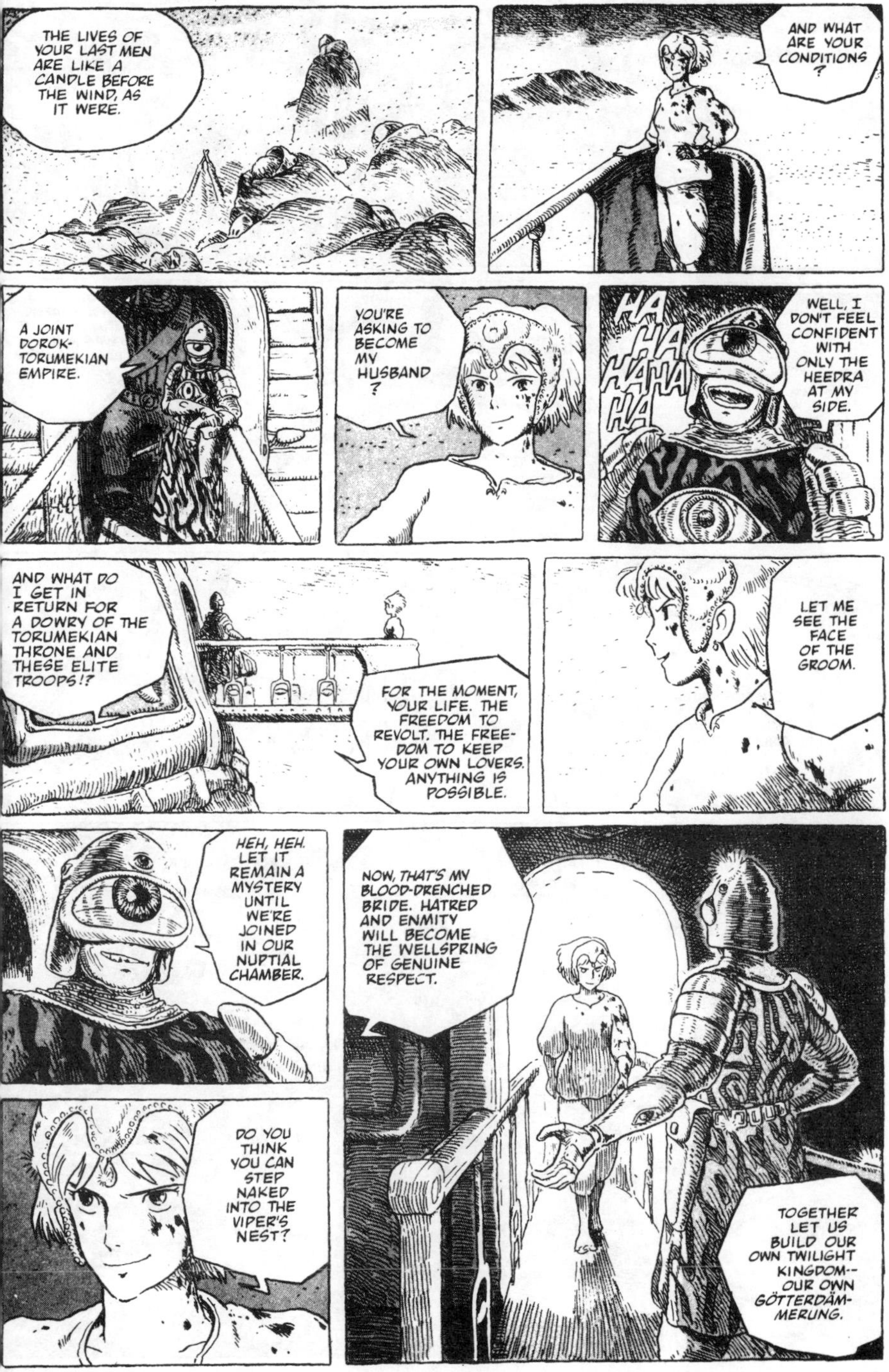
THE LIVES OF YOUR LAST MEN ARE LIKE A CANDLE BEFORE THE WIND, AS IT WERE.
AND WHAT ARE YOUR CONDITIONS ?
A JOINT DOROK-TORUMEKIAN EMPIRE.
YOU'RE ASKING TO BECOME MY HUSBAND ?
HA HA HA HA HA HA
WELL, I DON'T FEEL CONFIDENT WITH ONLY THE HEEDRA AT MY SIDE.
AND WHAT DO I GET IN RETURN FOR A DOWRY OF THE TORUMEKIAN THRONE AND THESE ELITE TROOPS!?
FOR THE MOMENT, YOUR LIFE. THE FREEDOM TO REVOLT. THE FREE-DOM TO KEEP YOUR OWN LOVERS. ANYTHING IS POSSIBLE.
LET ME SEE THE FACE OF THE GROOM.
HEH, HEH. LET IT REMAIN A MYSTERY UNTIL WE'RE JOINED IN OUR NUPTIAL CHAMBER.
DO YOU THINK YOU CAN STEP NAKED INTO THE VIPER'S NEST?
NOW, THAT'S MY BLOOD-DRENCHED BRIDE. HATRED AND ENMITY WILL BECOME THE WELLSPRING OF GENUINE RESPECT.
TOGETHER LET US BUILD OUR OWN TWILIGHT KINGDOM-- OUR OWN GÖTTERDÄM-MERUNG.

REPAIR DAMAGED AREAS IMMEDIATELY. PREPARING TO LAND.

YOU'VE LOOKED LONG ENOUGH, NOW. LET ME SHOW YOU TO THE GUEST'S QUARTERS.

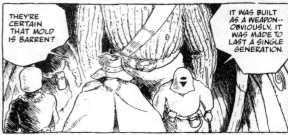

THEY'RE CERTAIN THAT MOLD IS BARREN?

IT WAS BUILT AS A WEAPON-- OBVIOUSLY, IT WAS MADE TO LAST A SINGLE GENERATION.

I HOPE YOU'RE RIGHT. BUT SOMETIMES A MUTATION HAS THE ABILITY TO ACTUALLY PROLIFERATE AT AN EXPLOSIVE RATE.

HEH, HEH. LUCKY FOR US, THEN, THAT THE OHMU HAVE SHOWN UP. THEY'LL EAT THE WHOLE MESS UP FOR US, NOW, WON'T THEY?

DIDN'T YOU SEE THE COLOR OF THE OHMU'S EYES?

THAT WASN'T THEIR ATTACK COLOR.

Hmph.

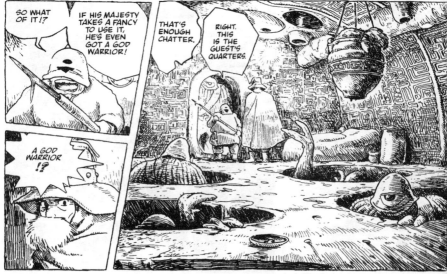

SO WHAT OF IT!?

IF HIS MAJESTY TAKES A FANCY TO USE IT, HE'S EVEN GOT A GOD WARRIOR!

THAT'S ENOUGH CHATTER.

RIGHT. THIS IS THE GUEST'S QUARTERS.

A GOD WARRIOR !?

124

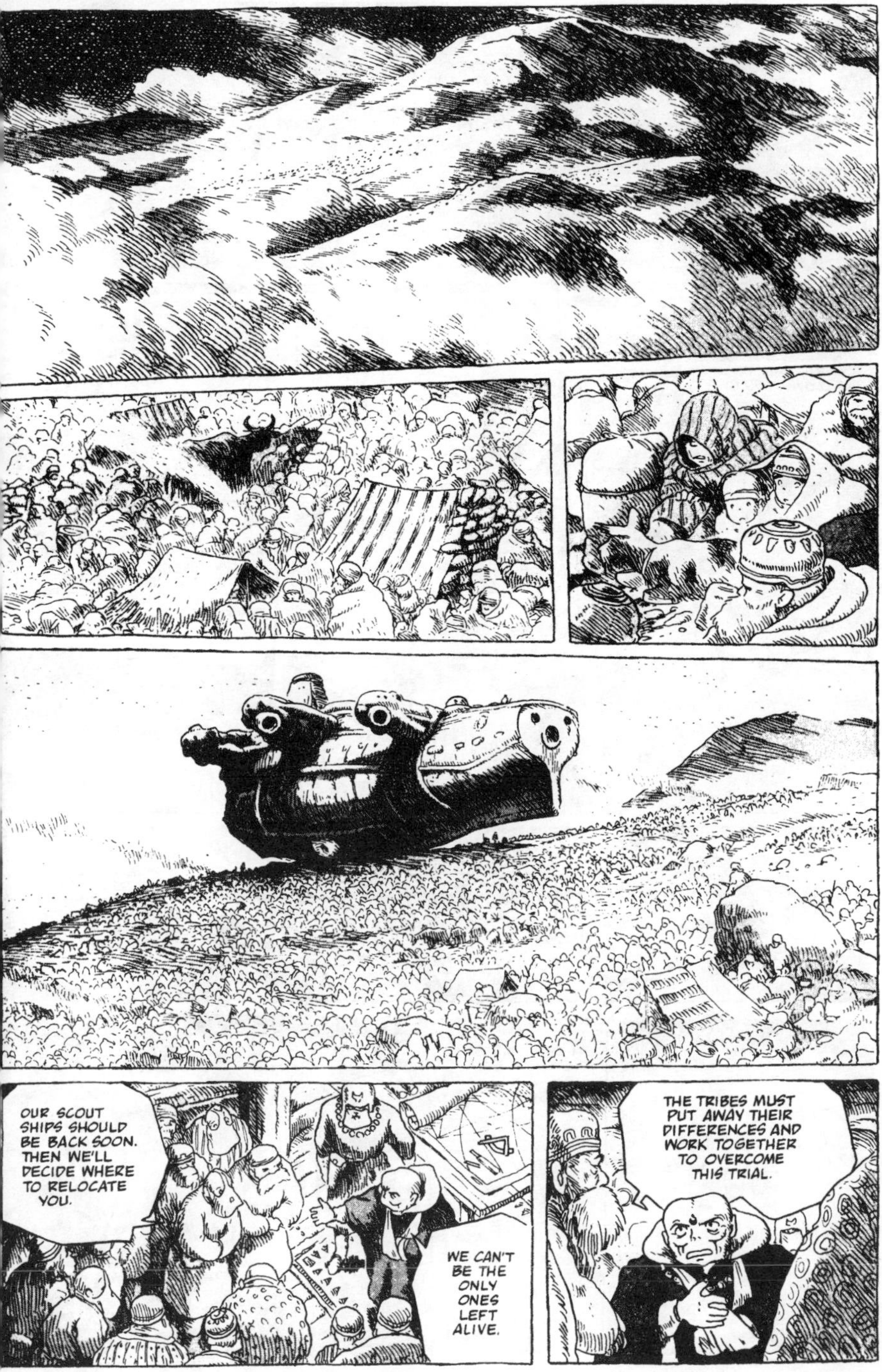
OUR SCOUT SHIPS SHOULD BE BACK SOON. THEN WE'LL DECIDE WHERE TO RELOCATE YOU.
WE CAN'T BE THE ONLY ONES LEFT ALIVE.
THE TRIBES MUST PUT AWAY THEIR DIFFERENCES AND WORK TOGETHER TO OVERCOME THIS TRIAL.

YOUR EMINENCE, THE BASE OF THIS MOUNTAIN IS OUR HOME. OUR PEOPLE WANT TO RETURN TO THEIR VILLAGES.

WHAT!?

EVEN IF WE MOVE TO ANOTHER PLACE, THAT LAND WILL STILL BELONG TO OTHER PEOPLE.

THERE'LL BE NO EXTRA GRASS TO FEED OUR LIVESTOCK, NO LAND TO TILL.

TO BE LEFT ALIVE ONLY TO LOSE EVERYTHING AND WANDER AIMLESSLY IN A STRANGE LAND CAN ONLY DEEPEN OUR MISERY.

WHAT FOOLISHNESS! ARE YOU SAYING YOU'D RATHER STAND BY HELPLESSLY AS THE MIASMA POISONS YOU AND THE MOLD SWALLOWS YOU UP!?

YOUR EMINENCE, YOU ARE FORGETTING THE SCRIPTURES.

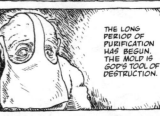

THE LONG PERIOD OF PURIFICATION HAS BEGUN. THE MOLD IS GOD'S TOOL OF DESTRUCTION.

THE END OF THIS WORLD OF SUFFERING HAS COME.

THAT IS WHY THE WHITE BIRD HAS COME TO LEAD THE WAY.

WE WILL BE LIBERATED FROM THE HEAVY TAXES, THE WARS, THE 'PETRIFYING DISEASE.'

PARENTS WILL NO LONGER HAVE TO SUFFER THE DEATHS OF THEIR CHILDREN.

THE OLD PAGAN FOLKLORE AND THE TEACHINGS OF THE COUNCIL OF PRIESTS HAVE BECOME JUMBLED TOGETHER!!

WHAT HAS THE COUNCIL OF PRIESTS DONE TO THESE PEOPLE? HAS IT DONE NOTHING BUT ALLOW NIHILISM TO THRIVE?

TH-THE VOICE! THE VOICE OF THE WHITE BIRD!

I-I CAN HEAR IT!

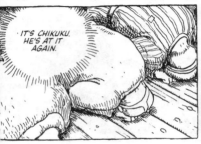

IT'S CHIKUKU. HE'S AT IT AGAIN.

CONFOUND IT!

DO YOU SEE NOW? YOU MUST GO ON LIVING!

THE VOICE IS TELLING YOU TO STAY HERE, ISN'T IT!?

Y-YES.

PLAYING GAMES WITH HIS SUPERNATURAL POWERS...

BLAST IT, CHIKUKU!

YOU WERE USING YOUR TELEKINESIS AGAIN, WEREN'T YOU? HOW MANY TIMES DO I HAVE TO EXPLAIN BEFORE YOU UNDERSTAND? WHAT WILL YOU DO IF THE SOLDIERS FIND YOU OUT?

THERE ARE LIMITS EVEN TO MY POWERS, YOU KNOW.

TAKE A LOOK.

!?

127

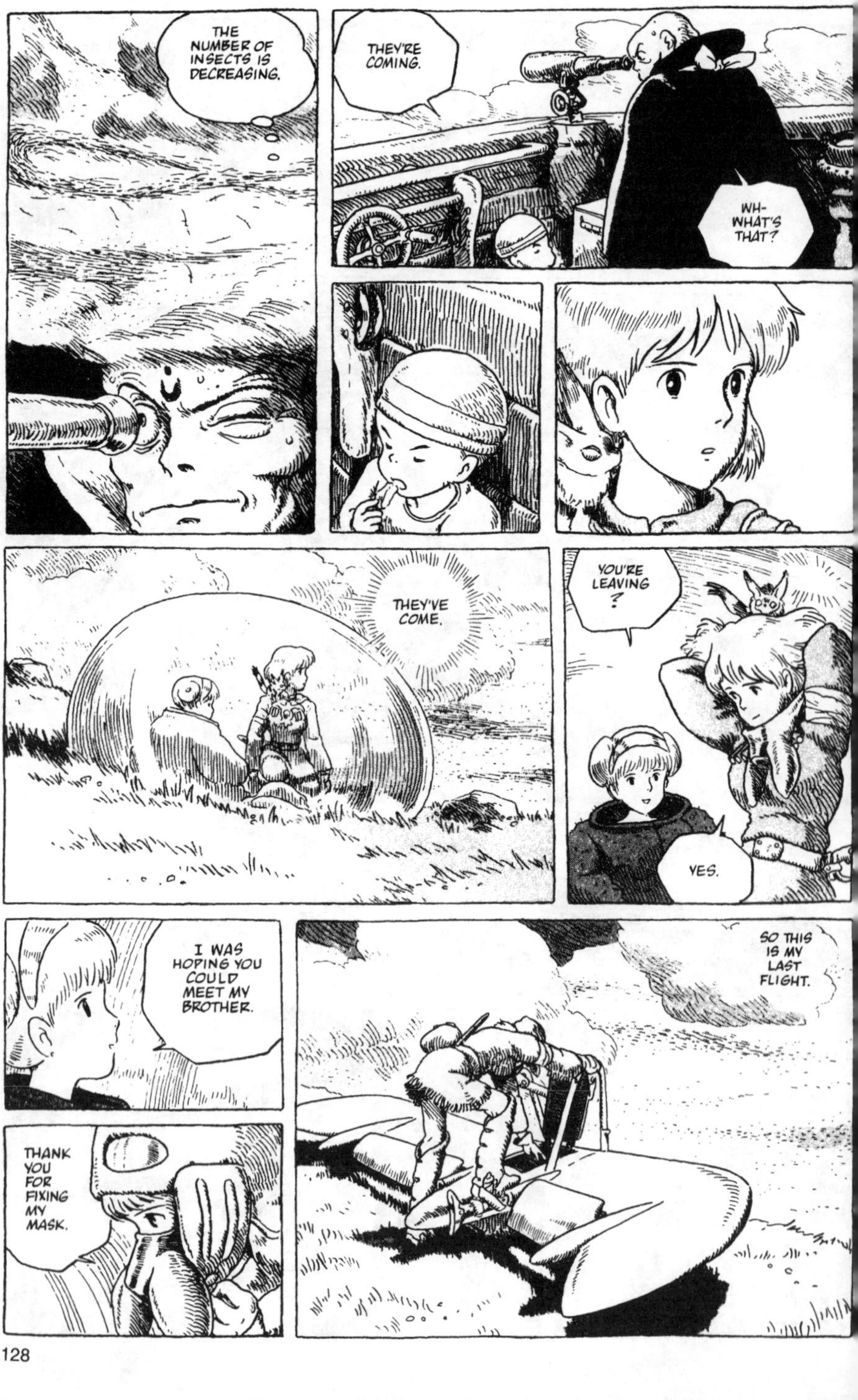
THE NUMBER OF INSECTS IS DECREASING.
THEY'RE COMING.
WH- WHAT'S THAT?
THEY'VE COME.
YOU'RE LEAVING?
YES.
I WAS HOPING YOU COULD MEET MY BROTHER.
SO THIS IS MY LAST FLIGHT.
THANK YOU FOR FIXING MY MASK.

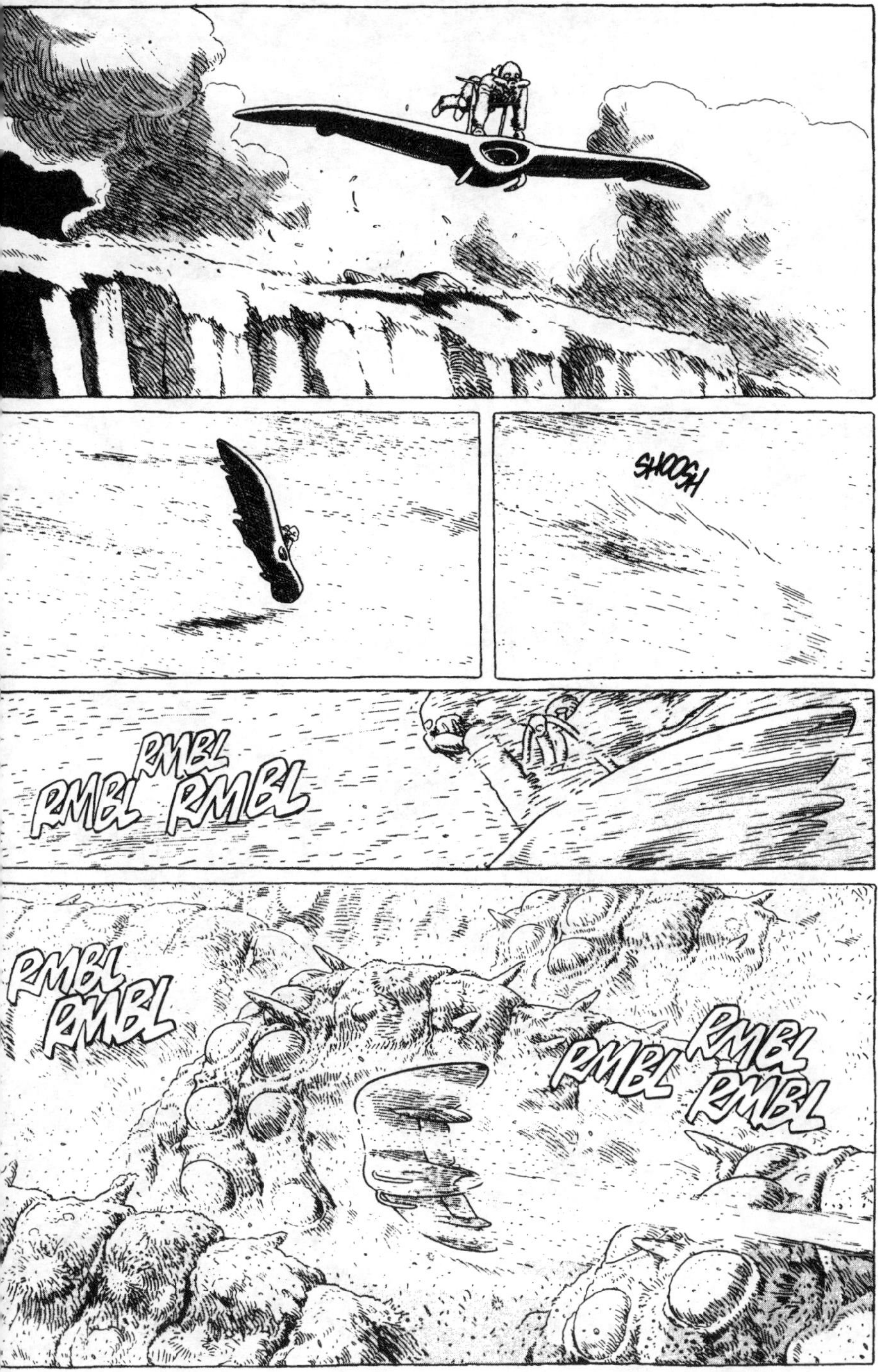
SHOOSH
RMBL
RMBL RMBL
RMBL
RMBL
RMBL
RMBL
RMBL

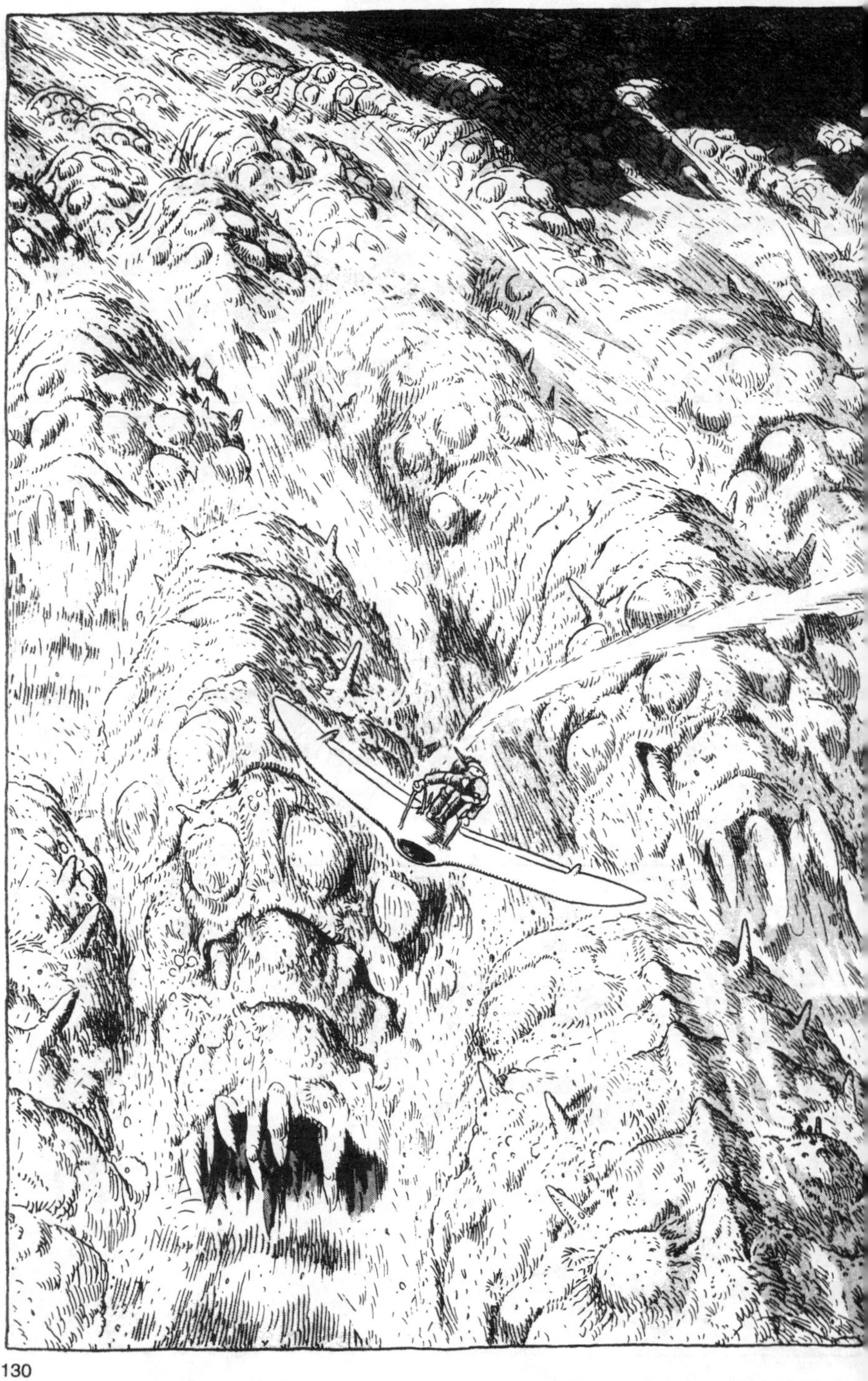

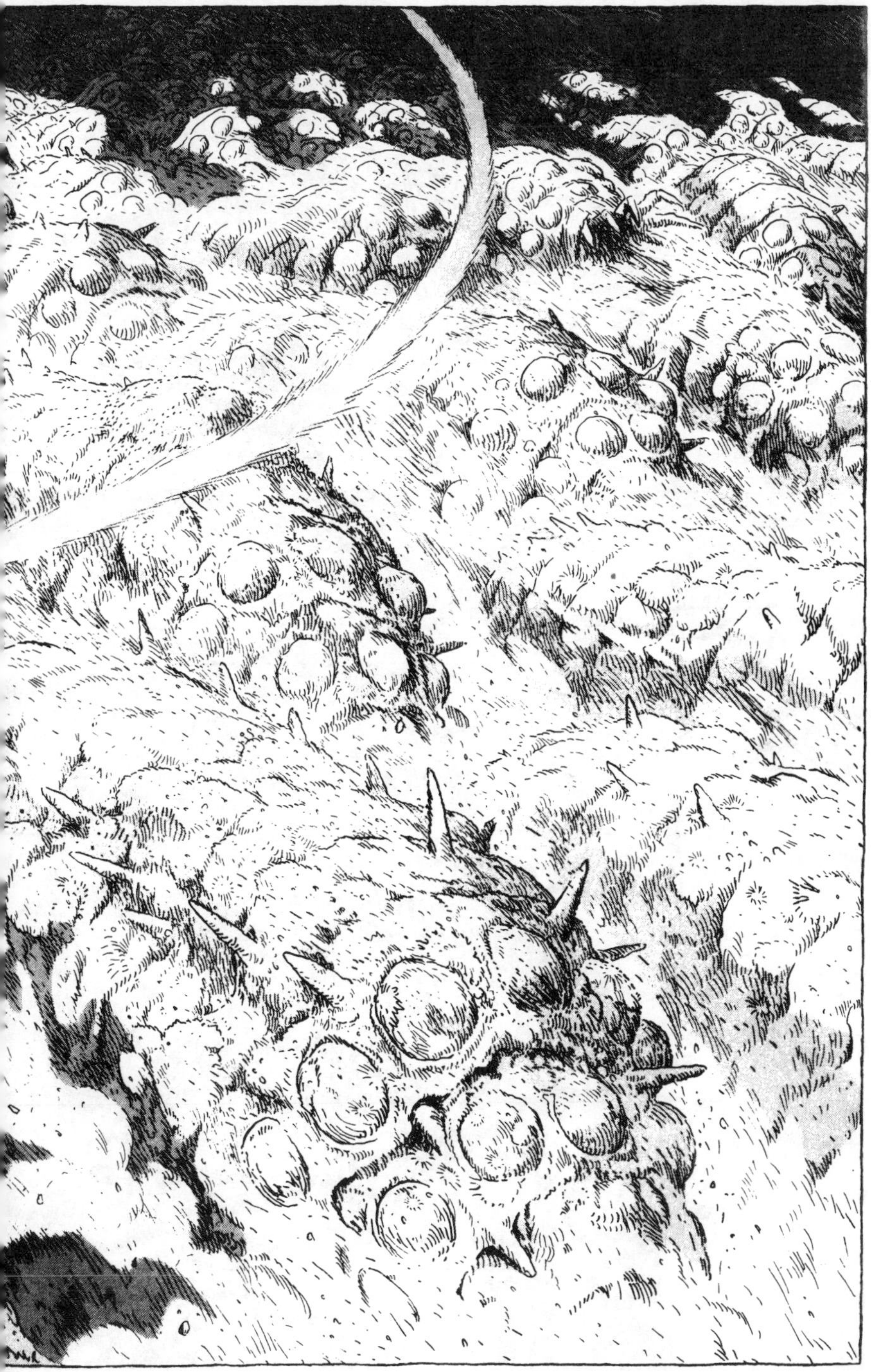

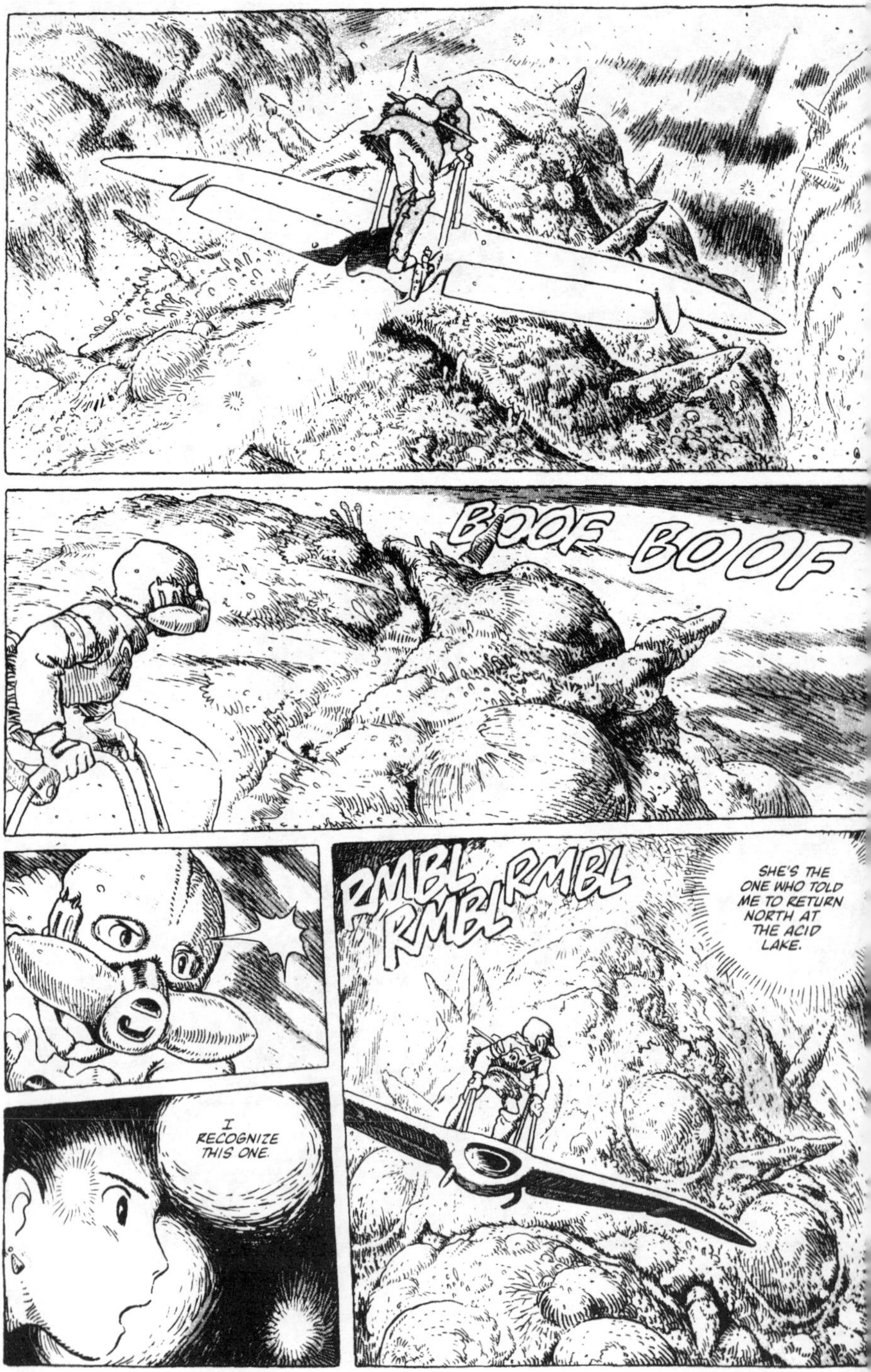
BOOF BOOF
RMBL RMBL
RMBL
SHE'S THE ONE WHO TOLD ME TO RETURN NORTH AT THE ACID LAKE.
I RECOGNIZE THIS ONE.

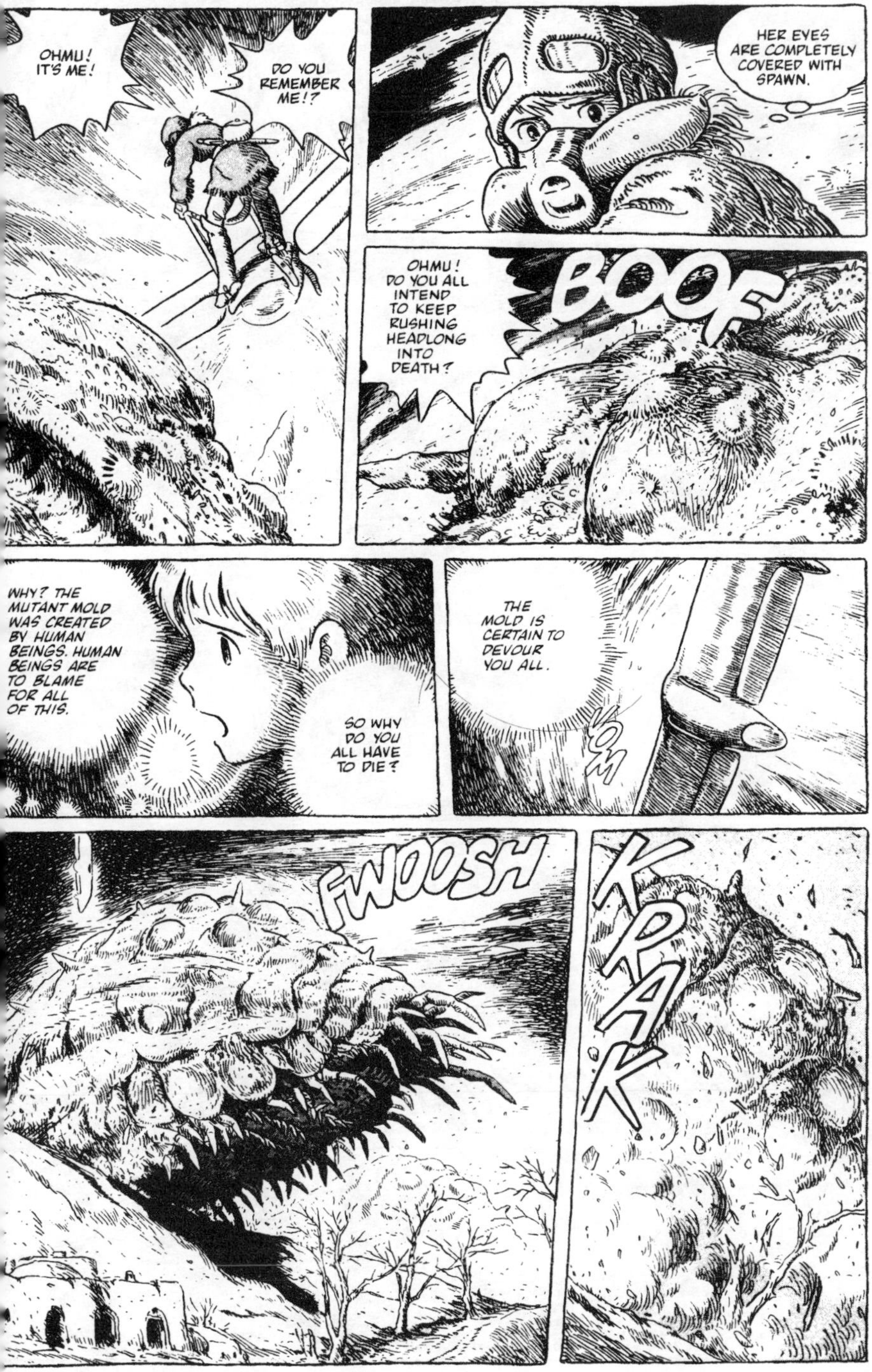

OHMU! IT'S ME!
DO YOU REMEMBER ME!?
HER EYES ARE COMPLETELY COVERED WITH SPAWN.
OHMU! DO YOU ALL INTEND TO KEEP RUSHING HEADLONG INTO DEATH?
BOOF
WHY? THE MUTANT MOLD WAS CREATED BY HUMAN BEINGS. HUMAN BEINGS ARE TO BLAME FOR ALL OF THIS.
SO WHY DO YOU ALL HAVE TO DIE?
THE MOLD IS CERTAIN TO DEVOUR YOU ALL.
VOM
FWOOSH
KRAK

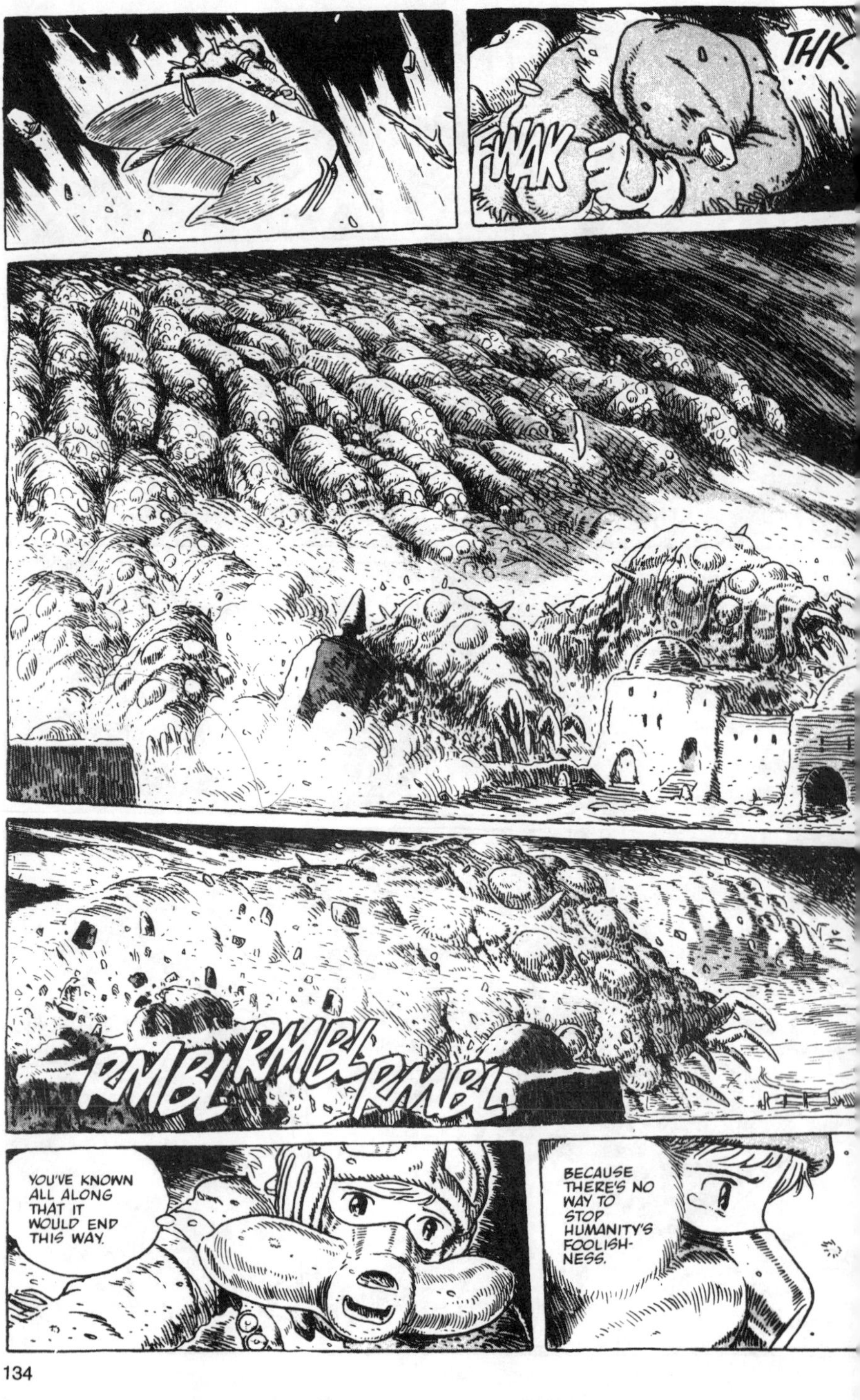
THK.
FWAK
RMBL RMBL RMBL
YOU'VE KNOWN ALL ALONG THAT IT WOULD END THIS WAY.
BECAUSE THERE'S NO WAY TO STOP HUMANITY'S FOOLISH-NESS.

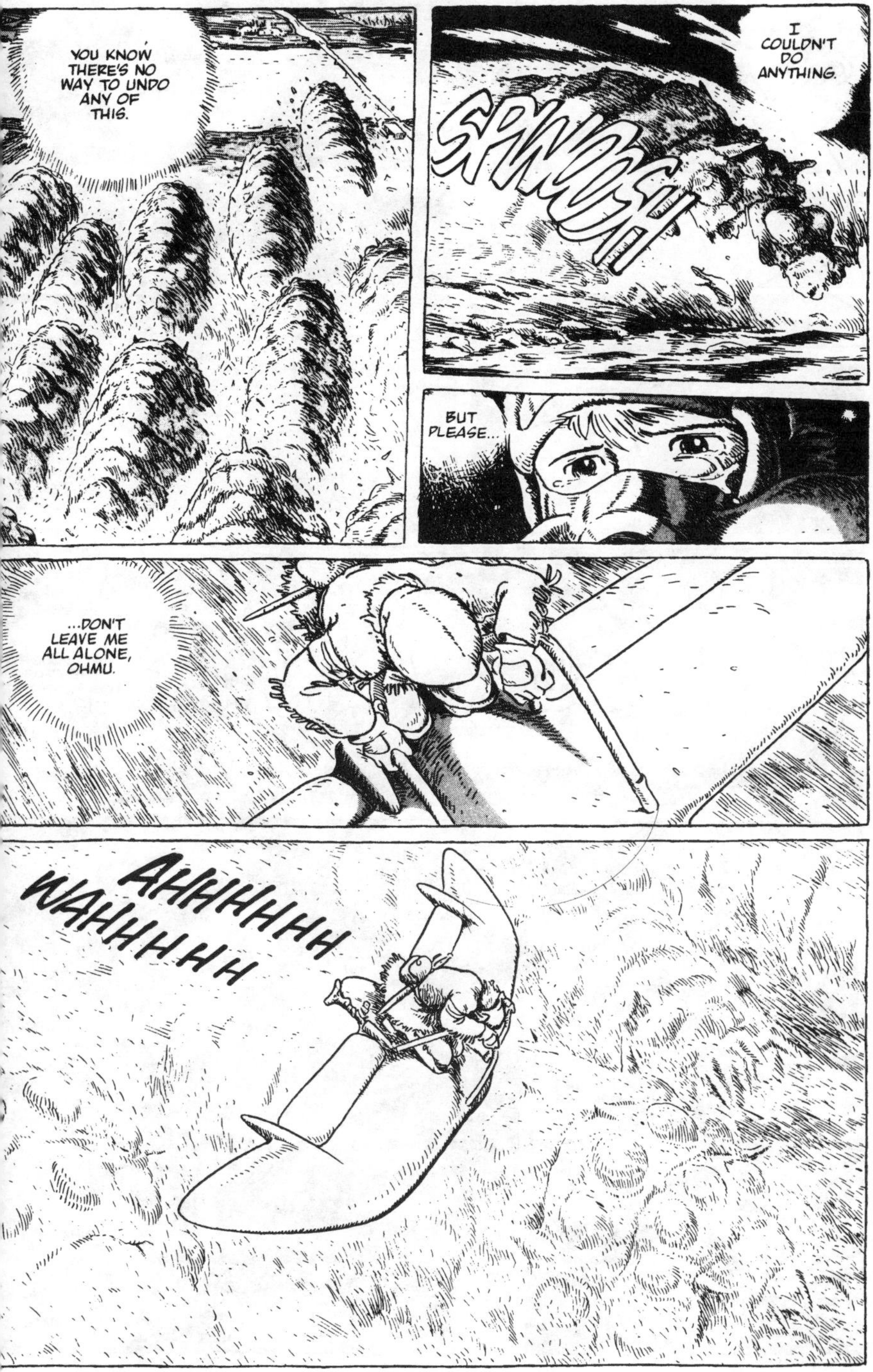
YOU KNOW THERE'S NO WAY TO UNDO ANY OF THIS.
I COULDN'T DO ANYTHING.
SPWOOSH
BUT PLEASE...
...DON'T LEAVE ME ALL ALONE, OHMU.
AHHHHHHH
WAHHHHHH

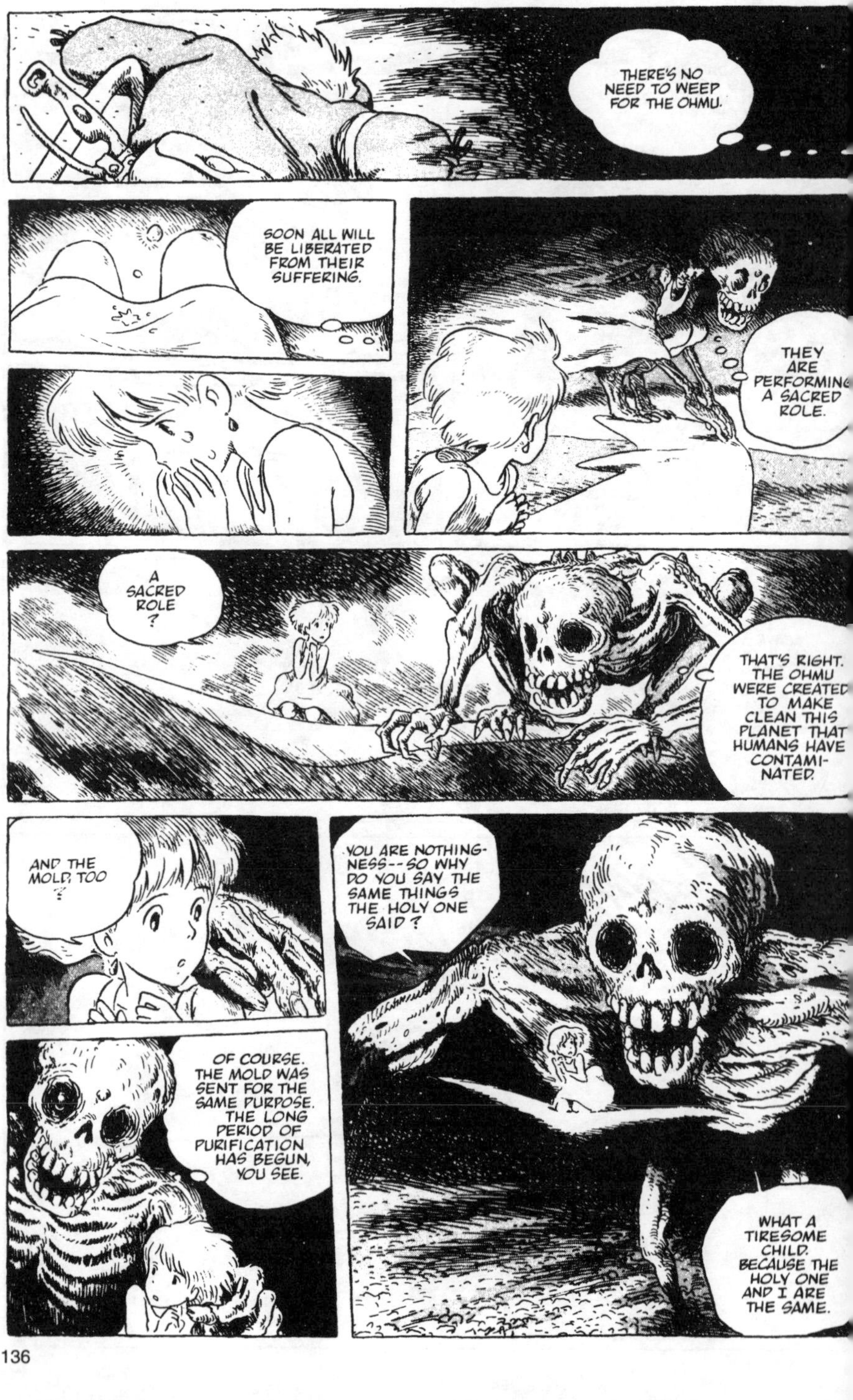
THERE'S NO NEED TO WEEP FOR THE OHMU.
SOON ALL WILL BE LIBERATED FROM THEIR SUFFERING.
THEY ARE PERFORMING A SACRED ROLE.
A SACRED ROLE ?
THAT'S RIGHT. THE OHMU WERE CREATED TO MAKE CLEAN THIS PLANET THAT HUMANS HAVE CONTAMINATED.
AND THE MOLD, TOO ?
YOU ARE NOTHINGNESS--SO WHY DO YOU SAY THE SAME THINGS THE HOLY ONE SAID ?
OF COURSE. THE MOLD WAS SENT FOR THE SAME PURPOSE. THE LONG PERIOD OF PURIFICATION HAS BEGUN, YOU SEE.
WHAT A TIRESOME CHILD. BECAUSE THE HOLY ONE AND I ARE THE SAME.

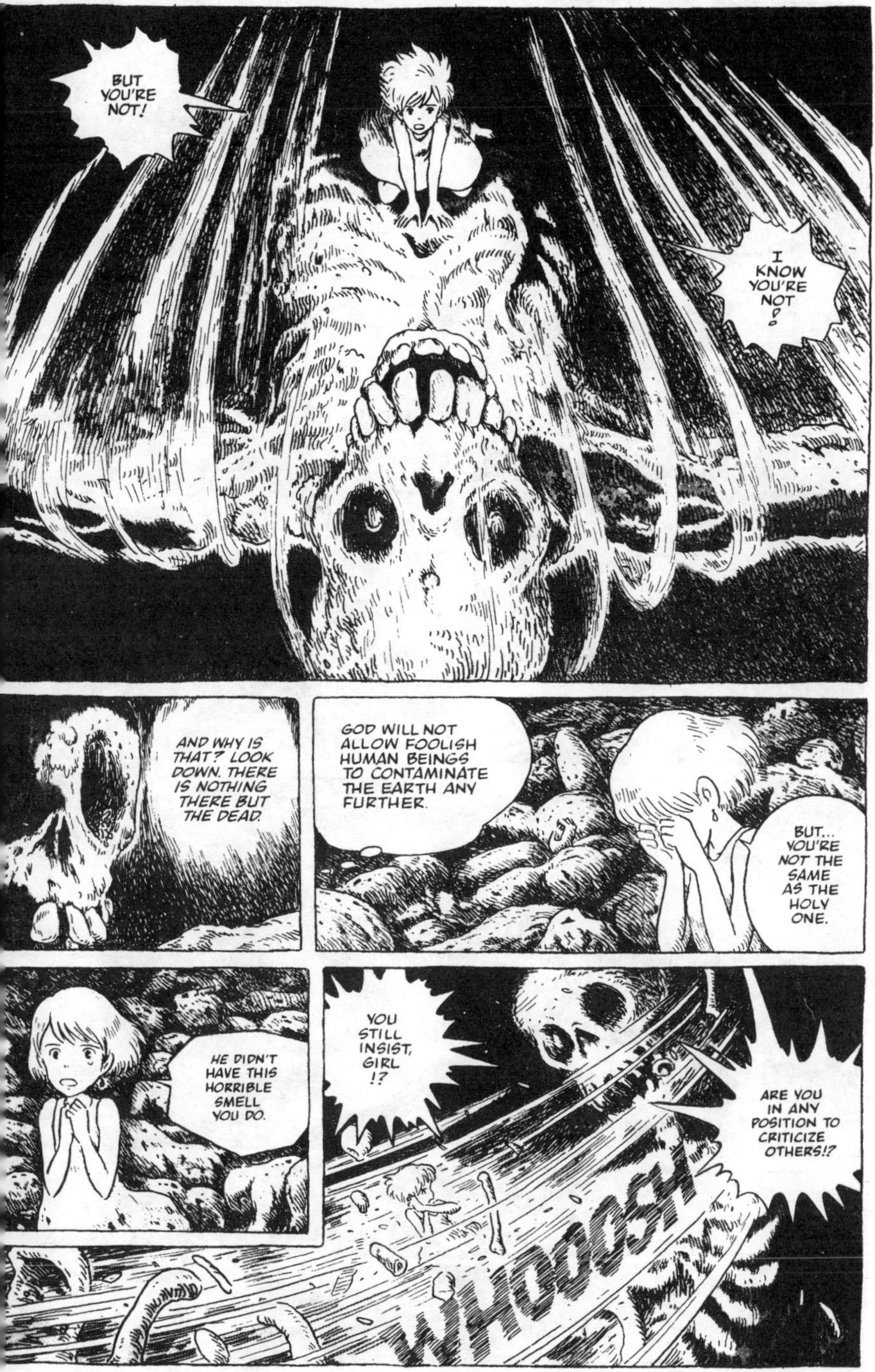
BUT YOU'RE NOT!
I KNOW YOU'RE NOT!
AND WHY IS THAT? LOOK DOWN. THERE IS NOTHING THERE BUT THE DEAD.
GOD WILL NOT ALLOW FOOLISH HUMAN BEINGS TO CONTAMINATE THE EARTH ANY FURTHER.
BUT... YOU'RE NOT THE SAME AS THE HOLY ONE.
HE DIDN'T HAVE THIS HORRIBLE SMELL YOU DO.
YOU STILL INSIST, GIRL!?
ARE YOU IN ANY POSITION TO CRITICIZE OTHERS!?
WHOOOSH

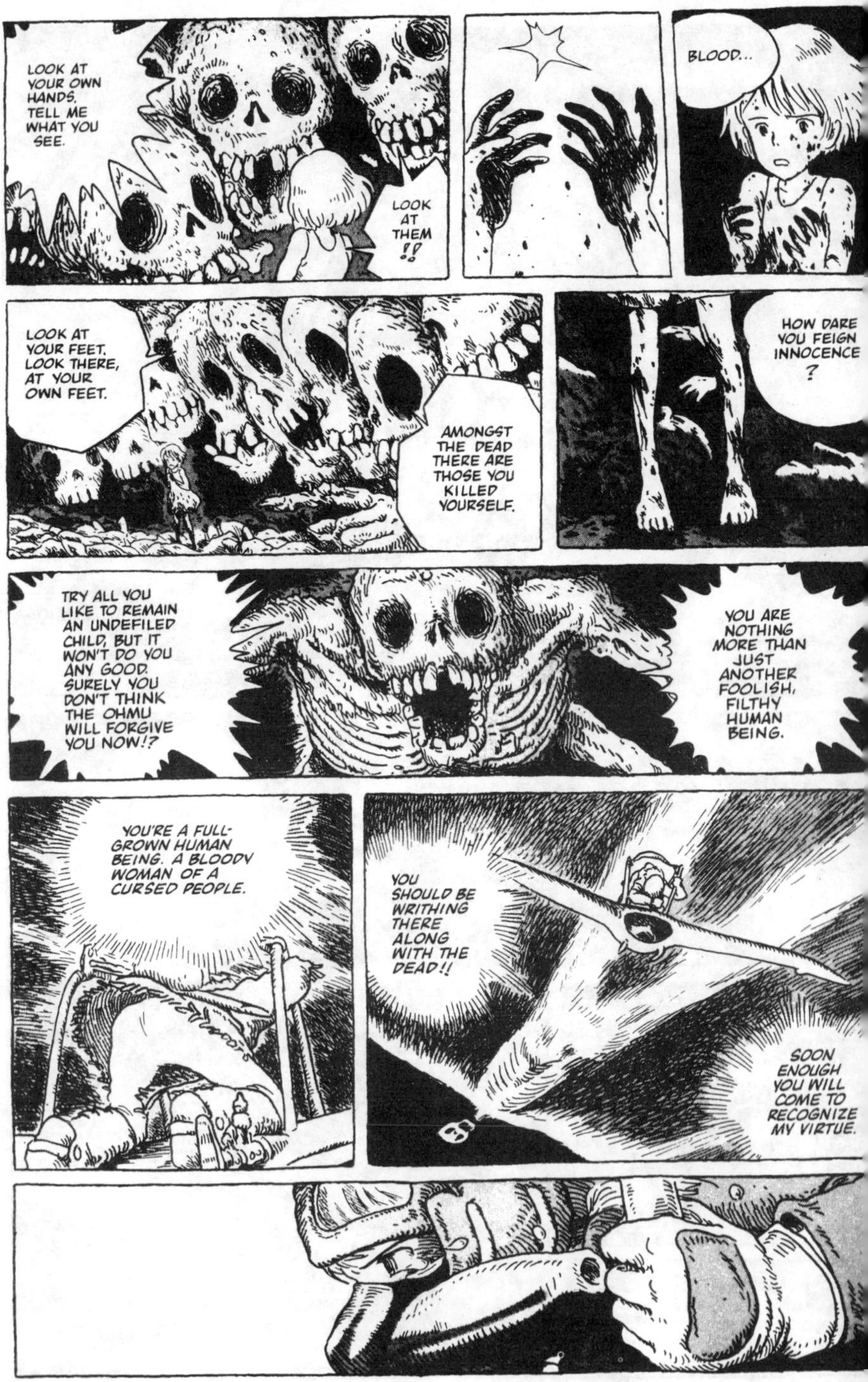
LOOK AT YOUR OWN HANDS. TELL ME WHAT YOU SEE.
LOOK AT THEM!?
BLOOD...
LOOK AT YOUR FEET. LOOK THERE, AT YOUR OWN FEET.
AMONGST THE DEAD THERE ARE THOSE YOU KILLED YOURSELF.
HOW DARE YOU FEIGN INNOCENCE?
TRY ALL YOU LIKE TO REMAIN AN UNDEFILED CHILD, BUT IT WON'T DO YOU ANY GOOD. SURELY YOU DON'T THINK THE OHMU WILL FORGIVE YOU NOW!?
YOU ARE NOTHING MORE THAN JUST ANOTHER FOOLISH, FILTHY HUMAN BEING.
YOU'RE A FULL-GROWN HUMAN BEING. A BLOODY WOMAN OF A CURSED PEOPLE.
YOU SHOULD BE WRITHING THERE ALONG WITH THE DEAD!!
SOON ENOUGH YOU WILL COME TO RECOGNIZE MY VIRTUE.

I DON'T NEED THE NOTHINGNESS TO TELL ME THAT WE ARE A CURSED PEOPLE.

WE'RE THE UGLIEST OF ALL CREATURES. WE DO NOTHING BUT HARM TO THE EARTH--PLUNDERING IT AND POLLUTING IT AND BURNING IT...

THE OHMU ARE FAR MORE BEAUTI- UL HAN E ARE.

WHAT GOOD IS IT TO BEG FOR FORGIVE- NESS NOW?

THE OHMU HAVE TRAVELLED A LONG, LONG WAY, HALF-BLINDED BY THE SPAWN FORMING OVER THEIR EYES, IN ORDER TO TRY TO HEAL THE WOUNDS THAT HUMANS HAVE INFLICTED.

AND NOW THAT JOURNEY IS ABOUT TO END.

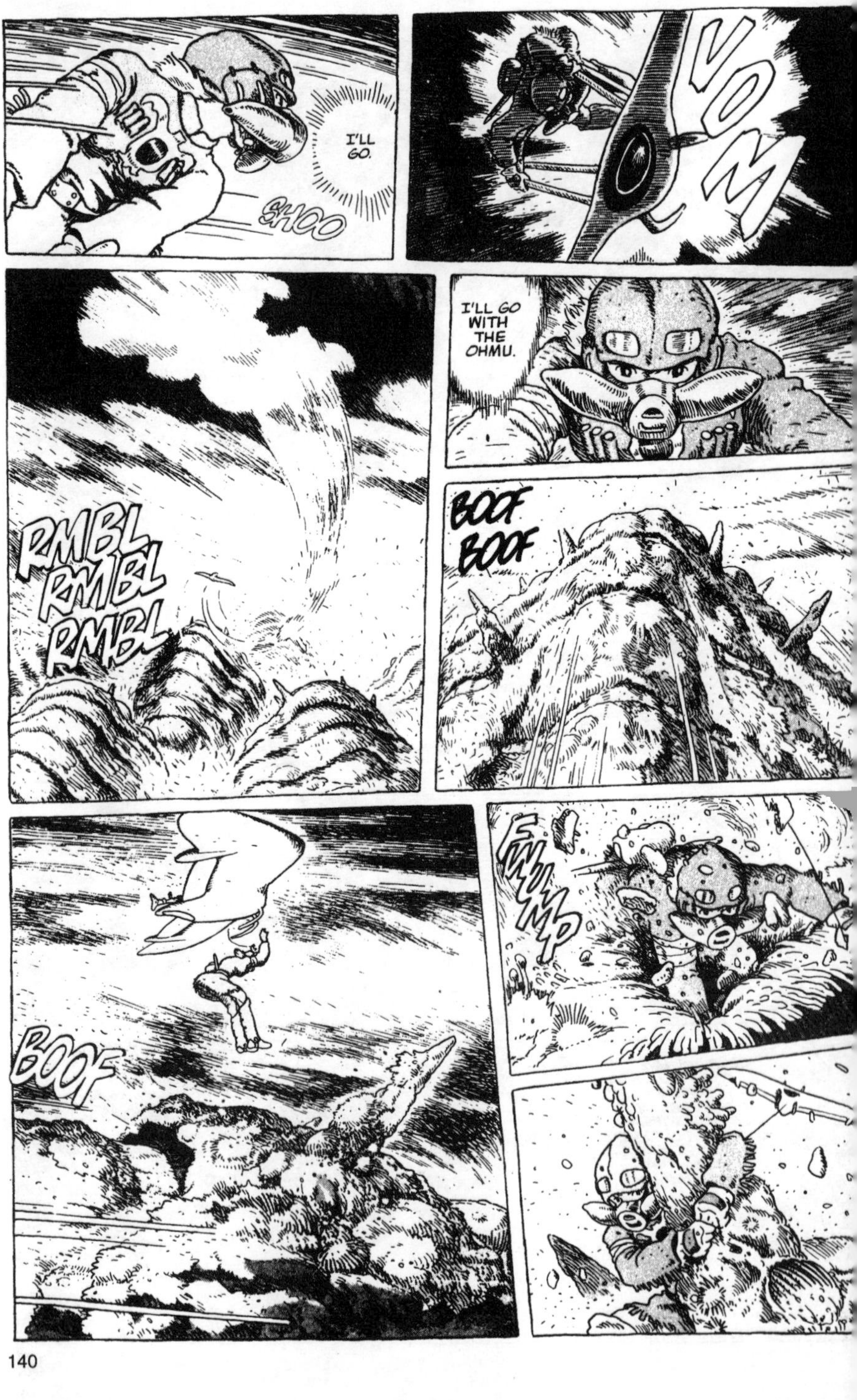
I'LL GO.
SHOO
VOM
RMBL RMBL RMBL
I'LL GO WITH THE OHMU.
BOOF BOOF
BOOF
FWUMP

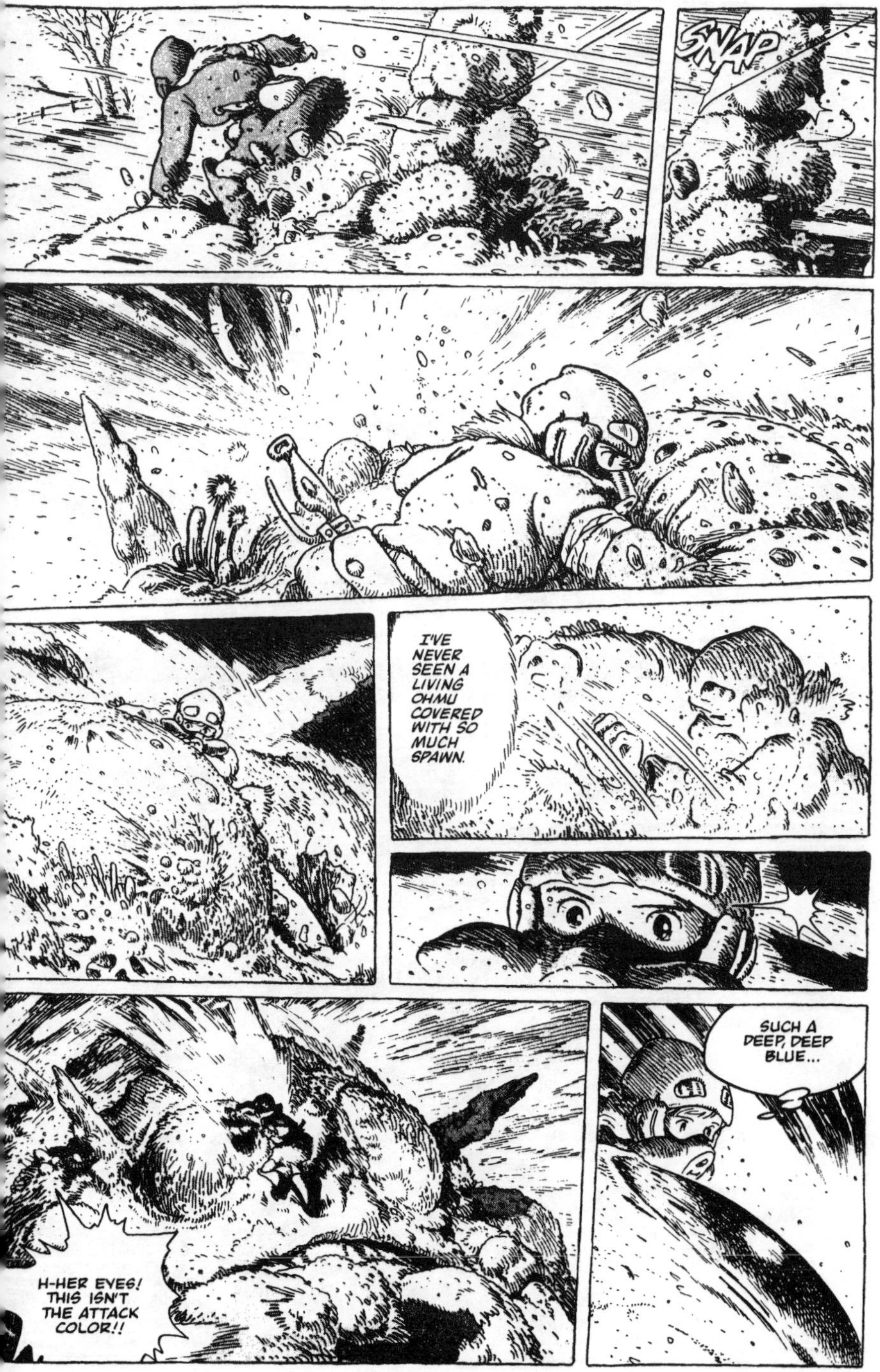
SNAP
I'VE NEVER SEEN A LIVING OHMU COVERED WITH SO MUCH SPAWN.
H-HER EYES! THIS ISN'T THE ATTACK COLOR!!
SUCH A DEEP, DEEP BLUE...

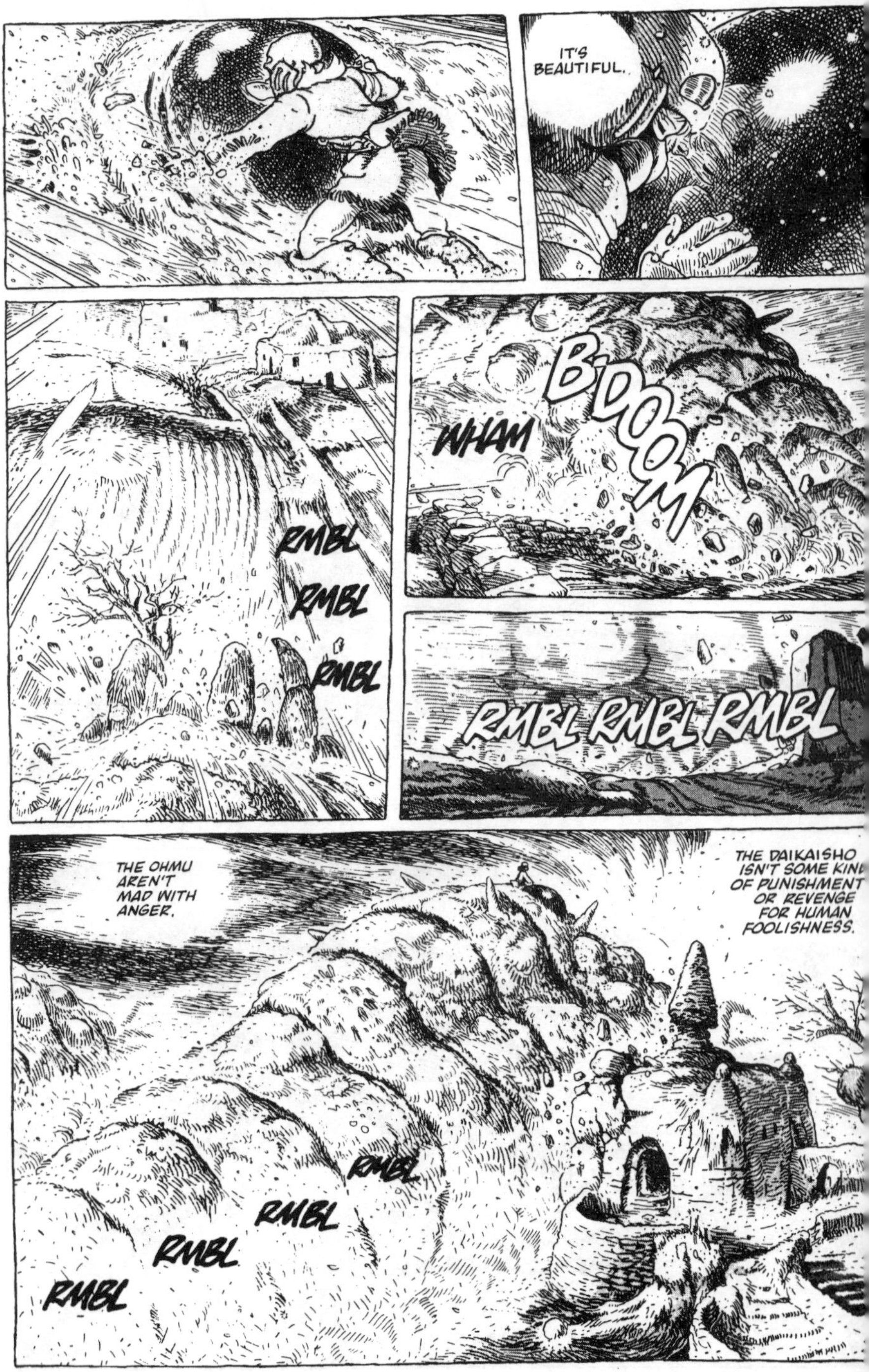
IT'S BEAUTIFUL.
B-DOOM
WHAM
RMBL
RMBL
RMBL
RMBL RMBL RMBL
THE OHMU AREN'T MAD WITH ANGER.
THE DAIKAISHO ISN'T SOME KIN
OF PUNISHMENT OR REVENGE FOR HUMAN FOOLISHNESS.
RMBL
RMBL
RMBL
RMBL

THE OHMU ARE SIMPLY TRYING TO HEAL THE EARTH'S WOUNDS...

...BY BECOMING LIVING SEEDBEDS FOR THE SEA OF CORRUPTION.

IT'S THE FOREST. THE SEA OF CORRUPTION ITSELF IS MOVING.

RMBL RMBL RMBL
RMBL RMBL

FAP

THEN I'LL BECOME PART OF THE FOREST, TOO.

TAP

A, HA. I GUESS IT WON'T STICK TO ME THE WAY IT DOES TO THE OHMU AS LONG AS I'M STILL ALIVE.

BUT I CAN'T TAKE MY MASK OFF YET.

IF ONLY I COULD TURN INTO A TREE WHILE I'M STILL ALIVE... AH!?

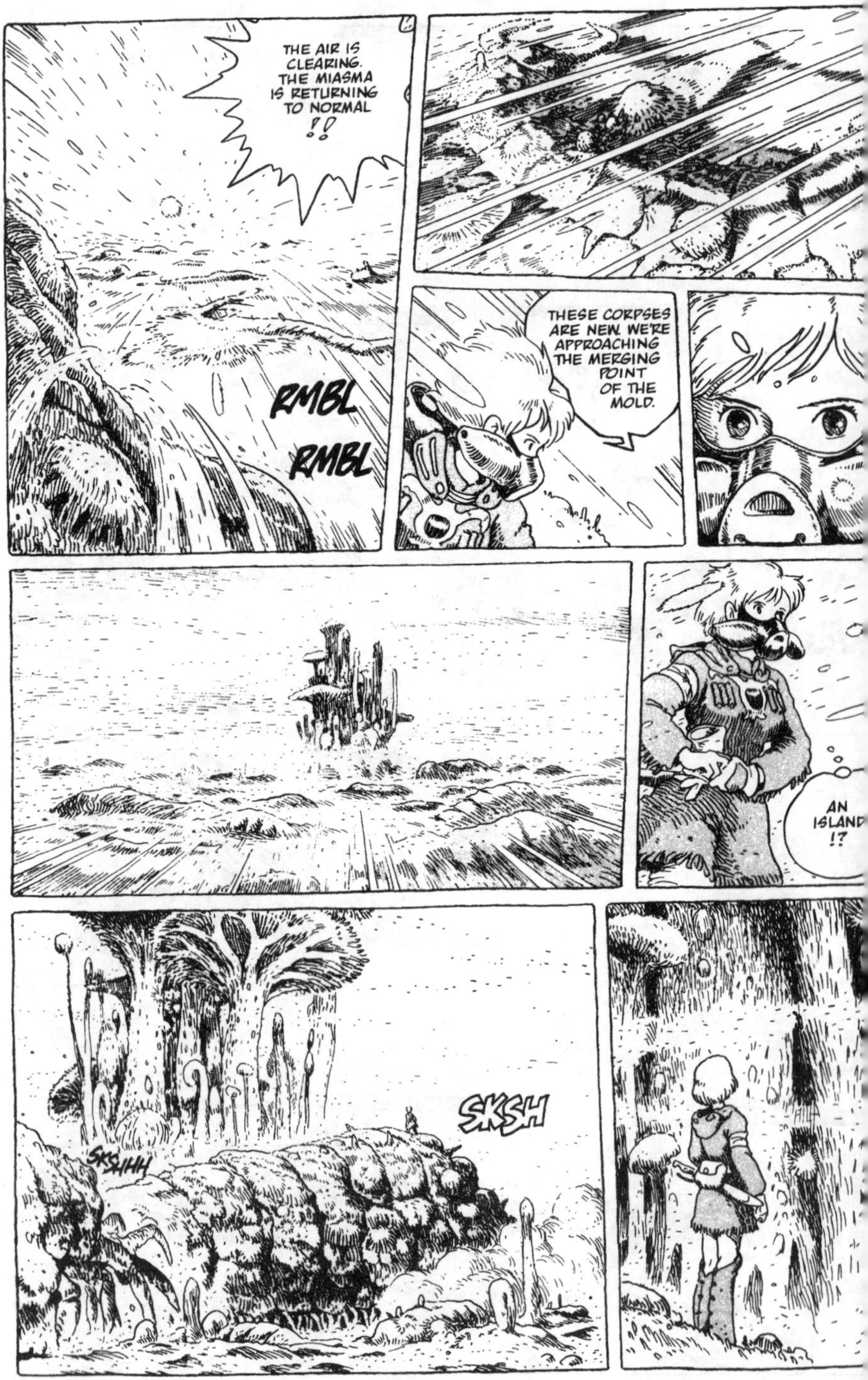
THE AIR IS CLEARING. THE MIASMA IS RETURNING TO NORMAL !!
RMBL
RMBL
THESE CORPSES ARE NEW. WE'RE APPROACHING THE MERGING POINT OF THE MOLD.
AN ISLAND !?
SKSH
SKSHHH

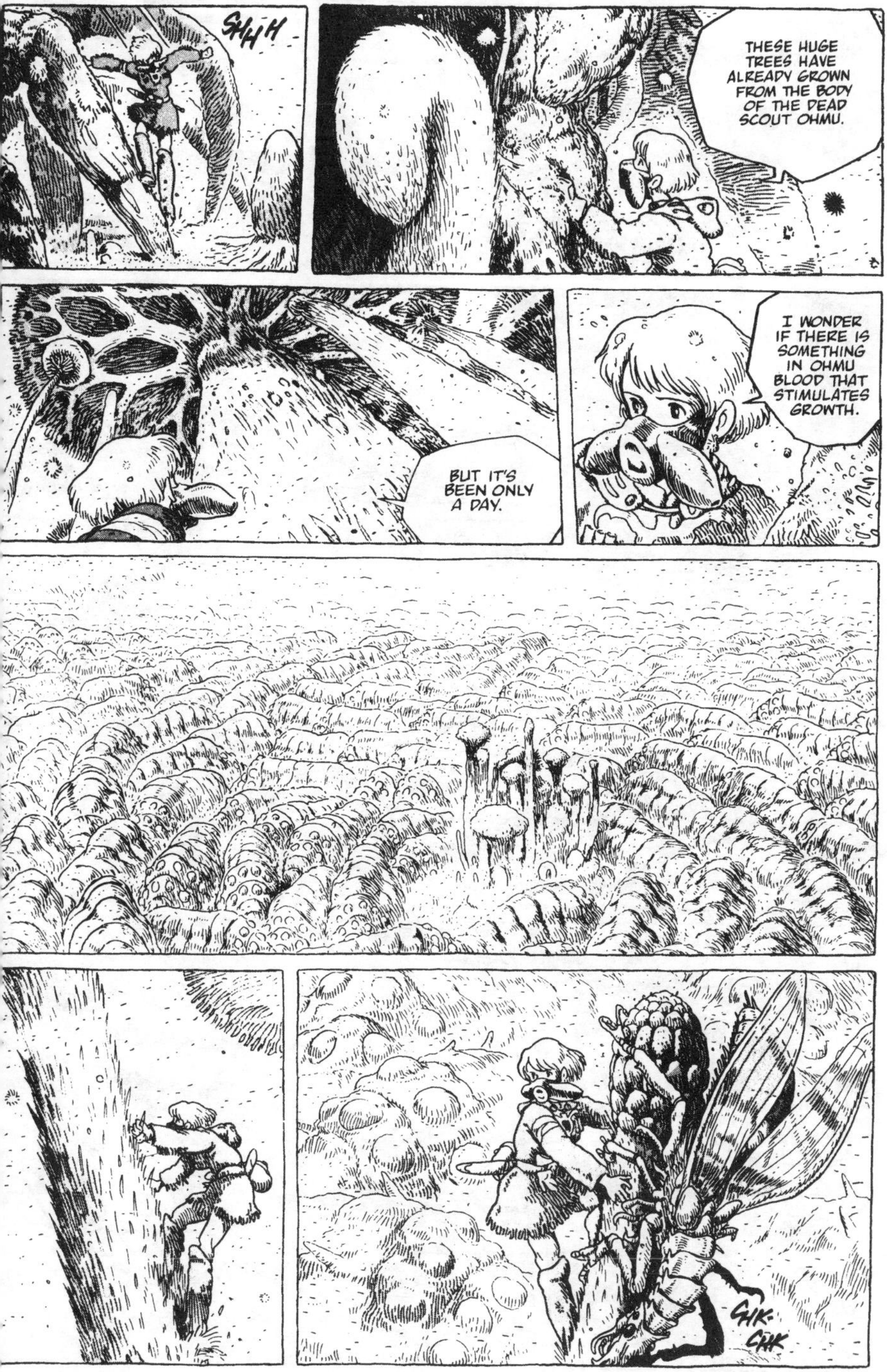
SHHH
THESE HUGE TREES HAVE ALREADY GROWN FROM THE BODY OF THE DEAD SCOUT OHMU.
BUT IT'S BEEN ONLY A DAY.
I WONDER IF THERE IS SOMETHING IN OHMU BLOOD THAT STIMULATES GROWTH.
CHK CHK

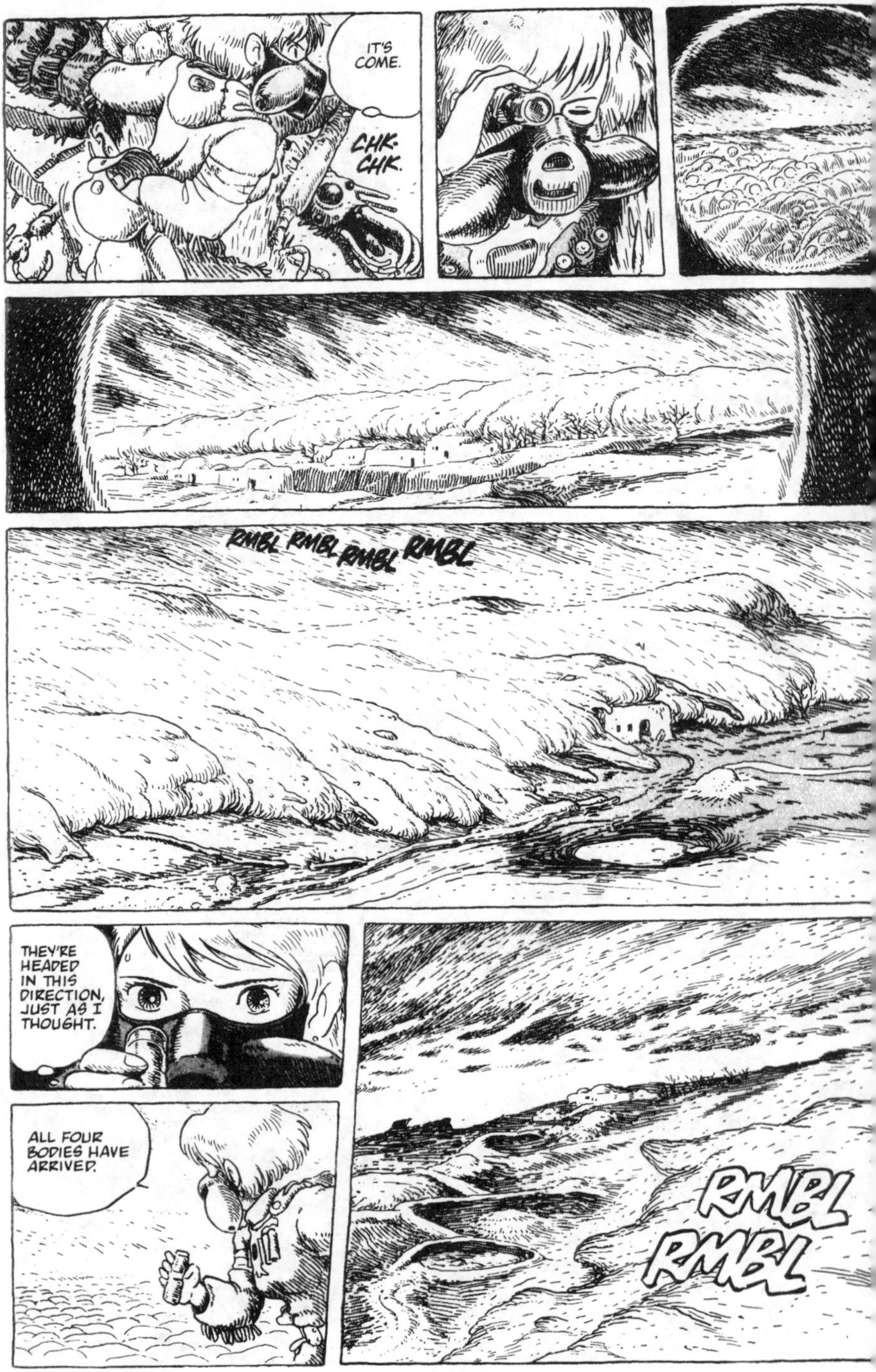
IT'S COME.
CHK-CHK.
RMBL RMBL RMBL RMBL
THEY'RE HEADED IN THIS DIRECTION, JUST AS I THOUGHT.
ALL FOUR BODIES HAVE ARRIVED.
RMBL RMBL

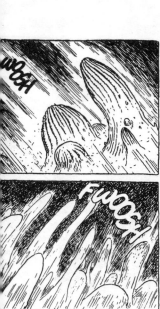

THEY'VE BEGUN TO MERGE.

CHK CHK

YOU'D BETTER FLY AWAY NOW, BEFORE THE MIASMA CHANGES.

WHY DO I FEEL SO PEACEFUL?

IT MUST BE BECAUSE I SAW YOUR EYE.

.....!!

......

......

I CAN SENSE THE SOUND OF THE TREES SPROUTING.

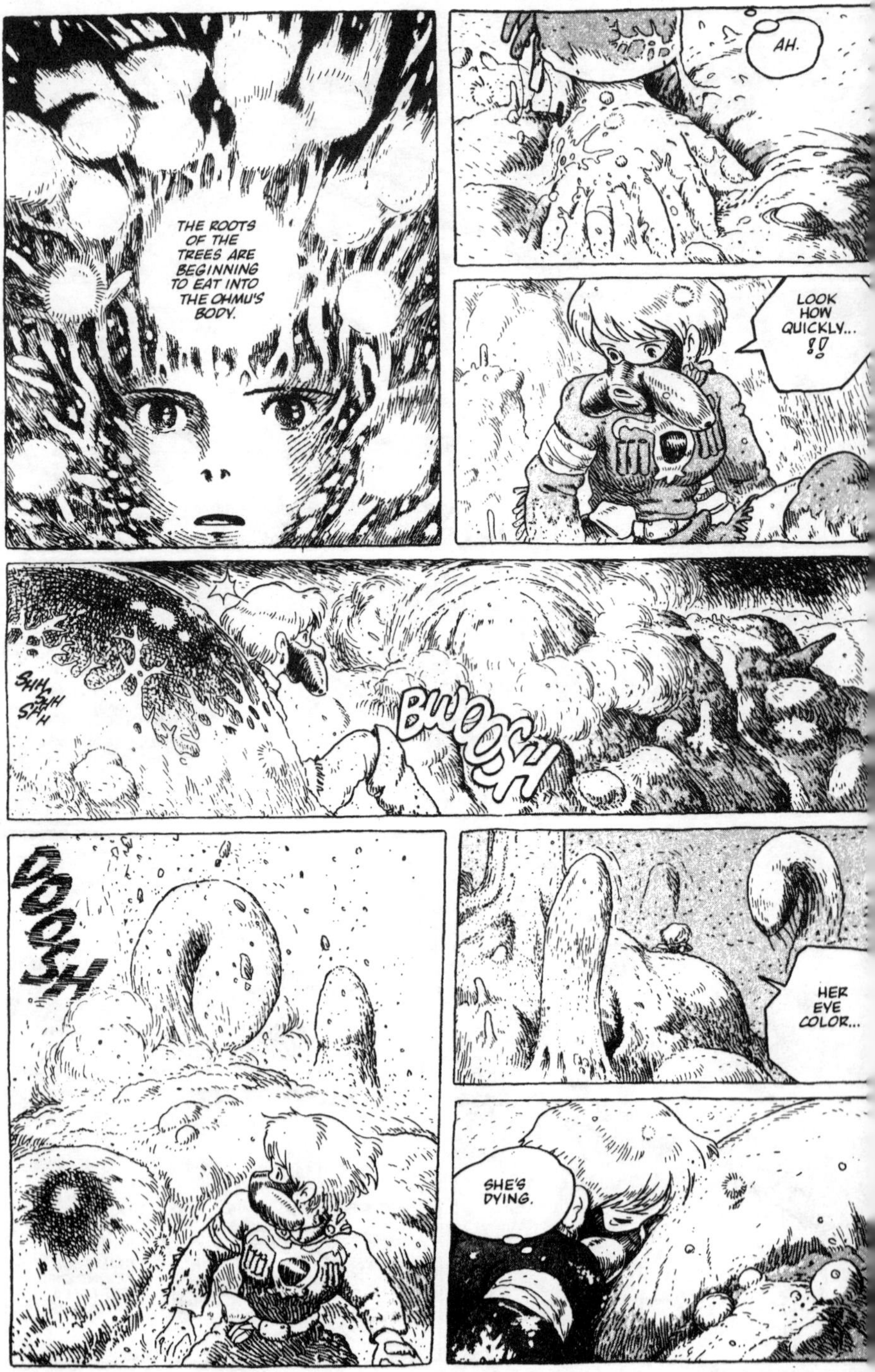
THE ROOTS OF THE TREES ARE BEGINNING TO EAT INTO THE OHMU'S BODY.
AH.
LOOK HOW QUICKLY... !!
SHH SHH SHH
BWOOSH
DOOSH
HER EYE COLOR...
SHE'S DYING.

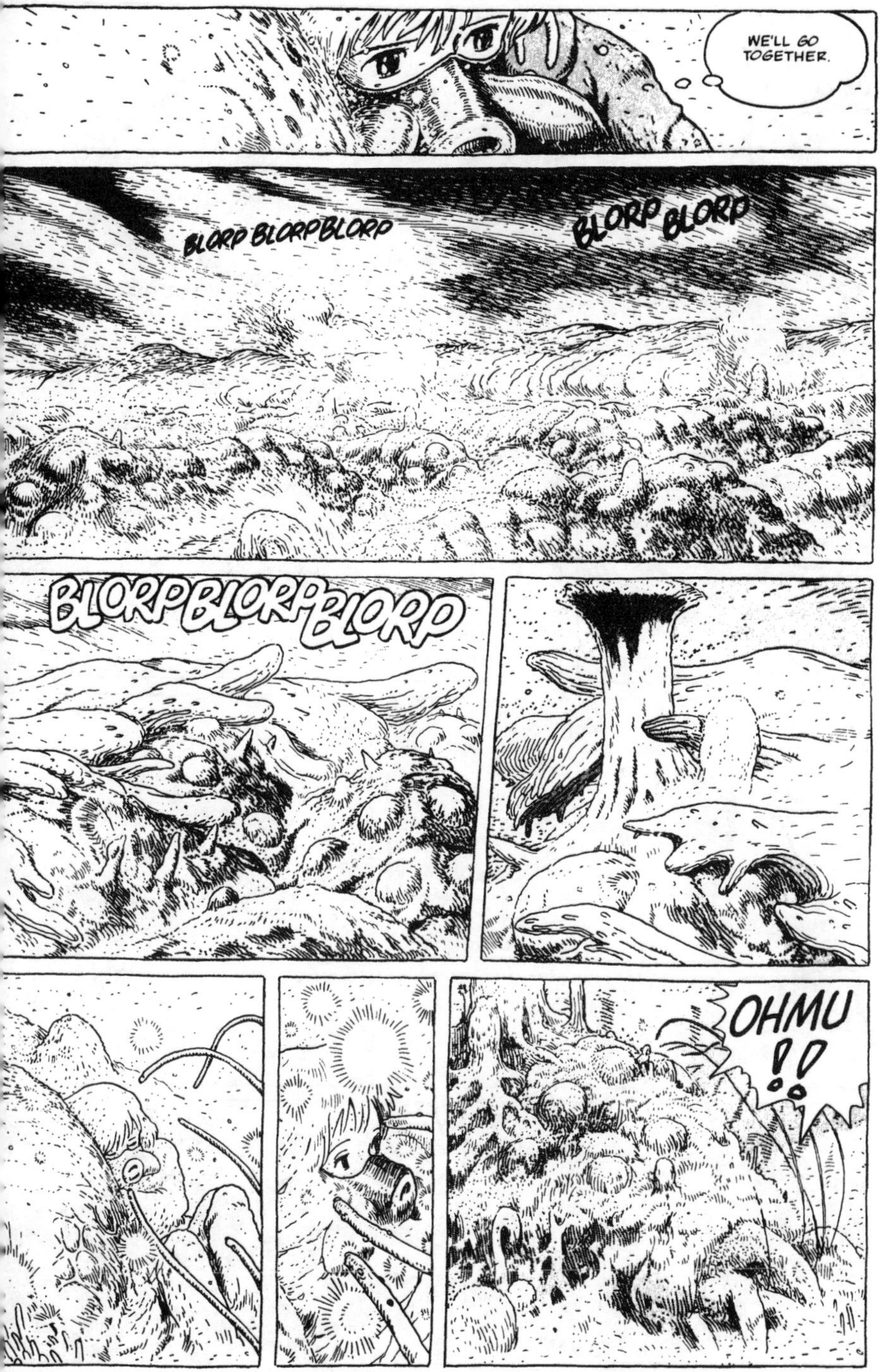
WE'LL GO TOGETHER.
BLORP BLORP BLORP
BLORP BLORP
BLORP BLORP BLORP BLORP
OHMU !!

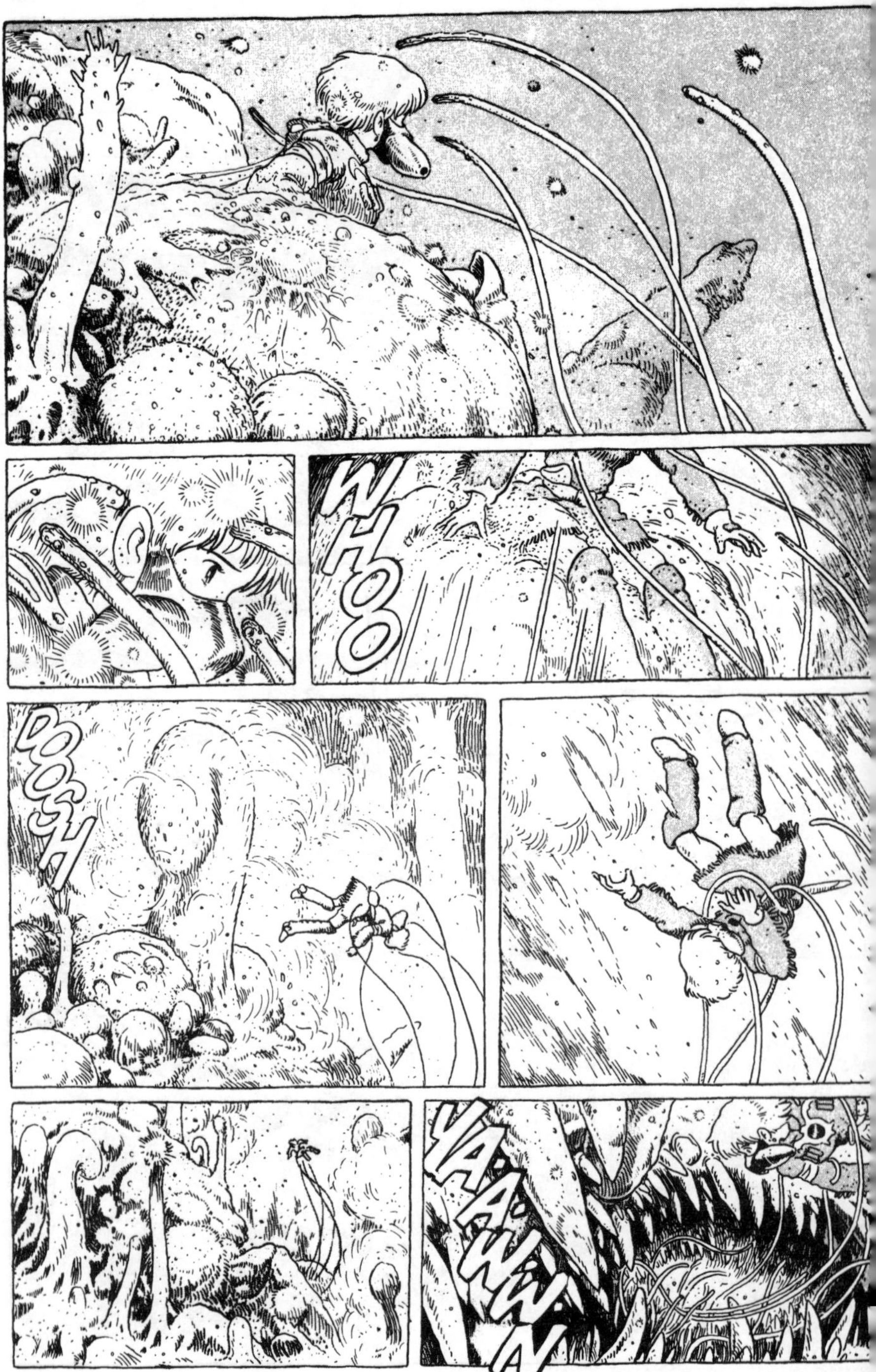
WHOO
DOOSH
YAAWWN

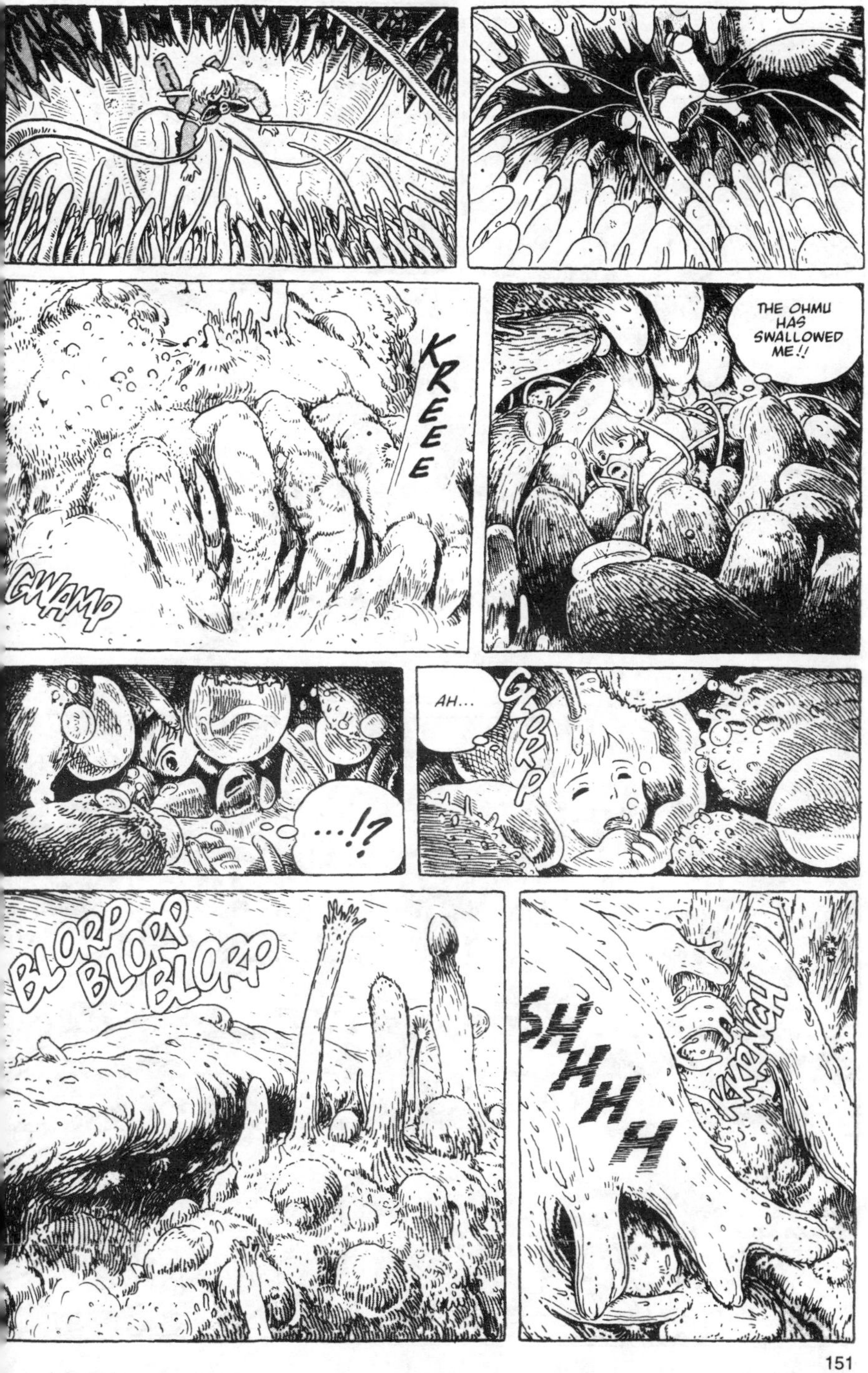
KREEEE
GWAMP
THE OHMU HAS SWALLOWED ME!!
...!?
AH...
GLORP
BLORP BLORP BLORP
SHHHHH
KRENCH

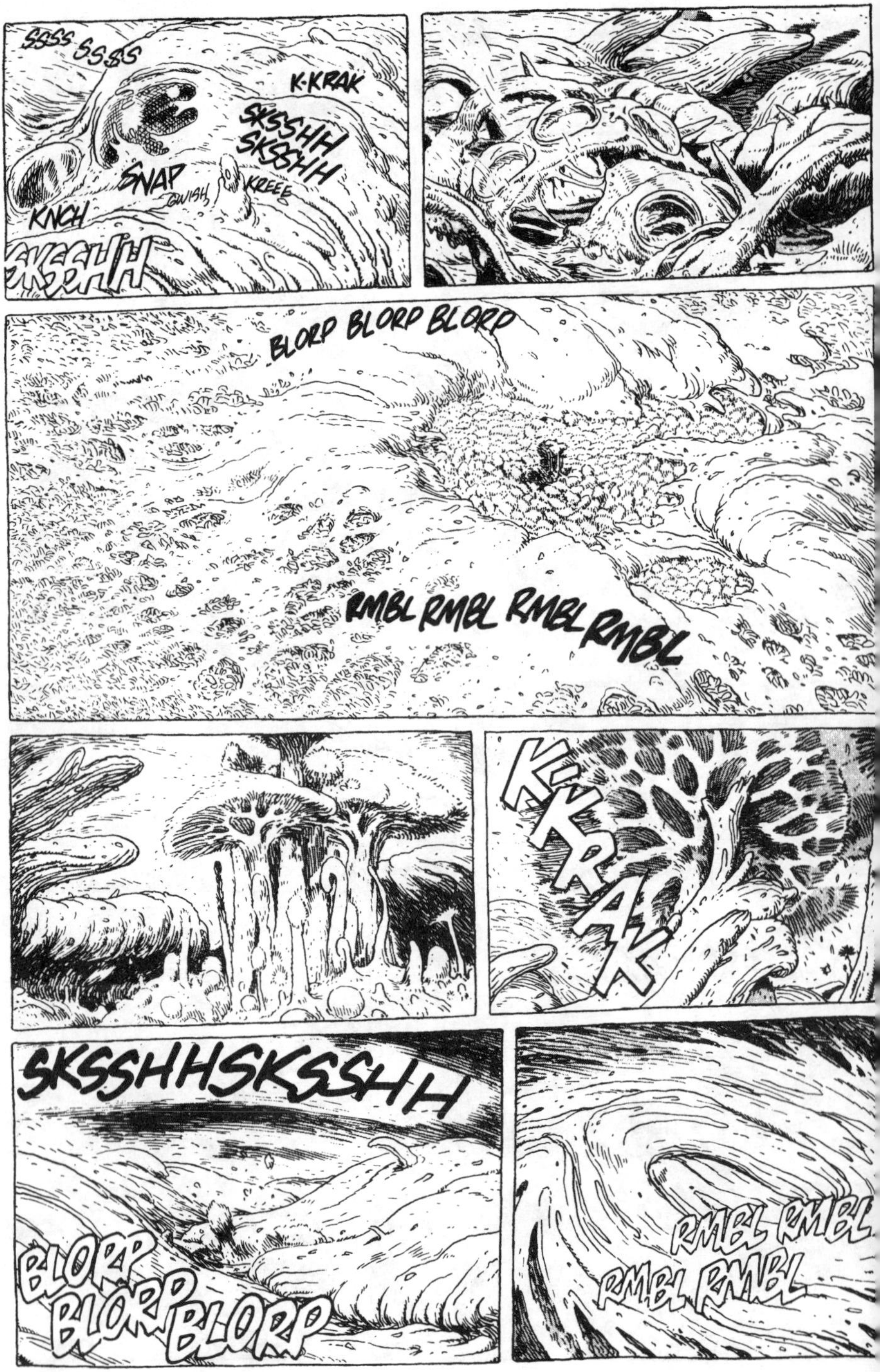
SSSS SSSS
K-KRAK
SKSSHH SKSSHH
SNAP
SWISH
KREEE
KNCH
SKSSHH
BLORP BLORP BLORP
RMBL RMBL RMBL RMBL
K-KRAK
SKSSHHSKSSHH
BLORP BLORP BLORP
RMBL RMBL
RMBL RMBL

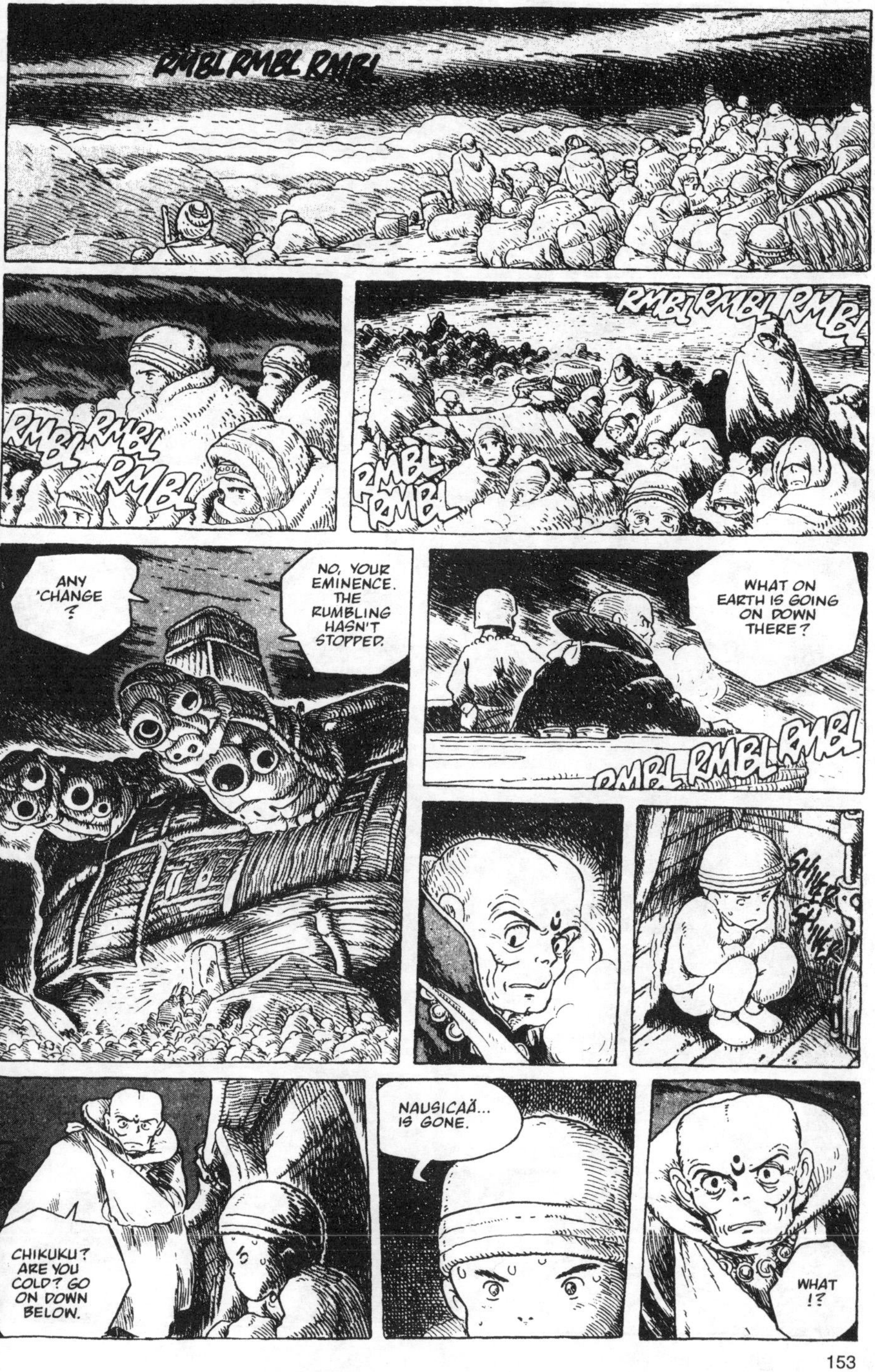
RMBL RMBL RMBL
RMBL RMBL RMBL
RMBL RMBL RMBL
RMBL RMBL
ANY 'CHANGE?
NO, YOUR EMINENCE. THE RUMBLING HASN'T STOPPED.
WHAT ON EARTH IS GOING ON DOWN THERE?
RMBL RMBL RMBL
SHIVER SHIVER
CHIKUKU? ARE YOU COLD? GO ON DOWN BELOW.
NAUSICAÄ... IS GONE.
WHAT!?

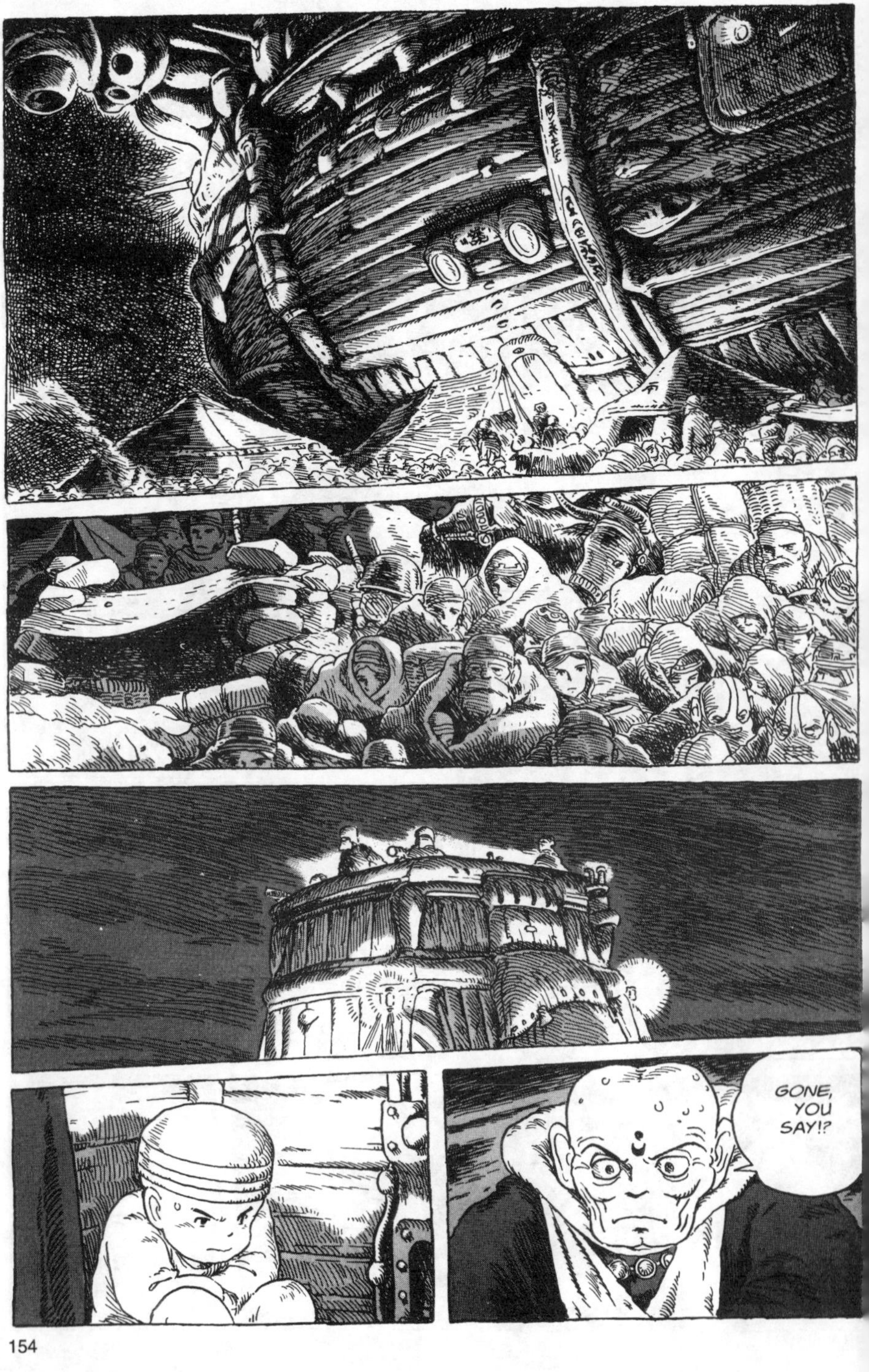
GONE, YOU SAY!?

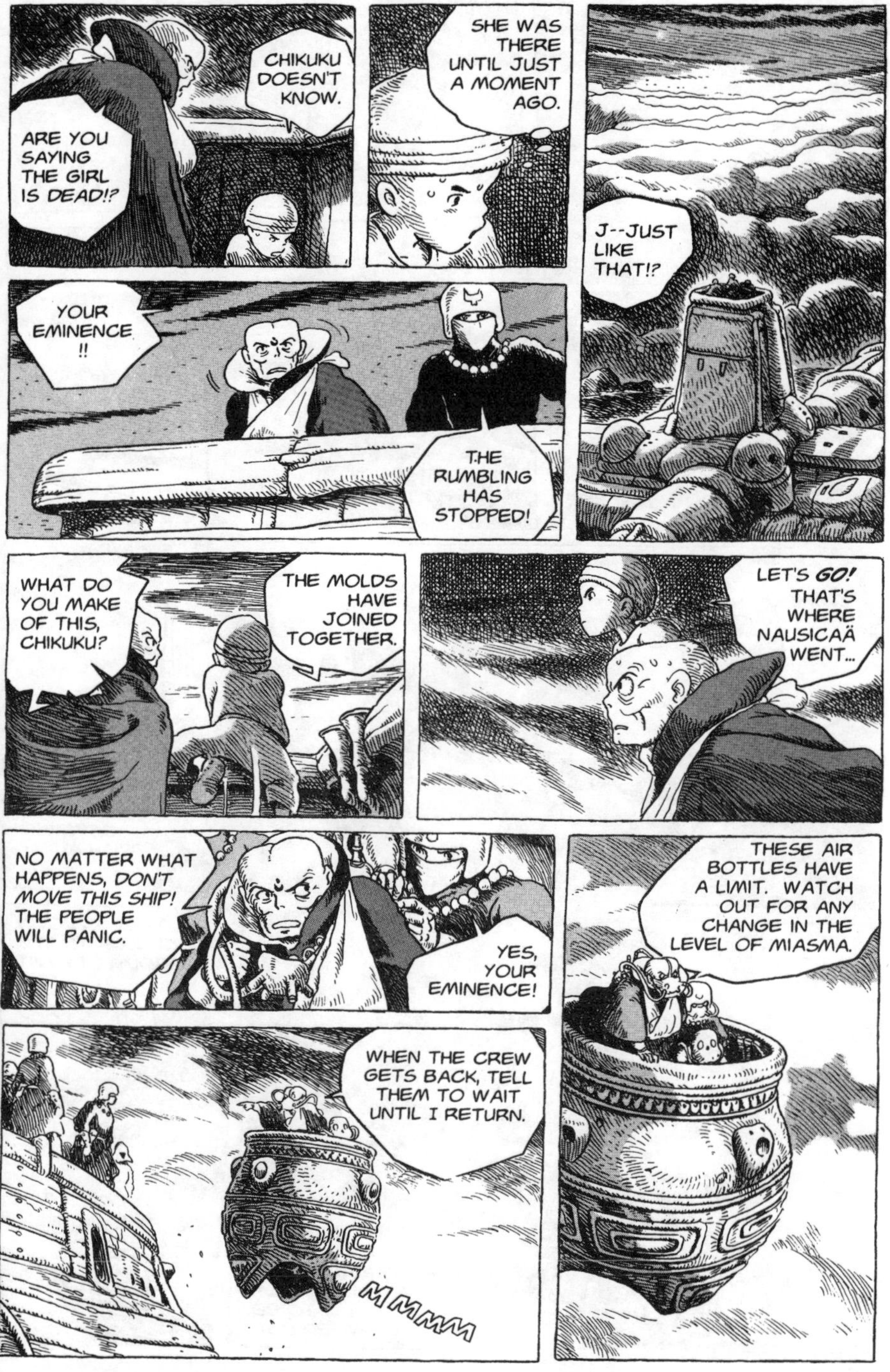
CHIKUKU DOESN'T KNOW.
ARE YOU SAYING THE GIRL IS DEAD!?
SHE WAS THERE UNTIL JUST A MOMENT AGO.
J--JUST LIKE THAT!?
YOUR EMINENCE !!
THE RUMBLING HAS STOPPED!
WHAT DO YOU MAKE OF THIS, CHIKUKU?
THE MOLDS HAVE JOINED TOGETHER.
LET'S GO! THAT'S WHERE NAUSICAÄ WENT...
NO MATTER WHAT HAPPENS, DON'T MOVE THIS SHIP! THE PEOPLE WILL PANIC.
YES, YOUR EMINENCE!
THESE AIR BOTTLES HAVE A LIMIT. WATCH OUT FOR ANY CHANGE IN THE LEVEL OF MIASMA.
WHEN THE CREW GETS BACK, TELL THEM TO WAIT UNTIL I RETURN.
MMMMM

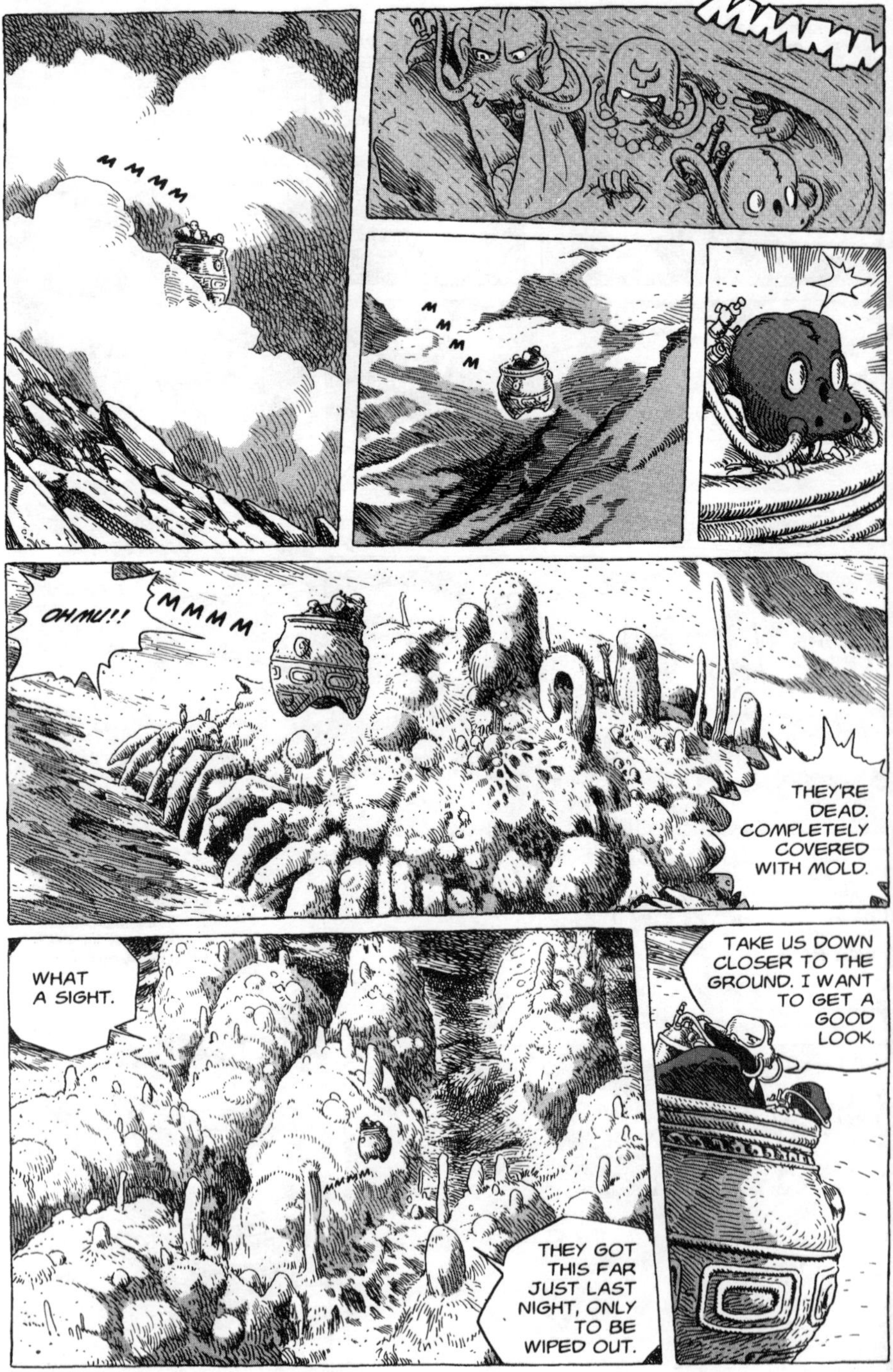
MMMM
MMMMMN
MMMM
OHMU!!
MMMM
THEY'RE DEAD. COMPLETELY COVERED WITH MOLD.
WHAT A SIGHT.
THEY GOT THIS FAR JUST LAST NIGHT, ONLY TO BE WIPED OUT.
TAKE US DOWN CLOSER TO THE GROUND. I WANT TO GET A GOOD LOOK.

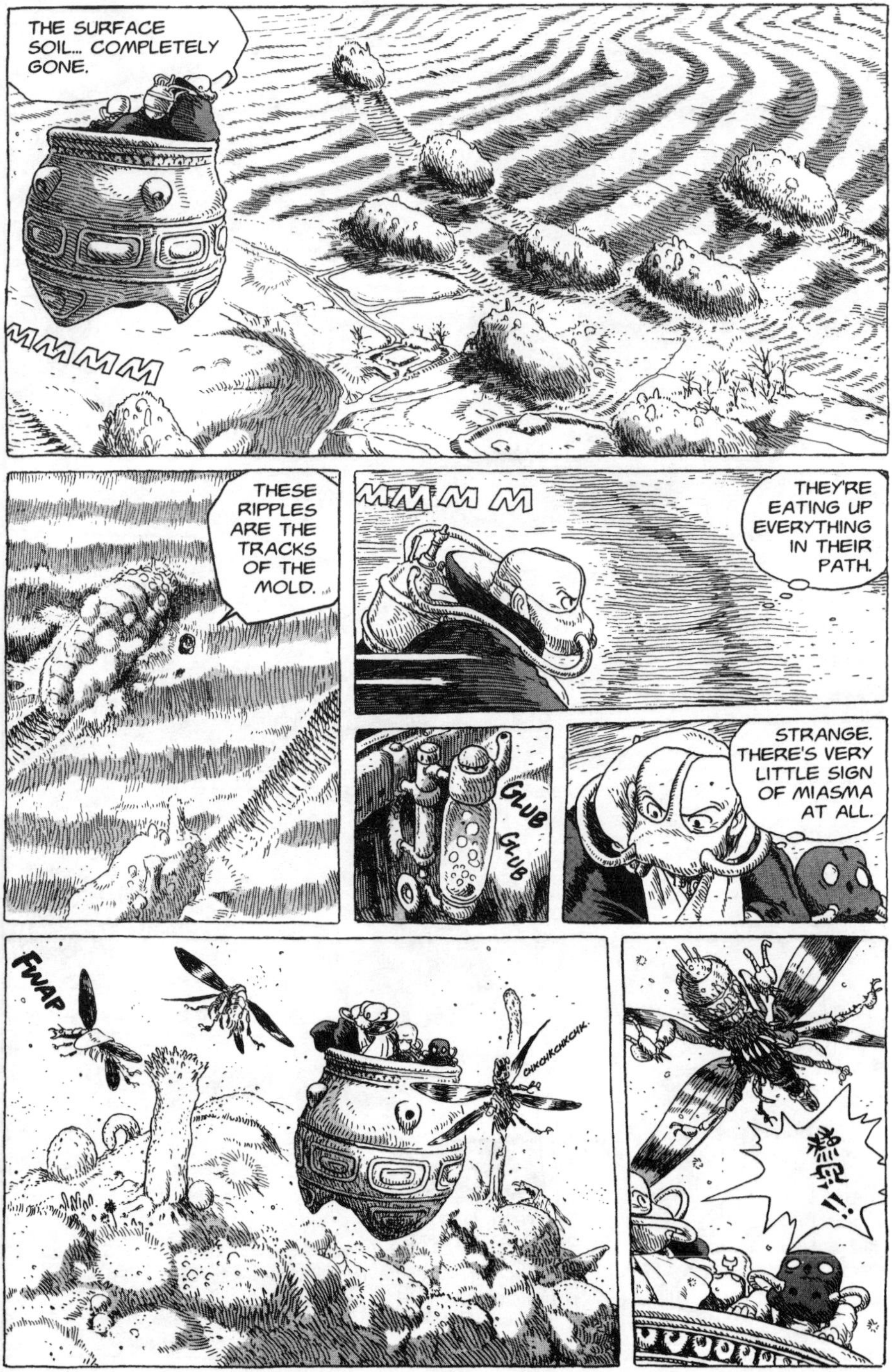
THE SURFACE SOIL... COMPLETELY GONE.
MMMMM
THESE RIPPLES ARE THE TRACKS OF THE MOLD.
MMMMM
THEY'RE EATING UP EVERYTHING IN THEIR PATH.
GLUB
GLUB
STRANGE. THERE'S VERY LITTLE SIGN OF MIASMA AT ALL.
FWAP
CHKCHKCHKCHK

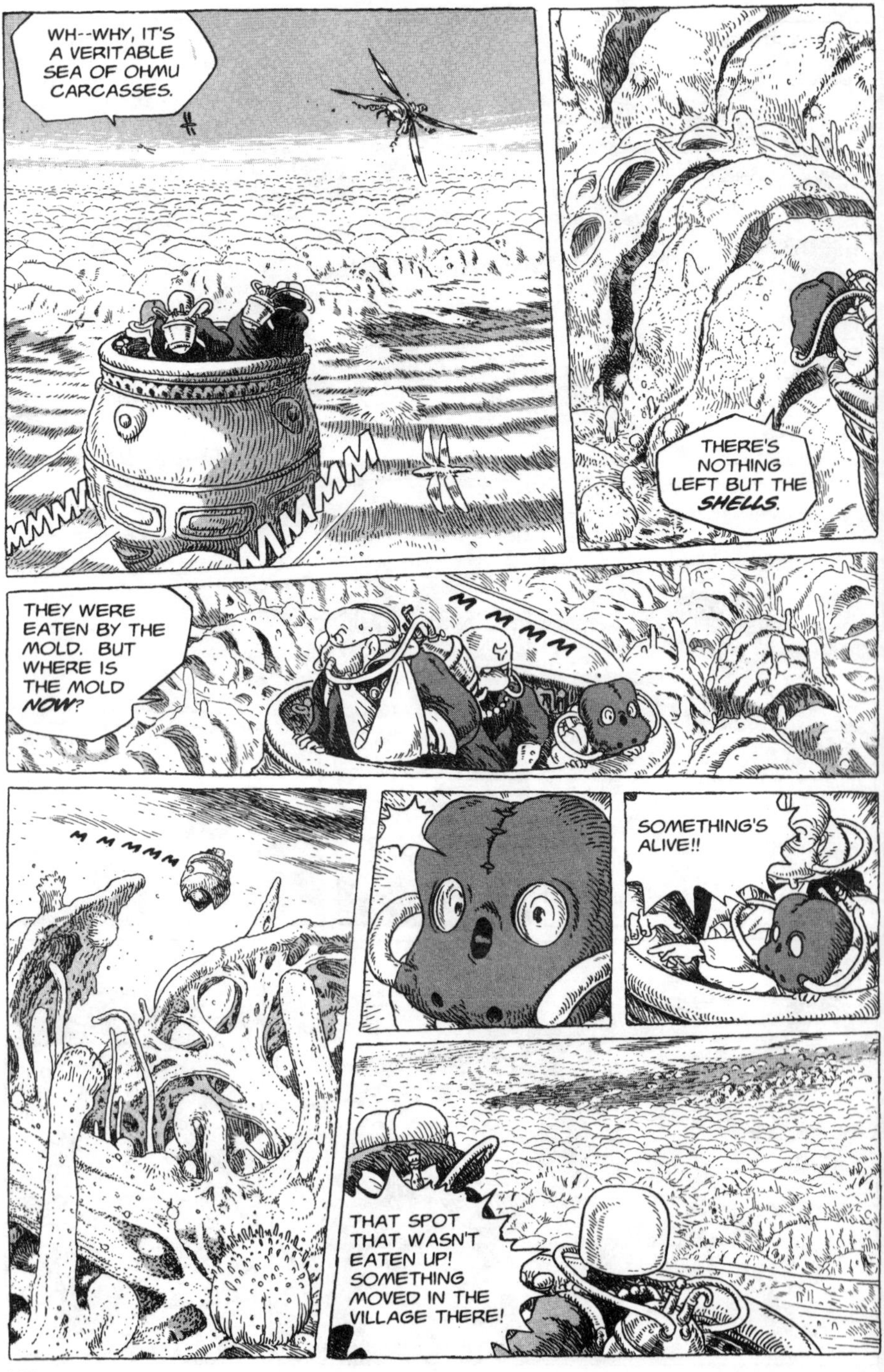
WH--WHY, IT'S A VERITABLE SEA OF OHMU CARCASSES.
MMMMM
MMMMM
THERE'S NOTHING LEFT BUT THE SHELLS.
THEY WERE EATEN BY THE MOLD. BUT WHERE IS THE MOLD NOW?
MMMMM
MMMMM
SOMETHING'S ALIVE!!
THAT SPOT THAT WASN'T EATEN UP! SOMETHING MOVED IN THE VILLAGE THERE!

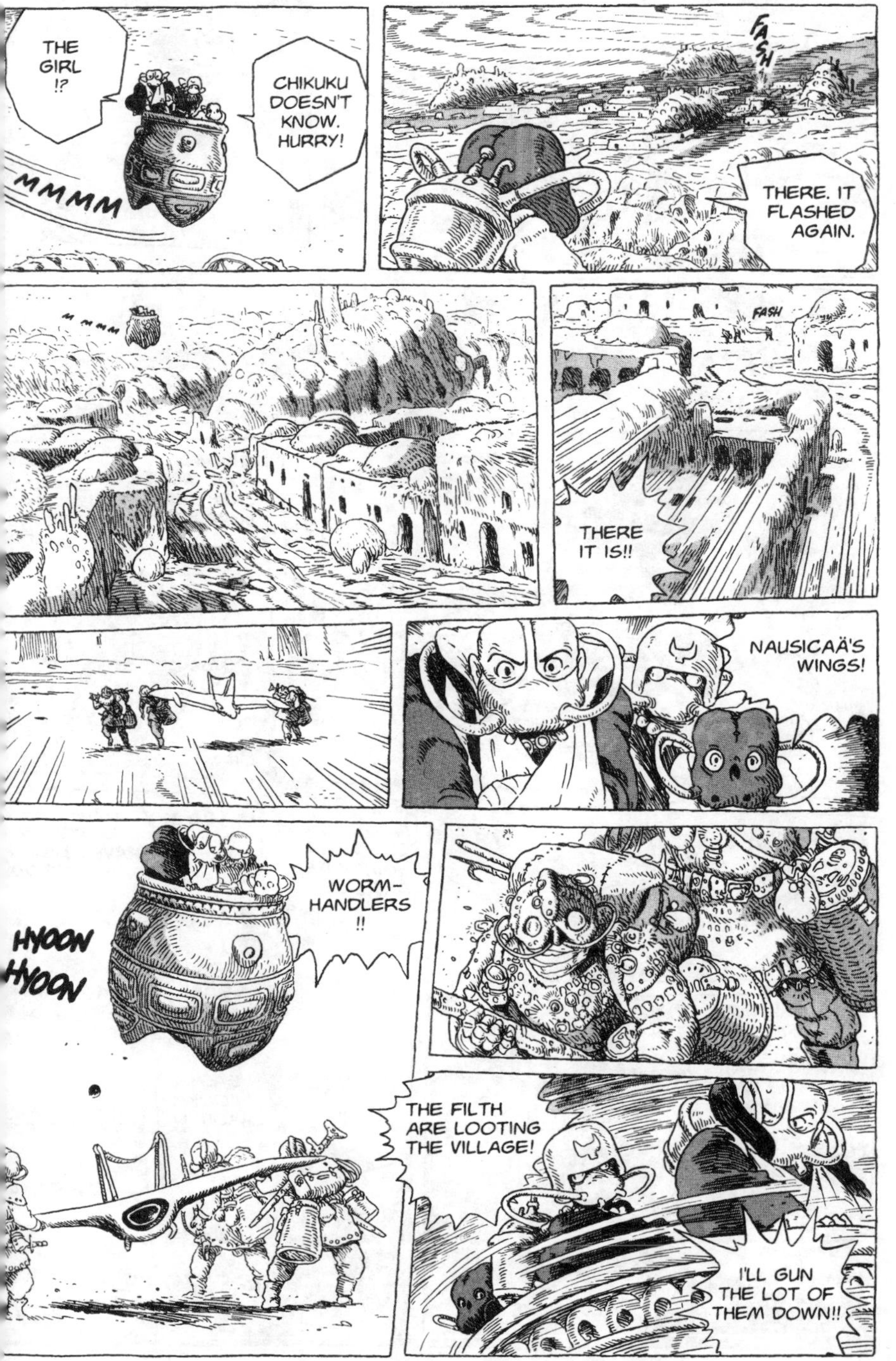
THE GIRL !?
CHIKUKU DOESN'T KNOW. HURRY!
MMMM
FASH
THERE. IT FLASHED AGAIN.
M MMM
FASH
THERE IT IS!!
NAUSICAÄ'S WINGS!
WORM-HANDLERS !!
HYOON HYOON
THE FILTH ARE LOOTING THE VILLAGE!
I'LL GUN THE LOT OF THEM DOWN!!

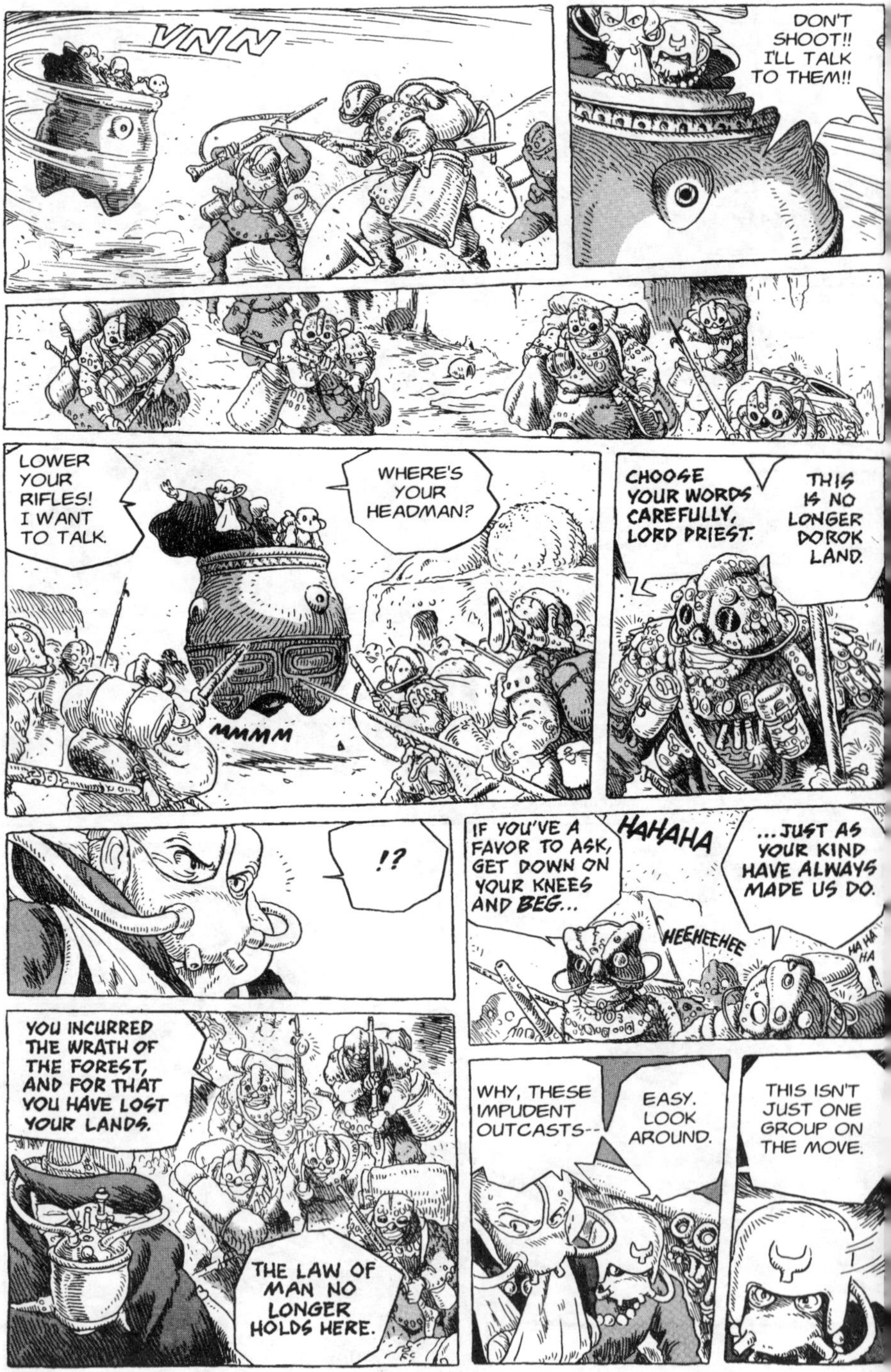
VNN
DON'T SHOOT!! I'LL TALK TO THEM!!
LOWER YOUR RIFLES! I WANT TO TALK.
WHERE'S YOUR HEADMAN?
MMMM
CHOOSE YOUR WORDS CAREFULLY, LORD PRIEST.
THIS IS NO LONGER DOROK LAND.
!?
IF YOU'VE A FAVOR TO ASK, GET DOWN ON YOUR KNEES AND BEG...
HAHAHA
...JUST AS YOUR KIND HAVE ALWAYS MADE US DO.
HEEHEEHEE
HA HA HA
YOU INCURRED THE WRATH OF THE FOREST, AND FOR THAT YOU HAVE LOST YOUR LANDS.
THE LAW OF MAN NO LONGER HOLDS HERE.
WHY, THESE IMPUDENT OUTCASTS--
EASY. LOOK AROUND.
THIS ISN'T JUST ONE GROUP ON THE MOVE.

WHERE IN BLAZES DID THEY ALL COME FROM?

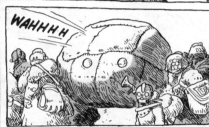
THEY FOLLOWED THE INSECTS.

THEY DON'T SEEM THE LEAST BIT AFRAID OF THE MOLD. COULD IT BE THEY JUST DON'T KNOW?

WAHHHH

WAIT! YOU THERE WITH THE BASKET!

EMINENCE!!

TMP

WAHHH

WHAT ARE YOU HIDING IN THERE? LET ME LOOK INSIDE!!

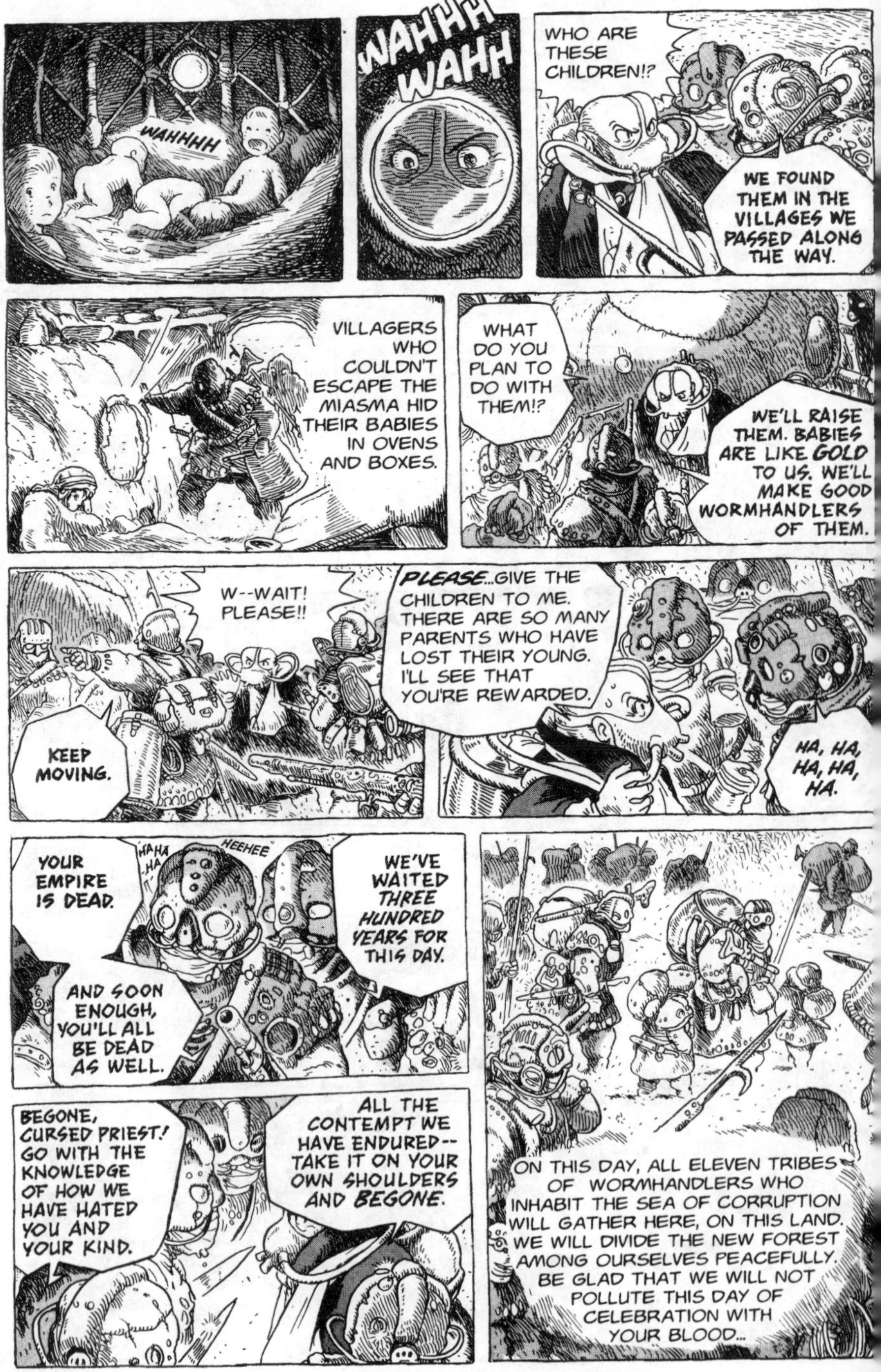
WAHHHH
WAHHH WAHH
WHO ARE THESE CHILDREN!?
WE FOUND THEM IN THE VILLAGES WE PASSED ALONG THE WAY.
VILLAGERS WHO COULDN'T ESCAPE THE MIASMA HID THEIR BABIES IN OVENS AND BOXES.
WHAT DO YOU PLAN TO DO WITH THEM!?
WE'LL RAISE THEM. BABIES ARE LIKE GOLD TO US. WE'LL MAKE GOOD WORMHANDLERS OF THEM.
W--WAIT! PLEASE!!
KEEP MOVING.
PLEASE...GIVE THE CHILDREN TO ME. THERE ARE SO MANY PARENTS WHO HAVE LOST THEIR YOUNG. I'LL SEE THAT YOU'RE REWARDED.
HA, HA, HA, HA, HA.
YOUR EMPIRE IS DEAD.
HA HA HA
HEEHEE
WE'VE WAITED THREE HUNDRED YEARS FOR THIS DAY.
AND SOON ENOUGH, YOU'LL ALL BE DEAD AS WELL.
BEGONE, CURSED PRIEST! GO WITH THE KNOWLEDGE OF HOW WE HAVE HATED YOU AND YOUR KIND.
ALL THE CONTEMPT WE HAVE ENDURED-- TAKE IT ON YOUR OWN SHOULDERS AND BEGONE.
ON THIS DAY, ALL ELEVEN TRIBES OF WORMHANDLERS WHO INHABIT THE SEA OF CORRUPTION WILL GATHER HERE, ON THIS LAND. WE WILL DIVIDE THE NEW FOREST AMONG OURSELVES PEACEFULLY. BE GLAD THAT WE WILL NOT POLLUTE THIS DAY OF CELEBRATION WITH YOUR BLOOD...

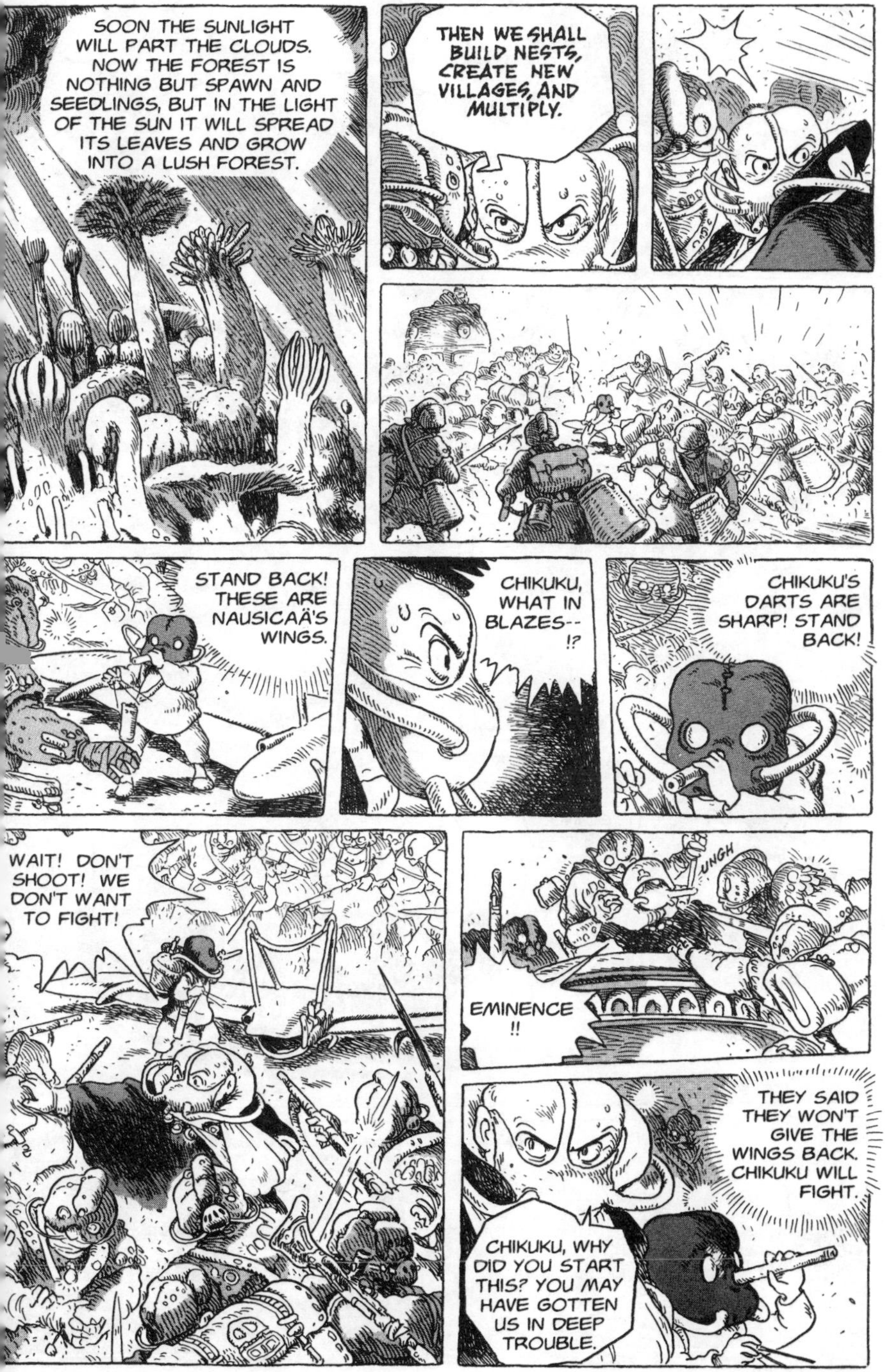
SOON THE SUNLIGHT WILL PART THE CLOUDS. NOW THE FOREST IS NOTHING BUT SPAWN AND SEEDLINGS, BUT IN THE LIGHT OF THE SUN IT WILL SPREAD ITS LEAVES AND GROW INTO A LUSH FOREST.
THEN WE SHALL BUILD NESTS, CREATE NEW VILLAGES, AND MULTIPLY.
STAND BACK! THESE ARE NAUSICAÄ'S WINGS.
CHIKUKU, WHAT IN BLAZES--!?
CHIKUKU'S DARTS ARE SHARP! STAND BACK!
WAIT! DON'T SHOOT! WE DON'T WANT TO FIGHT!
UNGH
EMINENCE!!
THEY SAID THEY WON'T GIVE THE WINGS BACK. CHIKUKU WILL FIGHT.
CHIKUKU, WHY DID YOU START THIS? YOU MAY HAVE GOTTEN US IN DEEP TROUBLE.

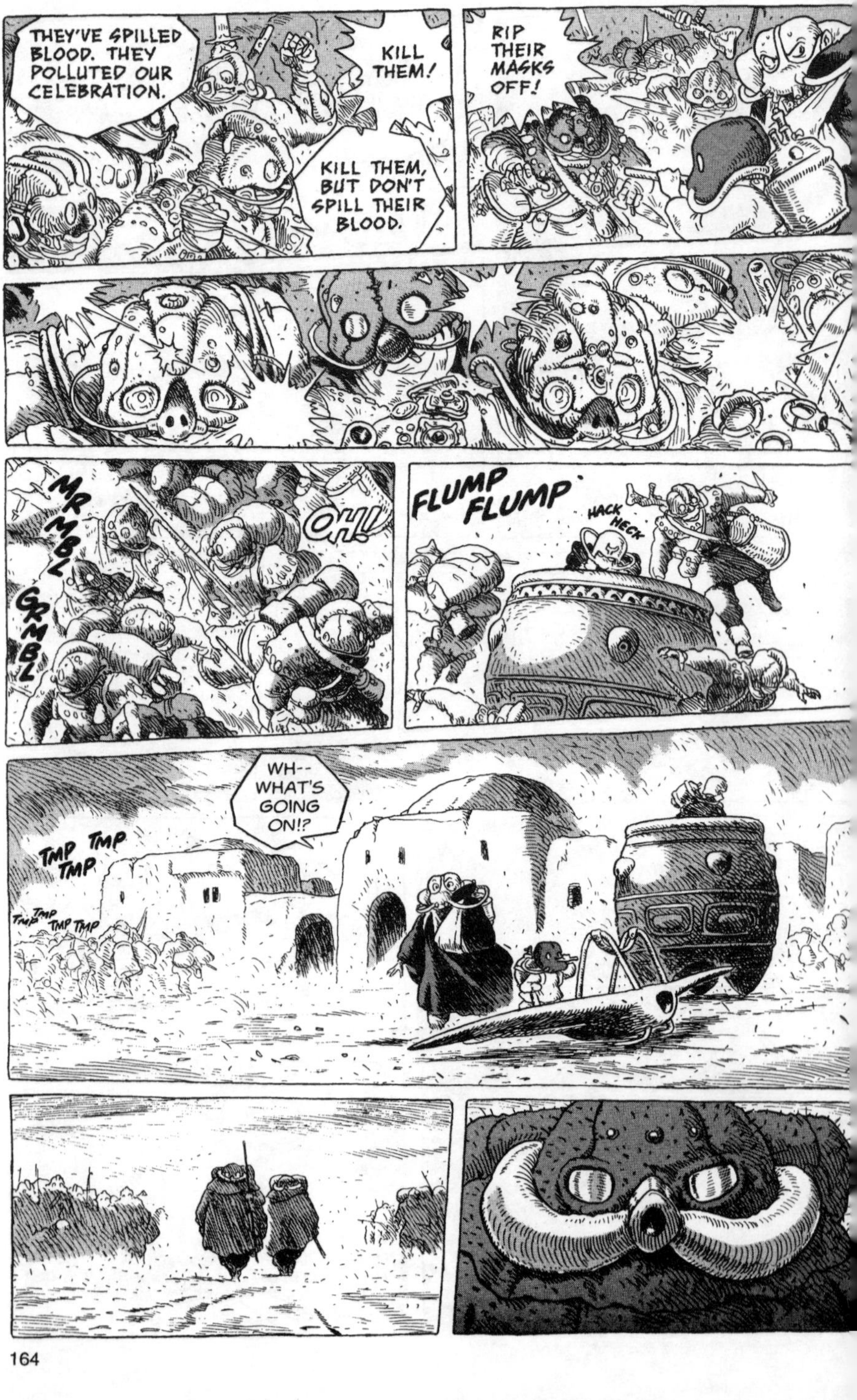
THEY'VE SPILLED BLOOD. THEY POLLUTED OUR CELEBRATION.
KILL THEM!
KILL THEM, BUT DON'T SPILL THEIR BLOOD.
RIP THEIR MASKS OFF!
MRMBL
GRMBL
OH!
FLUMP FLUMP
HACK HECK
WH-- WHAT'S GOING ON!?
TMP TMP TMP
TMP TMP TMP TMP

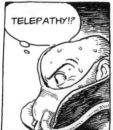

TELEPATHY!?

SHALL WE GO? WE MUST LOOK FOR NAUSICAÄ.

WHA--!?

I'M AFRAID YOUR MASKS WON'T BE SUFFICIENT.

FWA

PSSSSS

165

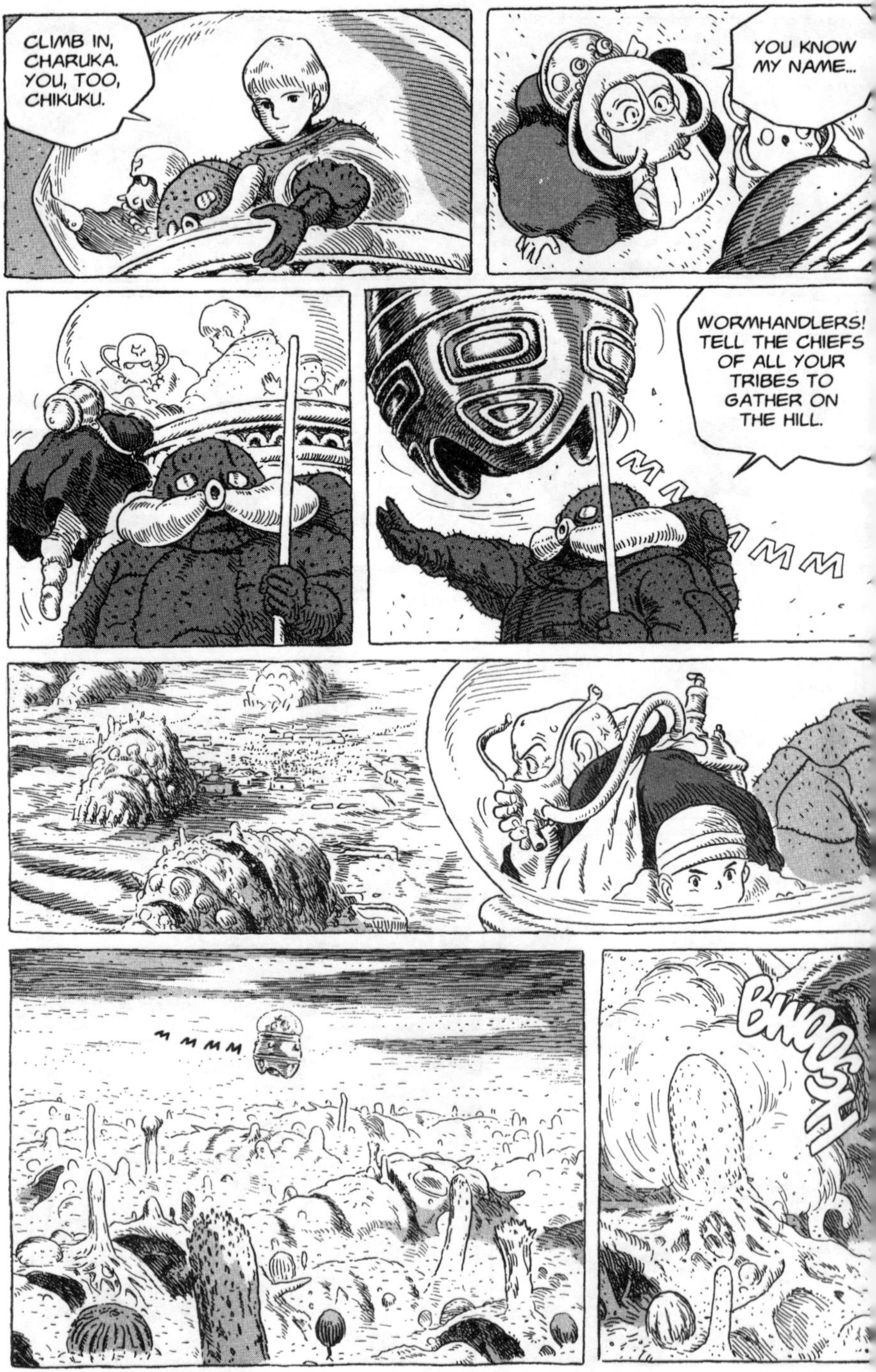
CLIMB IN, CHARUKA. YOU, TOO, CHIKUKU.
YOU KNOW MY NAME...
WORMHANDLERS! TELL THE CHIEFS OF ALL YOUR TRIBES TO GATHER ON THE HILL.
MMMMM
MMMM
BWOOSH

DOOSH DOOSH

B~DOOSH

THE SPORES THAT HAD ENTERED THE VAST SEA OF MOLD ARE STARTING TO SPROUT.

B--BUT WHERE HAS THAT ENORMOUS MASS OF MOLD DISAPPEARED TO?

THE MOLD IS THERE, AS WELL.

SEE THAT PATCH OF A DIFFERENT COLOR THERE? SOME MOLD IS STILL HOLDING OUT...

I CAN'T SEE IT. IT ALL LOOKS THE SAME TO ME.

IT WON'T BE FORMING INTO ANOTHER HUGE MASS LIKE THAT AGAIN. NOW THAT IT'S EATEN THE OHMU'S FOREST AND MINGLED WITH THE OTHER FUNGI, IT'S SETTLED DOWN.

IT MAY LOOK AS IF THE FOREST HAS COMPLETELY DISAPPEARED NOW, BUT THAT'S BECAUSE IT'S PUTTING ALL ITS ENERGY INTO SETTING DOWN ROOTS.

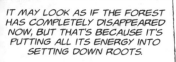

THE MOLD IS BECOMING THE SEEDBED FOR THE VERY TREES IT HAS EATEN. NOW IT WILL BE EATEN ITSELF.

MMMM

TO EAT AND TO BE EATEN... ONE AND THE SAME IN THIS WORLD. THE ENTIRE FOREST--ONE LIFE.

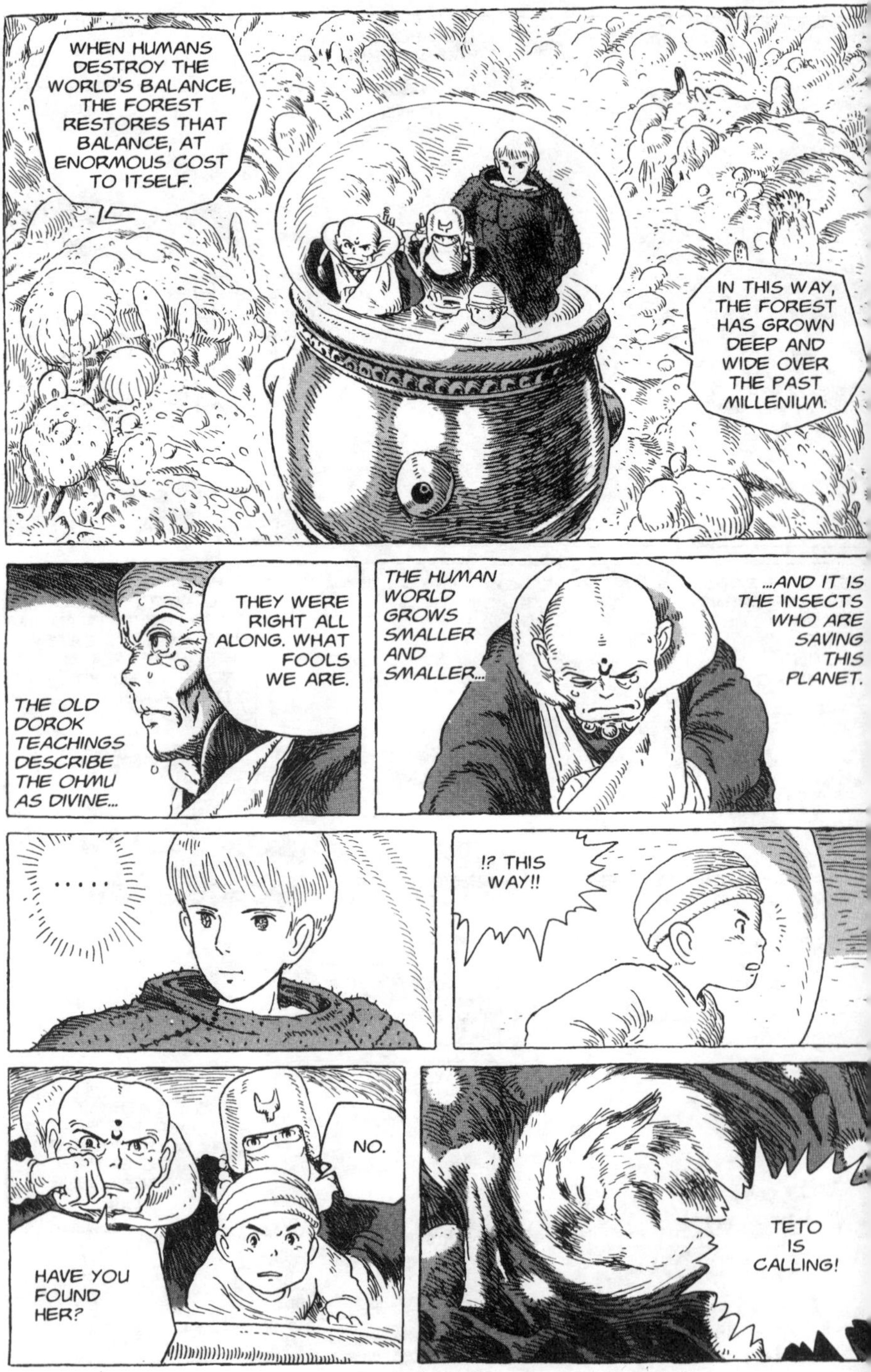
WHEN HUMANS DESTROY THE WORLD'S BALANCE, THE FOREST RESTORES THAT BALANCE, AT ENORMOUS COST TO ITSELF.
IN THIS WAY, THE FOREST HAS GROWN DEEP AND WIDE OVER THE PAST MILLENIUM.
THEY WERE RIGHT ALL ALONG. WHAT FOOLS WE ARE.
THE OLD DOROK TEACHINGS DESCRIBE THE OHMU AS DIVINE...
THE HUMAN WORLD GROWS SMALLER AND SMALLER...
...AND IT IS THE INSECTS WHO ARE SAVING THIS PLANET.
.....
!? THIS WAY!!
NO.
HAVE YOU FOUND HER?
TETO IS CALLING!

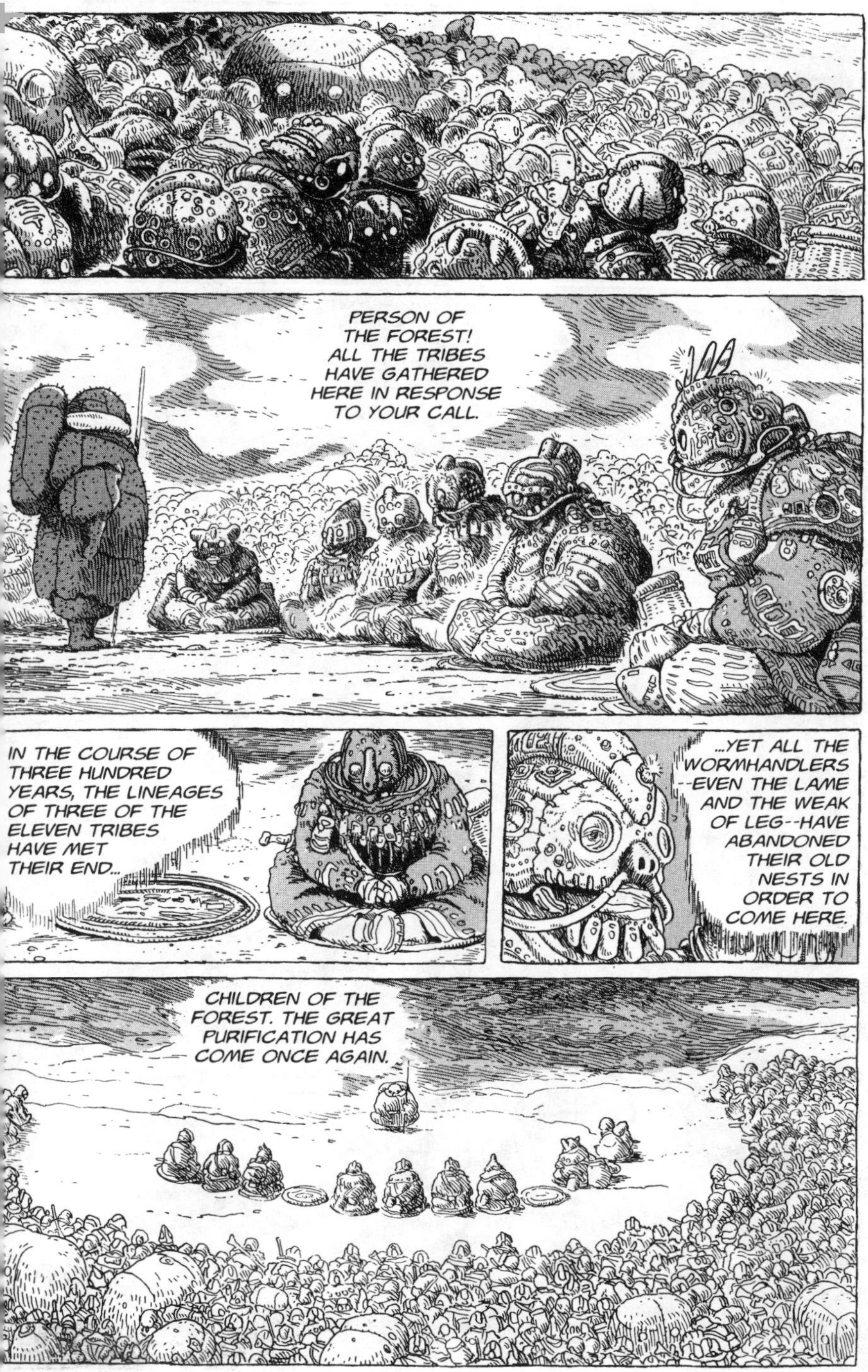
PERSON OF THE FOREST! ALL THE TRIBES HAVE GATHERED HERE IN RESPONSE TO YOUR CALL.
IN THE COURSE OF THREE HUNDRED YEARS, THE LINEAGES OF THREE OF THE ELEVEN TRIBES HAVE MET THEIR END...
...YET ALL THE WORMHANDLERS--EVEN THE LAME AND THE WEAK OF LEG--HAVE ABANDONED THEIR OLD NESTS IN ORDER TO COME HERE.
CHILDREN OF THE FOREST. THE GREAT PURIFICATION HAS COME ONCE AGAIN.

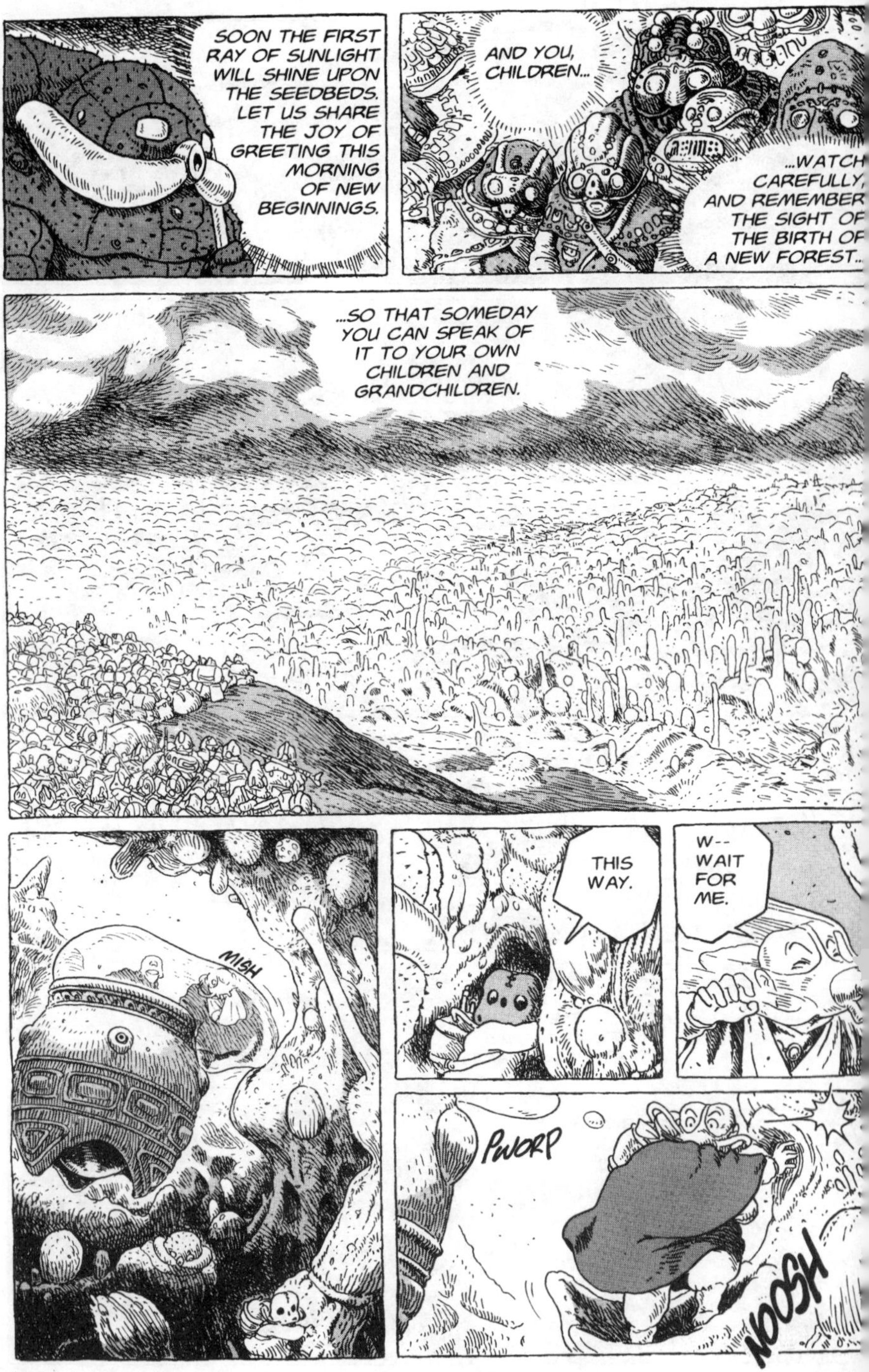
SOON THE FIRST RAY OF SUNLIGHT WILL SHINE UPON THE SEEDBEDS. LET US SHARE THE JOY OF GREETING THIS MORNING OF NEW BEGINNINGS.
AND YOU, CHILDREN...
...WATCH CAREFULLY, AND REMEMBER THE SIGHT OF THE BIRTH OF A NEW FOREST...
...SO THAT SOMEDAY YOU CAN SPEAK OF IT TO YOUR OWN CHILDREN AND GRANDCHILDREN.
MISH
THIS WAY.
W-- WAIT FOR ME.
PWORP
NOOSH

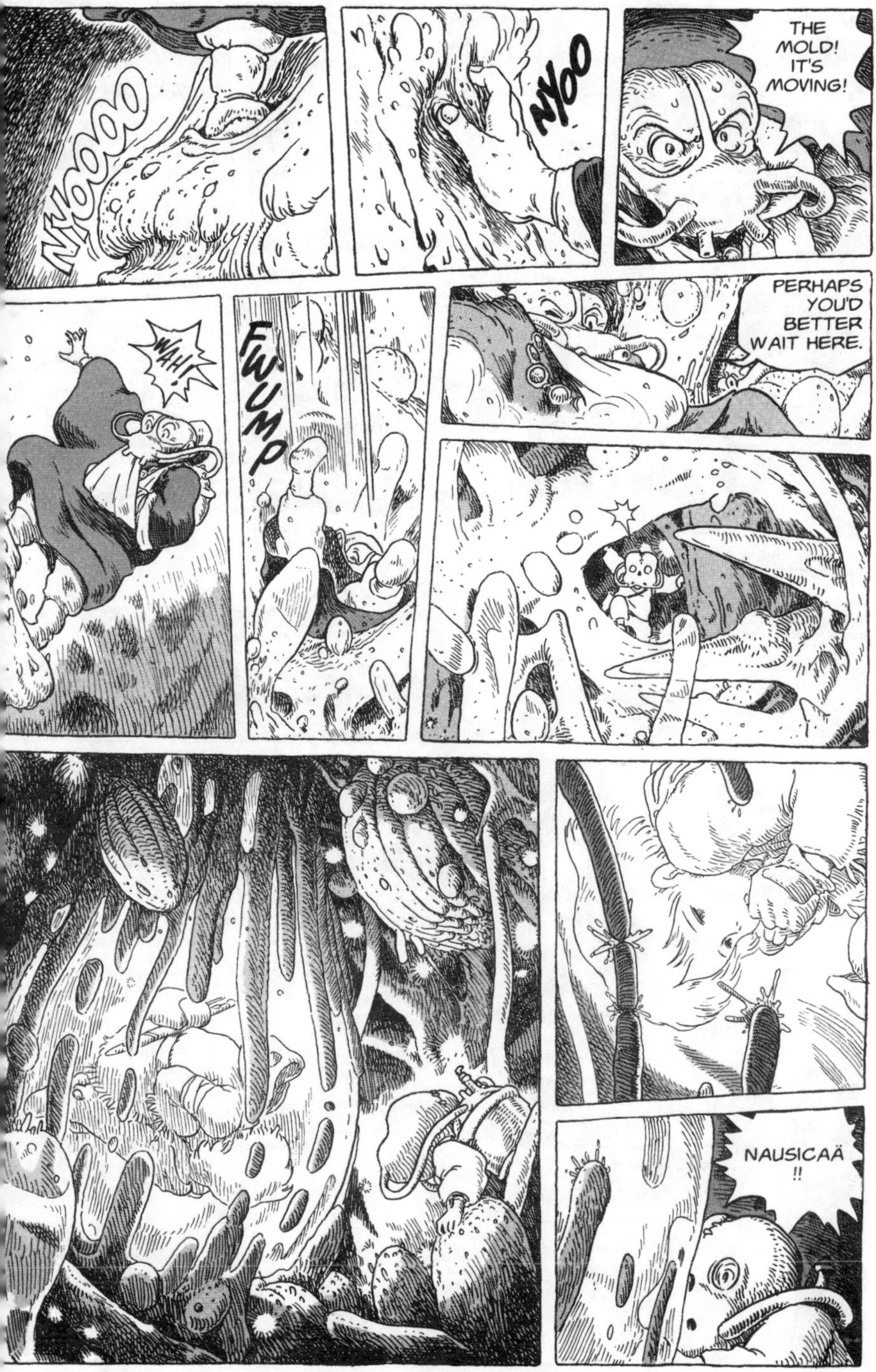
NYOOOOO
NYOO
THE MOLD! IT'S MOVING!
WAH!
FWUMP
PERHAPS YOU'D BETTER WAIT HERE.
NAUSICAÄ !!

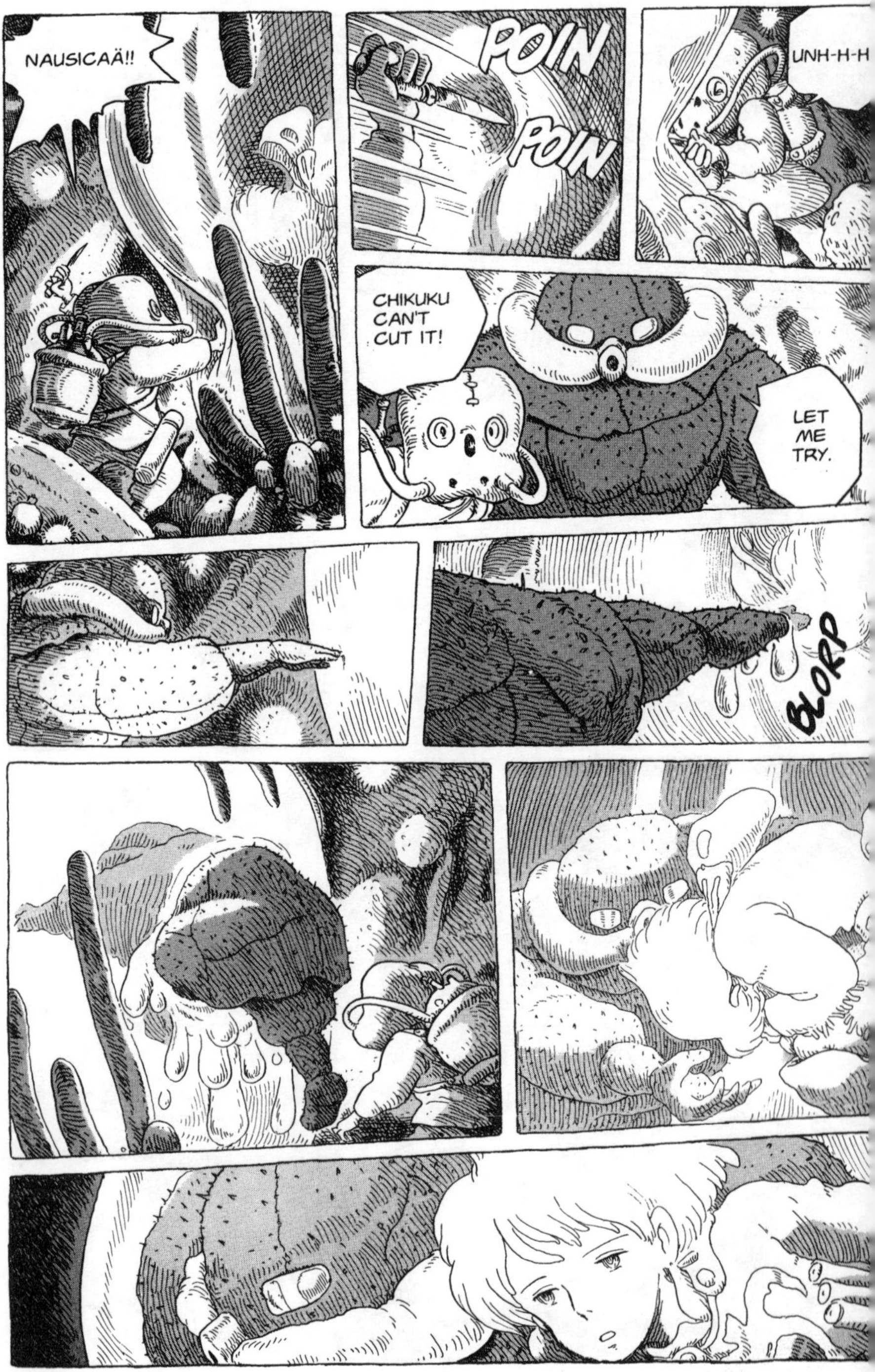
NAUSICAÄ!!
POIN
POIN
UNH-H-H
CHIKUKU CAN'T CUT IT!
LET ME TRY.
BLORP

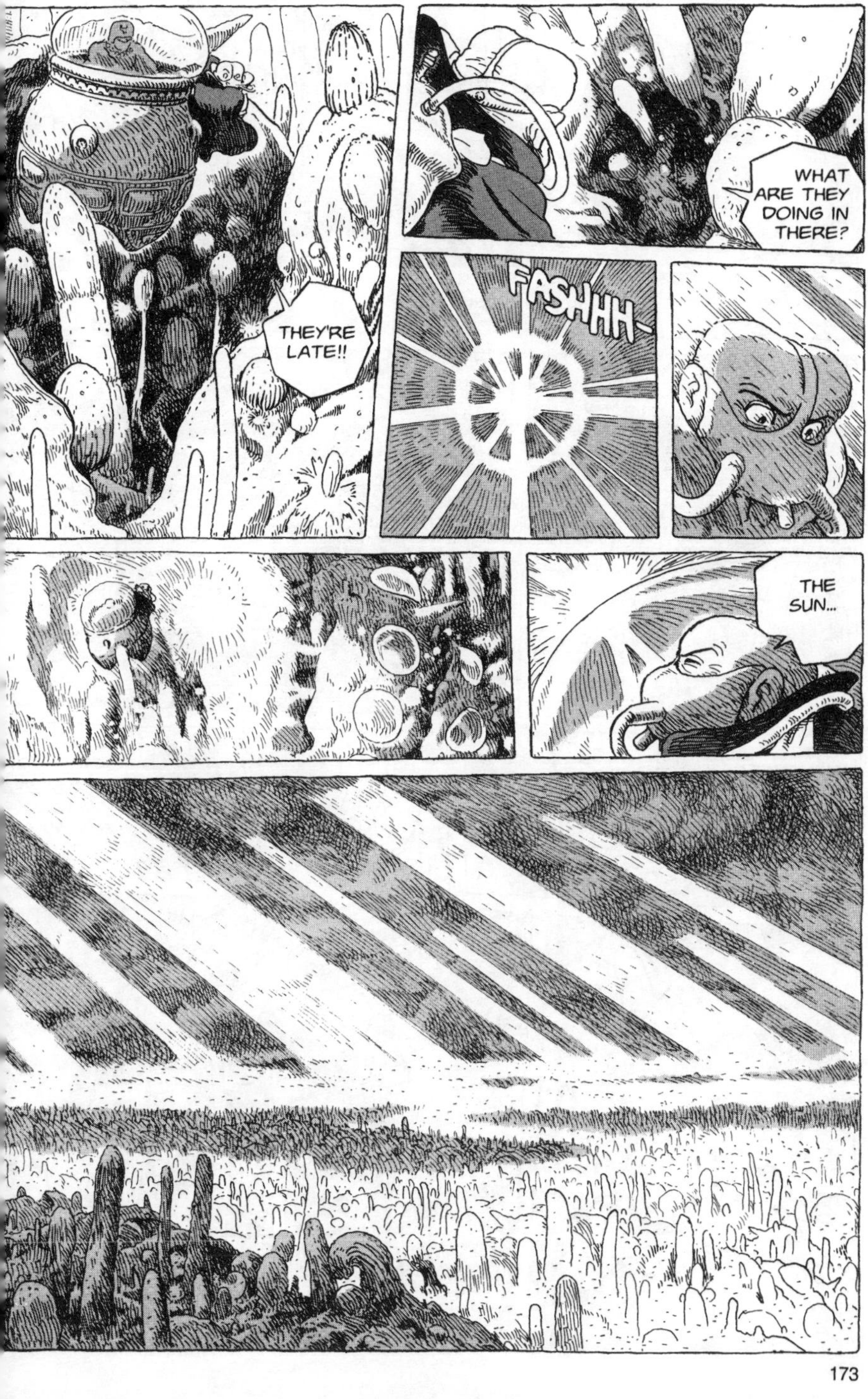
THEY'RE LATE!!
WHAT ARE THEY DOING IN THERE?
FASHHH-
THE SUN...

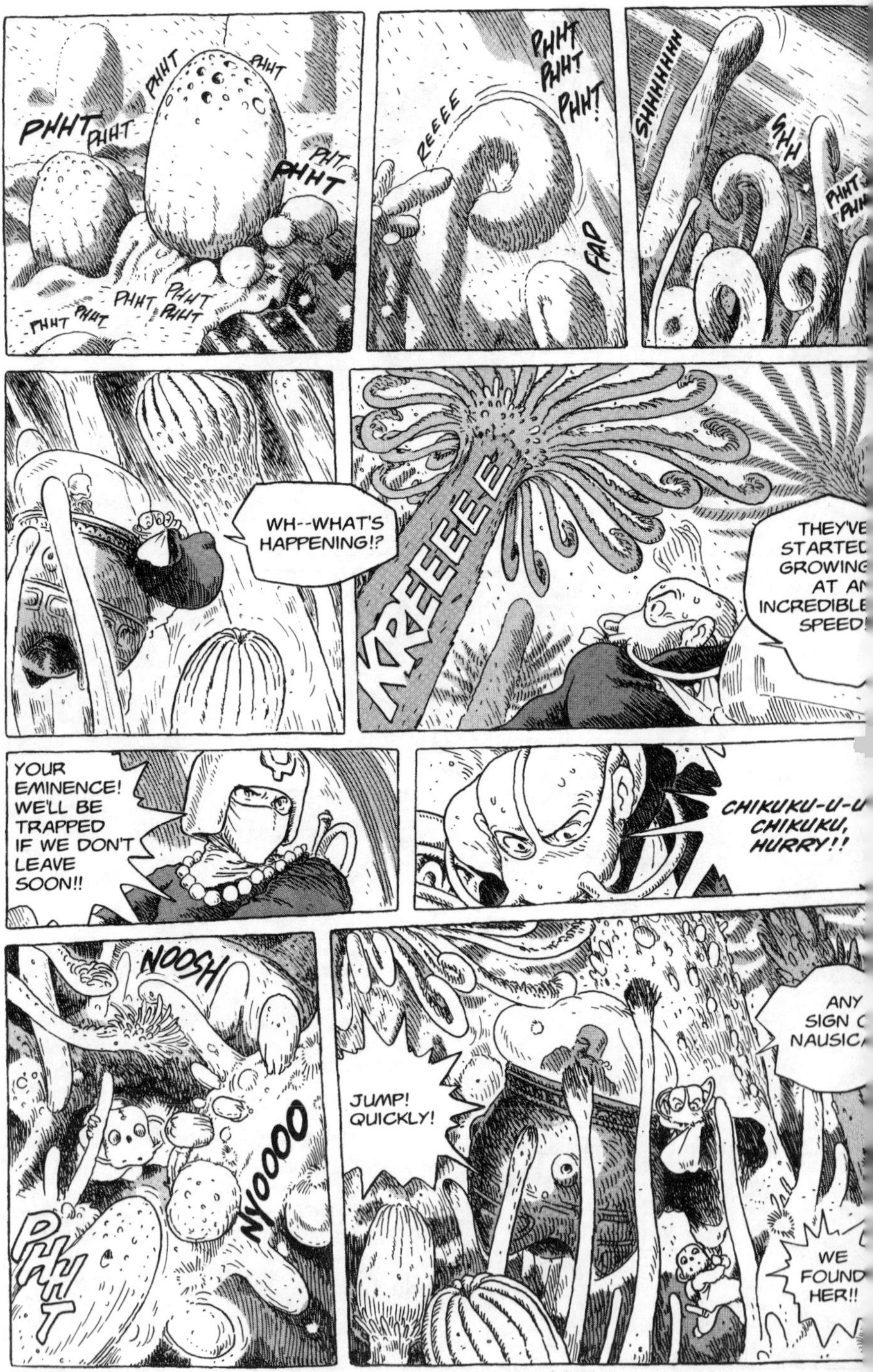
PHHT PHHT
PHHT
PHHT
PHT PHHT
PHHT PHHT PHHT PHHT PHHT
PHHT PHHT PHHT
REEEE
FAP
SHHHHHHH
SHH
PHHT PHH
WH--WHAT'S HAPPENING!?
KREEEEEE
THEY'VE STARTED GROWING AT AN INCREDIBLE SPEED!
YOUR EMINENCE! WE'LL BE TRAPPED IF WE DON'T LEAVE SOON!!
CHIKUKU-U-U CHIKUKU, HURRY!!
NOOSH
NYOOOO
PHHT
JUMP! QUICKLY!
ANY SIGN NAUSIC
WE FOUND HER!!

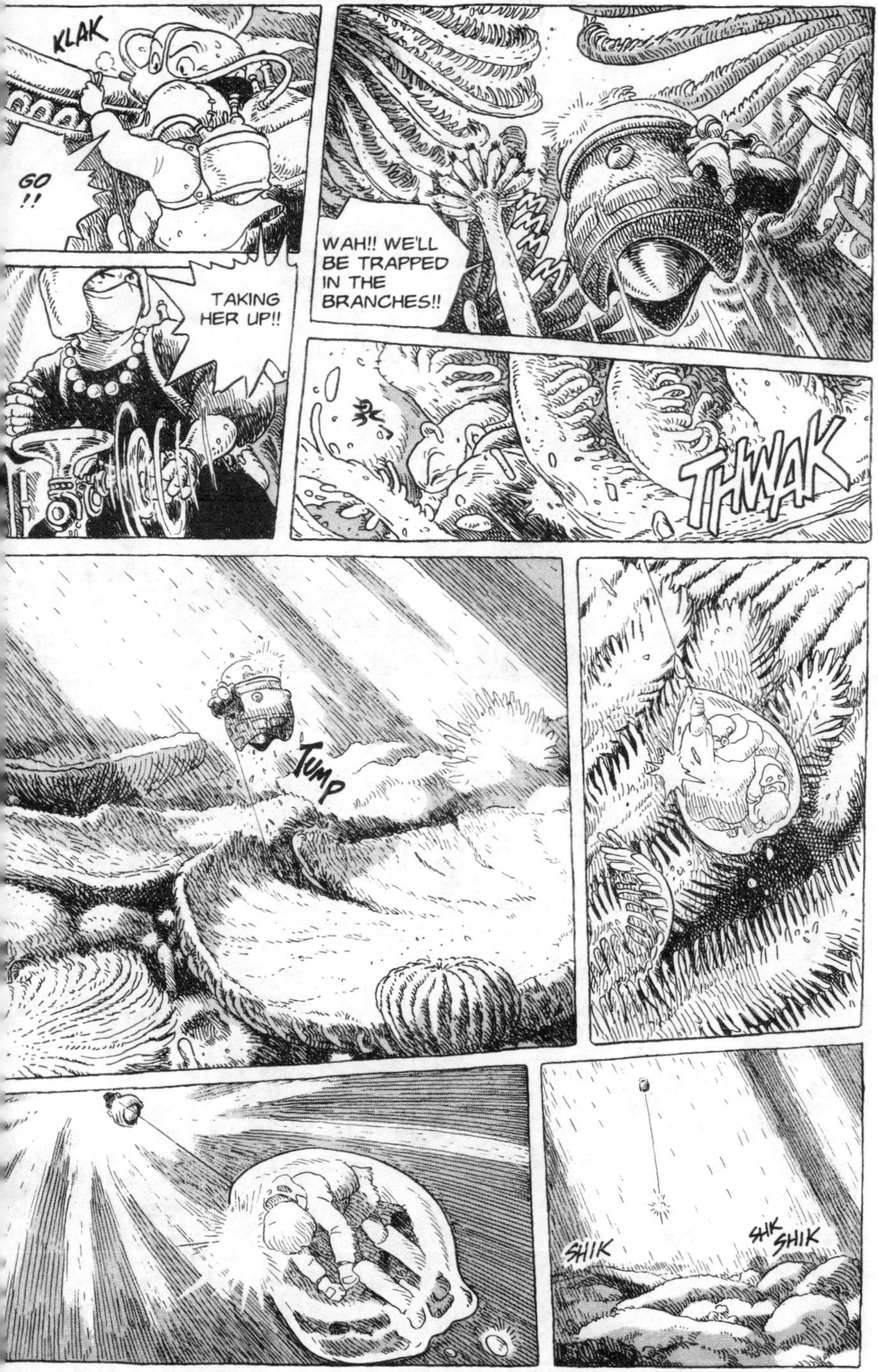
KLAK
GO !!
WAH!! WE'LL BE TRAPPED IN THE BRANCHES!!
TAKING HER UP!!
THWAK
TUMP
SHIK
SHIK SHIK

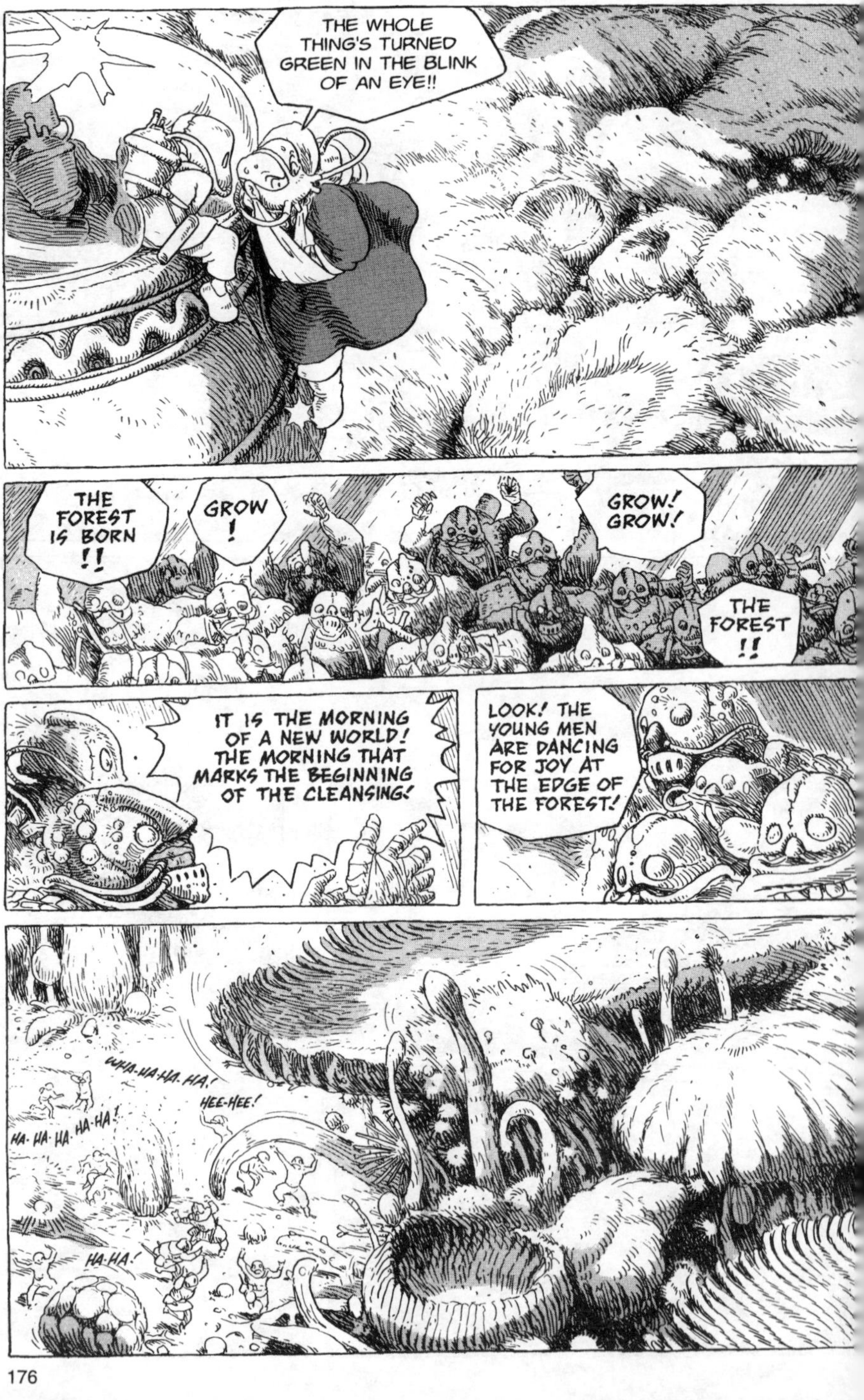
THE WHOLE THING'S TURNED GREEN IN THE BLINK OF AN EYE!!
THE FOREST IS BORN !!
GROW !
GROW! GROW!
THE FOREST !!
IT IS THE MORNING OF A NEW WORLD! THE MORNING THAT MARKS THE BEGINNING OF THE CLEANSING!
LOOK! THE YOUNG MEN ARE DANCING FOR JOY AT THE EDGE OF THE FOREST!
WHA-HA-HA. HA!
HEE-HEE!
HA-HA-HA. HA-HA!
HA-HA!

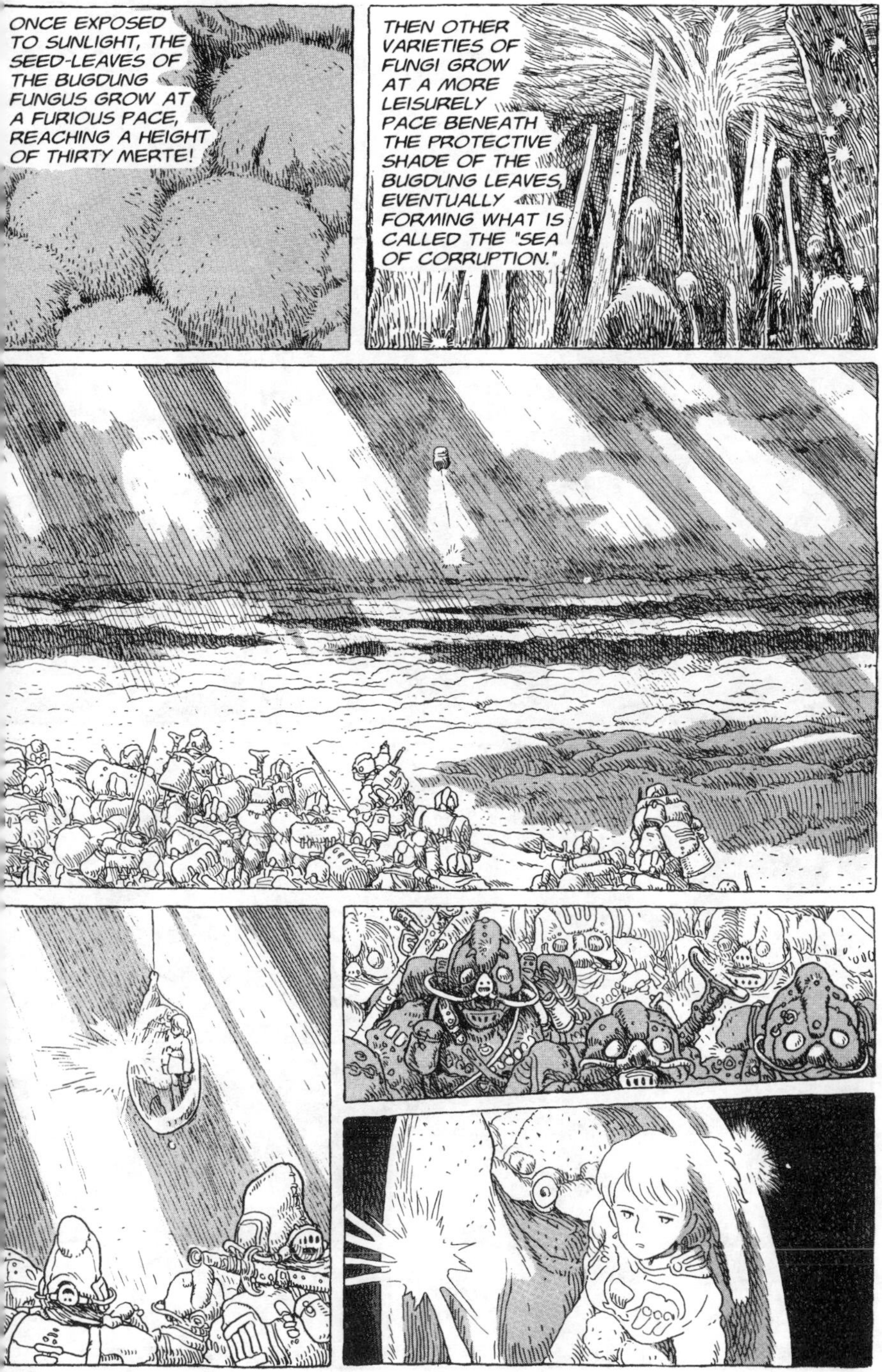
ONCE EXPOSED TO SUNLIGHT, THE SEED-LEAVES OF THE BUGDUNG FUNGUS GROW AT A FURIOUS PACE, REACHING A HEIGHT OF THIRTY MERTE!
THEN OTHER VARIETIES OF FUNGI GROW AT A MORE LEISURELY PACE BENEATH THE PROTECTIVE SHADE OF THE BUGDUNG LEAVES, EVENTUALLY FORMING WHAT IS CALLED THE "SEA OF CORRUPTION."

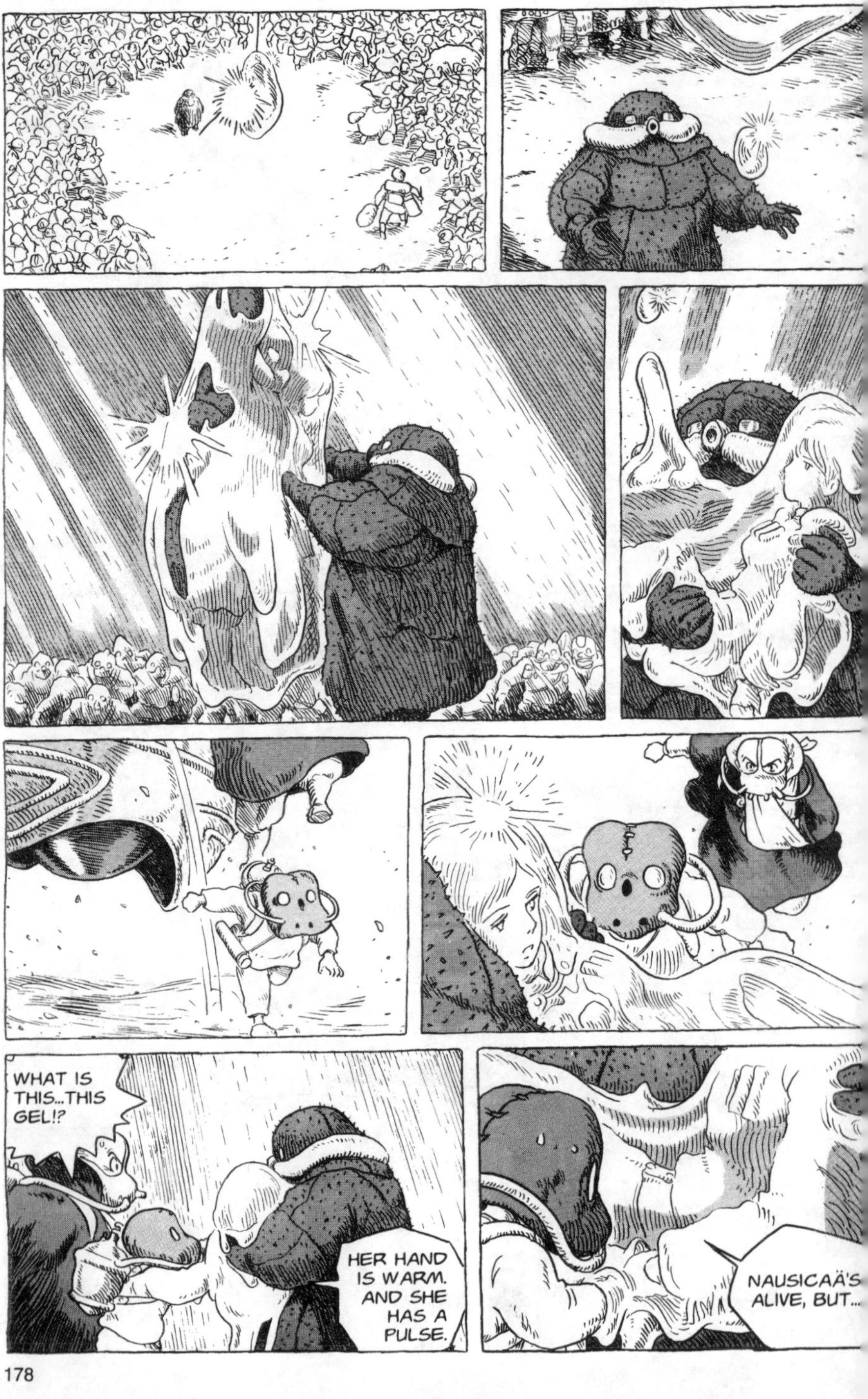
WHAT IS THIS...THIS GEL!?
HER HAND IS WARM. AND SHE HAS A PULSE.
NAUSICAÄ'S ALIVE, BUT...

THE SERUM OF THE OHMU PROTECTED HER.

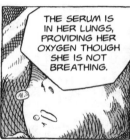

THE SERUM IS IN HER LUNGS, PROVIDING HER OXYGEN THOUGH SHE IS NOT BREATHING.

SERUM!!

CHIKUKU KNOWS. NAUSICAÄ TRIED TO HELP THE OHMU CALM THE MOLD.

SHE WANTED TO BECOME PART OF THE FOREST ALONG WITH THE OHMU.

SO THE OHMU TOOK HER AWAY...

NAUSICAÄ IS ALIVE, BUT SHE'S NOT HERE.

CHIKUKU IS SAD.

NO, CHIKUKU. THE OHMU WRAPPED NAUSICAÄ IN SERUM PRECISELY BECAUSE THEY DID *NOT* WANT TO TAKE HER AWAY.

S--SO THIS IS SERUM...

THIS IS THE FIRST I'VE EVER SEEN IT. WHAT A BLESS'D DAY!

...EOPLE OF THE ...OREST, THIS ...ONORED PERSON ... THE FOREST ...N HUMAN FORM. ...HE STANDS AT ...HE CENTER OF ...OTH WORLDS.

WE BEG YOU, PLEASE GIVE THIS HONORED PERSON TO US. WE SHALL MAKE HER THE GUARDIAN DEITY OF OUR PEOPLE.

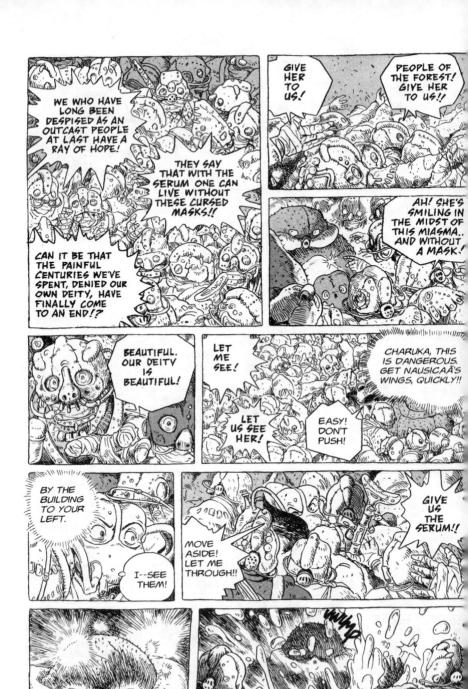

WE WHO HAVE LONG BEEN DESPISED AS AN OUTCAST PEOPLE AT LAST HAVE A RAY OF HOPE!

THEY SAY THAT WITH THE SERUM ONE CAN LIVE WITHOUT THESE CURSED MASKS!!

CAN IT BE THAT THE PAINFUL CENTURIES WE'VE SPENT, DENIED OUR OWN DEITY, HAVE FINALLY COME TO AN END!?

GIVE HER TO US!

PEOPLE OF THE FOREST! GIVE HER TO US!!

AH! SHE'S SMILING IN THE MIDST OF THIS MIASMA.. AND WITHOUT A MASK!

BEAUTIFUL. OUR DEITY IS BEAUTIFUL!

LET ME SEE!

LET US SEE HER!

EASY! DON'T PUSH!

CHARUKA, THIS IS DANGEROUS. GET NAUSICAÄ'S WINGS, QUICKLY!!

BY THE BUILDING TO YOUR LEFT.

I--SEE THEM!

MOVE ASIDE! LET ME THROUGH!!

GIVE US THE SERUM!!

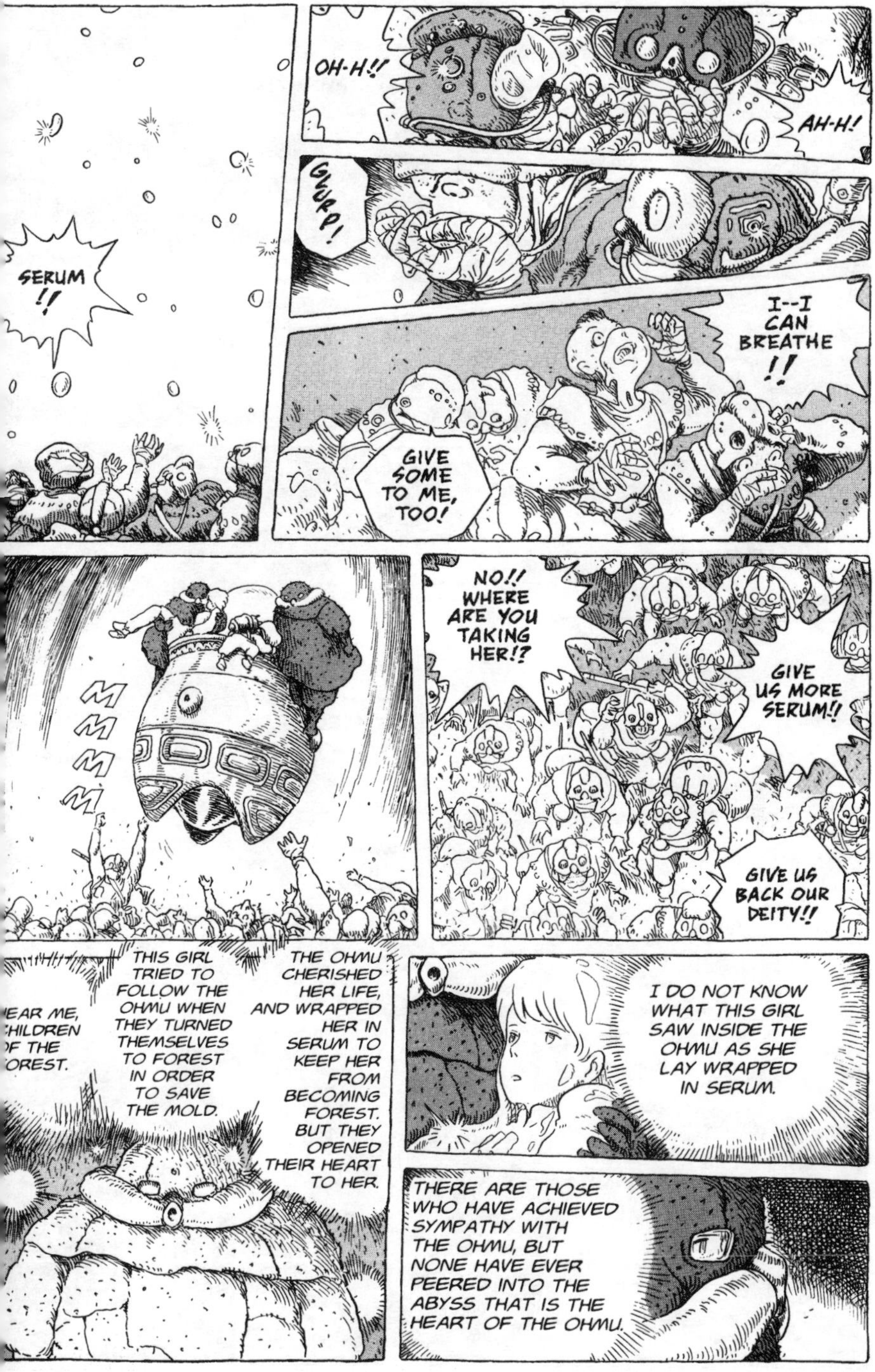
SERUM!!
OH-H!!
AH-H!
GLURP!
I--I CAN BREATHE!!
GIVE SOME TO ME, TOO!
MMMMM
NO!! WHERE ARE YOU TAKING HER!?
GIVE US MORE SERUM!!
GIVE US BACK OUR DEITY!!
HEAR ME, CHILDREN OF THE FOREST.
THIS GIRL TRIED TO FOLLOW THE OHMU WHEN THEY TURNED THEMSELVES TO FOREST IN ORDER TO SAVE THE MOLD.
THE OHMU CHERISHED HER LIFE, AND WRAPPED HER IN SERUM TO KEEP HER FROM BECOMING FOREST. BUT THEY OPENED THEIR HEART TO HER.
I DO NOT KNOW WHAT THIS GIRL SAW INSIDE THE OHMU AS SHE LAY WRAPPED IN SERUM.
THERE ARE THOSE WHO HAVE ACHIEVED SYMPATHY WITH THE OHMU, BUT NONE HAVE EVER PEERED INTO THE ABYSS THAT IS THE HEART OF THE OHMU.

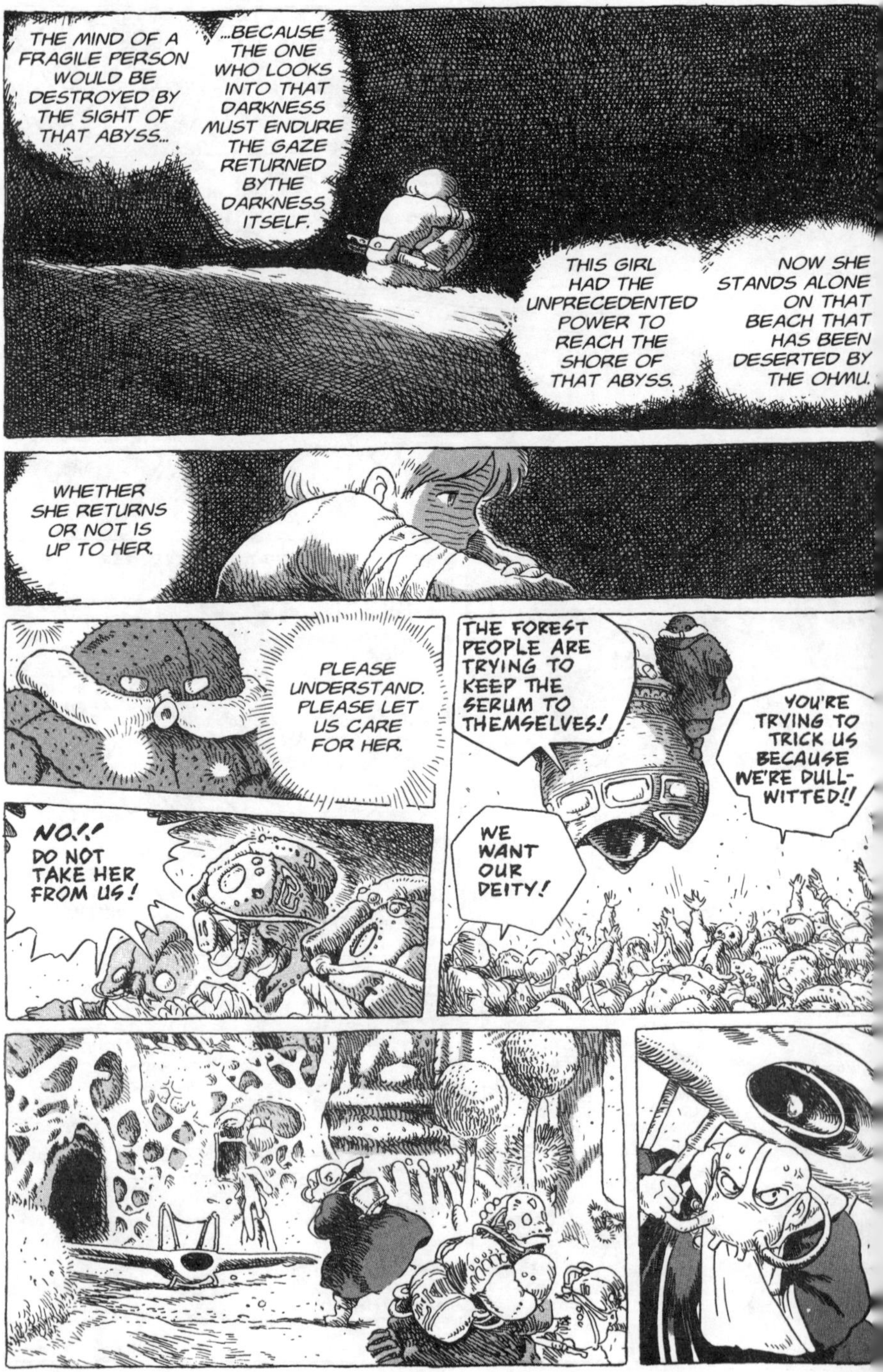
THE MIND OF A FRAGILE PERSON WOULD BE DESTROYED BY THE SIGHT OF THAT ABYSS...
...BECAUSE THE ONE WHO LOOKS INTO THAT DARKNESS MUST ENDURE THE GAZE RETURNED BYTHE DARKNESS ITSELF.
THIS GIRL HAD THE UNPRECEDENTED POWER TO REACH THE SHORE OF THAT ABYSS.
NOW SHE STANDS ALONE ON THAT BEACH THAT HAS BEEN DESERTED BY THE OHMU.
WHETHER SHE RETURNS OR NOT IS UP TO HER.
PLEASE UNDERSTAND. PLEASE LET US CARE FOR HER.
NO!! DO NOT TAKE HER FROM US!
THE FOREST PEOPLE ARE TRYING TO KEEP THE SERUM TO THEMSELVES!
YOU'RE TRYING TO TRICK US BECAUSE WE'RE DULL-WITTED!!
WE WANT OUR DEITY!

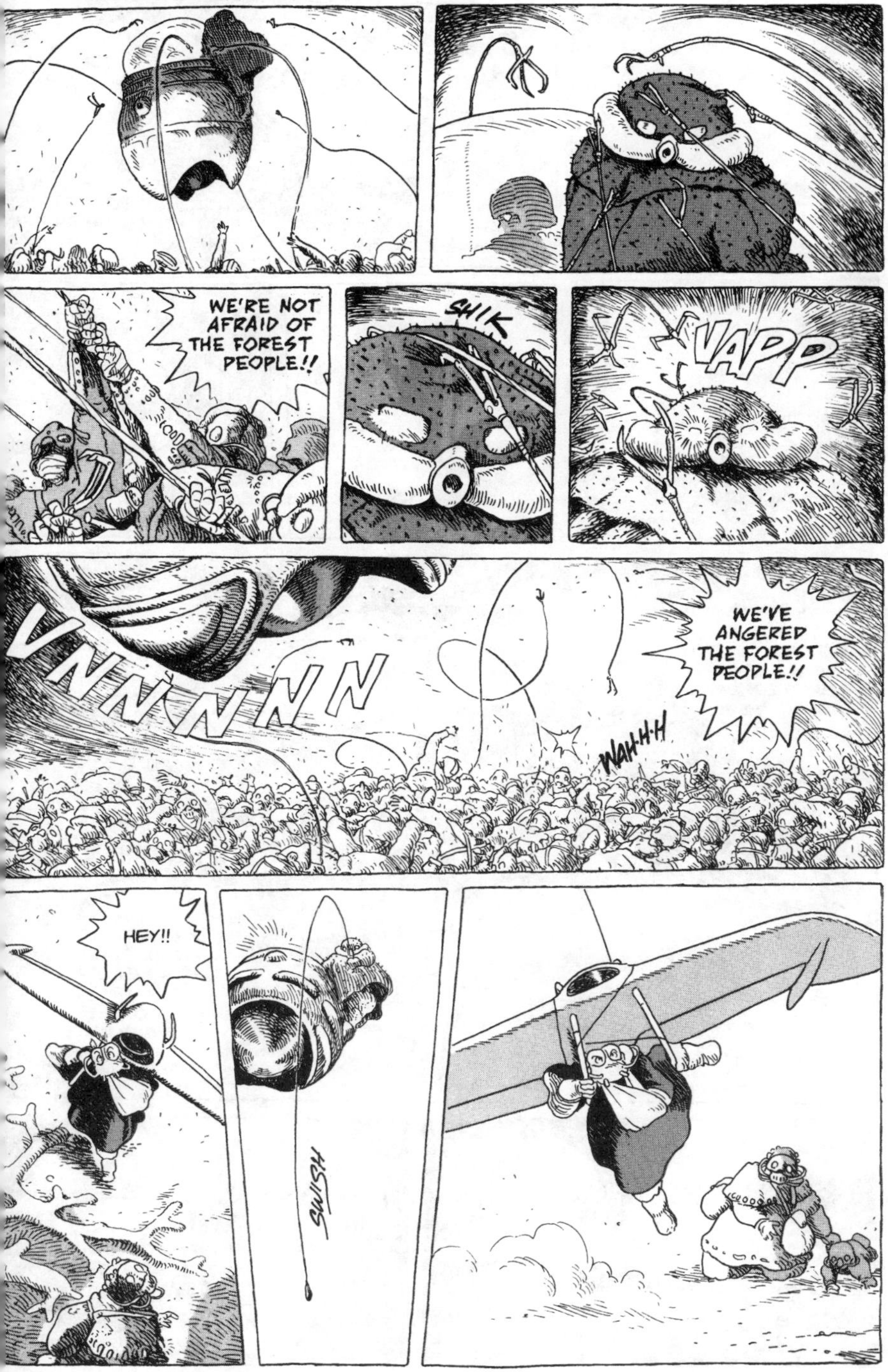

WE'RE NOT AFRAID OF THE FOREST PEOPLE!!
SHIK
VAPP
VNNNNNN
WE'VE ANGERED THE FOREST PEOPLE!!
WAHHH
HEY!!
SWISH

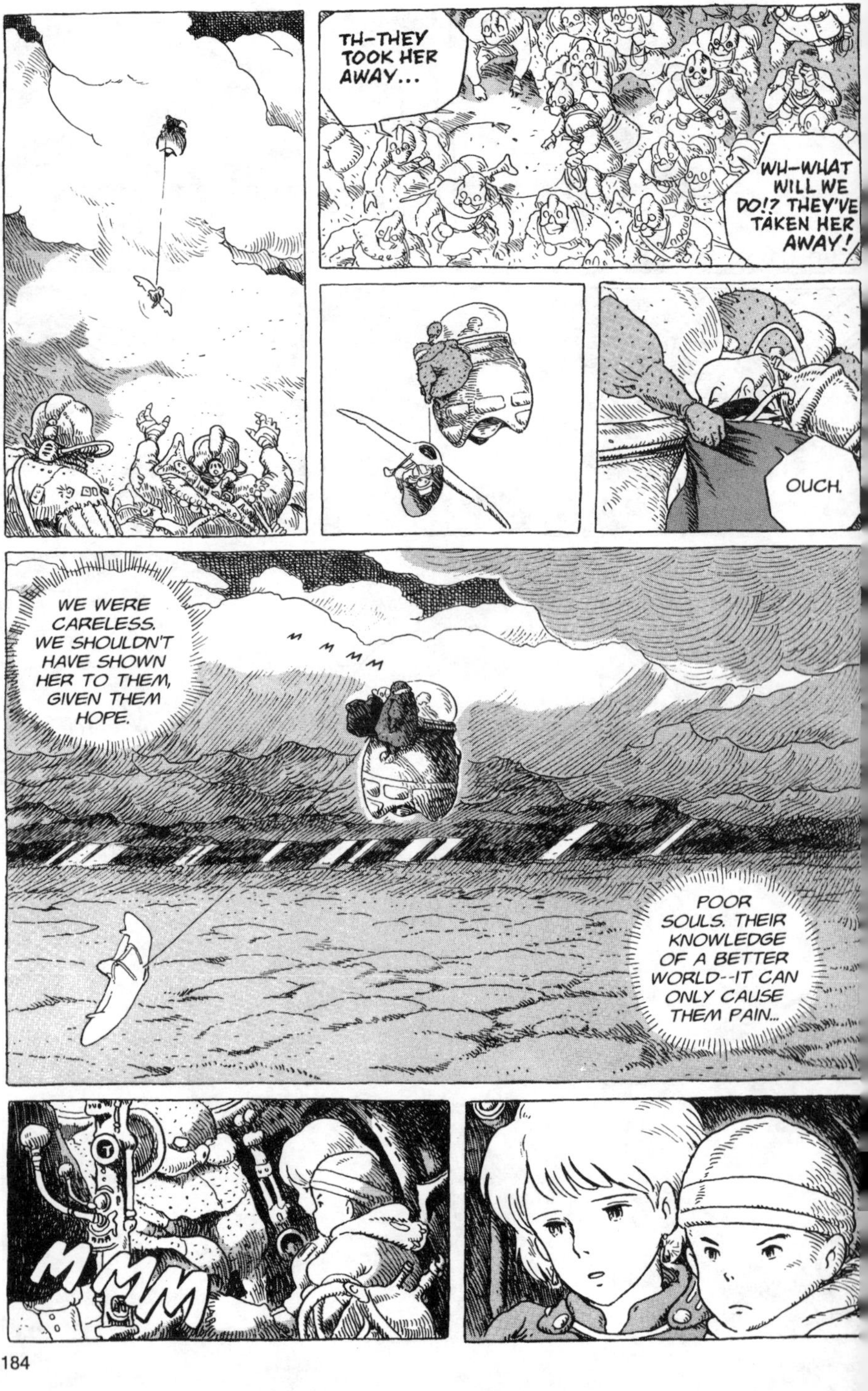
TH-THEY TOOK HER AWAY...
WH-WHAT WILL WE DO!? THEY'VE TAKEN HER AWAY!
OUCH.
WE WERE CARELESS. WE SHOULDN'T HAVE SHOWN HER TO THEM, GIVEN THEM HOPE.
M M M M
POOR SOULS. THEIR KNOWLEDGE OF A BETTER WORLD--IT CAN ONLY CAUSE THEM PAIN...
M MM

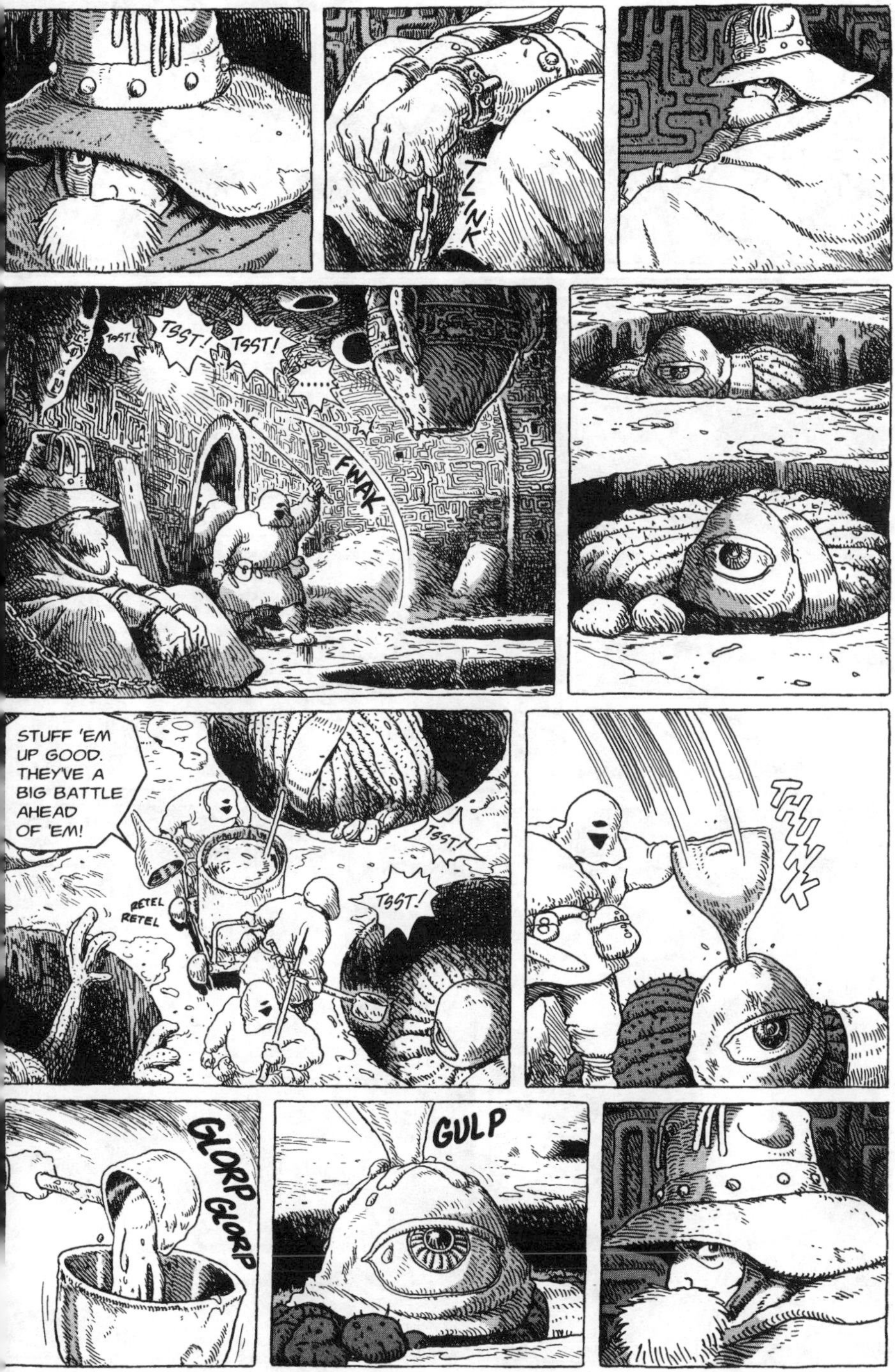
TLINK
TSST!
TSST!
TSST!
......
FWAK
STUFF 'EM UP GOOD. THEY'VE A BIG BATTLE AHEAD OF 'EM!
TSST!
TSST!
RETEL RETEL
THUNK
GLORP GLORP
GULP

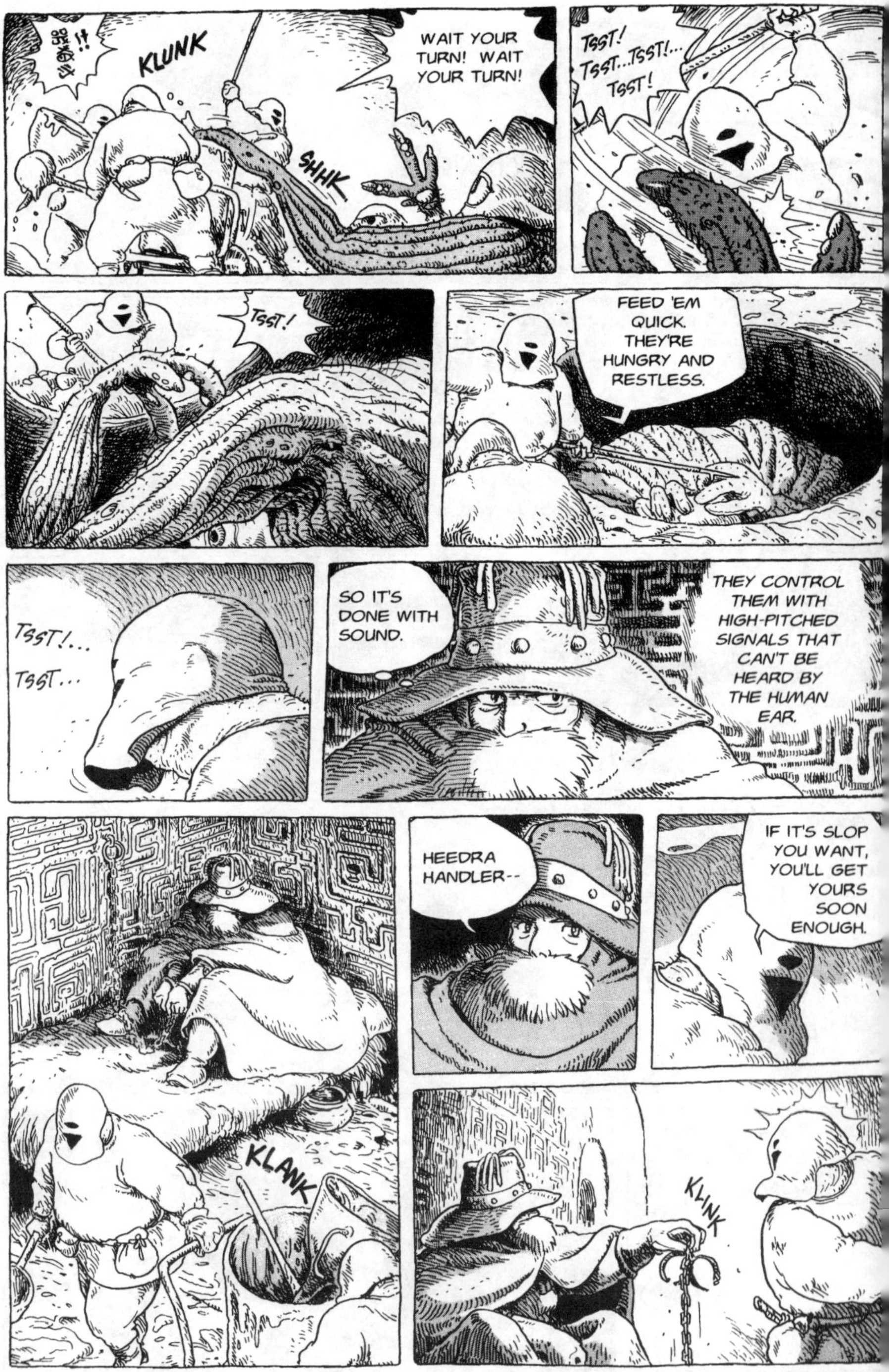
KLUNK
WAIT YOUR TURN! WAIT YOUR TURN!
SHHK
TSST! TSST...TSST!... TSST!
TSST!
FEED 'EM QUICK. THEY'RE HUNGRY AND RESTLESS.
TSST!... TSST...
SO IT'S DONE WITH SOUND.
THEY CONTROL THEM WITH HIGH-PITCHED SIGNALS THAT CAN'T BE HEARD BY THE HUMAN EAR.
KLANK
HEEDRA HANDLER--
IF IT'S SLOP YOU WANT, YOU'LL GET YOURS SOON ENOUGH.
KLINK

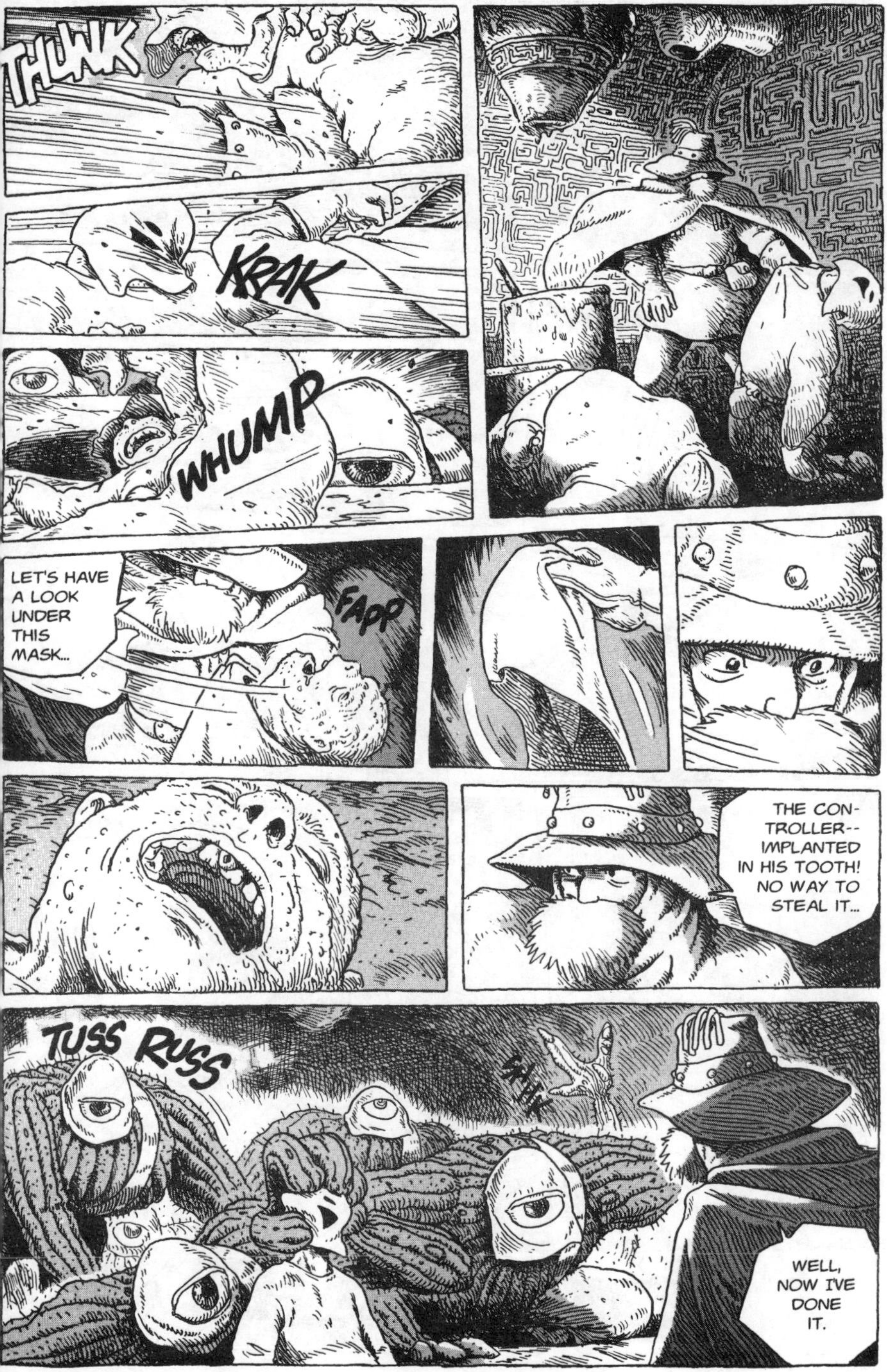
THUNK
KRAK
WHUMP
LET'S HAVE A LOOK UNDER THIS MASK...
FAPP
THE CON-TROLLER-- IMPLANTED IN HIS TOOTH! NO WAY TO STEAL IT...
TUSS RUSS
WELL, NOW I'VE DONE IT.

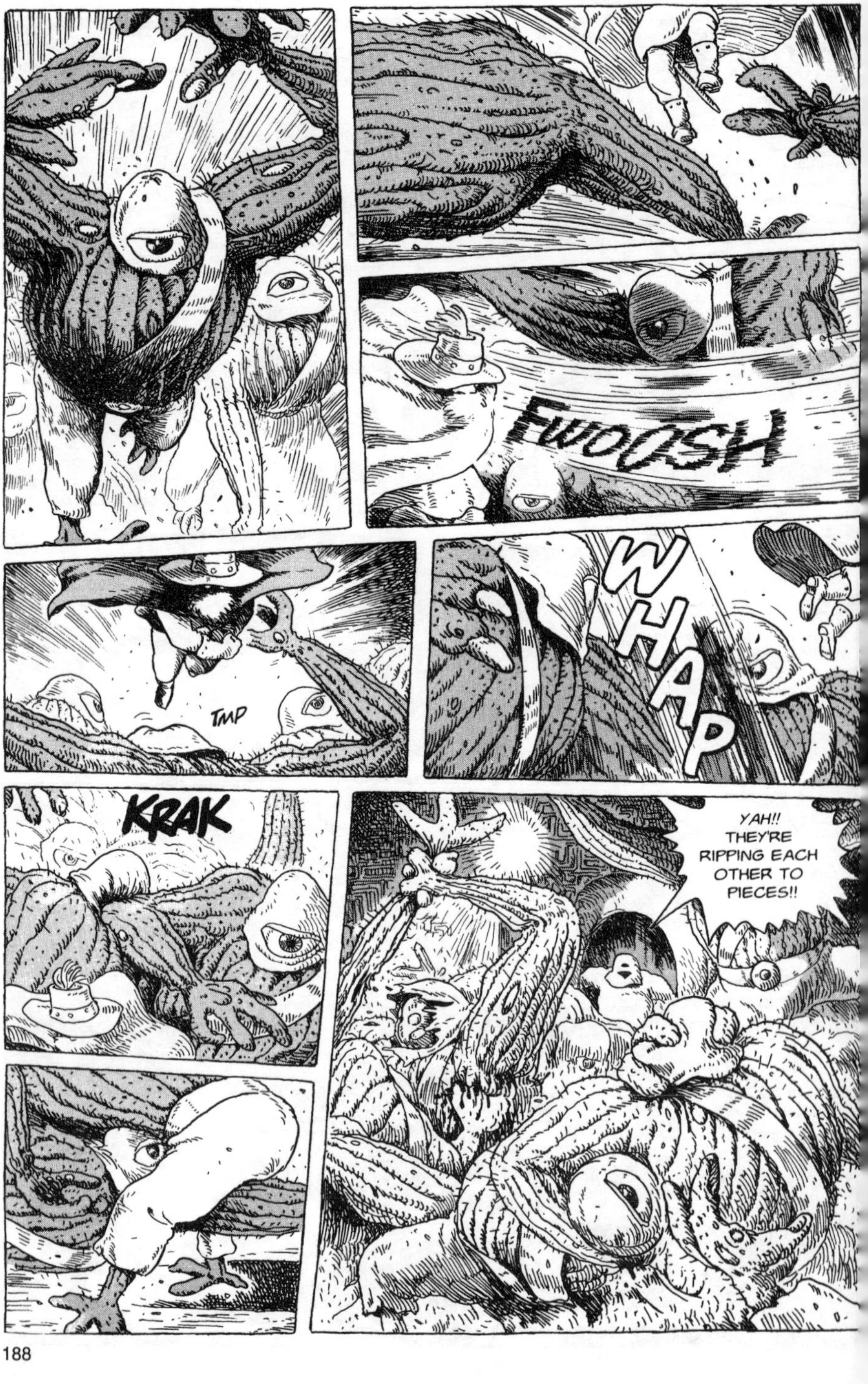
FWOOSH
TMP
WHAP
KRAK
YAH!! THEY'RE RIPPING EACH OTHER TO PIECES!!

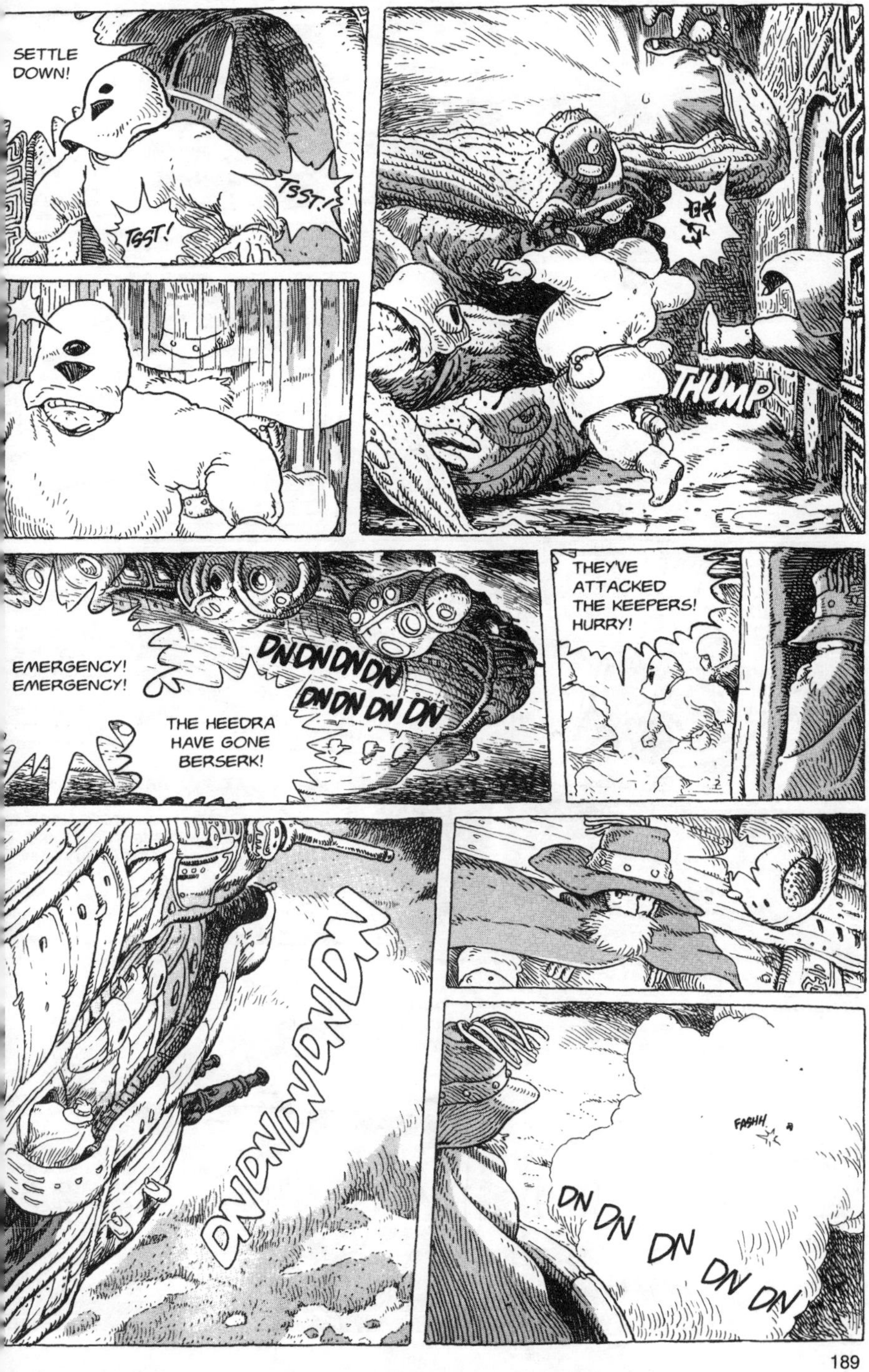

SETTLE DOWN!
TSST!
TSST!
THUMP
EMERGENCY! EMERGENCY!
DN DN DN DN
DN DN DN DN
THE HEEDRA HAVE GONE BERSERK!
THEY'VE ATTACKED THE KEEPERS! HURRY!
DN DN DN DN DN
FASHH
DN DN DN DN DN

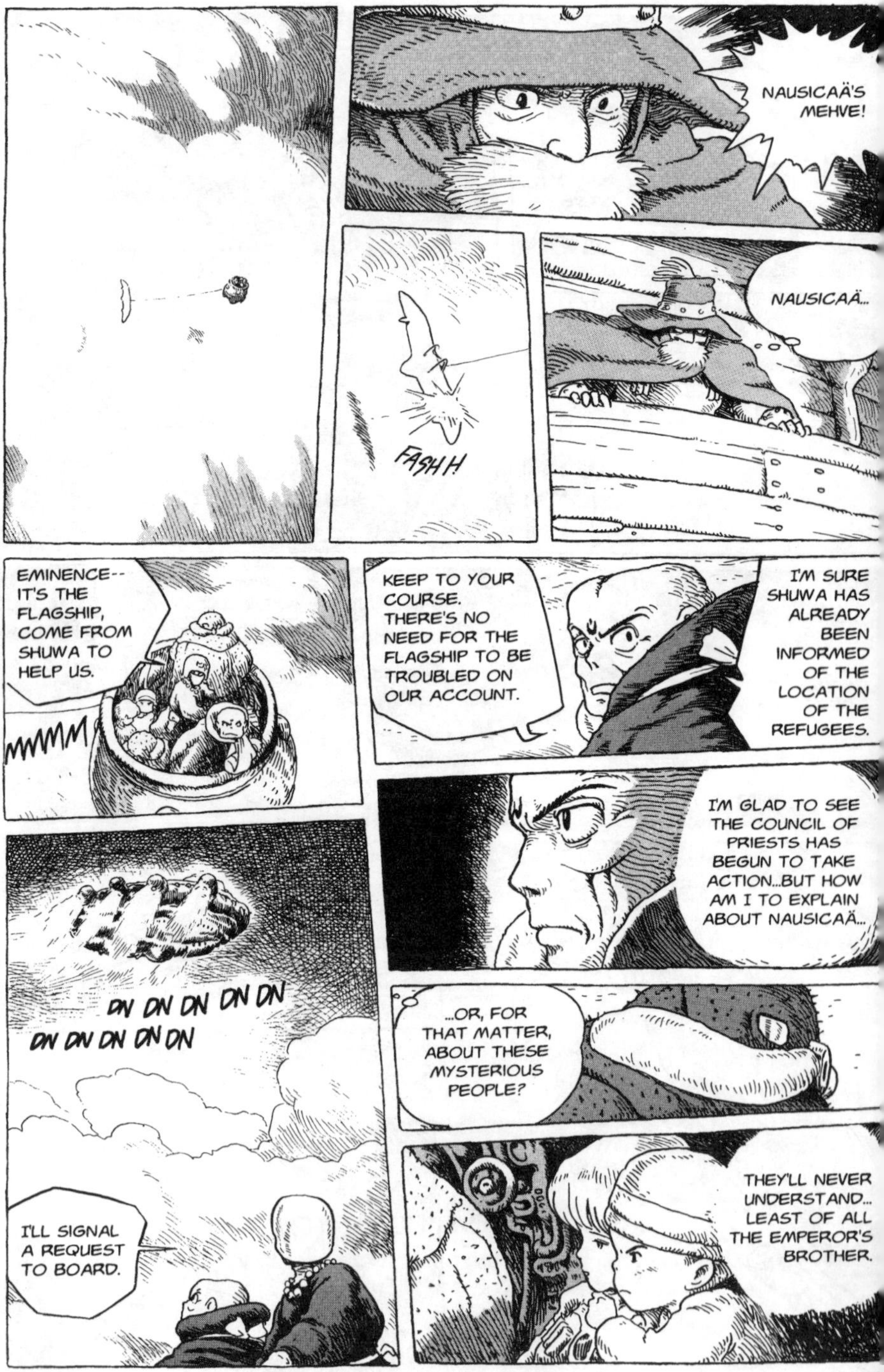
NAUSICAÄ'S MEHVE!
FASHH
NAUSICAÄ...
EMINENCE-- IT'S THE FLAGSHIP, COME FROM SHUWA TO HELP US.
MMMM
KEEP TO YOUR COURSE. THERE'S NO NEED FOR THE FLAGSHIP TO BE TROUBLED ON OUR ACCOUNT.
I'M SURE SHUWA HAS ALREADY BEEN INFORMED OF THE LOCATION OF THE REFUGEES.
I'M GLAD TO SEE THE COUNCIL OF PRIESTS HAS BEGUN TO TAKE ACTION...BUT HOW AM I TO EXPLAIN ABOUT NAUSICAÄ...
DN DN DN DN DN
DN DN DN DN DN
...OR, FOR THAT MATTER, ABOUT THESE MYSTERIOUS PEOPLE?
I'LL SIGNAL A REQUEST TO BOARD.
THEY'LL NEVER UNDERSTAND... LEAST OF ALL THE EMPEROR'S BROTHER.

CALM THE HEEDRA!

WHAT A MESS !

THERE'S NO SIGN OF THE *GUEST'S* BODY! HE'S ESCAPED!

HOW MANY HAVE BEEN DAMAGED?

TH--THREE ARE BEYOND REPAIR, YOUR MAJESTY. AND WE HAVE LOST FOUR KEEPERS.

HE CANNOT HIDE FOR LONG INSIDE THE SHIP. WE SHALL FIND HIM IN NO TIME, YOUR MAJESTY.

YES. THAT WOULD BE BEST...FOR YOU.

Y--YES, YOUR MAJESTY!

GLUB
GLUB

HA, HA, HA... THAT YUPA IS QUITE A MAN.

GLUB

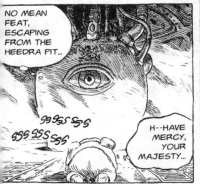

NO MEAN FEAT, ESCAPING FROM THE HEEDRA PIT...

H--HAVE MERCY, YOUR MAJESTY...

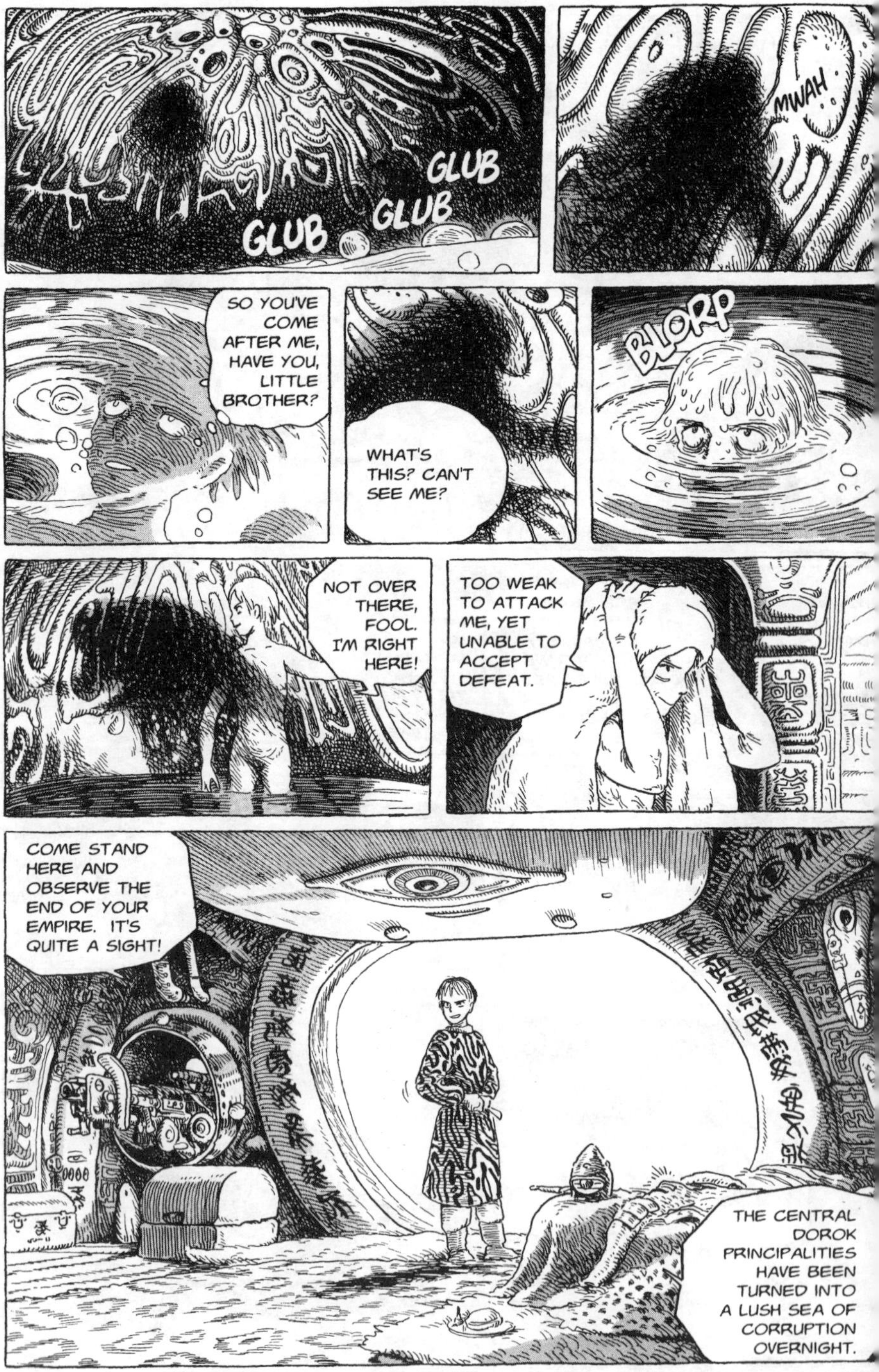
GLUB
GLUB
GLUB
MWAH
SO YOU'VE COME AFTER ME, HAVE YOU, LITTLE BROTHER?
WHAT'S THIS? CAN'T SEE ME?
BLORP
NOT OVER THERE, FOOL. I'M RIGHT HERE!
TOO WEAK TO ATTACK ME, YET UNABLE TO ACCEPT DEFEAT.
COME STAND HERE AND OBSERVE THE END OF YOUR EMPIRE. IT'S QUITE A SIGHT!
THE CENTRAL DOROK PRINCIPALITIES HAVE BEEN TURNED INTO A LUSH SEA OF CORRUPTION OVERNIGHT.

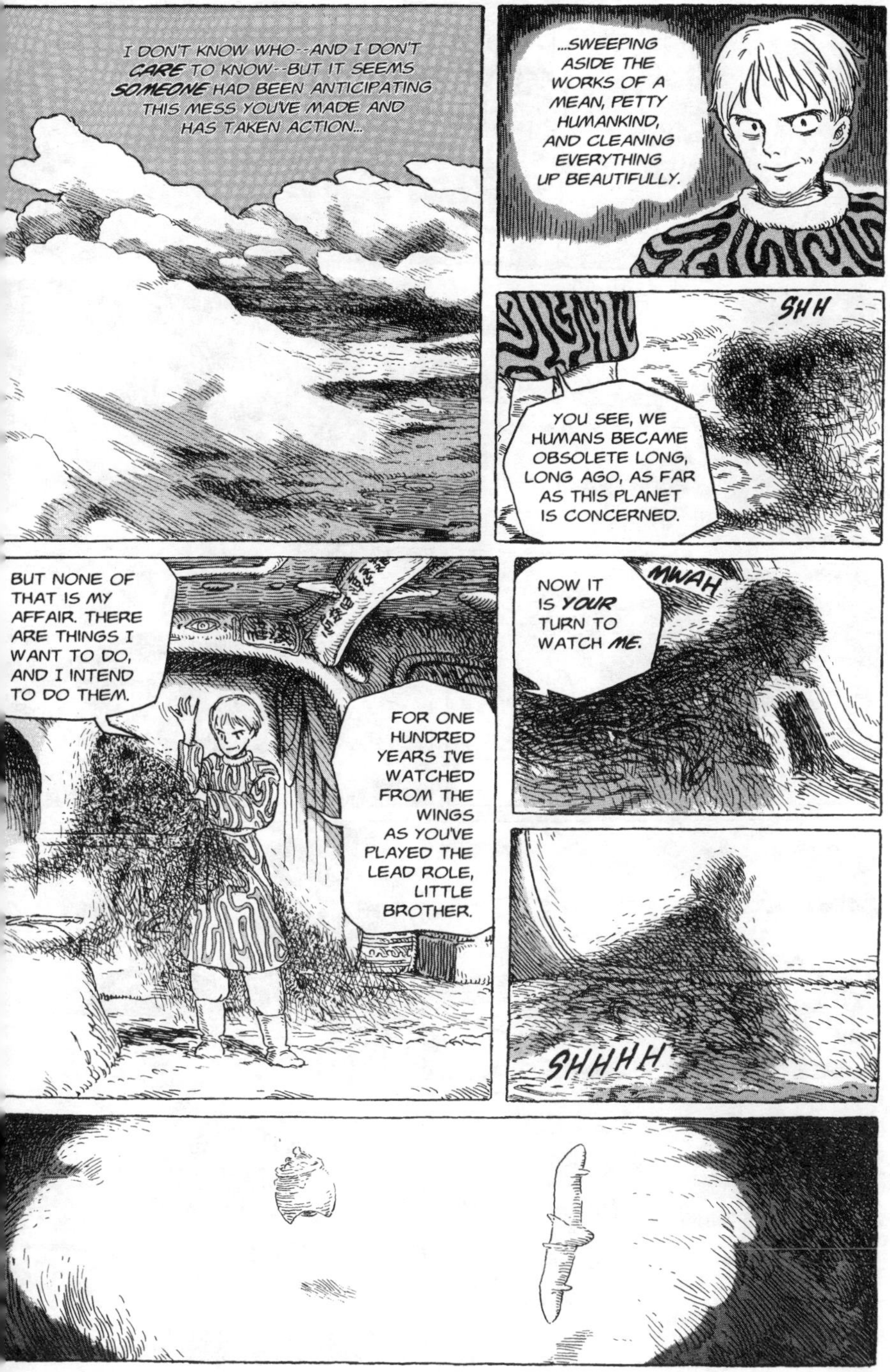
I DON'T KNOW WHO--AND I DON'T CARE TO KNOW--BUT IT SEEMS SOMEONE HAD BEEN ANTICIPATING THIS MESS YOU'VE MADE AND HAS TAKEN ACTION...
...SWEEPING ASIDE THE WORKS OF A MEAN, PETTY HUMANKIND, AND CLEANING EVERYTHING UP BEAUTIFULLY.
SHH
YOU SEE, WE HUMANS BECAME OBSOLETE LONG, LONG AGO, AS FAR AS THIS PLANET IS CONCERNED.
BUT NONE OF THAT IS MY AFFAIR. THERE ARE THINGS I WANT TO DO, AND I INTEND TO DO THEM.
FOR ONE HUNDRED YEARS I'VE WATCHED FROM THE WINGS AS YOU'VE PLAYED THE LEAD ROLE, LITTLE BROTHER.
MWAH
NOW IT IS YOUR TURN TO WATCH ME.
SHHHH

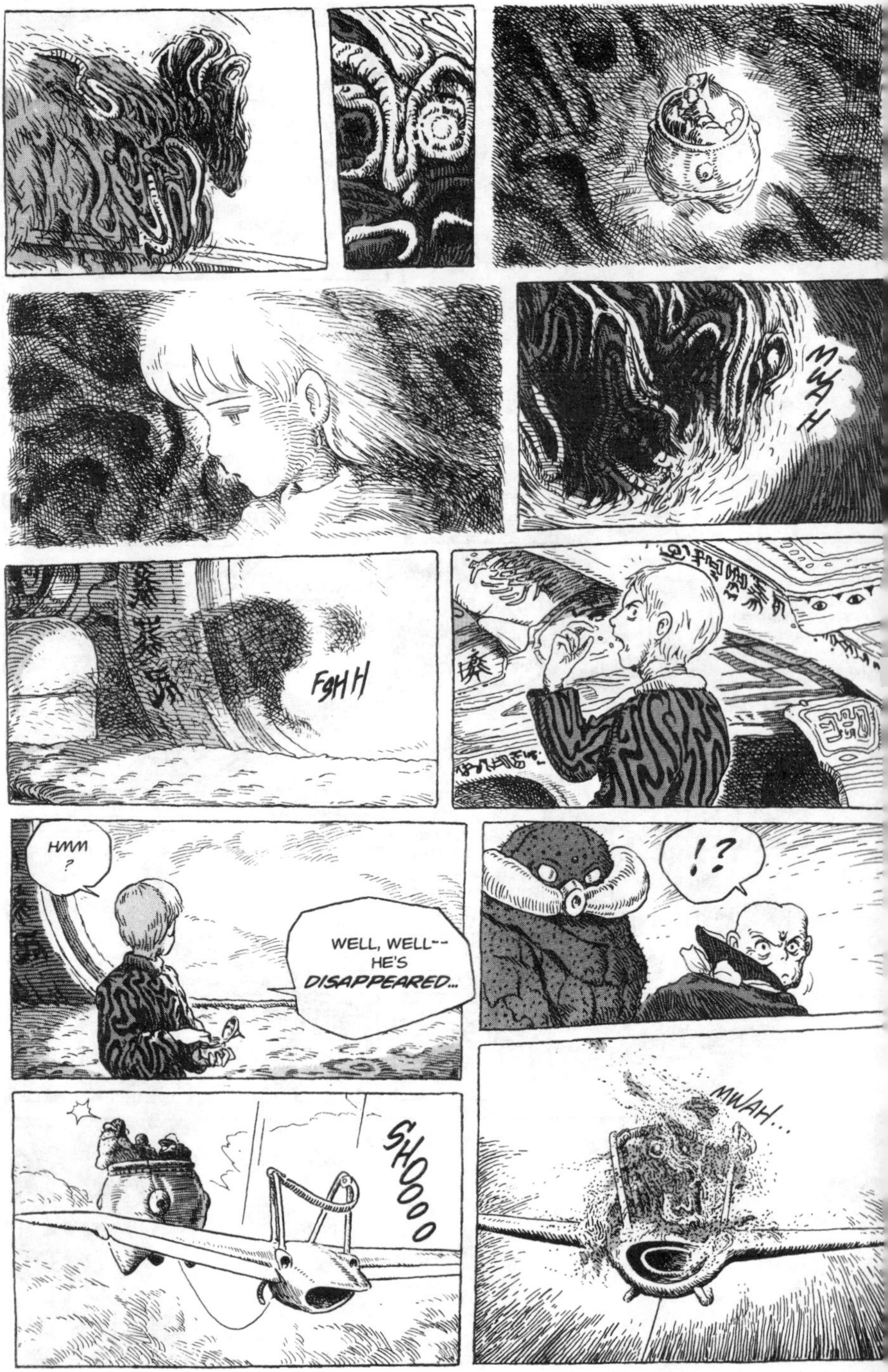
MWAH
FSHH
HMM ?
WELL, WELL--
HE'S DISAPPEARED...
!?
SHOOOOO
MWAH...

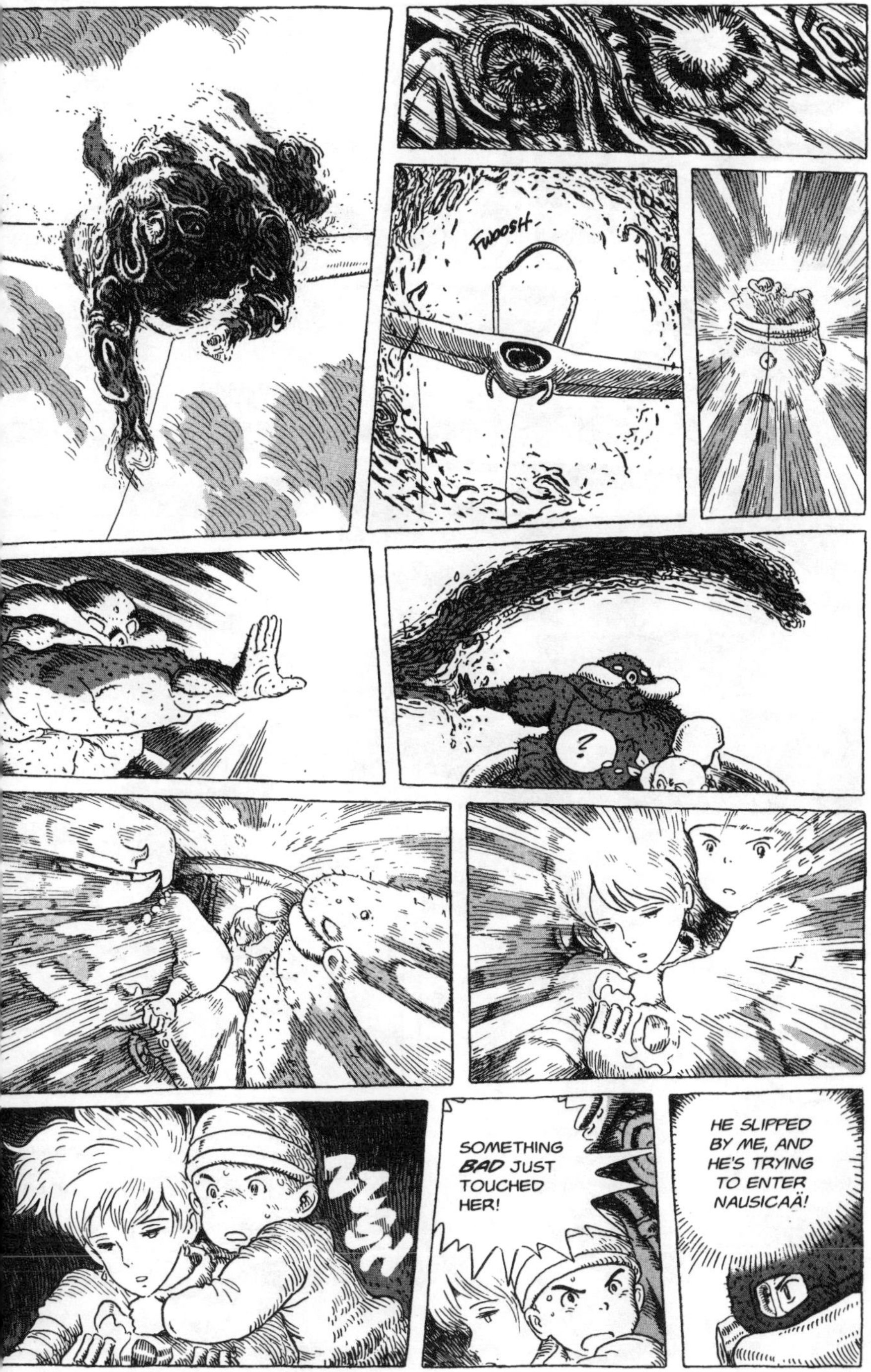
FWOOSH
?
SOMETHING BAD JUST TOUCHED HER!
HE SLIPPED BY ME, AND HE'S TRYING TO ENTER NAUSICAÄ!

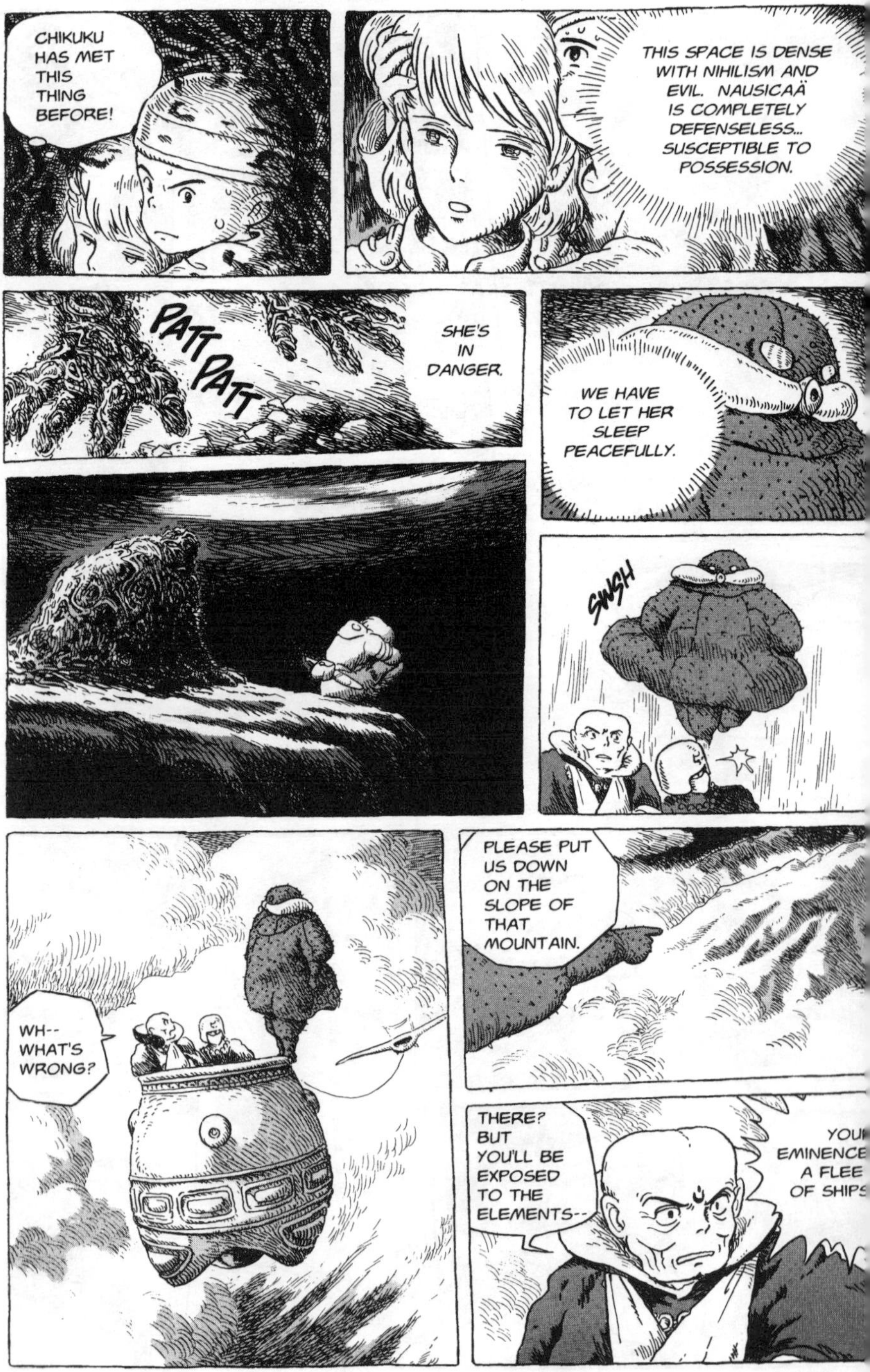
CHIKUKU HAS MET THIS THING BEFORE!
THIS SPACE IS DENSE WITH NIHILISM AND EVIL. NAUSICAÄ IS COMPLETELY DEFENSELESS... SUSCEPTIBLE TO POSSESSION.
PATT PATT
SHE'S IN DANGER.
WE HAVE TO LET HER SLEEP PEACEFULLY.
SWISH
WH-- WHAT'S WRONG?
PLEASE PUT US DOWN ON THE SLOPE OF THAT MOUNTAIN.
THERE? BUT YOU'LL BE EXPOSED TO THE ELEMENTS--
YOU EMINENCE A FLEE OF SHIPS

THESE AREN'T ONLY THE SHIPS PREVIOUSLY DISPATCHED THROUGHOUT THE LAND. THEIR NUMBERS HAVE GROWN!

DN DN DN DN DN DN
DN DN DN DN DN

I'M SURPRISED TO SEE THAT SO MANY REMAIN.

DN DN DN DN DN DN
DN DN DN DN DN

[N]OW WE'LL [B]E ABLE TO [E]VACUATE THE [R]EFUGEES ON [T]HE MOUNTAIN, [Y]OUR [E]MINENCE.

THAT'S THE COMMAND SHIP OF THE EASTERN MILITARY PARISH AT THE HEAD.

COULD IT BE THAT THE COASTAL REGIONS HAVE ESCAPED DAMAGE?

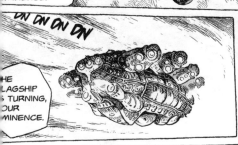

DN DN DN DN

[T]HE [F]LAGSHIP [I]S TURNING, [Y]OUR [E]MINENCE.

SHIK

HMPH.

[I] WAS HOPING TO LET THAT CURSED LITTLE BROTHER OF MINE SEE THIS, BUT HE'S DISAPPEARED.

DN DN DN DN

DN DN DN DN DN

VN N N N N

197

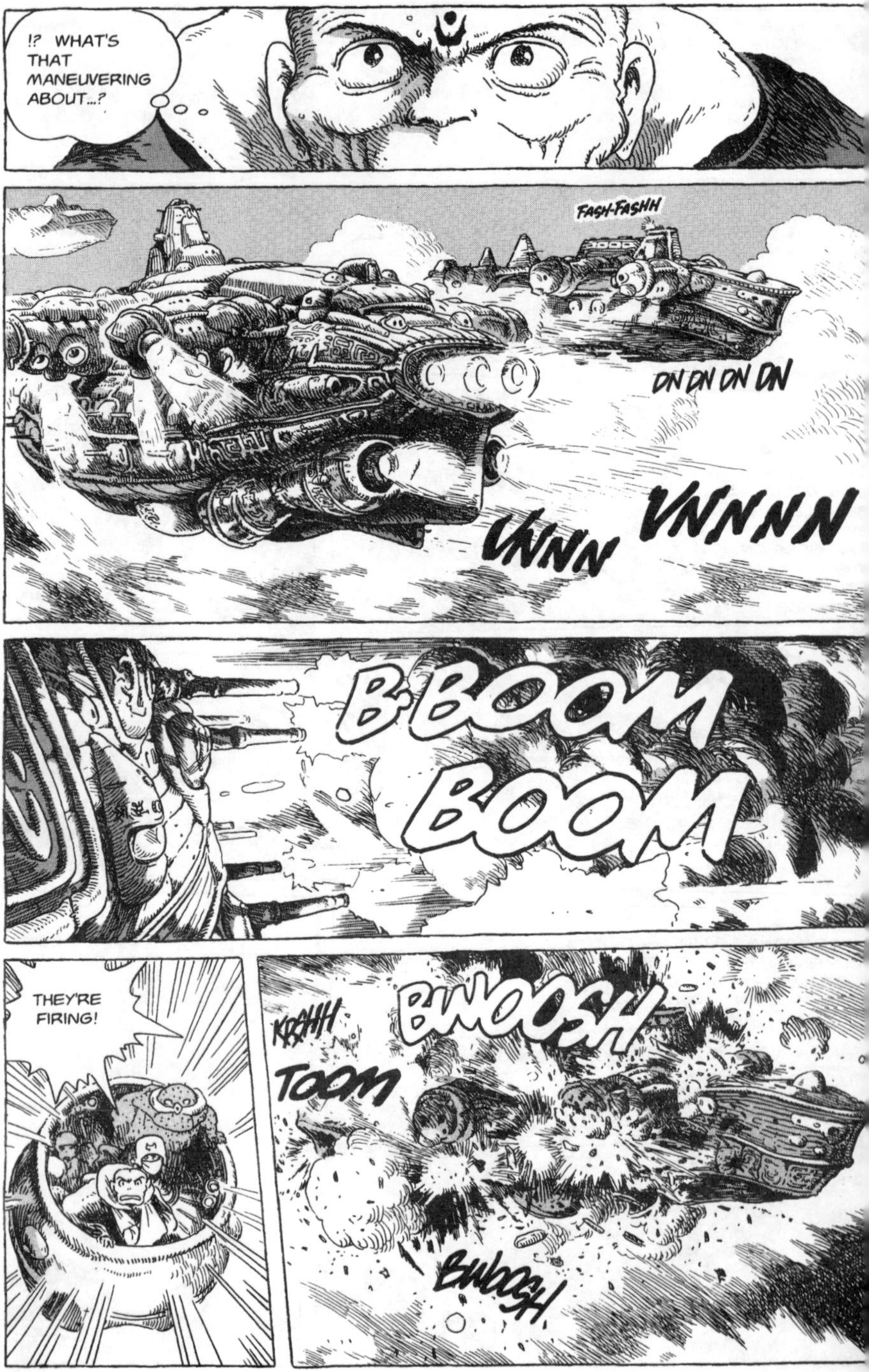
!? WHAT'S THAT MANEUVERING ABOUT...?
FASH-FASHH
DN DN DN DN
VNNN
VNNNN
B-BOOM
BOOM
THEY'RE FIRING!
BWOOSH
KRSHH
TOOM
BWOOSH

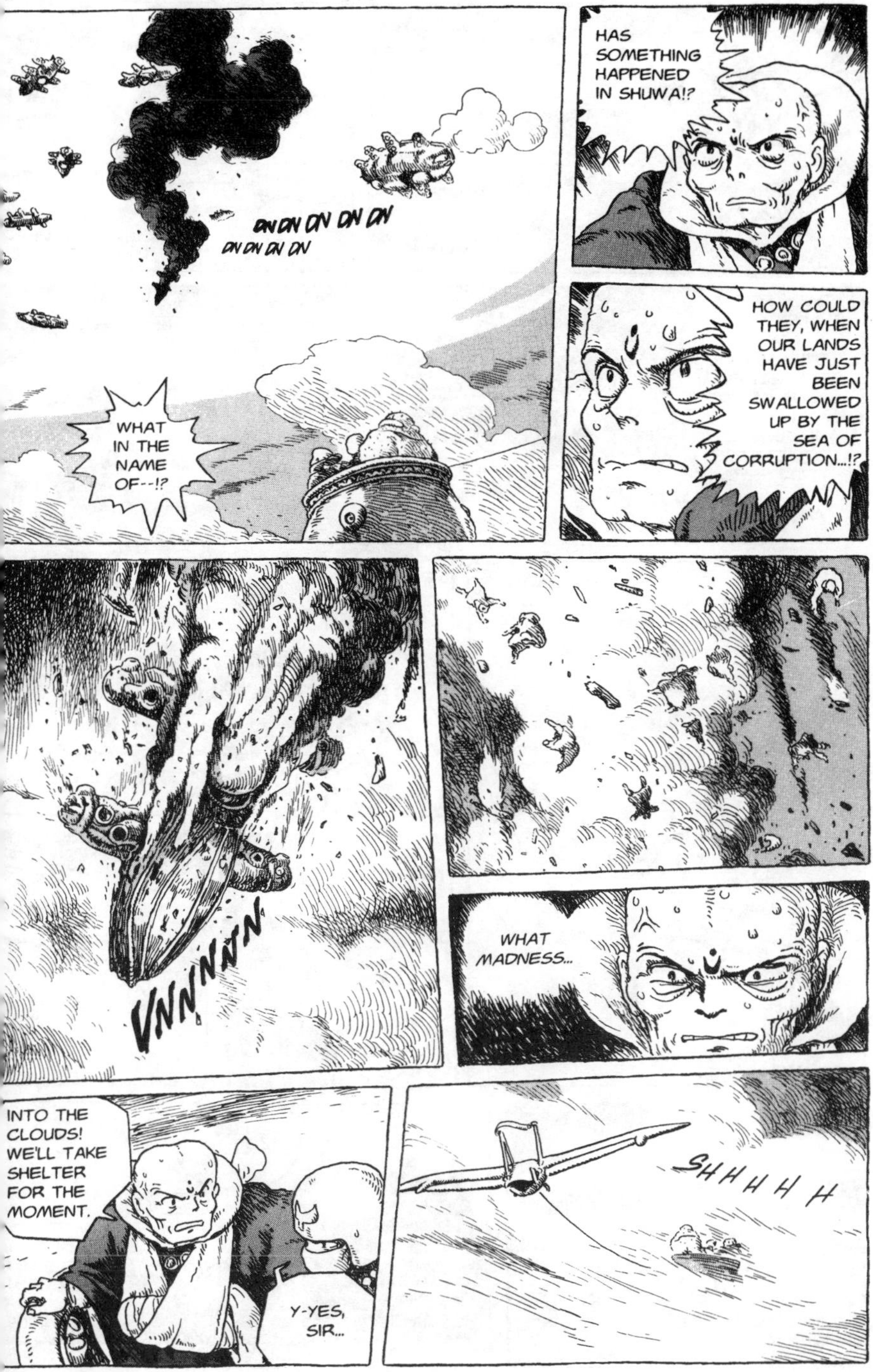

DN DN DN DN DN
DN DN DN DN
WHAT IN THE NAME OF--!?
HAS SOMETHING HAPPENED IN SHUWA!?
HOW COULD THEY, WHEN OUR LANDS HAVE JUST BEEN SWALLOWED UP BY THE SEA OF CORRUPTION...!?
VNNNNN
WHAT MADNESS...
INTO THE CLOUDS! WE'LL TAKE SHELTER FOR THE MOMENT.
Y-YES, SIR...
SHHHHH

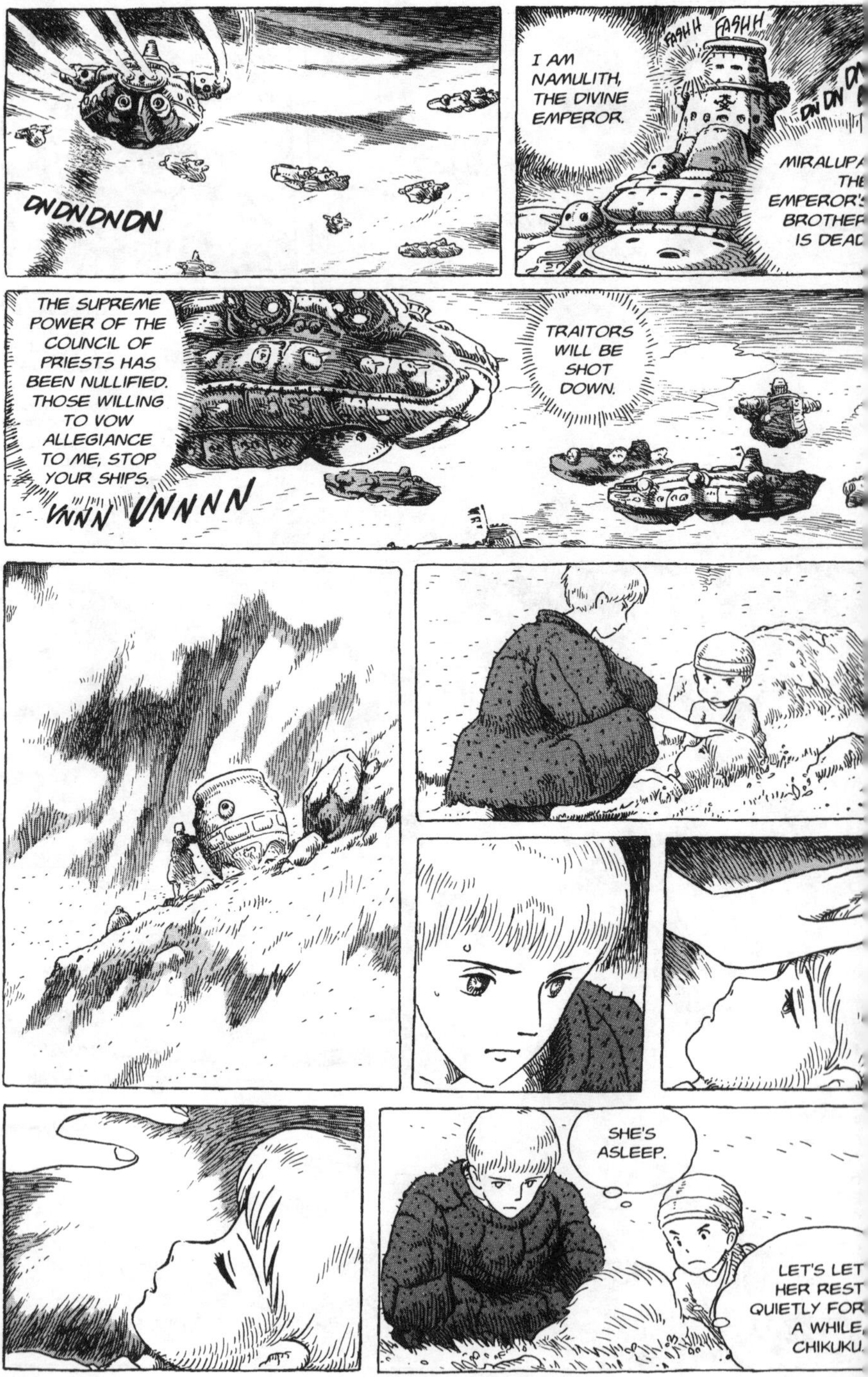
DNDNDNDN
FASHH FASHH
I AM NAMULITH, THE DIVINE EMPEROR.
DN DN DN
MIRALUPA THE EMPEROR'S BROTHER IS DEAD
THE SUPREME POWER OF THE COUNCIL OF PRIESTS HAS BEEN NULLIFIED. THOSE WILLING TO VOW ALLEGIANCE TO ME, STOP YOUR SHIPS.
TRAITORS WILL BE SHOT DOWN.
VNNN UNNNN
SHE'S ASLEEP.
LET'S LET HER REST QUIETLY FOR A WHILE, CHIKUKU.

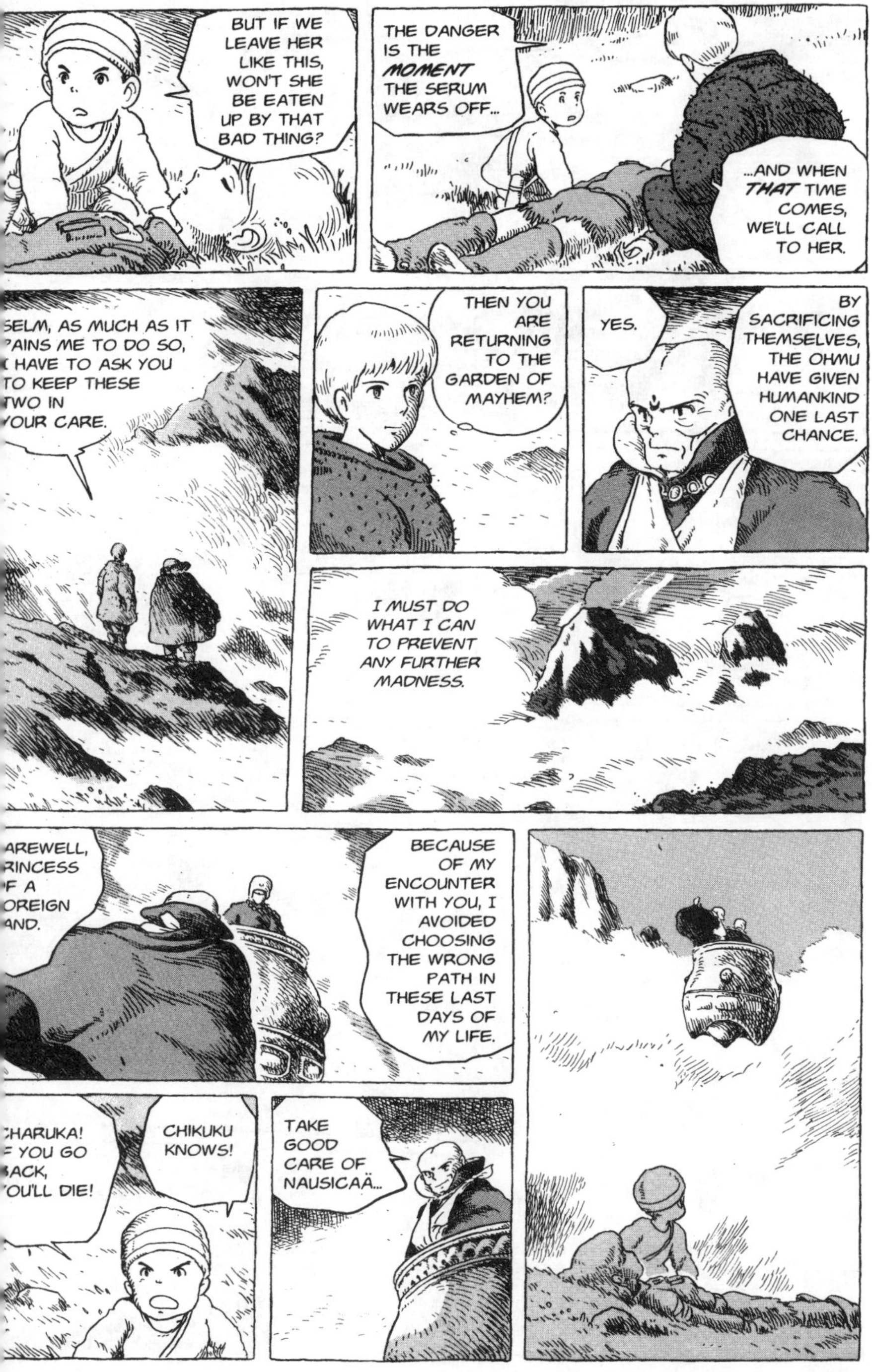
BUT IF WE LEAVE HER LIKE THIS, WON'T SHE BE EATEN UP BY THAT BAD THING?
THE DANGER IS THE MOMENT THE SERUM WEARS OFF...
...AND WHEN THAT TIME COMES, WE'LL CALL TO HER.
SELM, AS MUCH AS IT AINS ME TO DO SO, HAVE TO ASK YOU TO KEEP THESE TWO IN OUR CARE.
THEN YOU ARE RETURNING TO THE GARDEN OF MAYHEM?
YES.
BY SACRIFICING THEMSELVES, THE OHMU HAVE GIVEN HUMANKIND ONE LAST CHANCE.
I MUST DO WHAT I CAN TO PREVENT ANY FURTHER MADNESS.
AREWELL, RINCESS F A OREIGN AND.
BECAUSE OF MY ENCOUNTER WITH YOU, I AVOIDED CHOOSING THE WRONG PATH IN THESE LAST DAYS OF MY LIFE.
HARUKA! YOU GO ACK, OU'LL DIE!
CHIKUKU KNOWS!
TAKE GOOD CARE OF NAUSICAÄ...

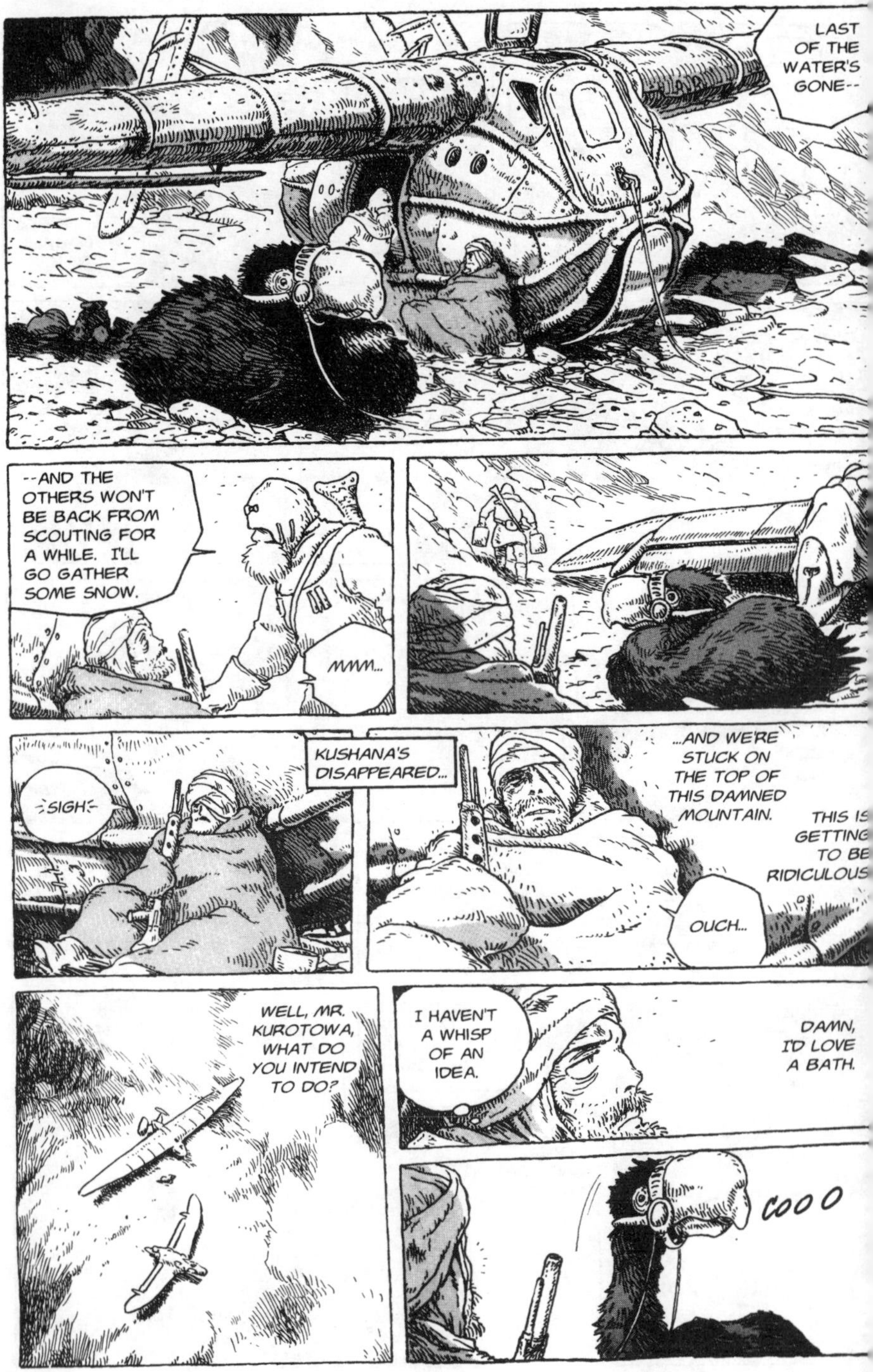
LAST OF THE WATER'S GONE--
--AND THE OTHERS WON'T BE BACK FROM SCOUTING FOR A WHILE. I'LL GO GATHER SOME SNOW.
MMM...
KUSHANA'S DISAPPEARED...
SIGH
...AND WE'RE STUCK ON THE TOP OF THIS DAMNED MOUNTAIN.
THIS IS GETTING TO BE RIDICULOUS
OUCH...
WELL, MR. KUROTOWA, WHAT DO YOU INTEND TO DO?
I HAVEN'T A WHISP OF AN IDEA.
DAMN, I'D LOVE A BATH.
COO O

KREE

H--HEY, NOW...?

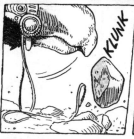

KLUNK

COO... COOOO

HOLD IT THERE! HEY!

TMP TMP TMP

WHERE DO YOU THINK YOU'RE GOING!? WHAT ABOUT YOUR EGG!?

YEOUCH!

WAIT!

OUCH!

TMP TMP

TRYING TO MAKE A FOOL OF ME, ARE YOU!?

STEADY, NOW, GIRL...

SOME REHABILI-TATION *THIS* IS.

HFF HFF

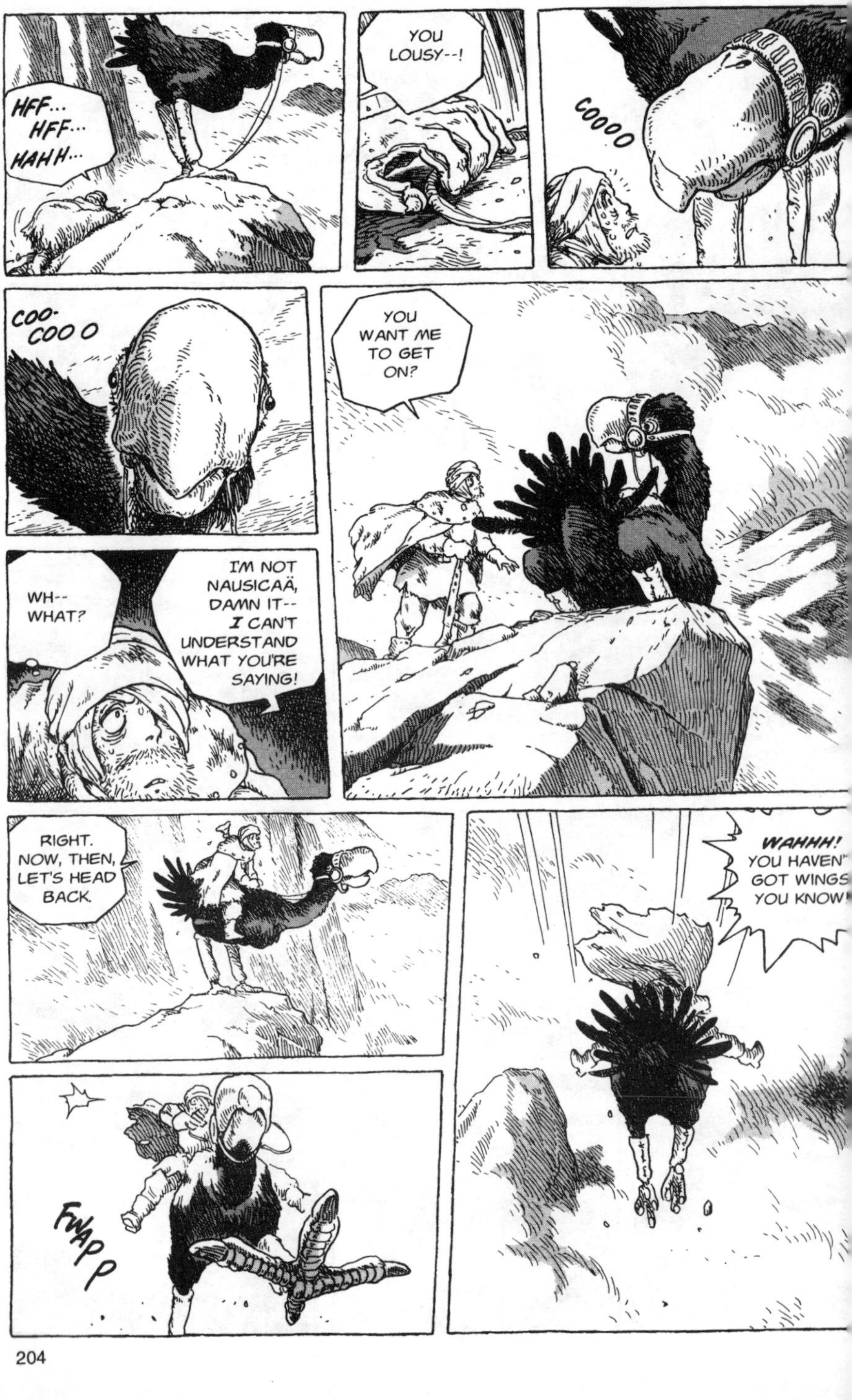
HFF... HFF... HAHH...
YOU LOUSY--!
COOOO
COO-COO O
YOU WANT ME TO GET ON?
WH-- WHAT?
I'M NOT NAUSICAÄ, DAMN IT-- I CAN'T UNDERSTAND WHAT YOU'RE SAYING!
RIGHT. NOW, THEN, LET'S HEAD BACK.
FWAPP
WAHHH! YOU HAVEN' GOT WINGS YOU KNOW

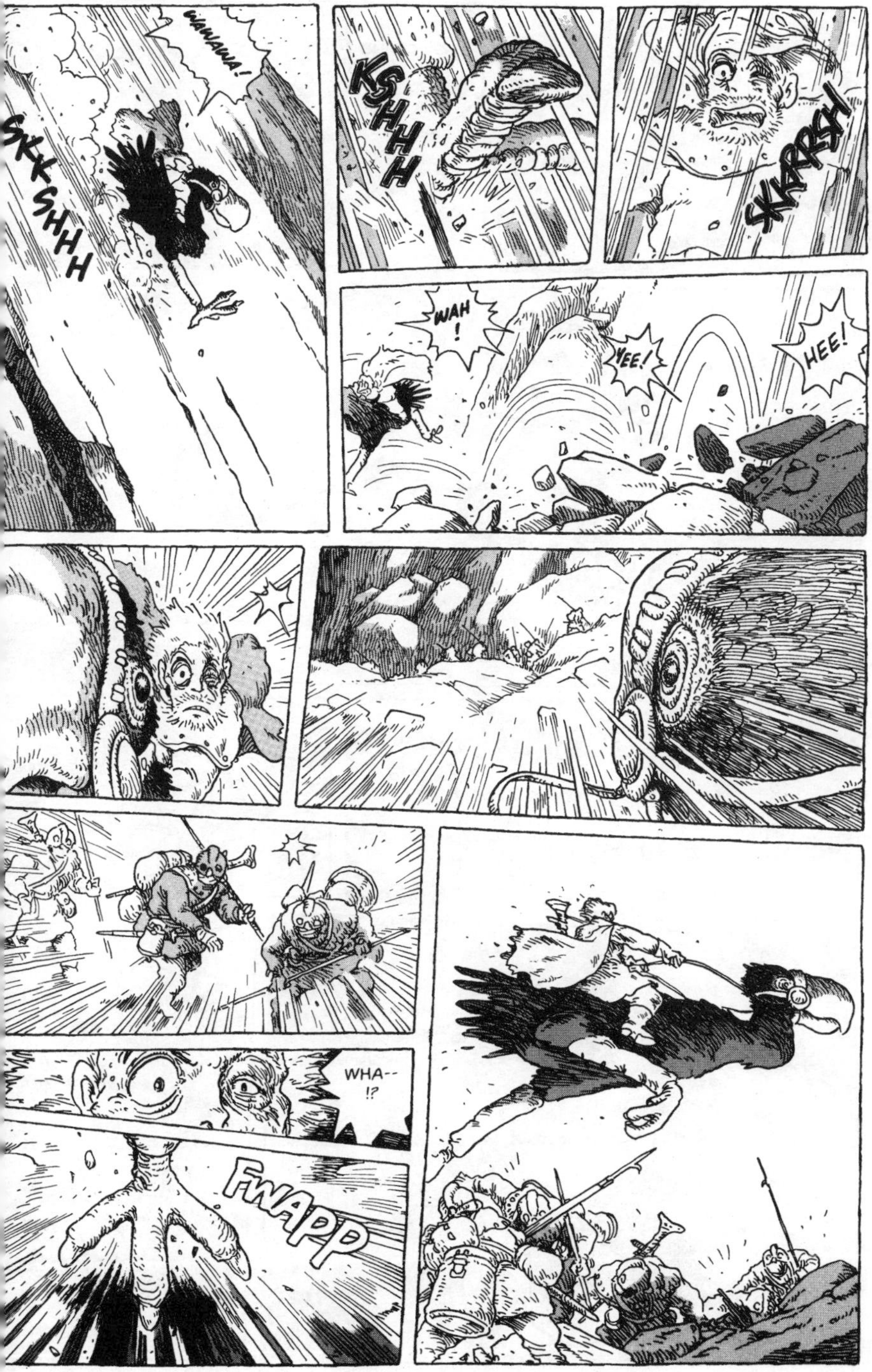
WAWAWAWA!
SKKSHHH
KSHHH
SKARRSH
WAH!
YEE!
HEE!
WHA--!?
FWAPP

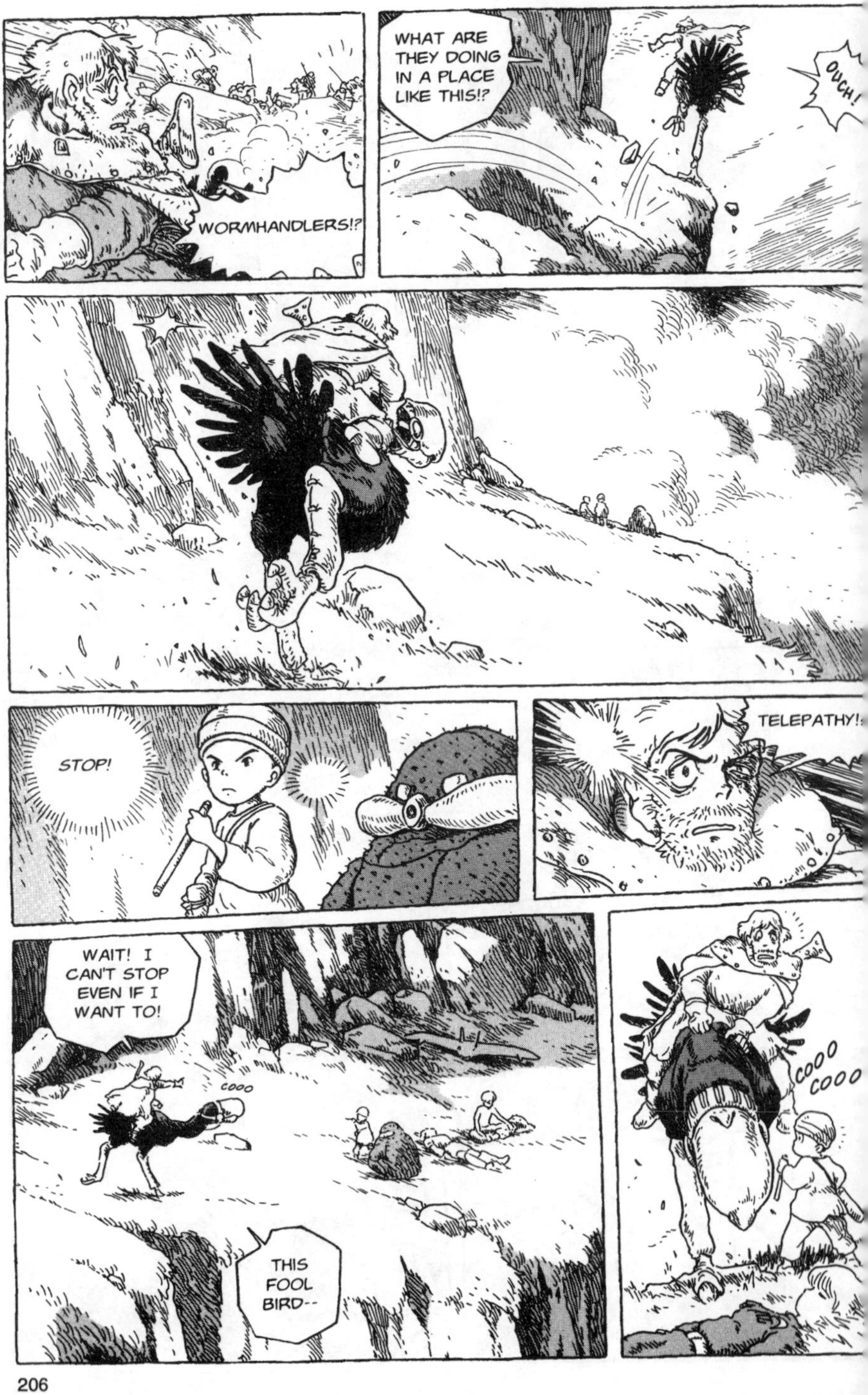
WORMHANDLERS!?
WHAT ARE THEY DOING IN A PLACE LIKE THIS!?
OUCH!
STOP!
TELEPATHY!
WAIT! I CAN'T STOP EVEN IF I WANT TO!
COOO
THIS FOOL BIRD--
COOO COOO

COO COOO

HEY! STOP!

IT'S ALL RIGHT, CHIKUKU. IT SEEMS THEY ARE OLD FRIENDS OF NAUSICAÄ'S.

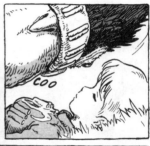

COO

WH--!? IT'S NAUSICAÄ!!

WHAT'S HAPPENED!?

IS SHE DEAD!?

SHE'S ASLEEP.

QUIETLY, PLEASE.

HMM? WHY THE GLOOMY FACE...?

SWISH
SWISH

KEE

HSSS

TETO'S AWAKE! THE SERUM'S WORN OFF!

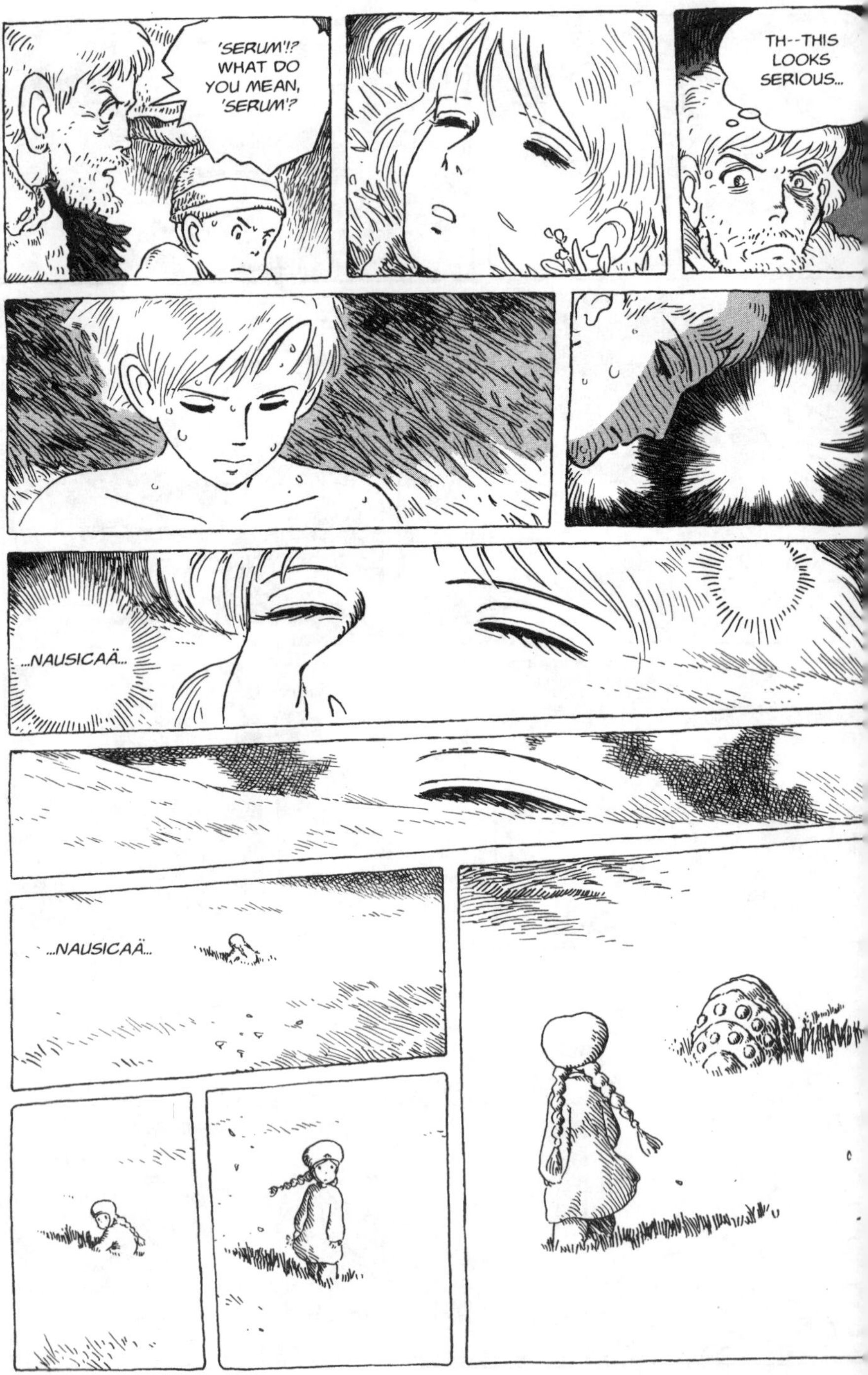
'SERUM'!? WHAT DO YOU MEAN, 'SERUM'?
TH--THIS LOOKS SERIOUS...
...NAUSICAÄ...
...NAUSICAÄ...

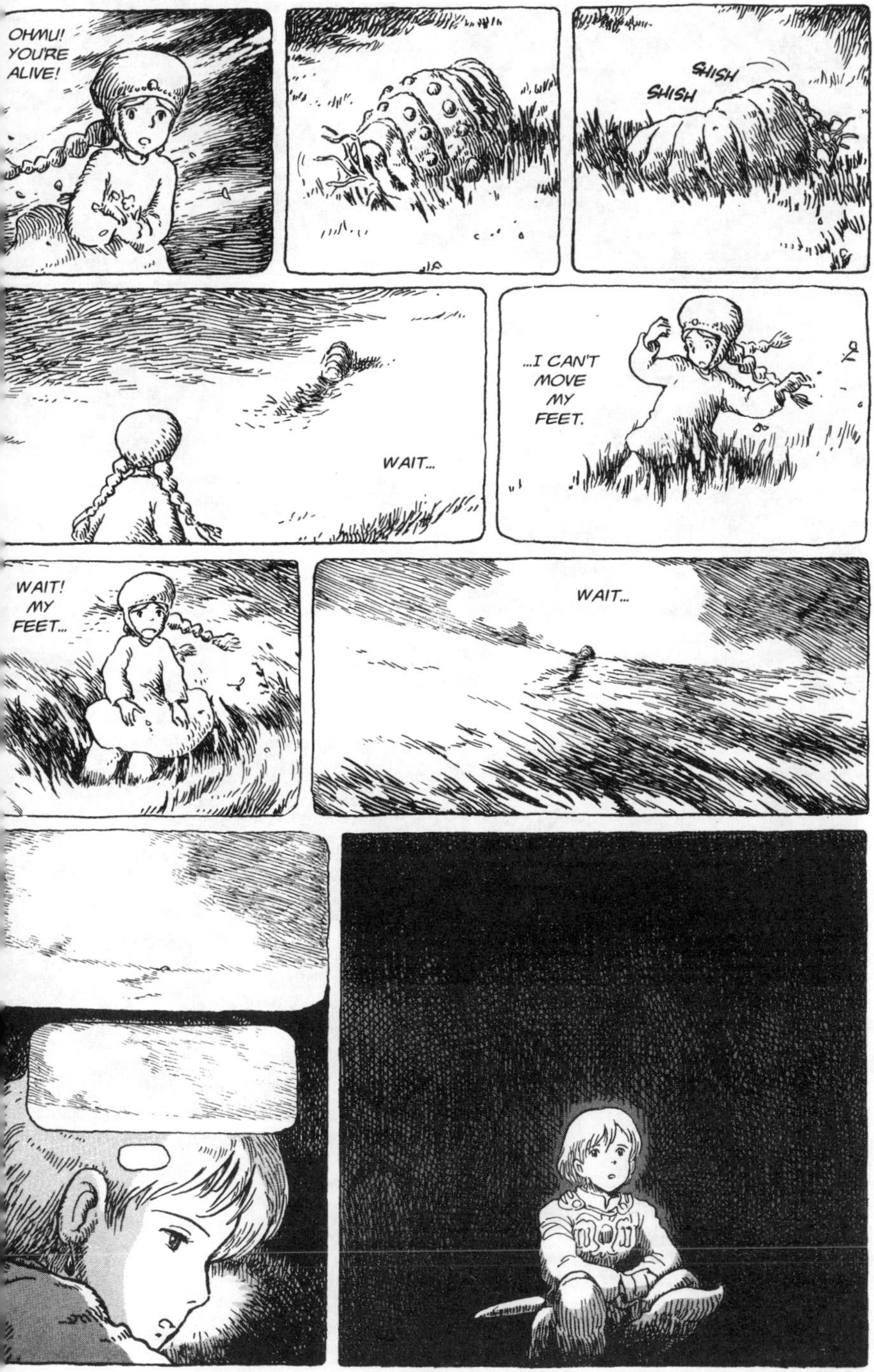
OHMU! YOU'RE ALIVE!
SHISH
SHISH
WAIT...
...I CAN'T MOVE MY FEET.
WAIT! MY FEET...
WAIT...

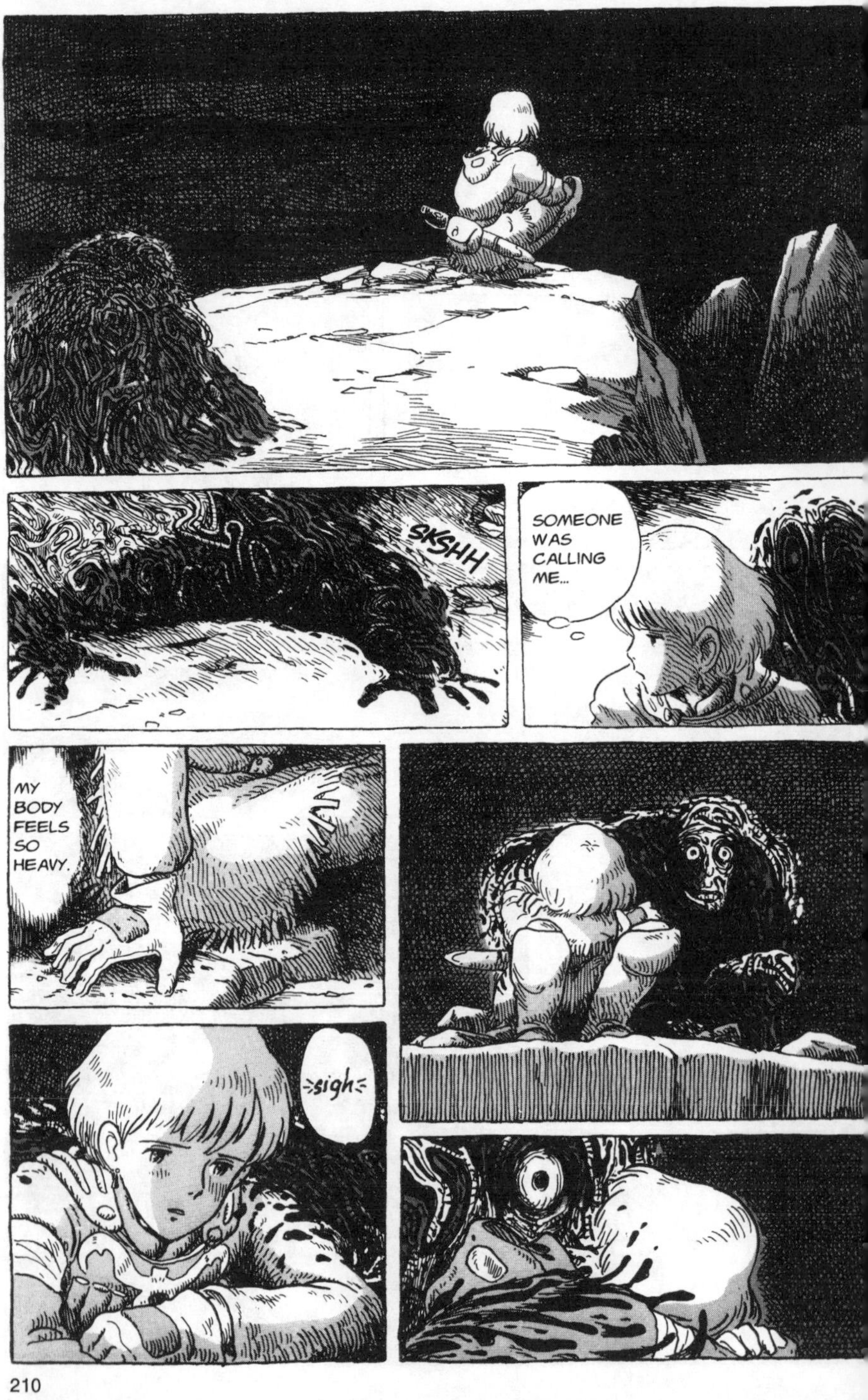
SKSHH
SOMEONE WAS CALLING ME...
MY BODY FEELS SO HEAVY.
sigh

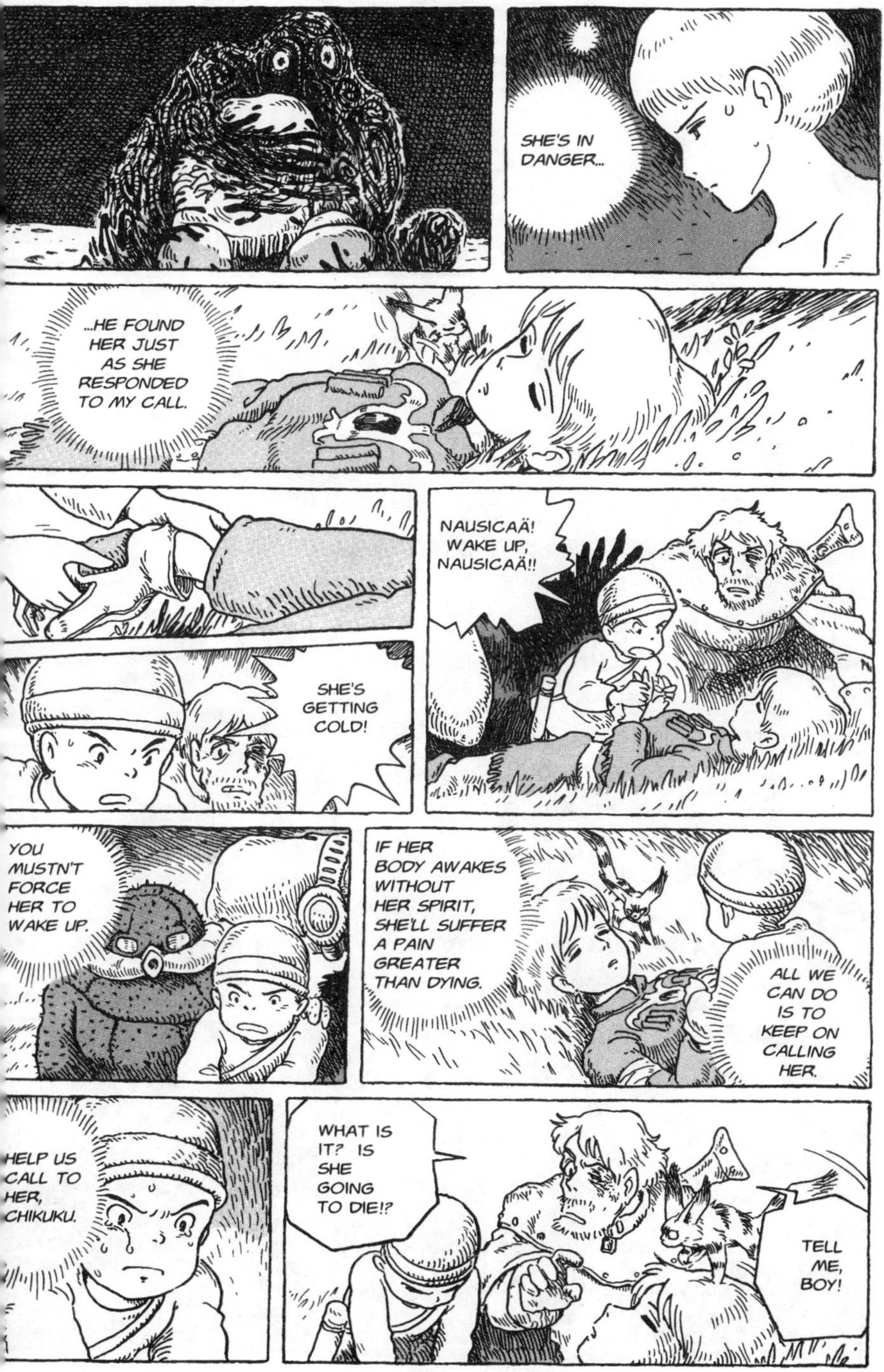
SHE'S IN DANGER...
...HE FOUND HER JUST AS SHE RESPONDED TO MY CALL.
NAUSICAÄ! WAKE UP, NAUSICAÄ!!
SHE'S GETTING COLD!
YOU MUSTN'T FORCE HER TO WAKE UP.
IF HER BODY AWAKES WITHOUT HER SPIRIT, SHE'LL SUFFER A PAIN GREATER THAN DYING.
ALL WE CAN DO IS TO KEEP ON CALLING HER.
HELP US CALL TO HER, CHIKUKU.
WHAT IS IT? IS SHE GOING TO DIE!?
TELL ME, BOY!

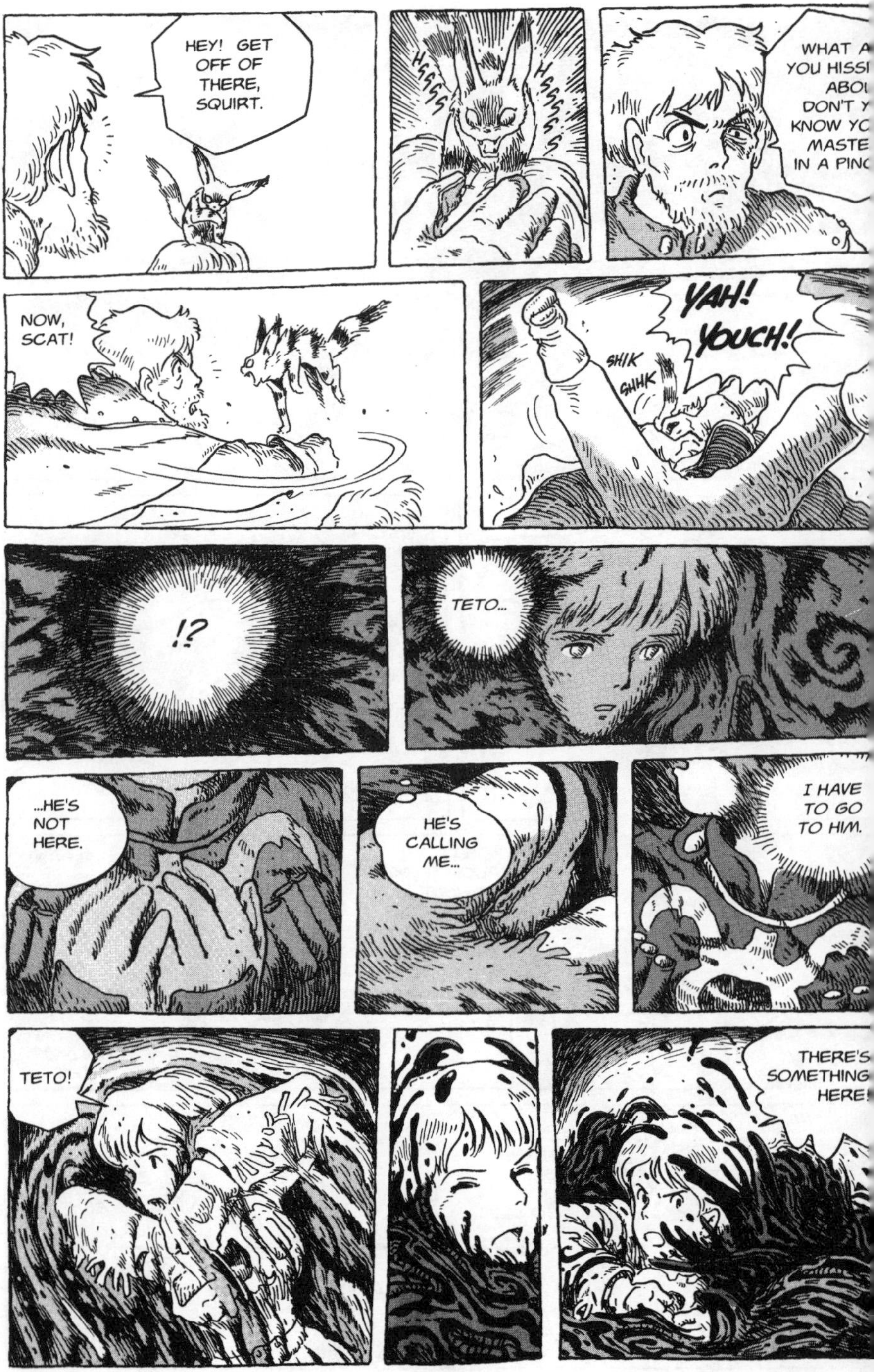
HEY! GET OFF OF THERE, SQUIRT.
HSSSS
WHAT A YOU HISSI ABOU DON'T Y KNOW YO MASTE IN A PIN
NOW, SCAT!
YAH! YOUCH!
SHIK SHHK
!?
TETO...
...HE'S NOT HERE.
HE'S CALLING ME...
I HAVE TO GO TO HIM.
TETO!
THERE'S SOMETHING HERE!

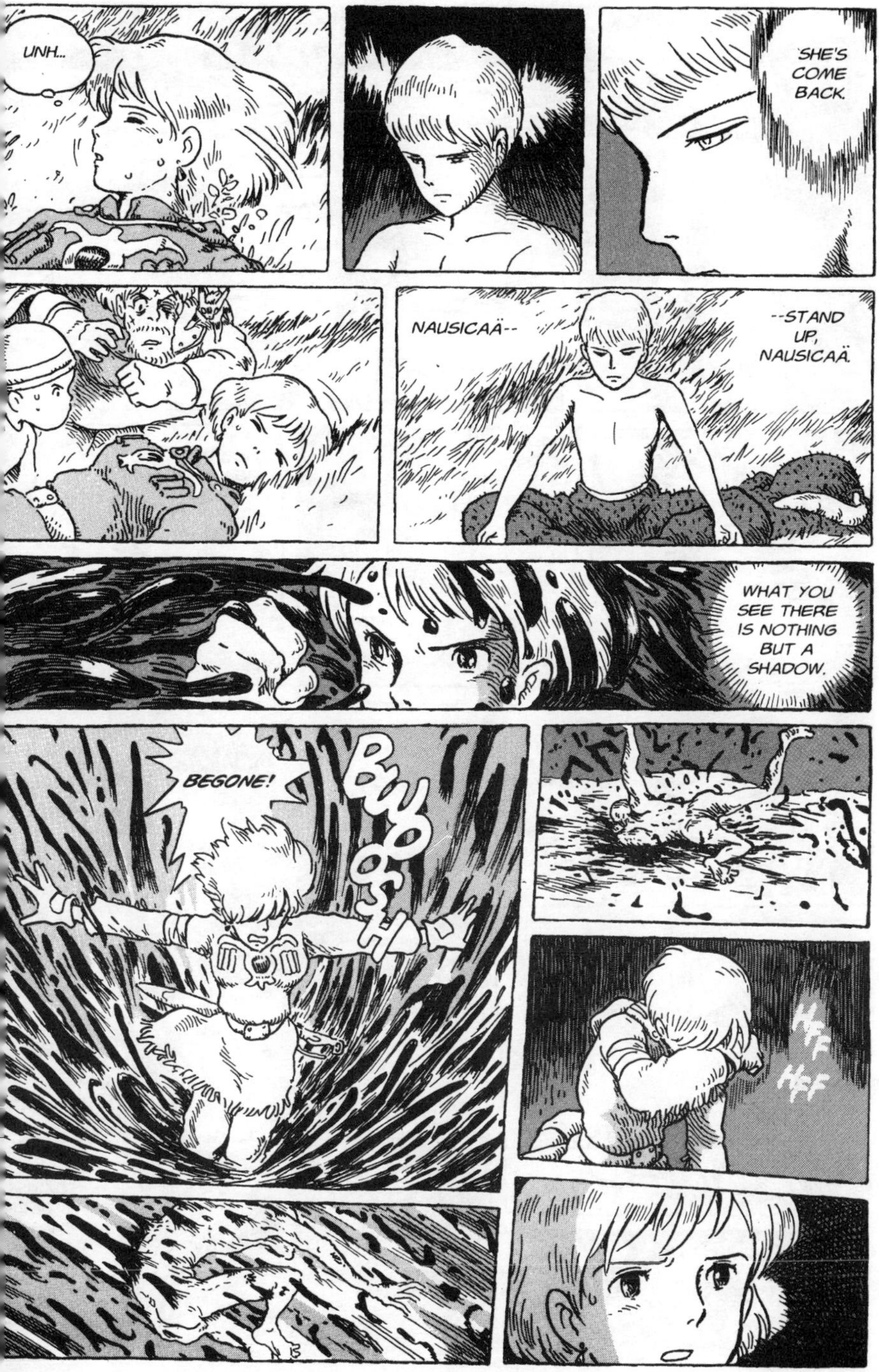

UNH...
SHE'S COME BACK.
NAUSICAÄ--
--STAND UP, NAUSICAÄ.
WHAT YOU SEE THERE IS NOTHING BUT A SHADOW.
BEGONE!
BWOOSH
HFF HFF

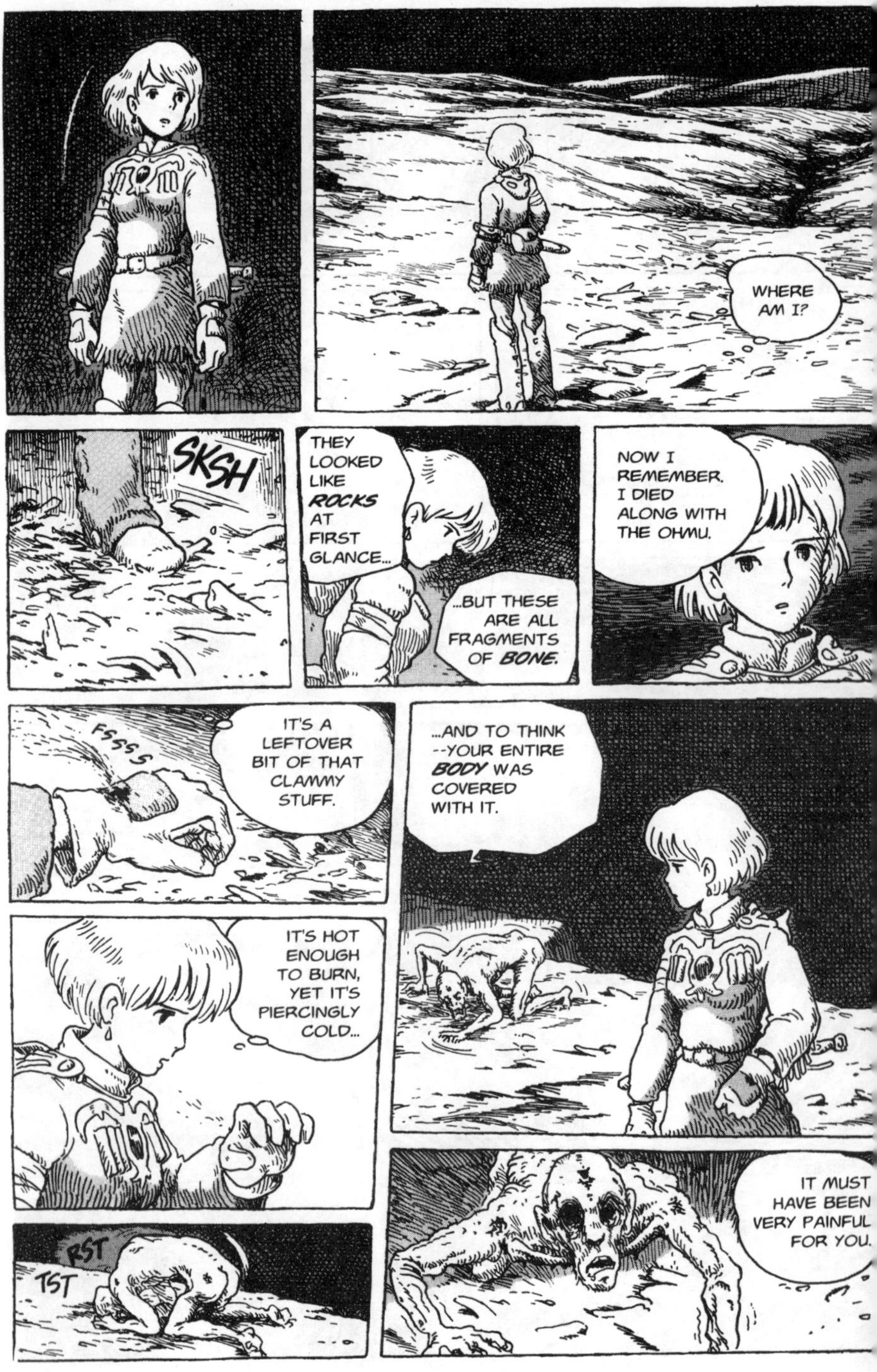
WHERE AM I?
SKSH
THEY LOOKED LIKE ROCKS AT FIRST GLANCE...
...BUT THESE ARE ALL FRAGMENTS OF BONE.
NOW I REMEMBER. I DIED ALONG WITH THE OHMU.
FSSSS
IT'S A LEFTOVER BIT OF THAT CLAMMY STUFF.
...AND TO THINK --YOUR ENTIRE BODY WAS COVERED WITH IT.
IT'S HOT ENOUGH TO BURN, YET IT'S PIERCINGLY COLD...
RST
TST
IT MUST HAVE BEEN VERY PAINFUL FOR YOU.

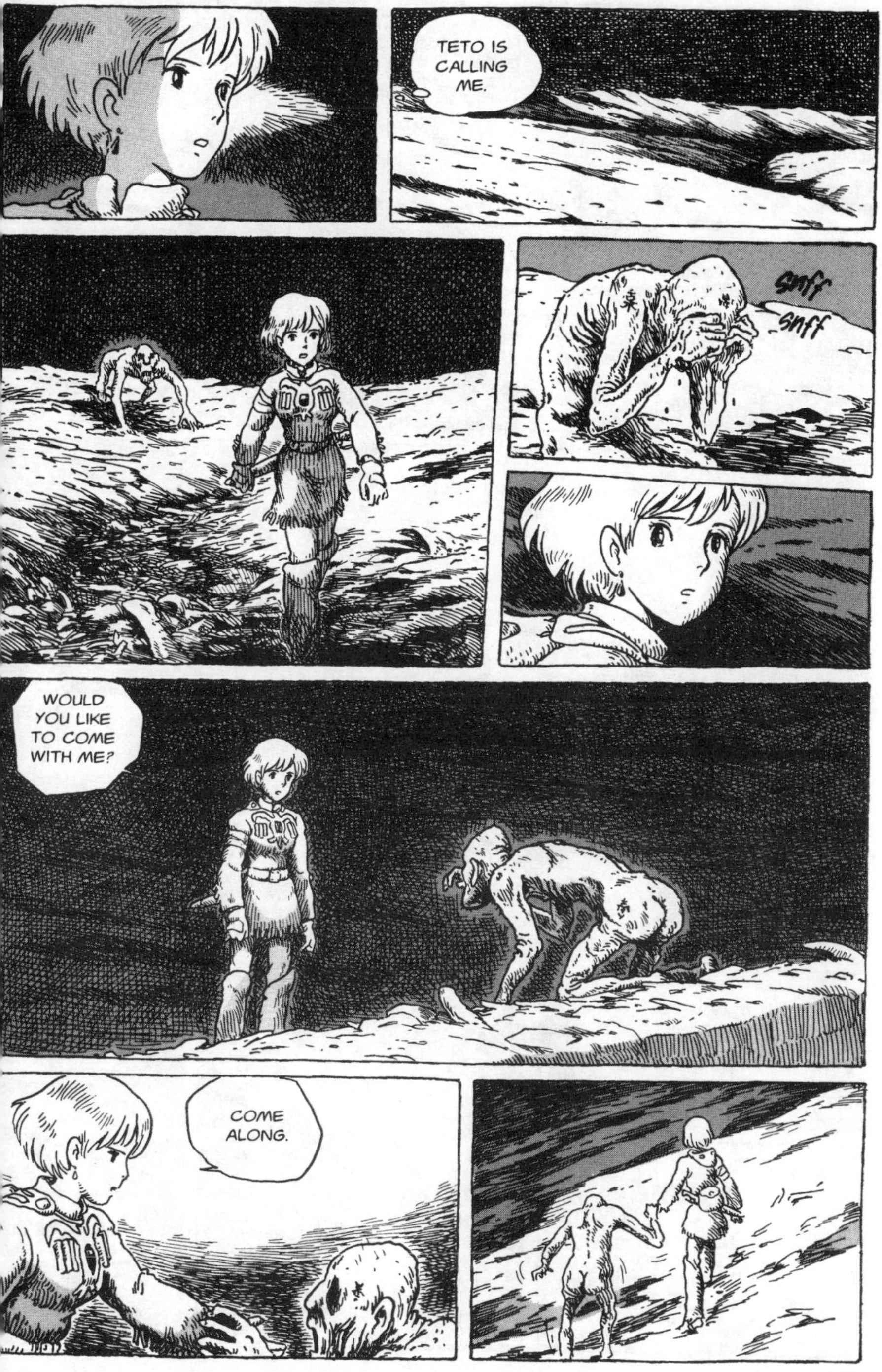
TETO IS CALLING ME.
snff
snff
WOULD YOU LIKE TO COME WITH ME?
COME ALONG.

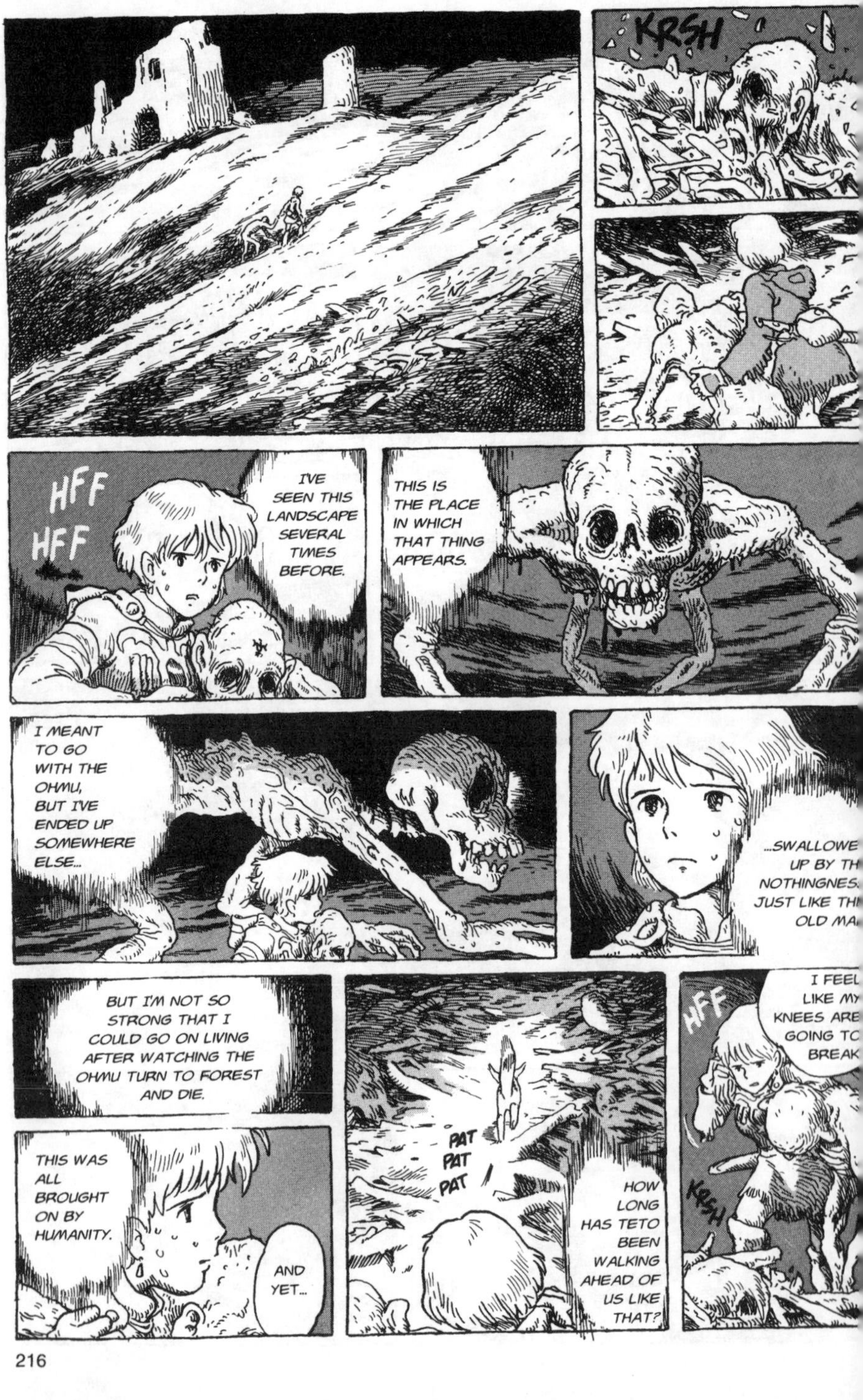
KRSH
HFF HFF
I'VE SEEN THIS LANDSCAPE SEVERAL TIMES BEFORE.
THIS IS THE PLACE IN WHICH THAT THING APPEARS.
I MEANT TO GO WITH THE OHMU, BUT I'VE ENDED UP SOMEWHERE ELSE...
...SWALLOWE UP BY TH NOTHINGNES JUST LIKE TH OLD MA
BUT I'M NOT SO STRONG THAT I COULD GO ON LIVING AFTER WATCHING THE OHMU TURN TO FOREST AND DIE.
HFF
I FEEL LIKE MY KNEES ARE GOING TO BREAK
KRSH
THIS WAS ALL BROUGHT ON BY HUMANITY.
AND YET...
PAT PAT PAT
HOW LONG HAS TETO BEEN WALKING AHEAD OF US LIKE THAT?

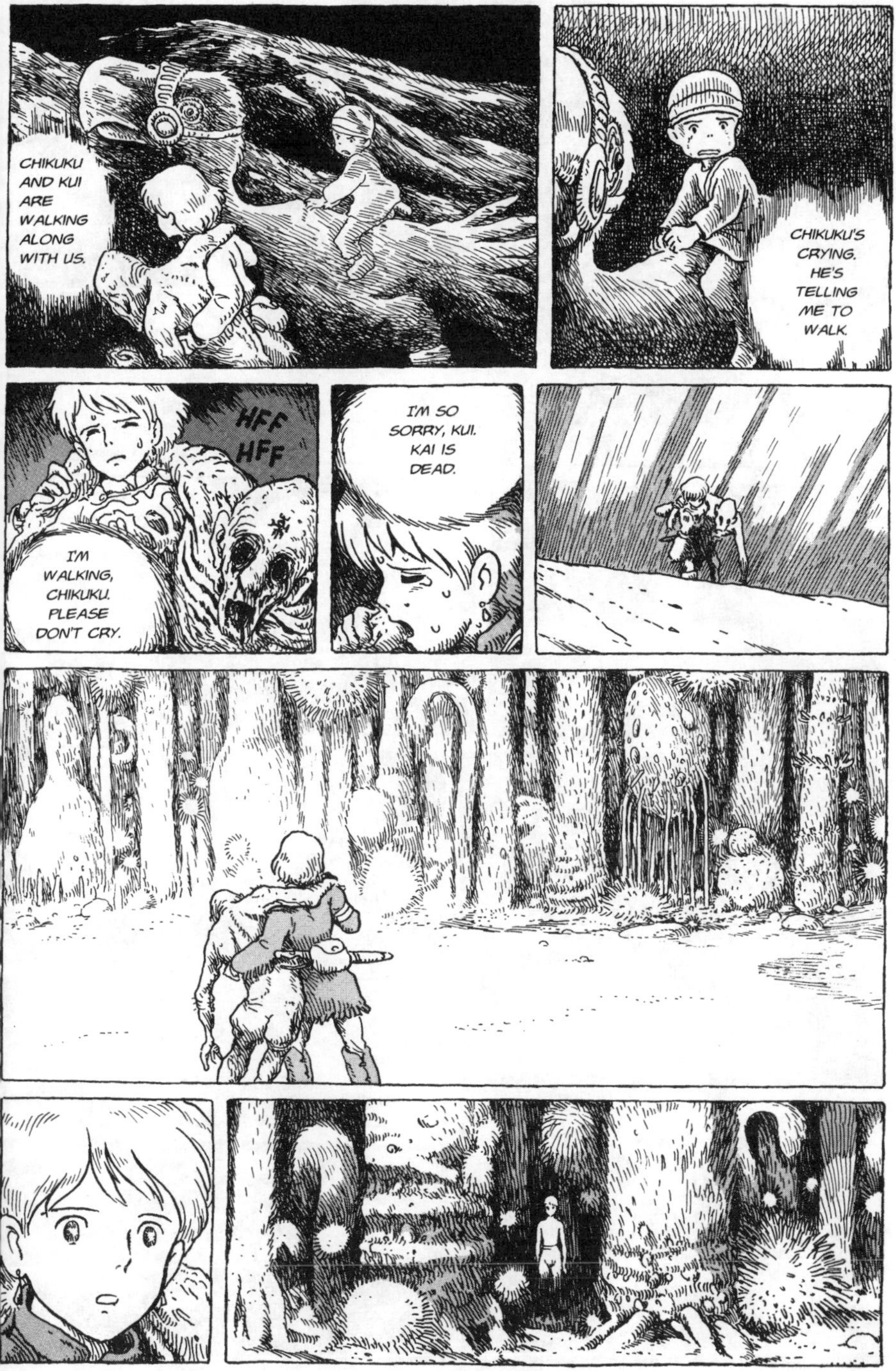
CHIKUKU AND KUI ARE WALKING ALONG WITH US.
CHIKUKU'S CRYING. HE'S TELLING ME TO WALK.
HFF HFF
I'M WALKING, CHIKUKU. PLEASE DON'T CRY.
I'M SO SORRY, KUI. KAI IS DEAD.

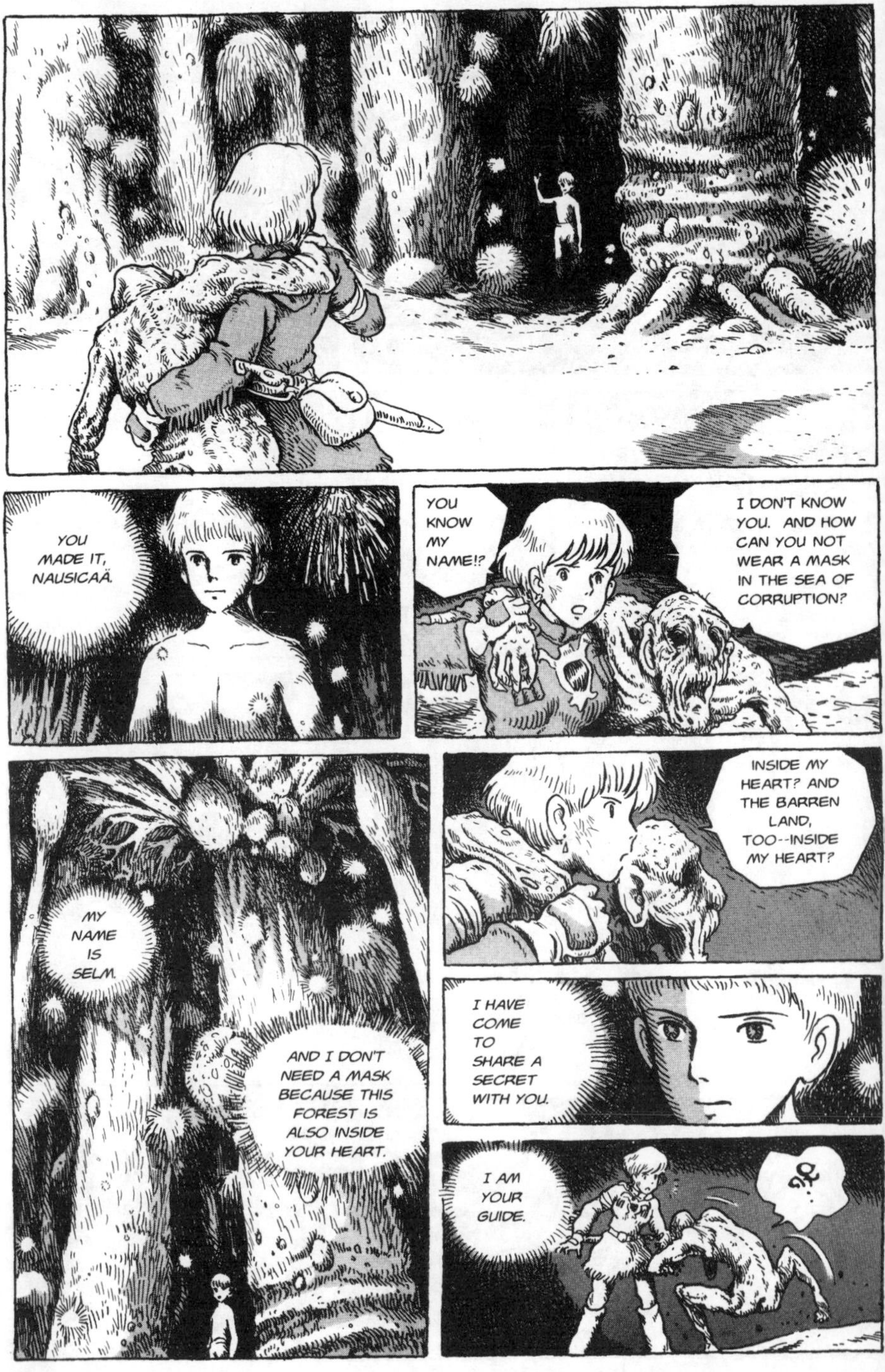
YOU MADE IT, NAUSICAÄ.
YOU KNOW MY NAME!?
I DON'T KNOW YOU. AND HOW CAN YOU NOT WEAR A MASK IN THE SEA OF CORRUPTION?
MY NAME IS SELM.
AND I DON'T NEED A MASK BECAUSE THIS FOREST IS ALSO INSIDE YOUR HEART.
INSIDE MY HEART? AND THE BARREN LAND, TOO--INSIDE MY HEART?
I HAVE COME TO SHARE A SECRET WITH YOU.
I AM YOUR GUIDE.
?!

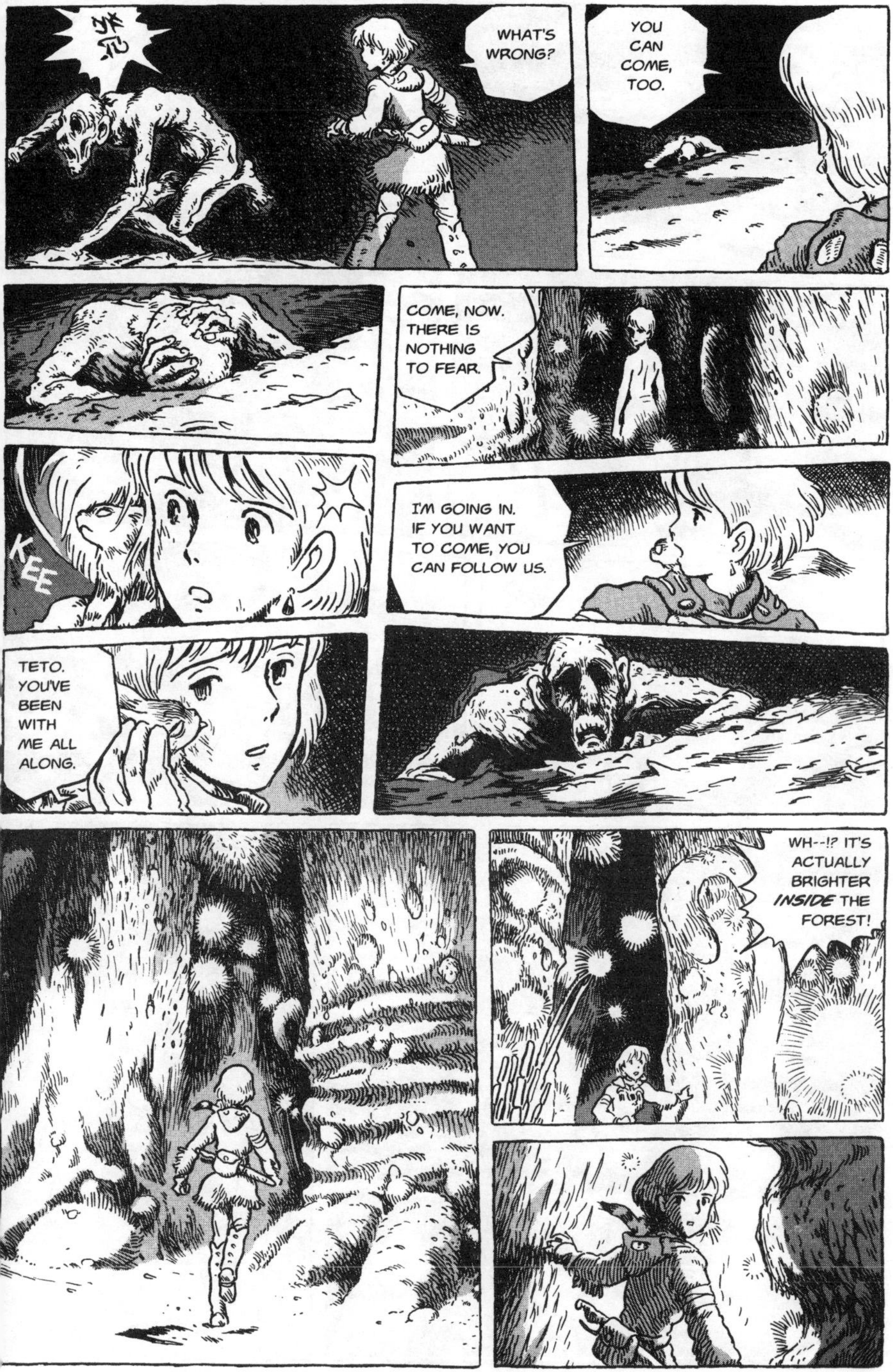
WHAT'S WRONG?
YOU CAN COME, TOO.
COME, NOW. THERE IS NOTHING TO FEAR.
KEE
I'M GOING IN. IF YOU WANT TO COME, YOU CAN FOLLOW US.
TETO. YOU'VE BEEN WITH ME ALL ALONG.
WH--!? IT'S ACTUALLY BRIGHTER *INSIDE* THE FOREST!

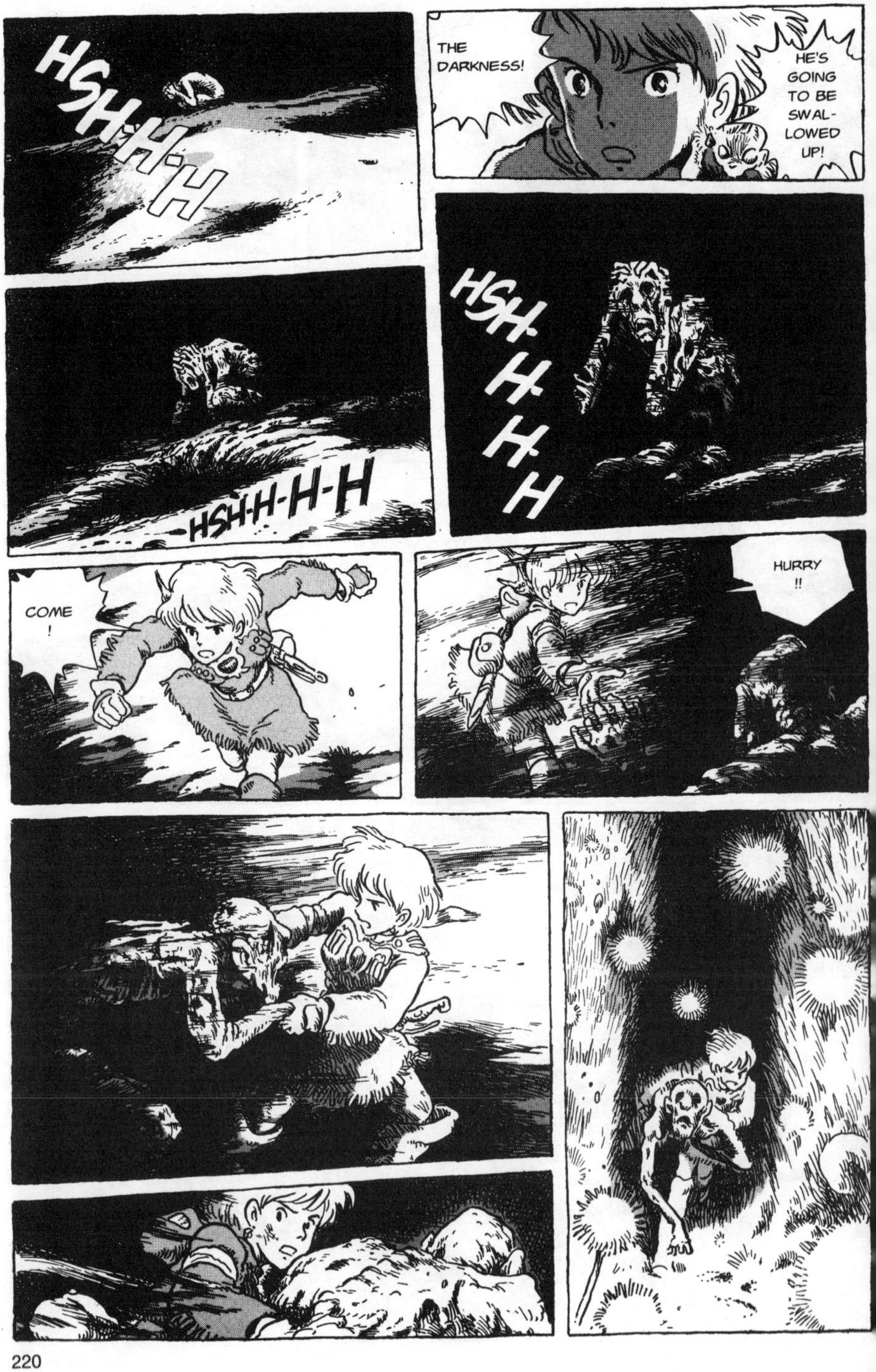
HSH-H-H-H
THE DARKNESS!
HE'S GOING TO BE SWAL-LOWED UP!
HSH-H-H-H
HSH-H-H-H-H
COME !
HURRY !!

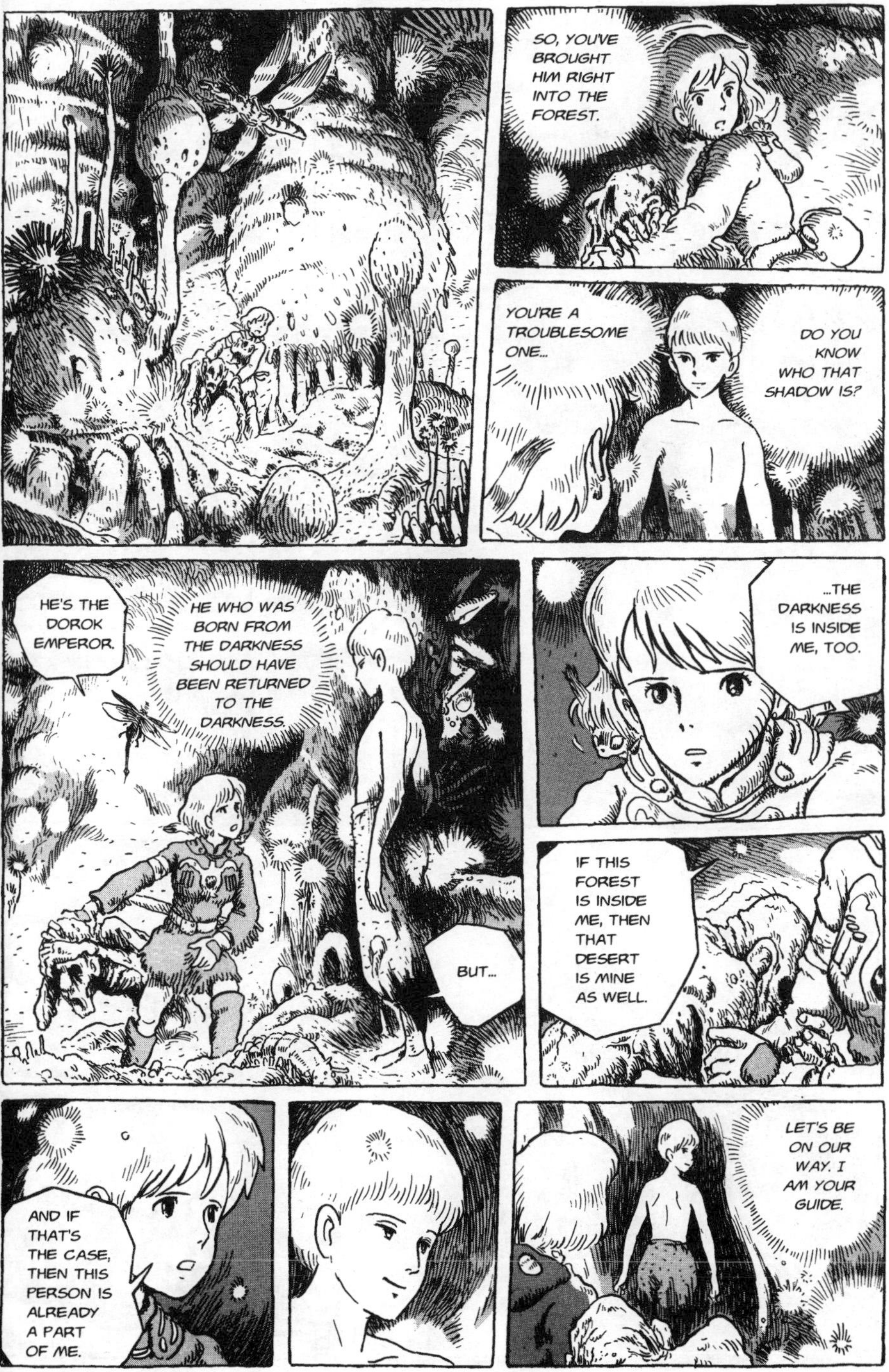
SO, YOU'VE BROUGHT HIM RIGHT INTO THE FOREST.
YOU'RE A TROUBLESOME ONE...
DO YOU KNOW WHO THAT SHADOW IS?
HE'S THE DOROK EMPEROR.
HE WHO WAS BORN FROM THE DARKNESS SHOULD HAVE BEEN RETURNED TO THE DARKNESS.
BUT...
...THE DARKNESS IS INSIDE ME, TOO.
IF THIS FOREST IS INSIDE ME, THEN THAT DESERT IS MINE AS WELL.
AND IF THAT'S THE CASE, THEN THIS PERSON IS ALREADY A PART OF ME.
LET'S BE ON OUR WAY. I AM YOUR GUIDE.

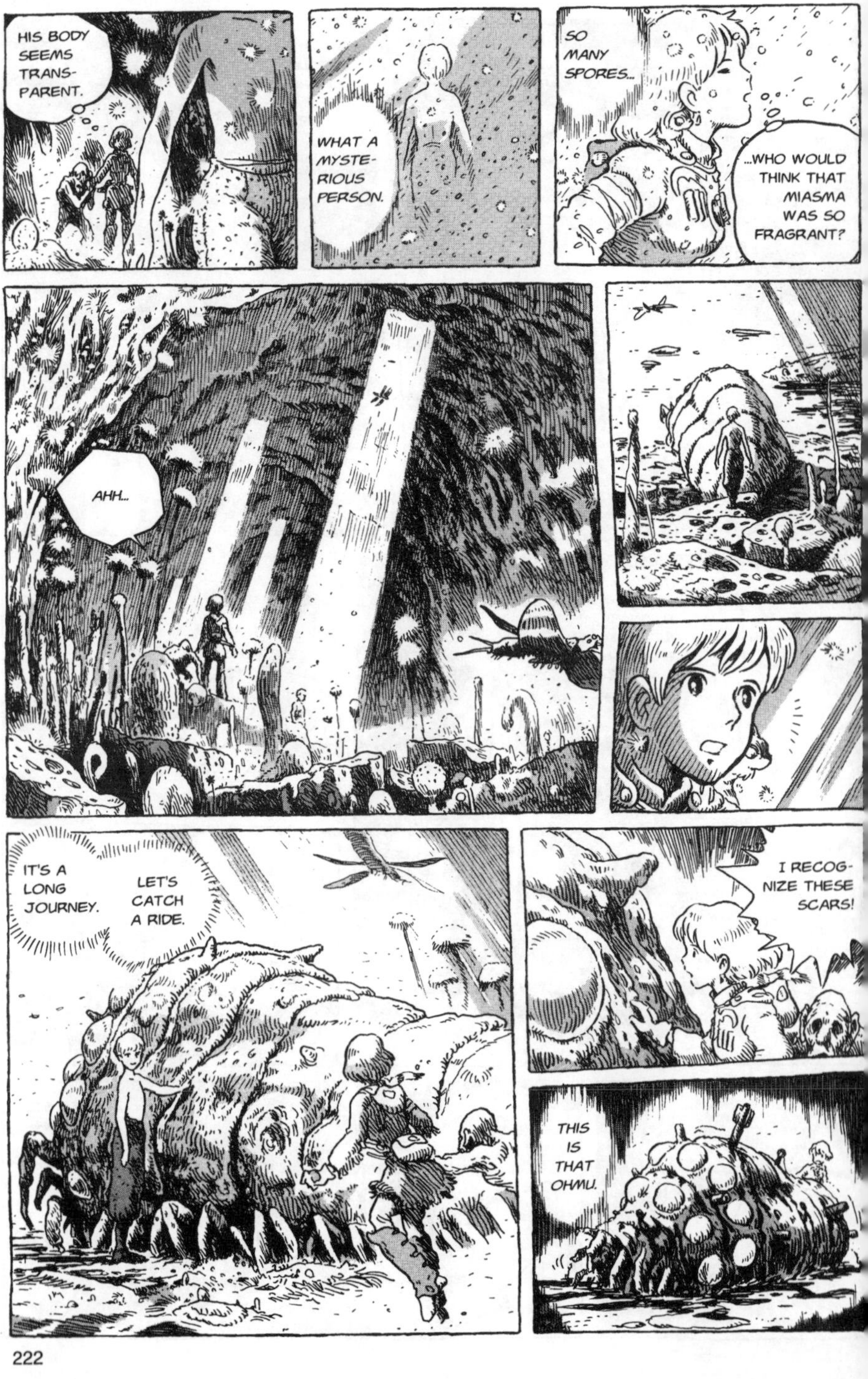
HIS BODY SEEMS TRANS-PARENT.
WHAT A MYSTE-RIOUS PERSON.
SO MANY SPORES...
...WHO WOULD THINK THAT MIASMA WAS SO FRAGRANT?
AHH...
IT'S A LONG JOURNEY.
LET'S CATCH A RIDE.
I RECOG-NIZE THESE SCARS!
THIS IS THAT OHMU.

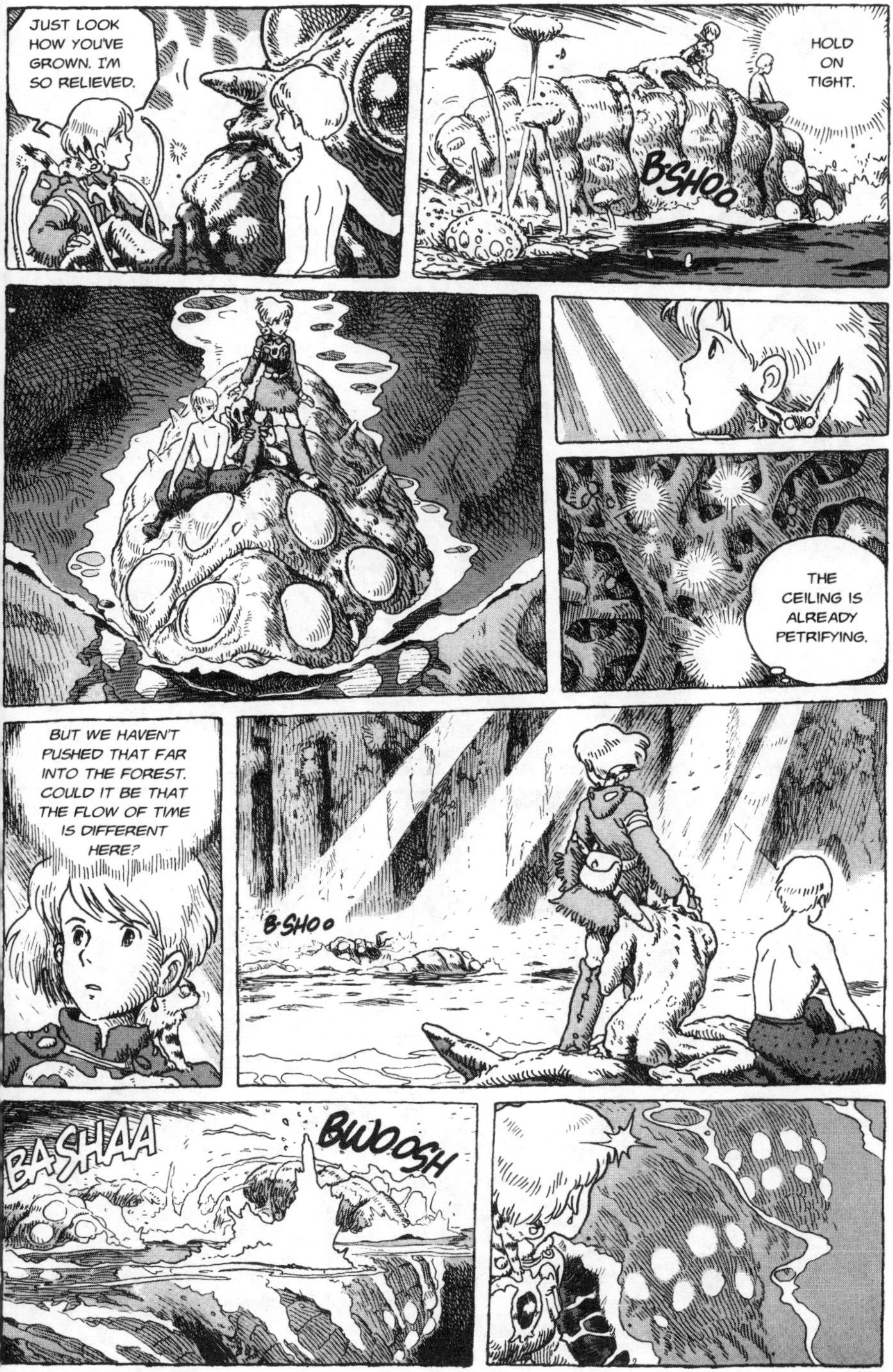
JUST LOOK HOW YOU'VE GROWN. I'M SO RELIEVED.
HOLD ON TIGHT.
B-SHOO
THE CEILING IS ALREADY PETRIFYING.
BUT WE HAVEN'T PUSHED THAT FAR INTO THE FOREST. COULD IT BE THAT THE FLOW OF TIME IS DIFFERENT HERE?
B-SHOO
BASHAA
BWOOSH

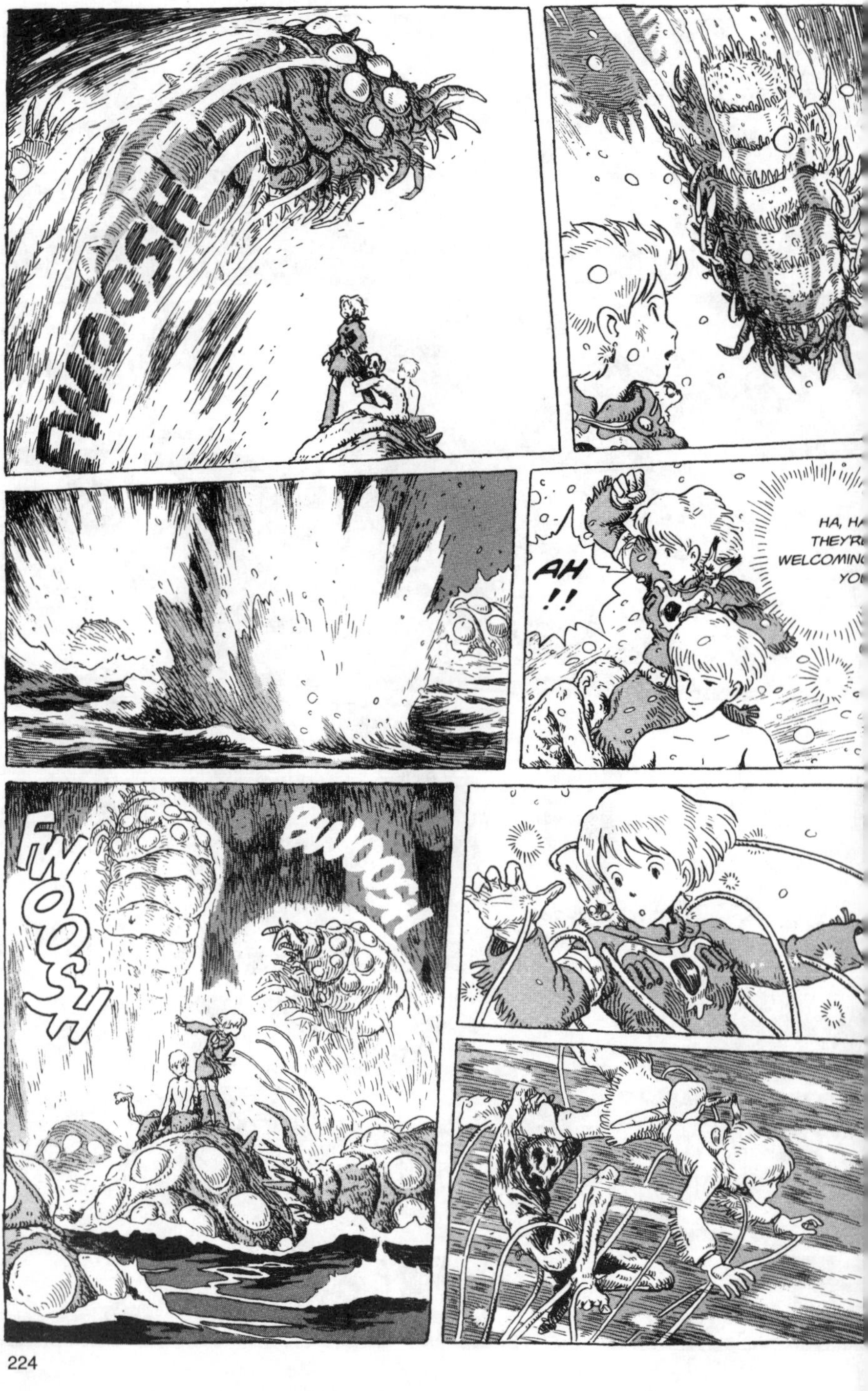
WHOOSH
AH !!
HA, HA
THEY'RE
WELCOMING
YO
FWOOSH
BWOOSH

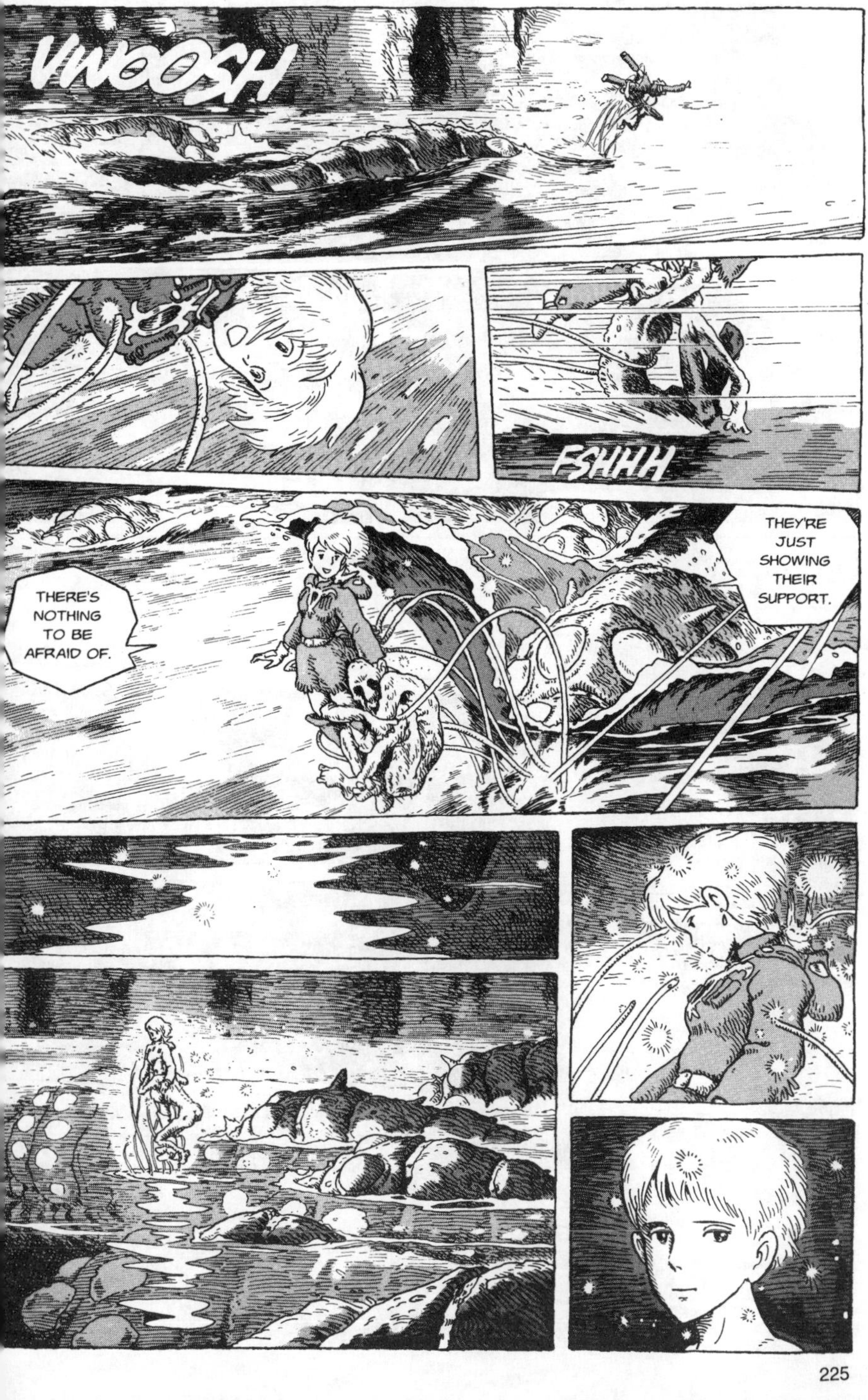
VWOOSH
FSHHH
THERE'S NOTHING TO BE AFRAID OF.
THEY'RE JUST SHOWING THEIR SUPPORT.

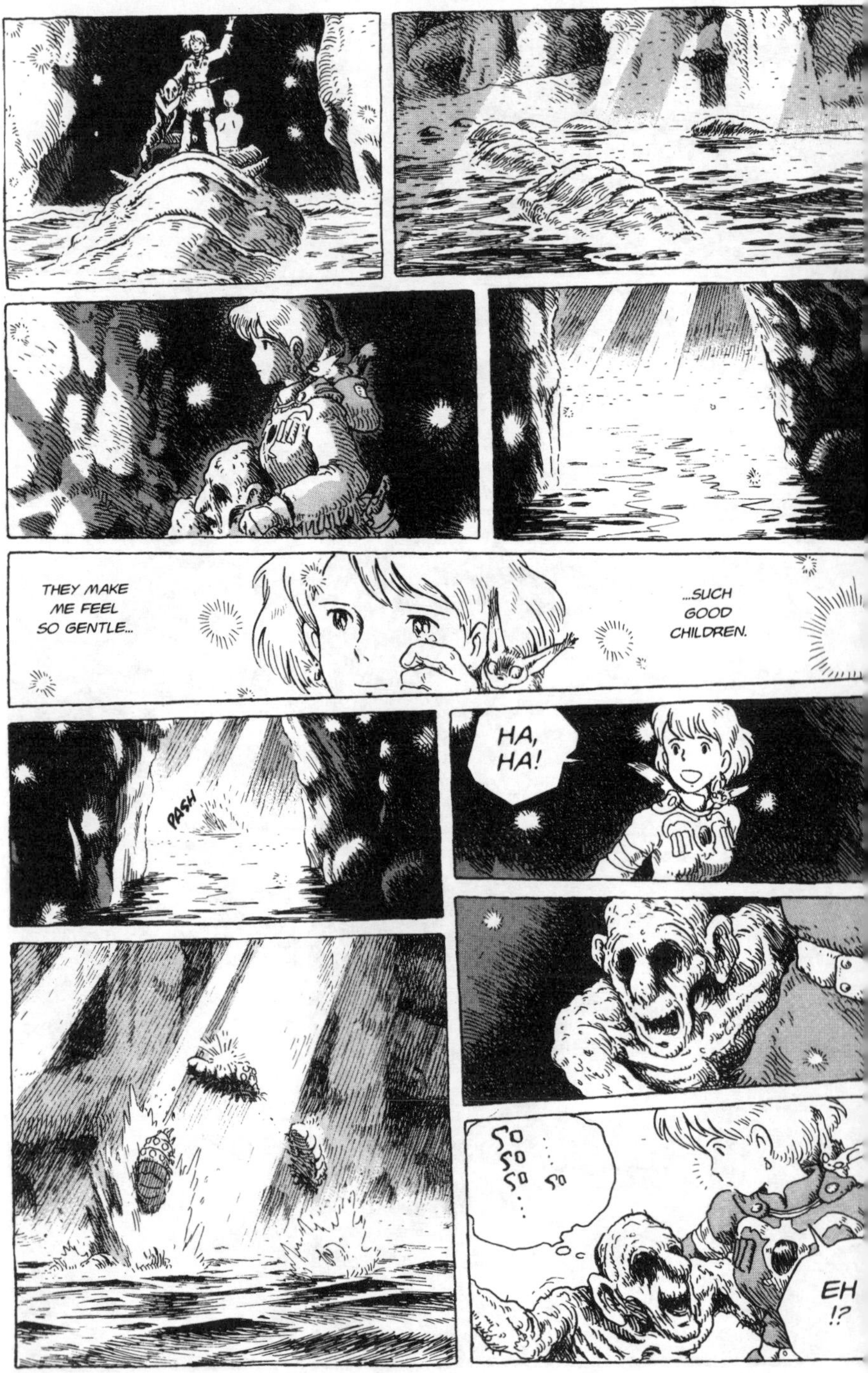
THEY MAKE ME FEEL SO GENTLE...
...SUCH GOOD CHILDREN.
PASH
HA, HA!
SO SO SO SO...
...SO
EH !?

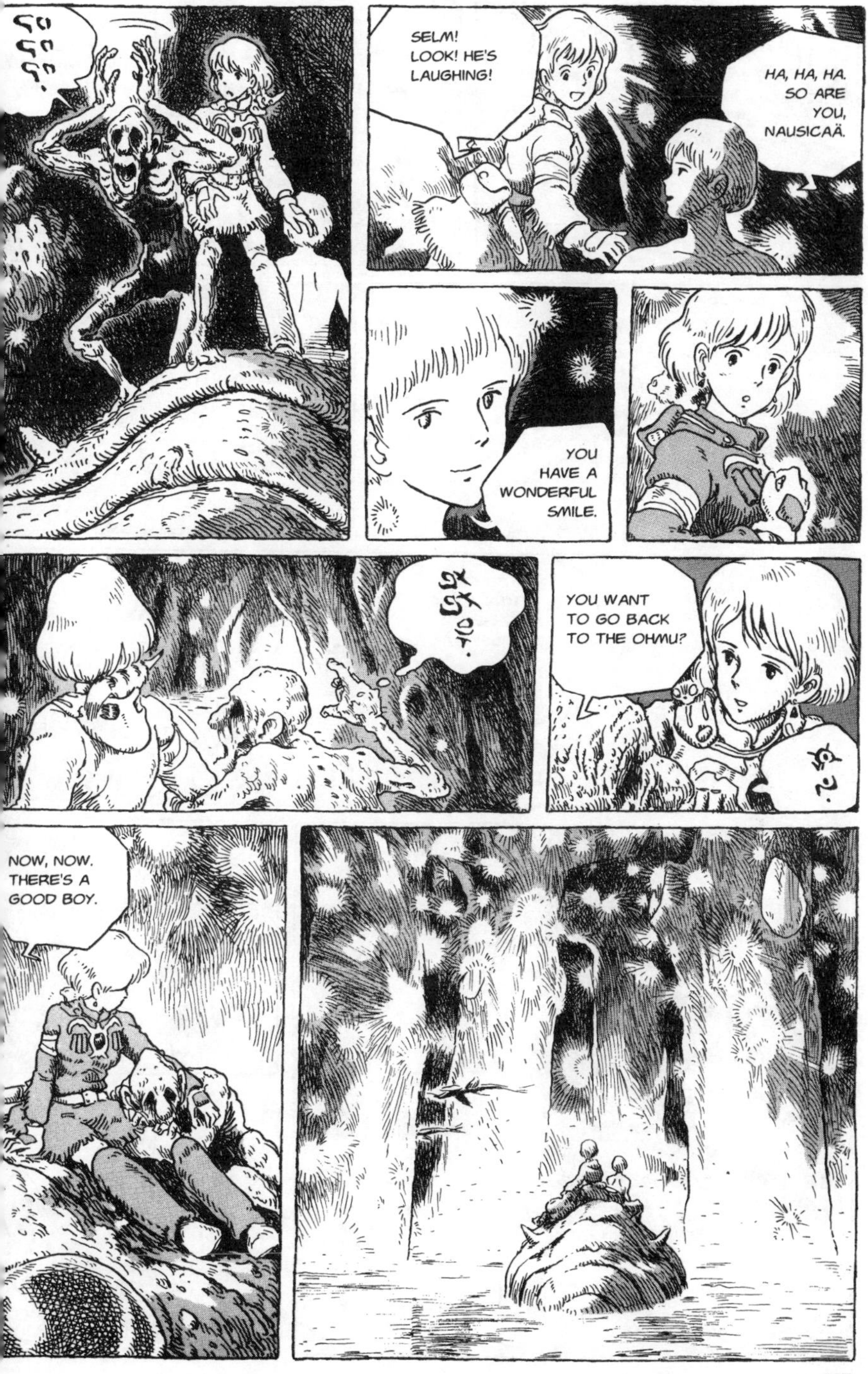
SELM! LOOK! HE'S LAUGHING!
HA, HA, HA. SO ARE YOU, NAUSICAÄ.
YOU HAVE A WONDERFUL SMILE.
YOU WANT TO GO BACK TO THE OHMU?
NOW, NOW. THERE'S A GOOD BOY.

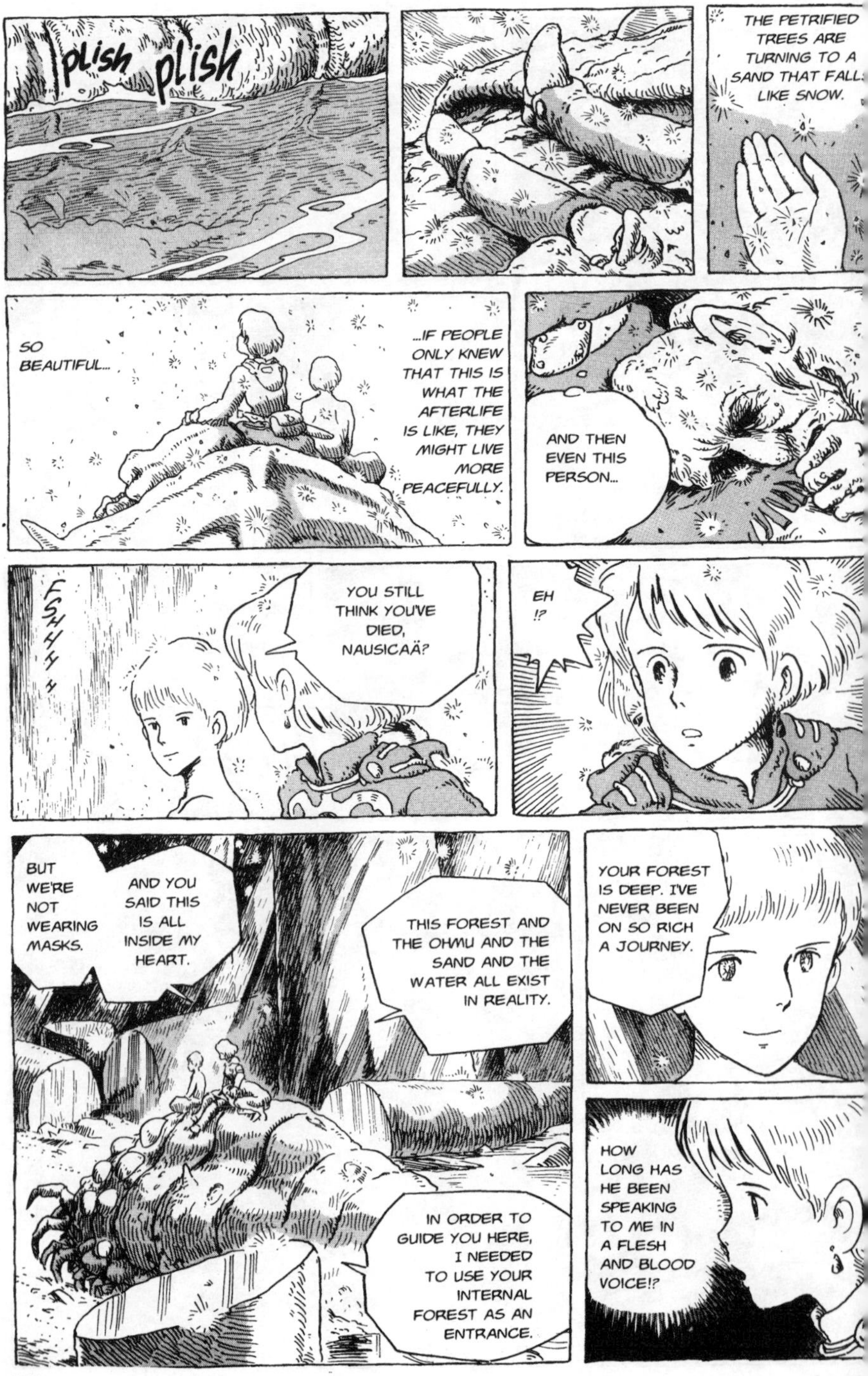

plish plish
THE PETRIFIED TREES ARE TURNING TO A SAND THAT FALLS LIKE SNOW.
SO BEAUTIFUL...
...IF PEOPLE ONLY KNEW THAT THIS IS WHAT THE AFTERLIFE IS LIKE, THEY MIGHT LIVE MORE PEACEFULLY.
AND THEN EVEN THIS PERSON...
FSHHHH
YOU STILL THINK YOU'VE DIED, NAUSICAÄ?
EH !?
BUT WE'RE NOT WEARING MASKS.
AND YOU SAID THIS IS ALL INSIDE MY HEART.
THIS FOREST AND THE OHMU AND THE SAND AND THE WATER ALL EXIST IN REALITY.
IN ORDER TO GUIDE YOU HERE, I NEEDED TO USE YOUR INTERNAL FOREST AS AN ENTRANCE.
YOUR FOREST IS DEEP. I'VE NEVER BEEN ON SO RICH A JOURNEY.
HOW LONG HAS HE BEEN SPEAKING TO ME IN A FLESH AND BLOOD VOICE!?

OUR BODIES ARE ON A DOROK HILL.

YOUR HAND.

HAND?

IT'S WARM. HE'S ALIVE.

YOU SEE? I'M NOT A GHOST.

AND I THOUGHT MY WISH HAD COME TRUE.

I'VE ALWAYS WANTED TO TAKE OFF MY MASK AND SLEEP PEACEFULLY ON THE FLOOR OF THE SEA OF CORRUPTION.

YOU CAN RETURN TO THE WORLD YOU CAME FROM.

BUT ONLY IF YOU WANT TO.

I...I THREW IT ALL AWAY ONCE.

ONCE YOU'VE LEARNED THE SECRET OF THE FOREST, YOU WILL CHOOSE YOUR PATH.

UNDERSTAND. YOU WERE CARRYING THE WEIGHT OF THE WHOLE WORLD ON YOUR SHOULDERS.

WE'LL WALK FROM HERE.

KREE KREE KREE

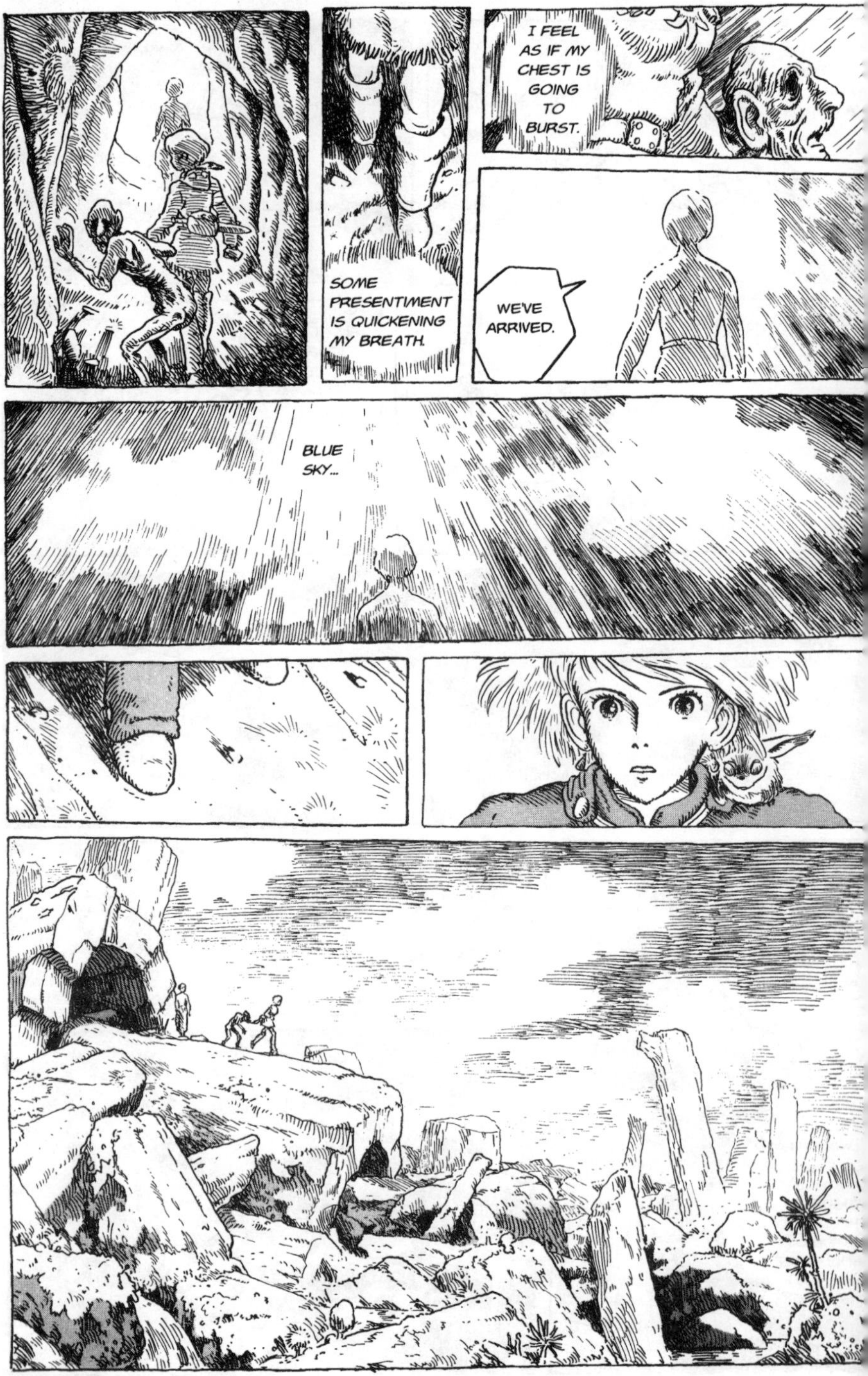
SOME PRESENTIMENT IS QUICKENING MY BREATH.
I FEEL AS IF MY CHEST IS GOING TO BURST.
WE'VE ARRIVED.
BLUE SKY...

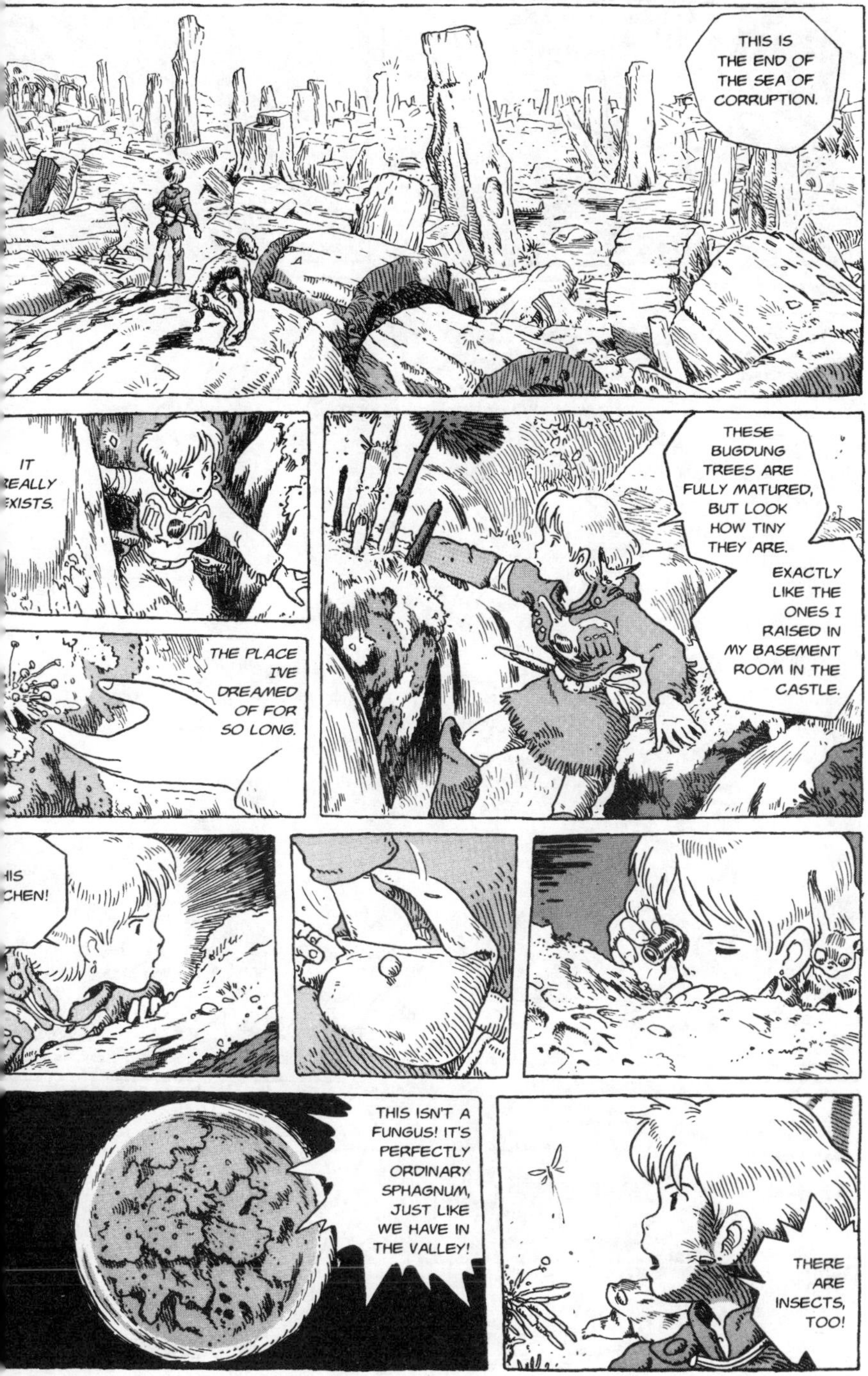
THIS IS THE END OF THE SEA OF CORRUPTION.
IT REALLY EXISTS.
THE PLACE I'VE DREAMED OF FOR SO LONG.
THESE BUGDUNG TREES ARE FULLY MATURED, BUT LOOK HOW TINY THEY ARE.
EXACTLY LIKE THE ONES I RAISED IN MY BASEMENT ROOM IN THE CASTLE.
HIS
CHEN!
THIS ISN'T A FUNGUS! IT'S PERFECTLY ORDINARY SPHAGNUM, JUST LIKE WE HAVE IN THE VALLEY!
THERE ARE INSECTS, TOO!

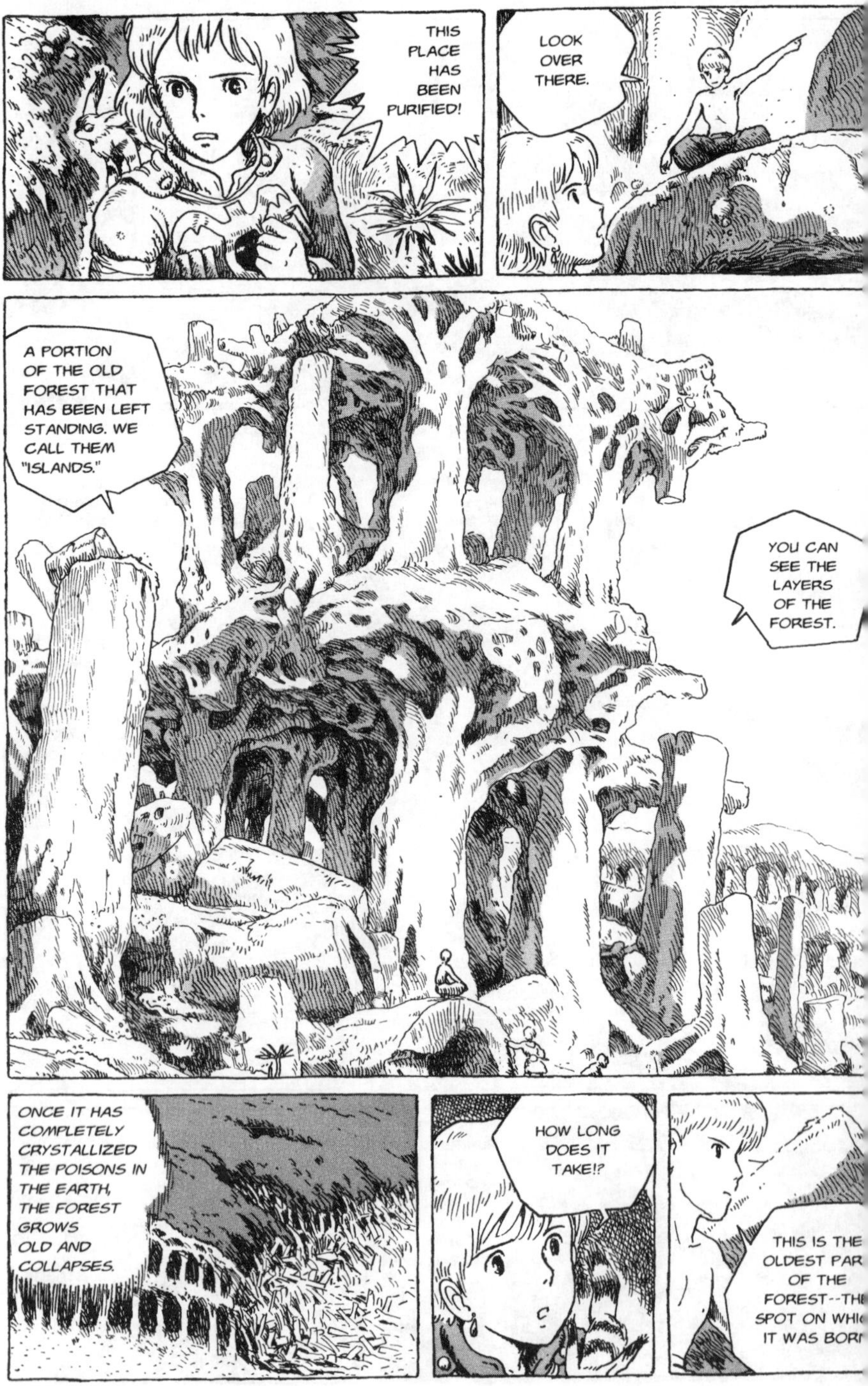
THIS PLACE HAS BEEN PURIFIED!
LOOK OVER THERE.
A PORTION OF THE OLD FOREST THAT HAS BEEN LEFT STANDING. WE CALL THEM "ISLANDS."
YOU CAN SEE THE LAYERS OF THE FOREST.
ONCE IT HAS COMPLETELY CRYSTALLIZED THE POISONS IN THE EARTH, THE FOREST GROWS OLD AND COLLAPSES.
HOW LONG DOES IT TAKE!?
THIS IS THE OLDEST PAR OF THE FOREST--TH SPOT ON WHI IT WAS BOR

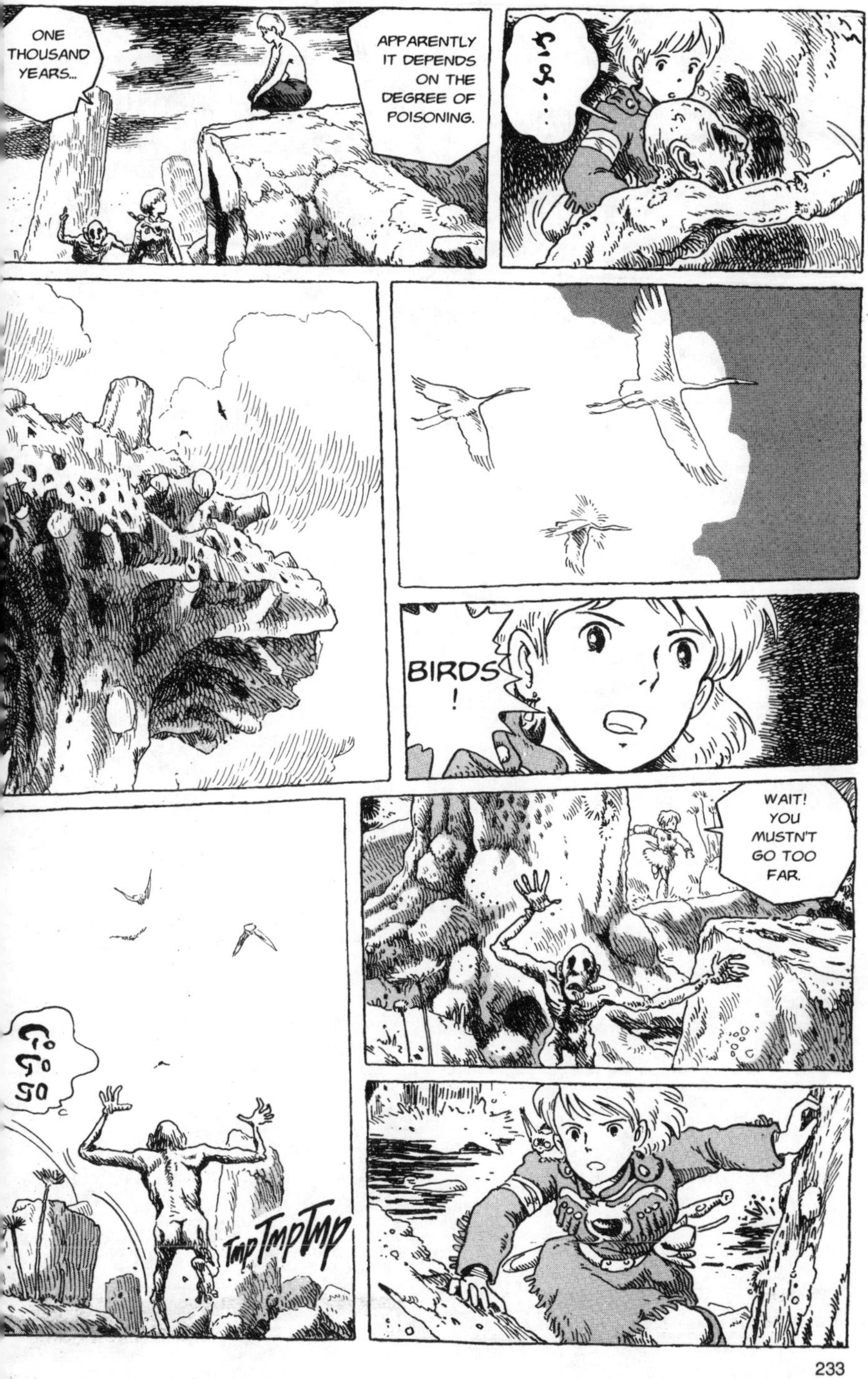
ONE THOUSAND YEARS...
APPARENTLY IT DEPENDS ON THE DEGREE OF POISONING.
BIRDS!
WAIT! YOU MUSTN'T GO TOO FAR.
TmpTmpTmp

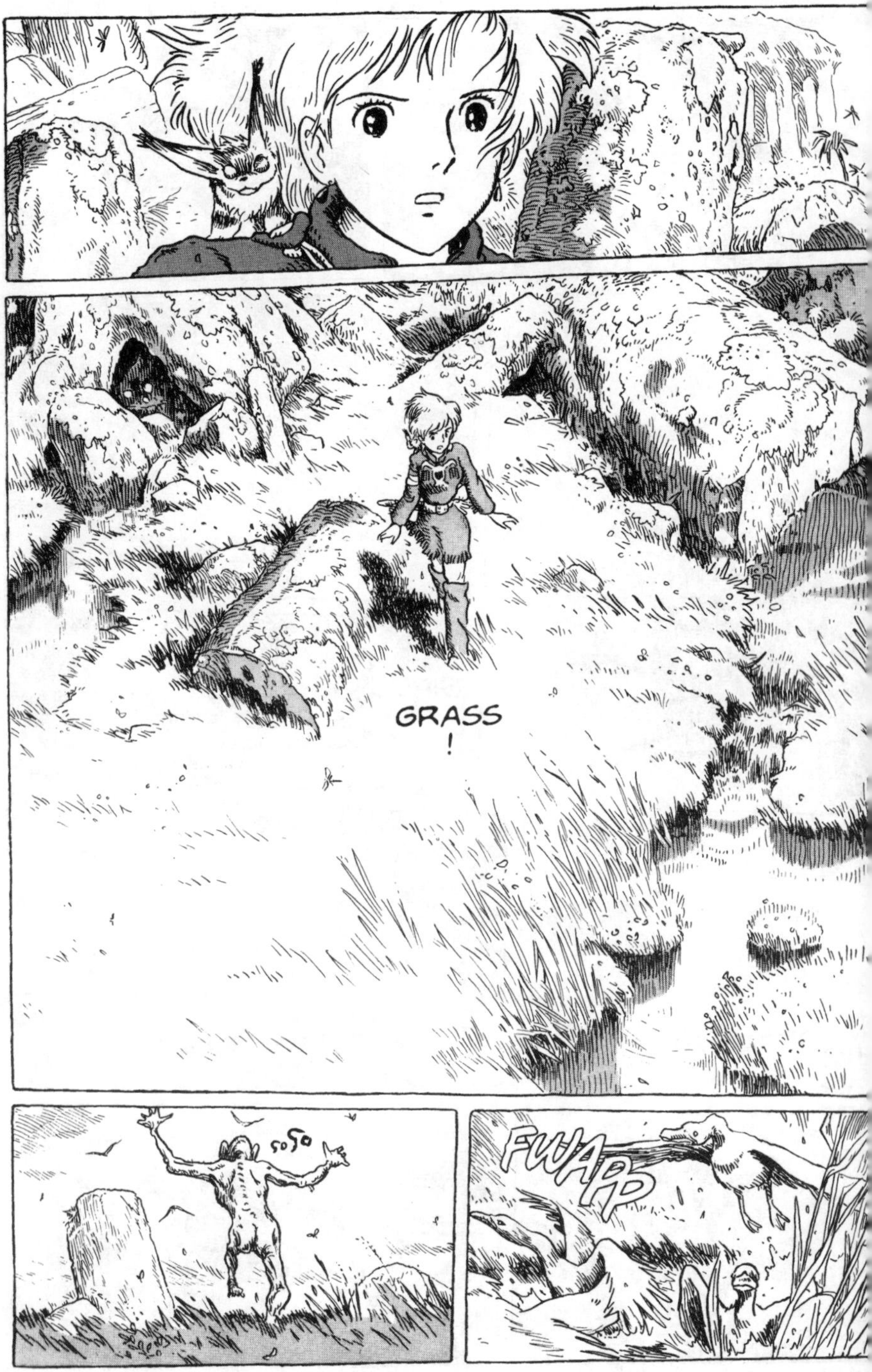
GRASS
!
FWAPP

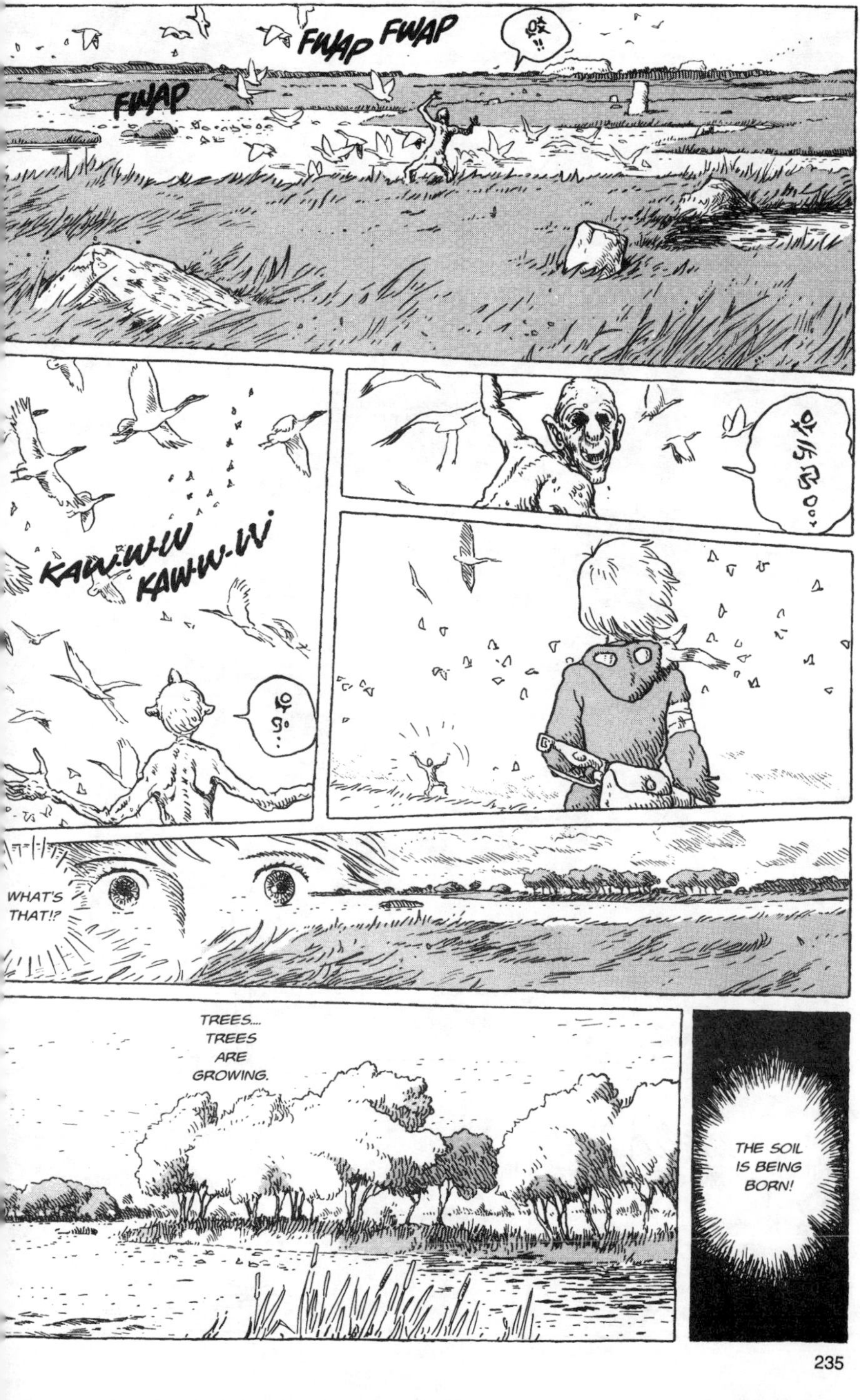
FWAP FWAP
FWAP
KAW-W-W
KAW-W-W
WHAT'S THAT!?
TREES.... TREES ARE GROWING.
THE SOIL IS BEING BORN!

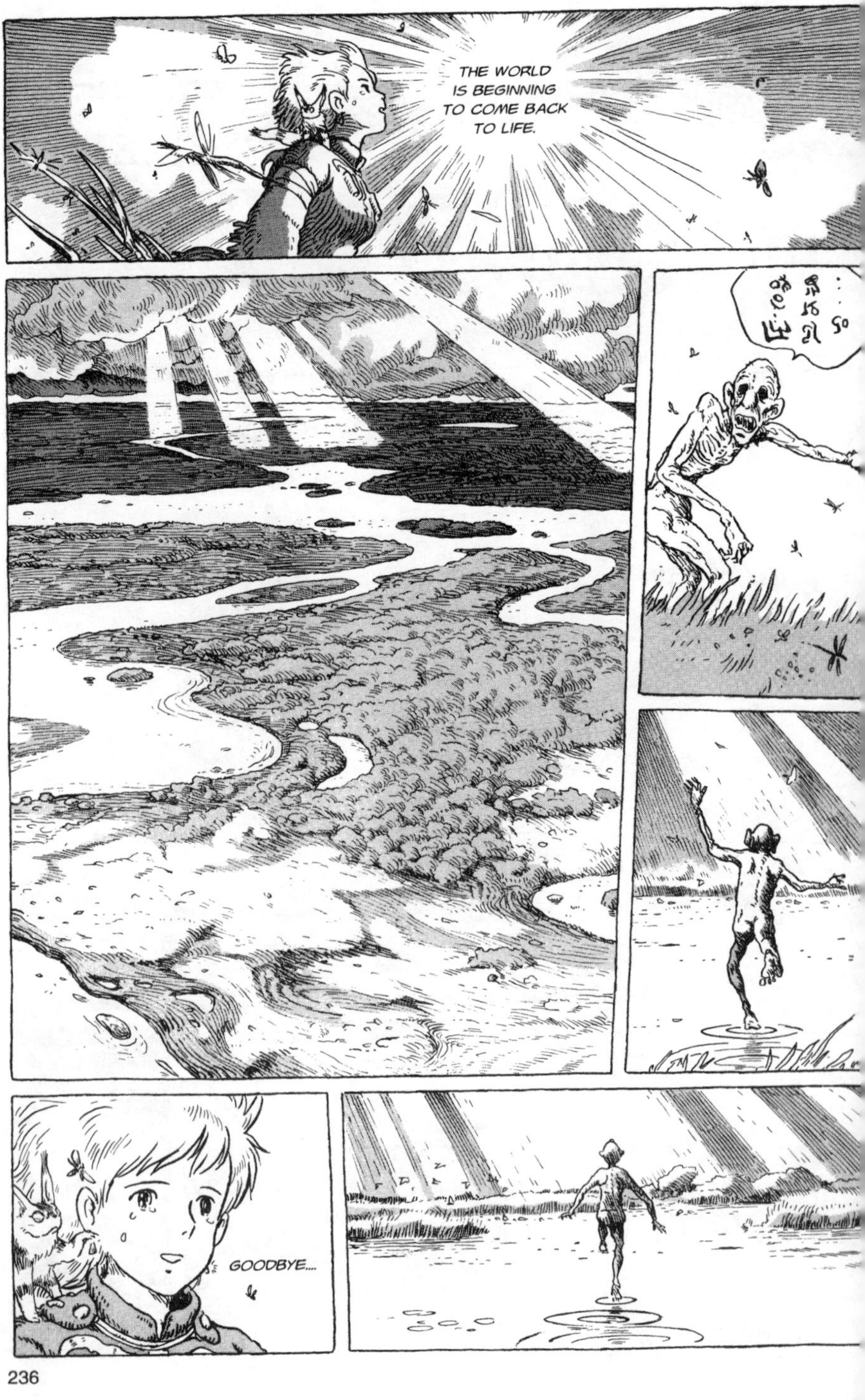
THE WORLD IS BEGINNING TO COME BACK TO LIFE.
GOODBYE....

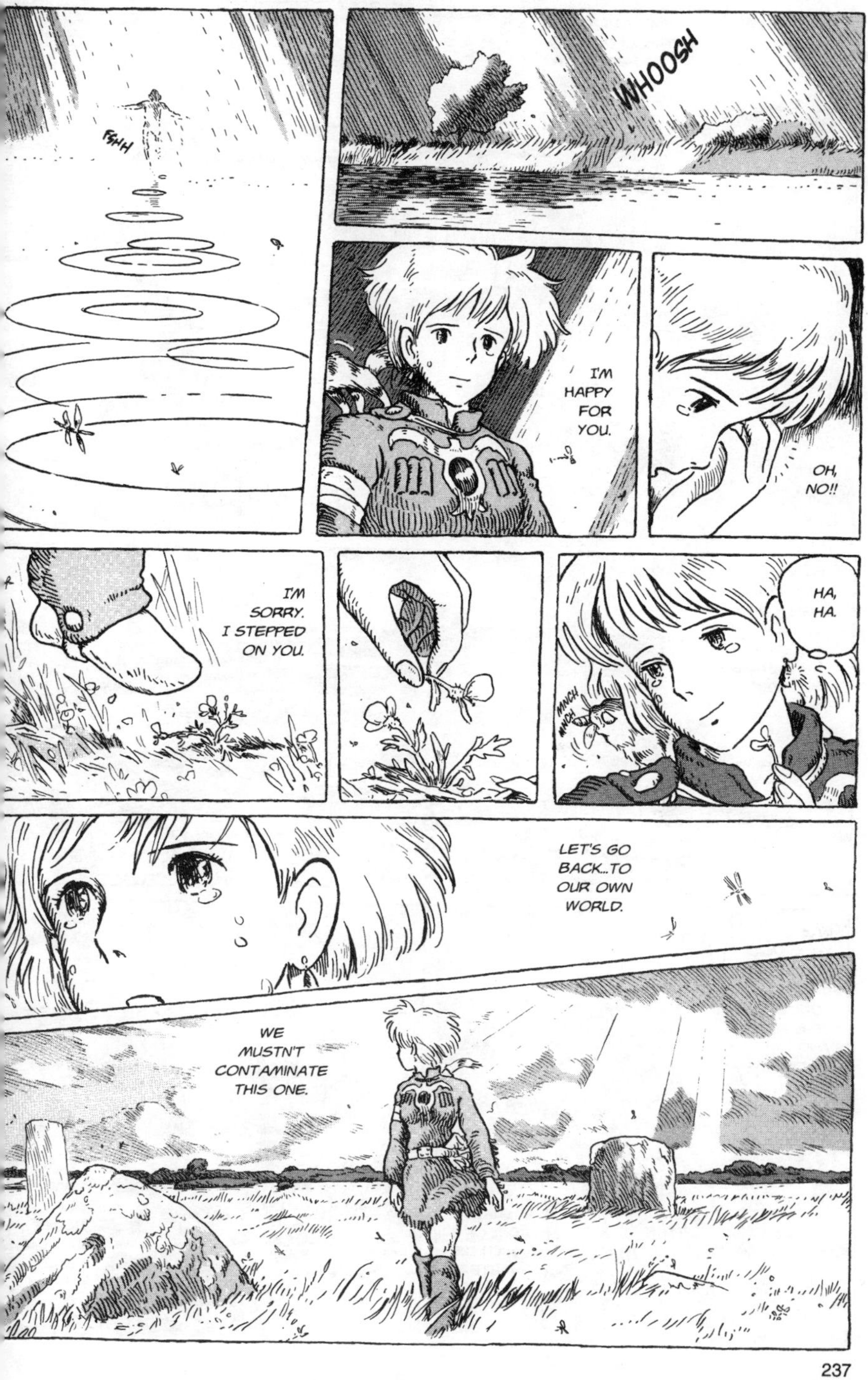
FSHH
WHOOSH
I'M HAPPY FOR YOU.
OH, NO!!
I'M SORRY. I STEPPED ON YOU.
HA, HA.
MNCH MNCH
LET'S GO BACK...TO OUR OWN WORLD.
WE MUSTN'T CONTAMINATE THIS ONE.

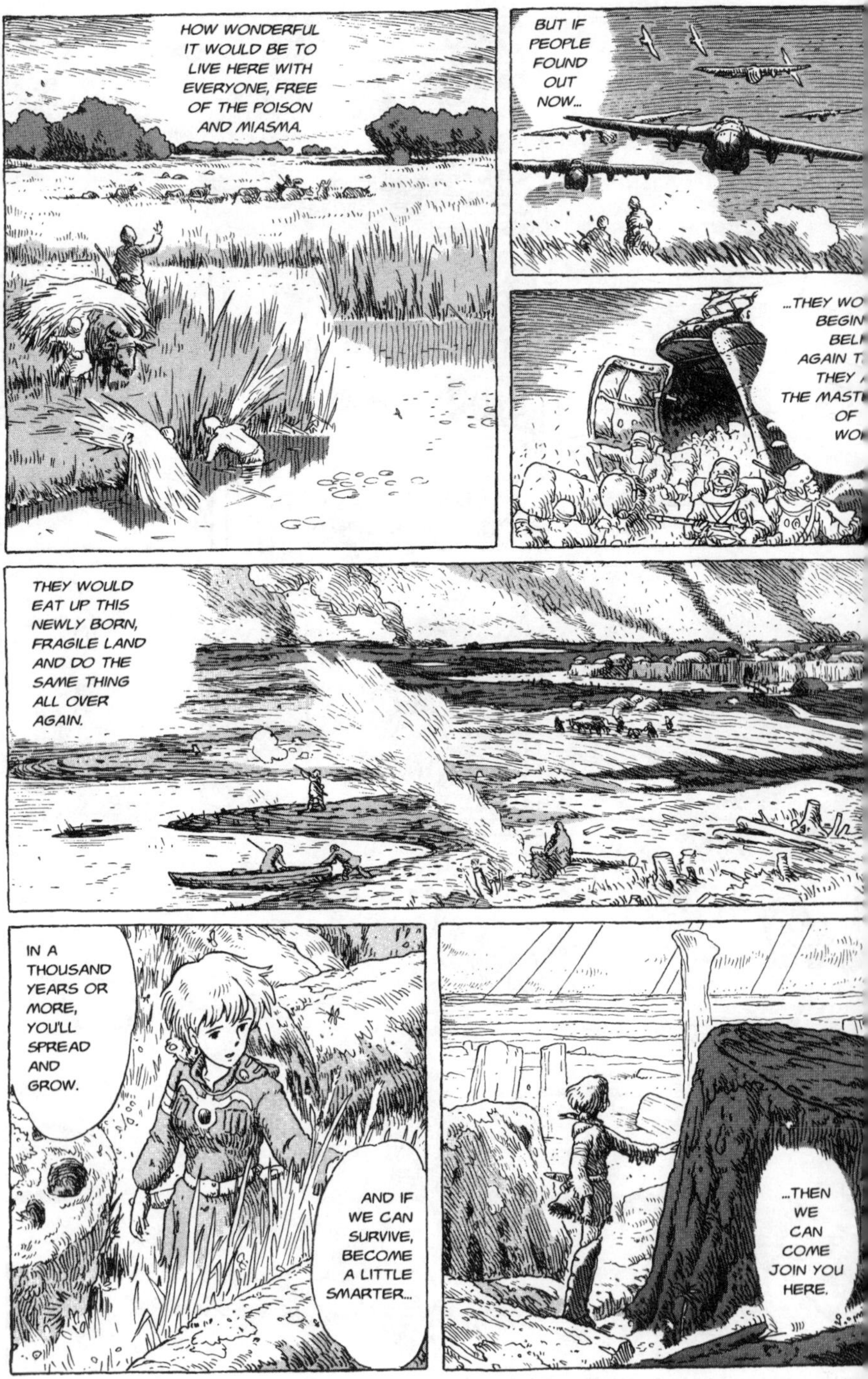
HOW WONDERFUL IT WOULD BE TO LIVE HERE WITH EVERYONE, FREE OF THE POISON AND MIASMA.
BUT IF PEOPLE FOUND OUT NOW...
...THEY WO BEGIN BEL AGAIN T THEY THE MAST OF WO
THEY WOULD EAT UP THIS NEWLY BORN, FRAGILE LAND AND DO THE SAME THING ALL OVER AGAIN.
IN A THOUSAND YEARS OR MORE, YOU'LL SPREAD AND GROW.
AND IF WE CAN SURVIVE, BECOME A LITTLE SMARTER...
...THEN WE CAN COME JOIN YOU HERE.

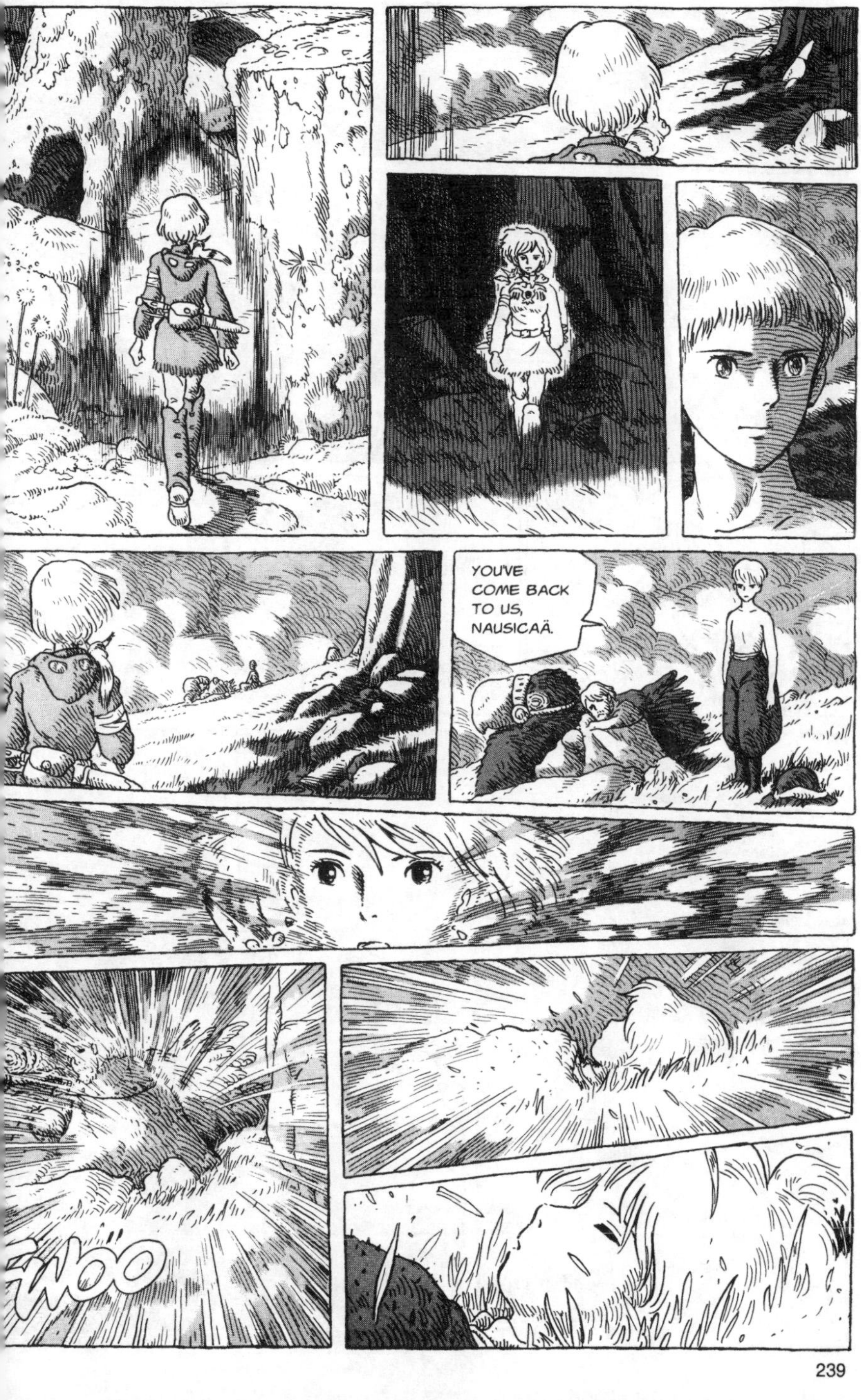
YOU'VE COME BACK TO US, NAUSICAÄ.
FWOO

HOW ARE YOU FEELING?

I FEEL SO STRANGE, AS IF THE INSIDE OF MY BODY HAS BECOME TRANSPARENT.

CHIKUKU AND KUI! AND KUROTOWA, TOO!

LET THEM SLEEP A LITTLE LONGER.

IT'S ALMOST DAWN.

IT'S BEAUTIFUL.

I FEEL AS IF I'VE BEEN REBORN.

I CAN'T STOP CRYING.

ARE YOU COLD?

NO. I WAS JUST WONDERING IF IT'S ALL RIGHT TO BE SO HAPPY.

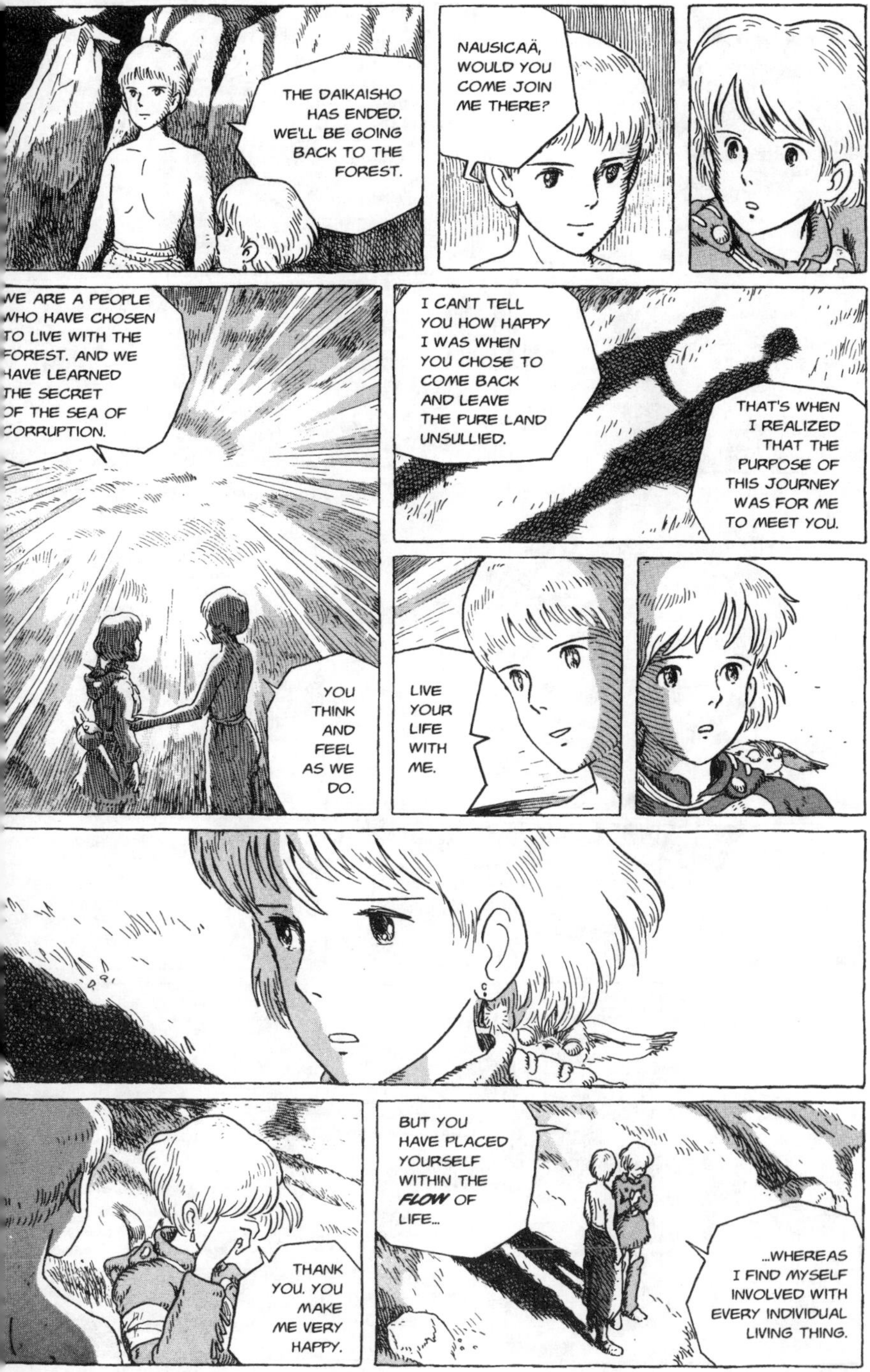
THE DAIKAISHO HAS ENDED. WE'LL BE GOING BACK TO THE FOREST.
NAUSICAÄ, WOULD YOU COME JOIN ME THERE?
WE ARE A PEOPLE WHO HAVE CHOSEN TO LIVE WITH THE FOREST. AND WE HAVE LEARNED THE SECRET OF THE SEA OF CORRUPTION.
I CAN'T TELL YOU HOW HAPPY I WAS WHEN YOU CHOSE TO COME BACK AND LEAVE THE PURE LAND UNSULLIED.
THAT'S WHEN I REALIZED THAT THE PURPOSE OF THIS JOURNEY WAS FOR ME TO MEET YOU.
YOU THINK AND FEEL AS WE DO.
LIVE YOUR LIFE WITH ME.
THANK YOU. YOU MAKE ME VERY HAPPY.
BUT YOU HAVE PLACED YOURSELF WITHIN THE FLOW OF LIFE...
...WHEREAS I FIND MYSELF INVOLVED WITH EVERY INDIVIDUAL LIVING THING.

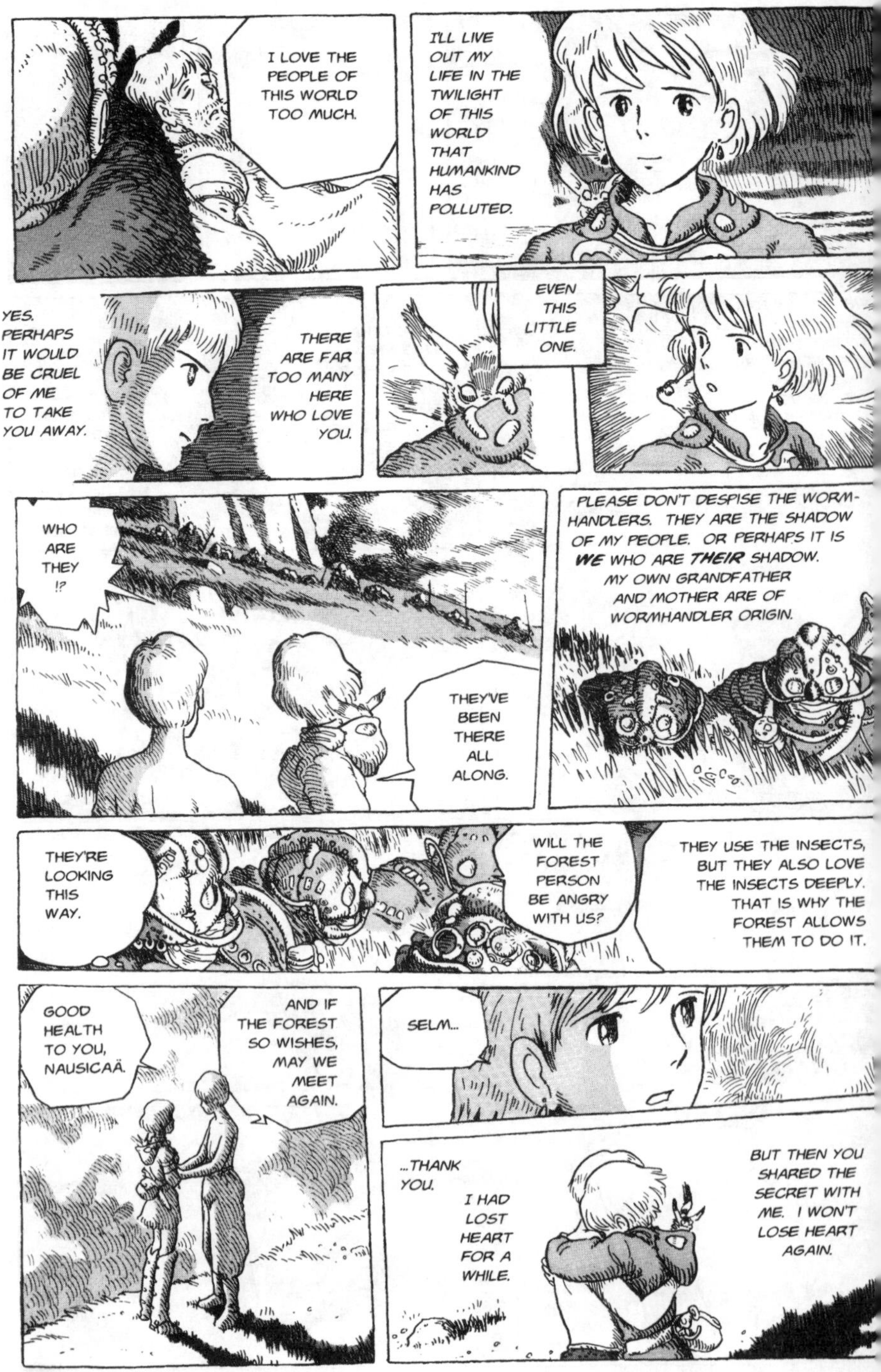
I LOVE THE PEOPLE OF THIS WORLD TOO MUCH.
I'LL LIVE OUT MY LIFE IN THE TWILIGHT OF THIS WORLD THAT HUMANKIND HAS POLLUTED.
YES. PERHAPS IT WOULD BE CRUEL OF ME TO TAKE YOU AWAY.
THERE ARE FAR TOO MANY HERE WHO LOVE YOU.
EVEN THIS LITTLE ONE.
WHO ARE THEY !?
THEY'VE BEEN THERE ALL ALONG.
PLEASE DON'T DESPISE THE WORMHANDLERS. THEY ARE THE SHADOW OF MY PEOPLE. OR PERHAPS IT IS ***WE*** WHO ARE ***THEIR*** SHADOW. MY OWN GRANDFATHER AND MOTHER ARE OF WORMHANDLER ORIGIN.
THEY'RE LOOKING THIS WAY.
WILL THE FOREST PERSON BE ANGRY WITH US?
THEY USE THE INSECTS, BUT THEY ALSO LOVE THE INSECTS DEEPLY. THAT IS WHY THE FOREST ALLOWS THEM TO DO IT.
GOOD HEALTH TO YOU, NAUSICAÄ.
AND IF THE FOREST SO WISHES, MAY WE MEET AGAIN.
SELM...
...THANK YOU.
I HAD LOST HEART FOR A WHILE.
BUT THEN YOU SHARED THE SECRET WITH ME. I WON'T LOSE HEART AGAIN.

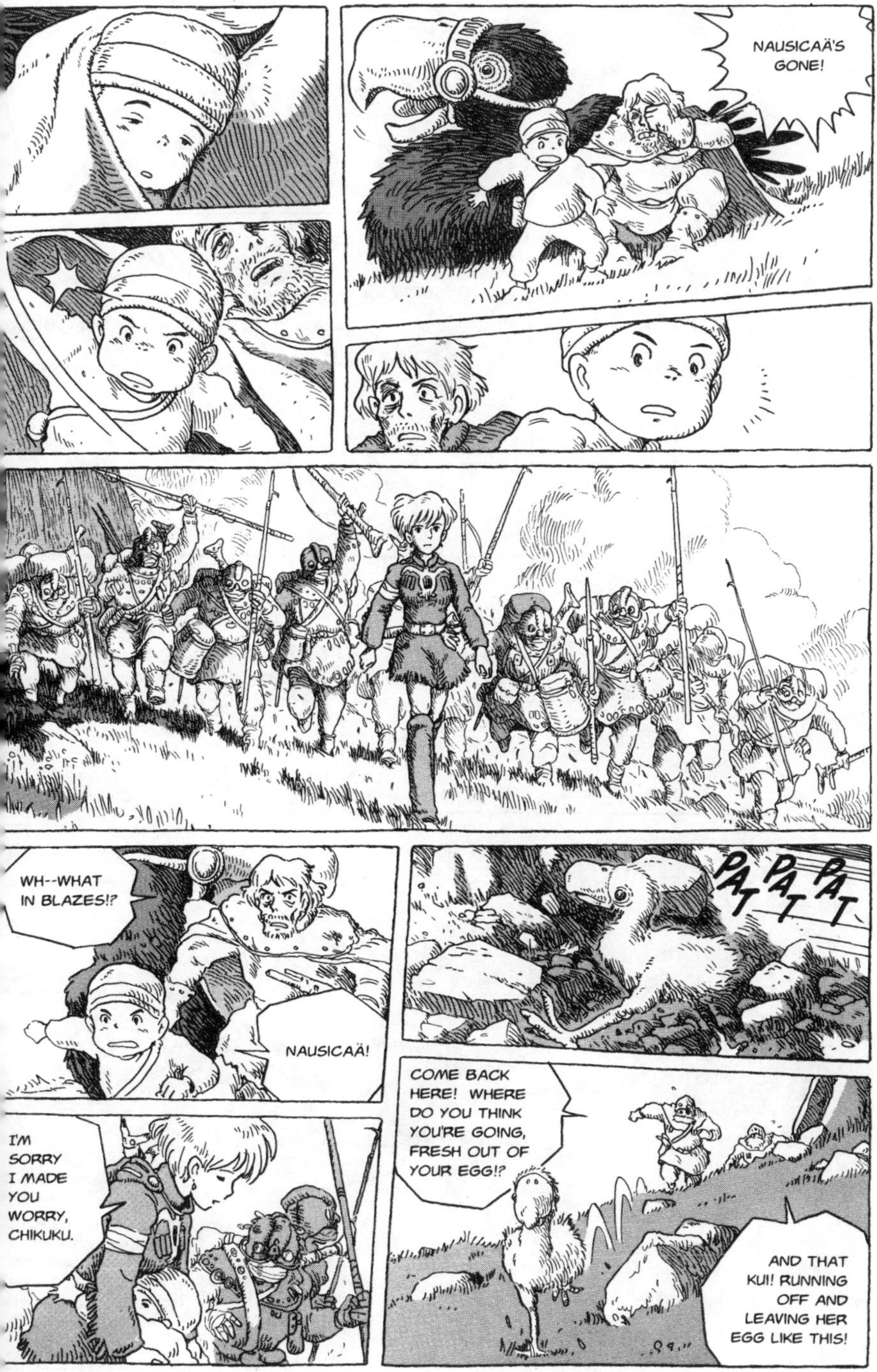
NAUSICAÄ'S GONE!
WH--WHAT IN BLAZES!?
NAUSICAÄ!
PAT PAT PAT
I'M SORRY I MADE YOU WORRY, CHIKUKU.
COME BACK HERE! WHERE DO YOU THINK YOU'RE GOING, FRESH OUT OF YOUR EGG!?
AND THAT KUI! RUNNING OFF AND LEAVING HER EGG LIKE THIS!

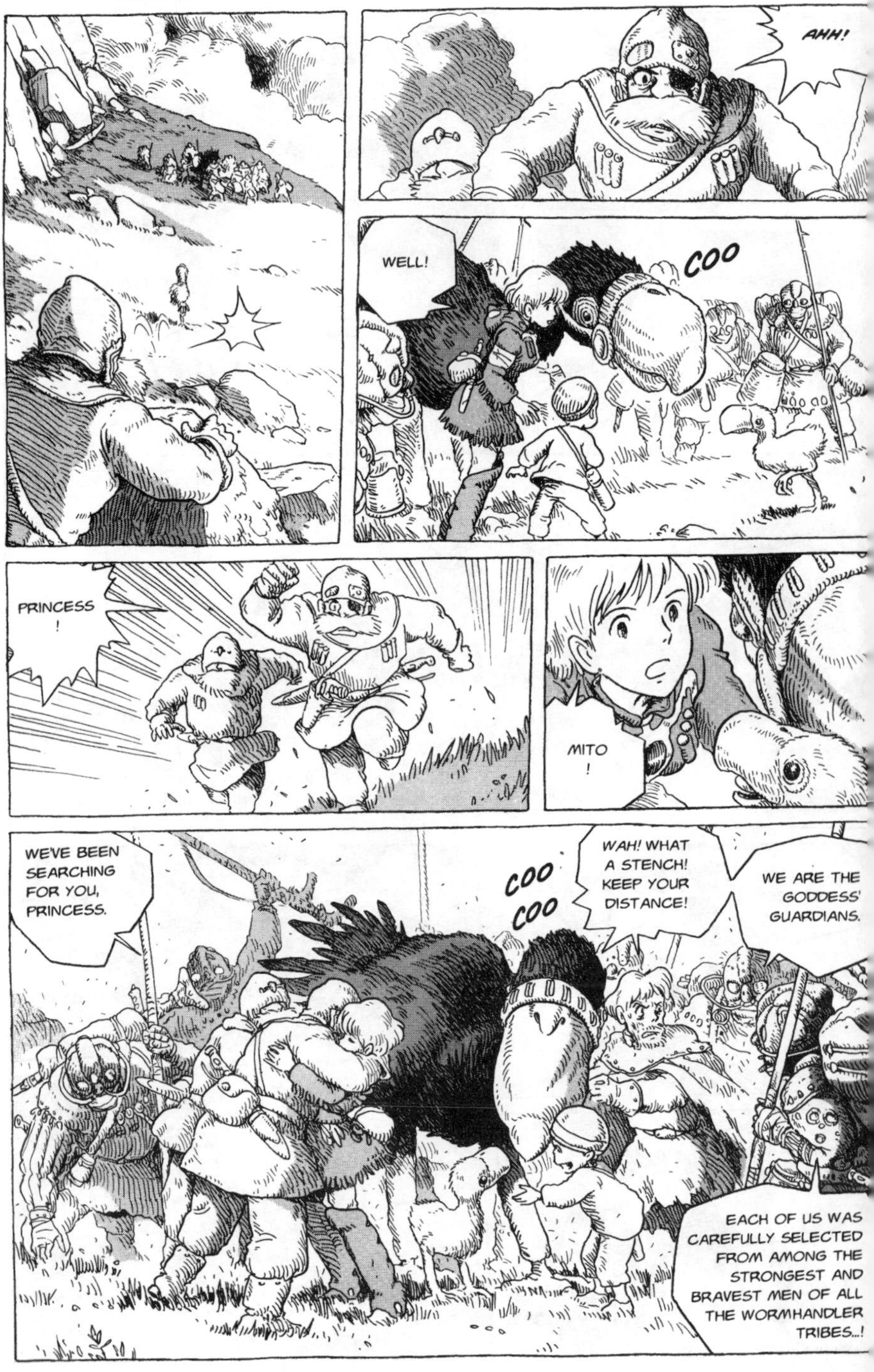
AHH!
WELL!
COO
PRINCESS !
MITO !
WE'VE BEEN SEARCHING FOR YOU, PRINCESS.
COO COO
WAH! WHAT A STENCH! KEEP YOUR DISTANCE!
WE ARE THE GODDESS' GUARDIANS.
EACH OF US WAS CAREFULLY SELECTED FROM AMONG THE STRONGEST AND BRAVEST MEN OF ALL THE WORMHANDLER TRIBES...!

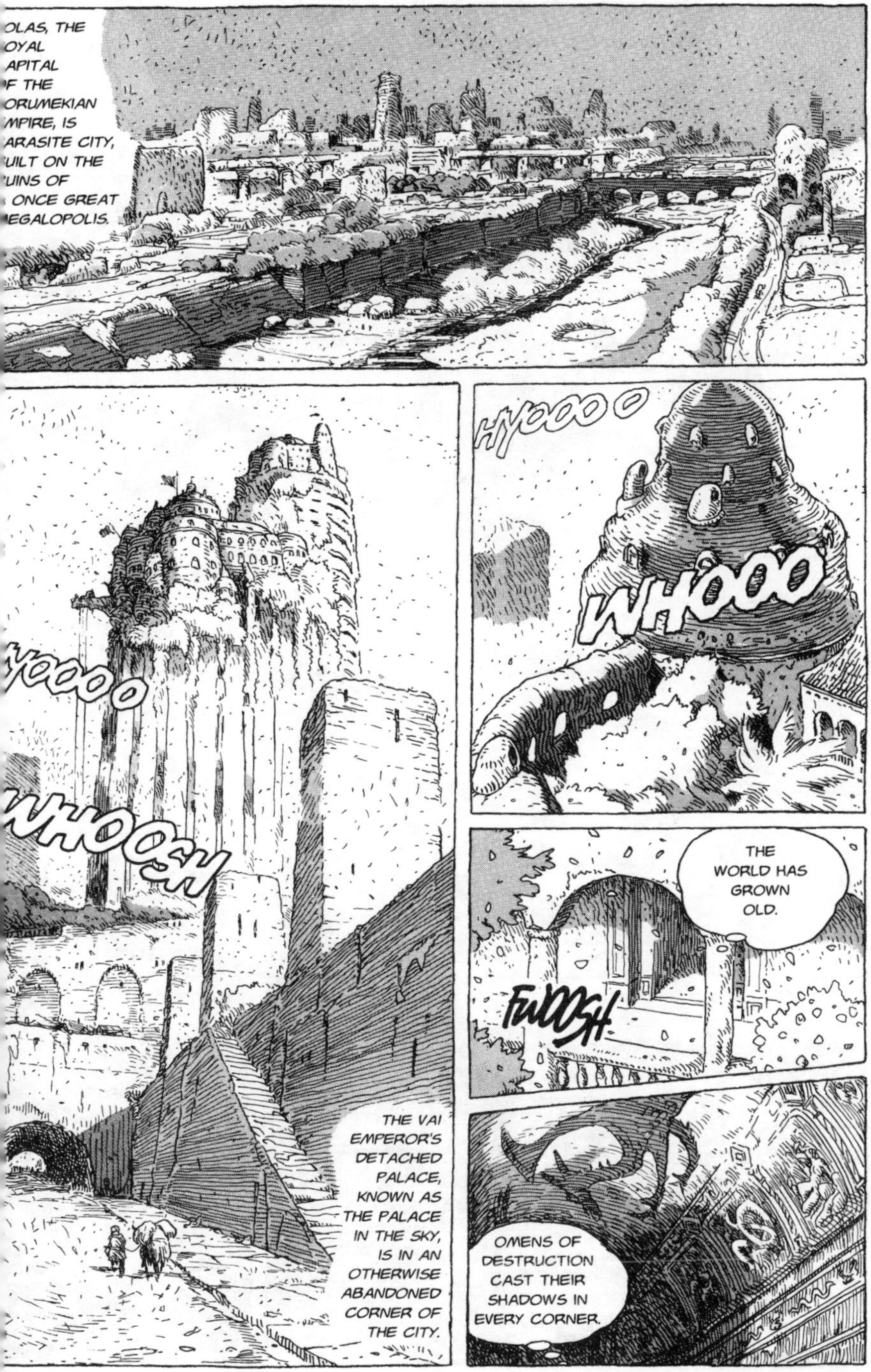
OLAS, THE OYAL APITAL F THE ORUMEKIAN MPIRE, IS ARASITE CITY, UILT ON THE UINS OF ONCE GREAT EGALOPOLIS.
YOOOO
WHOOSH
THE VAI EMPEROR'S DETACHED PALACE, KNOWN AS THE PALACE IN THE SKY, IS IN AN OTHERWISE ABANDONED CORNER OF THE CITY.
HYOOOO
WHOOO
THE WORLD HAS GROWN OLD.
FWOOSH
OMENS OF DESTRUCTION CAST THEIR SHADOWS IN EVERY CORNER.

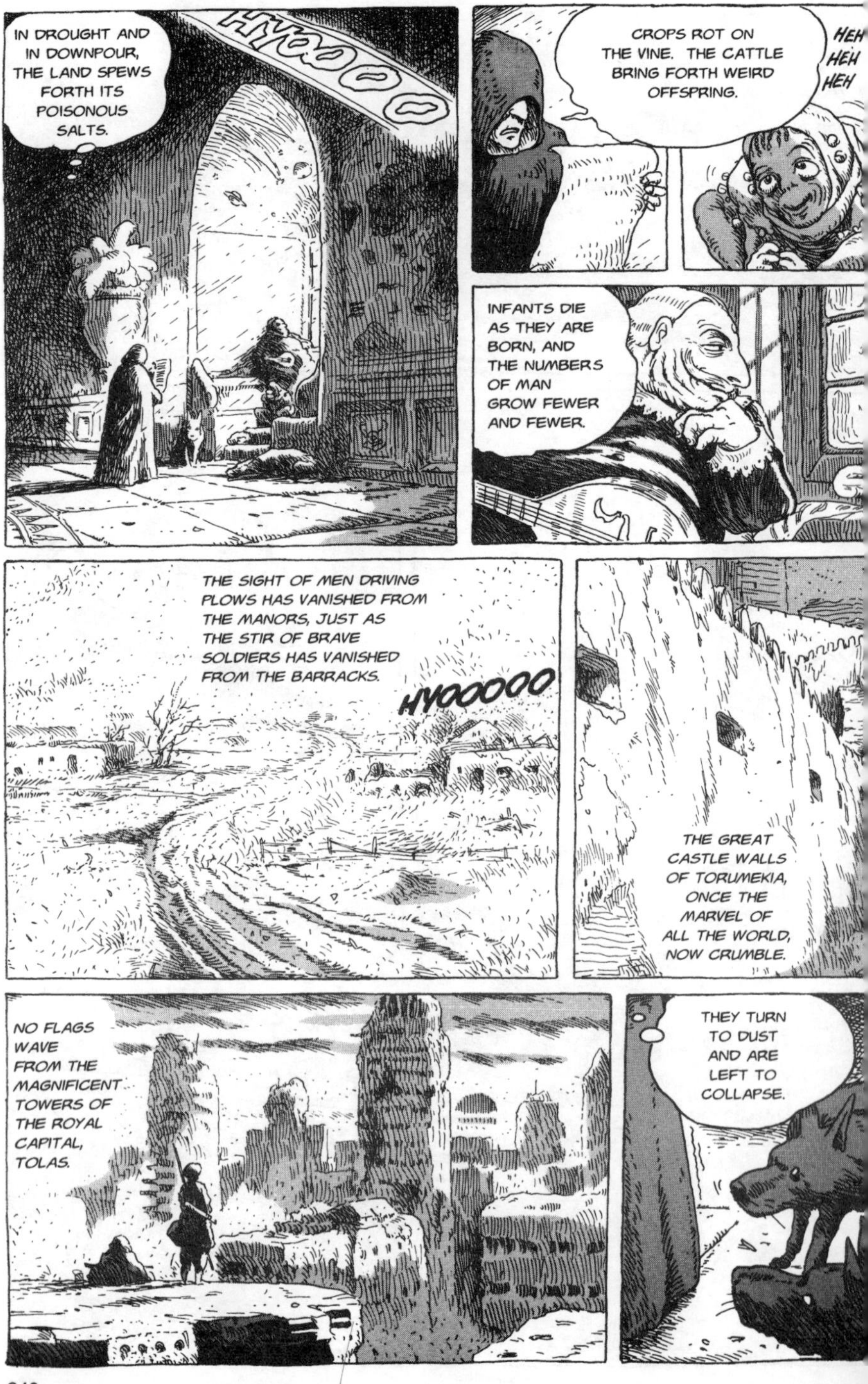
IN DROUGHT AND IN DOWNPOUR, THE LAND SPEWS FORTH ITS POISONOUS SALTS.
HYOOOO
CROPS ROT ON THE VINE. THE CATTLE BRING FORTH WEIRD OFFSPRING.
HEH HEH HEH
INFANTS DIE AS THEY ARE BORN, AND THE NUMBERS OF MAN GROW FEWER AND FEWER.
THE SIGHT OF MEN DRIVING PLOWS HAS VANISHED FROM THE MANORS, JUST AS THE STIR OF BRAVE SOLDIERS HAS VANISHED FROM THE BARRACKS.
HYOOOOO
THE GREAT CASTLE WALLS OF TORUMEKIA, ONCE THE MARVEL OF ALL THE WORLD, NOW CRUMBLE.
NO FLAGS WAVE FROM THE MAGNIFICENT TOWERS OF THE ROYAL CAPITAL, TOLAS.
THEY TURN TO DUST AND ARE LEFT TO COLLAPSE.

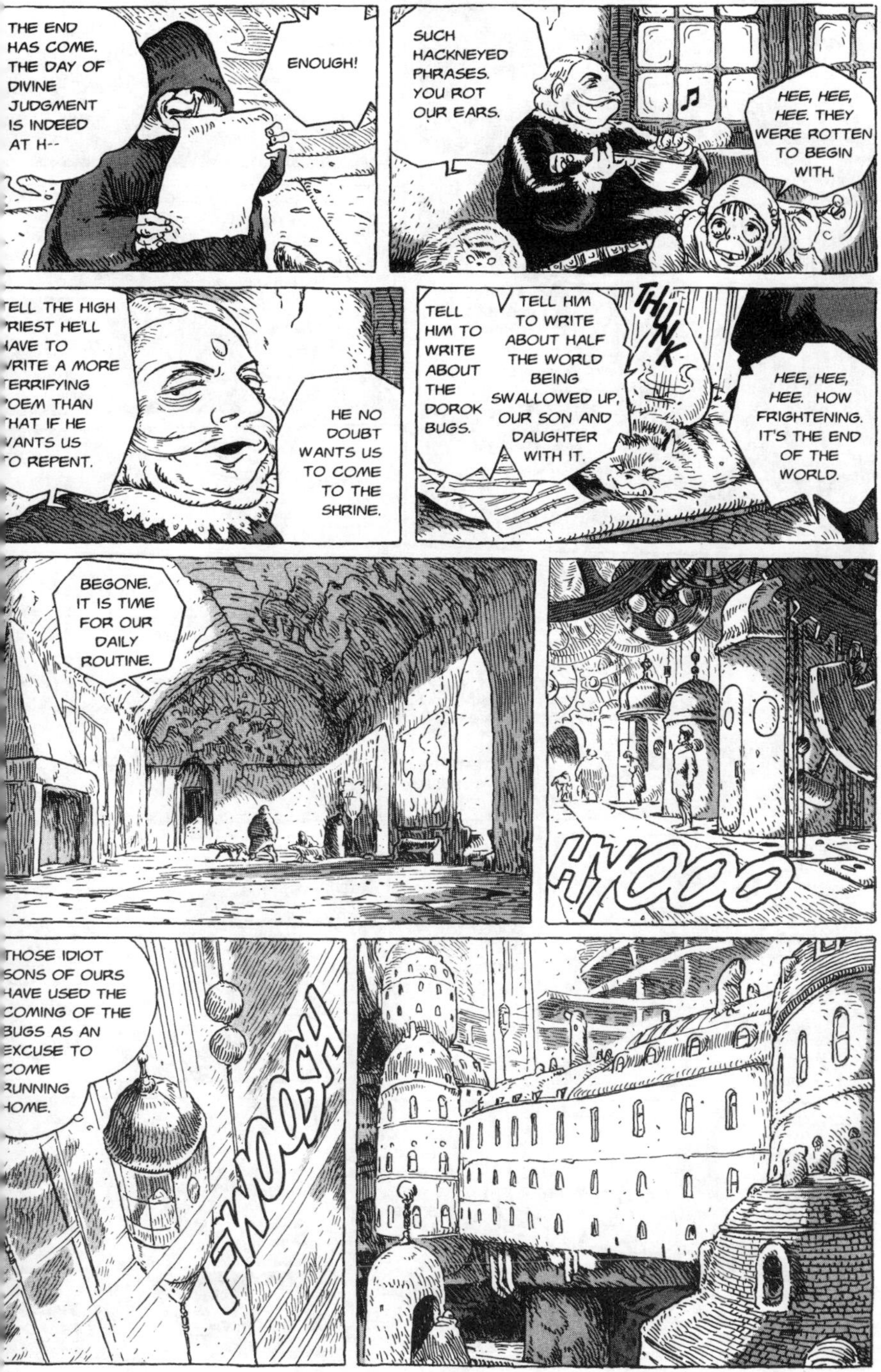
THE END HAS COME. THE DAY OF DIVINE JUDGMENT IS INDEED AT H--
ENOUGH!
SUCH HACKNEYED PHRASES. YOU ROT OUR EARS.
HEE, HEE, HEE. THEY WERE ROTTEN TO BEGIN WITH.
TELL THE HIGH PRIEST HE'LL HAVE TO WRITE A MORE TERRIFYING POEM THAN THAT IF HE WANTS US TO REPENT.
HE NO DOUBT WANTS US TO COME TO THE SHRINE.
TELL HIM TO WRITE ABOUT HALF THE WORLD BEING SWALLOWED UP, OUR SON AND DAUGHTER WITH IT.
TELL HIM TO WRITE ABOUT THE DOROK BUGS.
THUNK
HEE, HEE, HEE. HOW FRIGHTENING. IT'S THE END OF THE WORLD.
BEGONE. IT IS TIME FOR OUR DAILY ROUTINE.
HYOOOO
THOSE IDIOT SONS OF OURS HAVE USED THE COMING OF THE BUGS AS AN EXCUSE TO COME RUNNING HOME.
FWOOSH

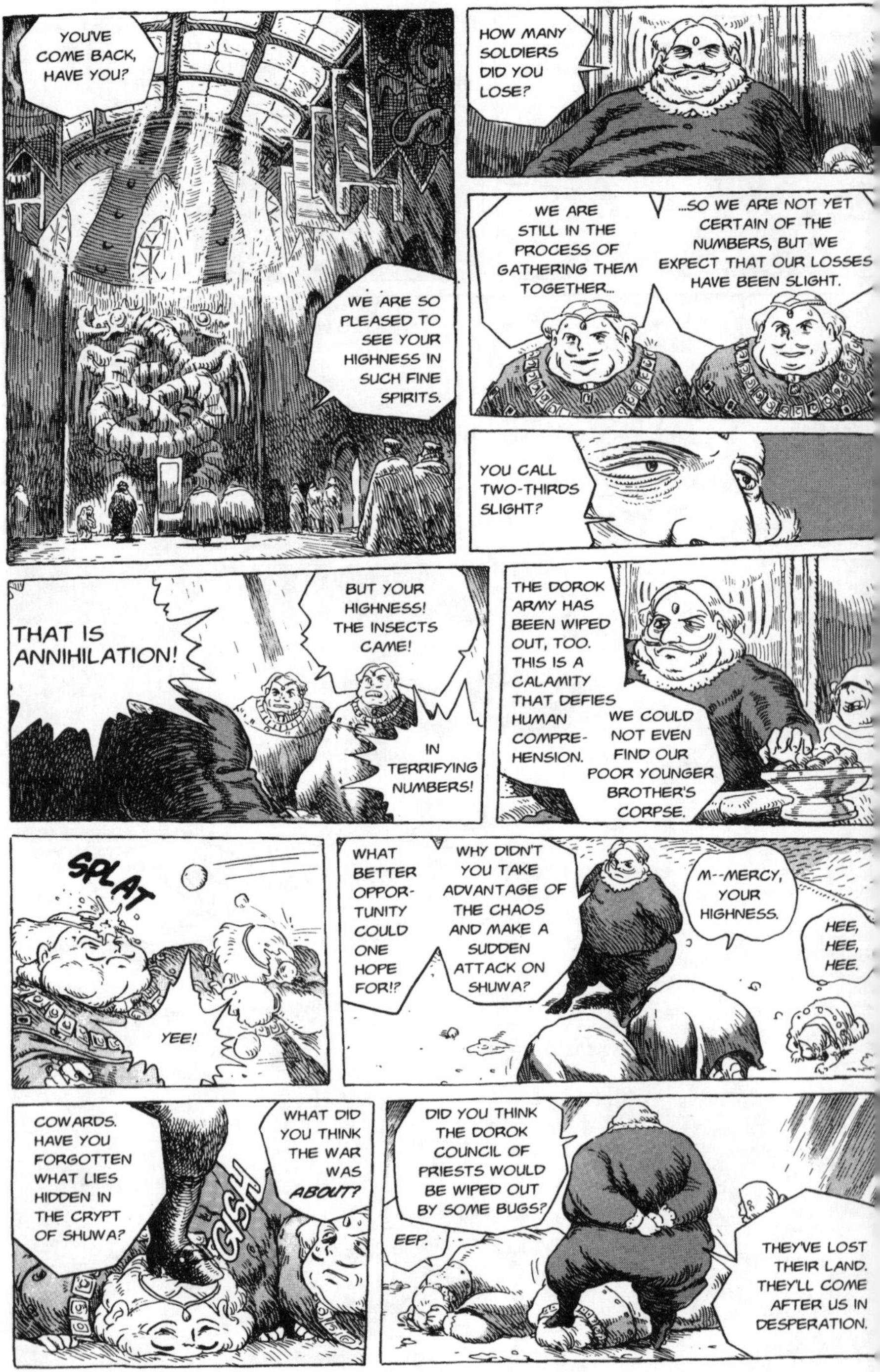
YOU'VE COME BACK, HAVE YOU?
WE ARE SO PLEASED TO SEE YOUR HIGHNESS IN SUCH FINE SPIRITS.
HOW MANY SOLDIERS DID YOU LOSE?
WE ARE STILL IN THE PROCESS OF GATHERING THEM TOGETHER...
...SO WE ARE NOT YET CERTAIN OF THE NUMBERS, BUT WE EXPECT THAT OUR LOSSES HAVE BEEN SLIGHT.
YOU CALL TWO-THIRDS SLIGHT?
THAT IS ANNIHILATION!
BUT YOUR HIGHNESS! THE INSECTS CAME!
IN TERRIFYING NUMBERS!
THE DOROK ARMY HAS BEEN WIPED OUT, TOO. THIS IS A CALAMITY THAT DEFIES HUMAN COMPRE-HENSION.
WE COULD NOT EVEN FIND OUR POOR YOUNGER BROTHER'S CORPSE.
SPLAT
YEE!
WHAT BETTER OPPOR-TUNITY COULD ONE HOPE FOR!?
WHY DIDN'T YOU TAKE ADVANTAGE OF THE CHAOS AND MAKE A SUDDEN ATTACK ON SHUWA?
M--MERCY, YOUR HIGHNESS.
HEE, HEE, HEE.
COWARDS. HAVE YOU FORGOTTEN WHAT LIES HIDDEN IN THE CRYPT OF SHUWA?
WHAT DID YOU THINK THE WAR WAS ABOUT?
GISH
DID YOU THINK THE DOROK COUNCIL OF PRIESTS WOULD BE WIPED OUT BY SOME BUGS?
EEP.
THEY'VE LOST THEIR LAND. THEY'LL COME AFTER US IN DESPERATION.

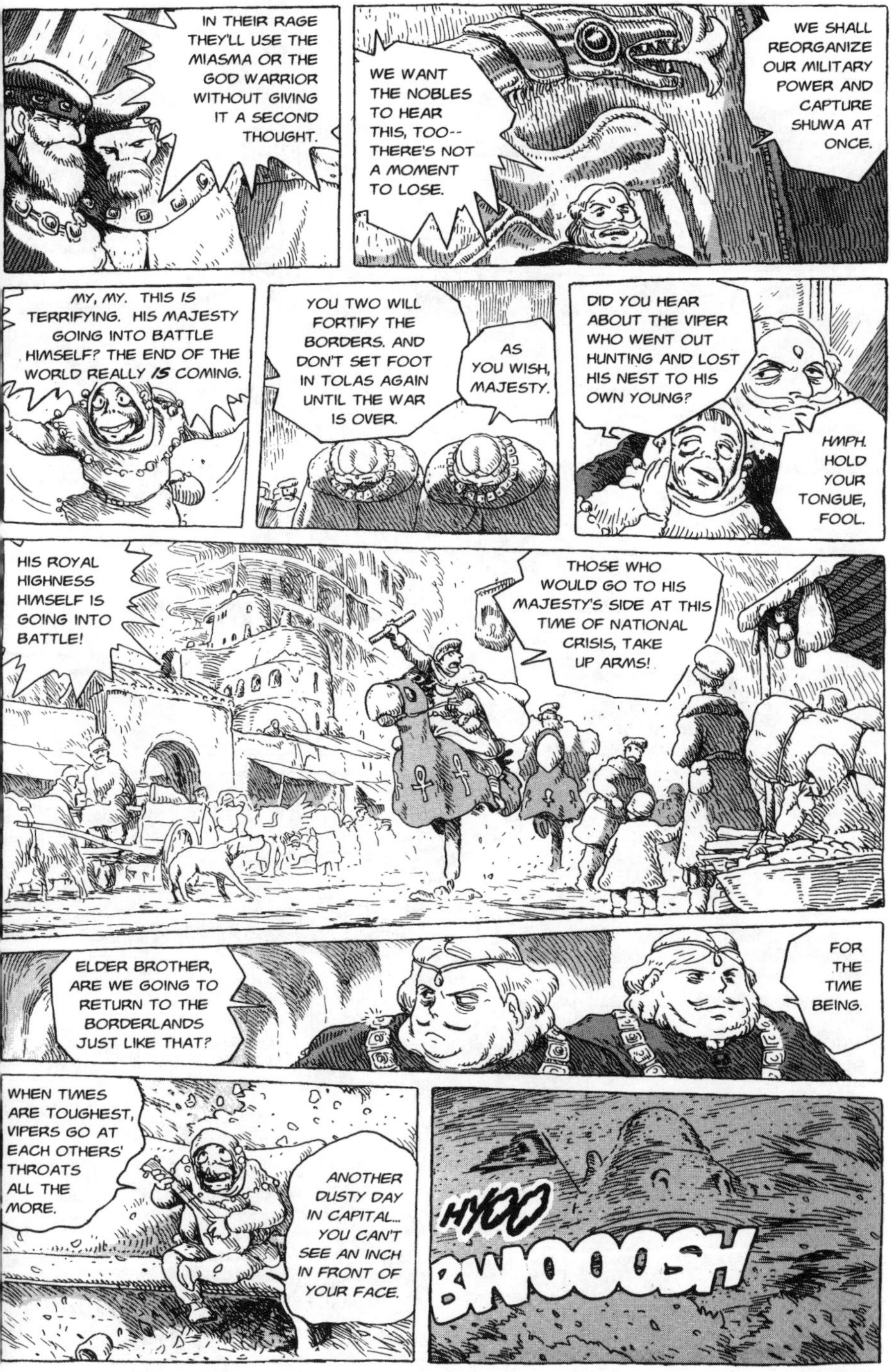
IN THEIR RAGE THEY'LL USE THE MIASMA OR THE GOD WARRIOR WITHOUT GIVING IT A SECOND THOUGHT.
WE WANT THE NOBLES TO HEAR THIS, TOO-- THERE'S NOT A MOMENT TO LOSE.
WE SHALL REORGANIZE OUR MILITARY POWER AND CAPTURE SHUWA AT ONCE.
MY, MY. THIS IS TERRIFYING. HIS MAJESTY GOING INTO BATTLE HIMSELF? THE END OF THE WORLD REALLY IS COMING.
YOU TWO WILL FORTIFY THE BORDERS. AND DON'T SET FOOT IN TOLAS AGAIN UNTIL THE WAR IS OVER.
AS YOU WISH, MAJESTY.
DID YOU HEAR ABOUT THE VIPER WHO WENT OUT HUNTING AND LOST HIS NEST TO HIS OWN YOUNG?
HMPH. HOLD YOUR TONGUE, FOOL.
HIS ROYAL HIGHNESS HIMSELF IS GOING INTO BATTLE!
THOSE WHO WOULD GO TO HIS MAJESTY'S SIDE AT THIS TIME OF NATIONAL CRISIS, TAKE UP ARMS!
ELDER BROTHER, ARE WE GOING TO RETURN TO THE BORDERLANDS JUST LIKE THAT?
FOR THE TIME BEING.
WHEN TIMES ARE TOUGHEST, VIPERS GO AT EACH OTHERS' THROATS ALL THE MORE.
ANOTHER DUSTY DAY IN CAPITAL... YOU CAN'T SEE AN INCH IN FRONT OF YOUR FACE.
HYOO
BWOOOSH

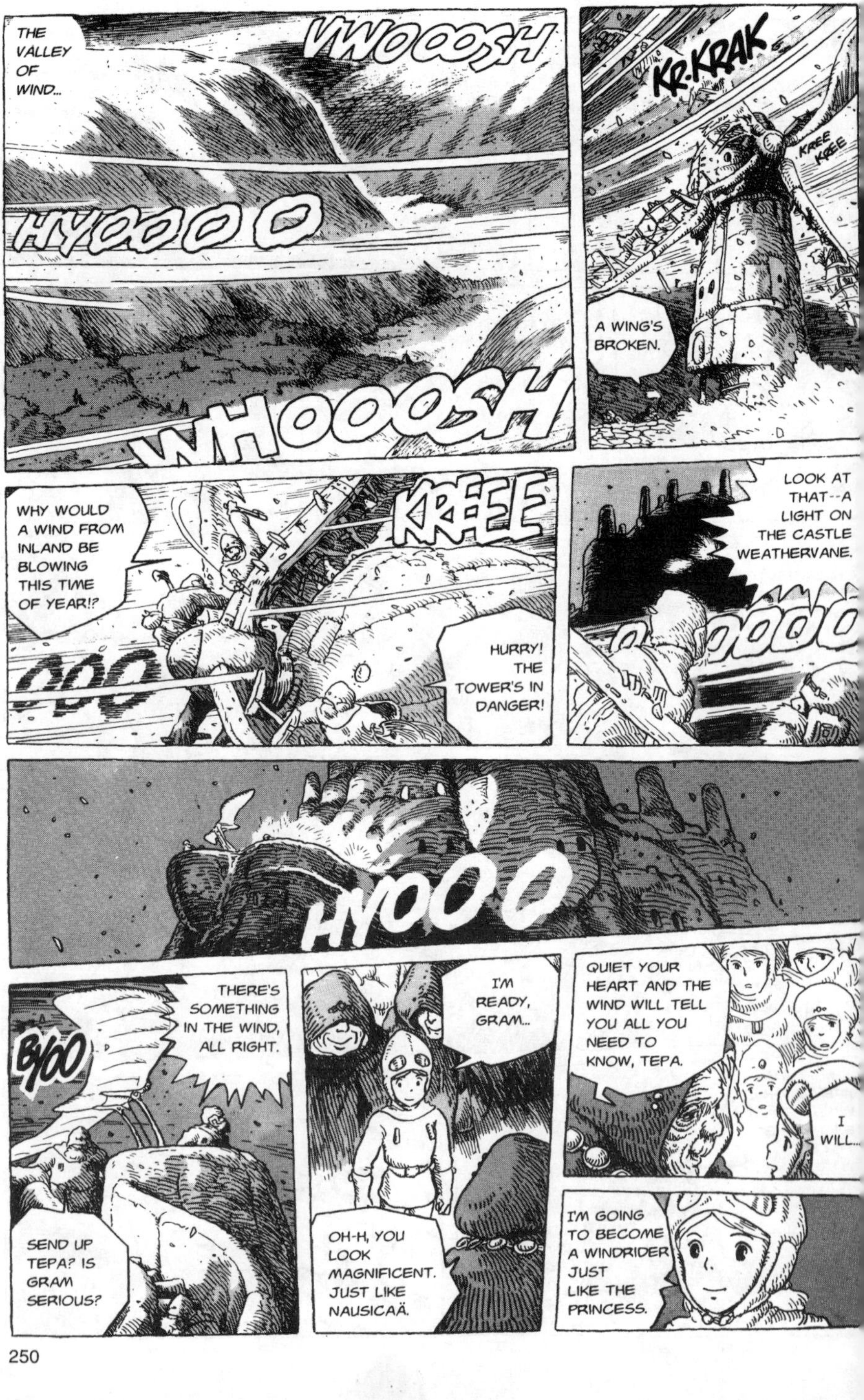
THE VALLEY OF WIND...
VWOOOSH
HYOOOOO
WHOOOSH
KR-KRAK
KREE KREE
A WING'S BROKEN.
WHY WOULD A WIND FROM INLAND BE BLOWING THIS TIME OF YEAR!?
KREEE
OOO
HURRY! THE TOWER'S IN DANGER!
LOOK AT THAT--A LIGHT ON THE CASTLE WEATHERVANE.
OOOOO
HYOOO
THERE'S SOMETHING IN THE WIND, ALL RIGHT.
BYOO
SEND UP TEPA? IS GRAM SERIOUS?
I'M READY, GRAM...
OH-H, YOU LOOK MAGNIFICENT. JUST LIKE NAUSICAÄ.
QUIET YOUR HEART AND THE WIND WILL TELL YOU ALL YOU NEED TO KNOW, TEPA.
I WILL...
I'M GOING TO BECOME A WINDRIDER JUST LIKE THE PRINCESS.

BYOOOO

FAPP
FAPP

TAKE CARE, NOW.

MAY THE WINDS BE KIND TO OUR PRECIOUS CHILD.

FLY!

WHAPP

CLIMB!

DON'T GET TANGLED IN THE WINDS WHIPPING AROUND THE CASTLE!

FAPFAPFAP

AH! A SUDDEN BLAST!

SHE'S AWAY!

HEEEEE

OOOO

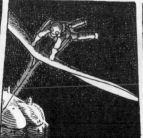

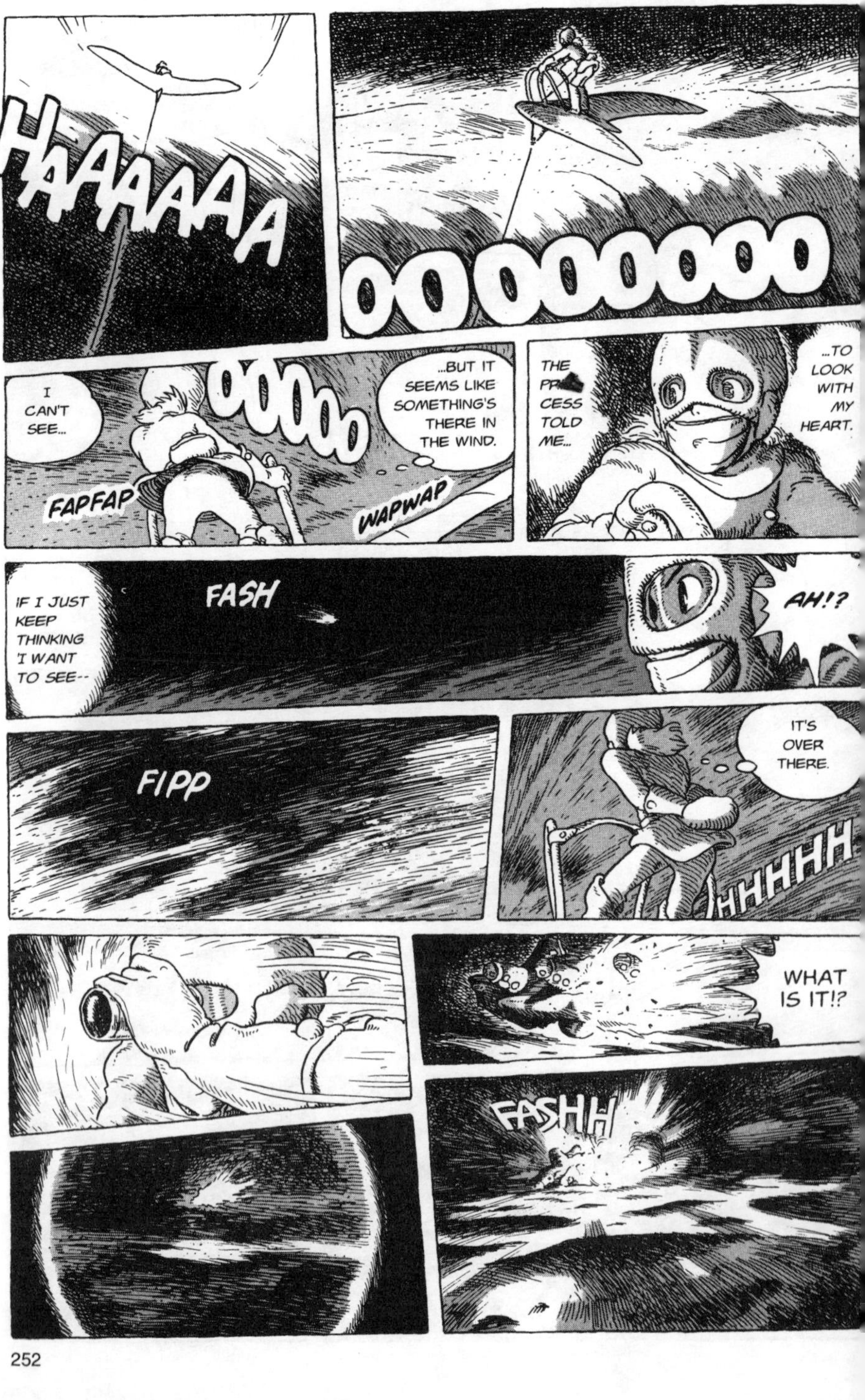
HAAAAAA
OOOOOOOOO
I CAN'T SEE...
OOOOOO
...BUT IT SEEMS LIKE SOMETHING'S THERE IN THE WIND.
FAPFAP
WAPWAP
THE PR CESS TOLD ME...
...TO LOOK WITH MY HEART.
IF I JUST KEEP THINKING 'I WANT TO SEE--
FASH
AH!?
FIPP
IT'S OVER THERE.
HHHHHH
WHAT IS IT!?
FASHH

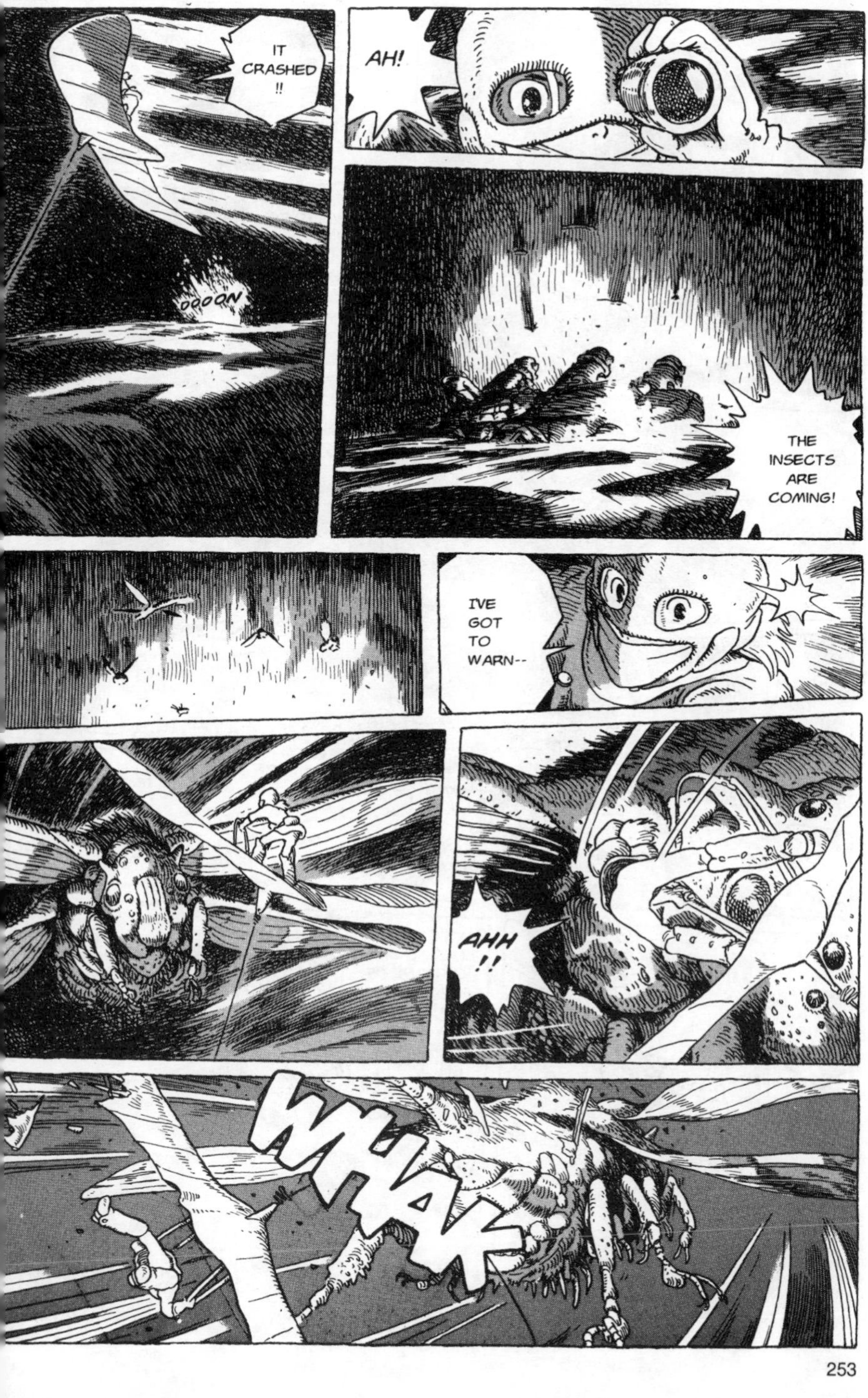
IT CRASHED !!
AH!
DOOON
THE INSECTS ARE COMING!
IVE GOT TO WARN--
AHH !!
WHAK

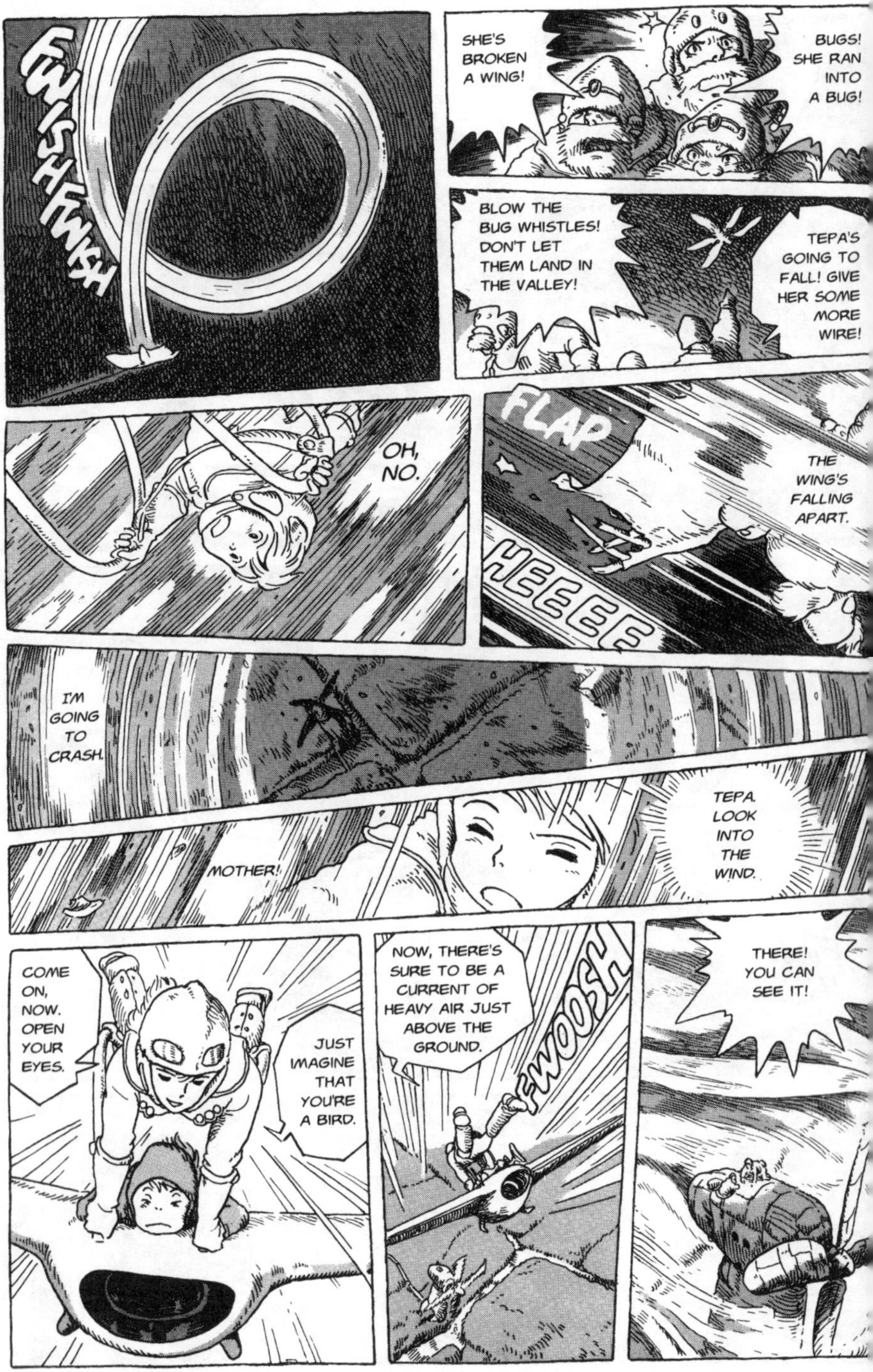
FWISHFWISH
SHE'S BROKEN A WING!
BUGS! SHE RAN INTO A BUG!
BLOW THE BUG WHISTLES! DON'T LET THEM LAND IN THE VALLEY!
TEPA'S GOING TO FALL! GIVE HER SOME MORE WIRE!
OH, NO.
FLAP
THE WING'S FALLING APART.
HEEEEE
I'M GOING TO CRASH.
MOTHER!
TEPA. LOOK INTO THE WIND.
COME ON, NOW. OPEN YOUR EYES.
JUST IMAGINE THAT YOU'RE A BIRD.
NOW, THERE'S SURE TO BE A CURRENT OF HEAVY AIR JUST ABOVE THE GROUND.
FWOOSH
THERE! YOU CAN SEE IT!

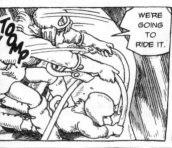

WE'RE GOING TO RIDE IT.

WHOOSH

SEE? AIR IS SPRINGY, LIKE A CUSHION.

PRINCESS, I CAN'T SEE ANYTHING.

THAT'S ALL RIGHT. SOMEDAY YOU'LL BE ABLE TO SEE IT, TOO, TEPA.

IT WAS THE SAME WITH ME AT FIRST.

HEE, HEE! MITO'S ANGRY.

NOW OPEN YOUR EYES WIDE AND DON'T BE AFRAID.

VWOO

WAH!!

SHE'S GOING TO CRASH!

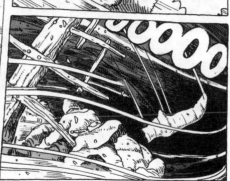

VOOOOO

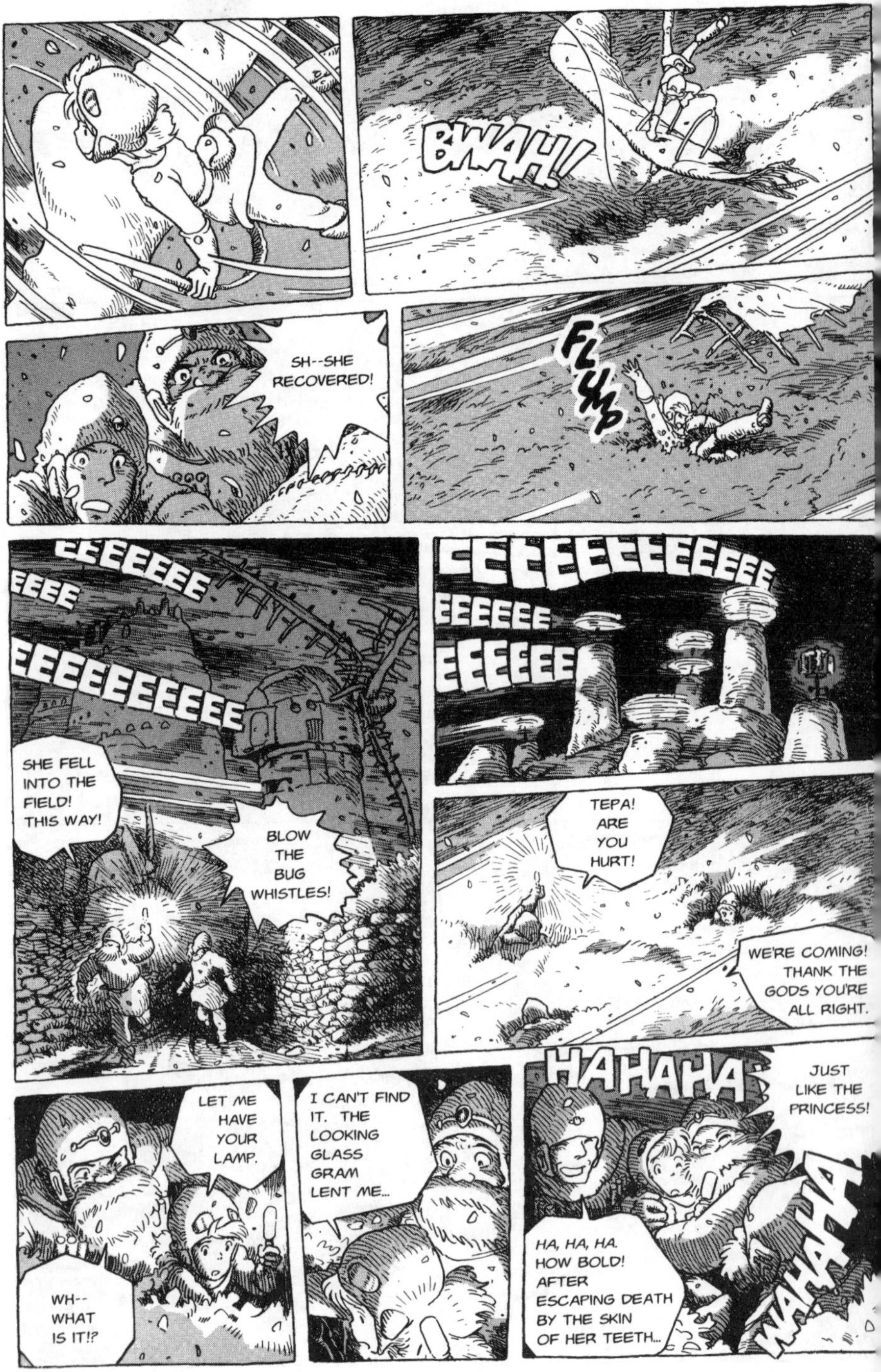
BWAH!!
SH--SHE RECOVERED!
FLUMP
EEEEEE
EEEE
EEEEEEEEEE
EEEEEEEEEEE
EEEEEE
EEEEEE
SHE FELL INTO THE FIELD! THIS WAY!
BLOW THE BUG WHISTLES!
TEPA! ARE YOU HURT!
WE'RE COMING! THANK THE GODS YOU'RE ALL RIGHT.
LET ME HAVE YOUR LAMP.
WH-- WHAT IS IT!?
I CAN'T FIND IT. THE LOOKING GLASS GRAM LENT ME...
HAHAHA
JUST LIKE THE PRINCESS!
HA, HA, HA. HOW BOLD! AFTER ESCAPING DEATH BY THE SKIN OF HER TEETH...
WAHAHA

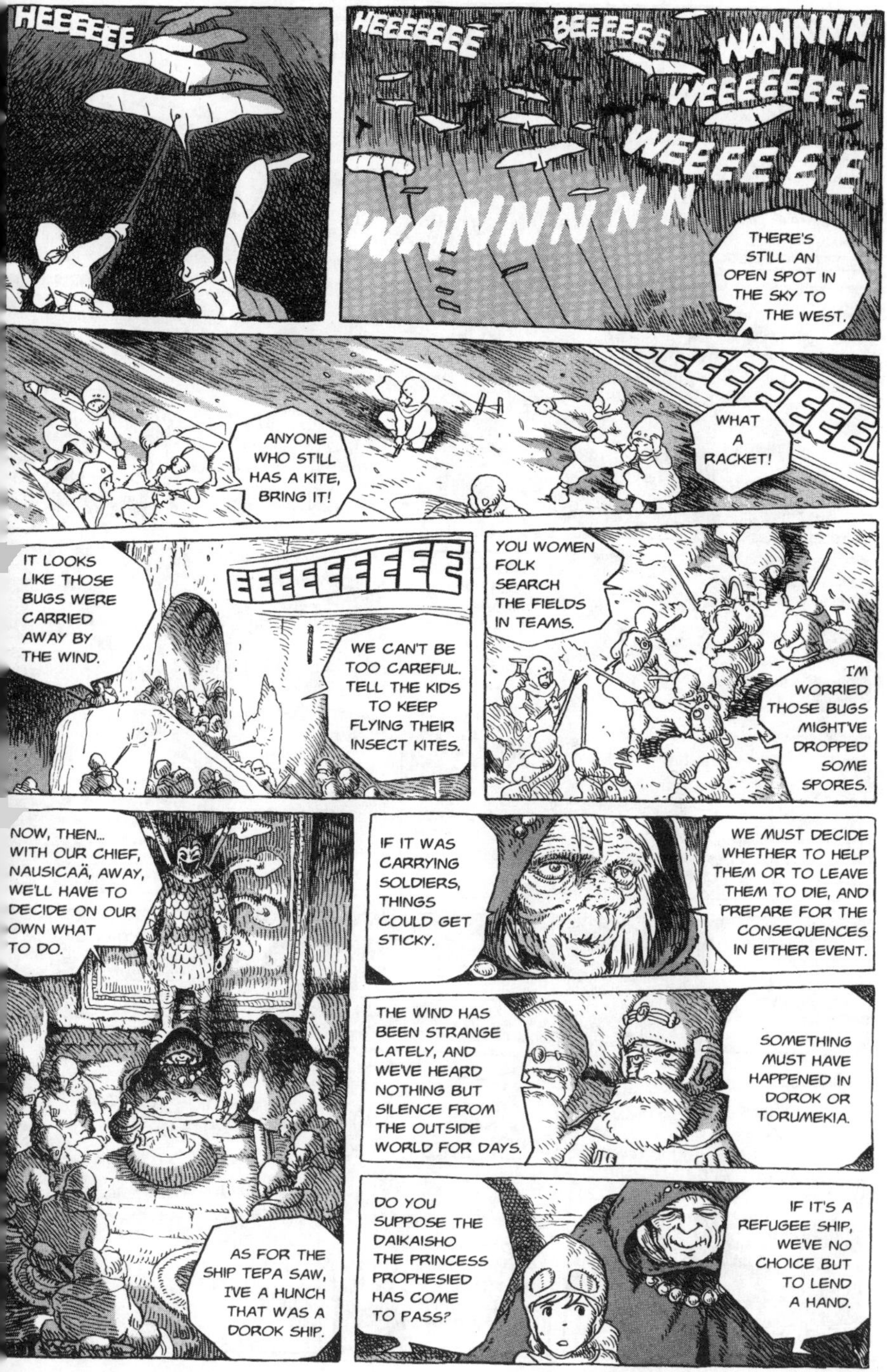
HEEEEEE
HEEEEEEE
BEEEEEE
WANNNN
WEEEEEEEE
WEEEEEE
WANNNNNN
THERE'S STILL AN OPEN SPOT IN THE SKY TO THE WEST.
EEEEEEEEE
ANYONE WHO STILL HAS A KITE, BRING IT!
WHAT A RACKET!
IT LOOKS LIKE THOSE BUGS WERE CARRIED AWAY BY THE WIND.
EEEEEEEEE
WE CAN'T BE TOO CAREFUL. TELL THE KIDS TO KEEP FLYING THEIR INSECT KITES.
YOU WOMEN FOLK SEARCH THE FIELDS IN TEAMS.
I'M WORRIED THOSE BUGS MIGHT'VE DROPPED SOME SPORES.
NOW, THEN... WITH OUR CHIEF, NAUSICAÄ, AWAY, WE'LL HAVE TO DECIDE ON OUR OWN WHAT TO DO.
AS FOR THE SHIP TEPA SAW, I'VE A HUNCH THAT WAS A DOROK SHIP.
WE MUST DECIDE WHETHER TO HELP THEM OR TO LEAVE THEM TO DIE, AND PREPARE FOR THE CONSEQUENCES IN EITHER EVENT.
IF IT WAS CARRYING SOLDIERS, THINGS COULD GET STICKY.
SOMETHING MUST HAVE HAPPENED IN DOROK OR TORUMEKIA.
THE WIND HAS BEEN STRANGE LATELY, AND WE'VE HEARD NOTHING BUT SILENCE FROM THE OUTSIDE WORLD FOR DAYS.
IF IT'S A REFUGEE SHIP, WE'VE NO CHOICE BUT TO LEND A HAND.
DO YOU SUPPOSE THE DAIKAISHO THE PRINCESS PROPHESIED HAS COME TO PASS?

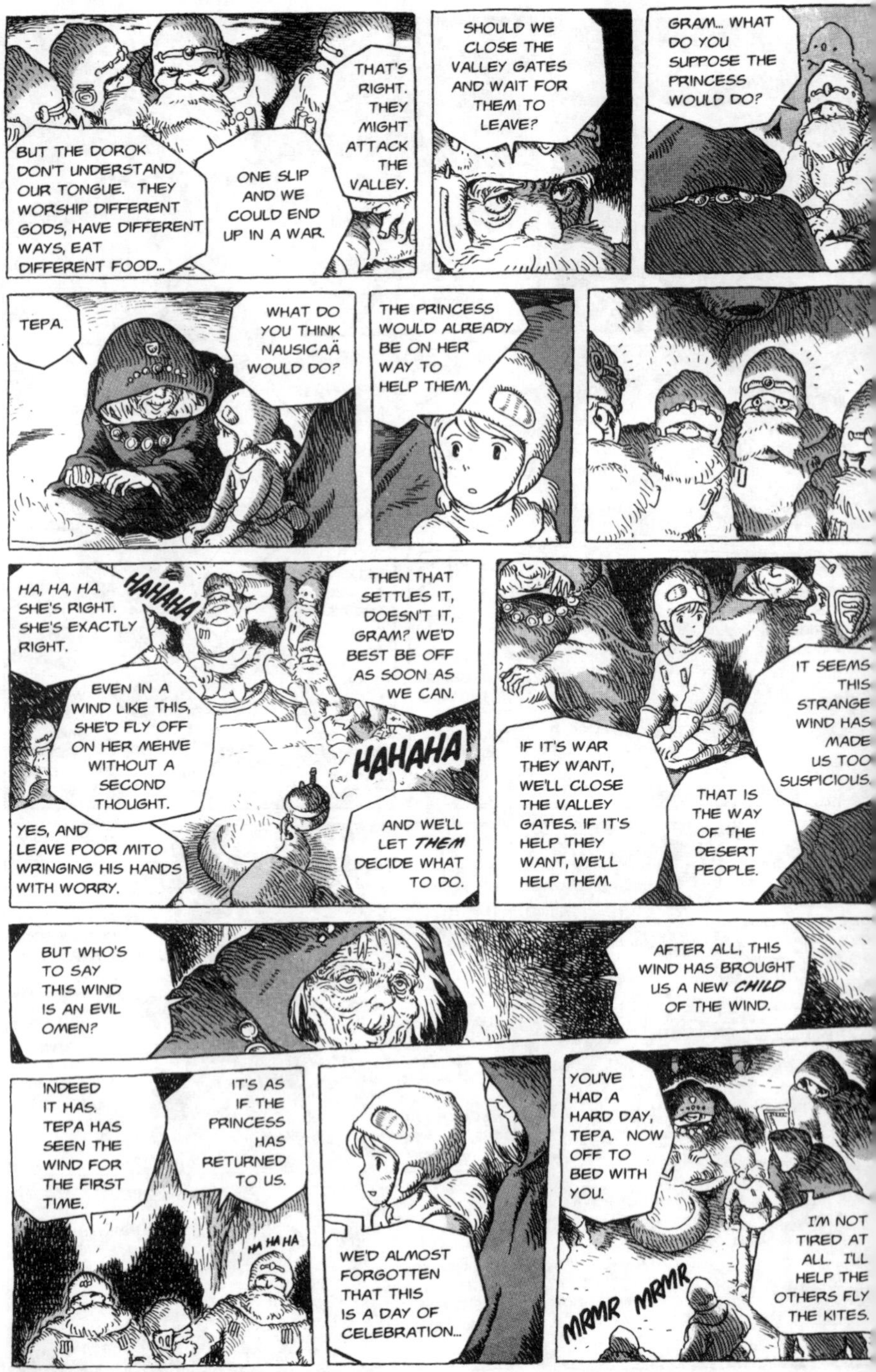
BUT THE DOROK DON'T UNDERSTAND OUR TONGUE. THEY WORSHIP DIFFERENT GODS, HAVE DIFFERENT WAYS, EAT DIFFERENT FOOD...
ONE SLIP AND WE COULD END UP IN A WAR.
THAT'S RIGHT. THEY MIGHT ATTACK THE VALLEY.
SHOULD WE CLOSE THE VALLEY GATES AND WAIT FOR THEM TO LEAVE?
GRAM... WHAT DO YOU SUPPOSE THE PRINCESS WOULD DO?
TEPA.
WHAT DO YOU THINK NAUSICAÄ WOULD DO?
THE PRINCESS WOULD ALREADY BE ON HER WAY TO HELP THEM.
HA, HA, HA. SHE'S RIGHT. SHE'S EXACTLY RIGHT.
HAHAHA
EVEN IN A WIND LIKE THIS, SHE'D FLY OFF ON HER MEHVE WITHOUT A SECOND THOUGHT.
YES, AND LEAVE POOR MITO WRINGING HIS HANDS WITH WORRY.
THEN THAT SETTLES IT, DOESN'T IT, GRAM? WE'D BEST BE OFF AS SOON AS WE CAN.
HAHAHA
AND WE'LL LET *THEM* DECIDE WHAT TO DO.
IT SEEMS THIS STRANGE WIND HAS MADE US TOO SUSPICIOUS.
IF IT'S WAR THEY WANT, WE'LL CLOSE THE VALLEY GATES. IF IT'S HELP THEY WANT, WE'LL HELP THEM.
THAT IS THE WAY OF THE DESERT PEOPLE.
BUT WHO'S TO SAY THIS WIND IS AN EVIL OMEN?
AFTER ALL, THIS WIND HAS BROUGHT US A NEW *CHILD* OF THE WIND.
INDEED IT HAS. TEPA HAS SEEN THE WIND FOR THE FIRST TIME.
IT'S AS IF THE PRINCESS HAS RETURNED TO US.
HA HA HA
WE'D ALMOST FORGOTTEN THAT THIS IS A DAY OF CELEBRATION...
YOU'VE HAD A HARD DAY, TEPA. NOW OFF TO BED WITH YOU.
MRMR MRMR
I'M NOT TIRED AT ALL. I'LL HELP THE OTHERS FLY THE KITES.

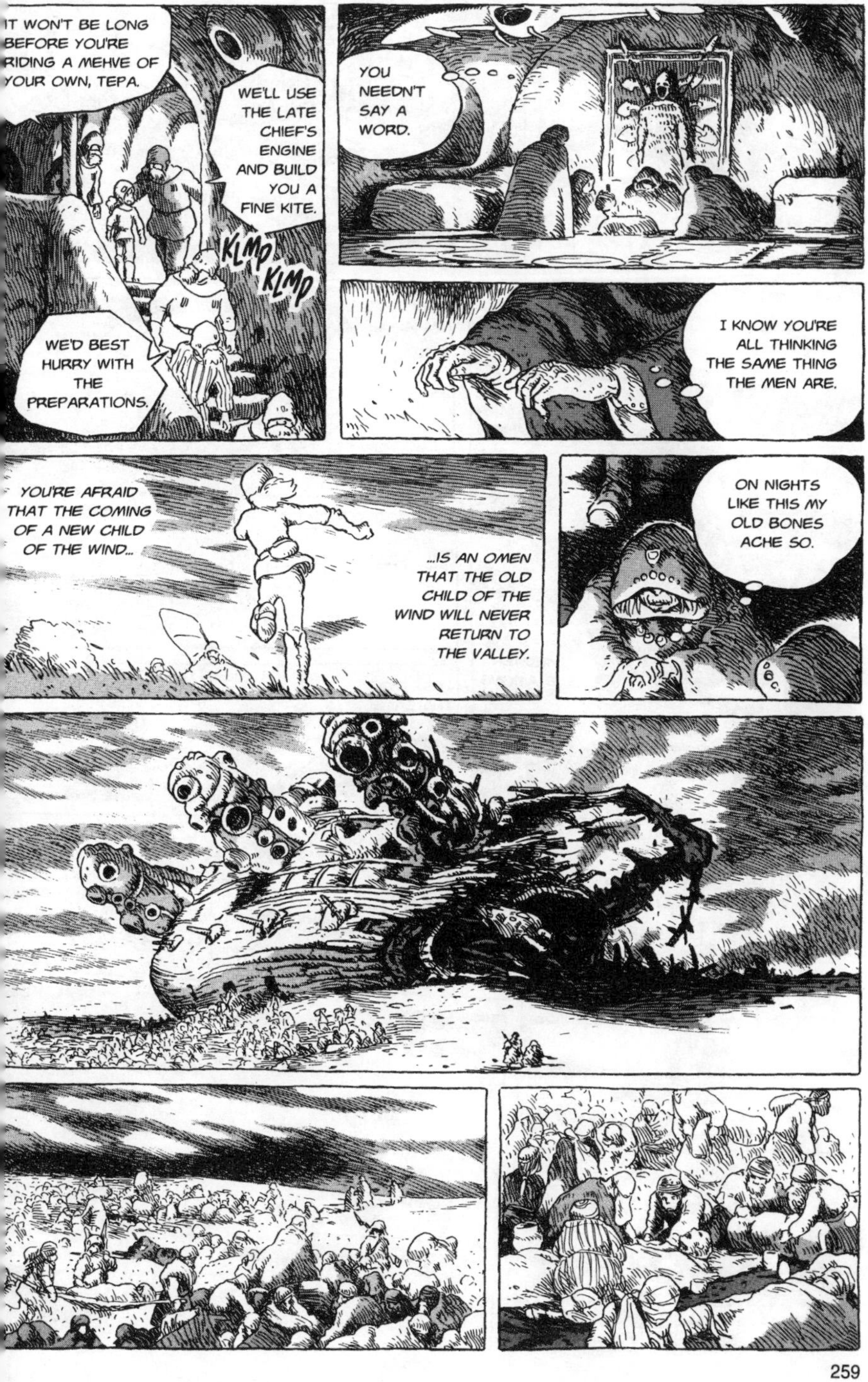
IT WON'T BE LONG BEFORE YOU'RE RIDING A MEHVE OF YOUR OWN, TEPA.
WE'LL USE THE LATE CHIEF'S ENGINE AND BUILD YOU A FINE KITE.
KLMP KLMP
WE'D BEST HURRY WITH THE PREPARATIONS.
YOU NEEDN'T SAY A WORD.
I KNOW YOU'RE ALL THINKING THE SAME THING THE MEN ARE.
YOU'RE AFRAID THAT THE COMING OF A NEW CHILD OF THE WIND...
...IS AN OMEN THAT THE OLD CHILD OF THE WIND WILL NEVER RETURN TO THE VALLEY.
ON NIGHTS LIKE THIS MY OLD BONES ACHE SO.

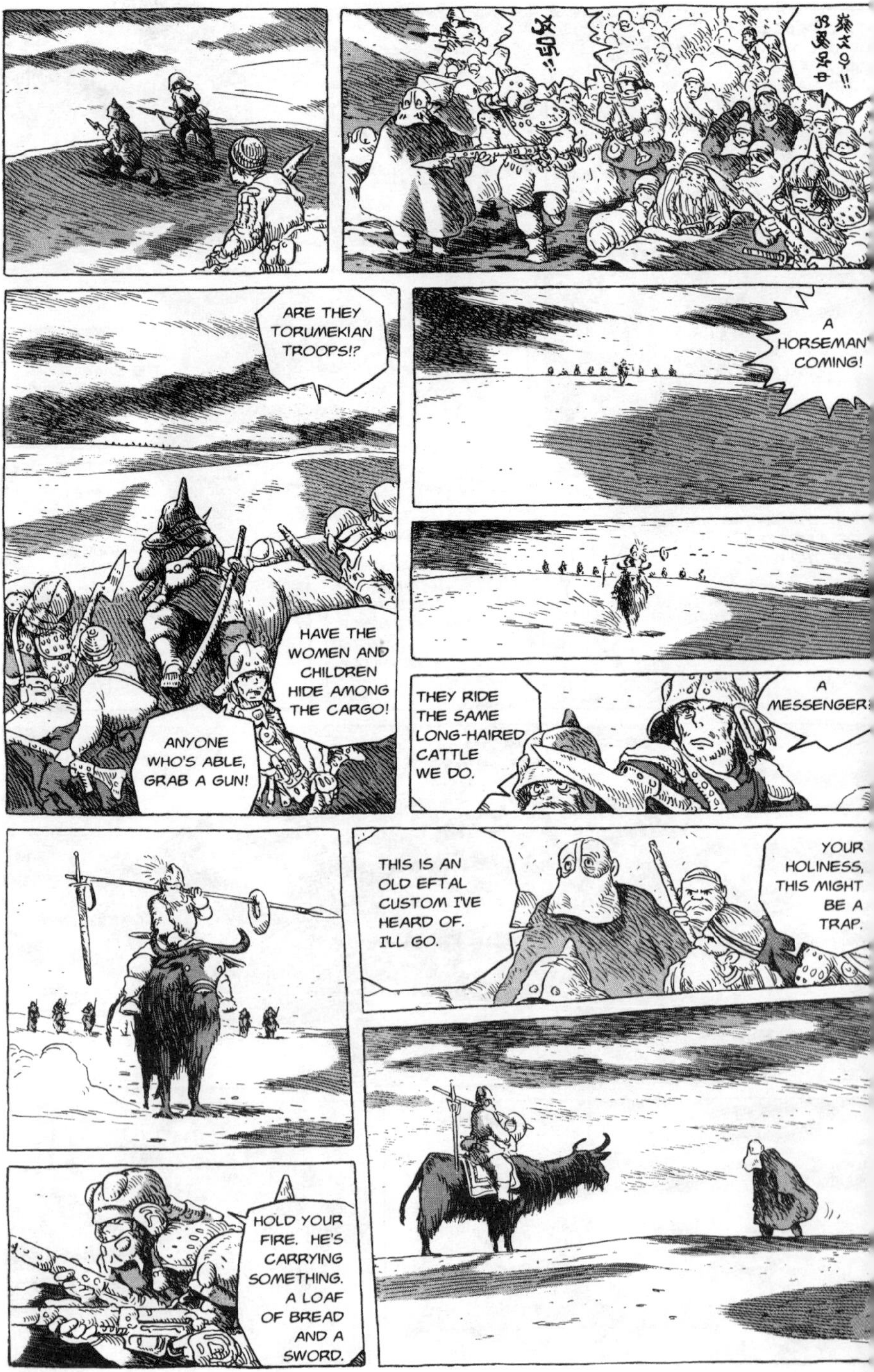
A HORSEMAN' COMING!
ARE THEY TORUMEKIAN TROOPS!?
HAVE THE WOMEN AND CHILDREN HIDE AMONG THE CARGO!
ANYONE WHO'S ABLE, GRAB A GUN!
THEY RIDE THE SAME LONG-HAIRED CATTLE WE DO.
A MESSENGER
THIS IS AN OLD EFTAL CUSTOM I'VE HEARD OF. I'LL GO.
YOUR HOLINESS, THIS MIGHT BE A TRAP.
HOLD YOUR FIRE. HE'S CARRYING SOMETHING. A LOAF OF BREAD AND A SWORD.

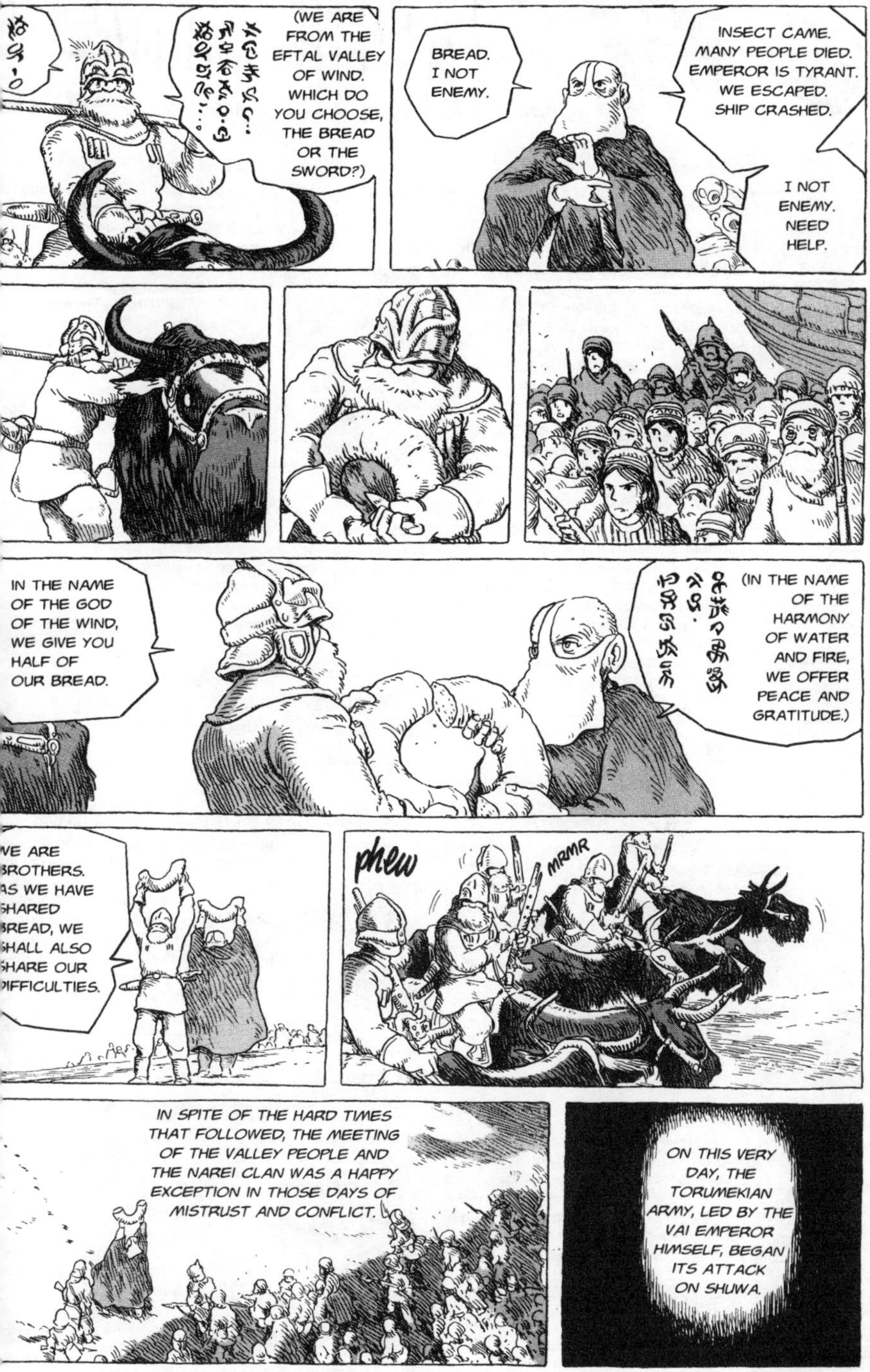
(WE ARE FROM THE EFTAL VALLEY OF WIND. WHICH DO YOU CHOOSE, THE BREAD OR THE SWORD?)
BREAD. I NOT ENEMY.
INSECT CAME. MANY PEOPLE DIED. EMPEROR IS TYRANT. WE ESCAPED. SHIP CRASHED.
I NOT ENEMY. NEED HELP.
IN THE NAME OF THE GOD OF THE WIND, WE GIVE YOU HALF OF OUR BREAD.
(IN THE NAME OF THE HARMONY OF WATER AND FIRE, WE OFFER PEACE AND GRATITUDE.)
WE ARE BROTHERS. AS WE HAVE SHARED BREAD, WE SHALL ALSO SHARE OUR DIFFICULTIES.
phew
MRMR
IN SPITE OF THE HARD TIMES THAT FOLLOWED, THE MEETING OF THE VALLEY PEOPLE AND THE NAREI CLAN WAS A HAPPY EXCEPTION IN THOSE DAYS OF MISTRUST AND CONFLICT.
ON THIS VERY DAY, THE TORUMEKIAN ARMY, LED BY THE VAI EMPEROR HIMSELF, BEGAN ITS ATTACK ON SHUWA.

TO BE CONTINUED…

VIZ GRAPHIC NOVELS

NEON GENESIS EVANGELION

The most controversial anime and manga of the 1990s! In the year 2015, half of the human race is dead, and the survivors face a terrifying last judgment from giant "Angels." Within Tokyo-3 and the headquarters of the secretive organization called NERV,

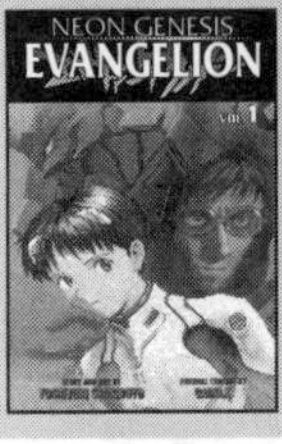
NEON GENESIS
EVANGELION

a handful of teenagers are trained to pilot the colossal superentities known as "Evangelions" and battle the Angels on their own terms...whatever the cost to their minds and souls.

by Yoshiyuki Sadamoto
168-176 pages each

VOLUME	PRICE
1 (Regular or Special Collectors' Edition)	$15.95
2 (Regular or Special Collectors' Edition)	$15.95

STRIKER

Violent, cinematic action-adventure! The Arcam Foundat ensures that deadly relics of an ancient civilization stay out of wrong hands. Against zombies, biological weapons, and cyb troops, one Arcam operative is always on the front lines. Ominae, overworked high school stuc and super-powered secret agent!

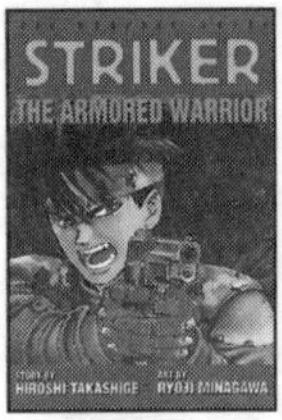
STRIKER
THE ARMORED WARRIOR

story by Hiroshi Takashige
art by Ryoji Minagawa
160-248 pages each

VOLUME	PRICE
The Armored Warrior	$16.95
The Forest of No Return	$15.95
Striker vs. The Third Reich *(available February '99)*	$15.95

INU-YASHA

When Japanese schoolgirl Kagome stumbles through a boarded-up well within an ancient shrine, she falls back in time to sixteenth-century Japan. There she becomes the master—and

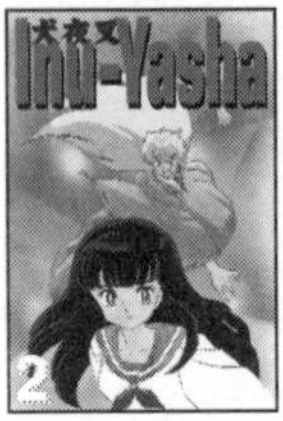
Inu-Yasha

friend—of the feral half-demon Inu-Yasha, and the protector of the magical Shikon Jewel against the demons of the present and past!

by Rumiko Takahashi
178-192 pages each

VOLUME	PRICE
#1	$15.95
#2	$15.95
#3	$15.95

EAT-MAN

Bolt Crank—aka Eat-Man—is a wandering explorer who e anything that may come in handy later, from weapons to rac to gasoline... becuase he can transform the flesh of his arm i

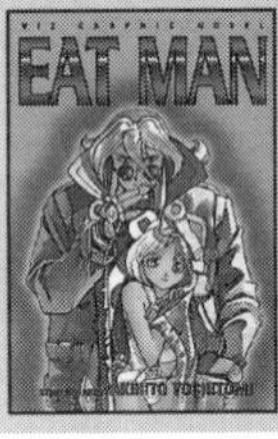
EAT MAN

the mechanisms he's consumed! A c customer with a penchant for attrac pretty girls, Eat-Man's life is packed v tall tales of dragons, princesses, and to grinding adventure!

by Akihito Yoshitomi
192-200 pages each

VOLUME	PRICE
Eat-Man	$15.95
Eat-Man: Second Course	$15.95

GALAXY EXPRESS 999

Aboard a train which travels the stars, a young boy named Tetsuro and a mysterious woman named Maetel must go on an

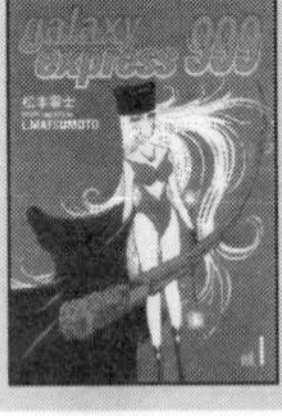

interstellar voyage to save the Earth—and all life in the universe—from a cosmic force of destruction. Meet the great space pirate Captain Harlock, the faithful Conductor, and many other classic characters in this new manga by a master of the form!

by Leiji Matsumoto
232 pages

VOLUME	PRICE
#1	$15.95

MOBILE POLICE PATLABOR

In the near future, tremendous advances in robotics make "Labor", or humanoid mecha, a common tool for heavy in

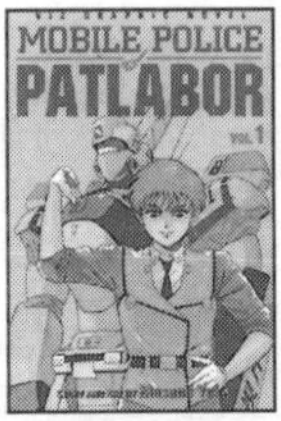
MOBILE POLICE
PATLABOR

trial work. But the great machines make great weapons for terrorists criminals, and the Tokyo Police must f a squad of Patrol Labors -- "Patlabors" fight fire with fire!

by Masami Yuki
184-192 pages each

VOLUME	PRICE
1	$15.95
2: Basic Training	$15.95

BLACK JACK

Tales of medical drama from Osamu "God of Manga" Tezuka, creator of ***Astro Boy*** and ***Adolf***! Black Jack is a brilliant, mysterious,

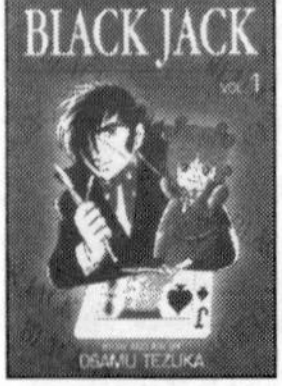
BLACK JACK

unlicensed surgeon, for whom no case is too bizarre and no operation is too risky. Includes Black Jack's first story, the origin of his "assistant" Pinoco, and more!

by Osamu Tezuka
184 pages

VOLUME	PRICE
1: Black Jack	$15.95
2: Two-Fisted Surgeon *(available March 1999)*	$15.95

STEAM DETECTIVES

Cliffhanging retro-future action! It is a past that never was— Age of Steam—where masked dandies, dastardly supervilla

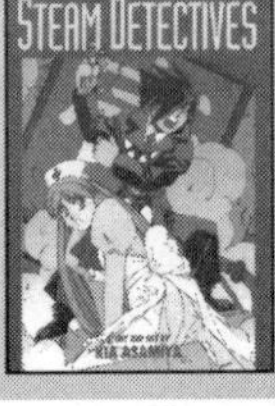
STEAM DETECTIVES

and sentient machines stalk the gc streets of Steam City by night. Are the and reflexes of wünderkind detec Narutaki, pretty nurse Ling Ling, and robot Goriki enough to thwart evil unravel the mysteries of this strange wc

by Kia Asamiya
200 pages

VOLUME	PRIC
#1	$15.9

Available at a comics store near you! Or order online at www.j-pop.com or by phone at (800) 394-30

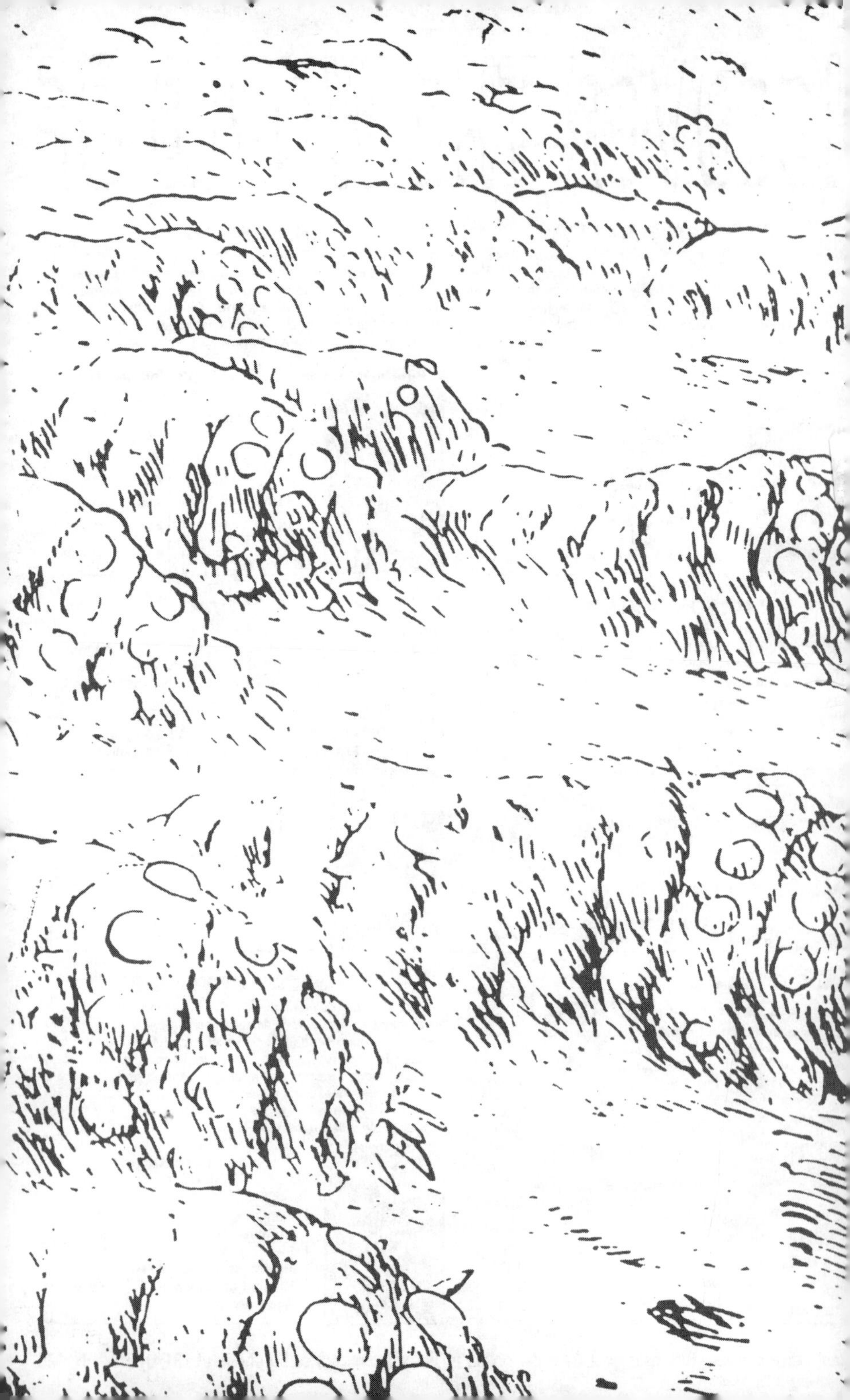